Memoirs of Modern Philosophers

Memoirs of Modern Philosophers
Elizabeth Hamilton

edited by Claire Grogan

broadview press

©2000 Claire Grogan

All rights reserved. The use of any part of this publication reproduced, transmitted in any form or by any means, electronic, mechanical, photocopying, recording, or otherwise, or stored in a retrieval system, without prior written consent of the publisher — or in the case of photocopying, a licence from CANCOPY (Canadian Copyright Licensing Agency) One Yonge Street, Suite 1900, Toronto, Ontario M5E 1E5 — is an infringement of the copyright law.

Canadian Cataloguing in Publication Data

Hamilton, Elizabeth, 1758-1816
    Memoirs of modern philosophers

(Broadview literary texts)
Includes bibliographical references.
ISBN 1-55111-148-9 (softcover)   ISBN 1-55111-311-2 (hardcover)

I. Grogan, Claire, 1961- . II. Title. III. Series.

PR4739.H164M4   2000   823'.6   C99-932657-0

Broadview Press Ltd., is an independent, international publishing house, incorporated in 1985

North America
Post Office Box 1243, Peterborough, Ontario, Canada K9J 7H5
3576 California Road, Orchard Park, NY 14127
Tel: (705) 743-8990; Fax: (705) 743-8353;
e-mail: customerservice@broadviewpress.com

United Kingdom:
Turpin Distribution Services, Ltd., Blackhorse Rd., Letchworth, Hertfordshire SG6 1HN
Tel: (1462) 672555; Fax: (1462) 480947; e-mail: turpin@rsc.org

Australia:
St. Clair Press, P.O. Box 287, Rozelle, NSW 2039
Tel: (02) 818-1942; Fax: (02) 418-1923

www.broadviewpress.com

Broadview Press is grateful to Professor Eugene Benson for advice on editorial matters for the Broadview Literary Texts series and to Professor L.W. Conolly for editorial advice on this volume.

Broadview Press gratefully acknowledges the financial support of the Book Publishing Industry Development Program, Ministry of Canadian Heritage, Government of Canada.

Typesetting and assembly: True to Type Inc., Mississauga, Canada.
PRINTED IN CANADA

Contents

Acknowledgements 6

Introduction 9

Elizabeth Hamilton: A Brief Chronology 27

A Note on the Text 29

Author's Advertisement to 3rd edition 1801 30

Memoirs of Modern Philosophers
    Volume I 31
    Volume II 149
    Volume III 277

Appendix A: Contemporary Works
    1. William Godwin
        A. *Enquiry Concerning Political Justice and its Influence on Modern Morals and Happiness* 391
        B. *The Enquirer* 395
    2. Mary Hays
        A. *Memoirs of Emma Courtney* 397

Appendix B: The Hottentots
    Fig 1. The "Hottentot Venus," George Cuvier 402
    Fig 2. A Gonoquais Hottentot 403
    Fig 3. Klaas, The Author's Favourite Hottentot 404
    Fig 4. Female Hottentot 405

Appendix C: Reviews of *Memoirs of Modern Philosophers*
    i. *Critical Review* (May 1800) 407
    ii. *British Critic* (October 1800) 408
    iii. *Anti-Jacobin Review and Magazine* (September 1800) 409
    iv. Anna Laetitia Barbauld *British Novelists* (1810) 413

Select Bibliography 415

Acknowledgements

While many people helped and encouraged me during the course of this project I specifically wish to thank Jean Porter, Cheryl Porter and Bonnie Stewart for typing assistance, Shelley King for her support and Holly Fedida for the distractions. I am also grateful to the Senate Research Committee at Bishop's University for financial assistance.

Elizabeth Hamilton (engraving by W.T. Fry, after a portrait by Henry Raeburn)

Introduction

When the *Anti-Jacobin Review* described *Memoirs of Modern Philosophers* as "the first novel of the day," and as proof "that all the female writers of the day are not corrupted by the voluptuous dogmas of Mary Godwin, or her more profligate imitators" such as "M[ar]y H[ay]s,"[1] they clearly situated her work within the revolutionary debate of the 1790s. In England, unlike in France, the debate was not accompanied by actual revolution but centred on intense discussion (and some rioting) about the political, social, legal and economic rights of the individual. Revolutionary ideas about a broader franchise, primogeniture, meritocracy, marriage and divorce found many sympathetic listeners—especially amongst the increasingly wealthy but politically disenfranchised middle-class dissenters and Catholics who were still denied power under the 1673 Test and Corporation Acts.[2] Revolutionary supporters, derogatorily labelled English Jacobins by their opponents, agitated for a broader franchise to force a redistribution of power and status to better reflect the economic and demographic realities of England in the 1790s. Those in power—the Loyalists—argued, not surprisingly, for a preservation of the *status quo*. The revolutionary debate engrossed people from all walks of life who used journals, magazines, newspapers, literary works and even sermons to participate.

Although women were denied a voice in parliament or the legislature they were not silent in the revolutionary debate raging in print. While Mary Wollstonecraft was somewhat unusual in publishing a political polemic (*Vindication of the Rights of Woman* 1792), most women, for social, economic and political reasons, wrote in the other genres of poetry, educational treatises, conduct books, fiction, children's literature, drama and miscellanies. All these genres offered women indirect access to the political discussions of the revolutionary debate. While the debate about female rights did not extend to enfranchisement (Thomas Spence alone suggested women should have the vote, Wollstonecraft only hinted at it) it was no less heated. The debate focused on demands for a decent education, gaining legal status, and means of economic independence for women. Given the wholesale disruption that might ensue from any increase in female rights, a woman's education, her reading material, her expectations in life and marriage, all became matters of increasing public concern.

---

[1] 7 (Sept 1800), 39; 7 (Dec. 1800), 375-6. See Appendix C for contemporary reviews of the novel.

[2] The Test and Corporation Act passed by the Cavalier parliament in 1673 was directed against Roman Catholics but also penalized Protestant Dissenters since it stipulated that all holders of civil and military offices had to be communicants of the Anglican Church, repudiate transubstantiation and take the Oath of Allegiance and Supremacy. It was finally repealed in 1829 and university religious tests were abolished in the 1870s and 1880s.

Fiction such as Elizabeth Hamilton's *Memoirs of Modern Philosophers* played an enormously important role, especially over the question of the rights of woman, since the wide availability of fictional works within circulating libraries, reading clubs and associations often meant novels reached a broader reading public than polemical and philosophical pieces. That writers were aware of this is evident in Anna Laetitia Barbauld's concluding comment to her Introductory Essay to the fifty-volume *British Novelists*: "Let me make the novels of a country, and let who will make the systems."[3]

The major polemical works in the revolutionary debate were Edmund Burke's *Reflections on the Revolution in France* (1790), Thomas Paine's *Rights of Man* (1791), Mary Wollstonecraft's *Vindication of the Rights of Woman* (1792) and William Godwin's *Political Justice* (1793) and *Enquirer* (1797). That these works and the sentiments expressed in them were common knowledge is apparent by the large number of references made to them by contemporary writers, cartoonists and journalists. It is clear upon reading *Memoirs of Modern Philosophers* that Hamilton expects her readers to be conversant with these works (or at least with a synopsis of them if not with the original) to relish her biting humour and satiric rendering of them since her novel contains an inordinate number of quotations, allusions, and parodies of such polemical pieces. Most especially, a detailed knowledge of Godwin's *Political Justice* and later *Enquiry* is crucial to fully savour her acerbic wit and political positioning. She has characters actually mouth passages from Godwin's works to point out the ludicrousness of much of his theory of perfectibility although she is clear to indicate that it is not the work in general that she despises but the uses to which it has been put. In the Introduction to *Memoirs of Modern Philosophers* we learn that the aim of the work is

> not to pass an indiscriminate censor on that ingenious, and in many parts admirable, performance, but to expose the dangerous tendencies of those parts of his theory which might, by a bad man, be converted into an engine of mischief, and be made the means of ensnaring innocence and virtue. (36)

Indeed, Godwin wryly noted in 1797 that "the cry spread like a general infection, and I have been told that not even a petty novel for boarding-school misses now ventures to aspire to favour unless it contains some expression of dislike or abhorrence to the New Philosophy."[4] Barbauld similarly summarized the situation: "no small proportion of modern novels have been devoted to recommend, or to mark with reprobation, those systems of philosophy or politics which have raised so much ferment of late years."[5] Indeed, "they [novels] take a tincture from the learning and

---

[3] Anna Laetitia Barbauld, *The British Novelists* (London: Rivington, 1810) 1: 59.
[4] "Thoughts Occasioned by Dr. Parr's Spital Sermon" (Qtd. in Brailsford *Shelley, Godwin and Their Circle* London: Williams and Norgate 1927) 156.
[5] Barbauld, *The British Novelists* 1: 50.

politics of the times, and are made use of successfully to attack or to recommend the prevailing systems of the day."[6]

That Hamilton participated in this raging battle is noted in the *Anti-Jacobin Review* (Sept 1800): "The public ... is infinitely obliged to *her* ... for her having given it in the form of a novel; for the same means by which the poison is offered, are, perhaps, the best by which their antidote may be rendered efficacious."[7] Hamilton's fictional editor Geoffrey Jarvis himself notes in his introduction:

> The ridiculous point of view in which some of the opinions conveyed to the young and unthinking through the medium of philosophical novels, is exhibited in the character of Bridgetina, appears to me as an excellent antidote to the poison; calculated to make an impression upon those to whom serious disquisitions would have been addressed in vain. (37)

The debate about female rights was centred in fiction because it was traditionally perceived as a feminine genre and because of the female's limited reading capabilities and accessibility to other forms of political discourse. Female readers were deemed to be especially receptive to fiction because of their limited activities, experiences and education, although opinion was divided as to whether females were (according to the Loyalist position) innately intellectually inferior to men because "there is a different bent of understanding in the sexes"[8] or (according to English Jacobins) "since there is no sex in the soul or mind"[9] merely limited by the poor education they received.

Educationalists of a liberal bent, such as Elizabeth Hamilton, held a middling position which espoused the view that females were intellectually capable but that an inadequate and poorly directed education system failed to develop the female's potential—although unlike the English Jacobins the potential is domestic in nature. In her early writings Hamilton subscribes to the position that "our sex is doomed to experience the double disadvantage arising from original confirmation of mind, and a defective education"[10] but a comment in her later *Series of Popular Essays* (1813) indicates a change of heart since she has not "been as yet convinced, that there is any subject within the range of human intellect, on

---

[6] Barbauld, *The British Novelists* 1: 2 For a fuller discussion of the political role of fiction see Gary Kelly, *The English-Jacobin Novel 1780-1805* (Oxford: Clarendon, 1976) and *Women, Writing and Revolution 1790-1827* (Oxford: Clarendon, 1993).
[7] See Appendix C.
[8] Hannah More, *Essays* (London: Dilly, 1777) 11.
[9] Mary Wollstonecraft, *A Vindication of the Rights of Woman*, 1792. (Ed. Carol H. Poston. New York: Scholars' Facsimiles and Reprints, 1975) 106.
[10] Elizabeth Hamilton, *Letters on Education* (London: G. and J. Robinson, 1801) 2.

which the capacity of any intelligent Being of either Sex, may not be profitably, or, at least, innocently employed."[11]

While the *Anti-Jacobin Review* aligns Hamilton with the Loyalist position and in opposition to English Jacobins such as Wollstonecraft, Hamilton was actually a liberal writer who sits midway between these two political extremes. Clearly her satirical rendering of "Modern Philosophers" distances her from the Godwin/Wollstonecraft/Paine group as she methodically indicates the limitations of the English-Jacobin position, its dangers to the status quo, and false championing of women's rights. However, she is equally unhappy to align herself with the Loyalist camp which argued that no reform was necessary and for which she satirizes it so mercilessly in *Memoirs of Modern Philosophers*. Hamilton engages in the revolutionary debate through her *Memoirs of Modern Philosophers* to teach the female reader how to improve herself, to act judiciously, appropriately and yet strive for economic and intellectual independence. She clearly points to the political import of her work when she has her fictional editor Jarvis remark that the design of *Memoirs of Modern Philosophers* is "evidently that of supporting the cause of religion and virtue." Hamilton's support of moderate reform determines that all female advances and more general social ones occur within a framework of middle-class morality and Christian faith and as such they reflect her own religious and socio-economic background.

Hamilton was born in Belfast in 1758, the third child and second daughter of a merchant and his wife. Her father's death, when she was six, prompted her removal to Stirling, Scotland, to live with her paternal aunt. It was in the Marshall household, composed of her Presbyterian aunt and Episcopalian uncle, that she imbibed the middle-class ideology of frugality, morality, meritocracy and tolerance. Her aunt regaled her with stories of the Hamilton family instilling in her a strong Scottish pride ("the Hamilton's of Woodhall [were] *one* of the first of the Saxon *family* established in Scotland"),[12] a distrust of people who judged on class and status rather than on merit, a strong sense of female independence and of the importance of self improvement. Hamilton wrote how her aunt "wished me to be self-dependent; and, consequently taught me to value myself upon nothing that did not strictly belong to myself, nor upon anything that did, which was in its nature perishable."[13] Educated at a boarding school in Stirling, Hamilton learnt to acquit herself in the traditionally feminine accomplishments of "hammering at the pianoforte,"[14] dancing, French and drawing. Less typical was her exposure to the experimental philosophy of Dr. Moyse, although even these early formative ventures

---

[11] Elizabeth Hamilton, *Series of Popular Essays* (London: Manners and Millar, 1813) 1: xxxi.
[12] Elizabeth Benger, *Memoirs of the Late Mrs Elizabeth Hamilton* (London: Longman, 1818) 1: 8.
[13] Benger 1: 43.
[14] Benger 2: 103.

into masculine areas of learning were quickly accompanied by feelings of anxiety about their appropriateness and fears of ridicule. Hamilton recalls, "Do I not well remember hiding Kaim's *Elements of Criticism*[15] under the cover of an easy chair, whenever I heard the approach of footsteps, well knowing the ridicule to which I should have been exposed, had I been detected in the act of looking into such a book?"[16] That she should have been anxious is not surprising given comments such as Dr. Gregory's warning in his popular *Father's Legacy to His Daughters*: "If you happen to have any learning keep it a profound secret, especially from the men, who generally look with a jealous eye on a woman of great parts, and a cultivated understanding."[17]

Contact with her mother was limited to brief visits until her death in 1767 after which Hamilton lived as a full-time companion to her aunt (who died in 1780) and uncle. The uncle's death in 1788 facilitated a reunion of the Hamilton siblings in London some sixteen years after their separation. Her sister, Mrs. Blake of Oran Castle, was over from Ireland and her brother Charles, who had briefly ventured into the world of business but quickly renounced it for a career in the army, was back in England on a five-year absence from India to publish his *Historical Relation of the Origin, Progress, and Final Dissolution of the Government of the Rohilla Afghans in the Northern Provinces of Hindostan* (1786) and then complete a translation of the *Hedaya*. Elizabeth had corresponded faithfully with Charles during his cadetship in India and regarded him as the "animating soul of [her] existence."[18] Although she had published an anonymous essay in the *Lounger* (1785), it was under Charles's tutelage and within his circle of friends that she flourished as a writer. Charles' Orientalist project[19] exposed Elizabeth to numerous members of the London Asiatic Society who were intellectuals, writers, and translators and some of whom became good friends and advisors. The current fascination with the impeachment trial of Warren Hastings, former Governor General of Bengal, also exposed her to the policies and procedures of the East India Company and William Jones's Orientalist project. Elizabeth sided with Hastings—to whom both she and Charles dedicated works—and used her *Letters of a Hindoo Rajah* to further exonerate his name after his acquittal. The unexpected death of Charles from typhus in March 1792 just prior to his return to the East severely shocked Elizabeth

---

[15] Henry Home, Lord Kames, *Elements of Criticism* (Edinburgh: A. Kinkaid and J. Bell, 1762).
[16] Benger 2: 31.
[17] John Gregory, *A Father's Legacy to His Daughters* (London: W. Strahan, 1774) 31-32.
[18] Benger 1: 185.
[19] The tradition of scholarship now defined as Orientalism was headed by the likes of Sir Warren Hastings and Sir William Jones whose overriding goal was the professionalisation of Imperial administration in the East. The promotion of intellectual studies of the Orient formed a major part of this project.

who turned to writing to express her love and respect for her brother. *Translation of the Letters of a Hindoo Rajah* (1796) is a fictionalised Oriental satire in which Hamilton incorporates her own extensive knowledge of Orientalism—learnt largely under her brother's tutelage. The final product, though an erstwhile novel, is part tribute, part memorialization and part continuation of her brother—and other Orientalists'—project of imperialism in the East. *Letters of a Hindoo Rajah* saw Hamilton broach the masculine field of Orientalism within the feminized genre of the novel and quickly established her as an author in her own right. *Letters of a Hindoo Rajah* was well received as critics felt she negotiated the path between female propriety and masculine assertiveness well.[20]

It is well documented that late eighteenth-century British society was structured around rigid gender roles that prescribed the intellectual and social capabilities of the sexes.[21] Educationalists used Nature and religion to explain "the mental and moral difference of sex"[22] and to prescribe corresponding activities for each sex. The male was defined as public, political, intellectual and rational while the female was defined as private, domestic, emotional and irrational, as illustrated in Dr. James Fordyce's *Sermons to Young Women* (1766): "War, commerce, politics, exercises of strength and dexterity, abstract philosophy and all the abstruser sciences, are most properly the province of men," while females, because they have been formed "with less vigour," must "command by obeying, and by yielding ... conquer."[23] Females were encouraged first and foremost to be "good daughters, good wives, good mistresses, good members of society, and good Christians."[24] Such demarcation of the sexes saw writing defined as a predominantly male activity. Female writers were tolerated so long as they restricted themselves to minor genres such as children's literature, educational treatises, polemics on household economy, and certain types of fiction. Women, because of their intellectual limitations, were deemed ill equipped to write in the major (and masculine) genres of political polemics, scholarship or philosophy.

That Hamilton was sensitive to the obstacles facing women writers is

---

[20] See *British Critic*, 8 (Sept. 1796), 237-241; *Critical Review*, ns 17 (July 1796), 242; *Analytical Review*, 24 (Oct. 1796), 431; *Monthly Review*, ns 21 (Oct. 1796), 176-79.

[21] Much recent scholarship considers the difficulties facing the eighteenth-century English woman as a result of inherent social sexism, a pervasive—albeit weakening—belief in the female's innate intellectual inferiority, and the improprieties of women publishing. See Kelly, *Women, Writing and Revolution 1790-1827*, and Janet Todd, *The Sign of Angellica: Women, Writing and Fiction, 1660-1800* (London: Virago, 1989).

[22] James Fordyce, *Sermons to Young Women* 2 vols (London: Millar and Cadell, Dodsley and Payne, 1766) 1: 175.

[23] Fordyce 1: 272, 1: 271, 2: 261.

[24] Hannah More, *Essays on Various Subjects, Principally Designed for Young Ladies* (London: J. Wilkie and T. Cadell, 1777) 133.

evident both in her private correspondence and in her published works. She apologizes in the preface to *Letters of a Hindoo Rajah* for her audacity in addressing the public since "it may be censured by others, as a presumptuous effort to wander out of that narrow and contracted path, which they have allotted to the female mind."[25] This apology is in part merely literary convention since she is writing in a designated masculine area (albeit in the feminized novel form). However, the reservations she felt as a female writer are evident in her *Memoirs*:

> The character of an author I have always confined to my own closet; and no sooner step beyond its bounds, than the insuperable dread of being thought to move out of my proper sphere (a dread acquired, perhaps, from early association,) restrains me, not only from seeking opportunities of literary conversation, but frequently withholds me from taking all the advantage I might reap from those which offer.[26]

After the success of *Letters of a Hindoo Rajah*, and despite failing health, Hamilton began work on her second project, which was the no less ambitious *Memoirs of Modern Philosophers*. Using fiction to enter the debate about individual rights and responsibilities in a period of social unrest, Hamilton parodied the New Philosophers and their cult, pointing out the dangers of their teachings. Although *Letters of a Hindoo Rajah* appeared with her name on the title page, Hamilton chose to present the *Memoirs of Modern Philosophers* anonymously, but packaged by the fictional editor Geoffrey Jarvis. Hamilton justifies her choice to publish anonymously in the Advertisement (dated 29 November 1800) attached to the third edition of *Memoirs of Modern Philosophers*: "The Author of the ... Memoirs resolved to introduce the first edition under a signature evidently fictitious" because "even the *sex*, of a writer may unwittingly bias the reader's mind."[27] In presenting her political satire in the feminized genre of the novel, Hamilton once again attempts to avoid criticisms of female impropriety.

Perhaps for these reasons Hamilton chooses to employ a male editor to introduce the "lodger's" three-volume work and hides behind his narrative voice throughout. The "editor" Jarvis explains how he obtained the partially damaged manuscript in his Paternoster Row lodgings from a recently deceased male lodger. The editor interrupts the narrative to direct the reader, whom he perceives to be largely female, to point out a moral or pass censorious comment, tactics which both educate the reader and draw attention to the art of writing and reading in the very act of doing both. In recognition of the predominantly female readership's limited education, Hamilton provides many footnotes and other indicators

---

[25] Elizabeth Hamilton, *Translation of the Letters of a Hindoo Rajah* (London: J. Johnson, 1796) 1: 1.
[26] Benger 2: 40.
[27] See 30.

to identify the work or idea being satirized and in so doing guides the reader to her moral or didactic purpose. As the work is meant to correct or modify the reader's behaviour, she attempts to prevent the reader escaping into a fictional reality by continually moving her/him back and forth between fiction and reality, between polemic and novel. The reader, both *in* the novel and *of* the novel, learns that romances are quite political and that political works are quite romantic. Hamilton writes a cautionary tale to warn her readers about embracing New Philosophical ideas and automatically rejecting old systems of governance and faith. The reader discovers how religious faith and political associations have far-reaching and dramatic implications for both the individual and for society at large. The personal impact is noted by Elizabeth Benger who relates that Hamilton was highly gratified to receive a letter from a reader who "confessed she had detected herself in Bridgetina, and instantly abjured the follies and absurdities which created the resemblance."[28]

Hamilton presents her ideas on appropriate female behaviour, aspirations and articulations of those aspirations in *Memoirs of Modern Philosophers* through the three female protagonists: Julia Delmond, Bridgetina Botherim and Harriet Orwell. She uses these three young women to articulate contemporary concerns about female capabilities and potential through each woman's reading skills, treatment of family and community members, and response to New Philosophical ideas.

Hamilton is not alone in blaming the New Philosophy for many of the current evils, joining the ranks of contemporaries such as Edmund Burke and Hannah More who blamed the New Philosophy and its disciples for the prevalence of disruptive concepts of sexuality and intellectual equality. More states that philosophical arguments in the 1790s have taken a "more serious turn" because they "bring forward political as well as intellectual pretensions."[29] Hamilton, like many liberals and Loyalists, is extremely nervous about the threat posed by the New Philosophy because it promotes a radical reshaping of existing society, values, institutions and division of power through its insistence on the individual's rights and caprice. Hamilton argues that one does not live in isolation or merely for oneself but that one's life in entwined with those of others towards whom one has duties and responsibilities. For Hamilton the New or Modern Philosophy encourages selfish, romantically self-indulgent and obsessive behaviour. As she notes in *Memoirs of Modern Philosophers*, the New Philosophy is suited for "gaining proselytes among the young, the unthinking, and the uninformed."[30]

The first of Hamilton's three heroines, Captain Delmond's young and beautiful daughter Julia, is just such an unthinking and uninformed vic-

---

[28] Benger 1: 133.
[29] Hannah More, *Strictures on the Modern System of Female Education* 2 vols. (London: T. Cadell and W. Davies, 1799) 2: 21.
[30] Hamilton, *Memoirs*, below, 60.

tim. The reader learns that Julia is receptive to New Philosophical ideas because of her limited education and her father's foolish doting upon her. Captain Delmond, like his father before him, openly castigates the established church and its doctrines, believing "religion a very proper thing for the common people, who, not having the advantages of military discipline, required a parson with some notion of hell, instead of a cat-of-nine-tails, to keep them in awe."[31] His misplaced pride in Julia accounts for her unguided use of free time and choice of reading material. She joins the local group of New Philosophers whose readings and discussions convince her to elope with a fellow philosopher Vallaton in a bid to further the "general utility" and advance women's rights. Vallaton, the villain, is in fact a vagabond who masquerades as a philosopher when he "perceived how much it would be to his advantage."[32] Julia is seduced both by her undisciplined reading of and by Vallaton's wilful misinterpretation of New Philosophical works and novels such as Rousseau's *La Nouvelle Héloïse*. Hamilton shows how undisciplined reading prompts Julia to comprehend everything, whether her attempt to reunite General Villers and his wife with their long lost son or her interpretation of General Minden's proposal of marriage, as instances of parental tyranny, or her response to Vallaton's flights of philosophic reasoning as the plot of a romance. She is also ruined by her own desire to be radical. Julia impetuously elopes with Vallaton only to be abandoned when pregnant and destitute in London. She resurfaces in the Unmarried Mother's and Destitute's home, a repentant and new-born Christian with just enough time to convince Bridgetina of the folly of enacting New Philosophical ideas before she dies. On her death bed she explains, "it was my own pride, my own vanity, my own presumption, that were the real seducers that undid me"[33] since she wished to lead the vanguard of women as they broke the shackles of convention. As Hannah More explains in her *Strictures* "preposterous pains have been taken to excite in women an uneasy jealousy, that their talents are neither rewarded with public honours nor emoluments in life; nor with inscriptions, statues or mausoleums after death" when in reality "each sex has its proper excellences, which would be lost were they melted down into the common character by the fusion of the New Philosophy."[34] The popular Loyalist novelist Jane West is similarly strident. She believes that female inferiority makes women ideal targets for New Philosophical devotees in what she terms the Anti-Christian conspiracy in Britain: "Women are very seldom deeply versed in any branch of philosophy; and a smattering of science is extremely apt to generate that dependence upon second causes, which is one of the

---

[31] Hamilton, *Memoirs*, below, 78-79.
[32] Hamilton, *Memoirs*, below, 60.
[33] Hamilton, *Memoirs*, below, 383.
[34] More, *Strictures* 2: 38, 22.

strong-holds of deism in weak minds." Thus it is crucial to "imbu[e] the juvenile mind with a sense of the divine authority of scripture."[35]

Hamilton differs from Loyalist writers such as More and West in that she does not categorically dismiss all of Godwin's New Philosophy but rather the improper use to which the ideas have been put. She also takes a more tolerant position over the question of sexual indiscretions. For Loyalist writers such as Jane West transgressions of a sexually and hence political nature are irreversible—the woman must die in ignominy. Hamilton, however, toys with various schemes for reintroducing the repentant Julia into society. Social pressures, however, prove too problematic and important to be ignored or sidestepped by even one fallen individual. As Julia herself observes:

> Whether the unrelenting laws of society with regard to our sex are founded in justice or otherwise, it is not for me to determine. Happy they who submit without reluctance to their authority! But first to set them at defiance, and then under false pretenses to shrink from the penalty, what is this but to add hypocrisy to presumption—to add an unjustifiable (because deliberate crime) to an error, which perhaps may receive some mitigation on the score of human frailty.[36]

Somewhat reluctantly, Hamilton concedes that transgressors must be punished to prevent other individuals from disregarding the law—both legal and social.

Julia's behaviour is contrasted with that of the exemplary Harriet Orwell who is guided by her aunt and father, assumes numerous responsibilities in the home and community, is a careful, considered reader and a committed Christian. The reader learns that Harriet's learning and self improvement are acceptable and indeed to be encouraged since they are founded upon her religious faith. Harriet Orwell has strong affections but is "able to controul the feelings of her well-regulated mind."[37] Harriet's self-control and dutiful nature are firmly attributed to her education in religious principles, something Bridgetina and Julia lack. Harriet exhibits great self-restraint in all her actions, none so clearly as over her love for Henry Sydney. Unlike Julia and Bridgetina, who both indulge their passions, Harriet restrains herself since any connection with Henry while in his penurious state would only impede his career and probably lead to unhappiness. This self-restraint is finally rewarded by Hamilton through the offices of Mrs. Fielding who settles an income upon the couple after they have proven themselves admirably restrained and thoughtful.

The obvious parodic source for the third heroine—Bridgetina Botherim—is found in both the English-Jacobin writer Mary Hays's person

---

[35] Jane West, *Letters to a Young Lady* (London: Longman, 1806) 1: 359.
[36] Hamilton, *Memoirs*, below, 375.
[37] Hamilton, *Memoirs*, below, 151.

and in her work *Memoirs of Emma Courtney* (1796). Hays' novel intermingles Hays's own correspondence with William Frend and the philosopher William Godwin with the fictional life of Emma—an unconventional heroine who (recognizing the social and economic oppression facing women) pursues the hero Augustus Harley to London where she eventually offers herself to him outside of marriage. This work was viewed by the Loyalist camp with horror and disgust as it epitomized all the sexual promiscuity and female forwardness they feared resulted from adopting "revolutionary principles." Despite Hamilton's Christian avowal of tolerance and openness, she is bitingly cruel in her depiction of Bridgetina. Although Wollstonecraft is treated with respect (several characters discuss the merits of her *Vindication of the Rights of Woman*) Hays, through the crude caricature of Bridgetina, is contemptuously mocked. Hamilton endows Bridgetina with a squint, a craggy short stature and a mop of hair, all of which make her the laughing stock of most people she meets. Hays and Hamilton had been associates, but the latter's animosity apparent in *Memoirs of Modern Philosophers* was prompted by Hays's negative response to *Letters of Hindoo Rajah*. Hamilton wrote that Hays paid "a strange sort of compliment" to Godwin "in taking it for granted" that he was the chief object of attack in *Letters of a Hindoo Rajah* and "that it is impossible to laugh at any thing ridiculous without pointing at him."[38] Clearly Hamilton left nothing to chance in *Memoirs of Modern Philosophers* and had characters speak actual passages from both Godwin and Hays's works.

Bridgetina, like Julia Delmond, also joins the local philosophical sect and embraces New Philosophical ideas which justify her contemptuous treatment of her mother, prompt her to pursue her beloved to London, openly declare her love and spout Godwinianisms at every opportunity. Like Captain Delmond's misplaced pride in Julia, Mrs. Botherim's awe and admiration of Bridgetina's accomplishments prompt her to overlook her daughter's slovenly and rude behaviour. Although Bridgetina is an avid reader she lacks any powers of discrimination. We soon learn that while she has a good memory she is unable to discuss issues in her own words since she has no comprehension of what she has read. Bridgetina's parrot-like learning is exactly what critics argue results from educating females. Dr. Fordyce writes "I do not wish to see [the female world] abound with metaphysicians, historians, speculative philosophers, or Learned Ladies of any kind,"[39] while Vicesimus Knox suggests that females should confine their education to approved areas so that "attainments [should not] occasion contempt or neglect;" those "sullied by obtruding arrogance, by a masculine boldness, a critical severity, and an ill-timed and injudicious ostentation deserve contempt."[40] Knox uses the

---

[38] Letter, Elizabeth Hamilton to Mary Hays, 13 Mar. 1797; original in the Carl H. Pforzheimer Library; Qtd in Kelly, *Women, Writing and Revolution 1790-1827*, 143.
[39] Fordyce 2: 102-03.
[40] Vicesimus Knox, *Essays, Moral and Literary* (London: Dilly, 1778) 2: 21.

term "masculine boldness" as a derogatory description of a female who has overstepped the bounds of propriety in an attempt to enter the domain of masculine learning.

Hamilton concurs that such "erudition" is despicable but clearly differentiates between it and the self-improvement undertaken by women such as Harriet. Hamilton had ridiculed false learning in *Letters of a Hindoo Rajah* through the philosophizing female Miss Ardent. As the prototype of Bridgetina, Miss Ardent, who "shook hands with masculine firmness" and prided herself on her "affectation of originality of sentiment, and an intrepid singularity of conduct,"[41] also neglected her person and treated others with contempt.[42] In Bridgetina, Hamilton perfects the "masculine woman" who is "possessed by the metaphysical mania and influenced by [an] inordinate desire to distinguish herself among her companions by the disgusting affectation of superior knowledge."[43] As the Loyalist novelist West explains, the "masculine woman" usually appears as a "petticoat philosophist, who seeks for eminence and distinction in infidelity and scepticism, or in the equally monstrous extravagancies of German morality."[44]

Unlike a true reformer (of the Christian kind) Bridgetina's theoretical prowess does not translate into practice. Despite her protestations of solidarity with the oppressed classes she refuses to sit in the same room as Julia's faithful retainer Quinten, and treats the harvest workers and London servants with utter contempt. Bridgetina reads to impress others but with no real understanding or appreciation of what she has read. Her reading of philosophical works does not translate into action of an acceptable sort since she has no real comprehension of the theories of equality being advanced. Like Vallaton, Bridgetina uses the New Philosophy in a purely self-serving manner.

That reading in general, and not just of philosophical texts, is an important factor is evidenced by Hamilton having both Julia and Bridgetina read a volume of *La Nouvelle Héloïse*. As an impressionable female reader, Julia immediately casts Vallaton as St. Preux and herself as Julie—the misunderstood and persecuted lovers. However, to prevent the reader empathizing with such a fantasy Hamilton has Bridgetina perform the same mental trick. The latter cuts such a ridiculous figure as a lover that the reader, and Julia herself, are reminded of the fallacious nature of daydreaming and mistaking fiction for fact.[45] Indeed, it is both Bridgetina's

---

[41] Hamilton, *Letters of a Hindoo Rajah* 2: 101.
[42] Loyalist and Anti-Jacobin writers suggest that inappropriate knowledge fosters delusions of masculine understanding in certain females because of the "superficial nature" of their education, "which furnishes them with a false and low standard of intellectual excellence" (More, *Strictures* 2: 3).
[43] West, *Letters to a Young Lady* 1: 17-18.
[44] West, *Letters to a Young Lady* 1: 18.
[45] See Claire Grogan, "The Politics of Seduction in British Fiction of the 1790s: The Female Reader and Rousseau's *Julie, ou la Nouvelle Héloïse.*" *Eighteenth-Century Fiction* 11: 4 (July 1999).

unquestioning devotion to Rousseau and her unrequited, but persistent, love for Henry Sydney that provide the novel's comic content. Bridgetina's attempt to woo the reluctant Henry with talk of *La Nouvelle Héloïse* meets with little success. Her assertion that "the example of Eloisa will prove a model to her sex"[46] is rejoindered by the sage Mr. Sydney's comment, "the example of Eloisa! ... was she not a wanton baggage, who was got with child by her tutor?"[47]

Hamilton's juxtaposing of the three young women invites the reader to draw her own comparisons between the protagonists. The reader's involvement in assessing appropriate and inappropriate behaviour reflects Hamilton's belief that females should learn to think rather than just to obey—a sentiment which aligns her with English-Jacobin writer Wollstonecraft rather than Loyalist writers West or More.[48]

Hamilton does not restrict herself to these three young heroines to question appropriate reading habits, social conformity or religious adherence. Other characters, whose actions and stories are presented in a variety of ways, provide a political critique of upper-class decadence and middle-class complacency in *Memoirs of Modern Philosophers*. The reader learns about Dr. Orwell, Dr. Sydney, Mrs. Fielding, Captain Delmond and the villain Vallaton through inset narratives, and about Lady Villers and Quinten the retainer through briefer life synopses.

The different styles employed in these narratives point to Hamilton's awareness of her audience's taste and need for distracting amusement. In this manner she tries to avoid losing the reader through boringly didactic summaries or digressions. She laments that "So very few young people read with any other view but that of amusement, that the hope of being useful must be confined within very narrow limits."[49] However, she is clearly not providing simple distractions when she repeatedly draws attention to the stylistic choices available to the author:

> It is necessary to give the reader a previous introduction into [Mrs Fielding's] acquaintance. A variety of methods presents itself for this purpose. ... [A]nother present[s] itself, which, while it indulges the indolence of the writer, will be equally conducive to our purpose of instruction. This is no other than transcribing, for our reader's perusal, a letter written some time previous to the period to which we have brought our history, from Mr. Sydney to his son.[50]

---

[46] Hamilton, *Memoirs*, below, 100.
[47] Hamilton, *Memoirs*, below, 101.
[48] See Mary Wollstonecraft, *A Vindication of the Rights of Woman*, Ed. Carol H Poston. "The Prevailing Opinion of a Sexual Character Discussed" Ch. 11.
[49] Benger 2: 48.
[50] Hamilton, *Memoirs*, below, 240.

The third-person narratives of Vallaton, Captain Delmond and Lady Villers are presented by an omniscient narrator who provides accompanying critical assessment on a narrative that has already been judged. There is no room left for reader empathy or decision making. Hamilton's use of third-person narrative distances her work from the first-person narrative associated with English-Jacobin texts. Hamilton does however use the first person in Dr. Sydney's personal rendition of his earlier association with Mrs. Fielding, which is presented in two letters to his son Henry. The epistolary form invites a more intimate involvement on the part of the reader since letters allow room for reader participation, although the didactic import remains strong. The letter, however, allows the reader to vicariously enter and engage with the subject rather than just observe it from a distance. The reader assesses the material provided and comes to a conclusion, albeit guided by authorial tone and comment. This type of first person narrative is meant to be less self-indulgent and more educational than the first-person narratives readers would associate with Mary Wollstonecraft's *Maria: or the Wrongs of Woman* (1798) and Mary Hays's *Memoirs of Emma Courtney* (1796) because Hamilton's letters serve an overtly didactic purpose. Unlike Emma's narrative, these are not self-indulgent since self-interest is shown to be carefully subordinated to social, religious and familial responsibilities and duties. That Hamilton disapproves of such pro-revolutionary texts and styles is evident in her parodying of Hays's novel through the burlesque character Bridgetina Botherim's speech and actions.

Hamilton's observations are not restricted to the actions of the young but are also drawn from those of older characters. She portrays a selection of older women who also manifest various skills and/or foibles. Hamilton depicts strikingly independent, confident and intelligent women through Mrs. Martha Goodwin and Mrs. Fielding, both of whom highlight the possibility of life outside of marriage. They instruct the reader how to manage a home, to arrange finances to provide for the poor and to protect oneself from unforeseen mishaps. That Hamilton models these women on her own experiences is probable since, like Mrs. Fielding, she too became "an active assistant in the promotion of the House of Industry, at Edinburgh, a most useful establishment for the education of females of the lowest class."[51] Hamilton managed the Edinburgh House of Industry which was "instituted for the purpose of affording assistance to aged females of respectable character, when thrown out of employment, and of training the young to habits of industry and virtue."[52] Her fictional counterpart, Mrs. Fielding, is well-read, indepen-

---

[51] Anne Elwood, *Memoirs of The Literary Ladies of England* (London: Colburn, 1843) 119.

[52] Benger 1: 193-4. As Kelly notes, "the description of the Edinburgh House of Industry is a separately paginated four-page notice bound at the end of Hamilton's *Exercises in Religious Knowledge*, originally written for the inmates" (*Women Writing and Revolution 1790-1827*, 277).

dent, learned, erudite but not pretentious. In contrast, Bridgetina's mother, Mrs. Botherim, is a proud but uneconomical housekeeper of very limited intellect, while Julia's mother, Mrs. Delmond, is an impersonal and selfish mother whose petty jealousies prevent her taking a serious interest in her daughter's well-being. Mrs. Villers, herself "the illegitimate offspring of a subaltern [and] the maid servant," values her aristocratic status above everything else and organizes shallow, superficial social gatherings in which gossip and intrigue predominate. These are gatherings quite unlike those of Mrs. Fielding to which people come to share the "the refined delight arising from the communication of ideas, the collision of wit, and the instructive observations of genius."[53]

Hamilton's observations are not restricted to women; men manifest similar flaws. The reader learns how the foolish and irresponsible Mr. Gubbles neglects his shop and abandons his wife and children when he adopts the New Philosophical ideas, while Bridgetina's uncle, who monitors and invests her money, is criticised for being too business and money oriented. Mr. Glib is yet another greedy, selfish and crooked individual who uses the New Philosophy to further his own desires. Even Julia's father Captain Delmond, who is generally depicted quite favourably, falls victim to his own contempt of religion and misguided reading. While stationed in the north of England as a young military officer, Delmond occupied his time reading "ponderous volumes of romances" and works by "free-thinking philosophers" which ridiculed the Bible. He becomes an avowed romantic and elopes with his fellow captain's intended bride, duels and then spends ten years in Gibraltar. Another spell serving in the far East ruins his health and he returns to England to a disaffected wife and a beautiful daughter to whom he has given no religious or moral instruction, only to die of grief at her elopement and a realisation of his folly.

On the other hand, Hamilton provides admirable characters such as Dr. Orwell, Dr. Sydney and his son Henry Sydney who are all well-read, open-minded, compassionate and civil, but for whom moral conduct and religious faith are lode stars. The enormous range of characters depicted, and Hamilton's refusal to reinscribe gender stereotypes, encourages the reader to judge people by their actions rather than on the basis of their sex or class. The reader of *Memoirs of Modern Philosophers* learns that not all men are trustworthy and not all women are foolish and simple.

For Hamilton, true reform clearly lies through the old, but sadly misread or neglected system posited in the the Bible rather than through any new system of ideas as encapsulated in the New Philosophy. The Bible does, she accepts, require careful and judicious reading to be an enlightening text.

Memoirs of Modern Philosophers is an entertaining and engaging political satire that also deftly negotiates social decorum. It is an erudite work,

---

[53] Hamilton, *Memoirs*, below, 285.

Hamilton's broad reading being reflected in the large number of quotations from popular literary works which head each chapter or are alluded to in passing. The epigrams hint at the events to follow, guide the reader as to the appropriate response to these events, suggest cultural and political affiliations and reinforce the range of Hamilton's knowledge. Hamilton has obviously read Godwin, both his fiction and polemic, Wollstonecraft and Hays, as well as numerous poets, contemporary and classical. Her breadth of reading is also suggested by the references to current works such as François Vaillant's *Travels from the Cape of Good Hope into the Interior Parts of Africa.* While she cites actual passages from Vaillant, she also uses his work to tap into prevailing opinions about foreigners, Hottentots in particular, their primitive culture and current status as objects of medical and sexual curiosity, to pass censorious comment on the New Philosophers.

Hamilton's extensive reading distances her from Loyalists, male and female, who felt censorship or closely controlled reading was the best course of action to prevent the dissemination of revolutionary ideas. It is tempting to connect Hannah More's refusal to read Wollstonecraft's *Vindication of the Rights of Woman* (because she felt there was "something fantastic and absurd in the very title" and its "metaphysical jargon"[54]) with Hamilton's quip in a letter to Miss J— B— in 1809: "You know that the very word metaphysical operates on weak nerves exactly as the word *bugaboo* in an English, or *bogle* in a Scotch nursery."[55] Hamilton suggests, by example, that since such texts will not go away and cannot be controlled it is imperative to teach the young how to read them circumspectly. All these factors indicate the importance of reading in Hamilton's novel and the instrumental role that she felt improved reading would play in bringing about female advancements. As Hamilton notes in *Memoirs:*

> It is only by the love of reading that the evils resulting from associating with little minds can be counteracted. A lively imagination creates a sympathy with favourite authors, which gives to their sentiment the same power over the mind, as that possessed by an intimate and ever-present friend: and hence a taste for reading becomes to females of still greater importance than it is to men, or at least to men who have it in their power to choose their associates.[56]

Hamilton defines her own goal thus:

> The object, however, that I have chiefly in view, is to lead conscientious, but unthinking minds, to reflect on the nature and tendency of party spirit, in all its branches, civil and religious.[57]

---

[54] Qtd in Doris Stenton, *The English Woman in History* (London: Allen, 1957) 313.
[55] Benger 2: 104.
[56] Benger 2: 142.
[57] Letter to Miss J— B— 1809 (Benger 2: 108-09).

Hamilton noted with pride in late 1800 of *Memoirs of Modern Philosophers:* "A third edition is now printing, the second having been disposed of in less than two months."[58] Such a successful reception of her novel afforded Hamilton "a passport to fame and distinction"[59] after which she continued to write, but in a variety of genres. She wrote only one more novel, the extremely popular *Cottagers of Glenburnie,* but was increasingly recognized as a writer of religious and educational pieces: *Letters on Education* (1801), *Letters Addressed to the Daughter of a Nobleman* (1806), *Exercises in Religious Knowledge* (1809), *A Series of Popular Essays* (1813), *Hints Addressed to the Patrons and Directors of Schools* (1815). It was for her "promulgation of religious sentiment" that she received a pension from George III in 1804. She also wrote a hybrid scholarly/fictional history, *Memoirs of the Life of Agrippina, Wife of Germanicus* (1804). Increasingly incapacitated by her gout, Hamilton nevertheless managed to meet many other writers of the day, even visiting Maria Edgeworth in Edgeworthstown, Ireland, in 1813.

Hamilton's contribution to the world of literature was noted by her contemporaries as "not only correcting the vulgar prejudices against literary women ... but ... giving a new direction to the pursuits of her own sex, and ... extending the sphere of female usefulness."[60] Maria Edgeworth assessed Hamilton as

> an original, agreeable, and successful writer of fiction; but her claims to literary reputation as a philosophic, moral and religious author, are of a higher sort, and rest upon works of a more solid and durable nature. ... She does not aim at making women expert in the wordy war; nor does she teach them to astonish the unlearned by their acquaintance with the various vocabulary of metaphysical system-makers: Such jugglers' tricks she despised; but she has not, on the other hand, been deceived or overawed, by those who would represent the study of the human mind as one that tends to no practical purpose, and that is unfit and unsafe for her sex.[61]

Positioning *Memoirs of Modern Philosophers* in the context of the revolutionary debate of the 1790s reveals the important role fiction played in shaping the social, political and economic role of women in the next century. Recontextualisation of *Memoirs of Modern Philosophers* restores its topicality and uncovers a literary sophistication not otherwise present in our reading of it. Hamilton rejected political extremes and wished instead

---

[58] Benger 2: 20-21; "R" is Robinson her publisher.
[59] Benger 1: 132.
[60] Qtd in Introduction by Gina Luria, ed. *Memoirs of Modern Philosophers* (New York: Garland Press, 1974) 10.
[61] Benger 1: 210-11. Maria Edgeworth's correspondence to Hamilton has not survived and she refused permission for it to appear in Benger's *Memoirs.*

to advocate moderate, calm reforms (especially of female education), and to warn people away from an uncritical adherence to new political, philosophical or religious groups because of the harm she perceived they did to the individual and to the nation. She is a writer adept in broaching masculine topics to champion women's rights in a quietly, persistent manner. Hamilton would be highly gratified to see her work reappearing in print at the beginning of the twenty first century because of what it reveals to the modern reader about the historic moment, the importance of educating women as readers and as members of society, and as an example of a liberal woman writer's negotiation around social prescriptions about female writers and political subjects. Although Elizabeth Hamilton and her female contemporaries were denied the vote, *Memoirs of Modern Philosophers* is one striking example of how an intelligent woman could actively participate in revolutionary debate and influence a broad segment of the public.

Elizabeth Hamilton: A Brief Chronology

1758 Born on July 25th in Belfast, third child of Charles and Katherine (Mackay) Hamilton

1759 Father dies of typhus fever

1762 Elizabeth is sent to Stirling to be raised by the Marshalls (her father's sister and brother-in-law). Sister Katherine and brother Charles remain in Belfast with mother

1764 Elizabeth, uncle and aunt visit family in Belfast

1766 Elizabeth enters boarding school in Stirling. Accompanied by servant Isabel Irvine. Six days at school, one day home. Educated by male schoolmaster Mr. Manson—three hours daily tuition in French, drawing and dancing. Mother visits Elizabeth in Scotland

1767 Mother dies

1769 Ends formal schooling although receives further guidance in drawing and music. Extended visit to Edinburgh and Glasgow where she receives lessons from various masters—most notably Dr. Moyse, lecturer on experimental philosophy

1772 Charles obtains a cadetship in the East India Company and sails for India. Elizabeth and Marshalls move to cottage at Ingram's Crook, near Bannockburn, where Elizabeth lives until her uncle's death. Solitary existence encouraged her writing. Kept a journal "Highland Tour" which aunt sent to a provincial magazine. Surprise opportunity to visit her sister in Ireland for six months

1780 Sister marries Mr. Blake the younger of Oran Castle and visits Stirlingshire on his quitting the army. Mrs Marshall dies

1783 Seldom leaves uncle's side. Declines Charles's proposal that she visit India

1785 Anonymously contributes essay "Anticipation" to *The Lounger* (#46, 17 December)

1786 Three-week trip to Glasgow. Charles visits Scotland on December 20th on a five-year leave to complete translation of the *Hedaya*, or Code of Mussulman Laws. Charles visits Katherine in Dublin then returns with her to London where his *Historical Relation of the Origin, Progress, and Final Dissolution of the Government of the Rohilla Afghans in the Northern Provinces of Hindostan; Compiled from a Persian Manuscript and Other Original Papers* is published. Both then travel to Ingram's Crook

1788 Charles and Elizabeth travel to London. Socialize among the Asiatic Society members. Elizabeth returns to Ingram's Crook for the summer but Mr. Marshall dies from an epidemic complaint. Elizabeth returns to London where she spends the next two years with her sister and brother

1791 *The Hedaya, or Guide: a Commentary on the Mussleman Laws* published. Charles appointed British resident at Oudh in India at the Vizier's court and begins preparations for departure. Katherine returns to north of England and Elizabeth to Ingram's Crook. Charles briefly visits Ingram's Crook. Illness keeps him in London until spring. Plans to visit Lisbon with Katherine but becomes too ill. Elizabeth joins them in London mid December

1792 14th March Charles dies.—Buried at Bunhill Fields; monument erected at Belfast. Elizabeth and sister (now widowed) retire to Hadleigh in Suffolk, then to Sunning in Berkshire. Elizabeth begins work on the *Letters of a Hindoo Rajah*

1796 *Letters of a Hindoo Rajah* published. Katherine leaves for Ireland and Elizabeth commences work on next project. Moves to Gloucestershire but illness forces her to London to seek medical assistance. Suffers from gout, although taking waters at Bath restores use of her limbs. Sisters settle together in Bath. Elizabeth's health gradually declines

1800 *Memoirs of Modern Philosophers* published; passes through two further editions before end of the year. Begins work on *Letters on Education*

1801 *Letters on Education* published

1804 *Memoirs of the Life of Agrippina, Wife of Germanicus* published. Settles in Edinburgh. Spends six months in home of nobleman educating his family—which prompts her next publication. Receives a royal pension from George III for "promulgation of religious sentiment"

1806 *Letters, Addressed to the Daughter of a Nobleman, on the Formation of Religious and Moral Principle* published

1808 *Cottagers of Glenburnie: A Tale for the Farmer's Ingle-nook* published

1809 *Exercises in Religious Knowledge; for the Instruction of Young Persons* published

1813 *A Series of Popular Essays, Illustrative of Principles Essentially Connected with the Improvement of the Understanding, the Imagination, and the Heart* published. Spends three months in Ireland, during which time she visits Maria Edgeworth at Edgeworthstown

1815 *Hints Addressed to the Patrons and Directors of Schools* published

1816 Travels to Harrogate for her health in May but dies on 23rd July. Buried in Harrogate

1818 Elizabeth Benger publishes a biography of Hamilton which incorporates various letters and the beginnings of an autobiography; a revised second edition is published the following year

A Note on the Text

This text is based on the first edition published in 1800. A second edition appeared before the end of the year and a third early in 1801. The only substantive change between the first and subsequent editions is the advertisement in the third edition revealing Hamilton as the author (reproduced here). A fourth edition appeared in 1804. Apart from the long "s", which has been modernised, the idiosyncratic spelling and punctuation of Hamilton's work have been retained. In the few instances when changes have been made to avoid confusion, they are explained in an accompanying footnote.

Hamilton's notes, indicated by asterisks, are incorporated with the editorial notes at the foot of the page.

Advertisement to Third Edition 1801

Conscious how much the judgement of friends is liable to be influenced by partiality; and sensible, that where partiality cannot operate, prejudice against the known opinions, or even the *sex*, of a writer may unwittingly bias the reader's mind; the Author of the following Memoirs resolved to introduce the first edition under a signature evidently fictitious. The various authors to whom this work has been attributed, will probably thank her now for acknowledging its real parentage; while the several persons who have been pointed out, by the sagacity of different readers, as the original Julias, and Vallatons, and Bridgetinas, will forgive the candid declaration that must for ever deprive them of the honour so kindly conferred upon them by their *friends*.

To divert the languor of sickness in the seclusion of a country retirement, FANCY first sketched the portraits in question; which were gradually formed, by tracing the probable operation of certain principles upon certain characters; necessarily divesting these principles of the adventitious splendour they have received, from the elegance and pathos that distinguish the language and sentiments of authors by whom they have been chiefly promulgated. For the other characters that appear in the work, the Author does not acknowledge the same obligation to Fancy. The happy effects of piety and benevolence, of prudence, good sense, and moderation, she has had too many opportunities of contemplating in the circle of her own acquaintances, to be obliged to have recourse to imagination for their delineation. Imagination, indeed, gave the colouring, but the outlines were drawn by Truth.

To many of the author's friends it is well known, that above twelve months of severe indisposition occasioned a delay in the publication, which deprived the plan of the advantage of appearing entirely original. On a perusal of the works which appeared in the interim, apparently written under similar impressions, she, however, did not find her own ideas so much anticipated by any of them, as to induce her to suppress the present work, or even to make the smallest alteration in its contents. Her chief design in the publication is so fully explained in the Introduction to the first edition—that she thinks it proper to present it to the reader in its original dress.

BATH
Nov. 29, 1800

MEMOIRS
of
MODERN PHILOSOPHERS.

In three volumes.

Vol. I.

"Ridiculum acri
"Fortius et melius magnas plerumque secat res."
HOR.[1]

"Ridicule shall frequently prevail,
"And cut the knot, when graver reasons fail."
FRANCIS.

BATH, PRINTED BY R. CRUTWELL,
FOR
G.G. AND J. ROBINSON, PATER-NOSTER-ROW LONDON.
1800.

---

1 Horace, *Satires* 1.10.14.

TO

MR. ROBINSON,[2]

BOOKSELLER, PATER-NOSTER-ROW.

SIR,

HAVING been lately dragged to London on the business of my ward, who is now (thank heaven!) nearly of age, it was my first care to look out for a pleasant situation. For this purpose I repaired to Pater-noster-Row, that birthplace of the Muses, that fountain of learning from which the perennial stream of literature for ever flows. The very name of the place has, from my earliest years, inspired my veneration; and I do assure you, the thoughts of visiting it tended to reconcile me to the journey more than any other consideration. Well, sir, though I must confess the first aspect of the place did not altogether answer my expectations, (being in point of airiness somewhat more confined than I could have wished) I was fain to put up with the only lodgings that were vacant, which, though not over and above convenient, were rendered pleasant to me from the view my chamber-windows afforded me of the numerous store-houses of learning, by which I was on all sides surrounded. My heart glowed within me as I contemplated the stupendous proofs of human genius, piled up in the opposite shops, or carried through the streets. For the space of several hours I continued, without interruption, to contemplate the interesting scene. Some porters passed sinking under the load of new-bound quartos, which they were carrying to your shop, Mr. Robinson; and it is not to be expressed how much I envied the feelings of the author. "Oh, that I could write a book!" cried I. "But, alas! of what subject am I master? All my old notions are, I find, by the Reviews,[3] quite exploded. Of the new fangled ones that are now in fashion, I can make nothing; and notwithstanding all I have heard to the contrary, I do suppose it is necessary to understand something of the subject one writes about. With regard to a work of imagination, that is quite out of the question; for I never could invent a lie in my life, not

---

[2] George Robinson, a London publisher, was renowned for the large proportion of English-Jacobin works that his firm published. Fictional works include Mary Hays's *Memoirs of Emma Courtney* (1796), William Godwin's *St. Leon* (1799) and the second and subsequent editions of *Caleb Williams*. Non-fictional works include Godwin's *Enquiry Concerning the Principles of Political Justice* (1793), *The Enquirer* (1797) and Mary Wollstonecraft's *Posthumous Works* (1798).

[3] For a comprehensive summary of contemporary reviews, periodicals, miscellanies and magazines see Robert D. Mayo, *The English Novel in the Magazines 1740-1815*, 159-358.

even to save me from being whipt at school, how then should I make one long enough to fill a volume?"

Just at this moment, and as I was about giving up all hopes of ever seeing my name in print, an incident occurred which saved me from despair.

A sudden and tremendous noise over my head interrupted my reverie, and drew me to the place from whence it proceeded, in order to learn the cause. Fire and robbery, the two evils which I had been taught to dread, were immediately present to my imagination; and greatly was I relieved on finding that the noise, which had so much alarmed me, proceeded only from the mistress of the house and her maid, who were both at work in cleaning down the garret-stairs. The former, whose voice was raised to what a musical friend of mine calls the *scolding pitch*, was severely chiding the latter for the time she had taken to sweep out the garret. The maid, indignant of rebuke, answered not in words but in deeds; making the dust fly before her broom in such a manner, as compelled me to meditate a quick retreat. Just as I turned round for that purpose, a manuscript, which the girl in her fury had twirled from the top of the stairs, fell at my feet. I instantly picked it up, and as soon as I could make myself heard, enquired of my landlady whether she knew any thing of its contents.

"Contents, sir," answered she, "it is the farthest thing in the world from contents, I assure you. I never had no contents about it. It is some of the scribbles of a scrubby fellor of an author, who, after lodging in my atticks for seven weeks, died all at once one morning when no one ever thought of such a thing; for though it is plain he knew all along of his being in a dying way himself, yet he was so good-humoured, and so cheerful, that no one would ever have suspected him."

'And pray had he no friend, no physician? I am afraid he must have been in great poverty.'

"In great poverty, sure enough!" returned my landlady, "that I knows to my cost; for the first five weeks he paid me regularly to a day, as often as the week was up; but for the two last weeks I never seed the colour of his money. Howsomever, as he was a very gentleman-like man, and so civil-spoken, I thought there was no fears of his behaving ungenteelly at the last, and so I gave myself no concern, till one morning that he desired me to speak with him, when, on going up to his room, I saw him, lack-a-day, so pale, and so altered! his voice, too, so low and changed, that I could hardly hear him. On seeing how I was astonished he smiled, and beckoning me to sit down, said he was sorry that it was not then in his power to pay me the small sum he was in my debt, but that in such a drawer I should find what would be sufficient to pay for that, as well as for the expences of his funeral; and what was over he begged me to accept of as a compensation for the trouble he had given me. He died in about half an hour after, and, to be sure, I thought I should have been quite made up with what he had left me, when on rummaging the drawers, I found all that load of writing; but on shewing it to a very learned gentlemen, a friend of mine, one who helps to make the almanacks, he laughed at me, and said it was a fair take-in, for that it was all stuff and good for nothing; and so it has been tossing about ever since."

This account of the author increased my curiosity to such a pitch, that I did not hesitate a moment upon making a purchase of the manuscript; and having fully satisfied my landlady, who willingly resigned to me her whole right and title to it, I retired to my apartment to examine its contents.

The first fifty pages having been torn off to kindle the morning fires, made a mighty chasm in the work; but the remaining fragment appeared to me so worthy of being laid before the publick, that I quickly conceived the design of becoming its editor. Not having the presumption to depend entirely on my own judgment in an affair of such importance, I had recourse to the advice of my friends, and accordingly submitted my manuscript to the perusal of several criticks of both sexes, to whom, through the favour of a certain learned acquaintance, I had the good fortune to be introduced. Alas! Sir, I now found myself more at a loss than ever. The opinions I received were so various, so contradictory, so opposite to each other, that I was quite bewildered, and should have dropt all thoughts of proceeding in the publication, had not my resolution been re-animated by the following letter, which I received from a gentleman of great worth and knowledge, to whom I had freely communicated all the objections of the criticks, and by whose opinion I determined finally to abide.

"SIR,

"ON a careful perusal of the whole of your manuscript, (for I pretend not to decide on the merit of a work from glancing over a few scattered passages) it appears to me not only praise-worthy in the design, which is evidently that of supporting the cause of religion and virtue, but unexceptionable in the means of executing this design; or at least less exceptionable than some other recent publications, which, like it, have avowedly been written in opposition to the opinions generally known by the name of the *New Philosophy*.[4]

"To impute evil intention to the author of every speculative opinion that has an evil tendency, is equally illiberal and unjust; but to expose that tendency to the unsuspicious, and to point it out to the unwary, is an office of charity, not only innocent, but meritorious. From the use that is made by Vallaton of some of the opinions promulgated in Mr. Godwin's Political Justice,[5] it appears to me to have been the intention of your

---

[4] A term to denote English supporters of the French revolutionary principles of equality, fraternity and liberty.
[5] William Godwin, *Enquiry Concerning Political Justice and its Influence on Modern Morals and Happiness* (1793).

author not to pass an indiscriminate censure on that ingenious, and in many parts admirable, performance, but to expose the dangerous tendency of those parts of his theory which might, by a bad man, be converted into an engine of mischief, and be made the means of ensnaring innocence and virtue.

"Of the keen weapon of ridicule, it must be confessed, your author has not been sparing. Were there the least appearance of its having been pointed by personal prejudice towards any individual, I should certainly advise you to consign the work to everlasting oblivion; but it is opinions, not persons, at which the shafts of ridicule are in the present work directed.

"Where'er the pow'r of ridicule displays
"Her quaint-ey'd visage, some incongruous form,
"Some stubborn dissonance of things combin'd,
"Strikes on the quick observer."
                    Akenside's *Pleasures of the Imagination*.[6]

"As the objections, which you tell me have been made to this part of the work by your friends, cannot be more fully obviated than by the author I have just quoted, I shall beg leave to transcribe the whole passage.

"Ask we, for what fair end th' Almighty Sire
"In mortal bosoms wakes this gay contempt,
"These grateful stings of laughter, from disgust
"Educing pleasure? *Wherefore, but to aid*
"*The tardy steps of Reason*, and at once,
"By this prompt impulse, urge us to depress
"The giddy aims of folly? Though the light
"Of Truth, slow-dawning on th' enquiring mind,
"At length unfolds, through many a subtle tie,
"How these uncouth disorders end at last
"In publick evil! Yet benignant Heav'n,
"Conscious how dim the dawn of Truth appears
"To thousands; conscious what a scanty space
"From labours and from care the wider lot
"Of humble life affords for studious thought
"To scan the maze of Nature; therefore stamp'd
"The glaring scenes with characters of scorn
"As broad, as obvious to the passing clown,
"As to the letter'd sage's curious eye."[7]

"The ridiculous point of view in which some of the opinions conveyed to the young and unthinking through the medium of philosophi-

---

[6] Mark Akenside, *The Pleasures of the Imagination* Bk II, 530-33.
[7] Mark Akenside, *The Pleasures of Imagination* Bk III, 259-77.

cal novels, is exhibited in the character of Bridgetina, appears to me as an excellent antidote to the poison; calculated to make an impression upon those to whom serious disquisitions would have been addressed in vain. Upon the whole, I do not hesitate to give it as my opinion, that in publishing this work, you will deserve the thanks of society.

"I am, Sir, &c."

Thus encouraged, I am resolved to submit it to the world; and that it may come forth with every advantage, I entrust it to your care; at the same time submitting it to your judgment, whether this letter (on which I have bestowed uncommon pains) may not appear as an Introduction.

With much impatience for the first proof-sheet, I remain,

Esteemed Sir,

Your most obedient servant,

GEOFFRY JARVIS.

---

*"The pudding is very good," replied Mr. Mapple, "and does great honour to my cousin Biddy, who, I dare say, is the maker."

'I have often told you,' cried the young lady in a resentful accent, 'that my name is not Biddy. Will you never learn to call me Bridgetina?'

"Well, well, Biddy, or Biddytiny, or what you please," rejoined the old gentlemen; "though, in my opinion, the world went as well when people were contented with the names that were given them by their godfathers and godmothers in their baptism. Bridget is a good christian name, and I pray the Lord make you as good a woman as your aunt Bridget, from whom you had it. She too was an excellent hand at making a plum-pudding."

'A pudding!' repeated Bridgetina, reddening with anger, 'I do assure you, sir, you are very much mistaken, if you think that I employ my time in such a manner.'

"And pray, my little cousin, how do you contrive to employ it better?"

To this question Miss Bridgetina disdaining reply, cast such a look of contempt upon her reverend relative, as but for the circumstance of the squint, which we have already noticed, must infallibly have discomfited him. But as her eyes, while in the act of darting indignant fire in his face, had every appearance of being directed towards the door, the poor gentleman escaped unhurt.

Mrs. Botherim now thought it time to astonish her old friend, by a discovery of the wonderful accomplishments of her daughter.

---

* Since the manuscript was partially destroyed by the maid, it begins in the middle of Chap V. See above, 35.

"You do not know, sir," she exultingly exclaimed, "that Biddy is a great scholar! You will find, if you converse with her a little, that she is far too learned to trouble herself about doing any thing useful. Do, Bridgetina, my dear, talk to your cousin a little about the *cowsation*, and *perfebility*, and all them there things as Mr. Glib and you are so often upon. You have no ideer what a scholar she is," continued the fond mother, again addressing herself to Mr. Mapple, "she has read every book in the circulating library, and Mr. Glib declares she knows them better than he does himself."

'Indeed, mamma, but I do no such thing,' cried Bridgetina, pettishly; 'do you think I would take the trouble of going through all the dry stuff in Mr. Glib's collection—history and travels, sermons and matters of fact? I hope I have a better taste! You know very well I never read any thing but novels and metaphysics.'

"Novels and metaphysics!" repeated her kinsman, casting up his eyes, "*O tempora! O mores!*"[8]

'Moses, sir,' rejoined the young lady, 'if indeed such a man as Moses ever existed, was a very ignorant person. His energies were cramped by superstition, and the belief of a God, which is well known to be the grand obstacle to perfectibility.'

"My poor child!" said Mr. Mapple, in a tone of compassion mixed with astonishment, "where hast thou got all this?"

'I told you so!' cried the delighted mother, 'I knew you had no ideer of her larning. She puts every one as visits us to a none-plush. The Doctor himself had as lief go a mile out of his road, as enter into an argument with her.'

"Truly, I make no doubt of it," returned Mr. Mapple, drily, "I am quite of his way of thinking; and as you have probably some preparations to make for the company you expect this evening, shall take my leave. You know I ride but slowly, and I should like to reach ***** before it grows dark."

'Nay, do pray now, sir, have a little more talk with Biddy before you go; for as to preparing for the company, I does all these there sort of things with my own hands. For though Nancy is a tolerable good cook in a plain way, she has no notion of nick-nacks. I am sure, if any one knew what a trouble it is for me to give suppers! Indeed, Mr. Mapple, you have no ideer. There had I this morning to make the tarts, and the custards, aye, and the pudding too, which you ate at dinner, and praised so much. And now I have only to put on the best covers on the drawing-room chairs, and to unpaper the fire-screens, and to fix the candles on the sconces, and to prepare my daughter's things; so that I shall soon be ready; meanwhile you may chat with Biddy—it will do your heart good to hear her talk."

Mr. Mapple seemed to be of a different opinion; and declining to enter into any controversy with an adversary whose prowess was so highly vaunted, he immediately took his leave.

---

[8] the times, the customs!

CHAP. VI.

Distrustful Sense with modest caution speaks,
It still looks home, and short excursions makes.
But rattling *Nonsense* in full vollies breaks;
And never shock'd, and never turn'd aside,
Bursts out resistless with a thund'ring tide.[9]

AS the principal families in the parish continued the same attentions to the widow of their late rector, which they had paid her as his wife, it will be concluded, to a certainty, by those who know any thing of the world, that she was left in possession of affluence.

It was not, however, to the extent of her fortune, so much as to the exertion of her talents, that Mrs. Botherim stood indebted for the civilities of her richer neighbours.

Whatever idea the reader may have formed of the negative strength of her intellects, she had sufficient sagacity to discover, that when she could no longer give dinner for dinner, and supper for supper, a compleat termination would, in the minds of many of her dear friends in the neighbourhood, be given to her existence. Effectually to keep herself alive in their remembrance, was a point which she might literally be said to *labour*. It required the incessant exertion of all the economy, and all the notability, of which she was mistress: nor would these alone have been sufficient, if they had not been assisted by the perfect knowledge of a science, which produced effects more delightful to many of her guests than all "Philosophy e'er taught."[10]

Though the science of cookery was the only one with which Mrs. Botherim was acquainted, it may be doubted whether it did not sometimes produce attractions as powerful as the metaphysical knowledge of her daughter.

Even Mr. Myope himself has been suspected of this preference; and has been actually known to leave his free-will opponent in possession of the last word, from the *necessity*[11] he felt himself under of devouring the good things set before him on Mrs. Botherim's table. Never shall I forget the eulogium I once heard him make on one of the good lady's currant

---

[9] Alexander Pope, *Essay on Criticism* Part III, 626-630.

[10] Dr. Samuel Johnson praised his acquaintance Elizabeth Carter for her scholarly achievements but still asserted "My old friend Mrs. Carter could make a pudding as well as translate Epictetus from the Greek and work a handkerchief as well as compose a poem" (James Boswell, *The Life of Samuel Johnson*, ed. G. Birkbeck Hill. Oxford: Oxford University Press, 1887) 1: 122 n.4.

[11] According to Godwin's philosophy of Necessitarianism, "Man is in no case, strictly speaking, the beginner of any event or series of events that takes place in the Universe, but only the vehicle through which certain antecedents operate, which antecedents, if he were supposed not to exist, would cease to have that operation" (*Political Justice*, Bk IV, ch. viii). See Appendix A.

tarts: a tart which, as he judiciously observed, could never have been so nicely sweetened, *if Alexander the Great had not set fire to the palace of Persepolis.*★[12]

To praise her cookery, or to praise her daughter, was at all times the most direct road to Mrs. Botherim's heart. When the tribute of flattery was on either of these subjects withheld, she quickly discerned the motive, and consoled herself by observing, "that it was better to be *envied* than pitied."

That she and her daughter were the objects of envy to many of her neighbours, she could not doubt. The rector's family, in particular, had given her many strong proofs of being possessed of this hateful passion: even the reverend gentleman himself had oftener than once dropt some hints about the needless expence of formal entertainments among friends and neighbours; and it was certain, that neither he, nor his sister, nor his daughters, appeared to enjoy half so much satisfaction at one of her feasts, as at the simple fare which was set before them when on a chance visit. The same *envious* disposition it was, which, in Mrs. Botherim's opinion, made them not only avoid the subject of metaphysics, on which her daughter could so far outshine them, but seem in pain when it was mentioned.

Of the visitors expected at the conclusion of the last chapter, the ladies of the family we have just mentioned, accompanied by the daughter of the dissenting clergy-man,[13] were the first that arrived. They were seated in the drawing-room before either Mrs. or Miss Botherim were ready to make their appearance.

At length the mother came curtseying into the room, and while she stroked down the obstinate folds of her well-starched apron, made a thousand apologies for not being sooner prepared for their reception. She was followed by Bridgetina, whose stiff turban and gaudy ribbons put the homely plainness of her countenance in the most conspicuous point of view.

Neither her dress nor person were, however, in any danger of criticism from the party present. They perceived not the prodigious fund of merriment that might have been derived from her wearing a blue gown and yellow slippers; a circumstance, which would have afforded a week's gigling to many misses, was altogether lost upon them. Their stupid insensibility to the pleasure of personal ridicule,

---

[12] ★See Godwin's Pol. Ins. vol. i. p.161.★ Godwin, *Political Justice* Bk I, ch. ii "History of Political Society".

[13] Dissenters was a blanket term for Presbyterians, Baptists, Congregationalists and other Protestants dissenting from and failing to conform to the Restored Church of England in 1662. Until 1828, Dissenters, along with Roman Catholics, were penalised by the Test and Corporation Acts passed by the Cavalier government in 1673. The Acts required holders of public office to receive the Anglican sacrament and reject the doctrine of transubstantiation.

will, no doubt, impress many readers with an unfavourable idea of their understanding. To the misfortune of never having been at a boarding-school, may perhaps be attributed this seeming want of discernment to those deformities of person, and incongruities of dress, to which so many ladies, and so many beaux, confine their whole stock of observation.

The compliments of both mother and daughter were received by these ladies with that unaffected complacency, which they had been taught to feel for the virtues of the heart. They were not insensible to the foibles or the peculiarities of either; but if those of Mrs. Botherim sometimes excited a smile, it was a smile unaccompanied by malice, and void of the ill-natured wish of exposing the object that excited it to the ridicule of others. What were their feelings with regard to Bridgetina, may, perhaps, appear here-after.

Personages of greater consequence now call for our attention. A loud knocking at the door announces the arrival of Sir Anthony Aldgate, his lady, and daughter.

Of her relationship to this great man Mrs. Botherim was not a little proud. She exulted in the honour of an annual visit from him, which he regularly paid on his way to Buxton every summer: and though the trouble and expense it cost him, to come so many miles out of the direct road, was always set forth in such terms, as might have disgusted a more fastidious mind; it acted upon Mrs. Botherim's exactly as it was intended, and only served to enhance the value of the visit. Mrs. Botherim was herself the daughter of a tradesman in the city, and had early acquired such a profound respect for wealth, that the sight of that sort of intoxication, produced by a full purse on a narrow heart and shallow understanding, was not so disgusting to her feelings, as it probably was to those of some of her present guests.

The two Mr. Gubbles', father and son, with their respective ladies, next appeared, and were formally introduced to Sir Anthony and his lady. In Miss Aldgate, the younger Mrs. Gubbles soon discovered a school-mate, and although the daughter of the city knight appeared not very willing to recognize the wife of the apothecary as an acquaintance, the claims of the latter were brought forward in too forcible a manner to be resisted.

"Locka me!" cried the bride of young Gubbles, "Miss Jenny Aldgate, I declare! Who would have thought of seeing you here? And you are not married yet! Well! I declare it is so odd that I should get married before you! Is n't it?"

Miss Aldgate bit her lips, while she declared, 'how vastly glad she was to see her old companion, and to wish her joy.' Without listening to her compliments, Mrs. Gubbles continued, "All the ladies at Mrs. Nab's school were so surprised when I went to see them, you have no ideer. Locka me! Do you remember our governess? How we quizz'd[14]

---

[14] Quizzes were odd-looking people or things, objects of ridicule.

her! I never think of our stealing the nice chicken from the fire, which she was having roasted for her own supper, without being ready to die with laughing. I told it all to Mr. Gubbles, and it so diverted him! And then the going over the garden-wall to get prog[15] at the pastry-cook's shop: was n't it excellent? And do you remember"—

Here followed a whisper, which called up something very like a blush in the cheeks of Miss Aldgate. Her friend proceeded—

"Oh, I assure you, upon my honour, I never told *that* to any one;" casting a significant glance at her husband. "I would not tell such a thing to any one for the world. But, locka me! I wager you won't guess what is become of Miss Bellfield, that was thought to be such a fortune: do guess, now, what is become of her: I lay that you don't?"

'Perhaps she is married,' said Miss Aldgate.

"She married, poor thing!" replied Mrs. Gubbles, "Locka me! She is only one of Mrs. Nab's teachers: is n't it very droll now, is n't it?"

'It is what I never should have thought of to be sure,' returned Miss Aldgate: 'though, as I heard pa say, her father was ruined. I suppose, poor thing, she was glad to do it for bread.'

"Aye, poor thing! you can't think how I feel for her! But," lowering her tone, "did you ever see such a fright as that Miss Botherim? I declare she is quite a *Guy*!"★[16]

'O dear,' cried Miss Aldgate, giggling, 'how can you be so droll? I protest you will make me die with laughing, you are so very comical." Here both ladies, holding up their fans before their faces, continued for some time tittering a duet, to the great edification of the Miss Orwells, who were placed beside them; but who, not having been at Mrs. Nab's school, were not, in boarding-school phraseology, to be *taken into the baby-house*.[17]

The entrance of their father, accompanied by his reverend friend Mr. Sydney, would, they hoped, give a more general turn to the conversation; but in this they were disappointed.

The disappointment of these young ladies arose, like most other disappointments, from the fallacy of their expectations. So ignorant were they of the world, as to imagine that those who were best qualified to speak, should, by the suffrage of the company, be called upon to speak the

---

[15] Food, victuals, provender—food generally, "grub".

[16] ★Alluding, as we suppose, to a grotesque effigy of Guy Faux, which is usually carried through the streets of London, by the rabble, on the anniversary of the Gunpowder-plot.★ Guy Fawkes night is celebrated every November 5th when his effigy is burnt on a bonfire amid fireworks to celebrate the discovery of the Popish Gunpowder plot to blow up the houses of Parliament in 1605. Godwin refers to a co-conspirator Everard Digby in his *Political Justice* (Bk II, ch. iv, "Of Personal Virtue and Duty").

[17] Like many female educationalists, Hamilton criticises boarding schools for their poor standards and unhealthy practices. See for example Wollstonecraft's chapter on "Boarding Schools" in *Thoughts on the Education of Daughters* (1787).

most. They did not know, that while those whose knowledge enables them to instruct, or whose genius qualifies them to enlighten, every circle in which they are placed, are restrained by the modesty and diffidence which are the usual concomitants of real merit, from taking the lead in conversation, it is without ceremony assumed by the self-assured, the vain, and the ignorant.

The characters of Doctor Orwell and Mr. Sydney were in many respects so strikingly similar, that the outlines might justly be described in the same terms. Both were benevolent, pious, unaffected, and sincere. The minds of neither were narrowed by party zeal, nor heated by prejudice. To this liberal turn of thinking were they indebted for the blessing of mutual friendship: a friendship, which received no interruption from the difference of their opinions in some speculative points, as each, conscious of the integrity that governed his own breast, gave credit for an equal degree of integrity to the other. Both delighted in literature and science; but in these, as in other pursuits, each took the walk most agreeable to his own peculiar taste, without contesting for its absolute superiority over that which was chosen by his friend. General literature, and the belles lettres, had greater attractions for Doctor Orwell, than the abstruser studies which engaged the attention of Mr. Sydney. The amusement of the one was gardening; of the other, botany: but the chief business of both was to promote the happiness of their fellow-creatures.

No sooner had these reverend gentlemen taken their seats, than they were addressed by Sir Anthony upon the late fall of stocks, a subject in which he well knew himself to be the only person in company at all interested. The confessed ignorance of his audience inspired him with an unusual flow of eloquence. He considered the portentous event in every point of view in which it could possibly be placed. He compared it with similar occurrences of former years, and recited, with great exactness, all the observations he had then made; observations which never failed to be verified by the event, so as to redound to the honour of his own sagacity.

Various were the effects produced by his discourse on the minds of his hearers.

When he spake of his mighty bargains of twenty thousand scrip,[18] and thirty thousand consols,[19] purchased in the course of one morning, his importance seemed to rise so high, in the estimation of the Messrs. Gubbles, that they exulted in the honour of being in company with so great a man.

"Bless me!" thought Mrs. Botherim, "with so many thousands of them there stocks, (if so be as how, that they are all like so many bank-notes) one might keep as good a table as my lord-mayor himself!"

---

[18] Fractional paper currency, a certificate of indebtedness issued as currency or in lieu of money.

[19] Abbreviation of Consolidated Annuities—government securities.

'Ah!' thought the lovely Harriet Orwell, a sweet blush rising with the thought, and playing for a moment on her beauteous cheek, "Ah! that such a fortune were in the possession of the noblehearted Henry Sydney! To what exalted purposes would he employ such a fund of superfluous wealth! How many would he make happy! But would Harriet Orwell be then the object of his attention?'

The deep sigh that followed was drowned in the sharp tones of the elder Mrs. Gubbles, who, impatient of the knight's long harangue upon a subject in which she could bear no share, had broken the painful restraint of silence; and in a hoarse whisper was giving to Lady Aldgate a minute and circumstantial detail of an intrigue, long suspected, but only that morning *brought to light*, betwixt the shopman and her favourite housemaid.

Long as was this history, and many as were the *says I's*, and *says she's*, which added to its length, when it was finished, Mrs. Gubbles found the knight just where she had left him.

"I tell you, sir," said he to Mr. Sydney, whose eye he at that moment caught, "I tell you, sir, it is the very best stock in which you can possibly purchase, and I will undertake to prove it to you in a moment. Supposing, I say, supposing now you to have only ten thousand pounds."

'Indeed, sir,' said Mr. Sydney, 'I never was, nor ever expect to be, worth the tenth part of the sum in my life.'

"Eh!" rejoined the knight, "not worth a thousand pounds! Pray, what did you begin with?"

'I began the world,' replied Mr. Sydney, 'with an education, which taught me that a man's riches consisteth not in the abundance which he possesseth—that he only is truly affluent, whose treasures lie where moths cannot corrupt, nor thieves break through and steal; and that a man worth fifty thousand pounds, if wanting these, is poor indeed!'

"Very true, very true, indeed," rejoined Sir Anthony, "no man can be called rich, till he is worth a plum."[20]

'There is one advantage,' resumed Mr. Sydney, 'attendant upon riches, which a good Providence has no doubt bestowed as a compensation for the degradation to which the glorious powers of intellect are forced to stoop in its acquirement, as well as for the cares, anxieties, and temptations, which inevitably accompany its possession; I need not name this advantage to you, sir,' continued the reverend old gentleman, 'but I think, if you had been witness to the scene which my friend Dr. Orwell and I have just come from, you would have declared you never had a more glorious opportunity of enjoying it.'

The eyes of Dr. Orwell glistened with pleasure, at the successful method taken by his friend to introduce a subject on which his thoughts

---

[20] The sum of 100,000 (slang).

incessantly dwelt, and which Mrs. Botherim's frequent praises of the knight's liberality made him anxious to bring forward.

"It was a scene of extreme misery, indeed!" cried he; "happy must be the person who could effectually relieve so worthy a family from at least one moiety of their present distress."

The knight took snuff, which occasioned a long fit of sneezing; at the conclusion of which, Dr. Orwell repeated the last sentence he had uttered, in a still more impressive manner, adding, "the struggle they have made has been noble, their resignation has been exemplary, and unbounded, I am sure, would be their gratitude."

'Gratitude, did you say, sir?' cried Miss Bridgetina, who had been all this while sitting screwed up for a metaphysical argument, 'Give me leave to tell you, sir, there is nothing so immoral as gratitude. It is, as Mr. Myope says, a vice, or rather a mistake, peculiar to minds who have imbibed certain prejudices, but which none who have energy to rise above them, are ever known to practice; it is, in short, the greatest obstacle to perfectability.[21] Whoever knew Mr. Myope grateful for any favour that he ever received?"

Just as Bridgetina had concluded this speech, which, though new to great part of the company, had been delivered in exactly the same words at least seventeen times before, a sort of general alarm was produced by the sudden entrance of Mr. Glib; but this is a subject well deserving a new chapter.

CHAP. VII.

"Spectatum admissi risum teneatis."

HOR. *ARS POET*.[22]

MR. Glib, who, like a true philosopher, despised all ceremony, took not the least notice either of Mrs. Botherim or her guests, but skipping at once up to Bridgetina, "Good news!" cried he, "citizen[23] Miss. Glorious news! We shall have rare talking now! There is Mr. Myope, and the Goddess of Reason, and Mr. Vallaton, all come down upon the top of the heavy coach.[24] There they are at my house taking a snack, all as hungry as so many cormorants. I was in such a hurry to tell you, that I left the

---

[21] See Godwin's *Political Justice* Bk II, ch. ii, "Of Justice".

[22] Horace, *Ars Poetica*: "Being admitted to the sight could you, my friends, restrain your laughter?"

[23] Hamilton has her modern philosophers ape the language of the French revolutionary *sans-culottes* whose hatred of the aristocracy or wealthy and their fierce devotion to equality led them to say "citoyen" instead of "monsieur" and to use the familiar "tu" instead of "vous".

[24] A stage wagon for the conveyance of goods.

shop to take care of itself, and off I ran. Just as I was at the door, up comes a wench for the patent styptic[25] for Mr. Plane, the carpenter, who, she said, had met with a doleful accident—but would not go back. Bid him exert his energies, my dear, said I: that's it! energies do all![26] And off I came, as you see, without gartering my stockings.[27] But never mind, come along. The Goddess of Reason longs to give you the fraternal embrace;[28] faith, and a comely wench she is, that's certain. But let us be off, I have not a moment to spare, and I can't go without you."

'Mr. Myope! and the Goddess of Reason! and Mr. Vallaton! and all!' exclaimed Bridgetina, 'you make me too happy! Lead me to the enlightened groupe,' continued she, rising from her chair, or rather getting off it, (for as she was rather taller sitting than standing, she could not well be said *to rise* when she assumed the latter posture) 'Lead me to the enlightened groupe; I would not lose a moment of their converse for the world; the injury would be incalculable.'

Mrs. Botherim observing her daughter's motion, laid down the teapot to expostulate.

"You would not go now, sure, my dear?" cried she; "you cannot possibly think of leaving this here company, who are all of our own inwiting: and who, though they may not be quite so larned in that there philosophy, seeing that it is but a new sort of a thing, as a body may say; yet you know, my dear, it would be one of the most rudest things in the world to run away from them."

To this expostulation, which was made in a low voice, Bridgetina replied aloud—

'And do you think I am now *at liberty* to remain here? I wonder, mamma, how you can speak so ridiculously? Have I not told you again and again, that I am under *the necessity* of preferring the motive that is most preferable?[29] The company, if they are not very ignorant indeed, must

---

[25] A medicant that arrests haemorrhage—a substance having the power of contracting organic tissue.
[26] See Godwin's *Political Justice* Bk IV, ch. viii, "Inferences from the Doctrine of Necessity". See Appendix A.
[27] Philosophers are often depicted as unkempt although it is a more serious failing in female philosophers. Of the five examples of female readers Vicesimus Knox presents in his *Essays, Moral and Literary* (1778) it is Sempronia who, after "ten years of magazine reading", feels "herself emancipated from the usual decorums of external forms" and completely disregards her personal appearance. Knox presents the shocking picture of Sempronia "with slipshod shoes, no apron, matted hair, a dirty face, cap awry, and fingers begrimed with ink" (2: 18).
[28] Hamilton cynically suggests that certain *citoyens* adopted "revolutionary" behaviour because it dispensed with established protocol and allowed improper acts of familiarity, such as embracing.
[29] According to Godwin's *Political Justice* each individual was "under *the necessity* of preferring the motive that is most preferable" (Bk IV, ch. viii, "Inferences from the Doctrine of Necessity"). See Appendix A.

know that my going instantly to Mr. Glib's is a link in the glorious chain of causation, generated in eternity, and which binds me now to act exactly as I do.' So saying, she put her arm in Mr. Glib's, and hurried off as fast as the shortness of her legs would permit.

Her conductor, soon tired of the slow pace at which she appeared to him to walk, though she had actually hopp'd and run her very best to keep up with him, proposed leaving her at the first turning, while he ran up to Captain Delmond's for Miss Julia, whose presence he knew was expected with much impatience by some of the party at his house.

He could not have left the hapless maiden at a more unlucky moment. She had not advanced many steps, till her passage was opposed by a mighty torrent, vulgarly called a kennel,[30] which was now swelled to an unusual size by the washing out of the shambles, it being market-day. While she stood meditating on the brink of this by no means pellucid stream, a sudden gust of wind whirled off the high-raised turban, and with it, O luckless destiny! went the flowing honours of her head. The stiff ringlets so well pomatumed,[31] and so nicely powdered, which Mrs. Botherim had with her own hands so carefully pinned on, together with the huge knots of many coloured ribbons; all, all were hurried down the black bosom of the remorseless stream!

"Smoke the lady's wig!"★[32] called out an unlucky boy to his companions, who instantly set up such a shout of laughter, that the discomfited Bridgetina, regardless of the danger she encountered, and forgetful of the irremediable ruin of her yellow slippers, dashed into the muddy torrent, which, in spite of many opposing obstacles, she made shift to waddle through. Arrived at Mr. Glib's, she slipt in through the shop and back-parlour to the kitchen; but there she found only the three children, busily employed in picking the bones that had been sent out upon the stranger's plates. She begged the eldest boy to go into the parlour for his mother: "No, but I wont though," returned the little half-naked urchin, "I would as soon go to church." She attempted to coax him, but in vain. At length her voice was heard by Mrs. Glib, who, coming into the kitchen, was soon informed of the dismal plight of Bridgetina, which she relieved as far as possible, by a necessary change of apparel; and having pinned up the petticoats to prevent their trailing on the ground, for Mrs.

---

[30] The surface drain of a street, a gutter.
[31] From Pomatum—a pomade. A scented ointment (in which apples are said to have been originally an ingredient) for application to the skin; used especially for the skin of the head and for dressing the hair.
[32] ★at the time the above was written, the author had probably no idea that wigs were so soon to become a reigning fashion amongst his fair country-women. He, poor man, would most likely have deemed it a slander upon the taste and understanding of the ladies of England—to suppose it in the power of *fashion* to introduce a custom so odious and absurd!★

Glib was rather above the middle size, she conducted her into the parlour.

Miss Botherim was received by Mr. Myope, and Mr. Vallaton, in a manner sufficiently cordial: each of them taking a hand conducted her up to the Goddess of Reason,[33] who was lolling in the easy chair, caressing that favourite monkey who acted such a conspicuous part at the Apotheosis of her Goddessship at Paris, as hath been already related in the third chapter of these memoirs.[34] Placing her companion upon the table, she rose to embrace the pupil of her dear Myope; but on observing the grotesque figure that was presented to her, she hesitated.

Mr. Pug was not quite so scrupulous, he without ceremony sprang forward, and clasping his paws round the neck of Bridgetina, gave her the fraternal embrace in due form; and then putting out his chin, chattered in her face in such a manner, that poor Miss Botherim, who was not accustomed to this sort of jargon, uttered a scream of terror.

It was with some difficulty that the Goddess of Reason prevailed upon Mr. Pug to quit his hold. While she was coaxing him for that purpose, Mr. Myope, provoked at the obstinacy of the little animal, seized his paw on purpose to force him to relinquish his grasp, which Mr. Pug, being an avowed enemy to the system of coercion, resented upon the finger of the philosopher by his teeth.

"D— ye!" cried the serene inculcator of non-resistance, "you little devil! If I don't break every bone in your body for this!"

'Ah! de poor little angel!' exclaimed the Goddess of Reason, hugging her little favourite close to her bosom, 'Has he frightened oo, lovey, has he? but oo sant be hurt, ittle dear! oo sant.'

"You are insufferably provoking," retorted Myope; "but don't think that the little devil shall escape a beating for this. He has bit my finger to the very bone!"

'Well,' returned the Goddess of Reason, 'and how could *pauvre cher* help dat? Had he no de motive?'

'The citizen Goddess is in the right,' said Bridgetina. 'As justly might you punish the knife for cutting your finger, as the monkey for biting it; since, according to you own sublime system, they are instruments equally passive.'*[35]

---

[33] The Festival of Reason, celebrated on 10 November 1793 (20 brum II), formed part of the new revolutionary year. In it Notre-Dame was renamed the "Temple of Reason" and the Goddess of Reason (played by Citizenness Maillard of the Paris Opera) appeared before assembled crowds. Reportedly, she "wore a long white dress, sat still in an impressive and graceful posture that commanded respect" (*Chronicle of the French Revolution*, Longman, 1989, 383). See note 50.

[34] The Memoirs actually begin mid-way through chapter v.

[35] *See Godwin's Pol. Justice, vol. i. b. 3d.* Godwin notes in *Political Justice* that "a knife is as capable as a man of being employed in purposes of utility; and the one is no more free than the other as to its employment" (Bk IV, ch. viii). See Appendix A.

"D— their passiveness," cried Myope in encreased agony, while Mrs. Glib applied some Fryer's Balsam[36] to the wound, "d— their passiveness: I tell you, I believe I shall lose my finger; I never felt such pain in my life."

"Exert your energies, my dear citizen," cried Mr. Glib, who had just entered, "exert your energies, my dear. That's it! energies do all! Cure your finger in a twinkling. Energies would make a man of the monkey himself in a fortnight."

The wound being now bound up, and the pain a little abated, Mr. Myope did exert his energies so far as to resume some degree of philosophical composure.

Not so Mr. Vallaton. Having twice changed his seat to different corners of the room, through the restlessness of impatience; he again, from the same impulse, drew near Mr. Glib, to re-question him concerning Julia; and was receiving from him, for the third time, a full and compleat recital of all that she had said to him, when the door opened, and Julia herself, the charming Julia, appeared.

Never did she look more lovely. The small straw hat which was carelessly tied under her chin with a bow of pink ribbons, had been so far driven back by the wind, as to display the auburn ringlets that in profusion played upon her lovely cheeks; those cheeks, where the animated bloom of nature set all poetical comparison at defiance. Mr. Vallaton was the last person to whom she addressed herself; but the blush that overspread her countenance, plainly denoted that he was not the most indifferent to her heart. Mr. Vallaton likewise reddened; but who, so little skilled in physiognomy[37] as not to have perceived, in the different shades of the colour that overspread each countenance, the difference of the sensation by which it was produced? Whilst the pleasure of beholding the object of an innocent affection heightened the glow in the cheek of modesty, and sweetly sparkled in the eye; the passions that flushed the countenance of the deep designer, were evidently of far grosser birth.

The fraternal embrace (that laudable institution, and most excellent contrivance for banishing all reserve betwixt the sexes) being over, Mr. Vallaton began to complain, in exaggerated terms, of the length of time she had kept him in suspense about her coming.

'I could not get away sooner, indeed,' cried Julia, eager to justify herself from the charge of unkindness. 'You know,' continued she, 'the general bad state of my father's health; but he has been indisposed even more than usual for this last fortnight: and when he is ill, nothing appears to soothe his pain so much as my reading to him; and knowing the pleasure it affords him, I cannot possibly be so undutiful as to deprive him of it.'

---

[36] Tincture of benzoin compound used as an application for ulcers and wounds; also inhaled and used internally as an expectorant.

[37] The judging of a person's nature by his/her features.

"Duty!" repeated Mr. Vallaton, "How can a mind so enlightened as Julia's talk of duty, that bugbear of the ignorant? I would almost as soon hear you talk of gratitude."

'Indeed,' answered Julia, 'I cannot help thinking that there is some regard due to duty. You know how kind my father has ever been to me. My mother, too; whose very soul seems wrapt up in me, who knows no pleasure but in promoting mine. It is possible that I do not owe them some duty? Gratitude you have convinced me is out of the question; but indeed I cannot help thinking that there is in this case something due to duty.'

"And is this," retorted Mr. Vallaton, in a chiding tone, "is this all the progress you have made in the new philosophy?*[38] Do you not know, that duty is an expression merely implying the mode in which any being may be best employed for the general good? And how, I pray you, does your humouring these old people conduce to that great purpose? Ah, Julia! there are other methods in which you might employ your time far more beneficially."

"Truth," said Mr. Myope, who had been attentively listening to their conversation, "truth, fair citizen, obliges me to declare, that Mr. Vallaton is in the right. We are not, you must remember, connected merely with one or two percipient beings, but with a society, a nation, and in some respects with the whole family of mankind. To esteem any individual above his deserts, because he is in some manner related to us, or has been in any wise serviceable in promoting our happiness, is the most flagrant injustice.[39] What magic is there in the word *my*, to overturn the decision of everlasting truth? Did the obligations, as you call them, conferred upon you by your parents, originate in the conviction of your being a being of more worth and importance than any other young female of their acquaintance? If they did not, they were founded in injustice, and therefore immoral; and whatever is so, your judgment should contemn."

---

[38] *The frequent plagiarisms of our author have been particularly objected to by some of my learned friends; who informed me, that by perusing the works of Mr. Godwin, and some of his disciples, I should be enabled to detect the stolen passages, which it would be but honest to restore to the right owner. Alas! they knew not what a heavy task they imposed on me. If I have failed in its execution, I humbly hope Mr. Godwin and his friends will accept of this apology; and while they recognize, in the speeches of Mr. Vallaton, the expressions they have themselves made use of, that they will have the goodness to forgive me, for not having always correctly pointed out the page from whence they have been taken.—Editor*

[39] See Godwin's *Political Justice* Bk II, ch. i, "Principles of Society" which describes how the correct moral response to a burning building containing the archbishop of Cambray, Fénelon, and his chambermaid "who might be my wife or mother" would be to save Fénelon as the "preferable" and most useful of the two. This example prompted criticism such that Godwin modified it in later editions to be Fénelon and his valet. See Appendix A.

"Yes," resumed Vallaton, "and as to your regard for them, philosophy should teach you to consider only—how can these old people benefit society? What can they do for the general good? And then placing beside them some of those whose extensive faculties, whose great powers enable them to perform the glorious task of enlightening the world; say, whether justice, pure unadulterated justice, will not point out where the preference ought to fall?"

'Well!' rejoined Julia, 'I declare I never thought of it in this light before. Every new proof of affection which I received from my father and mother, has always so endeared them to my heart, that I have thought, if I could lay down my life for them, it would be too little for all their goodness to me.'

"How unworthy of the enlightened mind of Julia is such a sentiment!" exclaimed Vallaton. "But I hope you will soon get the better of these remains of prejudice, and in ardent desire for the general good, lose this confined *individuality* of affection."

'Indeed I shall never lose my affection for my parents,' returned Julia; 'I should hate myself if I did.'

Mr. Vallaton, afraid of pushing the matter too far, changed the discourse; but in every subject that was introduced, artfully contrived to bring in such allusions to the purpose of his argument, as he thought best calculated to work on the ardent imagination of his fair and unsuspecting pupil.

CHAP. VIII.

"But some there are who deem themselves most free,
"When they, within this gross and visible sphere,
"Chain down the winged thought; scoffing ascent,
"Proud in their meanness; and themselves they cheat
"With noisy emptiness of learned phrase."
SOUTHEY.[40]

IN the sketch we presented to our readers, of the principal incidents which marked the life of Mr. Myope, we entered into a sort of promise to furnish a similar degree of information concerning his friend and associate, Mr. Vallaton.

As we hold every engagement of this nature sacred, and as it is probable that a more convenient opportunity than the present may not occur for discharging our obligation, we shall, without further loss of time, proceed to gratify the curiosity which we make no doubt we have excited.

Who were the parents of this illustrious hero, it is probable the most accurate research could not have ascertained; not that we shall take upon

---

[40] not found.

us to affirm that such research was ever made; it is more probable, that the discovery was left to that chance which is so obliging to the foundling hero of every novel. Similar as were the circumstances of Mr. Vallaton's birth, in point of obscurity, to that of the great men, whose lives and adventures have employed the pens of so many eminent writers, philosophers and sempstresses, authors by profession, ladies of quality, and milliners at their leisure hours; it was attended by some peculiarities, a relation of which will sufficiently exculpate us from the charge of plagiarism.

A woman who lodged in one of the subterraneous abodes, vulgarly denominated cellars, in a little alley of St. Giles's, was called his mammy; and to her, upon pain of whipping, he delivered all the halfpence which his infant importunity had extorted from the passengers in the street; but this woman, even at the foot of the gallows, denied being the mother of *the funny vagabond*, as her little charge was commonly called. To her instructions, however, was he indebted for the first rudiments of his education; and it is but justice to his early genius to observe, that there never was an apter scholar.

At six years old he could, with wonderful adroitness, adapt his tale so as best to work upon the feelings of his auditors. Sometimes, in a pitiful and whining tone, he would beg 'for God's sake, a single halfpenny to buy a bit of bread for six of them, who had not broke their fast to-day.'

One passenger he would follow with clamorous importunity for the length of a street. Another, from whose aspect he expected better things, he would attack with a tale of sorrow; his father had then a broken leg, and his mother was just that morning brought to-bed of twins; a story which he told so well, and with such apparent simplicity, that it more than once produced a sixpence. In this way were the talents of our hero employed till his ninth year, when the fatal exit of his mammy left him at his own disposal.

During the last weeks of the life of his benefactress, he so improved by the conversation of her fellow prisoners, that there were few of the choicest secrets in the science of pilfering, of which he did not acquire some idea; of all the more common modes of exercising the profession he became perfect master. Being thus initiated in the theory, we make no doubt that he would soon have become an adept in the practice, had not the last moments of his mammy produced a certain feeling of terror, which so forcibly operated upon his mind, as to deter him from accepting the overtures of a gang of thieves, who had conceived a just opinion of his talents.

That most great men have had their weaknesses, is an observation, which, however trite it may appear, is nevertheless founded in truth. Let not, then, our hero be derided for *his*; since it must be acknowledged, that many have trembled at phantoms less formidable than the gallows.

Whether the native strength of his mind might not have at length enabled him to conquer the dread of an evil from which he daily saw so many adventurers escape, and which he knew to be most despised by those on whom it was most likely to fall, we cannot take it upon us to determine. Before the power of existing circumstances had directed his energies into this channel, an incident occurred, which probably changed the colour of his future destiny.

While employed in sweeping the crossing, opposite the door of a charitable lady, in the neighbourhood of Bloomsbury-square,[41] he observed a squirrel make its escape from the house; and seeing two or three servants immediately run after it, judged that something might be got by recovering the fugitive. He accordingly engaged in the chace, and being either the most active, or the most zealous, of those who were employed in the pursuit, easily outstripped them all, and had the honour of securing the little runaway, who revenged the loss of liberty by biting the hand of its enslaver. Notwithstanding the pain occasioned by the wound, the little fellow bravely kept hold of his adversary, and returned with him in triumph to his mistress.

The good lady, delighted at the restoration of her favourite, demanded the name of his preserver. 'The boys calls me *the funny vagabond*,' replied he, 'and Ise never answers to no other name.'

"And where do your father and mother live?" enquired the lady.

'Ise have got no fathers nor mothers,' returned he, beginning to whimper.

"Poor thing!" said the lady, "and were you never at school?" The negative to this question, and the apparent wretchedness of the little object, so wrought upon the compassionate heart of this good woman, that she immediately conceived the intention of taking him under her protection. He was accordingly cloathed, and put to school by the name of *Alphonse Vallaton*; for so the good lady, who was a great reader of novels, chose to construe the appellation of *funny vagabond*, which, though probably but a nick-name, was all that he had any remembrance of possessing.

If our hero's progress in literature did not keep pace with his adroitness in other pursuits, yet even here he found apparent smartness an imposing substitute for more solid understanding. So plausibly could he retail scraps of the lessons of others, that with all, but the master, he passed for a promising scholar; and the master had something else to do than to attend to the real progress of a boy who was indebted to the support of charity. When, at the desire of her lady, the housekeeper would sometimes condescend to listen to the young Alphonso, while he read to her a lesson in his school-book, she acknowledged herself astonished at the manner in which he acquitted himself. He did not then (as a boy of inferior genius in the same circumstances certainly would have done) proceed to spelling and putting together, but went boldly on without stop or hesitation, so artfully manag-

---

[41] A fashionable area of central London later associated with the Bloomsbury group of Virginia Woolf, Leonard Woolf, Vanessa Bell, Lytton Strachey and Leslie Stephen.

ing the tones of his voice, as to remove all suspicion of deceit. When memory failed, invention was always at hand to supply the deficiency.

Indeed the wonderful dexterity with which he brought these powers of the mind to contribute to each other's assistance, was, through life, one of the most conspicuous as well as most useful of our hero's accomplishments.

At twelve years old being, by the report of the housekeeper, which was corroborated by the testimony of his schoolmaster, qualified to read, write, and cast accounts, he was taken from school, and promoted to the employment of footman's assistant. Here every talent that he had received from nature, every habit that he had acquired among the companions of his early life, were placed in a soil suited to their expansion and improvement. Here that inventive faculty, which not only furnished him with a ready excuse for every fault he himself committed, but which was ever at the service of his friends, found daily opportunities of exercise. Nor was it in words alone that his superior genius was displayed. Each of his fellow-servants received, in their separate departments, convincing proofs of his abilities. To John, his immediate superintendent, he quickly endeared himself, by the dexterity with which he assisted him to carry off a greater quantity of wine from the cellar and the sideboard, than he had ever before ventured to appropriate to his own use. By the cook, his knowledge in the art of making up accounts was put in a continual state of requisition. So acutely did he perceive where the additional charge could best be made, that while her bills had the appearance of being less extravagant, they were actually more productive to her than ever. The coachman likewise experienced the benefit of his good offices, in a more advantageous disposal of the oats bought for his horses; one half of which he now contrived to sell for little less than half of what they had cost his mistress. In short, during the two years of our hero's abode in this family, the system of peculation was so compleatly organized, that it is thought to have given the first hint to Mr. Myope of his notion of perfectibility.[42]

Here we think it is necessary to stop, and to enter a caveat against any invidious application of our account of the above transactions. For which purpose we do most solemnly declare and aver, that we did not mean to insinuate the most distant allusions to the practices of any man, or bodies of men, in any public office, or department of the state, in this or another country; and particularly beg we may not be understood as intending any thing in the least disrespectful to those gentlemen who are called "*servants of the public*," either in this or the sister kingdom. With which asseveration of the purity of our intentions, we shall conclude the chapter.

---

[42] Mr. Myope is taken to be a caricature of William Godwin.

CHAP. IX.

"Ha! soft! 'twas but a dream,
"But then so terrible it shakes my soul:
"Cold drops of sweat hang on my trembling flesh;
"My blood grows chilly, and I freeze with horror."
SHAKESPEARE.[43]

THAT "fortune favours the brave,"[44] is a remark almost proverbial; but, alas! the truth of the observation is not always justified by experience. The most shining abilities are not at all times crowned with equal success: and in the warfare of life, there are some contingencies placed beyond the reach of human foresight to prevent, of human vigilance to elude.

While our hero was flourishing the pride and darling of the kitchen, an event was ripening in the womb of fate, which threatened to deprive him of all the comforts he there so liberally enjoyed.

The suspicions of his mistress, with regard to the depredations on her wine cellar, were at length aroused. They were communicated to a friend, and this friend, who possessed talents for circumventing fraud, and detecting villainy, far beyond what the good lady herself could boast, laid such a train as, at the moment least suspected, produced a full and complete discovery. As the false keys were found in the possession of our hero, his fellowservants thought to screen themselves by throwing all the blame on him, and with one voice voted his impeachment. The young gentleman did not hesitate to recriminate, and brought such convincing proofs of the knavery of his accusers, as the friend of the lady wisely observed, left her no choice but to *dismiss them all*.

In the benignity of his patroness, however, our hero still found a powerful advocate; which, in spite of the remonstrances of her friend, prevented her from throwing destitute upon the world, a creature she had once taken under her protection. Instead, therefore, of dismissing him with those to whose bad example she attributed all his share of guilt, she resolved to expose him no more to similar temptations. She desired him to choose a trade for his future support, and, in consequence of his preference, had him bound to a hair-dresser; taking upon herself to pay the customary premium, and to provide him with clothes during the period of his apprenticeship.

In the dexterous management of the comb, and the curling irons, our hero soon excelled; nor in the more subtle and recondite arts of his new

---

[43] cf: Shakespeare, *Richard III* V. 2. in the exchange between Richard and the ghost: "Have mercy, Jesu! Soft! I did but dream/.../Cold fearful drops stand on my trembling flesh."

[44] Terence (c190-159 BC), "Fortis fortuna adiuvat", *Phormio* 203.

profession did he less ably distinguish himself. In the latter part of the above account, we are, doubtless, anticipated by the judgment of the reader, which will at once conclude, that a proficient in lying, would soon be an adept in flattery. With such accomplishments he could not possibly fail of becoming a favourite with the ladies. In fact, his services were in such request, that long before the expiration of his apprenticeship, the house of his master attained celebrity with the fair sex, from the name of Vallaton.

During this period, the amours of our hero would, of themselves, be sufficient to fill a volume; and much do we wish it were in our power to gratify the laudable curiosity of our reader with a circumstantial and minute detail of this part of his history. Convinced as we are, from authority the most respectable, that it is from works like these the modern philosopher seeks the materials with which he builds his system of the human mind, we feel distressed at withholding from him information so desirable as that which we certainly have it in our power to bestow. But, alas! in spite of all our efforts, we find ourselves still so much the slaves of a certain weakness, called *delicacy*, as to be withheld from the description.

However derogatory the above confession may be to our fame, we are happy to learn, that the world is not likely to lose any thing by our infirmity. A full and complete account of the life and atchievements of our hero being now preparing for the press by one of our *female philosophers*, who will, no doubt, amply fill up every chasm, which the weakness above alluded to has forced us to make. To return to our narrative.

It was not in the favour of the ladies alone, that the young Vallaton found means to ingratiate himself; nor was it to them that his attentions were exclusively confined. In a certain three-penny spouting club,[45] his oratorical talents had already been so conspicuously displayed, as to obtain the unbounded applause of all the apprentices, journeymen, and shop-sweepers, who were there assembled. They did more; they attracted the notice of a gentleman who was particularly desirous of being considered *the patron of genius*: and from him our hero received such infor-

---

[45] Sarcastic reference to clubs such as the Society for Constitutional Information, the Constitutional Society and the London Corresponding Society, which encouraged political discussions, promoted ideas of reform amongst working-class men and facilitated the exchange of ideas and agendas with other like-minded clubs throughout Britain. Thomas Hardy, a Scottish shoemaker, founded the London Corresponding Society in January 1792 when he invited thirteen artisan friends to meet and discuss "parliamentary reform". The society's object was to "enlighten the people, to show the people the reason, the ground of all their sufferings" and membership was set at a penny a week. The London Corresponding Society expanded rapidly and within six months had a membership of 2,000, reaching a peak of 30,000 in 1795. Literary members included such dissenters as John Thewall, Horne Tooke and Thomas Holcroft. Loyalists despised these associations because they helped disseminate revolutionary ideas.

mation, with regard to some speculative points, as in some degree obviated the inconvenience to which he was exposed by his own consummate ignorance.

He soon had his ambition gratified by a little circle of applauders, who received, without comment or contradiction, whatever opinions he chose to advance. In short, he soon became the oracle of his district, and who has not observed with what despotic sway these oracles preside in the circle that acknowledges their supremacy? The subjects, over whom Vallaton began his reign, were distinguished by one uniform sentiment of enmity towards religion and religionists of all denominations. His towering genius quickly discerned, that by advancing one step beyond what any of his contemporary oracles had ventured to soar, he should infallibly procure for himself the most enviable distinction. He, therefore, boldly professed himself an ATHEIST.

To account for this wonderful display of mental energy, let it be remembered, that our hero enjoyed advantages from his early education, equal to any that the most enlightened philosopher has ventured to prescribe.

He reached his ninth year without having even heard of a GOD, but through the medium of blasphemy; and the words "God have mercy on your soul," pronounced by the judge in giving sentence on his mammy, was the first expression that conveyed to his mind any sort of idea of a future state. It is true that, by the directions of his patroness, he had been taught to repeat the creed, the catechism, and the Lord's-prayer; but in the repetition, not a single idea obtruded itself upon his mind, that could tend to injure it by any religious prejudice or impression whatever. The value of these manifest advantages we leave it to our philosophical readers to calculate; it is our business to point out the effects.

The breast of our hero now glowed with an ambition, which not all the praises bestowed upon his pretty taste as a *friseur*, had power to gratify.

The applause he had met with as an orator, enflamed his desire to figure as an author. To the uninitiated in the art of book-making, such a design, in a person of our hero's slender stock of information, may, perhaps, appear temerarious and absurd. To those who are better acquainted with such matters, a sufficient number of precedents will occur to exculpate Mr. Vallaton from the charge of singularity.

As it fell to the lot of the writer of these memoirs to correct the orthography and grammar of the volume of metaphysical essays, which was the first production of his pen, he may, perhaps, be supposed to arrogate to himself some of the merit of its success; and will, therefore, pass it over in silence.

Whatever reception this production met with from the world, it appears to have effected a compleat revolution in its author's views. For the pen, the comb, and the curling-irons, were from thenceforth forsaken; and the task of adorning the heads of his fair country-women gave place to the more dignified employment of enlightening their understandings. In which of the occupations, whether as an author or a friseur, our hero was most conducive to the real benefit of society, it may perhaps be difficult to determine.

To enlarge the sphere of his utility, Mr. Vallaton thought it necessary to have recourse to politics, and took upon himself (for we never heard that it was conferred upon him by the public) the appellation of *Vallaton, the patriot.*[46]

Should the reader be inclined to suppose, that the patriotism of Vallaton bore any resemblance to that which has appeared in some distinguished characters of our own and former days, he will labour under an egregious mistake.

To that generous and disinterested love of liberty, which glowed in the breasts of a Russel[47] and a Sydney;[48] to that zeal for the glory, and jealousy for the honour, of his country, which animated a Chatham;[49] or to the effect of all these principles, as they appear combined, invigorated, and improved in the capacious minds of some distinguished characters of our own day, our hero was a perfect stranger. The only shape in which patriotism ever appeared to the mind of Vallaton, was in that of a ladder, by the assistance of which, he might be enabled to climb a few steps higher on the hill of fame. But, alas! his courage by no means kept pace with his ambition. At the very second step in his career he stumbled. A threatened prosecution for sedition struck such terror to his heart, that he resolved to quit the kingdom, and hastened to communicate his intentions to the only friend, on whom, in such a juncture, he could depend for support or assistance.

This gentleman, whom we have already mentioned as the patron of his rising genius, and from whom he had already received many pecuniary obligations, cordially entered into his views; and told him that he would most cheerfully bear his expences to Paris, provided he took charge of a sum of money, which he greatly wished to convey to a

---

[46] Sarcastic reference to the fact that non-titled commoners assumed revolutionary titles despite their professed hatred of hereditary titles.

[47] The Russells were a great English Whig house of earls and dukes of Bedford who rose under the favour of Henry VIII. The allusion is most likely to John Russell (1710-71) who opposed Sir Robert Walpole as a recognised leader of the Whigs, was Lord-Lieutenant of Ireland in the Duke of Devonshire's administration and lord high constable at the coronation in 1760.

[48] Algernon Sidney, the seventeenth-century nobleman, commonwealth man, and martyr to court government and religious persecution, who remained a hero for eighteenth-century Dissenters and who was often cited in the 1790s as a model for modern patriots (Caroline Robbins, *The Eighteenth Century Commonwealthman*, repr. New York 1968, 46).

[49] Either William Pitt, the Elder, 1st Earl of Chatham or his son John, 2nd Earl of Chatham, 1st Lord of the Admiralty in 1788.

brother then residing in that city. To this proposal Vallaton gave a cheerful consent, and having so artfully concealed the seven hundred guineas committed to his care, as to avoid detection, set out upon his journey. The route he was obliged to take, though circuitous, was safe; so that without material accident or interruption, he, in less than a fortnight, reached the French capital.

The first public ceremony to which he was a witness, was the Apotheosis of the Goddess of Reason;[50] where, as has been already related in the second chapter of these memoirs, he met with Mr. Myope. The circumstances of their meeting, together with all the events of that memorable day, have there been given as such full length, that we shall not weary the reader by a repetition; suffice to say, that the friendly behaviour of Mr. Myope, upon that occasion, seemed to excite in the breast of Vallaton feelings of the most lively gratitude. He was profuse in his acknowledgments, and having formerly known Myope in the character of an itinerant preacher, he took care to season his speeches with such pious phrases, concerning his wonderful deliverance, as he thought would be pleasing to the ears of his benefactor.

Mr. Myope quickly convinced him of his mistake. He informed him of his having become a convert to the new philosophy; and by the enthusiastic warmth of his eulogium, convinced him, that if he wished to ingratiate himself in his affection, he could not take a more effectual method than by espousing the doctrines he had embraced.

Had Mr. Myope continued a religionist, it is difficult to say whether the complaisance of Vallaton would have been able to carry him so far as to profess himself a proselyte to his opinions. For though the speculative points that had successively excited the zealous support of that doctrinal Proteus, had little or no connection with that religion which "purifies the heart;" they were all attended with the inconveniency of being attached to certain notions of a Supreme Being,[51] and a future state, which it was by no means agreeable to our hero to take into his account.

The new opinions embraced by Mr. Myope, were happily free from this encumbrance. They were, moreover, possessed of an advantage

---

[50] Part of the dechristianisation campaign in France saw the introduction of a new revolutionary calendar in 1792 and all churches in Paris ordered closed in November 1793. Instead the Festival of Reason was celebrated on 10 November 1793 (20 brum II) in which Notre-Dame was renamed the "Temple of Reason". See note 33.

[51] Robespierre, who loathed the dechristianisation campaign of the *sans culottes,* partly on religious grounds and partly because it upset Catholics and created enemies of the revolution, attempted to unite all Frenchmen under a new religion called the Cult of the Supreme Being. He persuaded the convention to accept this cult in a decree of 7 May 1794 (18 flor II) and the Festival of the Supreme Being was held in Paris, 8 June 1794 (20 prair II), staged by the artist Jacques Louis David and presided over by Robespierre.

which, to a person of Mr. Vallaton's education, gave them a manifest superiority over such doctrines as require the trouble of study, or stand in need of the support of knowledge.

Vallaton quickly perceived how much it would be for his advantage, to become the strenuous advocate of a system which nature had so eminently qualified him to support: a system, which, soaring to a higher region than experience has ever reached, might be despised by the wise, but could never be refuted by the learned. Nor were these the only advantages attendant upon the new theory. While a shallow plausibility rendered it admirably calculated for gaining proselytes among the young, the unthinking, and the uninformed, the boldness of its assertions was not likely to incur the censure of the legislative authority; since, however thy might tend to warp the heart and mislead the understanding, they neither excited to tumult, nor recommended immediate reform.

After a due consideration of all these weighty arguments, Mr. Vallaton acknowledged himself not only to be convinced, but enraptured, by the enlightened reasonings of his new friend; and from thenceforth never opened his lips, but in the language of the new philosophy.

Our hero had been several days in Paris, before the object of his mission once occurred to his recollection. At length the money which he had received from his friend for travelling expences being exhausted, the bag of gold, which was concealed in his portmanteau, presented itself to his thoughts. Why should he not supply himself from thence? How should he know whether the proprietor was dead or alive? Perhaps the guillotine[52] had ere now put an end to his existence. Were that, indeed, happily the case, who could call him to account? Not the original proprietor, who had violated the laws of his country by sending it thence. Must not the money, in that event, be certainly his own? This thought seemed to inspire our hero's breast with a new degree of animation. He looked at the gold: its value appeared enhanced, and his desire of possessing it to increase at every glance. It was not without difficulty that he tore himself from the contemplation of this tempting object; but at length having taken out twenty guineas for his immediate use, he restored the rest to their place of concealment; resolving, that if their owner did not seek them, they should never seek their owner.

The more he considered the subject, the more fully was he convinced of the expediency of his silence. He was quickly persuaded, that any enquiry concerning the brother of his friend might, at this time, be attended with real danger to himself. "This person was known to be an Englishman. He, through the good offices of one of the servants of the American Ambassador, who had been his fellow-apprentice, passed for an

---

[52] Proposed by Dr. Guillotin as a novel and humane method of execution 10 October 1789.

American.[53] To have any connection with a native of England, would inevitably involve him in suspicions." Such were the reasonings of our hero; and considering that this was the very height of the reign of terror,[54] they may, perhaps, be thought sufficiently cogent. It is, however, a little remarkable, that the same reasonings never occurred to prevent him from forming an acquaintance with any other person of his own country, except this unfortunate gentleman. Of this gentleman, however, he was at length obliged unwillingly to hear. One day, when he happened to call upon his friend at the ambassador's, he received the unwelcome intelligence, that a person had just been there to enquire for him, who was very urgent to receive his address: that his friend had at first scrupled to comply with the request of the stranger, but remarking the mildness of his deportment, and the genteel air which not even a dress that bespake the extreme of indigence could conceal, he had at length yielded his belief to the story which he told of his being brother to Mr.—, and of his expecting, from that gentleman, the remittance of a considerable sum through the hands of Mr. Vallaton. Our hero used his best endeavours to conceal from his friend the chagrin which this information occasioned, and quickly took his leave.

As he was on his return, ruminating on the method he might best employ to elude the restoration of the precious deposit, a croud advanced towards him, in the midst of which he presently discovered the fatal cart, which had, alas! become too familiar to the eyes of the inhabitants of Paris, and which was now loaded with victims for the guillotine: he stood aside to observe them as they passed. Various were the expressions which might be read in the different countenances of these unhappy persons. On some was depicted the meekness of resignation; on others, the sullenness of despair.

A youth of about seventeen or eighteen years of age, whose air of manly fortitude expressed maturity of virtue, appeared to exert his utmost efforts to comfort and support an aged mother, whose enfeebled mind was lost in the horrors that surrounded her. A young woman, who was placed in the most conspicuous part of the machine, still more forcibly attracted the notice of the spectators. A gleam of satisfaction illumined each fine feature of her beautiful countenance; and as she turned

---

[53] Many English remained in Paris in this manner—Mary Wollstonecraft assumed American status through her association with her lover Gilbert Imlay.

[54] Generally accepted as the period from August 1792 to July 1794, the Terror took three forms. There was the official Terror, controlled by the Committees of Public Safety and of General Security, which was centred in Paris and whose victims came before the Revolutionary Tribunal. There was Terror in the areas of federal revolt, where the worst atrocities took place, and there was also the Terror in other parts of France, which was under the control of watch committees and representatives-on-mission, and the revolutionary armies (Duncan Townson, *France in Revolution*, London: Hodder and Stoughton, 1990, 82-83).

her lovely eyes to heaven, they appeared animated with the sweet enthusiasm of hope and joy.

This young lady was the last remains of an honourable and happy family; she had, in the beginning of the reign of terror, seen her father, mother, and brother, perish on the scaffold; and last of all, a lover, to whom from childhood her heart had been united, was doomed to the same fate. After the death of this beloved youth, she seldom spake, but to repeat the French translation of the lines of our English poet,

"*This* is the desert, *this* the solitude;
"How populous, how vital is the grave!"[55]

Which words having been overheard by the reporter of the commune, she was accused of incivism, denounced, and sent to the guillotine.

The person who imparted these circumstances to our hero, seemed willing to favour him with an equal degree of information concerning the rest of the unhappy groupe; but he was too much occupied by his own thoughts to listen to such uninteresting details, and hastily stepped on.

"What a charming contrivance is this guillotine!" said he to himself, as he went along. "How effectually does it stop the mouths of troublesome people. Would that this good-for-nothing old man had made such a desirable exit! And why should he not? Of what utility is his life to society? Why should he deprive me of these seven hundred guineas? Does not the philosophy, I now profess, teach that there is no such thing as right? From thence the inference is plain, that the gold ought in justice to be disposed of in the way that will be most conducive to the general interests of society. If I give to this foolish old man the six hundred and fifty guineas which are now left, what will be the consequence? Will he not claim the remainder; and asperse my character, if I refuse to comply with his demand? And would not this be to deprive me of my utility? Thus it is evident, that one of us must inevitably be destroyed; and surely, of the two, it is fitting that the one most useless to society should suffer.

"My promise has been passed to his brother. True; but in the interval, betwixt the promise and my fulfilling it, a greater and a nobler purpose offers itself, and calls, with an imperious voice, for my cooperation.★[56] Which ought I to prefer? That, surely, which best deserves my preference. A promise, says my friend Myope, can make no alteration in the case. Ought I not be guided by the intrinsic merit of the objects, and not by any external and foreign consideration? And what merit has this old man to boast? It is said, that he has passed an innocent and inoffensive life; but innocence is not virtue. It is great passions that bespeak great powers, and

---

[55] Edward Young, *The Revenge* (1721), Act IV. Hamilton substitutes "this" for "life".
[56] ★See Pol. Jus. vol. i.★ Godwin, *Political Justice* Bk III, ch. iii "Of Promises", 216-230.

great powers are but another expression for great energies, and in great energies the whole of virtue is comprised; I, then, am a more virtuous, and consequently a more useful, individual than this person; therefore it is I whose utility ought not to be interrupted."

In this manner did Vallaton continue to reason with himself, till every doubt vanished, and hope and confidence once more took possession of his mind.

The greediness with which denunciations were at this time received by the tribunal, whose decrees were written in blood, and the slender evidence that was necessary for the conviction of the accused, were circumstances well calculated to facilitate the success of that plan which had suggested itself to the mind of our hero. He hurried home, and shutting himself up in his chamber, soon scrawled over such a letter as he thought best suited to the important service for which he intended it. This letter, which was addressed to the owner of the seven hundred guineas, bore a fictitious signature, but purported to be from an intimate correspondent; and was written as if in answer to one which had communicated the plan of an intended assassination of some of the members of the Revolutionary Tribunal,[57] and treated the gentleman as head of the conspiracy.

No sooner has our hero finished this epistle, than he went in search of the person to whom it was addressed.

Having, at length, with some difficulty, found out the obscure and shabby habitation at which he lodged, he was told by the owner, (whose poverty would not permit her to maintain a servant) that the good citizen he enquired for was not then within, but that she expected him every minute.

Vallaton's eye flashed with the triumph of success: he begged leave to wait the return of his friend, to which the good woman of the house readily consented, and ushered him into the dirty and half-furnished chamber, which she called *the apartment of Monsieur*.

"You are an Englishman, I presume," said the woman, while she reached him a chair, "and, *apparemment*, you bring some good news for Monsieur. Alas! he has been so often disappointed! And after the straits to which he as been reduced, disappointment sits so hard! And what is the hardest matter of all is, his having a fortune of his own too, though he has been so many months without having the value of a single sous.[58] But, *qu'importe*? Monsieur is so good, and so amiable, that he shall share a bit of bread with me and my children, as long as we have a morsel to eat." Here a knock at the door gave notice of Monsieur's return. The woman

---

[57] Victims of the Committees of Public Safety and of General Security came before the Revolutionary Tribunal centred in Paris. Up to September 1793 the Tribunal heard 260 cases and pronounced 66 deaths, but thereafter the Tribunal became the scene of endless trials and death sentences.

[58] French currency.

flew to open it, and our hero, rejoicing in her absence, dexterously deposited the feigned letter beneath the cover of an old broken sopha, which stood in a corner of the room.

The gentleman entered, and Vallaton announced himself as the friend of his brother. An emotion of pleasure seemed to reanimate the old man's pallid countenance. He saluted his visitor with the most cordial satisfaction, listened to his apology for not having waited on him sooner with complacency, and heard of the safety of the seven hundred guineas with delight. Vallaton then presented him with a letter from his brother, the perusal of which brought tears (though not such bitter ones as he had of late been accustomed to shed) down his furrowed cheek; and again, and again, he repeated his fervent thanks to **God** for the happy period that was thus put to his distresses.

Having appointed the day after the following for returning with the money, Vallaton took his leave, loaded with the gentleman's thanks for his goodness in taking so much trouble.

In the evening he again sallied forth, and directing his steps to the office of the Revolutionary Tribunal, he threw into it an anonymous billet, notifying that "a conspiracy, of which ✱ ✱ ✱ ✱ ✱ ✱ ✱ ✱, a lodger in the house of a female citizen in Le Rue ✱ ✱ ✱ ✱, was the contriver and the head, had come to the knowledge of a *bon patriot*, who desired that a thorough search might be made in the apartment of the conspirator for further information." He retreated unobserved, and took the nearest road to his own lodgings.

Never, till this moment, did the legs of Vallaton shake under their master's weight. He attempted to tread firm, but in vain, his knees bent under him at every step; and a certain flutter of spirits, which he had never before experienced in the same extent, seemed alternately to accelerate and to arrest the motion of his heart.

Ashamed of this weakness, he retired to his chamber to avoid the observation of his fellow-lodgers; he there recalled to his recollection every dogma of the philosophy that was most eminently calculated to reassure his mind. What he had just done would, it was true, probably be the means of making an old man lose his head. What then? he was but the passive instrument: no more to blame than the guillotine which should behead him. His actions had, of necessity, followed their motives. And to whom was he accountable? There was no GOD to whose allseeing eye the secrets of his heart were open; no judge to condemn; no hell to punish; no state beyond the grave, where retribution could possibly await him.

While the idea of death and judgment glanced along his mind, a cold sweat broke upon his forehead; he found it was not by meditation, that his agitated spirits were to be restored to composure; and hastily leaving his apartment, he sought in wine and revelry to forget the events of the day.

The morning came on which he was, by appointment, to wait on Mr. ✱✱✱✱ with his money; but some hours before it would have been necessary to have attended him, he read, in *Le Jounal de Paris*, of his having been arrested as a conspirator. Not all the energies of our hero were sufficient to quell the anxiety which, for some days after this event, continued to haunt his mind. It was not long, however, till doubt was lost in certainty. As he was one morning of the following week hastily walking along the *Pont Neuf*, without knowing where he intended to proceed, his ears were stunned by the vociferous pronunciation of that name, which he had of late so assiduously laboured to banish from his thoughts. Scarcely knowing what he did, he suffered the hawker, who was bellowing it, to put a paper into his hands; it was the list of those who had on that morning expired by the guillotine; and the first upon this list was the unfortunate old gentleman, who was there termed *the organizer of a bloody and atrocious conspiracy against the guardians of liberty!*

The paper dropt from our hero's hand. "This morning!" said he to himself, "this very morning! But what have I to say to it? I am but a machine in the hand of fate. Nothing but what has happened, could have happened. Every thing that is, must inevitably be; and the causes of this old man's death were generated in the eternity that preceded his birth.[59] What then have I to say to it?" Absorbed in these reflections our hero returned home.

He found Mr. Myope, and the Goddess of Reason, and two gentlemen, who were their guests, sitting down to dinner. 'O gemini!' exclaimed the Goddess of Reason, 'how pale Mr. Vallaton is! he look for all de world as if he had seen a ghost.'

"Do I?" said Vallaton, with a forced smile; "I have, indeed, been haunted with a violent head-ache all the morning, and have, besides, tired myself to death with walking, but a bumper of burgundy will recover me;" so saying, he filled a bumper to the lady's health, and so frequently repeated the prescription, that before the end of dinner he was completely restored to his complexion.

The accidental mention of a ghost gave to Mr. Myope an opportunity, of which he was ever willing to avail himself, of inveighing against priests and priestcraft. A momentary pause in his harangue permitted one of the strangers to get in a word. 'I admit,' said this gentlemen, 'that to superstition many of the terrors which haunt the imagination and enervate the mind, may certainly be traced; but feeble would have been the powers of superstition, if they had not been armed by the string of guilt. What apparition did fancy ever form, or credulity ever listen to, that did not originate in a guilty conscience?'

"And what, pray, is this bugbear of a guilty conscience?" retorted Myope. "What is it, I say, but one of the creatures of priestcraft? Have I not already proved that there is no such thing as crime? How, then, can there by any guilt? The most atrocious *crime* (as it is vulgarly termed) that

---

[59] See Godwin's *Political Justice* Bk IV, ch. vii, "Of Free Will and Necessity", for his views on predestination and fate.

ever was perpetrated, amounts to no more than mere mistake; and whose conscience ever smote him for a mistake? Our mistakes ought, on reflection, to excite in our minds the emotion of pleasure rather than of pain. Error once committed cannot be recalled; and regret, and sorrow, and repentance, are the extremes of folly. It is this fruitless and childish waste of time, which conduces to an habitual abuse of our faculties; and it is this abuse of our faculties which creates the bugbear of remorse and conscience, and all that nonsense, which priests know so well how to manage for their advantage."

'Whatever use may have been made of it,' returned the stranger, 'I cannot believe that that awful monitor, which Heaven has implanted in the breast of man, was bestowed upon him in vain; or that, after the perpetration of any atrocious crime, it is in the power of sophistry to silence its imperious voice. Pray, sir, what is your opinion?' added the stranger, turning to Vallaton, who sat next him.

Vallaton drank off another glass of wine, got up hastily from the table, complained of increased indisposition, and retired.

The indisposition of Vallaton was not altogether feigned. He felt a sickness at his heart, which he persuaded himself was occasioned by the unusual quantity of wine which he had swallowed, operating on a empty stomach. The open air would dissipate these fumes, and a walk would, by supper-time, restore his appetite: he went out. With hasty steps he hurried along the streets without observing which way he went, nor did any object attract his attention, till he found himself in the midst of *La Place de Carousal*. He there looked up; but never were the energies of a philosopher put to a severer trial than those Vallaton underwent, on beholding himself at the foot of the instrument of death—the blood-stained guillotine! He started with horror, yet had he not the power of instantly turning from it; he seemed arrested to the spot; he gazed upon the scaffold; he fancied he there beheld the placid countenance of the meek old man smiling upon him, as when he pressed his hand at parting. Again he thought he saw his silver hairs grasped by the hand of the executioner, and the blood-streaming head held up to his distracted sight. His knees smote against each other, a chilly coldness crept along his whole frame, and his emotions became so apparent, as to attract the notice of the passengers.

An honest sans-culotte[60] came up to him. "My good citizen," said he, "I would have you remember, that this is no place to indulge your melancholy. You have, probably, had some friend sent to heaven by this short bridge; but who, in Paris, has not? If you stay here till your grief be taken

---

[60] Although *sans culotte* was originally a vulgar expression ridiculing the Parisian revolutionaries they themselves adopted it as a mark of pride. They were comprised mainly of urban workers, wage earners and small property owners, who did not wear knee breeches like the aristocrats but rather trousers held up by suspenders, a short jacket or *carmagnole*, a Phrygian cap (the sign of liberated slaves in antiquity), a tricolour cockade, and wooden shoes.

notice of, it may create some suspicions of incivism, which may get you into a disagreeable predicament."

Vallaton thanked his monitor, and using his utmost endeavours to recollect himself, returned to his home.

The inventions of priestcraft had never implanted a prejudice in the breast of Vallaton. He laughed at the terrors of superstition, and derided the folly of those who could believe in the existence of conscience. Yet would he now have given, not only the bag of gold which was contained in his portmanteau, but all which the wide world could furnish, to have been restored to the same tranquillity which, but a fortnight ago, he had enjoyed.

Whether he sought the conversation of his friends, or mixed in the scenes of revelry and riot; whether he basked in the mid-day sun, or covered himself up in the darkness of night; still the trunkless head of the old man pursued him. To his "*mind's eye*,"[61] in every place, in every situation, the haggard vision appeared. In this frame of mind, it may be believed, that he readily acquiesced in Myope's proposal of leaving Paris. All that happened to him from this period, is so interwoven with the history of Mr. Myope, that it must still be fresh in the reader's recollection. Here, therefore, we shall close this tedious chapter.

CHAP. X.

"Hard is the fortune that your sex attends!
"Women, like princes, find few real friends.
"Hence, oft from reason heedless beauty strays,
"And the most trusted guide the most betrays;
"Hence by fond dreams of fancy oft amused."
LYTTLETON.[62]

IT was a late hour before the philosophers, assembled at Mr. Glib's, thought of separating; and long after Mrs. Botherim's usual time of breakfast on the following morning, before Bridgetina issued from her apartment.

They had just began the repast, which the fond mother had been at much pains to prepare, and to keep warm for her darling child, when Julia Delmond entered the parlour. The pallid countenance and languid air of their fair visitor plainly spoke her want of rest; and the visible impatience with which she waited for the finishing of the tedious meal, evidently denoted the perturbed state of her spirits.

No sooner had Mrs. Botherim left the room, than Julia, seizing the hand of her friend, said she was extremely anxious for her opinion con-

---

[61] Commonly used to suggest the imagination.
[62] Lord George Lyttleton, *Advice to a Young Lady* (1731).

cerning an affair of some moment, but could not have that satisfaction without betraying the secrets of another, and feared it was not justifiable to do so.

"Not *justifiable!*" returned Bridgetina, "surely you cannot have forgotten, that *the facts* with which you are acquainted are a part of your possessions, and that you are as much obliged, with respect to them as in any other case, to employ them for the public good. *Have I no right to indulge in myself the caprice of concealing any of my affairs; and can another person have a right, by his caprice, to hedge up and restrain the path of my duty?*[63] You may take down the book, if you please, but I know I have quoted it word for word; you know I am seldom wrong in a quotation."

'Well, then,' said Julia, 'I shall tell you all. You must know, that last night Mr. Vallaton gave me his whole history.'

"How!" cried Bridgetina, "while he escorted you home?"

'No!' returned Julia, while a crimson blush overspread her countenance, 'not exactly as we were walking home, but afterwards. For you must know,' continued she, blushing still deeper than before, 'that having offended him by something I said at Mr. Glib's, he told me, as we were going to my father's, he plainly saw that, instead of being enlightened by the principles of the philosophers, I was still the *slave of prejudice*. I denied the charge, and he retorted it. At length he said he would put me to the proof. If I had energy sufficient to dare to meet him in the arbour at the bottom of the garden, after the family were retired to rest, he would acknowledge his error, and adore me. I for some time hesitated, but at length I could not bear the thought of appearing despicable in his eyes by my *want of energy*. I went. Think, Bridgetina, what an interview! how extraordinary! how interesting!'

"Ah! how charming!" exclaimed Bridgetina, heaving a deep sigh; "ah! what a dear man Mr. Vallaton is!"

'Dear, indeed!' rejoined Julia, 'he is the most amiable of men, and, alas! the most unfortunate. Had you but heard how feelingly he deplored the mystery that hung over his birth!'

"Good gracious!" cried Bridgetina, interrupting her, "a mystery over his birth! how delightful! how did it happen?" drawing her chair still closer to Julia's, "Pray tell me all."

'Why you must know,' proceeded Julia, 'that it was on a fine summer's morning, in the month of July, that his dear deceased patroness (a lady of great family and fortune) being induced, by the beauty of the morning, to take a walk in the thick shade of a sequestered grove, heard the cries of an infant, and turning her eyes, beheld a white basket, lined with

---

[63] Godwin writes that "Duty is the best possible application of a given power to the promotion of the general good" (*Political Justice* Bk VII, ch. v).

quilted pink satin, and a covering of white peelong,[64] richly embroidered, thrown lightly over it. She approached; and lifting up the covering, beheld a lovely boy, who sweetly smiled in her face. She immediately resolved on taking the charming infant under her protection, and bringing him up as her own son. As he grew up, her affection for him, as you may easily imagine, increased; and her whole fortune would undoubtedly have been settled upon him, had she not suddenly died one morning without having made a will, so that poor Mr. Vallaton was left without any other provision than two or three thousand pounds; which she had put into the funds for his college expenses. These circumstances, he said, unfortunate as they might appear in the eyes of vulgar minds, were to him matter of great satisfaction, till he saw me. His mind had sufficient energy to rise above every existing circumstance, but that of hopeless love. It was now that he first deplored those circumstances of his birth and fortune, which he knew the illiberal prejudices of my father would consider as an obstacle—an invincible obstacle to our union. 'Accursed prejudices!' exclaimed he, 'what misery do ye not create in society! Why, my Julia,' he continued, in a voice *so* tender and *so* impressive, 'why were we not born in a more enlightened period? In that blest time, so happily approaching, when the sentiments of nature shall be omnipotent, when no absurd institution shall stand in the way of the happiness of lovers, and no cruel father's sanction be necessary for its completion!' O Bridgetina! had you seen how he was agitated, while he pronounced these words, I am sure you would have pitied him. For my share, (continued Julia, while a pearly drop stole drown her check) I was quite melted into compassion; but though I said all I could to comfort him, the dear youth was so overwhelmed with affliction, that it made me truly wretched.'

"Happy Julia!" exclaimed Bridgetina, "how I envy you for being the object of such a passion as that which inspires your Vallaton! But, pray, was Vallaton the name of his adopted mother, or was it only given him by her?"

'In several parts of his infant robes,' replied Julia, 'as well as in the covering of the basket, the initial letters A.V. were most beautifully embroidered, from which his patroness bestowed upon him the name he at present bears. It is from this circumstance, Bridgetina, that a ray of hope has darted upon my mind; and an idea occurred, which, though it may at first sight seem romantic, is far from improbable, and the more I think of it, appears the more likely to be true. What would you think, if I should make a discovery of his real parents?'

"Think!" cried Bridgetina, "I should think it extremely wonderful, to be sure."

'Well, wonderful as it is,' said Julia, 'I think I have hit upon them. You

---

[64] A kind of material used for gowns worn in southern India.

know my father's friend and patron, Gen. Villers. He and his lady were for some years privately married, or at least promised to each other, before they durst acknowledge it, for fear of his father the old lord. What can be more likely than that he should be their son?'

"Nothing, certainly, can be more probable," returned Bridgetina. "Nay, it is quite obvious; for the General's name is Andrew, which you know begins with an A; I wonder it did not occur to me from the first. If you take my advice, you will make your father write immediately to the General a full account of the whole affair."

'Alas!' said Julia, sighing, 'my father, as Mr. Vallaton justly observes, has his prejudices. It would, perhaps, be a difficult matter to make him view the affair in the very light we do. Besides, I should rather have the pleasure of making the discovery myself. Good heavens! what extatic delight I shall feel in seeing the amiable Vallaton clasped in the fond arms of his venerable parents! They weeping over him tears of joy, and thanking me by their looks, a thousand times more expressive than words, for restoring to them their long lost-son. My poor father, too! how happy he will be to see me united to the son of his friend. It is too much,' continued she, covering her face with both hands, 'I can never deserve such a torrent of felicity.'

Here the entrance of Mrs. Botherim put an end to the *tête-a-tête*, and Julia, whose imagination was too much heated to descend to the common topics of the good lady's discourse, took her leave. She was no sooner gone, than Bridgetina (who measured her progress in philosophy by the degree of contempt which she felt for the ignorance of her parent) left the room, and muttering an ejaculation upon the misfortune of being subjected to the society of a person whose pursuits were so dissimilar, retired to her own apartment.

"Happy Julia!" cried she, throwing herself into a chair, "Happy Julia, to have such a lover! Why do I not experience the same delightful sensations? Why have I not likewise inspired the breast of some fond youth with a similar passion? Is it because I am not quite so handsome? But are not moral causes superior to physical? And in philosophy I have surely made a greater progress than she. I am, therefore, a fitter object for admiration. It is true, I am not quite so tall—but all men do not admire may-poles; and though I have a little cast in my eyes, and a little twist in my left shoulder, these defects are no moral obstacles to love. Nothing but the unjust prejudices of an unnatural state of civilization, could make Julia loved in preference to me. But Henry Sydney loves her not. Happy thought! Henry, the beloved object of my soul's tenderness, may not be insensible to those soft effusions of a tender sensibility which he shall find to flow from my heart; and incessantly shall I—" Here the soliloquy of the loving maiden was interrupted by the maid-servant, who came to inform her that Mr. Sydney and his son were in the parlour. She instantly went to the glass to adjust her morning cap; and now first felt the mortifying consequences of the disaster of the preceding evening. To appear before Henry Sydney without the flowing braid and frizzled curls, was distressing; but to remain in her chamber while she knew he was below, was more so; she, therefore, only staid to pin an additional bow to the bright pink ribbon that bound her cap, and then, in the slow step which she thought best suited to the expression of extreme sensibility,[65] she moved towards the parlour.

She was met at the door by young Sydney, who, with easy and unaffected good-nature, expressed his pleasure at seeing her, and his hopes that she had enjoyed her health during his absence.

"I thank you, sir," she replied, with a sigh; "the interest you are so good as to take in my health, should certainly make it precious to me."

'I hope, indeed,' said Mr. Sydney, 'that my son will never be so basely interested, as not to rejoice in the health of his friends, notwithstanding his profession.'

"His profession, sir," said Bridgetina, "is a noble one; and I dare say will, by Dr. Sydney, be directed to the noblest purposes. When mankind are sufficiently enlightened to cure all diseases by the exertion of their energies, I doubt not, that despising what he may in point of fortune suffer from it, he will have sufficient philanthropy to rejoice in such a sublime proof of the perfectibility of his species."[66]

A question which had been put to the old gentleman by Mrs. Botherim, relative to the culture of some of her garden-stuff, prevented his hearing the latter part of this observation; which, however, attracted the notice of his son, who was well enough versed in the language of the new philosophy, to know at least from whom she now quoted.

He would have answered her in her own stile, but recollecting how unpleasant, as well as unprofitable, it is to enter into an argument with one possessed of a shallow understanding, and a mind totally occupied by two or three ideas, on which the changes are eternally to be rung, he only observed, that he found Miss Botherim had not misspent her time in his absence.

"I hope, sir," said she, in as soft a tone as the natural shrillness of her voice would permit, "that that time which has appeared so insupportably tedious to your friends, has been spent agreeably by you."

Henry only bowed.

"I know not how it happens," resumed Bridgetina, "seeing that moral causes are always superior to physical ones, I say I know not how it happens, that the pain of separation appears to be always more severely felt by our sex than by yours. It is more than probable, that since you left your native village, no painful sensation, excited by the tender recollection of the friends you left behind you, has ever disturbed your bosom's peace. Ah! how different have been the feelings of those friends!"

---

[65] Books on etiquette and decorum stress the steady, slow entry for dramatic effect!
[66] See Godwin's *Political Justice* Bk VIII, Appendix, "Of Health, and the Prolongation of Human Life". See Appendix A.

Henry, who instantly suspected that the secret of his attachment to Harriet Orwell, which he, till then, imagined confined to his own breast, had been some how or other discovered by Miss Botherim, coloured, and with an impressive accent, but faultering voice, said, 'he was much indebted to the friends who in his absence had so kindly remembered him.'

Joy diffused itself through the bosom of Bridgetina. In the looks, in the words of Henry, she discovered the tender sensibility of his soul; and exulting in the idea that she too had a lover, she resolved to return his passion with tenfold tenderness, and cast upon him a glance which she hoped would have been sufficiently expressive of her sentiments. But, alas! the unfortunate squint rendered the charitable design abortive. Henry, following, as he thought, the direction of her eyes, cast his towards the door, which was at that moment opened by a little dirty-looking urchin kept by Mrs. Botherim to attend her cow upon the common.

"Here be miss's wig," cried he, in a loud voice, "the boy be come with it as picked it out o' the kennel; what a slush o' wet it is!" holding up the dishonoured tresses of the enraged Bridgetina; who, pushing the little wretch from the door, entered into a warm expostulation with her mother on keeping so unenlightened a domestic.

Mr. Sydney and his son, not wishing to take any part in the altercation, took their leave; and left the mother and daughter to settle the dispute by themselves.

CHAP. XI.

HAD the inclination of Henry been consulted, the first visit which had been paid that morning, would have been to the rectory; but as his father proposed calling first on Mrs. Botherim, whose house lay directly in their way, he could not with any propriety object to it.

The words that had fallen from Bridgetina added fuel to his impatience. That he had some interest in the heart of Harriet Orwell, he fondly flattered himself: but that she should make a confidante of Miss Botherim, of one who possessed a mind so uncongenial, in every way so unlike her own, was equally irreconcilable with her extreme delicacy and good sense. Yet how otherwise could he interpret the speech of Miss Botherim?

While the mind of Sydney was occupied with these reflections, his father, who had stood for some moments contemplating the beauty of a tree in full blossom, was expatiating on the charms of nature; and as the association of his ideas led "from Nature up to Nature's GOD,"[67] was making observations on the striking proofs of the divine benevolence with which we are every where surrounded; a benevolence which, he

---

[67] Most likely used by Hamilton to echo Pope's *Essay on Man*, Epistle iv, line 331.

observed, makes the beauteous cradle of the embryo fruit a feast no less delightful to the eye, than the fruit itself is to the palate. Happily this was a subject which never failed to elevate the heart of this good old gentleman in a degree that totally engrossed every faculty, otherwise he could not but have observed, how much the monosyllable answers of his son indicated the total absence of his mind.

As they approached the door his agitation increased, and it is probable would no longer have escaped the notice of his father, had not the old gentleman's attention been attracted to another object. A moth butterfly, of rare and uncommon beauty, happened to alight on a neighbouring honey-suckle; and to discover whether it was the **** **** of Linnaeus, or the **** **** of Buffon, was a matter of too great importance, in Mr. Sydney's estimation, not to deserve the most serious attention. While he went in pursuit of the butterfly, his son, attracted by beauty of a different kind, hastily advanced to the saloon where he knew the family of Dr. Orwell usually spent the mornings.

It was now past twelve o'clock. Already had the active and judicious Harriet performed every domestic task, and having compleatly regulated the family economy for the day, was quietly seated at her work with her aunt and sister, listening to Hume's History of England,[68] as it was read to them by a little orphan girl she had herself instructed.

Here some notable housewife, who may, peradventure, chance to sit long enough at a time to catch the last paragraph as it is read by some of her family, will probably exclaim, "a few hours' attention regulate a family, indeed! a pretty story, truly! what nonsense these *men authors* speak! but how, indeed, should they know any thing of the matter! I wish any of them saw how I am employed from morning till night. I wonder how I should get time to listen to books?" Softly, good lady, and for once take the trouble to calculate. Be so good as fairly to set down, at the end of every day, the time employed in repeating directions imperfectly given, or in revoking those that were given improperly; the time wasted in again looking at that which you have looked at before; the time thrown away in peeping into corners, without object or end in view; the time misspent in perplexing your domestics with contradictory orders; and the time abused in scolding them;—and casting up the sum total, please to consider the amount; and then candidly confess, whether Miss Orwell, whose enlightened intellect, and calm and steady judgment, deprived her of all those admirable methods of evincing her notability, might not have time sufficient for the cultivation of her understanding, and the fulfilment of every social as well as every domestic duty. But to return—

The surprise occasioned by the unexpected appearance of Henry was announced by a general exclamation. Unaffected pleasure sparkled

---

[68] David Hume, *History of England* (1754-62).

in every eye; and if those of Harriet beamed with a superior expression of delight, that delight was so regulated by the transcendant delicacy of her mind, that it required a delicacy similar to her own to read its full extent. Dr. Orwell, who had heard the name of Henry from his study, quickly joined the friendly groupe, and with heart-felt pleasure welcomed the return of his young favourite. He enquired for his father: at that moment the old gentleman entered with a joyful countenance, holding out his pocket-handkerchief, in which the captive butterfly was safely lodged. Nor let this circumstance excite the contempt of any peevish critic, till after a mature investigation of the intrinsic value of his own favourite pursuits, of every object which engages his attention, and every care which disturbs his rest, he can lay his hand upon his heart and say, that all are in the eye of reason more truly estimable.

Happy in themselves and in each other, the time slipt so imperceptibly away with this little party, that though their conversation was not *relieved* by one word of scandal, nor enlivened by any of the news of the village, the clock announced the hour of dinner before they thought of separating: nor would they have done so then, but for the sake of Miss Sydney, who was at home alone.

The old gentleman, whose temper made every thing easy to him, would soon have been prevailed upon to accept of Dr. Orwell's cordial invitation, but Henry, who knew the disappointment it would give his sister, and was too just and too generous to inflict a moment's pain on another for the sake of his own gratification, was peremptory in his refusal. On going through the garden, which afforded a nearer way to the house of Mr. Sydney, Dr. Orwell pointed out to his friends some improvements he had lately planned. "And all this," says he, "should have been done this summer, but for the folly of my daughter Harriet, who has such a strange fancy for that good-for-nothing bush," (pointing to a moss-rose tree,[69] which grew in the middle of a small plat) "that I was silly enough, at her entreaties, to put if off till another season."

No chromatic air ever raised such soft emotion in the breast of any Grecian youth, as those words of Dr. Orwell's excited in the heart of Henry. That rose tree he had, sometime previous to his last departure for college, planted with his own hands. The charge of rearing it he had given to Harriet, and the pretence of seeing how it throve had given occasion for many a delightful *tête-a-tête*. His eyes now met hers—need we tell the reader they were both sufficiently expressive?

---

[69] A garden variety of the cabbage rose, *rosa centifolia*; so called from the moss-like growth of its calyx and stalk.

CHAP. XII.

"When I see such games
"Play'd by the creatures of a Power, who swears
"That he will judge the earth, and call the fool
"To a sharp reck'ning, that has liv'd in vain;
"And when I weigh this seeming wisdom well,
"And prove it in th'infallible result,
"So hollow and so false—I feel my heart
"Dissolve in pity."

COWPER.[70]

WHILE the daughter of Dr. Orwell was enjoying the happiness with which the return of Henry Sydney had inspired her breast, a happiness rendered doubly dear by the approving smiles of her respected parent; emotions of a less placid nature agitated the fair bosom of her sister beauty. In the breast of Julia Delmond all was turbulence and perturbation. While following the course of an unreined imagination, she experienced that deluding species of delight, which rather intoxicates than exhilarates, and which, by its inebriating quality, gives to the sanguine votary of fancy a disrelish for the common enjoyments of life; the eagerness with which her mind grasped at the idea of an extraordinary extatic felicity, agitated her whole frame, and deprived her of peace and rest. Still she pursued the flattering dream of fancy, and kept her mind's eye so fixt upon its airy visions, that she at length believed in their reality, and what appeared at first the mere suggestion of imagination, seemed in the sequel the certain dictates of truth.

That in General Villers Mr. Vallaton should find a father, at first seemed barely possible; then probable; then more than probable; it was next to certainty, or rather *certainty itself.*

All that now remained was to find means for effecting the discovery in a manner the most striking and pathetic. For this purpose she called to her remembrance all the similar events in her most favourite novels; in these instructive books the discovery of the hero's parents had always appeared to her a catastrophe particularly interesting, and the idea that she should now have it in her power, not only to witness, but to be a principal actor in so tender a scene, filled her heart with extacy.[71] After much deliberation, she at length fixed upon a most delightful plan for introducing Vallaton to the house of his long-lost parents; but as part of it depended on the indulgence of her father, she found it necessary immediately to procure his consent to its execution.

---

[70] William Cowper, *The Task* (1785), Book III, "The Garden", 176-83.
[71] Examples such as Henry Fielding's *Tom Jones* (1749) and Frances Burney's *Evelina* (1778).

In order to conceal the agitated state of her mind, she had, on pretence of indisposition, absented herself from breakfast, and begged to be excused from her usual attendance in her father's chamber; nor did she now approach it with that cheerful alacrity which had hitherto led her steps to his door.

Instead of lightly tripping, in her usual manner, to make the fond enquiry after his health, she now stole through the passage as if afraid of being seen; and on opening his door was seized with such a palpitation and embarrassment, that he had twice demanded who was there, before she mustered sufficient courage to advance towards the couch on which he lay. For the first time in her life she now feared to meet the scrutinizing eyes of her father, for, for the first time of her life, she had something to conceal. The shame of being suspected to be the dupe of prejudice had prompted her assent to the clandestine meeting with Vallaton; to that shame she had sacrificed her feelings of propriety, and now felt a consciousness of deserved blame, which not all the applauses bestowed upon her conduct by her enlightened preceptor could palliate or remove.

While Vallaton spoke, his arguments appeared irrefutable, and the light in which he placed the prejudices of her father, made them sufficiently contemptible in her eyes; but the instant she found herself in her father's presence, a mingled sentiment of affection and respect took possession of her mind; the high sentiments of honour he had so carefully inculcated, recovered their influence in her breast; and the shame of having swerved from them, by encouraging the clandestine addresses of the philosopher, overwhelmed her with mortification and disquiet.

It is now time to introduce the father of Julia to the reader's acquaintance, for which purpose we hope the following sketch of his life will not be deemed an impertinent digression.

HISTORY OF CAPTAIN DELMOND.

CAPTAIN DELMOND was the son of an officer of distinguished merit, who lost his life in the field of battle, leaving to his only child the inheritance of his sword, his honour, and his valour. The young man was then in his seventeenth year, an ensign in his father's regiment. The same ball which tore in pieces the body of the gallant father, struck the standard from the hands of the no less gallant son; who, starting from the ground, bravely recovered the colours as they were about to be taken possession of by a party of the enemy.

The spirited behaviour of young Delmond upon this occasion happened, fortunately for him, to be mentioned at the table of a certain General, in the very moment when the successful efforts of his cook, in dressing a turbot of uncommon excellence, had extorted his warmest approbation. The praise of the turbot and of the ensign were repeated alternately; and it was, perhaps owing to the happy association of ideas thus produced, that the memory of the noble General, which, upon such occasions, was very apt to be imperfect, now served him so well, that he remembered young Delmond in the next promotion. He was by this circumstance raised to the rank of lieutenant.

The two nations then at war, having at length sacrificed such a quantity of human blood, and expended such a portion of treasure, as was deemed sufficient for the amusement of the governing powers on either side, thought proper to make a peace; and after a few preliminaries, in which the original cause of dispute was not once mentioned, and things were put as nearly as possible into the same state in which they were at the commencement of hostilities, its ratification was formally announced.

The wretched remains of those numerous armies which in the beginning of the contest had marched forth, elate with health and vigour, were now returned to their respective countries; some to languish out their lives in hospitals, in the agony of wounds that were pronounced incurable; some to a wretched dependence on the bounty of their families, or the alms of strangers; and the few whose good fortune it was to escape unhurt, according to the seniority of their regiments, either disbanded to spread habits of idleness and profligacy among their fellow-citizens, or sent into country quarters to be fattened for fields of future glory.

The regiment to which young Delmond belonged, was disposed of in the last-mentioned way. It was ordered into the north of England; and the division of it to which he was attached, quartered at a small village in a very remote situation, and above ten miles distant from the rest of his military associates.

As it was a fine sporting country, the diversions of hunting and shooting afforded for some time sufficient employment to his active mind; but the winter setting in earlier than usual, and with uncommon severity, he was not only deprived of these sources of amusement, but by the badness of the roads cut off from all communication with his brother officers, whose society he had hitherto occasionally enjoyed.

In this dilemma he had recourse to reading, and soon discovered that books were really capable of affording some degree of entertainment. The pleasure which resulted from this discovery daily increased, and he soon found it little inferior to that which is derived from any of the methods usually employed by the modern sons of Mars to murder that worst of enemies, Time. If it lost in comparison with the lounge at the milliner's-shop, it was, at least, fully as amusing as *looking over the bridge*, that never-failing resource for every vacant hour; and though less exhilarating than drinking, gambling, or intriguing, it was, perhaps, as good for the fortune, and safe for the constitution, as any of these approved methods of killing time.[72] The important discovery made by this young soldier, we should

---

[72] Coleridge repeats this sentiment in his witticism that "reading novels is not so much to be called pass-time as kill-time" (*Coleridge on Shakespeare*, London: Routledge, 1971, 46).

here strenuously recommend to the serious attention of those whom it particularly concerns; did we not apprehend, that to recommend books, through the medium of a book, to those who never look into one, would not probably be attended with any great effect. From the example of many great divines and moralists, we might, indeed, infer that this ought to be no obstacle; but as the advancement of our own character for superior wisdom, in the eyes of our own adherents, is not the object at which we aim, we shall reserve our instructions for those whom they may have a chance of reaching.

The place of young Delmond's residence, in the village to which we conducted him, was at an old manor-house, now occupied by the farmer who rented the adjoining lands. The family to whom the estate devolved, had on the death of the late possessor removed from the house all the valuable pieces of furniture, leaving to the present tenant such articles of lumber as they did not deem worthy of removal: of this description was an old book-case with its contents.

Doomed to dust and obscurity, here lay mouldering many ponderous volumes of romances, which had, in the days of their glory, afforded ample amusement to the fair readers of former times; and the works of many free-thinking philosophers, whose labours alarmed the pious zeal of our fathers, but whose names are now forgotten, or only known to those who make it their laudable employment to present to the world under new titles, what they have pilfered from their contents. Of these it may be conjectured that the romances first engaged the attention of the young soldier. Happily his taste had not as yet been sufficiently formed to the more perspicacious stile of modern writers to render him fastidious. The stories were of a nature calculated to excite an interest in his breast. The sentiments of honour were congenial to those he had been early taught to entertain; and the wonderful instances of fortitude, constancy, and valour, displayed in the lives of those illustrious heroes, excited his most ardent admiration. With unwearied patience he laboured through every huge folio in this collection, and was not a little mortified at the conclusion of the Grand Cyrus, to find that not one new adventure remained to excite or to gratify his curiosity.

The ground was still covered with snow, and the inclement skies continued to pour forth their vengeance on the world. What could he do? To read over again the books, which had afforded him so much pleasure, was, indeed, an obvious resource; but like other young people, he had too great a thirst for novelty to relish any story as well a second time as a first. From the works of the philosophers he had been deterred by the professions of regard to religion, with which, in compliance to the prejudice of the times, some of these old authors had thought proper to commence their essays, and which produced in his mind a very proper degree of contempt. Religion he had heard his father talk of as a very proper thing for the common people, who, not having the advantages of military discipline, required a parson with some notion of hell, instead of a cat-of-nine-tails, to keep them in awe, but was quite beneath the notice of a gentleman. From this consideration Mr. Delmond would probably have for ever remained in ignorance of the treasure in his possession, had it not been for an accident which presented to his view, in the middle of a volume, a delicious piece of ridicule on the bible. The wit and pleasantry of this passage, which has indeed raised the reputation of every succeeding author by whom it has either been stolen or borrowed, highly delighted the young soldier, and so effectually excited his curiosity with regard to the rest of the books, that in less than a fortnight he was in complete possession of all that ever has, and probably all that ever will be, said against the Christian faith.

Great and manifold were the advantages resulting to Mr. Delmond from this circumstance. Besides strengthening his contempt for the weak votaries of religion, it furnished him with weapons for attacking their belief. Early taught to class all professors of piety into two divisions, viz. fools, and hypocrites, he exulted in the superior information which made him look down with pity on the one, and regard the other with a becoming degree of detestation.

We do not think it necessary to follow the young gentleman through all the towns and villages in which, for the four ensuing years, he was successively quartered.

At the end of that period, being then on garrison duty in the west of England, he happened to accompany a brother officer to his father's seat, where he received a pressing invitation to spend a few weeks of the summer.

Among other visitors at S—hall, was the sister of the lady of the house, and with her a niece, the heiress of her fortune, and the intended bride of Captain S—, who, on the very first interview, appeared charmed with the dazzling prize his parents had so kindly provided for him.

The young lady was indeed, what she was universally esteemed, a compleat *beauty*; her features formed a model of the most perfect symmetry; a symmetry, which seemed never to have been discomposed by any impulsive emotions of joy or grief, pain or pleasure. She even appeared (for we will not take upon us to pronounce that it was really so) to be totally unconscious of her own superior charms, and was quite free from that affectation and conceit, which is the portion of so many beauties.

That such a charming creature should attract the notice of the gentlemen, will not appear at all surprising; but that she should escape the envy of the ladies may, perhaps, be deemed somewhat more extraordinary. Yet so it was. She was universally cried up by them as a *sweet girl*— the *sweetest* girl in the world! and as to beauty, she was declared to be *quite a picture*.

Captain S—soon found the latter part of the encomium to be more literally true than he could have wished.

The young lady received him without scruple as the husband chosen for her by her aunt; but how far her own heart acquiesced in her guardian's choice, it was utterly impossible for him to conjecture. She was at all times equally sweet, and equally silent. She received every mark of his attention with the most enchanting smile; but smiled just as enchantingly when he forbore to take any notice of her. Fatigued with her insipidity, he was not ill pleased at the opportunity of emancipating himself from an attendance which he found insupportably irksome, and willingly agreed to make one of a grouse-shooting party, who were to be absent for two or three weeks. Delmond, who was prevented by a sprained ancle from accompanying his friend, at his desire remained to take care of the ladies in his absence.

Whether the young lady was piqued at the neglect her lover manifested in thus leaving her, or whether the superior personal attractions of his friend had really made an impression on her heart, we cannot absolutely determine. She, indeed, found means to convince Delmond of the latter part of the position; but as a cold and sullen pride is generally found to be the sole animating principle in the race of insensibles, we are rather inclined to believe the former. However it was, her preference for Delmond, whether real or feigned, made such an impression on his heart, that he easily persuaded himself his *honour* was concerned in protecting so much worth and beauty from the cruelty of a forced marriage. The fair nymph sweetly accepted his proffered services, and the very night before the expected return of her lover, set out under the conduct of her new champion on an hymeneal excursion to Gretna-Green.[73]

Though the heart of Capt. S. received no very deep wound from the loss of his mistress, the imperious voice of honour demanded that it should be revenged. The honour of Delmond was no less forward to give satisfaction to his friend for the supposed injury; three days after his return to head-quarters, they met by appointment, and after mutual salutations, and declarations of perfect good-will, took aim at each other's heart, and fired their pistols. The first shot missed, but the second was more successful; it took effect on each; and each, after receiving his adversary's ball, declared that he was *satisfied*.[74] The seconds interposed, and prounced that nothing could be more *gentleman*-like than their whole behaviour.

Neither of the wounds proved mortal, though both were painful in the extreme, and very tedious in their cure. The long confinement was attended with very unpleasant consequences to Delmond, whose

---

[73] In Scotland all that was required of contractory parties was a mutual declaration before witnesses of their willingness to marry, so that elopers reaching the parish of Graitney (Gretna-Green), or the village of Springfield, could get legally married without licence, banns, or priest. The declaration was generally made to a blacksmith (*Fowler's Dictionary of Phrase and Fable*).

[74] Godwin describes the "despicable practice" of duelling in *Political Justice* (Bk II, Appendix ii, "Of Duelling").

finances were so much exhausted by his Gretna-Green expedition, that he was under the necessity of borrowing a considerable sum of money from a brother officer. The friends of his bride remained inexorable; nor would her aunt ever be prevailed on to see her, or to grant the least pecuniary assistance.

The regiment was now ordered to Gibraltar; and during the ten years that it remained there, Mr. Delmond on the scanty income of a lieutenant contrived, by the exertion of a rigid economy, to support his wife and family. His fortune remained stationary, but his family received the yearly addition of a fine thriving child. Happily, the poor things, by dint of bad management, bad nursing, improper food, and measles, and the small-pox, were one by one sent to heaven, so that Mr. Delmond and his wife returned to England without encumbrance.

Here they had not long remained, when Mr. Delmond had the offer of a company in a corps then about the embark for the coast of Africa. The climate was unhealthy, the season was unpropitious; but as he had no friend that could command a vote at a borough election,[75] it was the only offer of promotion he was ever likely to experience; it could not, therefore, be rejected.

The knowing reader, when he calls to mind the beauty of Mrs. Delmond, will think, from many respectable examples, that a subaltern possessed of so handsome a wife need not to have been at a loss for the road to preferment. It would seem, however, that such a path never presented itself to the mind of Delmond; whose sole care was to place his wife in such a situation during his absence, as might be at once safe, private, and respectable. His solicitude upon this head was soon terminated by the friendship of a very worthy man, who had formerly been quarter-master[76] in the regiment, and had, at the time it was ordered for Gibraltar, retired to the cultivation of the farm which his father-in-law had formerly occupied.

The wife of this respectable farmer, who in soundness of judgment and goodness of heart greatly resembled her husband, joyfully received Mrs. Delmond into her house, and took unwearied pains to render her situation there agreeable. How far her endeavours to please were successful, she never had from Mrs. Delmond the satisfaction to learn. That sweet woman went to the place appointed by her husband without gainsaying, but without one word expressive of approbation or content.

When the hour of his departure arrived, she behaved with a philosophy that would have done honour to any sage of the stoic school; and as soon as he rode from the door, quietly betook herself to the embroidery of a work-bag. Mrs. Hurford, who knew from experience what it was to

---

[75] A vote at a borough election could obtain one a civil position or even advancement to parliament.
[76] A non-commissioned officer in a company who takes charge of the company stores.

endure the sharp pang of separation, thought it prudent to suffer the first unconquerable emotion to get vent in solitude. A considerable time elapsed before she could bring herself to intrude upon the sorrows of her guest. At length, her heart overflowing with compassionate tenderness, she ventured into her apartment. Mrs. Delmond looked up from her work, and seeing the tears ready to start from the eyes of her hostess, enquired if any thing was the matter?

"Nothing, madam," replied Mrs. Hurford, struck with such an uncommon instance of fortitude, "I only came to see whether it would be agreeable to you to walk in the garden, but I perceive you are engaged."

'Yes,' replied Mrs. Delmond, 'you know how I have been hindered all the morning, and I was set upon having this tulip done to-night; does it not look very natural?'

Mrs. Hurford said she was no judge of such work, and left the room, with feelings of compassion not altogether so tender as those which had filled her breast on entering it.

Under this peaceful roof the fair eyes of Julia first opened on the world; and to the judicious management of its mistress was she indebted for the health and happiness of her infancy. The good couple under whose auspices she was reared, experienced for her all the tenderness of the fondest parents. As they were confessedly strangers to all systems of education, the learned reader will undoubtedly suppose that the child must infallibly be lost; but though they knew nothing of any system, they had a sufficiency of that, which, seldom as it enters into the composition of any of them, can amply supply the place of all—sound common-sense. This principle supplied the use of volumes: it fashioned the clothes, regulated the diet, and even dictated the amusements of the little Julia. The sportiveness of infancy was unchecked by the harsh restraints which render a town-nursery a house of bondage. The love of novelty, that source of happiness and instruction to the infant breast, was here gratified, not by the destruction of costly toys, but by the sublime and every-changing scenes of nature. Instead of tedious and unimpressive lessons upon the beauty of truth and virtue, while, as it often happens, every action of the speaker is a libel on the speech, she saw truth and virtue exemplified in the actions of those around her. She was never cheated into obedience, nor had she the seeds of deceit and cunning sown in her mind by promises or threatenings never meant to be performed.

The natural indolence of Mrs. Delmond led her very readily to resign the trouble attending the management of her little charge; she was nevertheless mortified at finding herself the only object of the child's indifference. Mrs. Hurford, perceiving her resentment, wisely obviated its consequences, by contriving to make her the medium through which every gift was to be dispensed, and every little treat bestowed; thus was all jealously on the part of the mother effectually prevented, and the little heart of the daughter inspired with a proper degree of gratitude and affection.

The interest which Mrs. Hurford took in the happiness of her little favourite, inspired her with an idea, which, as it turned out, was essentially conducive to her future fortune. She no sooner mentioned the scheme to her husband, which was indeed the moment it was thought on, than it had his warm approbation. Without hinting at the object they had in view, they asked Mrs. Delmond's consent to carry the little Julia with them on a visit to a relation, who resided at a certain village at the distance of twenty miles; the name of the place they did not mention to Mrs. Delmond; it was the residence of her aunt; and to this lady it was the design of Mrs. Hurford to introduce her lovely charge.

The design succeeded to her wish. The old lady, who lived on terms of great intimacy with Mrs. Hurford's friend, was attracted by the beauty, and charmed with the sprightliness and good-temper of her little visitor. The name of Julia, which belonged to herself, still more endeared her. She questioned her concerning her age.

"She was as old as the little Brindle, and pa Hurford says, that Brindle will be six years old next grass."

'Had she any other papa besides pa Hurford?'

"O yes; but poor papa was far, far away!"

'And mamma?'

"Own mamma lived with t'other mamma, at Rush-mead."

'And what was mamma's name?'

"Own mamma was mamma Delmond."

The old lady was equally shocked and affected by this discovery. The vow she had made never to see her niece, was not to be broken: but it extended not to her offspring; and from this time to the day of her decease, she at her own desire received an annual visit from her grand-niece.

Julia had nearly reached her tenth year, before she had the happiness of beholding her father; he then returned. But how returned? No longer that blooming and handsome figure, whose manly beauty attracted universal admiration. Bent down to disease, pale, infirm, and emaciated; the vigour of health, the life of life was gone. The only surviving victim of the ungenial climate, where,

"'Mid each dank stream the reeking marsh exhales,

"Contagious vapours and volcanic gales,"

His gallant companions were doomed to meet the poisoned shafts of death. He, it is true, returned to his county—but returned to linger out a life of pain, and to experience the protracted sufferings of premature old age.

The reader, we hope, is well convinced, that under a wise and uncorrupt government the advantages to be thus purchased at the expence of so many useful and valuable lives, must be far from problematical or uncertain. If the said reader enjoys, or is likely to enjoy, a snug sinecure from the government of a fortress in these regions of pestilence, or has a prospect of pocketing any of the various emoluments arising from contracting for the same, we need say nothing to convince him of its utility, and shall therefore proceed in our narrative.[77]

With an agitation of joy, almost too powerful for his enfeebled frame to support, Capt. Delmond embraced his wife and daughter. With the latter he was truly charmed; she was more than his most sanguine hopes had painted, or his fond heart had dared to wish. To her he resolved to dedicate the remainder of his life, and to spare no pains on her instruction and improvement.

In the once beautiful face of Mrs. Delmond time had produced an alteration no less conspicuous than that which climate and disease had wrought upon the person of her husband. To beauties of Mrs. Delmond's description Time is, indeed, a most formidable foe. Where no spark of animation supplies the place of youth's bewitching, but alas! transient glow; where, when the roses die and the lilies fade, no trait of *mind*, no vivid expression of sensibility shoots along the desolated waste, every wrinkle is triumphant, and the conquest over beauty is compleat.[78] The alteration thus effected in the countenance of Mrs. Delmond, though apparent to the eye, reached not the heart of her faithful husband. His attachment to her was not, it is true, either sentimental or sublime; it was, nevertheless, cordial and sincere. As an helpless object depending on his protection, he had been accustomed to cherish her. As *his own*, he had considered her with that regard which self-love attaches to property;[79] and even the very sufferings she had occasioned to him, were, perhaps, an additional motive of his affection. Habit made him experience uneasiness from the want of her presence, (*society* we can scarcely term it) and that delight with which the human mind returns to those deep-worn channels, where it has long been accustomed to flow, made him experience in this re-union emotions of the most lively joy.

As for Mrs. Delmond, the meeting and the parting kiss were given by her with the same frigid composure. Without any alteration in the tone of her voice, or in one muscle of her countenance, she said 'she was *glad*

---

[77] Perhaps a reference to the general animosity against servicemen overseas despite the financial rewards reaped by those at home.

[78] Educational treatises such as Hamilton's own *Letters on Education* (1801) and Wollstonecraft's *Thoughts on the Education of Daughters* (1787) warn about relying on looks alone. In the latter Wollstonecraft notes "It is true, regular features strike at first; but it is a well ordered mind which occasions those turns of expression in the countenance, which make a lasting impression" (33).

[79] Sir William Blackstone's *Commentaries on the Laws of England* (4 vols., 1765-69) explain that "by marriage, the husband and wife are one person in law, that is, the very being or legal existence of the woman is suspended during the marriage, or at least is incorporated and consolidated into that of the husband: under whose wing, protection and *cover*, she performs every thing" (430; bk.1, ch. 15). The wife literally was the husband's property.

to see him.' And as we never heard of her being addicted to falsehood, we are bound to believe her.

Capt. Delmond having, through the interest of General Villers, obtained leave to retire upon half-pay, took a small house in a village near that gentleman's seat, and with the prudence of which he was always master, regulated his economy in exact conformity to his circumstances.

The mind of Julia, which had been suffered to expand in the freedom of the country, was now eager for instruction. It was perhaps no less adapted to receive it, than if it had gone through the regular course of emulation, jealousy, envy, and hatred, which so regularly succeed each other in the breast of a boarding-school miss. She received the lessons of her father with delight, and soon became mistress of all he thought necessary for her to learn. Her temper, which had never been spoiled by the alternate application of indiscreet indulgence and unnecessary severity, was open, ardent, and affectionate. To every species of cunning and deceit she was quite a stranger. The happiness which glowed in her own bosom, she wished to communicate to every thing around her.

The cheering influence of her light and buoyant spirits penetrated the breast of her father. It soothed his pains, re-animated his spirits, and gave a charm to his otherwise miserable existence. He regarded his Julia as a being of a superior order. Her capacity he thought almost supernatural. The inferiority of the female understanding he had hitherto considered incontrovertible, and had treated every attempt at the cultivation of the mental powers of that sex with the most sovereign contempt.[80] But his Julia was an exception to the general rule: an understanding so capacious as hers ought to have every advantage. He, therefore, encouraged her insatiable appetite for knowledge with a free command of all the books which either the private collections of his friends or the circulating library could furnish.[81] He laid no restraint upon her choice, for from the pains he took to form her taste, and from the opinion he entertained of the amazing maturity of her judgment, he was convinced she would of her own accord choose only what was proper.

Had a due allowance for the power of imagination in young minds entered into Capt. Delmond's calculation, he would perhaps have been less sanguine. In fact, though Julia read with pleasure books of philosophy, history, and travels to her father, she found a pleasure still more poignant in devouring the pages of a novel or romance in her own

---

[80] Debate raged in educational treatises over whether females were innately intellectually inferior or merely limited by the poor education they received.

[81] Many educationalists warned about the dangers of unsupervised reading habits, especially given the ready availability of novels in circulating libraries.

apartment.[82] Her feelings were alive to all the joys and all the sorrows of the heroes and heroines, whose adventures she had the delight of perusing. The agitation they excited was so animated, so intoxicating, that she felt a void in her breast when not under the influence of strong emotions. In vain did her reason revolt at the absurdities which abounded in these motley tales; in the kindling passions of her youthful bosom they found a never-failing incentive to their perusal.[83]

Imagination, wild and ungoverned imagination reigned paramount in her breast. The investigation of truth had no longer any charm. Sentiment usurped the place of judgment, and the mind, instead of deducing inferences from facts, was now solely occupied in the invention of extravagant and chimerical situations. In these, to do her justice, the most noble and heroic virtues were uniformly displayed. Of the immense fortunes of which she was the ideal mistress, she reserved to herself but a very slender share. All the poor of the country were in one moment enriched by her bounty, all were made happy by her power. Tender and faithful lovers were released from unheard-of-miseries, and put in possession of the most exquisite felicity. Her father, quite cured of his gout, was the lord of an immense domain, whose various beauties fancy painted in more lively colours than the pencil of Raphael was ever dipt in. In short, Julia was an adept in the art of castle-building.

With the education of her daughter Mrs. Delmond never presumed to interfere. She had before her father's return, indeed, taken the trouble to teach her her sampler, and had besides endeavoured to initiate her into the mysteries of cross-stitch, chain-stitch, and gobble-stitch,[84] the last of

---

[82] Critics conflated the female appetite for books, especially novels, with an unhealthy appetite for food and sex. Hence many educationalists decried the practice of reading alone "unsupervised". John Bennett explains in his *Letters to a Young Lady* (1789):
   Plays, operas, masquerades, and all other fashionable pleasures have not half so much danger to young people as the reading of these books. With *them*, the most delicate girl can entertain herself, in *private*, without censure; and the poison operates more forcibly, because unperceived. (2: 72)
In a similar vein, Vicesimus Knox complains that "books are commonly allowed with little restriction, as innocent amusements; yet these often pollute the heart in the recesses of the closet, inflame the passions at a distance from temptation, and teach them all the malignity of vice in solitude" (*Essays, Moral and Literary*, 2: 71).

[83] Many concurred with the educationalist Thomas Gisborne that "the perusal of one romance leads, with more frequency than is the case with respect to works of other kinds, to the speedy perusal of another. Thus a habit is formed ... the appetite becomes too keen to be denied; and in proportion as it is more urgent, grows less nice and select in its fare. ... The produce of the book-club, and the contents of the circulating library are devoured with indiscriminate and insatiable avidity" (*Enquiry into the Duties of the Female Sex*, 1797, 215-17).

[84] Needle-work stitches. The first was characterised by two stitches crossing each other, the second a kind of ornamental stitch resembling the links of a chain and the third a stitch made too long through haste or carelessness.

which only seemed to suit the genius of the little romp, who did not much relish the confinement necessary for these employments. As to mental improvement Mrs. Delmond wisely judged it to be altogether out of her sphere: nor was it with any view to produce such an effect, that she taught her to get by heart the same portion of the church catechism, and the same number of psalms from Sternhold and Hopkins,[85] as she herself had learned; all of which she took care that Julia should regularly repeat every Sunday evening at the same hour and in the same manner which she herself had done when at the same age. To poor Julia the sabbath was indeed a day of bondage and dismay. Happy was she when it was over, and nothing more was to be got by heart for a week to come.

Indeed all the religious duties of Mrs. Delmond were very properly confined to that day which is appointed by the church for their especial performance; every Sunday she very regularly went to church, as her aunt had done before her. And there she was so far from missing any part of the service, that she very audibly repeated the whole of it, absolution and all, after the clergyman, to the great edification of those who had the happiness of sitting in the same pew. By this means she obtained the appellation of a mighty devout good-sort-of- lady from all the neighbours; nor did she at all displease her husband by the practice of this devotion. But though Captain Delmond thought it proper to encourage this weakness in his wife, he wished the mind of his daughter to soar above the vulgar prejudice.

Virtue, he told her, required no incentive to its performance, but its own innate loveliness. The doctrine of rewards and punishments was only adapted to weak and slavish minds. Honour, he said, was the inspiring motive of the great and noble. As to the notion of revelation, it was involved in absurdities which all truly-enlightened men treated with a proper degree of contempt; it was only the tool of knaves and priests, which they made use of to excite the reverence of fools, the more easily to impose upon them.

The beauty and the peace of virtue Julia found enshrined in her own breast; but had that breast ever been taught to glow with devotional sentiment, to expand in grateful adoration of Divine beneficence, and to wrap itself in the delightful contemplation of a future state of felicity, fairer colours would probably have marked its future destiny!

As the heart of Julia was not altogether insensible to vanity, she was exceedingly pleased to find herself so much wiser than the rest of the world. Thus prepared, it is not surprising that she was charmed with the tenets of the new philosophers, which taught her that denying revelation is but one step towards that state of perfection to which the human mind

---

[85] Thomas Sternhold (1500-49) and John Hopkins (d. 1570) wrote the English version of the Psalms in 1562 that was included in the Book of Common Prayer and was for two centuries almost the whole hymnod, of the Church of England.

is so speedily advancing. Her introduction to the philosophers, and all that happened subsequent to that event, the reader has already been made acquainted with. It is high time the fair petitioner whom we left at the door of her father's chamber, should now speak for herself, which she shall have an opportunity of doing in the next chapter.

CHAP. XIII.

"Hence to the realms of night, dire demon, hence!
"Thy chain of adamant can bind
"That little world, the human mind,
"And sink its noblest powers to impotence."

ROGERS.[86]

CAPT. Delmond's spirits, sunk by a restless and painful night, revived at the sight of his lovely daughter; he kissed her with even more than usual tenderness, and anxiously enquired concerning the indisposition which had so long detained her from him. She said, her head had ached violently, which she attributed to the want of exercise, and had no doubt that a little air would entirely remove it.

"And why, my darling, do you confine yourself so much; I shall insist hereafter upon your going out regularly every day. The air of this apartment is injurious to you, and my dear girl must not be allowed to suffer from her too great kindness to her old father."

The open and susceptible heart of Julia, hitherto a stranger to every species of artifice and concealment, felt this tenderness as a reproach too poignant to be borne. Her eyes filled with tears. She dared not trust her voice, but with an air of the most emphatic gratitude and affection she kissed the hand which had fondly taken hold of hers.

At length the importance of the projected enterprize rushed upon her recollection; when stifling her emotion, and assuming an air of cheerfulness, she said she had been thinking that a ride into the country would be of service to her. She had long promised a visit to Castle-Villers, and with her father's permission thought she might now accomplish it.

"Certainly, my love, as soon as ever you please: you shall yourself write a note to Mrs. Villers to inform her of your intention, and she will, I make no doubt, send the carriage to fetch you."

'I was thinking,' replied Julia hesitatingly, 'I was thinking whether I could not go without giving her that trouble. You remember Dr. Orwell's gig. I am sure he would be so good as let me have it for a day, and I would not wish to stay longer.'

"But you cannot go alone in the gig, my dear?"

---

[86] Samuel Rogers (1763-1855) "Ode to Superstition" (1785), I.i.1-4.

'O no, I—I would get some one to drive me.'

"If Dr. Orwell goes himself, and I know he sometimes visits there, I shall have no objection. He is a very respectable man, and I believe the worthiest man of his profession. He, I make no doubt, will take proper care of you. Go then, my dear, and make the request yourself, a walk will do you good; and I shall not suffer you to read to me this morning, it would not be proper for you after being so much indisposed, so GOD bless you, my child—good-bye."

Half defeated in her purpose, though not quite discomfited, Julia left her father's room without having suffered the name of Vallaton to pass her lips. She could not prevail upon herself to encounter the prejudices of her father, and this timidity led her to practice a deceit, which, though contrary to her feelings and repugnant to her judgment, she hoped the plea of necessity would sufficiently excuse.

The admireers of amiable weakness, who consider the virtues of fortitude and courage as inimical to every charm of the female character, reflect not how impossible it is for the mind that is deprived of their support, firmly to tread the "onward path" of sincerity; nor how often the timid and irresolute will be prompted by their fears "*to take dissimulation's winding way.*" Fortitude and courage are, however, only the companions of undeviating rectitude. They had hitherto been constant inhabitants in the gentle breast of Julia; whose soft and winning manners clearly evinced that those virtues, masculine as they are generally deemed, are far from being incompatible with modesty and gentleness. In once having permitted herself to tread the path of error, short as were the steps she had as yet taken, she found she had already lost the firm supporters of her mind; and to extricate herself she had recourse to their unworthy substitutes, art and concealment.

In her father's name she wrote a note to Dr. Orwell to request the gig for the following day; and desiring the answer to be delivered into her own hands, and strictly charging the messenger to say nothing of where he had been to either of her parents, she took the road to Mr. Glib's.

Mr. Vallaton, who did not expect to see her till the evening, was charmed at a circumstance, which he did not fail to interpret to his own advantage. And still more was he delighted, when she informed him that she had come on purpose to request a favour of him.

"A favour of me, Julia! impossible. You know not how exquisitely it would delight me to oblige you. I hope it is something that may require the exertion of all my energies, that you may see what power you have over me."

'It is only to drive me a few miles in a gig. I wish to call at Castle-Villers tomorrow; and thought perhaps you would have no objection to accompany me. The General is very hospitable, and will be happy to receive any friend of my father's; for as such I mean to introduce you. You do not know,' continued she with an enchanting smile, 'what good may arise from this introduction.'

Vallaton was profuse in his acknowledgments, which Julia interrupted by saying she had still another request to make, which she hoped he would have as little hesitation in complying with.

"Can my lovely Julia fear that any request of hers should meet with a refusal? Impossible. Let her but name her wish; and were it to pluck her kerchief from the horned moon, it should be done."

'I greatly wish, then,' replied Julia, 'nay, I would give the world to see the embroidered covering of the basket which formed your infant cradle. Have you it not with you.'

"No, I believe not; it is not with me at present."

'Nor any of your infant robes.'

"No, I—I unfortunately left them in the care of a very particular friend in town."

'How unlucky! indeed, indeed you ought never to go any where without them. Are they not the blessed instruments by which the strange mystery of your birth will most undoubtedly be developed. I must chide you for trusting so precious a deposit in any hands but your own. You can, however, write for them, and your friend may send them to you by the mail-coach.'

Vallaton, who could hardly suppress a smile at the earnestness with which Julia made this unforeseen request, took from it a hint, which effectually relieved his present embarrassment. He promised to write to his friend by that night's post; and doubted not, but that in a few days he should receive the credentials of his noble birth in safety. It is probable that his mind's eye at that moment cast a retrospective glance to the cellar of St. Giles's, where his first blanket, whose embroidery was certainly of no Tyrian dye,[87] after having done its duty as a mop, and gone through the process of decomposition on a dung-hill, had probably long since lent its aid to enrich its native soil. How much soever Mr. Vallaton's patriotism might lead him to glory in the certainty of his first rags having been thus useful to his country, his modesty prevented his assuming any merit upon this head; and Julia, whose memory furnished her with a thousand similar examples, was quite satisfied that the little embroidered vestments, he had so particularly described, would lead to the happy discovery her ardent imagination had so fully planned.

Mr. Vallaton, willing to change a subject which was rather becoming too interesting, enquired whether the excursion to Castle-Villers was with her father's knowledge.

'Oh yes,' replied Julia, 'my dear papa is always so indulgent that he never objects to any thing that will give me pleasure, unless fears for my safety, or doubts concerning propriety, should suggest the objection.'

---

[87] Purple or crimson dye anciently made at Thyre, an ancient Phoenician city on the Mediterranean, from certain molluscs.

"Propriety! in what vocabulary of prejudice did you pick up that offensive word? What can be improper that does not rebel against the great commands of nature? It is these worldings 'gorged with misanthropy,' who have by this term *propriety* forged the most galling fetters for the amiable period of youth. Would that my Julia were superior to the ignoble bondage!"

'Indeed, indeed now, Mr. Vallaton, you do my father wrong. He never wishes to subject my mind but to the bondage of reason. If you knew his affection for me, and how good to me he has always been, you would not wonder that I should love him.'

"And pray tell me from whence does his affection for you proceed? If it appears, that the circumstance of being his daughter has any influence upon your father's mind, such a weak and foolish prejudice is more deserving of your contempt than veneration."

'Your argument is, indeed, very forcible; I know not how to answer it; but still I cannot so far conquer that prejudice which I have hitherto considered as virtuous, and which makes me feel it improper too strictly to scan the imperfections of a parent. If I were dependent on his bounty, I should perhaps be less scrupulous; but since, through my aunt's partial affection, I have come to the command of an independent fortune, I feel as if it were not only ungrateful but ungenerous to examine the motives of an affection, for which I confess (and do not hate me for the confession) it is my most anxious wish to make a suitable return.'

"And pray what has this old gentleman done for you?"

'Done! how can you ask the question? Did he not, during the period of my infancy, and even before he had ever seen me, part with more than half his income for mine and my mother's support? Was it not for our sakes that he endured the horrors of that detested climate; sacrificed his ease, his health, his comfort? And then on his return: what tender affection! what unremitting care! To procure for me the accomplishments which he himself could not teach, and to enable me to make an appearance equal to my companions of larger fortune; how often has he and my mother denied themselves every little comfort to which they had been habituated? Oh! how happy am I now in having it in my power to restore to them these innocent enjoyments, to make their old age as easy and as comfortable as that period of life will admit! Till your arguments convinced me that there could not possibly be a GOD, I could hardly refrain from the superstitious persuasion, that a sort of Providence had interposed to send me this legacy at the very time when, by the loss of the small pension which my father, in addition to his half-pay, had hitherto enjoyed, it became almost impossible to support his family, and keep up the rank in life he had been accustomed to maintain. In giving up this fortune to his disposal, I experienced the sweetest pleasure of my life!'

"And have you actually given it up to his disposal?" cried Vallaton with great earnestness, and in a tone fully expressive of the virtuous horror he felt as such a flagitious proof of the destructive vice of gratitude.

'No,' rejoined the fair philosopher, 'my father would not accept the gift. He said he would do no more than act as my steward. It was evidently the intention of my aunt, that I should be independent before the period affixed by law, and he would not frustrate her intentions. He said, he surely had no cause to be less confident in my prudence than she had! And by saying so he doubly bound me to give myself up to his direction in every article of my conduct.'

"Dear enchanting enthusiast!" cried Vallaton, somewhat recovered from his alarm. "The false views in which things appear to your understanding is truly to be regretted. And so you are indebted to this gentleman, because, forsooth, *in the hateful spirit of monopoly, he chose by despotic and artificial means to engross a pretty woman to himself;*[88] and even in absence unjustly to prevent his neighbour from enjoying a good which he could not himself continue to possess; for was not this the true motive of his care of your mother? As for you, whatever he bestowed previous to his knowledge of your real worth, was a glaring proof of the most odious selfishness. Was it not because he believed himself your father, that he thus provided for you? In what a contemptible light does philosophy teach us to view this prejudice? *I ought to prefer no human being to another, because that being is my father, my wife, or my son, but because, for reasons which equally appeal to all understandings, that being is entitled to preference. In a state of equality, it will be a question of no importance to know who is the parent of each individual child. It is aristocracy, self-love, and family pride, that teach us to set a value upon it at present.*★[89] And for this offspring of aristocratic prejudice, this selfish affection which your father had for you because you were *his*, and not the offspring of some other man, haply more worthy than himself, he is entitled to your duty and your gratitude! Mistaken Julia! I wish you would exert the energies of your mind, to conquer prejudices so unworthy of your understanding."

Poor Julia had not now one word to say in her own defence. Abashed at the conviction of her filial weakness, she cast her lovely eyes upon the ground. The enlightened philosopher tenderly seized her hand, and changing his voice to the soft tone of supplication, entreated she would pardon him for his zeal in the cause of truth. He wished to remove every obstacle to *perfectibility* in one so near perfection: she had but to conquer a few of those remaining prejudices to reach the goal. "By this fair hand I swear," said he, pressing it to his lips, "that all I say proceeds from the strength and disinterestedness of my affection." The entrance of the

---

[88] Godwin wrote that "marriage as now understood, is a monopoly, and the worst of monopolies" in which a man "by despotic and artificial means, maintain[s] ... possession of a woman" (*Political Justice* Bk VII, "Of Co-operation, Cohabitation and Marriage"). See Appendix A.

[89] ★See Pol. Jus. Vol. ii.★ Godwin *Political Justice* Bk IV, ch. x, "Of Self-Love and Benevolence".

Goddess of Reason, Mr. Myope, and Mr. Glib, prevented her reply. She soon took her leave, and her heart palpitating with various contending emotions, returned to her father's house.

CHAP. XIV.

"Mortals, in vain ye hope to find,
"If guilt, if fraud have stain'd your mind,
"Or saint to hear, or angel to defend."
So Truth proclaims. I hear the sacred sound
Burst from the centre of her burning throne,
Where aye she sits, with star-wreath'd lustre crown'd;
A bright sun clasps her adamantine zone.
So Truth proclaims, her awful voice I hear,
With many a solemn pause it slowly meets my ear.[90]

IN the personification of the virtues, Sincerity ought certainly to be delineated as the most vindictive of the whole groupe. Inflexible in her decrees, and jealous of her authority, she hedges round her white domain with so many thorns, that it is impossible to depart from it for a single moment with impunity. In endeavouring to effect his escape, the poor fugitive gets so entangled, that should he even succeed in avoiding the disgrace of detection, he cannot avoid the stings of shame and dishonour, which, if he have any feeling, will pierce him to the quick.

Alarmed lest the answer of Dr. Orwell should by mistake have been delivered to her father, Julia's first care was to seek the messenger it was sent by. He was not yet returned. Indeed the boy thought he never could have a better opportunity of taking his own time. The injunctions laid upon him by his young mistress to conceal his errand from her father, made him quickly sensible that she was in his power. Why should he not indulge himself in a game at marbles? If he staid ever so long she durst not inform on him for her own sake. And if Miss told a lie, by saying she sent him any where else, why should he not tell her another? Could he pretend to be better than Miss.

Vexed at his delay, and trembling lest it should occasion a discovery, Julia began to feel the thorns which strewed the path on which she had so lately entered. The boy at length arrived, and brought with him a polite answer from Dr. Orwell, who willingly granted her request. She hastily put the note in her pocket, and then went to the parlour, where she found Mrs. Gubbles, senior, sitting with her father and mother.

"Well, my love," said Capt. Delmond, "what says Dr. Orwell to your request? Did you find all the family at home?"

---

[90] not found.

'Dr. Orwell is kind enough to let me have the gig whenever I please, and desires his compliments to you and my mamma.'

'And pray,' said Mrs. Delmond, 'did you see Mrs. Goodwin? I wonder she did not give you the receipt for the elder wine which I sent to beg of her this morning. She told Nanny she would write it out for me before dinner. Did not she mention it to you?'

'No,' replied Julia, 'I—I did not see Mrs. Goodwin.'

"Aye, but I warrant," cried Mrs. Gubbles with an arch smile, "I warrant Miss saw somebody better worth looking at. There was young Mr. Sydney just come home from the colleges; I saw him with his father a going to the parsonage just before Miss went out; one would be astonished to see what a great, tall, proper man he is grown. Good lack! it was but yesterday, as I think, since he was quite a little baby; and now to be sure he is one of the most handsomest and most genteelest young men I ever seed in my life. Don't you think so, Miss?"

'I don't know, I did not see him.'

"Not see him! well that is the most extraordinary thing as ever I knew. He could not possibly come back without my seeing him. You know I am quite in the way, and notices every body as goes by: not a foot on the street, I warrant you, but I knows of. There is that heathenish set as come to Mr. Glib's, who are all (heaven preserve us!) said to be no better than so many atheists; I see'd them go by this morning; there they are, all living at rack and manger. A good hot supper last night, and a fine dinner to-day. I wonder what will come on it at last? A pretty thing, truly, for folks in their way to entertain at such a rate! If it was only their own neighbours and townsfolks, it would be a different thing; but to be throwing away their substance upon authors and such scum, it is a shame to hear of it!"

'I should suppose, ma'm,' said Julia with some warmth, 'that Mr. Glib knows his own affairs best: I believe the party you allude to are very respectable people, and do Mr. Glib great honour by their visit.'

"It may be so, Miss. They may be very respectable people, to be sure, for aught I know; though I don't think it's the most respectablest thing in the world, for people to be sneaking about the streets all night, that have no honest calling to take them out of their warm beds."

'Do the people at Mr. Glib's keep such late hours?' enquired Capt. Delmond.

"I don't know for all of 'em," replied the loquacious Mrs. Gubbles, "but betwixt four and five this morning, as my husband was a going to Mrs. Dunstan's, (who, as I was telling you as Miss there came in, has got a fine thumping boy) he passed that there tall one just at your garden-gate, I don't know his name, but there he was a perambulating through the street, and I leave you to judge, whether at that late hour it was likely he had been building churches?"

In the loud laugh to which Mrs. Gubbles was excited by her own *wit*, Julia felt no inclination to join. The consequences of Vallaton's having been seen in his retreat from the arbour, filled her with terror and dismay. To conceal the inquietude of her mind, she made a pretence for quitting the room, and did not return till the visitor was gone and dinner put upon the table.

In places far removed from the great and crouded theatre of the metropolis, the scenes of life (if we may be permitted to carry on the hacknied allusion) come so near the eye, that every little wheel and pulley becomes visible to the audience. The actors are there indeed so few, and so seldom do any incidents occur in the rural drama of sufficient importance to excite a general interest, that if the good people in a country town were not to find a substitute for more important articles of intelligence in the minutiae of family transactions, they must either be condemned to silence, or laid under the dreadful necessity of cultivating internal resources. No such miserable alternative awaits the happier inhabitant of the metropolis. There day unto day furnishes an everlasting fund for talk, and the insatiable thirst for news is gratified by such a succession of great events, that though petty scandal may serve as a relish, it is by no means an absolute necessary of life. In the country, where the appetite for news is not a whit less voracious, it is obligated to put up with a more limited bill of fare: the minutest action of every neighbour is there, indeed, very liberally served up, while conjectures on its cause and its consequences serve as sauce to the entertainment.

The valetudinary state of Captain Delmond's health, which deprived him of those resources for killing time to which he had formerly been accustomed, made him glad to fill the vacuum by any piece of intelligence that offered: even a visit from Mrs. Gubbles was on this account acceptable, as no one possessed more information concerning the state of affairs in the village and its neighbourhood than that good lady. Wherever she went, she generally left heads of discourse to occupy the remainder of the day; so it appeared likely to be at present. The birth of Master Dunstan, the fortune he was likely to inherit, the age of his mother, and the question of who was most likely to be asked to stand god-father upon the important occasion, having been all successively discussed; the return of Henry Sydney came next under consideration.

Had Julia heard nothing of him at the parsonage?

It was very extraordinary. Who did she see there? Julia, at a loss for a reply, hesitated, and then said she had only seen Dr. Orwell.

"Were you in the saloon?"

'No.'

"Oh! then the matter is plain enough; the ladies wished to have the gentleman all to themselves, and so the Doctor did not invite you to go in? Ay, ay, let the parson alone. He did not choose to trouble his daughters with a female visitor, when he knew they were more agreeably engaged."

'Indeed, sir, Dr. Orwell was to-day as he always is, very kind and polite. I am sure he and his daughters are equally above every little jealousy.'

"Well, well, it may be so; but who are those people at Glib's? You spoke to Mrs. Gubbles as if you had known something of them."

'I believe it is Mr. Myope, the great author, and his lady; I have met them at Mrs. Botherim's: they are very genteel, well-informed people.'

"And the tall young man who was seen lurking about the streets at that unseasonable hour; what is he?"

'I don't know indeed,' replied Julia, looking at the same time out of the window, 'I can't tell who Mrs. Gubbles meant.'

"Some idle fellow of an author too, I suppose," rejoined her father; "one who I dare say would be very properly employed in carrying a musket.[91] Really, my dear, I am somewhat afraid that Mrs. Botherim is not quite difficult enough in regard to the choice of her guests. Authors and these sort of people may be very good in their way, but they are by no means proper acquaintances for my Julia."

'But, my dear sir, ought we not to pay some respect to talents and genius, even though destitute of fortune?'

"Fortune!—I despise fortune as much as any man; but will talents and genius make a gentleman? And are not all the authors who have talents or genius known to be democrats in their hearts. Talk not to me of such people, my dear, they ought to be the dread and detestation of every loyal subject."

This was a theme on which Julia was ever fearful of entering. She knew her father's prejudices to be unconquerable. It was this circumstance which had hitherto prevented her from bringing him acquainted with Vallaton, whose patriotism so pure, so disinterested, so enlightened, must be shocked at sentiments so opposite to his own! Even should his respect for her impose upon him a silence repugnant to his generous principles of hazarding all for truth, he could not fail to be wounded at the expression which, if the subject of politicks was started, would infallibly drop from her father's tongue. She had, therefore, most carefully concealed her knowledge of him from Capt. Delmond, who she well knew would on his part be equally shocked at the enlightened system of her new preceptor.

This concealment she at first imagined would have been a very easy matter; but she soon experienced the torment which, in a generous mind, attends the least attempt at disingenuity. The entrance of Henry Sydney and his sister relieved her present embarrassment. The latter came to request the favour of Miss Delmond's company to a rural feast in the hayfield, to which the Captain, who considered the symptoms of indisposition he had lately remarked in his daughter to originate in too much confinement, readily acquiesced; and Julia, who now for the first time of her life was happy in any excuse that could relieve her from the burthen of her father's presence, hastily prepared herself to attend her amiable friend.

---

[91] Captain Delmond believes all idle hands should be conscripted.

CHAP. XV.

"Where the sense of the speech is but ill understood,
"We are bound to suppose it uncommonly good."
                                            SIMKIN'S LETTERS.[92]

IT is now time to return to Miss Botherim, whom we left very properly rebuking her mother for the fault committed by her domestick. In reply to a very long and very learned exhortation, which had, however, nearly exhausted the good lady's patience, "I tell you, Biddy," said Mrs. Botherim, "that though coming into the parlour and speaking of your wig before the gentlemen was not his business, to be sure, yet he is a very good boy for all that. He takes such care of the cow, and is so kind to all the dumb creatures, that he must be good."

'Good!' repeated Bridgetina with great indignation, 'It appears, madam, that you know very little of the nature of goodness. What is goodness but virtue? *Considered as a personal quality, it consists in the disposition of the mind, and may be defined a desire to promote the benefit of intelligent beings in general, the quantity of virtue being as the quantity of desire. Now desire is another name for preference, or a perception of the excellence, real or supposed, of any object; and what perception of excellence can a being so unenlightened possibly possess?*'[93]

"You know very well, daughter," rejoined Mrs. Botherim, "that I cannot answer you in all them there argumentations; but I can tell you that it will be long enough before we get a better boy than Bill, and that there is not a cow upon the common half so well fed as ours."

'It is a strange thing, mother,' rejoined Bridgetina, 'that you never will learn to generalize your ideas. The boy may take very good care of your cow, and by leading her to the best pasture, promote both her benefit and yours; *but if he derives this benefit, not from a clear and distinct perception of what it is in which it consists, but from the unexamined lessons of education, from the physical effect of sympathy, or from any species of zeal unallied to and incommensurate with knowledge, can this desire be admitted for virtuous?*[94] If your prejudices were not invulnerable, you would not hesitate to acknowledge that it ought not; and if his actions cannot be admitted for virtuous, how can he be called good?'

To this Mrs. Botherim was incapable of making any reply. A silence of some minutes ensued, which the mother at length broke; "I was thinking," said she, "my dear, whether we might not drink tea with Miss Sydney this evening; now that her brother is come home, the compliment

---

[92] Ralph Broome, *Letters from Simkin the Second to his Dear Brother in Wales* (1789), modification of Letter v.
[93] See Godwin, *Political Justice* Bk IV, ch. ix, "Of the Mechanism of the Human Mind".
[94] See Godwin, *Political Justice* Bk IV, ch. ix, "Of the Mechanism of the Human Mind".

will be expected; and you know next week is the week of our great wash, when I never goes from home, and to-morrow I must look over your things to prepare for it; so as it will be a long time before I have an other day, I think we had as well go this.'

The proposal was too agreeable to Miss Botherim to be rejected. A messenger was dispatched to notify their intention; and while Mrs. Botherim betook herself to the task of combing out the unfortunate tresses, whose luckless fate hath already excited the reader's commiseration, Bridgetina retired to her library to study for the discourse of the evening.

CHAP. XVI.

"These gentle hours that plenty bade to bloom;
"Those calm desires that ask'd but little room;
"Those healthful sports that graced the peaceful scene,
"Liv'd in each look, and brighten'd all the green."
GOLDSMITH.[95]

OUR heroine bestowed so much time on the tedious labours of the toilet, that the little party at Mr. Sydney's had enjoyed nearly an hour of each other's society before she and her mother appeared. They found the house deserted of its inhabitants, but were conducted by a little girl through the garden into a meadow which beautifully sloped towards the river. On the lower part a groupe of hay-makers were at work; Mr. Sydney, and his friend the rector, were cheerfully conversing with the rustick band, and encouraging the innocent merriment which lightened all their toil. At the upper part of the field was Mrs. Martha Goodwin and her nieces, together with Julia, Maria Sydney, and her brother, all at work; some settling the camp stools which they had carried in their own hands, some depositing their share of the tea equipage upon the table which Henry had just fixed beneath the shade of a spreading elm, and in a spot from which the most delightful prospect of the country opened to the view. All was hilarity and ease, cheerfulness and good-humour.

Ceremony, that tiresome and ineffective substitute for true politeness, found no admittance here. Necessary as her presence is deemed, and necessary as it in reality may be, to preserve the decorum of a city rout, it could be dispensed with by the present party without any apprehension of inconvenience. Where confidence of mutual good-will and congenial harmony of sentiment influence every breast, and the polish of the manners proceeds from the polish of the mind, the forms of ceremony are as useless as impertinent.

If the art of making every one around feel easy and comfortable be

---

[95] Goldsmith, "The Deserted Village" (1770), lines 69-72.

accounted a mark of true politeness, Miss Sydney must be confessed to do the honours of her table as an adept. She had seen little of what is called the world, but the few acquaintances with whom she was accustomed to associate, were all well-bred and sensible.

Ever attentive to the wants, and observant to the manners of others, she would have conducted herself with propriety in any scene or upon any occasion that could possibly have occurred. Her good breeding was indeed of that sterling sort that might pass current in any country of the civilized world; and must be confessed in this respect to possess some advantage over that of the frivolous votaries of fashion, whose knowledge of the artificial forms of ceremony, like the paper money of a country bank, has only a circumscribed and local value.

The natural vivacity of Maria's temper had been long suppressed by an unremitting and painful attendance on the death-bed of her mother. Time had worn off the sharp edge of sorrow, but had not quite restored her usual cheerfulness, when the return of her darling brother gave new animation to her spirits, and once more turned her heart to joy.

She had the pleasure of seeing her happiness diffusive. Every eye seemed to sparkle with a delight responsive to that which glowed in her own breast. Even Julia, whose once gay and lively spirits had of late been chilled and frozen in the cold region of metaphysics, seemed reanimated by the participation of pleasures congenial to youth and nature. She entered into the amusements of her friends, joined in the light-hearted laugh, retorted the inoffensive raillery, and was one of the most busy in preparing for the rural feast. She and Harriet Orwell had just finished decorating a basket of strawberries with a wreath of flowers which Henry had gathered, and were with light and graceful steps bearing it betwixt them to the table, while Henry, keeping his seat upon the grass, was with eyes of rapture following every motion of the lovely pair, when the small shrill voice of Miss Botherim accosted his ears, and drew his attention from these engaging objects.

'So Doctor,' cried she, 'I perceive that you have retired to taste the pleasures of abstract speculation. How I admire a taste so similar to my own! Divine congeniality of sentiment! it is thou alone can'st give a taste of true felicity to enlightened minds!'

Henry, whose contemplations of whatever nature they were, seemed little disposed to relish this interruption, made no other reply than the common form of salutation; but suddenly rising and placing himself by the side of Mrs. Botherim, he begged to attend the ladies to his sister.

Bridgetina, who humanely resolved to treat her chosen lover with all imaginable tenderness, immediately went round to his side, and instantly began her well-conned conversation.

'I have just been renovating my energies,' said she, 'by the impressive eloquence of Rousseau. I need not ask whether the sublime virtues of his Eloisa do not enrapture your soul? Was any character ever drawn so natural, so sublime, so truly virtuous?'

"I am sorry that I cannot perfectly agree with you," replied Henry; "but here are the ladies, they had almost despaired of seeing you."

Maria then came forward, and politely led her guests to the seats she had prepared for them; while Henry slipt round to the opposite side of the table, and took possession of a little turfy knoll, which separated the seats of Harriet and Julia.

Though the conversation that commenced between these young people was, if we may judge from the smile of satisfaction that played upon their countenances, sufficiently entertaining to themselves, it might probably be with justice considered beneath the dignity of history. Happily for the edification of the learned reader, it received an interruption from Bridgetina, who, as she never trusted to the spontaneous effusion of the moment, might always be said to speak for the press.

The bustle of the tea-table, and the playful contention which attended the distribution of fruit, cakes, &c. for some time stopt the torrent of her eloquence; but it was only stopt to pour forth at the first opportunity with redoubled force.

'Dr. Henry Sydney,' cried she, in a voice sufficiently audible, 'I must call upon you for an explanation of the words you uttered before tea, which seemed to my apprehension to cast a doubt upon the sublime virtue of Eloisa. If it be to that part of her conduct which seems to have been dictated by her prejudices as a religionist that you object, I have nothing to plead in her defence. But as to her affair with St. Preux, it was surely the most sublime instance of abstract virtue! A virtue superior to the fantastic prejudices of a distempered civilization; and which, in the wild career of energetic feeling, nobly pursued the sentiments of nature. Is it possible that you can perceive no charms in such a conduct?'

"Situated as St. Preux," replied Henry, (while an ingenuous modesty heightened the colour of his expressive countenance) "I will not pretend to answer for myself. No such situation, however, can possibly occur; for never will there be an Eloisa such as Rousseau's vivid imagination has described. The different parts of her character are indeed incompatible with each other."

'In what respect?' asked Bridgetina.

"In minds of a certain cast," returned Henry, "the licentious passions may revel in the heart, while the imagination is forming the most sublime conceptions of exalted virtue. But the virtues of Heloise are not the transient effusions of this species of enthusiasm, they are represented as the steady and dignified offspring of reason. With such principles a part of her conduct is utterly inconsistent, and therefore, in my opinion, unnatural and absurd."

'Indeed, Doctor,' replied Bridgetina, 'I should not have expected to have found you infected by the prejudices which are engendered by the unnecessary institutions of a depraved society. But when sublimer notions of things have been sufficiently generated by philosophy, depend upon it the example of Eloisa will prove a model to her sex.'

"The example of Eloisa!" repeated old Mr. Sydney; "was she not a wanton baggage, who was got with child by her tutor? I remember reading an extract from the book in an old review; and I must say the world was very little obliged to Mr. Rousseau for publishing such a story. He might intend it, and if he was a good man he doubtless did intend it, as a warning to young women to beware of falling into the snares of men; but, alas! I am afraid it has done little good."

'I never read the book in question,' said Dr. Orwell, 'but of Rousseau's system of female education, I think the circumstance you allude to might very naturally be the result. A creature instructed in no duty but the art of pleasing, and taught that the sole end of her creation was to attract the attention of the men, could not be expected to tread very firmly in the paths of virtue.'

"I wonder," said Mrs. Martha Goodwin, "what Rousseau would have done with all the ordinary girls, for it is plain his system is adapted only for *beauties*; and should any of these poor beauties fail in getting husbands, GOD help them, poor things! they would make very miserable old maids."[96]

'Beauty, madam,' cried Bridgetina, 'is a consideration beneath the notice of a philosopher, as the want of it is no moral obstacle to love: will not the mind that is sufficiently enlightened always behold the preferableness of certain objects?' continued she, drawing up her long craggy neck so as to put the shrivelled parchment-like skin which covered it upon the full stretch. 'In a reasonable state of society women will not restrain their powers, they will then display their energies; and the vigour of their minds exerted in the winning eloquence of courtship, will not be exerted in vain. There will then be no old maids, or none but fools will be so. As to Rousseau, it is plain that he was a stranger to the rights of women.'

"The inconsistency and folly of his system," said Henry, "was, perhaps, never better exposed than in the very ingenious publication which takes the Rights of Women[97] for its title. Pity that the very sensible authoress has sometimes permitted her zeal to hurry her into expressions which have raised a prejudice against the whole. To superficial readers it appears to be her intention to unsex women entirely.[98] But—"

'And why should there be any distinction of sex?' cried Bridgetina, interrupting him; 'Are not moral causes superior to physical? And are not

---

[96] Rousseau actually received a letter from a woman who agreed with his devised role for women but asked that since no one would marry her what her role in life should be. Rousseau was reportedly flabbergasted and unable to reply coherently since he could envisage no extra-domestic, merely human solution to her existential dilemma.

[97] Mary Wollstonecraft, *Vindication of the Rights of Woman* (1792).

[98] A criticism levelled by Richard Polwhele in his poem *The Unsex'd Females* (1798) in which he lambastes Wollstonecraft, among other women, as masculine and "unsex'd" who "vaunt the imperious mien". The anonymous author of the *Female Jockey Club* (1794) describes such women as letting their charms whither in time rather than submit "to the *rude mercy* of that *odious monster* man".

women formed with powers and energies capable of perfectibility? Ah! miserable and deplorable state of things in which these powers are debased by the meanness of household cares! Ah! wretched woman, restrained by the cruel fetters of decorum! Vile and ignoble bondage! the offspring of an unjust and odious tyranny, a tyranny whose remorseless cruelty assigns to woman the care of her family! But the time shall come when the mind of woman will be too enlightened to submit to the slavish talk!'

"Indeed, Miss Botherim," said Harriet, "I do not think that there is any thing either slavish or disagreeable in the task: nor do I think a woman's energies, as you call them, can possibly be better employed. Surely the performance of the duties that are annexed to our situation, can never be deemed mean or ignoble?[99] For my share, so far from feeling any derogation of dignity in domestic employment; I always feel exalted from the consciousness of being useful."

'I hope you will never cease to do so, my dear,' said her father, 'and you will ensure to yourself a never-failing source of happiness and contentment. It appears to me that each sex, in every situation in life, has its peculiar duties assigned to it by that good Providence which governs all things, and which seems to delight in order.[100] For the preservation of this order, the inferior creation are endowed with an instinct which impels them to the peculiar mode of life best suited to their species. To man a higher behest is granted; to him reason is given as the sovereign director of his conduct. Alas! that pride and passion should so often render the precious gift of no avail! It is these which, under various disguises, have generally influenced all the system-makers who have taken upon them to prescribe the duties of the sex. These have, according to their several prejudices, laid down the law which was to govern the whole. The best of these have only given rules of conduct where they ought to have infused principles of action: the few who have not treated women as mere machines, incapable of reason, have made it their business to pervert that reason by turning it into a principle of revolt against the order

---

[99] Such views were shared by the educationalist Hannah More who argues "it appears that the mind in each sex has some natural kind of bias, which constitutes a distinction of character and that the happiness of both depends, in a great measure, on the preservation and observance of this distinction (*Essays*, 13). She rails in *Strictures on the Modern System of Female Education* (1799) against those such as Bridgetina who wish to "lift" their sex "from the important duties of [their] allotted station" or "who seek to annihilate distinctions from which a female deserves advantage, and to attempt innovations which would depreciate her real value" (2: 21-22; ch. 13).

[100] A sentiment shared by Hannah More who stated in 1799 that "each sex has its proper excellencies, which would be lost were they melted down into the common character by the fusion of the New Philosophy.... Why should we do away with distinctions which increase the mutual benefits and enhance the satisfactions of life" (Strictures on the Modern System of Female Education, 2: 22; ch. 13).

of Providence, exciting to a spirit of murmuring and discontent, as distant from true wisdom as it is inimical to real happiness. One philosopher, and one only, has appeared, who, superior to all prejudices, invariably treated the female sex as beings who were to be taught the performance of duty, not by arbitrary regulations confined to particular parts of conduct, but by the knowledge of principles which enlighten the understanding and improve the heart."

'And pray what was the name of this philosopher, sir?' said Bridgetina, 'I wonder whether he is an acquaintance of Mr. Myope's, I never heard him speak of him.'

"Very probably not," rejoined Dr. Orwell; "his name was JESUS CHRIST. He was the first philosopher who placed the female character in a respectable point of view. Women, we learn from the gospels, frequently composed a great part of his audience: but to them no particular precepts were addressed, no sexual virtues recommended. He knew that by whomsoever his doctrines were sincerely received, the duties annexed to their situation would be fully and conscientiously fulfilled. His morality was addressed to the judgment without distinction of sex. His laws went not to fix the boundaries of prerogative, and to prescribe the minutiae of behaviour, but to fix purity and humility in the heart. And believe me, my children, the heart that is thus prepared, will not be apt to murmur at its lot in life. It will be ready to perceive, that true dignity consists not in the nature of the duty that is required of us, but in its just performance. The single woman whose mind is embued with these virtues, while she employs her leisure in cultivating her own understanding, and instructing that of others, in seeking for objects on which to exert her charity and benevolence, and in offices of kindness and good-will to her fellow-creatures, will never consider her situation as abject or forlorn. Nor will she who is the mother of a family, consider its humblest duties as mean, or void of dignity and importance. The light of the mind is necessary for the performance of every duty; and great is the mistake of those who think ignorance the guard of innocence and virtue."

'What you have said, my good friend,' said old Mr. Sydney, 'well explains the cause, why minds destitute of the solid principles of religion no sooner get a smattering of knowledge than they renounce the respectable duties of their sex; flying from the post assigned them by nature and Providence,[101] they vainly attempt to seize the command of that which it is impossible they can ever reach. It is, indeed, as you justly observe, in the lessons of our great Master alone that a preservative is to be found against this folly. They offer a sovereign antidote against the swellings of pride and the effusions of vanity; they effectually prepare the

---

[101] Opponents of educational reform for females argued that Nature and God not Man determined the female's role.

mind, not merely for moving in one particular sphere, but for acting with sense and propriety in every situation. Whether married or unmarried, the woman who is thus instructed, will sustain her part with dignity; and the man who is influenced by the same principles, will behave to her with the respect that is due to a joint heir of immortality.'

"Yes," rejoined Dr. Orwell, "if the sublime truths of the gospel had their proper influence upon our sex, women would have little reason to complain. It is impossible that a real Christian should ever be a tyrant. To gratify the passion for dominion, or to exercise the pride of power, can never be an object with him who has imbibed the spirit which pervades the philosophy of JESUS. He can never form the wish of degrading the partner of his bosom to the condition of a slave."

'Alas!' said Mrs. Martha, 'I am afraid, brother, that such sort of Christians are very rare. When I have heard you, and our good friend Mr. Sydney here, expatiating upon the exercise of Christian virtues, I have often thought it a great pity that the heads of our church had not, instead of prescribing confessions of faith with regard to abstruse and speculative points of doctrine, confined themselves to those which are chiefly insisted upon in the discourses of our Saviour. The creed universally enjoined should then have begun with "I believe it is my duty to love my neighbour as myself, and to do to others as I would have others do to me on the like occasion;"[102] and so gone on through the virtues of humility, meekness, and charity; brotherly love, forgiveness of injuries, &c. &c. which articles might have been signed by the most tender conscience, and might probably have been repeated with as much advantage to the soul as the most incomprehensible mystery.'

"It is a very ingenious thought, Madam," said Mr. Sydney, "and would have done more towards coalescing the different sects into which the Christian world is so unhappily divided, than any mode that has yet been adopted. I fear, however, that the measure would meet with some opposition from the zealots of every party. The confession of charity and brotherly love would be justly deemed an innovation big with alarm, and quite inimical to the spirit of party zeal. But come, Maria, here we are talking away about loving our neighbours as ourselves, and never thinking of our thirsty friends in the hayfield. Go, my dear, and order them some refreshment; let them have the best cheese of the dairy, and the best ale that our cellar affords, and see that it be given them by yourself. Never depute another to do an office of kindness which you may yourself perform. Be assured that the manner of doing it is more than half its value."

With cheerful alacrity Maria rose to obey her father's commands: Harriet insisted on accompanying her; Julia would not be left behind; and Henry probably thought his presence would be necessary to assist his sister, for he too chose to be of the party. Bridgetina seeing the motion of

---

[102] *Leviticus* 19:18.

Henry would have likewise followed, but before she could contrive to sidle down from her seat, which was rather the highest, the active groupe were more than half-way to the house. Mr. Sydney, apprehensive from her moving that she was tired of her seat, proposed their taking a walk down the field, which was assented to the more readily by Bridgetina as she there hoped for an opportunity of introducing some philosophical observations with which she had indeed come ready prepared, but which the untoward turn the discourse had taken, had prevented her from introducing.

The approach of Mr. Sydney and his party was observed with pleasure by the hay-makers, who knew that he was no hard task-master, that where reproof was necessary he reproved with gentleness, but that he never withheld from the deserving the just tribute of applause. In truth, their labour being divided among many more hands than was necessary was by no means hard; many found employment here who would have been rejected by more scientific farmers.

> "E'en stooping age is here; and infant hands
> "Trail the long rake, or with the fragrant load
> "O'ercharg'd amid the kind oppression roll."[103]

The glee of the rustics was soon still further animated, on beholding Maria and her friends advancing in gay procession with a profuse supply of refreshments. Maria carried the goblet which, like another Hebe,[104] she presented to all around, and which was plentifully replenished from the pitcher borne by Henry. Harriet and Julia took upon themselves the distribution of the bread and cheese, giving, at the desire of Mr. Sydney, a double portion to such as had left any part of their family at home. Every face wore the appearance of cheerfulness and contentment.

'Miserable wretches!' exclaimed Bridgetina; 'how doth the injustice under which you groan, generate the spirit of virtuous indignation in the breasts of the enlightened.'

"What d'ye say, Miss?" said an old man who imagined her eyes were directed toward him, though in reality she was stedfastly looking in Henry's face. "What d'ye say, Miss," repeated he, "about any one's being miserable?"

'I say,' returned Bridgetina, 'that you ought to be truly wretched.'

"And why so, Miss? what has I done to deserve to be wretched? I works as hardly, and I gets as good wages, as any man in the parish; my wife has good health, and we never lost a child. What should make me wretched?"

'Miserable depravity!' cried Bridgetina, 'how abject that mind which can boast of its degradation! Rejoice in receiving wages! No wonder that

---

[103] James Thomson, *The Seasons* (1726-39) "Summer" 358-60.
[104] The daughter of Zeus and Hera, Goddess of Youth and Spring, who as cup bearer on Mount Olympus was able to restore health and youth to the aged.

gratitude, that base and immoral principle, should be harboured in such a breast!'

"Why, Miss," returned the man, considerably irritated by her harangue, "I would have you to know as how that I don't understand being made game of; and if you mean for to say that I have no gratitude, I defy your malice. I am as grateful for a good turn as any man living. I would go ten miles at midnight upon my bare feet to serve young Mr. Sydney there, who saved my poor Tommy's life in the smallpox: poor fellow, he's remembers it still — don't ye Tommy? Aye that a does; and if thou ever forgets it thou art no true son of thy father's."

Here Mrs. Martha interposed, and by a few kind words allayed the resentment which the declamation of Bridgetina had enkindled. She then invited our heroine to walk with her, and as soon as they were out of the hearing of the labourers, asked her what was her motive for thinking that poor man so miserable.

'And are not all miserable?' said Bridgetina. 'Are not all who live in this deplorable state of distempered civilization miserable, and wretched, and unhappy?'

"Indeed, my dear Miss Botherim," rejoined Mrs. Martha, "I have the comfort of assuring you that you are very much mistaken. In the dwellings of the poor I am no stranger. As fortune has not put it in my power to do much towards removing their wants, I consider myself doubly bound to do all I can towards relieving their afflictions. For this purpose I make it my business to enquire into them; and in the course of these enquiries I have found frequent cause to admire the order of Providence, in distributing the portion of happiness with a much more equal hand than on a slight view we could possibly imagine. I question, whether any lord in the land enjoys half the share of content and satisfaction that falls to the lot of that industrious labourer to whom you spoke. You shall, if you please, accompany me some evening to his cottage, which is one of the neatest and pleasantest little habitations you ever visited in your life. You may there, towards sunset, see the poor man sitting in his nicely-dressed little garden, and perhaps singing some old ballad for the amusement of his children, while their mother is preparing their supper."

'Preparing their supper!' repeated Bridgetina. 'In that one expression you have given an ample description of the misery of their state. Preparing supper! Yes, ye wretched mortals, *the whole of the powers you possess is engaged in pursuit of miserable expedients to protract your existence. Ye poor, predestined victims of ignorance and prejudice! Ye go forward with your heads bowed down to the earth in a mournful state of inanity and torpor. Yet like the victims of Circe, you have the understanding left to give you ever and anon a glimpse of what ye might have been.*★[105] Wherever these poor wretches cast their eyes, they behold nought but cruel aggravations of their affliction.

---

[105] ★Godwin's Enquirer.★ *Enquirer*, Part II, Essay 1, "Of Riches and Poverty", 161-67.

'Suppose them at their homely meal, and that the sumptuous carriage of the peer, whose stately mansion rises on yonder hill, should pass their cottage. When they behold my lord and lady lolling in the gilded coach which is conveying them home to the luxuriant repast prepared by twenty cooks, what effect will the grating sight produce in their tortured bosoms? Will not a sense of the inequality of their conditions wring their wretched hearts? With what horror and disgust will they then view the smoking dish of beans and bacon? Will not their mouths refuse to swallow the loathed food, which the thoughts of the tarts and cheese-cakes that cover the great man's table has converted into bitterness? Will they not leave the untasted meal, and retiring to their bed of chaff, or at best of hen's-feathers, spend the gloomy night in drawing melancholy comparisons betwixt the happy state of the peer and their own miserable condition?'

"And do you really believe all this, my dear?" said Mrs. Martha, laughing. "How in the name of wonder did such strange notions come into your head? Be assured," continued she, "that these poor people see the equipage of my lord and lady with the same indifference that they behold the flight of a bird; and would as soon think of grieving at the want of wings as at the want of a carriage. Were you to follow that lord and lady to their banquet, you would soon be sensible that it was at their luxuriant feast, and not at the cottager's supper the spirit of repining and discontent was to be found. At night, when tossing on their separate beds of down, they might very probably be heard to envy the sound sleep of the peasant; while the contented cottager in the arms of his faithful wife, and surrounded by his little babes, enjoyed the sweets of sound and uninterrupted repose."

'And so,' said Bridgetina, 'your religion, I suppose, teaches you to be callous to the miseries of the poor?'

"GOD forbid!" returned Mrs. Martha, "but my understanding teaches me to discriminate betwixt the natural evils that are incident to poverty, and the fantastic and imaginary ones which have no existence but in the dreams of visionaries. It is one of the blessings belonging to a life of labour, to be exempted from the disquietude of fancied ills. You mistake me, however, if you think I am insensible to the abundance of real ones that falls, alas! too frequently to their lot. But in visiting their afflictions, in advising and consoling them in their distresses, I conceive that I conduce more effectually to the alleviations of their misfortunes, than if I were to indulge myself in the most gloomy reveries, or by exaggerated descriptions of their calamities excite in the wretched objects of my compassion the spirit of discontent. Let us not forget, my dear Miss Botherim, that the essence of charity is very apt to evaporate in the bitterness of declamation. The result of our active benevolence is, on the contrary, attended with the happiest effects, not only to the objects of our bounty but to ourselves:— it returns to our own breasts, extinguishes the sparks of discontent, quenches the flame of pride, and keeps alive that spirit of kindness and goodwill, which is the very bond of peace and source of social happiness."

'You are right, my sister,' said Dr. Orwell, who had heard the latter part of the conversation; 'even the benevolence of a Howard[106] might have degenerated into misanthrophy, if it had only been employed in abstract speculation upon human misery. Far be it from me, however, to speak of the sufferings of the poor with levity or indifference. I too well know the daily increasing misery of their situation, and too sincerely deprecate the causes which have produced it. These we may, without difficulty, trace to the accelerated progress of luxury and its concomitant vices. But can the feeble voice of declamation stem the mighty torrent? As well might it arrest the career of the winds, or stop the fury of the raging elements. He alone who governs the elemental strife, and from "seeming evil still educes good,"[107] can, by some great national calamity, chastise the haughty pride of luxury, and open the eyes of the ignorant and misguided croud, who estimate national prosperity by the superfluous riches heaped upon *thousands* at the expence of the accumulated wretchedness of *millions* of their fellow-creatures. All we have to do as individuals, is to exert our utmost efforts to ameliorate the condition of all within our reach.'

"What you observed, sir," said Henry, addressing himself to Dr. Orwell, "concerning the exact proportion betwixt the increase of luxury and of poverty, I had frequent occasion of remarking in my late tour through Scotland."[108]

'And may we not be favoured with an account of this tour?' said Harriet. 'Let us seat ourselves down upon this bank, where we shall have a charming view of the setting sun, and while we feast our eyes upon its beauties, you shall entertain us with an account of Scotland.'

The motion was instantly agreed to; but Henry, far from availing himself of the advantages which the spot afforded for beholding the most splendid spectacle with which nature has vouchsafed to favour the inhabitants of this terrestrial sphere, turned his back upon the kindling glories of the sky, and contented himself with a full view of Harriet's lovely face. Having placed himself to his liking, he began as may be read in the following chapter.

---

[106] The philanthropist and prison reformer John Howard (1726-90), remembered for his efforts to improve the conditions of prisoners.

[107] James Thomson, *A Hymn on the Seasons* (1730) 114.

[108] Hamilton often uses her works to advance the reputation of Scotland over that of England.

CHAP. XVII.

"—Nor ye who live
"In luxury and ease, in pomp and pride,
"Think these lost themes unworthy of your ear:
"Such themes as these the *rural* Maro sung
"To wide imperial Rome, in the full height
"Of elegance and taste, by *Greece* refined."

THOMSON.[109]

"IF you consider the journal of my tour worthy your perusal," said Henry, "it is very much at your service; you will there find the description of a variety of objects which have escaped the notice of travel-writers, who have seldom gone out of the beaten path.[110] I, on the contrary, was seldom to be found in one.

"As I traversed the country on foot, I had a more ample opportunity for observing its romantic scenery. How many sublime prospects did I enjoy from hills that had never echoed the rattling of a carriage? How often did I find the most extraordinary instances of picturesque beauty in steep and woody glens, which would have been equally dangerous to the horse and his rider? Sometimes I botanized along the margin of a pellucid stream; sometimes I pursued my mineralogical researches, and gratified myself with specimens from the grand Museum of Nature; but it was the manners, the character of the inhabitants that chiefly attracted my attention.

"I made no use of the many introductions I received from my friends in Edinburgh to the country gentlemen near whose seats I was to pass, I trusted to the hospitality of their tenants, and I was not disappointed."

'Well,' cried Mrs. Botherim, 'I vow I am quite astonished how you could think of trusting yourself among them there Scotch savages, I would not have wondered if they had murdered you. Why I heard my late dear Mr. Botherim declare, that them Scotch presbyterians were the most horridest, wickedest people in the world.[111] And then the wretches are so very poor! not one of them with rags to cover their nakedness; faugh! I wonder how you could enter into their stinking houses?'

"Believe me, Madam, that in the course of one morning, in visiting the out-patients of the London Dispensary, I have met with more numerous and striking instances of the extremes of poverty and

---

[109] James Thomson, *The Seasons*, "Spring", 52-57.

[110] Travel journals such as William Gilpin's *Observations, Relating Chiefly to Picturesque Beauty, on several parts of England, particularly the Mountains and Lakes of Cumberland and Westmoreland* (1786).

[111] Hamilton is joking about herself since she is a Scottish Presbyterian. Since the insult comes from the foolish Mrs. Botherim the reader knows better than to take it seriously.

wretchedness, than were to be seen from the Banks of the Tweed to Johnny Groat's house."

'That is just what I should have expected,' said Dr. Orwell, 'as every enjoyment of luxury is purchased by the extraordinary labour of the poor, the effects must be chiefly seen in the spot where she has fixed her empire. There too the poor man comes within the vortex of her vices. He learns to scorn frugality, and the hard earnings of his extraordinary labour is dissipated in intemperance. But I interrupt you, sir; pray proceed.'

"Every step I travelled, whether in England or in Scotland," resumed Henry, "tended to elucidate your assertion. As I receded from the capital, I found simplicity gradually supplying the place of low and loathsome vice, till a decent cleanliness in poverty took place of squalid wretchedness. The reverse of this gave me notice of my approach to some great manufacturing town.[112] There the manners again became corrupted, and brutal ignorance and impudent depravity again became the inmates of the poor man's hovel.

"Soon as I was surrounded by a ragged and clamorous gang of young beggars, I looked out for the stupendous cotton-mill, or other great work where the parents of the little wretches were earning, it may be, three times the wages of the laborious cottager, whose honest pride would rather that himself should suffer starvation, than that his children should submit to the mean trade of beggary. But sentiment is lost in the society of the vicious, and of every species of vice untutored minds quickly catch the contagion.

"Untutored, very untutored, indeed! did I every where find the minds of our English peasantry.

"In situations remote from the influence of luxury, I found the poor cleanly and industrious; but still I found them involved in almost brutal ignorance.

"How superior in this respect did I find the peasantry of Scotland![113] Their reading (for there all can read) was, it is true, often confined to the Bible; but it would seem, that the knowledge of the Bible alone can have a wonderful effect in enlightening the understanding and invigorating the intellect. The explanation given them by their teachers of the obscure and difficult passages that occur to them in their perusal of the sacred volume, sets their faculties to work. The investigation rouses those powers of the mind, which, when suffered to lie dormant, degenerate into impenetrable stupidity. In this point of view, every dogma they are taught to discuss, whether, when in itself abstractedly considered, it be true or false, is to them of real and important use.

---

[112] Comtemporaries such as William Wordsworth, Mary Robinson and Jane West noted that the urban poor were more squalid and had less dignity than the rural poor.

[113] This is explored more fully by Hamilton in her later novel *Cottagers of Glenburnie* (1808).

"When on coming out of one of their country churches, I have observed a groupe of grey-headed rustics in such earnest conversation as excited my curiosity to know the subject of their discourse, I have constantly found it to be engaged on some of the doctrinal topics that had been discussed in the preceding sermon. But would the intellect thus set at work, expand itself into no other channels? Would the perceptions thus quickened be entirely confined to subjects of speculation?

"It is not improbable that zeal for the favourite dogmas they have embraced, may sometimes lead them too far; and that it would be still better for the people, if, instead of being taught a profound veneration for speculative opinions, they were more fully instructed in the unchangeable principles of morality; but, alas! where is not the gratification of the teacher's pride more attended to than the real advantage of the pupil?

"Whose child are you, my pretty maid? said I one day to a little girl, who was sitting on a tomb-stone in the church-yard betwixt the hours of divine service."

'I am the child of GOD, sir;' returned she, with great simplicity.[114]

"And how did you become the child of God;" enquired I.

'I became the child of GOD by adoption and regeneration,' rejoined she with great solemnity, crossing her little hands upon her breast, and dropping me one of her best curtseys.

"But have you no other father besides GOD?" said I.

'O yes; I am Jamie Thomson's *bairn*.'

"I now discovered my error, and while I smiled at the simplicity of the child, could not help wondering at the folly of her instructors; who, by a vain attempt to inculcate doctrines so far beyond her capacity, had taught her to repeat words to which it was impossible she could affix a single idea."

'That there is some foundation for your remark,' said Mr. Sydney, 'I will readily allow, but that the fear of exceeding the capacity of children in their religious instructions has produced consequences of a still more fatal tendency, I am well convinced. And though I am far from being an advocate for enthusiasm, yet I think it must be confessed, that the general sobriety of manners and orderly conduct of the lower classes in North-Britain is a strong testimony in favour of their instructors; but, indeed, where have not Christian principles been found efficacious under whatever form administered?'

"Did the care of their teachers extend no farther than to their instruction in orthodoxy," replied Henry, "I am afraid they would have less cause to boast of its efficacy upon the moral character of their disciples; but to the honour of these good men be it spoken, they are, as far as I could judge, no less assiduous in watching over the morals of their flocks, than

---

[114] cf: William Wordsworth, "We are Seven", *Lyrical Ballads* (1798).

in inculcating a regard to the peculiar tenets of their faith. Dr. Orwell will, I am sure, pardon me for observing, that in this respect the lower orders in Scotland enjoy many peculiar advantages.

"There the clergyman resides in the bosom of his flock. He is intimately acquainted with the situation and character of every individual that composes it. He visits, he instructs, he advises, and comforts them. Every breach of morals comes under his inspection, and is punished by his censure. The individual that has gone astray is exhorted, reasoned with, and more than probably reclaimed. The stipend of the clergyman being there fixed and permanent, no squabbles concerning tithes sow the seeds of discord, or render him odious to his parishioners. His situation is sufficiently elevated to command respect, without exalting him too much above the level of his congregation. He is not, like too many of our poor curates, seen pining in degrading indigence; nor like our proud and full-fed dignataries, is he rolling in that affluence which elevates him above the performance of his duty. Perhaps no situation is more favourable to virtue; and perhaps in no situation is more real virtue to be found. In the course of all my tour, and on the most minute and particular enquiry, I did not meet with one clergyman whose character was sullied with the imputation of any vice."

'Unhappy men!' cried Bridgetina, '*obliged by their profession to the constant appearance of sanctity! how miserable must be their course of self-denial! how formal and uncouth their manners! What a constrained and artificial seeming must this attention to a pious exterior necessarily give to their carriage!*'★[115]

"Indeed, Madam," said Henry, "you are very much mistaken. I never saw more unaffected cheerfulness, more natural gaiety and innocent mirth, than at the meeting of the divines of a certain district called a presbytery. They favoured me with an invitation to dinner, and I never spent a day more pleasantly."

'Pray, sir,' cried Mrs. Botherim, 'may I ask what was the bill of fare? It must doubtless have been very good to give you so much satisfaction; one would think, to hear you speak, it had been quite a turtle feast. Well, I vow and declare, I had never no ideer that them there Scotch people knew so well how to live.'

"I am extremely sorry, madam, that my memory serves me so very ill with regard to such matters, that I am quite unable to give you the particulars. All I know is, that the salmon of the river, which washes the walls of the town in which this presbytery was held, is excellent; and that the mutton which comes from the neighbouring hills, is the best I ever ate in my life. But the enjoyment of this feast was not confined to the good things set upon the table. It was harmony of sentiment, the good-humour and intel-

---

[115] ★See Enquirer.★ *Enquirer*, Part II, Essay V, "Of Trades and Professions". See Appendix A.

ligence which prevailed throughout the company, that gave the peculiar zest to the entertainment."

'I am particularly sorry to be obliged to contradict you, sir,' said Bridgetina, with great solemnity; 'but truth obliges me to declare, that the thing is utterly impossible. How can a priest, (I beg pardon of Dr. Orwell and Mr. Sydney, but no respect for persons ought to stop the promulgation of truth)—How then, I say, can a priest in any part of the world, or under any form of what is called religion, be a man of liberal mind or amiable manners? *Do we not know, that all his schemes and prospects depend upon the perennial stationariness of his understanding; and that the circumstances of every day tend to confirm him in a dogmatical, imperious, illiberal, and intolerant character? Is not the most reputable clergyman timid in enquiry, prejudiced in opinion, cold, formal, the slave of what other men may think of him, rude, dictatorial, impatient of contradiction, harsh in his censures, and illiberal in his judgments?*'★[116]

"Good heavens!" exclaimed Mrs. Martha, "was ever judgment so illiberal? Was ever censure so harsh as that you have at this moment pronounced? Is this the boasted liberality of your philosophy? Where is the priest, however narrow his heart, however strong his prejudices, that could, in such an arrogant and dogmatical manner, pass sentence on a whole body of men without exception or reservation?"

'Wherever he be,' said Dr. Orwell mildly, 'if, indeed, the man who has imbibed so little of the spirit of his Master is to be found within the pale of any church, he is the object of pity and contempt. The language of invective and abuse is best answered by silence. Let us not, therefore, interrupt Dr. Sydney any further. It grows late, and I wished to be informed concerning the mode of maintaining the poor in a country where there are neither work-houses nor poor's-rates.'

"In the country parishes," resumed Henry, "the few paupers that are to be found, are supported from the collection made at the church-door every Sunday, aided, where necessary, by the voluntary contributions of the inhabitants. The sum you may imagine is not very large; but there no part of it is swallowed up by parish-feasts, no part embezzled by avaricious and hard-hearted overseers, but all carefully and conscientiously distributed according to the necessities of every individual—distributed by the hands of those to whom these necessities are perfectly well known; who do not think that when they have contributed their quota of the general collection, they have done their duty to their poor brethren, but who very judiciously consider a portion of their time, as well as of their money, to be the right and property of the indigent.

"In my perambulatory excursions through the country, I often visited the labourer's cottage. The furniture was in general much more

---

[116] ★See *Enquirer,* by Godwin.★ Part II, Essay V, "Of Trades and Professions". See Appendix A.

plentiful, and of a better quality, than is to be found among the same class of inhabitants in this opulent country; but there, in proportion to the price of provisions, the labourer is better paid. He is considered as a more respectable member of the community. His family I commonly found tolerably well provided with, what are there deemed, the necessaries of life. The nerves of the women are not there, as with us, unstrung by the destructive and debilitating habit of tea-drinking.[117] A hearty breakfast of wholesome oatmeal pudding and good milk enables the wife to perform her share of the domestic duties. To provide the family in food is the exclusive care of the husband: to furnish them with clothes, is the business of the wife; and so well does she perform her part, that the general decency of their apparel is very striking to a stranger. Shoes and stockings, indeed, do not come within their list of necessaries for children; and his circumstance has generally conveyed to our countrymen the idea of compleat wretchedness. An ancient Roman, however, would have found nothing shocking in the custom.

"It was once my fate to be overtaken in a thunder-storm, when I was happy in finding a timely shelter from the tempest, in such a cottage as I have been describing. I was received very hospitably by the good woman of the house, and invited to a seat in her kitchen, which I found extremely well occupied. In one corner sat two taylors[118] cross-legged upon their board, stitching away at a great rate, while two fine little boys seemed intent upon watching the progress of their work. Two girls, of about twelve and fourteen years of age, were industriously employed at their spinning-wheels, which, soon as they found they had attracted my notice, they turned with redoubled speed.

"A man with an expressive and pallid countenance, and whom I observed to be somewhat lame, sat at the small and only window with a book in his hand, which at my entrance he was reading aloud. I entreated him to resume it, which after some entreaty and much formal preparation he proceeded to do, and though it must be confessed he held forth with rather "more of emphasis than good discretion," gave much pleasure to his attentive audience, by reading a long chapter of the Pilgrim's Progress. While he was thus employed, the good woman of the house was busied in preparing oat cakes, which she baked on an iron plate called a girdle; and which, as I found to my cost, required no small share of dexterity in the management. Ashamed of being idle where all were

---

[117] Tea had been drunk in England since the seventeenth century. Pepys records drinking his first cup of tea in 1660. Imports of tea increased dramatically throughout the eighteenth century. While coffee drinking was associated with males, tea drinking was a private, feminine domestic activity (See Elizabeth Kowaleski-Wallace, *Consuming Subjects: Women, Shopping and Business in the Eighteenth Century* [New York: Columbia UP, 1996], 19-36).

[118] i.e. tailors.

employed, I begged permission to assist her in what I thought a very simple operation, and taking up the wooden trowel with which she turned the cakes, I fell to work; but, luckless me! at the very first attempt I broke the cake, dropt the trowel in the fire, and burned my fingers!"

'How charmed I am,' exclaimed Harriet Orwell, 'to find that the beautiful description given by Burns in his "Cotter's Saturday Night,"[119] was not the mere child of fancy, but an original picture taken from truth and nature.'

"It is, indeed," replied Henry, "so true a picture, and so justly drawn, that it has been repeatedly called to my remembrance by similar scenes."

'Pray who was the reader in your cottage?' said Julia. 'From his pallid but expressive countenance, I should suppose him to be the lover of one of the peasant's daughters.'[120]

"I believe the poor man made no such pretensions," rejoined Henry; "he was the schoolmaster, who, according to the simple manners of the people, resides alternately with the peasants whose children he instructs. In the time of harvest, which is the universal vacation, he changes his ferule for a sickle, and reaps more pecuniary advantage from the one employment in the course of a few weeks, than he derives from the other during the remainder of the year. It was now his month of residence with these good people; which as night advanced without any abatement of the storm, was mentioned by both the husband and wife with great regret, as it prevented the possibility of my accommodation.

"This obstacle was at length removed by the schoolmaster himself, who observed, 'that peradventure the stranger's journeying in a mirksome night, where the path was dubious, and moreover encompassed with many floods, might be perilous; he therefore begged humbly to propose to relinquish (that is, give up) his bed to him, while he himself should go to sleep in the barn with the taylors!' The proposal was agreed to, and at that moment the little boys announced the finishing of their new coats, which they instantly got on, and strutted about with as much self-importance and complacency, as ever was experienced by a courtly beau when he first viewed himself in full dress for a birth-day drawing-room. Nor did the looks of the mother display a less degree of satisfaction. She took care to inform me that all the cloth was of her own spinning and dyeing; and that she had got it made up in haste that the children might make a decent appearance at the *examin*, which was to take place next day at the Elder's house. We then sat down to supper, which long fasting and excessive fatigue made appear to me the most luxurious I ever tasted.

"Soon as our repast was over, the bibles were handed round. The

---

[119] Robert Burns, "The Cotter's Saturday Night" (1786).
[120] Julia perceives everything as a love story.

schoolmaster again held forth, and to shew his dexterity, chose to read the account that is given of numbering the tribes of Israel by Nehemiah. He ran no risk of conjuring up the dead by the pronunciation of their names; for I dare swear not an Israelite among them would have known his own. But he went on, to the great admiration of his audience, without stop, pause, or spelling, to the end of the chapter. Burns has given an exact description of the ceremony that followed:

"Then kneeling down to heav'n's eternal King,
   "The saint, the father, and the husband prays.
"Hope springs exulting on triumphant wing,
   "That thus they all may meet in future days;
   "There ever bask in uncreated rays,
"No more to sigh, or shed the bitter tear;
   "Together hymning their Creator's praise,
"In such society, yet still more dear;
"While circling time moves round in an eternal sphere.
"Compar'd with this, how poor religion's pride!

   "In all the pomp of method and of art;
"When men display to congregations wide
   "Devotion's every grace— except the heart.
"The pow'r incens'd the pageant will desert,
   "The pompous strain, the sacerdotal stole;
"But haply in some cottage far apart,
   "May hear well pleas'd the language of the soul,
"And in his book of life the inmates poor inroll."[121]

"Curiosity led me next day to the examination. I accompanied my host and his family to the Elder's barn, which was already occupied by a very numerous assemblage of country people of each sex and all ages, decently dressed, and devoutly attentive.

"Every one rose at the entrance of the minister, who after going the round, like the king at a levee, and like him finding something kind and agreeable to say to every individual, began the business of the day by a short prayer. All the children were then called up by name, and questions put to each, suited to their respective ages and capacities. Where any instance of ignorance or neglect appeared, not only the children, but the parents were rebuked and admonished. The seniors next formed a circle round their pastor, and underwent a very long and strict examination concerning their knowledge in the articles of faith and principles of conduct. Another short but well-adapted prayer concluded the ceremony."

'Well,' cried Mrs. Botherim, 'I declare I never heard the like of all this;

---

[121] Robert Burns, "The Cotter's Saturday Night" 144-61.

why it is no better than downright methodism![122] My dear late Mr. Botherim would ha' given no encouragement to such practices, I assure ye. He would no more have prayed in the middle of the day in that there manner than he would have ate a pig without pruen sauce, and every one knows how nice he was in that particular.'

"With what emotions the Rev. Mr. Botherim might have viewed the scene I have been describing," said Henry, "I know not, but I confess it afforded me much pleasure. Happy people! said I, as I pursued my walk, ye are only ignorant of your own happiness from having never seen its contrast in the miseries of the vicious. Farewell! ye respectable, though lowly children of virtue! Never may the fiends of avarice and luxury find their way to your humble dwelling! Never may the voice of philosophy shake your confidence in Heaven, or annihilate in your hearts the cheering hope of immortal felicity."

'And are all the people in Scotland so good and so happy?' cried the youngest daughter of Dr. Orwell. 'Oh! how I should like to go there!'

"My dear child," replied her father, "you must recollect that a good description is like a fine painting, where whatever would disgust the eye is thrown into shade. To be able to admire a virtuous simplicity of manners through all the disadvantages of a coarse and homely dress, and to discriminate betwixt that simplicity and vulgar brutal ignorance, requires a judgment ripened by experience, and a mind enlarged by contemplating the effect of circumstances in the formation of human character. Let us know from Dr. Sydney, whether the virtuous simplicity so justly the object of your admiration was universal, or confined to rural life."

'Alas!' replied Henry, 'It must indeed be confessed, that wherever commerce and manufactures have spread their golden wings, innocence and simplicity of manners have fled before them. In their neighbourhood, according to Miss Martha's favourite poet,

"The town has ting'd the country, and the stain
"Appears a spot upon a vestal's robe."
                              COWPER.[123]

When after the contemplation of such scenes as I have been describing, I have in the close of evening come to a manufacturing town, and observed the crouds of pallid wretches who issued from the huge piles of buildings that were it pride and boast—the men, riotous, profane, and brutal; the women, bold, squalid, and shameless—all flying with eagerness to recruit their worn-out spirits by drafts of liquid fire; how often have I

---

[122] The system of religious doctrine and organisation of Methodists. Methodist was the term originally applied to a religious society (the Holy Club) at Oxford University in 1729 by John and Charles Wesley, having for its object the promotion of piety and morality.

[123] William Cowper, *The Task* (1785) Bk IV "The Winter Evening" 553-54.

been tempted to deplore the introduction of these boasted blessings, which, while they bestowed wealth on a few fortunate individuals, were to thousands the destruction of health and innocence. How much better, have I said to myself, how much more usefully would these poor wretches have been employed, had the men been engaged to cultivate some of the many thousand acres of waste land which presents its desart hue on every side! And the women—how had they been preserved from vice and misery in the bosom of domestic industry!"

'I am afraid,' said Dr. Orwell, 'that few converts will be made to your opinion. There is something so fascinating in the idea of wealth, that it can never be deemed too dear a purchase. The ostentatious display of the riches acquired in any branch of commerce or manufacture presses on the senses, and inflames the imagination, while the misery it has been the means of introducing into the families of the poor, in the loss of health, of vigour, and of virtue, is screened from observation; or if observed, is thought unworthy of being taken into the account.'

"And yet," rejoined Henry, "this sudden influx of wealth into a poor country, may be aptly compared to the torrent which astonishes by its magnificence, and gives an appearance of grandeur to the very scene it desolates; while the improvements of agriculture, like the perennial stream which holds on its silent course, is the unobserved dispenser of fertility and verdue.

CHAP. XVIII.

"—Well-dress'd, well-bred,
"Well-equipag'd, is ticket good enough
"To pass us readily through ev'ry door.[124]
"—She that asks
"Her dear five hundred friends, contemns them all,
"And hates their coming. They (what can they less)
"Make just reprisals; and with cringe, and shrug,
"And bow obsequious, hide their hate of her."[125]
COWPER.

BRIDGETINA was by no means satisfied with the small degree of attention that was paid her by Henry. Of Harriet Orwell, however, she was by no means jealous. In such contempt did she hold her prejudices, and so meanly did she think of her understanding, that to consider her as a rival she would have deemed injustice to her own superior powers. Besides, on entering the field, did she not find Henry retired from the rest of the company, evidently to indulge his meditations on some absent

---

[124] Cowper, *The Task* Bk III, "The Garden", 97-99.
[125] Cowper, *The Task* Bk II, "The Time-Piece", 642-46.

object? Who so likely to be that object as herself? 'Does he then love me?' cried she, soliloquising in the manner of all heroines. 'Have my mental attractions power to charm his soul? Oh! the soft, the tender, the extatic thought! But why did he not sigh? Why did he not press my hand? Perhaps I was too distant. Perhaps I awed the youth to silence. Perhaps—"

"I wish to goodness, Biddy," said Mrs. Botherim, "that you would talk in a way that a body could understand. When you get into one of them there tanterums, there is no getting any good of you. I had as lieve be in a room all by myself. Come now, let us have a bit of social chat: you knows I never bids you do any thing for me the whole day long, nor any thing for yourself neither. I loves to see you take so to your book, as to be sure it makes you wiser than any body; but I do think you might chat a little with your poor mother now and then; yes, that I do think."

'How can you break the chain of my reflections in this manner?' replied Bridgetina. 'Betwixt you and I it is impossible there should be any conversation that deserves the name. No; I pant for the society of the enlightened, and your taste, you know, is very dissimilar.[126] So since you have thought fit to disturb the course of my mental reverie, I must have recourse to my book till bed-time, and I beg that I may not be again interrupted.'

Leaving Bridgetina to her studies, let us return to her sister pupil in philosophy—-the fair, the lovely Julia; whose spirits had, during the latter part of the evening, lost that transient glow of sprightliness, which had for a short time shed its enlivening influence over her breast.

As she drew towards home, the uneasiness and agitation of her mind increased. She dreaded lest Dr. Orwell should propose stepping in with her to enquire for her father; and anxiously obviated the proposal, by declaring him too much indisposed to receive any visit.

She did not forget to thank the Doctor for his promise of the carriage, in which she said a friend of her father's was to drive her, who would, if the Doctor pleased, call for it at one o'clock. Dr. Orwell said it should be ready, and he and his daughter, after having conducted her to her father's door, wished her good-night.

The knock which announced the return of Julia, was music to her father's ears. So much did he doat on this darling daughter, so necessary was her presence to his happiness, that the effort he made in parting with her, if but for a few hours, was extremely painful. His spirits, which always sunk at her departure, seemed to receive new animation on her approach. But no longer did she fly to his apartment on the swift wings of undivided affection. With painful anxiety he watched her slow and languid

---

[126] That many educated young females learned to despise their parents' lowly origins was remarked upon by many contemporary novelists. The Muggleton parents in Jane West's *Infidel Father* (1802) provide their daughter with a fashionable but useless education from which she "imbibed a sovereign contempt for her father and mother" (1: 40).

steps. With regret he perceived the distraction of her thoughts, the frequent fits of absence which supplied the place of that lively prattle with which she had been wont to amuse him after every little absence. Fears for her health took possession of his mind; but unwilling that she should perceive his apprehensions, under pretence of wishing to retire to rest at an early hour, he dismissed her. As he wished her good-night, tears of paternal tenderness mixed with his parting embrace, and with more than usual emphasis he pronounced his heart-wished blessing.

Julia went to bed, but the undisturbed and peaceful slumbers that had heretofore been the companions of her pillow, were not to be found. In vain she sought for the soothing balm of sleep. Sleep, which kindly comes to the relief of sorrow, sternly refuses its wished-for aid to the agitations of anxiety.

Imagination was now at liberty to run its wild career. In vivid colours it painted the extacy of Vallaton in discovering his parents, the raptures of the parents in beholding their accomplished son. Now she beheld the General present him to her father, and saw the gleam of joy which beamed in her father's face, while he united her hand with the son of his most honoured friend. As Fancy painted the happiness of her lover, the warmth of his gratitude, the excess of his tenderness, her breath became quick, and burning blushes flushed her modest cheek. But if the reverse of all this should happen, said Judgment; if your father should discover that you have been carrying on a clandestine correspondence with a man he considers as your inferior? Imagination took the alarm, and instantly delineated the consequences of her father's displeasure in such dreadful lines, as to make her shudder with horror. Her blood then ran cold, and terror and dismay drew the deep sigh from her agitated bosom.

In this manner did Julia pass the night. Her first care, when she arose, was to step down to Mr. Glib's with the necessary instructions for Mr. Vallaton. The shop was still shut, though every other in the town had long been opened. After knocking a considerable time, Mr. Glib himself came to the door. "Ah! glad to see you, citizen Miss," cried he; "find me too much of a philosopher to be tied to hours. Nothing so bad for energies as order: eat when I please, sleep when I have a mind. That's it! my dear, that's the way to have energies."★[127]

'It's not the way to have customers, though, let me tell you, master,' said a gentleman's servant, who just then came into the shop. 'Here have I been waiting this hour past,' continued the man, 'for a parcel of stationary for my master, and a change of novels for the young ladies. If I were them, I know I should rather send to the next town than trouble you again.'

While the man was speaking, Julia slipped a note for Vallaton into Mr.

---

[127] ★See Pol. Jus. vol ii.★ Godwin, *Political Justice* Bk VIII, ch. VIII, "Objection to this System from the Inflexibility of its Restrictions".

Glib's hand, and hastily returned home, where she arrived before any one had taken notice of her absence.

Anxiously did she wait for the appointed hour. The hour at length arrived; and from the window of her father's apartment she saw her Vallaton nimbly driving the parson's gig up towards the door. She instantly announced its arrival; and saying she would not let the Doctor wait for her, took a hasty leave of her father, (her mother she then knew to be employed in a room above) and without calling on any servant to attend, she herself opened the street-door, lightly sprang into the carriage, which instantly drove off, and was out of sight in a moment.

Fondly did her heart now exult in the auspicious commencement of her important enterprize; and hardly could she refrain from giving her happy lover a hint of the hopes which fluttered in her bosom; but the idea of making the discovery more interesting, from its being totally unexpected, sealed her lips, and charmed her into silence.

The morning was very fine, and the country through which they passed was beautiful; but neither to the fineness of the morning, nor to the beauty of the country, was Julia or her lover at all indebted for any part of the pleasure they experienced in the course of their delightful ride.

On arriving at Castle-Villers, Julia heard with pleasure that both the General and his lady were at home, though her pleasure received some abatement on being told that they had company with them. She however sent up her name, and was instantly admitted.

On entering the drawing-room, she found Mrs. Villers surrounded by a party of ladies, some of whom she recollected to have seen on a former visit at the castle, the others were strangers to her. They were all talking at once, and all directing their discourse to one little effeminate-looking gentleman; nor did the entrance of Julia give even a momentary interruption to their conversation.

Mrs. Villers herself appeared so much engaged, as not to have heard the servant who pronounced Miss Delmond's name, as he threw open the folding-doors of the drawing-room, though he uttered it in a voice so loud, as not a little discomposed the blushing Julia. She advanced with timid steps and shrinking diffidence to the upper end of the room, where Mrs. Villers at length noticed her approach, and received her with a very gracious curtsey.

Julia, somewhat reassured by this reception, with faultering voice begged leave to introduce the gentleman who accompanied her, who was, she said, a particular friend of her father's. Mrs. Villers cast a look on Vallaton, made him a slight curtsey, and then, with a stately and cold formality, desired him to be seated.

'You have been a great stranger, Miss Delmond,' said she; 'I should indeed have sent the carriage for you, or taken you up myself some morning, but that I have been so much engaged with company of late, that I have not had one moment to spare. I hope Capt. Delmond has got the better of that lameness—a broken leg I think it was.'

"It is the gout, Madam, to which my father has been many years a martyr."

'Aye, so it is the gout, now I remember; and your mother, I hope she is very well. Does she go to any watering-place this summer?' Then, without waiting for the answer which Julia was preparing to give, she turned to the lady who sat by her on the sopha, and observed, 'that Sir Jeremy and the General had taken a very long ride.'

"And why were not you of the riding party, Colonel?" lisped a young lady, whom Julia recognized as the daughter of a Mr. Mushroom, an army agent, and sole heiress to the immense wealth which in the several occupations of clerk, deputy commissary, member of parliament, and contractor, her father had contrived to amass. The gentleman to whom Miss Mushroom addressed herself, regarding her with an air of great astonishment, replied in a tone so full of affection, as to excite an involuntary smile in the countenance of Julia. 'Me ride Ma'am? How could you petrify me by the mention of any thing so horrid? Getting on horseback is the greatest bore in nature. I wish the savages who first invented it had been all put to the guillotine.'

"I wonder, Colonel," replied Miss Mushroom, 'as you dislike riding so much, that you do not exchange into a regiment of foot."

Before the Colonel could reply, he was called upon by two voices from the other side of the room.

"I know it was a blue domino," said one.

'Colonel Goldfinch will tell you it was a Turkish habit,' said the other; 'was it not, Colonel, A Turkish habit which Lady Lovelife wore when she eloped from the masquerade with Major Swindle.'

"It petrifies me to contradict Miss Page," said the Colonel with great gravity, "but I am obliged to say she is for once mistaken."

'There now,' cried the other young lady, 'I told you that I had a full account of the whole from the very best authority. Lady Lovelife slipt on the blue domino, as I was saying, over her muslin pilgrim. And'—

"Pardon me, Madam," said the Colonel, "I see you have been egregiously misinformed. I myself saw Major Swindle conduct her to the carriage in a Spanish dress."

'You saw them!' said both ladies at once. 'O then we shall now have the *certain* account of the whole affair.'

"And a very shameful affair it was," said Mrs. Villers. "It is astonishing how a woman of Lady Lovelife's family and connexions, could demean herself by an intrigue with so *low* a fellow. He was once a drummer in General Villers' own regiment."

'A drummer was he,' said Lady Page, who was set by Mrs. Villers on the sopha, 'I always understood he had been a *hairdresser.*'

As her ladyship concluded this sentence, she cast a look (whether by accident or design cannot now be ascertained) full in the face of Mr. Vallaton. Something very like a blush diffused itself over the countenance of that gentleman, as his eyes met hers; but calling his energies into action, he drew out his pocket-handkerchief, and applying it to his nose, made the room resound with the noise occasioned by the application, which was somewhat longer and louder than perfect politeness could well warrant in such company. Mrs. Villers appeared disconcerted, but turning to Lady Page she hastily renewed the conversation, which the vociferous action of Vallaton had of necessity suspended.

"Did your Ladyship ever see Lady Lovelife?"

'I never did,' returned her ladyship, 'but I am told she is amazingly handsome.'

"She handsome!" said Miss Mushroom; "well, I wonder how any one can think so, she is the very picture of Miss Mordaunt; but she too may be thought handsome by some people, for ought I know."

'The man who thinks her handsome,' said Col. Goldfinch, 'must have a strange predilection for thread-papers. She had no more shape than a walking-stick.'

"And no more ease than the poker," said Miss Page.

'And then that eternal riding-habit,' said the Colonel. 'It quite petrifies me to see her in that dress. It is as tiresome as Lady Wellwyn's yellow turban, which sickened half the town last winter.'

"Or as Miss Wingrove's salmon-coloured slippers," said Miss Page.

'If Miss Mordaunt's waist had what Miss Wingrove's ankle could spare,' said the Colonel, 'what an advantage would it be to both!'

"I hope she at least is sufficiently *en bon point* to please you, Colonel," said Miss Mushroom.

'Miss Wingrove!' exclaimed the Colonel. 'It is enough to suffocate any Christian to look at her. I don't know any thing so petrifying as to see her go down a country-dance, shaking all the way like a bundle of dirty linen.'

"Or like Lady Mary Metcalf's plume of white feathers," said Miss Page.

'Her ladyship's plumage, I think, has been pretty well plucked by the hand of Pharo last winter,' said Lady Page; an observation which changed the giggle that had before prevailed into a general laugh, in which all but Julia joined with great appearance of satisfaction; her ignorance of high life rendered her ladyship's allusion altogether unintelligible: nor was this the only disadvantage under which she laboured. Having never been initiated into the amusements of the beau monde, she had no relish for that elegant and exalted species of wit, which consists in throwing into a ridiculous point of view some little peculiarity in the dress, the person, or the manners of absent friends. In one word, she had no idea of polite conversation.

The vivid imagination of Julia painted the figures that had been described as more diverting caricatures than her confined acquaintance with the world had ever presented to her observation. When, therefore, the footman announced the name of Miss Mordaunt, she prepared herself for beholding an object that would powerfully excite her risibility.

"A thread-paper in a riding-habit," said the Colonel, imitating the voice of the servant.

'A may-pole, with a long story of its mamma's cough,' said Miss Page; 'but I vow I shan't stay to hear it. I shall make my escape, that's certain.' Then running up to Miss Mordaunt, who that moment entered, 'My dear Miss Mordaunt,' cried she, 'how rejoiced I am to see you! What an age it is since I had the pleasure of meeting you! I protest I was speaking of you this very moment to Mrs. Villers.'

"So we were, indeed, my dear," said Mrs. Villers; "I rejoice in your good fortune in finding me surrounded by so many of your friends."

'And I have brought two gentlemen to add to the number,' said Miss Mordaunt, 'Sir Charles Wingrove and Major Minden,' presenting them to Mrs. Villers.

"Miss Mordaunt makes her visit doubly acceptable by coming so accompanied," said Mrs. Villers. "We should have been quite a female party this morning, if Col. Goldfinch had not taken compassion on us."

'My very best of good stars has predominated this morning,' said the Colonel, bowing first to Mrs. Villers, and then to Miss Mordaunt; 'but my dear Miss Mordaunt, you positively must have some compassion upon our sex, and not go on improving in beauty at this rate. You were killing enough in all conscience before these morning rides had given such an additional lustre to your complexion.'

Surely, thought Julia, this cannot be the Miss Mordaunt of whom the Colonel so lately spoke so slightingly! This is no thread-paper, no poker, no walking-stick; but a very pretty sweet-looking girl, with more gracefulness in her manner, and more affability and good-humour in her look, than is visible in any of the company. The Colonel too seems quite of my opinion. No, no, it must certainly be some other lady of the same name of whom they spoke.

Alas! poor Julia, how deplorably ignorant was she of the nature of those exaggerated descriptions, which constitute the Attic wit of modern conversation!

The arrival of Miss Mordaunt relieved the mind of Julia from some uneasy doubts which she had harboured concerning the propriety of introducing Vallaton. That young lady had brought with her two gentlemen, of whom one at least was evidently a stranger to Mrs. Villers, who nevertheless seemed to receive their visit as a favour. Capt. Delmond had, she believed, a greater claim upon the friendship of the General, than the father of Miss Mordaunt; and his friend must of course be at least equally acceptable. The difference, then, which she remarked in the reception given by Mrs. Villers to the friends of Miss Mordaunt, could only be the effect of accident. It could be nothing else; for surely the appearance of Vallaton was infinitely more prepossessing than that of either of the other gentlemen.

In this manner did Julia make up her mind upon the subject; nor did it once occur to her, that the very thing which may be esteemed a favour from a person of a certain rank, is deemed a very unwarrantable and improper liberty from one who has not the happiness of being numbered in that privileged order.

Miss Mordaunt, who was niece and grand-child to an earl, and who had always moved in the first circles of fashion, could have no attendants in her train, who were not of that description of the human species, to which only, in the opinion of Mrs. Villers, the urbanity of people of fashion ought to extend.

Miss Delmond, on the contrary, though sprung from a good family, (a point on which Mrs. Villers was remarkably tenacious) and consequently one whom it was no disgrace to be civil to *in the country*, was of an order of beings, who, though they are frequently admitted upon sufferance to the tables of persons of rank, are there considered rather as appendages to the company than as any part of the company itself. To express ourselves at once to the comprehension of our genteel readers, she was *one whom nobody knew*. For Miss Delmond, therefore, to presume to being another person of the same description to the house of the Hon. Mrs. Villers—a person perhaps of mean birth and low extraction, of no stile, no fashion—was a breach of all decorum, and deserved to be punished accordingly.

With regard to all points of etiquette, Mrs. Villers was indeed a woman of the nicest sensibility. The smallest breach of the rules by authority of fashion established, was in her opinion an offence far more heinous than the breach of every commandment in the decalogue. Indeed a strict attention to the prohibitions of the latter was by no means a necessary recommendation to her esteem. For instance: though Colonel Goldfinch had, just before his arrival at the castle, been cast in damages for *crim. con.*[128] with the wife of his benefactor and friend; though Sir Charles Wingrove had killed a man in a duel; and though Mr. Mushroom had been threatened with a black charge of peculation, which was well known to have been only averted by a timely application of its fruits; yet these were all received by Mrs. Villers with the most distinguished complacency. The two first had the passport of birth as well as fortune to recommend them to her favour; and the latter had, by his long-established reception into the most fashionable circles, obtained a sort of prescriptive right to the same distinction. His deficiency of birth was moreover on

---

[128] Criminal conversation (illicit sexual intercourse). Passage of a private divorce act followed a series of procedures. The petitioner had to first obtain a separation from a church court for reason of his wife's adultery before claiming damages from his wife's accomplice in her adultery. The damages for *crim. con.* were based on the principle that a married woman was her husband's property, and that by having intercourse with her any other man trespassed on the husband's property and owed him damages. See Roderick Phillips, *Untying the Knot: a Short History of Divorce* (Cambridge: Cambridge UP, 1991), 64-65.

the eve of being expiated by a peerage. The title of Right Honourable being in the esteem of Mrs. Villers an infallible panacea, which, like the advertized drugs of the empirics, clears the blood from all impurities. But though a title could operate thus powerfully, it was quite otherwise with the qualities of great virtue, extraordinary talents, or any species of excellence: for these, when of plebean birth, she felt so little respect, that it never once entered her imagination to calculate their value.

To account for the uncommon fastidiousness of Mrs. Villers with regard to birth and rank, it is perhaps only necessary to observe, that she was herself of very mean extraction; pride, like a good general, never neglecting to put a double guard upon the weakest part. The same happy instinct to which is to be ascribed the outrageous *virtue* of prudes, the insulting *courage* of coxcombs, and the tenacious *honour* of certain fine gentlemen, excited in the breast of the General's lady an insuperable aversion to people of ignoble birth.

Mrs. Villers was the illegitimate offspring of a subaltern, by the maid-servant of the inn at which he was quartered. At nine years of age she was apprenticed by the charity-school to a respectable milliner, to whose instructions she was indebted for a better education than would otherwise have fallen to her lot.

From this good woman she passed to the service of the Countess of Villers, in which situation her beauty attracted the attention of the General, who privately married her, and at the death of his father publicly acknowledged her as his wife.

It was these circumstances, ever present to the recollection of Mrs. Villers, which produced that extraordinary degree of pride by which she expected to *command* the world into forgetfulness of what she wished to obliterate even from her own remembrance.

To the advantages of illustrious birth General Villers was not less sensible than his lady, though he did not find it necessary to assert its prerogative with the same jealous ardour. Having from infancy been taught to value himself on his high descent, he considered it as a thing of course; and as the antiquity of a family which could be traced beyond the Conquest was not to be disputed, he deemed family-pride a part of his inheritance.

It is true, that in the long line of ancestors boasted by this noble family, no one person eminent for talents or for virtue was to be found. Undistinguished by any deed of valour, ungraced by any act of virtue, their names alone remained; but these, though consigned to oblivion by the world, which had never been benefited by their existence, were sufficiently numerous to justify the pride of their descendants.

The General partook of the mediocrity which characterized his family. He was an easy good-natured man, more disposed to kindness than to generosity, and less inclined to investigate prejudices than to entertain a bad opinion of all who opposed their authority. To the gallantry of Capt. Delmond he was indebted for his life in his first campaign; and as

Captain Delmond proved to be a man of family, he did not think it beneath him to acknowledge the obligation. His feelings were, however, too obtuse to lead him to make any great exertion in favour of his benefactor. A small pension, indeed, he did procure for him, on his return from the coast of Africa; and not long after he had done so, actually harboured an idea of conferring on him a still greater benefit, by nominating him to a lucrative sinecure, which by some parliamentary manoeuvring had come into the gift of his family. This idea, however, was soon relinquished, and the place in question more properly disposed of to a gentleman of some celebrity in the fashionable world, who had lost a large fortune at the gaming-table; and not being possessed, after this loss, of one quality which could give him a claim to the notice of society, must have sunk into inevitable obscurity, but for this well-timed appointment.

As this gentleman was one whom *every body knew*, the generosity of Gen. Villers became the subject of conversation in all the parties he frequented; and so great were the applauses he received upon the occasion, that he could not help congratulating himself on the preference he had given to one in whom so many people of quality were deeply interested. Still, however, he preserved for Capt. Delmond all the appearance of the sincerest friendship: frequently called at his house, and since Julia had been put in possession of an independent fortune, made a point of honouring her with his particular attention. By no mark of his regard could he so warmly have excited the gratitude of Capt. Delmond.

In about half an hour from the arrival of Miss Mordaunt, General Villers and Sir Jeremy Page returned from their ride, and brought with them the intelligence of an approaching thunder-storm, which soon came on with great violence.

The entrance of the General was a great relief to poor Julia, whose feelings were too acute to be insensible to the mortifying circumstances of her present situation.

Mrs. Villers spoke but little at any time, and the little she had now to say was not directed to Julia. To the rest of the party she was unknown, and but for a broad stare which she now and then received from the gentlemen, and which by no means tended to alleviate her confusion, she was totally unnoticed.

There are many who would have submitted to all this, and much more than all this, with pleasure, for the opportunity it would have afforded them of obtaining a paltry gratification to vanity, by the boast of having been in such a party. But the mind of Julia had too much real dignity to be solicitous for this species of importance. She had acquired a turn of thinking, which is extremely hostile to the adventitious advantages of rank and fortune. In listening to a conversation, she never considered the dignity of the person who spoke, but the truth or falsity, the wisdom or folly, of the sentiment that was uttered. By these, and these alone, she measured the quantity of her contempt or admiration.

Now it so happened, that since her entrance into this brilliant party, not one syllable had struck her ears, which in the utmost extent of charity, she could possibly attribute either to good-sense or good-nature. So that while Mrs. Villers and her honourable guests considered the poor unnoticed Julia as filled with silent awe, and envious admiration of their wit and gaiety, she was contemplating with pitey the emptiness of their minds and the perversion of their understandings.

From the entrance of the General, Julia no longer experienced the mortification of neglect. He not only made it a point to treat her with particular attention, but extended his politeness to the gentleman who accompanied her. Soon as the rain, which came in torrents, began to descend, he begged leave to order up their carriage, which he had seen at the door as he came in; and politely observed, that Mrs. Villers and he were much obliged to the storm, which procured them the honour of such an addition to their dinner-party. Mrs. Villers could not avoid bowing assent to the General's proposal, which Julia returned in the same manner, and felt internally satisfied at the circumstance, which might eventually furnish her with an opportunity of fulfilling the great object of her visit.

She now began attentively to compare the physiognomy of the General with that of his supposed son.[129] Their eyes then were of the same colour. Their noses too both approached the Roman; though the General's was somewhat more prominent, the similarity was still sufficient for a family likeness. She had before observed a similar degree of resemblance in the mouth of Mrs. Villers; and that making a proper allowance for the alterations produced by time, their foreheads had exactly the same characteristics. These casual resemblances were to her prepossessed imagination, 'confirmation strong as proofs of holy writ.'[130]

To hit upon a proper method of making the discovery, was a point of equal delicacy and importance. After revolving in her mind a variety of plans for this purpose, she was at length obliged to trust to chance for an opportunity of disclosing the important secret. It was, indeed, no time for indulging in reflection. The most abstracted philosopher must now have been roused from his reverie by the pretty squals of Miss Mushroom, reiterated, every time the low murmurs of the distant thunder reached her ears, with increasing vociferation. That young lady, perhaps conscious of the inherent insignificance of her character, wisely took the only practicable method of bringing herself into notice, whenever an opportunity presented itself for an ostentatious display of her silly fears. Her plan was generally successful; and so conscious was she of its success, that she with triumph watched the slow approach of the spider or the earwig, which,

---

[129] Studies such as Johann Lavatar's *Physiognomische Fragmente* (1775-78), translated as *Essays in Physiognomy*, attempted to elevate physiognomy into a science. Such efforts were extremely popular.

[130] Shakespeare, *Othello*, III.iii.

when it came within screaming distance, was to make her the object of soothing attention to a whole company. The noise of thunder (for of the danger of the lightning she entertained not the slightest apprehension) was a circumstance productive of still greater effect. By frequent repetition, she at length actually caught the terrors she at first affected; and by indulging these terrors, brought her mind into a state little short of frantic delirium, usually relieved by a regular hysteric fit. Happily the thunder kept at too great a distance for producing any thing so interesting in the presence of Julia, who had not the least idea that any creature, ranking in the list of rationals, could form a wish of being distinguished for pre-eminence in weakness.

By the time dinner was announced, the sky retained not the appearance of a single cloud which could present an apology for further alarm; so that poor Miss Mushroom was obliged to make the most of what was passed, and live it over again in description.

By the help of her papa's arm, for she still trembled too much to support herself, she contrived to accompany the party to the dining-room, where, as Julia happened to be placed betwixt the terrified fair one and her father, she had the pleasure of receiving a minute and accurate account of all the silly things which the former had either said or done during every thunder-storm within the period of her remembrance.

Julia had never witnessed an entertainment so splendid and profuse as that which now covered the General's table. It consisted of every delicacy of the season, made inviting to the appetite by all the studied refinements of Epicurean luxury.

Mrs. Villers desired the servants to hand the *brown barley-bread*[131] along with the white, observing that she always made a point of using a little of it every day at her own table, by way of setting a good example. "And yet, would you believe it," addressing herself to Lady Page, "the poor people are so saucy as not to like it."

'I am sure, then, they deserve to starve,' returned her Ladyship, sending her plate for some more jelly-sauce to the nice slice of venison; 'I never ate any thing better in my life; but the poor are really now become so insolent they are quite insufferable.'

"Yes, indeed," rejoined Mrs. Villers, while she helped herself to another plate of turtle-soup, "I think those who murmur at such bread as that, do not deserve any compassion."

'I thought so, too,' said Miss Mordaunt, 'till I heard from Dr. Orwell, who dined the other day at our house, that the poor wretches had really nothing but bread to eat. Only think how shocking, to having

---

[131] Any bread of a brown colour—darker than ordinary white bread since it contains the bran or outer skin of the grain as well as fine flour. Bread made of a rye or mixed rye and wheat.

nothing but a dry morsel of bread for one's whole dinner! One can scarcely wonder that they should wish that to be good.'

"I dare say that Dr. Orwell is a democrat," said Mrs. Villers. "It is these people who encourage the poor in all their insolence; to hear them speak, one would think there was nothing but misery in the world."

'For my share,' said Lady Page, 'I believe all the rout that is made about scarcity is mere talk. I am sure I never saw less appearance of it.'[132]

"I do not remember a better venison season in all my life," said Mr. Mushroom. "Nor do I believe a better haunch ever came to any table. I must, however, have a cut at the stewed carp, which appears delicious," sending his plate to Mr. Vallaton, who happened to be placed near this favourite dish; and who fortunately made so judicious a choice of the nicest part, as impressed Mr. Mushroom with a very favourable opinion of his understanding.

Soon as he had finished, he asked the gentleman's name of Miss Delmond, and when he had obtained it, "Mr. Vallaton," said he in an audible voice, "I must beg the honour of drinking a glass of wine with you. Vallaton!" repeated he, as the servant was filling the wine, "I certainly have had the pleasure of meeting with some of that family abroad: your family is of French extraction, I presume, sir?"

Vallaton bowed assent.

"O yes; a great many Vallaton's in France formerly—all emigrated now—every thing turned upside down in that miserable country."

As Vallaton put down his glass, his eyes again encountered those of Lady Page. The remark which, from the encouraging overtures of Mr. Mushroom, he was about to make, died upon his lips, and while the ladies remained in the room, he continued to observe a strict silence.

Miss Mushroom, who had now completely fastened upon Julia as a listener, continued her persecution to the drawing-room, and had got about half through the tedious history of the horrors she had once experienced from the direful prodigy of a frog hopping along one of the gravel-walks in the garden, when Mrs. Villers, who had been for some time in earnest conversation with Lady Page at a distant bow-window, advanced towards Julia, and in a voice almost suffocated with agitation, begged to speak with her in the adjoining room.

When Julia beheld the flushed countenance of Mrs. Villers, when she perceived the emotion that quivered on her lip, the idea of her having made some discovery concerning Vallaton rushed upon her mind. Her heart bounded with expectation, and as she lightly tripped into the withdrawing-room, elate with hope and joy, she knew not that she touched the ground.

Mrs. Villers followed, apparently struggling to subdue an extreme degree of agitation. Having carefully shut the door of the apartment she

---

[132] Britain actually suffered a series of devastating famines and food shortages between 1790 and 1820.

turned to Julia: "Miss Delmond," said she, in a solemn but tremulous voice, "I cannot imagine that your father would permit any person to accompany you to Castle-Villers, with whose previous history he was not thoroughly acquainted. Tell me then," continued she, with increased agitation, "tell me what you know of the young man who came with you to-day?"

'Good Heavens!' exclaimed the delighted Julia, 'and is it indeed possible that I should have guessed the truth? And have you really discovered any thing concerning Mr. Vallaton?'

"Discovered! Miss Delmond; yes, I have made a discovery, indeed! I wonder you are not ashamed of yourself, for having concealed a circumstance so—so—but I will, if possible, command myself: do not expect, however, that either the General or myself can ever possibly forgive you."

'Ah! Madam, can you believe, that if I had really been certain of the circumstance you have so unaccountably discovered, that I should for a moment have concealed it? Did you but know the interest I take, the joy, the satisfaction I at this moment feel, you would not thus accuse me.'

"What do you mean?" said Mrs. Villers, in an angry tone. "Satisfaction, indeed! Is this your gratitude for the notice I have condescended to take of you? Is this your return for the friendship General Villers has shewn to your father, to tell me to my face, that you have a satisfaction in a circumstance which will be considered by all my friends as an irremediable disgrace? I must say, Miss Delmond, your behaviour is intolerable."

'Dear Madam!' returned Julia, in the mildest accent, 'surely no one can attach the idea of disgrace to you on account of this affair. In *his* birth there is nothing dishonourable, *he* was not the produce of an illicit amour, but the dear pledge of hallowed love. *His* parents need not blush to own him to the world for their child.'

The scarlet hue which had hitherto overspread the countenance of Mrs. Villers, now gave place to the livid paleness of rage; while all the circumstances of her own birth, to which she thought Julia alluded, rushed upon her recollection.

"Do you dare to insult me?" cried she, in a voice almost choked with passion. "And do you imagine you shall insult me with impunity? But I will not bear it; no, Miss, I will not tamely submit to be insulted by your insolence. I will—I will— but you are beneath my resentment. If your father has dared to affront General Villers, he shall suffer for it as he ought!"

Julia, overwhelmed with astonishment and horror, sat trembling and motionless; totally unable to account for a catastrophe so unexpected, her faculties were for some time entirely suspended. At length she was awakened, as if from a confused dream, by Mrs. Villers' violently ringing the bell, and ordering Miss Delmond's carriage to the door. She then made an effort to speak, but her voice refused its assistance. Seeing Mrs. Villers move towards the door, she caught hold of her gown, and throwing herself on her knees before her, burst into a violet flood of tears.

The distress of Julia, the mildness of her looks, and the humility of her supplicating posture, somewhat assuaged the wrath of the enraged lady, who nevertheless continued to maintain the dignity of silence.

'However I have unknowingly incurred your displeasure,' said Julia, as soon as tears and sobs would permit her utterance, 'I on my knees assure you that my offence extends not to my father. He is an utter stranger to Mr. Vallaton. He knows nothing of the mystery of his birth; he never heard of the embroidered covering of the basket; and if any circumstances unfortunately exist, which would induce you to wish that the affair should be still concealed, you may confide in my secrecy and discretion. Believe me, I would sooner suffer death than betray you.'

"Heavens!" cried Mrs. Villers, regarding Julia with a mixture of horror and apprehension, "the girl has certainly lost her senses!" Then gently disengaging her gown from Julia's grasp. "Compose yourself, Miss Delmond," said she, in a soothing tone, "sit down upon the sopha, and compose your-self."

'I cannot be at ease,' said Julia, 'till I know how I have been so unfortunate as to offend you. Alas! in the distant contemplation of this event, I have fondly flattered myself, that should my conjectures prove true, should he indeed prove to be what you have now discovered him, you would have considered the discovery as the happiest moment of your existence. I thought I should have seen him clasped to your breast in the fond agony of maternal tenderness. Oh! did you but know how worthy he is of your affection! were you but acquainted with the greatness of his mind, the strength of his powers, the sublimity of his virtue! you would bless the day that gave him to your arms!'

"Hush! hush!" said Mrs. Villers, making her a motion to be silent, "you had better sit quiet, and recover yourself." Then softly slipping towards the door that opened into the drawing-room, she gently pushed it so far open, as should secure her a speedy retreat, in case Julia, whom she now saw to be quite light-headed, should suddenly become outrageous.

Julia on her part considered the behaviour of Mrs. Villers as no less unnatural and extraordinary. Many and various were the descriptions she had read of the behaviour of parents on discovering a long-lost child, but nothing to equal the conduct of Mrs. Villers occurred to her recollection. She could by no means account for it.

'I hope, Madam,' said she, after a short pause, 'you will not deem my curiosity impertinent, if I confess I am anxious to know by what means this interesting discovery has been effected.'

"By means of Lady Page," replied Mrs. Villers, happy to see her beginning to talk rationally; "and I hope, Miss Delmond, it will serve as a warning for you in future, to be extremely careful of making acquaintance with people while ignorant of their family and connexions; for I am now well convinced that you would not willingly have brought this man to Castle-Villers, if you had really known him to have been a hair-dresser."

'A hair-dresser!' repeated Julia, who in her turn began to suspect the brain of Mrs. Villers to be a little affected, 'I know nothing of any hair-dresser, I never was in company with a person of that description in my life.'

"Do you not know, then," returned Mrs. Villers, in astonishment, "that Mr. Vallaton is a London hair-dresser, a common friseur, a fellow who—good heavens! that such a fellow should ever have the impudence to sit at my table! He richly deserves that my servants should kick him down stairs."

'Mr. Vallaton a hair-dresser!' exclaimed Julia, 'it is a gross deception, a most egregious mistake! His whole life has been devoted to the sublime pursuits of philosophy. His writings have enlightened the world; and his virtues are the most illustrious comment on the glorious doctrine of perfectibility. Is this, then, the discovery you have made? And are you yet ignorant of the interesting mystery of his birth?'

"Indeed, I neither know, nor desire to know, any thing of the birth of such a person," said Mrs. Villers, drily; "it is enough for me to be convinced that Lady Page cannot possibly be mistaken, as he dressed her ladyship every day for a whole season."

'Her ladyship does, however, most assuredly labour under a very great mistake,' returned Julia. 'Mr. Vallaton is the adopted son of a lady of great rank and fortune, who bestowed upon him an education suited to the supposed dignity of his birth, which, from the circumstances of his infant dress, the casket of jewels which was deposited in the satin-lined basket in which he was laid; above all, from the elegant covering of pelong, with the letters A.V. richly embroidered in every corner, which served as a canopy to the whole, was evidently of no vulgar origin. Their can be no doubt that he is the off-spring of some noble but unhappy pair, who may yet live to glory in their accomplished son.'

Julia, all the time she spoke, kept her eyes stedfastly fixed on the countenance of Mrs. Villers, which, to her great surprise, betrayed not the least emotion at her lively and animated detail; to which she coolly replied, "All this, Miss Delmond, might make a very pretty story in a romance, but I believe such things very seldom happen in real life; but as you assure me Mr. What's-his-name has had the education of a gentleman, I must suppose Lady Page has made some mistake, and shall be glad to convince her of it. But pray who introduced this gentleman to your father?"

No question could possibly have been more *mal-apropos* to poor Julia. She was totally at a loss for an answer, and looked to the servant, who most seasonably entered to announce her carriage, as to a deliverer from the worst of punishments. She instantly arose to take leave, and though Mrs. Villers now condescendingly entreated her to stay to tea; she resolutely refused the invitation, and with a firm but modest dignity persisted in her immediate departure.

She found Mr. Vallaton, who had been informed by the servant of her intention, at the bottom of the stairs. He handed her into the carriage, placed himself beside her, and from the rate at which he drove, seemed no less eager than herself to lose sight of Castle-Villers.

CHAP. XIX.

"Assert it for a sacred truth—
"That sorrows such pursuits attend,
"Or such pursuits in sorrows end;
"That all the wild advent'rer gains,
"Are perils, penitence, and pains."

COTTON.[133]

CAPT. Delmond had been for some time watching the progress of the declining sun, whose setting ray he expected to light home his darling daughter. When the splendid orb had compleatly sunk beneath the horizon, and the effulgent glories which its last beam had kindled in the western clouds, began gradually to lose their vivid hues, and at length to exchange the living purple and the burnished gold for the sober livery of night, uneasiness and anxiety crept upon his mind.

"Is it not strange that Julia does not return?" said he to his wife. "I wonder how Dr. Orwell can be so imprudent as to stay thus late."

'Yes, it is very late, to be sure,' returned Mrs. Delmond; 'I cannot even see to knit my stocking.'

"I hate these open carriages," said the Captain, "and wonder how I consented to Julia's going in one. I protest it is quite dark."

'It is, indeed,' replied Mrs. Delmond; 'but here is Nancy with the candles, I shall now see to take up my stitch.'

The apprehensions of Capt. Delmond were suddenly suspended by the entrance of Dr. Orwell.

"Dr. Orwell," said he, "I am truly happy to see you. I was beginning to think that you were staying out rather later than was perfectly adviseable in an open carriage. But it is a sign that your time has passed agreeably. How did you find the General and his Lady? I hope they are both well."

'It is a considerable time since I have been at Castle-Villers,' replied Dr. Orwell.

"Oh, I suppose you drove directly home, then?" said the Captain. "You were quite right; but where is Julia, did she not return with you?"

'I have not yet seen Miss Delmond,' replied the Doctor; 'but I can tell you she is safe.'

"Safe!" repeated the Captain, "did she not return with you from Castle-Villers?"

---

[133] Nathaniel Cotton, *Visions in Verse, for the Entertainment and Instruction of Younger Minds* (1751), "Pleasure", Vision II, 41-46. Hamilton omits line 42 "That pleasures are the bane of youth".

'I did not go to Castle-Villers,' said Dr. Orwell; 'I never thought of it."

"Did not go!" repeated Capt. Delmond, in great surprise. "Who then went with my daughter? Did not you promise to escort her? Dr. Orwell, this is not what I should have expected from you."

'Indeed, my dear sir, you very much surprise me,' returned the Doctor. 'I had yesterday a note from you, requesting the use of my gig, in which, as Miss Delmond informed me in the evening, a friend of yours was to drive her. The gentleman called, as she said he would, about one o'clock, and had it accordingly.'

"Great GOD!" exclaimed the Captain, "how you astonish me! Julia, my Julia, go off with a gentleman of whom I know nothing! Who is he? How came he acquainted with my daughter?"

'I really know nothing further of the gentleman, than that I believe him to be a visitor of Mr. Glib's,' replied Dr. Orwell, 'and took it for granted that he was your acquaintance. I am sorry, heartily sorry to find it otherwise.'

"Where are they now? Where is my daughter? Why is she not returned? Oh! I read it in your face—I have lost my child, and am for ever miserable!"

Here the poor father sunk back in his chair in speechless agony.

'Dear me!' said Mrs. Delmond, laying down her knitting.

"My dear friend," said Dr. Orwell, taking the father's hand, "things are not so bad as you apprehend. Your daughter is within two miles of us, but must necessarily be detained there for some little time by an unlucky accident, from which she has, however, escaped better than could be expected."

'What is it?' said the Captain eagerly. 'Tell me all? Let me know the worst? I will bear it like a man, you shall see I will.'

"Then you shall know the very worst," said Dr. Orwell. "In coming down the hill just above the turnpike, which you know to be very steep and stony, the gig was unfortunately overturned. Miss Delmond and the gentleman were both thrown out by the shock, and both considerably hurt; but neither of them, I hope, dangerously. They were carried to the farm-house which is just by the turnpike, and there both Dr. Sydney and Mr. Gubbles are now attending them. Finding I could be of no service to them, I hastened here; as, however unwilling to be the messenger of bad news, I thought it better to obviate the possibility of your receiving it through the medium of sudden and exaggerated report. After going home to give some necessary directions, I shall return to the farm, and bring you back a full account how I find matters there."

'GOD bless you!' said Capt. Delmond, bursting into tears. 'Forgive this weakness; but, alas! I am now every way a child! I never felt the loss of my limbs till now. My poor Julia! my sweet, my darling child, I shall, perhaps, never see thee more!'

At sight of her husband's tears, Mrs. Delmond took out her pockethankerchief, "If you take on so, my dear," said she, "what is to become of me? Julia may not be so bad as you think; but I wonder who she has got with her? I never heard of this man, no, not I; and I wonder how she could have a sweetheart, and I not know."

The idea was torture to the father's heart. Julia! whom he had ever treated as a friend, a companion. Julia! in whose soul he had so carefully implanted sentiments of the nicest honour; on whose integrity he had ever relied with the most implicit confidence; that she should be capable of a train of falshood and deceit! It was a death-wound to a father's soul; and the soul of Capt. Delmond fully felt its force.

Dr. Orwell was too much affected by the scene, to be able for some time to speak; as soon as his feelings would permit, he said what he could to sooth and comfort the unhappy father, and with a promise of returning as speedily as possible, he took leave.

CHAP. XX.

WE cannot but suppose the lovely Julia to have created such an interest in the breast of the reader, as must excite some anxiety for her present situation, and some desire to be acquainted with the circumstances that led to it. Out of pure good-nature we shall therefore satisfy him in these particulars, before we return to Bridgetina, the true and proper heroine of this our history.

As she departed from Castle-Villers the breast of Julia swelled with the emotion of wounded pride, overwhelming shame, and cruel disappointment. Mortified as she was at the total failure of her well-planned project, she was yet sufficiently sensible of the ridicule to which an acknowledgment of her romantic views must inevitably expose her, to dare to confess her mortification. Her confusion did not escape the penetrating eyes of Vallaton. He had been too sensible of the scrutinizing glances of Lady Page, to be at any loss to guess the cause; but trembled for the effect of an explanation, which not all his confidence in the philosophy of his pupil could assure him would be favourable to his wishes. After proceeding about half a mile in silence, "How rejoiced I am," said Vallaton, "that you contrived to make your escape so soon from these silly people; I was absolutely tired to death with their impertinence."

'Did you ever see any of the party before?' said Julia.

"Why do you ask?" returned Vallaton, alarmed at the question, "did any of them talk of knowing me?"—-'Yes,' replied Julia, 'that Lady Page, it seems, does you the honour of claiming you for an acquaintance.'

"Does she, indeed? I cannot say that I have any recollection of her: but in London one sees so many faces, and meets so many people of the same general description, that it is impossible to remember them all."

'But you do not know half the honour Lady Page did you,' said Julia; 'she was so kind—but I am absolutely ashamed to repeat it.'

"Do not be afraid to tell me any thing she could say," returned Vallaton, firmly. "I am neither afraid nor ashamed to hear it."

'Well, then,' relied Julia, (while her countenance flushed at the recollection of the indignity) 'she told Mrs. Villers, that you were once a hairdresser.'

"Very likely," returned Vallaton, carelessly; "I may have amused myself in that way sometimes."

'You surely cannot be serious?' said Julia, in a faultering accent.

"Yes, indeed, but I am," returned Vallaton. "My dear adopted mother happening to read the Emilias of Rousseau, while I was in my fourteenth year, became so enamoured of his system, that she immediately determined to have me initiated into some handicraft employment, that in case of any revolution in fortune, I might be enabled to earn my bread. I dare say you will laugh at my choice, as she did very heartily, though she was at length kind enough to indulge me in the whim. As I grew up I used sometimes to bribe the person who instructed me, to permit me to go in his stead to some ladies of fashion; and in one of these frolics I may have dressed the head of this Lady Page, for aught I know, though I have no recollection of her face."

'Well,' cried Julia, 'I wonder how your dear adopted mother could permit you to exercise so mean an employment.'

"I cannot say it was altogether with her inclination," replied Vallaton; "the good lady had not strength of mind to rise above the silly prejudices of society."

'Indeed,' replied Julia, 'her prejudices in this instance were very allowable; and I only wonder how she could ever indulge you in a fancy so strange and unaccountable.'

"A mere juvenile extravagance," said Vallaton, carelessly, "not worth a serious thought; though perhaps after all it may be found, that as an occasional relaxation from severe study, it answered the end every bit as well as the work of either a turner or joiner. As to real dignity all manual labour is upon a par."

'Well, I protest I cannot think so,' said Julia. 'You may call it prejudice, and perhaps it is so, but there are some employments one cannot help considering as derogatory to the dignity of a gentleman.'

"If you said to the dignity of *man*," returned her companion, "I should willingly agree with you. In a society that has made any advances towards perfectibility, no man will do work for another of any kind, every man will then labour for himself; and when things are come to this desirable state, it will no doubt be disgraceful to employ the energies of one percipient being in adjusting the hair of another; but no more disgraceful than to join together pieces of wood to form his cabinet, or to turn buttons for his coat; all are in the eye of reason equally derogatory to the real dignity of *man*. As to the dignity of a *gentleman*, I thought my dear Miss Delmond had been more of a philosopher than to hint at such an absurd and unnatural distinction."

'You always get so much the better of me in argument,' replied Julia, 'that I am forced to yield to your superior judgment. But still in this instance—'

"Ah! that my lovely, my sensible Julia would exert those superior powers of which she is possessed, to conquer those hateful prejudices, which may be excusable in a weak and uninformed mind, but which are disgraceful to a soul like hers. Would you but consider—" At this moment the horse, which was going full speed down the hill, stumbled over a loose stone; he made an effort to recover himself, but in vain; he only fell with greater violence, and in his fall overturned the carriage, from which both Julia and Vallaton were thrown out upon the road. The horse was the first to rise: the shafts of the chaise having been broken in the fall, he found means, by a few kicks, to extricate himself from the harness, and galloped off so quickly as to elude the vigilance of the keeper of the turnpike, who saw him out of reach before he got to the gate.

The frightened animal continued his career, till perceived by Dr. Orwell and Henry Sydney, who were returning from a charitable visit to a poor family in the neighbourhood, where the eldest son was ill of a fever, for which the good Dr. Orwell had prevailed upon his young friend to prescribe. Great was the consternation of the two gentlemen, when they perceived the horse; whose appearance left no room to doubt of the catastrophe by which it was occasioned.

While Dr. Orwell employed himself in catching the horse, lest his arrival in town should occasion a premature alarm to the friends of Miss Delmond, Henry ran swiftly forward to give assistance to the sufferers; and arrived at the scene of their misfortune before Julia could be removed from the spot. Vallaton, notwithstanding his bruises, had been raised by the assistance of the people who kept the gate, and was standing lamenting over Julia, whose situation appeared far more deplorable. From the excessive pain of which she complained on every attempt to move, Henry judged the assistance of a surgeon must be necessary, and instantly dispatched a messenger for Mr. Gubbles; while he, having with equal presence of mind and dexterity, formed a litter of an old door which he forced from its hinges, contrived to have her conveyed as easily as possible to the farm-house, where the people, by his directions, prepared a bed for her reception.

On the arrival of Mr. Gubbles, Henry's apprehensions were found to be but too well verified. The knee-pan was discovered to be broken. The pain of setting it was excessive, but not so dreadful to Julia as the idea, conveyed by the hints and shrugs of Mr. Gubbles, that she would probably be lame for life. Henry did all in his power to quiet her apprehensions, and to re-animate her sinking spirits. He supported her by the assurance, that if she had resolution patiently to endure the torture of the tight bandage for four-and-twenty hours, she had nothing to fear; and at length, by the confidence he expressed, and by the numerous instances he adduced of compleat recovery from the consequences of a similar misfortune, he effectually succeeded in tranquillizing her dejected mind.

So entirely did the situation of Julia engross the attention of the spectators, that till she was composed to rest, no one so much as thought of Vallaton. He was at length observed by the farmer's wife, where he had sunk down upon a low chair in the kitchen, and was apparently very near fainting. The good-natured woman instantly ran into the room where Doctor Sydney and Mr. Gubbles were still with Julia.

"La me!" cried she as she entered, "if here ben't more broken bones yet! I lay my life the gentleman be worser than Miss, thos we none of us never thought o'n."

'Good GOD!' exclaimed Julia, 'Mr. Vallaton is then hurt, though he denied to me that he was. What misery has my folly occasioned!' She now burst into a flood of tears, which in all the pain she had suffered, her resolution had hitherto restrained.

While Henry used his endeavours to compose her, Mr. Gubbles proceeded to examine into the condition of Vallaton. In answer to his interrogatories, Vallaton replied, "that he was indeed very much hurt, that the pain of his arm and shoulder was intolerable."

'From the manner in which the arm hangs,' replied Mr. Gubbles, 'I should indeed apprehend a complicated fracture; but perhaps it may not be quite so bad.'

The sleeve of the coat being ripped of, the man of science congratulated his patient on his very extraordinary good fortune. 'It is a mere trifle, my dear sir, nothing but a dislocation of the humerno, and a simple fracture of the lower extremity of the ulna.'

While he dexterously replaced the arm in its socket, poor Vallaton could not suppress a groan. 'It is impossible I can hurt you,' said the learned operator; 'nothing was ever done with greater ease; and as for this other little business, it is a mere nothing. I never met with a more elegant fracture in my life—sure I don't hurt you?'

"Indeed but you do,' cried Vallaton, "you put me to very exquisite pain."

'It is impossible, my dear sir, quite impossible; the swelling of the adjacent muscles may indeed create some trifling uneasiness; but it is nothing to what I have met with in the course of practice.'

"La me!" exclaimed the landlady, who attended to supply the necessary bandages, "if you Doctors have more heart than a stone! I am sure the poor gentleman had need o' patience to hear you."

The good woman having offered her son's bed for the accommodation of Vallaton, he was immediately conveyed to it, and there we shall leave him to his meditations, while we return to the afflicted Julia.

Henry Sydney beheld with anxiety the agitated state of his fair patient's mind, and sensible how necessary repose was to her recovery, he prevailed upon her to swallow some quantity of an opiate which Mr. Gubbles had the precaution to bring.

Julia felt with gratitude the humane attention of her young physician, but was still deploring the want of a friend of her own sex, whose presence would, she thought, afford a support still more grateful, when a soft step approached her bed, and the figure of Harriet Orwell glided before her eyes.

"Is it possible!" said Julia, in a faint voice. "Is Miss Orwell indeed so good as to come to see me here, at this time of night?"

'Hush! hush!' said Harriet, putting her finger to her lips, 'we shall talk of every thing to-morrow; I only beg you would give me leave to do things in my own way to-night, without taking any notice of me, except merely to ask for what you want.'

"But you do not intend to stay with me all night?" said Julia; "that would be too much."

'Indeed I shall not leave you while you remain in this house,' replied Harriet; 'and as to sitting up all night, it is what I like of all things: but no more speaking; and I suppose we may now dismiss this gentleman here, who will attend my father home.'

Julia could only express her thanks by tears. Nor did Henry behold unmoved this fresh proof of Harriet's goodness. While she lightly glided round the bed of her friend, procuring for her a thousand little comforts which her active mind suggested, and her gentle hand supplied, he thought he beheld a guardian-angel on its work of mercy. When he was about to leave the room, she softly opened the door for his departure: he did not speak, but seizing the hand which hung down, he pressed it to his lips with an emphatic expression of admiration and respect.

On walking into the farmer's apartment, Henry there found Dr. Orwell, who was receiving from Mr. Gubbles a scientific description of the fractures, of which indeed the good Doctor did not comprehend one syllable. The explanation of Henry, however, soon made the matter perfectly intelligible, to the no small indignation of Mr. Gubbles; who, from the plain and simple language made use of by the young physician, conceived a sovereign contempt for his knowledge and capacity.

Henry persisted in his resolution of taking up his abode by the farmer's fire-side all night, which after a little opposition was agreed to by Dr. Orwell, who proceeded to acquaint the parents of Julia with the particulars of her misfortune.

CHAP. XXI.

"No argument like matter of fact is.
"And we are best of all led to
"Men's principles, by what they do."
                                    BUTLER.[134]

---

[134] Samuel Butler, *Hudibras* (1663), Second Part, Canto III, 193-95.

THE day which proved so unfortunate to poor Julia, was by Bridgetina considered as one of the most auspicious aeras that marked the period of her existence. It was indeed a day of much importance; a day which opened upon her mind the grandest view, the most extatic prospect, that was ever presented to an enlightened imagination.

It happened, that among several sets of new books which Mr. Glib about this time received from his correspondent in London, was a copy of the translation of Mons. Vaillant's Travels into the interior parts of Africa.[135] The first volume of this book Mr. Glib ran hastily over, without experiencing any degree of pleasure from the perusal. Neither the sprightliness of the author's manner, his zeal in the pursuit of natural history, his unbounded philanthropy, nor the novelty of his animated descriptions, had the power of captivating the fancy of Mr. Glib; but the second volume made very ample amends for the time thrown away upon the first. When he came to the account of the Gonoquais Hottentots, his delight and admiration increased at every line, till at length, no longer able to contain his rapture, he ran hastily with the book in his hand to the back parlour, where Bridgetina, who had just then happened to call, was sitting with Mr. Myope and the Goddess of Reason. "See here!" said he, "See here, Citizen Myope, all our wishes fulfilled! All our theory realized! Here is a whole nation of philosophers, all as wise as ourselves! All enjoying the proper dignity of man! Things just as they ought! No man working for another! All alike! All equal! No laws! No government! No coercion! Every one exerting his energies as he pleases! Take a wife today: leave her again to-morrow! It is the very essence of virtue, and the quintessence of enjoyment!"

'Alas!' replied Mr. Myope, 'I fear this desirable state of things is reserved for futurity. Ages must elapse before mankind will be sufficiently enlightened to be sensible of the great advantage of living as you describe.'

"No, no," cried Glib, "ages need not elapse. It is all known to the Hottentots. All practised by the Gonoquais hoard. Only just listen."

"In a country where there is no difference in birth or rank, (as is the case in Gonoquais) every inhabitant is necessarily on an equality."[136]

'The very ground-work of perfectibility!' cried Bridgetina, 'that is certain; but go on.'

"Luxury and vanity, which in more polished countries consume the largest fortunes, create a thousand unhappy distinctions entirely unknown to these savages; their desires are bounded by real wants, nor are they excluded from the means of

---

[135] François Le Vaillant, *Voyage dans l'interieur de l'Afrique*. Various English translations were available, including one published by G.G. and J.J. Robinson. References in footnotes are to *Travels from the Cape of Good-Hope into the Interior Parts of Africa*, translated by Elizabeth Helme. 2 vols. Lane: London, 1790. See Appendix B.

[136] Le Vaillant, *Travels from the Cape of Good-Hope*, 2: 67.

gratifying them; and these means may be, and are effectually pursued by all: thus the various combinations of pride for the aggrandizement of families, all the schemes of heaping fortune on fortune in the same coffer, being utterly unknown; no intrigues are created, no oppressions practised, in fine no crimes instigated."[137]

'O learned and amiable Hottentots!' exclaimed Bridgetina, 'by what means—'

"Stay a little, Miss, and only listen to this passage about their marriages," said Glib, resuming his book.

"The formalities of these marriages consist in the promises made by each party to live together as long as they find it convenient; the engagement made, the young couple from that moment become man and wife.—"[138]

'O enviable state of society!' exclaimed Bridgetina, 'O—'

"Do not interrupt me, Miss, till I have finished the passage.—*As I have hinted before, they live together as long as harmony subsists between them; for should any difference arise, they make no scruple of separation, but part with as little ceremony as they meet; and each one, free to form other connections, seeks elsewhere a more agreeable partner. These marriages, founded on reciprocal inclinations, have ever a happy issue; and as love is their only cement, they require no other motive for parting than indifference."*[139]

"Mark that, citizens! *No other motive for parting than indifference.* Who would not wish to live in that blessed country? But here is a still further proof of their progress in philosophy. *You never meet among the Gonoquais with men who apply themselves to any particular kind of work, in order to satisfy the caprice of others. The woman who desires to lie soft, will fabricate her own mat. She who has a wish to be clothed, will instruct a man to make a habit. The huntsman who would have good weapons, can depend on those of his own making; and the lover is the only architect of the cabin that is to contain his future mistress."*★[140]

'Why this is the very state of perfection to which we all aspire!' cried Mr. Myope, in extacy. 'It is the sum and substance of our philosophy. What illustrious proofs of human genius may we expect to find in a society thus wisely constituted, a society in which leisure is the inheritance of every one of its members?'

"It is evident," cried Bridgetina, "that the author of our illustrious system is entirely indebted to the Hottentots for his sublime idea of the Age of Reason. Here is the Age of Reason exemplified; here is proof sufficient of the perfectibility of man!"

'Yes,' said Mr. Myope, 'and as we well know mechanical and daily

---

[137] Le Vaillant, *Travels from the Cape of Good-Hope,* 2: 67-68.
[138] Le Vaillant, *Travels from the Cape of Good-Hope,* 2: 69.
[139] Le Vaillant, *Travels from the Cape of Good-Hope,* 2: 68-69.
[140] ★The curious reader may, if he please, compare the passage quoted from Vaillant with the eighth chapter of the eighth book of Political Justice, vol. ii. octavo edition; and he will not be surprised that Citizen Glib should be struck with the coincidence★ Le Vaillant, *Travels from the Cape of Good-Hope,* 2: 85-86.

labour to be the deadliest foe to all that is great and admirable in the human mind, to what a glorious height of metaphysical knowledge may we expect a people to soar, where all are equally poor and equally idle! What attainments must they have doubtless made in science? What discoveries in philosophy?'

"As to science," said Glib, "it does not at least appear that they know much of arithmetic, for Mr. Vaillant here tells us, that *they cannot reckon above the number of their fingers. They count the time of the day by the course of the sun, saying, it was there when I departed, yonder when I returned.*"

'Astonishing proof of the progress of mind!' cried Bridgetina.

"Yes," said Glib, "and see further: *With calm tranquillity they behold the rising and the setting sun, unknowing and regardless of the pointed hour upon the time-piece.*[141] Do you mark that, citizens? No getting up at seven in the morning to open shop; no making up accounts; no care about business. Well, if before another year goes round I do not become a Hottentot, may I never more behold the face of a philosopher!"

'And if,' said Myope, 'every other particular in the character of this illustrious people, be found to correspond with what we have already learned, every philosopher must, like you, long to be received into the bosom of a society arrived at a state of civilization, which but to imagine has been justly considered as the most glorious effort of the sublimest genius!'

"You do not yet know the half of their perfections," returned Glib; "but here is the key-stone of the grand arch of perfectibility: only listen to this, and confess whether you ever heard of so wise a people. *Modes of divination are the usual appendages of superstitious worship, but how can this exist where they have no religion, no idea of a superior Being? In these hordes,* (do you take notice) *in these hordes they have neither physician, nor priest, nor superiority of degree, nor any word in the Hottentot language that signifies in any manner these distinctions.*"[142]

'Admirable!' exclaimed Myope.

"The very perfection of modern philolosophy!" cried Bridgetina.

'Vere do dese wise people live? enquired the Goddess of Reason. 'Have dey no fete, no grand spectacle, no ball, no concerta?'

"Yes, yes, they have balls, Madam," returned Glib, "and concerts too. But you are not to imagine, that in the reasonable state of society to which they are advanced, that any man will condescend to perform the compositions of another. All compose for themselves; all play their own tune; no two in the same key!"

'Vat be dere ball dress?' said the Goddess. 'De fashions of so enlightened a people be ver elegant, to be sure. Do dey rouge, like de French lady; or be dey pale-faced, like de lady of England?'

---

[141] Le Vaillant, *Travels from the Cape of Good-Hope*, 2: 104.

[142] Le Vaillant, *Travels from the Cape of Good-Hope*, 2: 107.

"Their taste in dress is equal to their other refinements," replied Glib. "Every one painted; not a pale face to be seen. All covered with grease, and soot, and ochre, from head to heel; bears' guts for bracelets, and cloaks of asses' skins. Their heads are ornamented with blown bladders, and a sheep's bone hangs about their necks instead of a locket."

'What strange fashions dis foreign nation of philosophers do follow!' said the Goddess.

"What elegant simplicity of taste!" cried Myope. "But I must beg leave to peruse the whole of this extraordinary account. It has already generated an idea in my mind, which may be productive of the most extraordinary consequences to the interests of society."

Mr. Myope then took the book, and proceeded to read the whole account of the Gonoquais in an audible voice, though not without receiving many interruptions from the exclamations of delight that frequently burst from his admiring audience. When he had finished, "Here," said he, "here, my friends, is the place—the only place to which, in this distempered state of civilization, a philosopher can resort with any hopes of comfort. Let us seek an asylum among these kindred souls. Let us form a horde in the neighbourhood of Haabas, and from the deserts of Africa send forth those rays of philosophy which shall enlighten all the habitable globe."

'Go with all my heart,' cried Glib; 'leave shop, and wife, and children, and all. Get a wife among the Gonoquais; meet when we please, separate when we have a mind. That's it! that's the way to have energies!'

The proposal of Mr. Myope appeared equally charming to Bridgetina, who had no doubt, that among the numerous philosophers of England a party would be formed every way agreeable to her wishes. Mr. Myope assured her, that the idea of emigration had for a considerable time prevailed; and that the difficulty of finding a place agreeable to their views presented the only obstacle to its execution. That obstacle was now happily removed; as no one could read the account of the Gonoquais Hottentots, and not be sensible that in the bosom of a people who had so fully adopted all their plans for the improvement of society; who had no trade, no commerce, no distinctions of rank, no laws, no coercion, no government; who had among them no physicians, no lawyers, no priests, and who, to crown all, *believed in* NO GOD! they must find that congeniality of sentiments and dispositions which they would in vain expect among the corrupt societies of Europe.

The more Mr. Myope considered the subject, the more was he impressed with an idea of its importance. His mind, ever under the influence of some one darling idea, which, during the period of its reign, excluded every other thought, was soon kindled into enthusiasm. It must be confessed, however, that the enthusiasm of Mr. Myope differed very materially from that which distinguishes certain great minds in the pursuit of some favourite object; it was of a nature very distinct from that sublime energy of the soul which, on the most extensive and comprehensive views, concentrates all its powers towards the accomplishment of some grand design. Indeed, no two principles of action are more opposite to each other in their nature, origin, progress, and consequences, than the two different species of enthusiasm here described. The first, born of reason and directed by judgment, is noble, discriminating, and effective. The other, the produce of an inflammable imagination, is blinded by the glare of its own bewildering light, expends itself upon any object that chance puts in its reach, and is usually unsteady as it is abortive.

Such was the enthusiasm of Mr. Myope.

While he was a religionist, it inflamed his zeal for the minutiae of every dogma of the sect to which he then happened to belong. As a Quaker,[143] it made him tenacious of the broad-brimmed hat, and all the peculiarities of dress and manner which distinguish that *apparently* plain and simple people. He then groaned at the sight of a coloured ribbon, and was moved by the spirit to denounce the most dreadful judgments against the crying sin of long trains and hair-powder.

As an Anabaptist,[144] in his eagerness for dipping all that came in his way, he very narrowly escaped being drowned along with a poor woman, of whom he had unfortunately made a convert in the time of a great flood. And when his energies were directed to Calvinism,[145] the state of the reprobate engrossed every faculty of his mind, and his whole soul was poured out in describing the nature of the dreadful tortures, which assuredly awaited all who did not embrace every article of his then faith, all whose intellectual optics happened to view things in a different light.

Nor when Mr. Myope changed his opinions, did his mind become more enlarged by the change. He wandered from maze to maze, in the intricate labyrinth of polemical divinity, without having once caught a glance of the sublime views, the simple but elevating principles of that religion, from which each of the different sectaries he embraced professed to be derived.

As a convert to the new philosophy, his zeal was no less conspicuous. We have already given some striking proofs of its effects; and perhaps may yet have occasion to relate some farther instances of it, no less memorable and extraordinary.

The account of the Gonoquais Hottentots had now inspired this philosopher with a flow of eloquence which produced the greatest

---

[143] Members of The Religious Society of Friends founded by George Fox in 1648-50, and distinguished by its stress on the "inner light" and rejection of sacraments, ordained ministry and set forms of worship; also noted for its pacifist principles and simplicity of life, in particular for plainness of dress and speech.

[144] Name of a sect which arose in Germany in 1521 and became a Protestant religious body known as Baptists.

[145] Followers of the theological doctrines of John Calvin (1509-64), the Protestant reformer.

effects upon his audience. Both Bridgetina and Mr. Glib, struck with the force of his irresistible arguments, promised to turn their serious thoughts to his proposal. They agreed to renew their consultations upon the subject as frequently as possible; but till their plan was more fully digested, thought it best not to drop a hint of it to the unenlightened; as such persons, being totally incapable of estimating its advantages, might maliciously endeavour to obstruct its success.

END OF THE FIRST VOLUME.

Vol. II.

CHAP. I.

"Folks prone to leasing
"Say things at first, because they're pleasing;
"Then prove what they have once asserted,
"Nor care to have their lye deserted;
"Till their own dreams at length deceive 'em,
"And oft repeating, they believe 'em."

PRIOR.[1]

THE miseries of war, of famine, and of pestilence, had all been experienced by Captain Delmond; but the combined horrors of this triple scourge of human kind fell short of what he endured the night of Julia's misfortune. At one time, exasperated into madness at the idea of her clandestine correspondence with a person whom, as a visitor of Glib's, he could not imagine to be a gentleman, he breathed forth threatenings and invectives. The artifice she had used to deceive him—the ingratitude which gave birth to that artifice—was a thought which rankled in his soul, and like the barbed dart peculiar to some savage tribes, could not even be touched without the extreme of torture. Anon he saw his darling child in pain! her life perhaps in danger! In a moment her errors were forgotten, and his whole soul melted into an agony of tenderness.

The sharp pangs of bodily pain were soon added to the poignancy of mental suffering. By the agitation of his mind the gout was thrown into his stomach, and he became so dangerously ill, that about four in the morning Mrs. Delmond was obliged to send for Mr. Gubbles, who administered a cordial draught, which tended to quiet the pain; and, as day advanced, exhausted nature sought relief in sleep.

He awoke somewhat more composed, and instantly enquired for Julia. No account of her had yet been received. Fretted at his wife's neglect, in not having dispatched some one to know how she had passed the night, he desired that Mrs. Delmond might herself instantly set out to see her daughter, and to order her every necessary attendance, and every comfort, that it was possible to administer in her present situation.

"I have, perhaps, blamed my poor girl too much," said he. "She told me she had seen this gentleman at Mrs. Botherim's; it may be only accident that has now thrown him in her way. Do not, therefore, drop a hint of my having suspected her of deceit; it would wound the poor child too severely to think that I could impute to her a deviation from those principles of honour which I have so carefully inculcated, and which she has ever so invariably maintained. Give her my blessing, and tell her that I live but in her happiness and safety."

Mrs. Delmond hastily prepared to obey her husband's orders. She

---

[1] Matthew Prior, *Alma* (1718), Canto iii, lines 10-14.

indeed felt more anxiety herself concerning Julia than she had ever experienced on any former event of her life. Though sometimes inclined to be a little jealous of the manifest partiality of her husband for his daughter, which extended so far, that though she could seldom please him in settling the little accommodations with which his valetudinary state required him to be surrounded, no sooner did Julia place the footstool, or adjust the cushion, than all was right; and such praises bestowed on the dexterity of the daughter, as glanced a reproach upon the wife. Yet was the jealousy thus excited divested of its sting by the demeanour of Julia. Such was the sweetness of her temper, such the generous pains she always took to put every thing her mother did in the most advantageous point of view, and such her solicitude to soften the little asperities that sometimes fell from her father, that she could not fail to endear herself to her mother, so as entirely to engross her affections.

The affections of Mrs. Delmond were not, it is true, of that ardent nature which is for ever tremblingly alive—ever ready to torment itself with the extreme of anxiety and disquiet. Mrs. Delmond took things more calmly;—she very implicitly relied on the assurances of Dr. Orwell, that Julia would completely recover the consequences of the accident she had so unfortunately met with; and but for the illness of Captain Delmond, she would have slept very soundly on the faith of these assurances. There was, however, one circumstance on which Doctor Orwell could not give her the satisfaction she wished for; her curiosity concerning the gentleman who accompanied her daughter was still unsatisfied. In the hope of obtaining information upon this point, she pursued her walk with unusual alacrity.

On her arrival at the farm, she was conducted to the apartment where poor Julia was suffering an extreme degree of pain, but suffering it with heroic fortitude and resolution. The shabbiness of the apartment was the first thing that attracted the attention of Mrs. Delmond. 'Dear me!' said she to Miss Orwell, as she entered, 'what a pitiful place this is! White-washed walls! check curtains! to be sure it is very wretched; but how is Julia?'

"Is that my mother's voice?" cried Julia, in feverish agitation.

'Yes, my love! said Miss Orwell, 'but you know the doctor strictly prohibits your speaking. Both Doctor Sydney and Mr. Gubbles think Miss Delmond will do very well, if she keeps herself quiet; and I dare say you, Madam, will agree with me in enforcing a strict observance of their injunctions.'

"Oh yes;" said Mrs. Delmond, "she certainly must not speak, if they forbid it; but how long is she to be confined to his place?"

'Let me but see my mother,' said Julia, 'and I will be satisfied.'

Mrs. Delmond approached the bedside, and put out her hand, which was eagerly grasped by Julia. 'My mother! you are too kind in coming to see me; but oh, my father! is he not enraged at his Julia?'

Mrs. Delmond would have replied, but Harriet insisted so much on the injunctions of the physicians, which the apprehensions of fever rendered it necessary punctually to observe, that she prevented her from speaking, and in a short time prevailed on her to quit the room.

She was led by Harriet into a small stone-floored parlour, which, in lieu of the white sand with which it had been strewed, was now neatly covered with a carpet. This was the work of Harriet, who had, in her quiet but active manner, already made such improvements in the appearance both of this room and of that which was occupied by Julia, that they now assumed a very different aspect from that which they had worn the preceding evening. Having early in the morning sent to her aunt for such things as she thought most wanted, she received, by the provident attention of that good lady, an abundant supply of every necessary, and of every article which she thought could in any wise contribute to the ease or comfort of the poor sufferer. These Harriet had so judiciously arranged, that the apartment of Julia no longer appeared incommodious or uncomfortable; and yet so softly had she glided about the performance of her operations, that the noise of her footsteps had never reached the ears of her unfortunate friend.

Mrs. Delmond was no sooner seated, than she began to enquire of Miss Orwell what she knew of the gentleman who had accompanied her daughter to Castle-Villers; but to her great mortification found that Harriet could give her little information on the subject, except the account of his misfortune.

"I am sure it has been a sad business for me," said Mrs. Delmond; "I was obliged to be up the greatest part of the night with the Captain, who made himself so ill, I had to send for Mr. Gubbles to give him some stuff. It was very ill done of Julia, to be sure, to go with a person we none of us knew; I thought it would have killed her father, the very thoughts of it. I dare say, now, he will be quite cross the whole day."

Harriet had, from some hints dropped by Julia in the course of the night, learned that all was not just as it should be. She evidently saw, that some mystery hung over the subject of the expedition, and that the mind of Julia suffered from the secret consciousness of some act of indiscretion. But so little had Harriet of the prying spirit of curiosity, so easily could she controul the feelings of her well-regulated mind, that so far from diving into the source of Julia's disquiet, she had been at much pains to turn her thoughts from the subject of uneasiness. The same spirit of animated benevolence made her now use all her endeavours to persuade Mrs. Delmond, that Julia would be fully able to vindicate herself, and to give such an explanation of the circumstances that had incurred her father's displeasure, as would prove entirely satisfactory.

"Aye, to be sure," said Mrs. Delmond, "she can easily get about him at any time. The very last word he said to me was, to be sure to give her his blessing." She then entered on a querulous lamentation concerning the length of time that must necessarily elapse before Julia could be brought home; "which," she said, "she was sure would be a sad time to her, as the

Captain would be so cross all the while, that nobody could please him."

To this Harriet found it impossible to make any reply; a silence of some minutes ensued, after which Mrs. Delmond, having coldly thanked Miss Orwell for her kindness, took her departure, to the great satisfaction of Harriet, whose warm and generous heart revolted at the cold selfishness which was too visibly displayed in the course of the conversation to escape her observation. When she returned to the poor pain-racked Julia, she softly whispered, that she had dismissed her mother, who would, however, come again to see her, as soon as she was better able to support conversation.

'She is then gone,' said Julia; 'gone, without speaking a word to me concerning my father! Alas! I fear he is too much displeased with me to bear the mention of my name.'

"On the contrary," said Harriet, "he charged your mother with his dearest blessing for you. Make yourself easy, then, my dear Julia! be assured that your father is only anxious concerning your recovery."

'Perhaps, then, he does not know who accompanied me?' cried Julia, seeming to revive at the thought.

"Perhaps not," said Harriet, "so make yourself easy; and here is something good for you, which it is now time for you to take," pouring out a draft which had been ordered by the Doctor. Julia swallowed the medicine, and somewhat reanimated by the hopes inspired by her friend, she continued in silent patience to endure the pain which the tight ligature every minute rendered more intolerable.

While the amiable Harriet was personally engaged in attending upon her companion, she did not forget the stranger who had shared in her misfortune. He experienced the benefit of her considerate attention in a number of little comforts, of which the sick nurse who had come to wait on Julia, but whom Harriet had sent to Vallaton, would never of herself have thought.

He kept his bed the whole day, and had, about five in the afternoon, fallen into a profound slumber, from which he was roused by the noise of many tongues; a noise sufficiently loud not only to disturb the repose of Vallaton, but to awaken the nurse, who was sweetly snoring in the easy chair.

This uprorious[2] din was soon explained by the entrance of Mr. Myope and Mr. Glib, accompanied by Bridgetina, and followed by the mistress of the house, who expostulated with great emphasis upon the impropriety of so many people going altogether into the sick chamber, when both the old Doctor and the young one had particularly desired her to see that no more than one at a time was permitted to enter it. "But I am sure, sir," said she, hastily drawing the curtains, and elevating her voice to a still higher key, "I am sure you must do me the justice to free me from any blame, if so be, as how, that the noise do you any harm. I

---

[2] *sic* (uproarious).

am sure I did all I could to hinder it; and so I hope you will tell the young Doctor, for to be sure he is so civil, one would not disoblige un for the world."

While the landlady attacked the ears of Vallaton from one side of the bed, Citizen Glib assailed him from the other. 'Sad mishap, Citizen Vall! hast got a cursed tumble, broke half a dozen bones, eh? Vile things them gigs, but never mind: no gigs among the Hottentots. No breakneck curricles in the Gonoquais horde. Every one trusts to his own legs. That's it! The Hottentots are the only true philosophers after all.'

"But how did the accident happen?" said Mr. Myope, addressing him from the foot of the bed.

'What motive,' said Bridgetina, (who had now taken the place of the landlady at the right side) 'What motive could induce the horse to act in such a reprehensible manner?'

In this tumult of tongues, it was some time before Mr. Vallaton, who was somewhat weakened by a slight degree of fever, could exert his voice sufficiently to be heard. He at length proceeded to answer the interrogatories of his friends, by giving an account of the manner in which the accident happened, laying the blame of the whole catastrophe entirely upon the poor horse.

In this it however appears, that Mr. Vallaton did the noble animal great injustice. To clear the character of this deserving creature, and to wipe away those aspersions so unjustly thrown upon his reputation, we shall proceed to throw such light upon the subject, as may, perhaps, serve to shew him more deserving of pity than of censure.

Be it then known to the reader, that the groom, who received the General's orders for putting up the carriage, had been brought up in a strict observance of the rules of military discipline: those rules which, according to the opinion of the great monarch to whom mankind are indebted for the greatest improvements *en l'art militaire*, may in time, if properly practised, bring a great part of the human race into the desirable state of automatons.[3]

This well-trained groom no sooner received the orders of his master, than he gave a prompt obedience to his commands; but as these commands only extended to putting up the chaise, and as taking off the harness, rubbing down the horse, and giving him either food or water, made no part of his orders, he very properly stopped short at the point of literal obedience, and presumed not to harbour a single thought of the consequences.

However agreeable the conduct of the groom might have been to some veteran theorists, the poor horse did not much relish the effects of this perfection of discipline. He felt encumbered with the weight of his

---

[3] Probably referring to Frederick the Great, King of Prussia (1740-86) who continued his father's military reforms and established the Prussian army as an efficient instrument of war and one of the most powerful in Europe.

harness, and was soon tired of champing the bit of his bridle, which he would willingly have exchanged for a mouthful of hay, or a few oats. But in vain did he utter his complaints, in vain did he neigh to every passing footstep; he was unheard, or at least unheeded, by any servant in the family. The domestics of General Villers were indeed all inspired with such lofty sentiments, as to conceive no small contempt for such of their master's visitors as came unaccompanied by a train of lacqueys; how then could they be expected to pay any regard to an animal that meanly condescended to draw an unattended gig?

Notwithstanding the honour of having passed the day in a stable which cost some thousand pounds in the erection, the parson's horse was extremely happy when he found himself on the way to his own comfortable home. He went on with eagerness; but alas! his strength did not second his inclination. Though a horse ecclesiastic, he had not been accustomed to keep Lent; and fasting agreed so ill with his constitution, that it occasioned a weakness which made him altogether incapable of recovering the fatal trip which was productive of such deplorable consequences.

From a description of the accident, Mr. Vallaton was led to mention the pain he had sustained by the broken arm, the dislocated shoulder, and the bruises which he felt all over his body.

"I cannot but congratulate you," said Bridgetina, "on the glorious opportunity you now enjoy of proving the omnipotence of mind over matter.[4] What is pain to those who resolve not to feel it? Physical causes sink into nothing, when compared with those that are moral. Happy had it been for the world, if not only your arm, but every bone in your body had been broken, so that it had been the means of furnishing mankind with a proof of the perfectibility of philosophical energy!"

'Nothing can be more truly philosophical than the observation of Citizeness Botherim,' said Mr. Myope; 'and I make no doubt, from the known powers of my friend Vallaton, that if every bone in his body had been broken, he would have effected a reunion of the parts by his own exertion. As for pain, it is a mere vulgar prejudice; a weakness which will vanish before the light of philosophy, and, in a more advanced state of society, be utterly unknown.'

"It most unfortunately happens, though, (replied Vallaton, writhing in great agony, from an attempt to move) it unfortunately happens, that one's energies are apt to desert one, at the very time they are most wanted. I think I have seen you make wry faces at the rheumatism before now; but no rheumatism in the world ever occasioned half the pain I feel."

---

[4] Godwin explains that "the human mind ... is nothing else than a faculty of perception" (*Political Justice*, Bk I, ch. v, "The Voluntary Action of Men Originate in their Opinions") and "that mind would one day become omnipotent over matter" (Bk VIII, Appendix, "Of Co-operation, Cohabitation and Marriage"). See Appendix A.

'I grant you,' returned Myope, 'that even a philosopher may sometimes be taken by surprise. Besides, in a corrupt state of society, where many people believe in a GOD, the existence of laws and government generates weakness, which no one can entirely escape; the energies cannot arrive at that state of perfection to which they will be found to approximate, as soon as these existing causes of depravity have been entirely removed.'[5]

"All removed among the Hottentots!" cried Glib. "No obstacles to perfectibility among the Gonoquais. No priests! No physicians! All exert their energies.—Broken bones healed in a twinkling."

Here Mr. Glib was interrupted by a loud groan from Vallaton, whose pillow the energetic citizen had, in the vehemence of his action, drawn from under the lame shoulder; which, in spite of the mind's omnipotence, resented the loss of its supporter in a manner that made the tears find their way into the sufferer's eyes. Mr. Myope no sooner observed the misfortune, than he good-naturedly went round to remedy it, by adjusting the pillow; in which charitable office he was employed, when Henry Sydney, who was with his sister on the way to Julia's apartment, hearing the groans of Vallaton, hastily entered the room, to enquire the cause. Having received information on that head, he began to make other enquiries, which he concluded by asking the patient whether he had had any sleep?

To this Vallaton replied, that "he had been prevented by pain from closing his eyes all the night and morning; but that he had just fallen into a very profound slumber a little before the arrival of this friends."

'Charming proof of perfectibility!' said Bridgetina. 'I sincerely congratulate you on being able for so long a time to ward off the great foe of human genius, the degrader of the noblest faculties of the mind! How fortunate it was that we should arrive in time to save you from falling into that torpid and insensible state, from which it will be the glory of philosophy to free the human race!'[6]

"I hope philosophy will pardon me," said Henry, "if I take the liberty of declaring, that a good sound sleep will be very serviceable in the present instance; and that I must therefore entreat the gentleman may be left at liberty to enjoy it."

'To one who has not accurately investigated the powers of the mind,' said Mr. Myope, 'sleep may doubtless appear useful, nay, in some degree necessary; but to those who have carried their enquiries further, it is evident that mind, being omnipotent over matter, may exert that omnipotence over every part of the animal œconomy; and that not only sleep, but death itself, may yield to its controul.'

---

[5] See for example Godwin, *Political Justice*, Bk VI, ch. 2, "Of Religious Establishments".
[6] Godwin, *Political Justice*, Bk VIII, Appendix, "Of Health, and the Prolongation of Human Life" in which he argues that "if the power of intellect can be established over all other matter, are we not inevitably led to ask why not over the matter of our own bodies?" See Appendix A.

"If the investigators of mind took the trouble to extend their investigations to the nature of organized bodies," replied Henry, "they would probably arrive at very different conclusions."

'What a lamentable thing it is,' said Bridgetina, 'that a mind like Doctor Sydney's should be thus warped by prejudice! Yes, my amiable friend, you are possessed of powers which might generate happiness to the human race; and it can only be attributed to the present unjust and odious constitutions of society, that these powers are, by the prevalence of vulgar errors, obstructed in their progress to perfection. Miserable prejudice! which shuts its eyes against the truth; which listens to arguments that would impress conviction upon every impartial hearer, and is astonished at their futility! To any unprejudiced understanding, would not the circumstance of Mr. Vallaton's having wanted sleep for a period of more than forty hours incontestibly prove the possibility of living without it altogether? Would not any impartial person be at once convinced, that if, by the exertions of his mind, he could ward off the sluggish foe to mental energy for such a length of time, he might, by a continuation of the same exertion, ward it off for ever? And yet such are the deplorable prejudices of the greater part of mankind, that the very length of time he has been kept awake, would to them appear an argument in favour of the necessity of his now indulging in repose.'

"The statement of Citizeness Botherim is equally judicious and profound," said Mr. Myope. "But though it be impossible to set any bounds to the operations of mind, it is not in the present miserable state of society, that her operations can be expected to arrive to such perfection. Vulgar prejudices are in their nature so obstinate, that it is possible some ages may elapse, before sleep will be considered as altogether unnecessary. And therefore as every wise man would wish the progress of improvement to be gradual and moderate, it may be more adviseable not to urge the citizen to a further exertion of his energies, in refraining from sleep entirely. It is sufficient that he has already given a proof of what may be done; and I hope that by exerting his powers towards knitting the broken bones, he will soon give a still more illustrious evidence of the omnipotence of mind."

'Ay,' said Glib, 'that's it! Energies are the only true doctors. Energies do all. Energies cheat the undertaker, and make a man live for ever.[7] Never mind broken bones. All trifles to philosophers.'

The philosophy of Mr. Vallaton was put to a severe trial by the length of this conservation, which was at last happily concluded at the earnest request of Henry, whose prejudices were very strong in favour of the patient's obtaining a little repose.

Henry now proceeded to enquire for Julia, and was followed by Bridgetina into the parlour, where Harriet Orwell waited to receive them. She had left Maria with the fair sufferer, into whose room Henry was

---

[7] Godwin, *Political Justice*, Bk VIII, "Of Health, and the Prolongation of Human Life". See Appendix A.

introduced. He found her so low and feverish, that he requested Miss Botherim to postpone her intended visit to some other opportunity. Bridgetina then enquired, whether he would not walk home with her?

"He was extremely sorry that it would not be in his power, as he waited for Mr. Gubbles, and should not depart till he saw how Miss Delmond was after the ligature had been relieved."

'Did not Miss Orwell and Miss Sydney go home that night?'

"No: Maria intended sitting up with Miss Delmond, and Harriet was to sleep in a settee bed, which had been put up for her in the parlour."

Bridgetina, to whom the idea of a moonlight walk with Henry was very charming, expressed her desire to wait for him, in terms that ought to have been sufficiently flattering; but unfortunately, Henry either wanted sense to take her hints, or gallantry to avail himself of them. He cruelly urged her departure with the philosophers, on pretence of the appearance of rain; and as Miss Orwell did not invite her stay, she found herself obliged to comply with his entreaty, with which, as his regard for her health was the ostensible motive, she could not be displeased.

Myope and Glib had already advanced some paces on the road, and Bridgetina was too well pleased with the opportunity of enjoying her meditations upon the conduct of Henry, to be very anxious to overtake them.

'Yes,' said she, aloud, 'it is evident he loves. Whence, but from the transporting source, could the solicitude he evinced for my health be possibly derived? How anxious did he seem for my departure? How did his fine eyes sparkle with pleasure, when he saw me about to comply with his request? How eager was his solicitude? How tender his regard for my safety? How did he watch the clouds, as if apprehensive of their injuring the object of his wishes? This tide of tenderness enchants my very soul! It tingles through my veins, and wraps my senses in delirium! And shall I not indulge the sweet sentiments of nature that now inspire my breast? Shall a false regard for the debasing and immoral institutions of a corrupt society deter me from making a suitable return to his enchanting tenderness? No: forbid it philosophy! forbid it love! From this moment—'

Here the soliloquy of Bridgetina was unfortunately interrupted; and never did the soliloquy of a love-sick maiden receive interruption from a more indignified source. While pouring out the effusions of her tender heart in the middle of the highway, she was too much occupied by her *feelings* to observe the approach of a drove of pigs, which at length advanced upon her so fast as to prevent the possibility of retreat. She was surrounded on all sides in a moment. The obstreperous and unmanageable animals, not contented with terrifying her by their snorting and grunting, (a species of music very little in unison with the tender feelings) pushed her about from side to side in a most ungentle manner. She, however, contrived for some time to keep her ground, calling out to the pig-drivers for assistance. Alas! the pig-drivers were no less deaf to her supplications than were the pigs they drove. Both seemed wickedly to enjoy her distress; nor was the grunting of the one species of brutes more unpleasant to her ears, than the loud laugh which was set up by the other. At length a violent push from a huge untoward beast laid her prostrate on the ground, and completed the climax of her misfortune.

The pig-drivers now came to her relief, and quickly raised her from the ground. She had happily received no bodily injury from her fall, but was not a little mentally hurt by the grin which was visible in the countenance of her deliverers. 'Are ye not ashamed,' cried she, with great warmth, 'to rejoice in an accident which has befallen a fellow-mortal by your negligence? Miserable and unhappy wretches! Ye have indeed the shape of men, but ye want all the more noble distinguishing characteristics of the species. As far as relates to any intellectual improvement, ye might as well have been born in Otaheite.'[8]

The answer of the pig-drivers would have impelled Bridgetina to an immediate retreat, but that one of the men had still hold of an umbrella which she had dropped in her fall, and with which he refused to part without some compensation.

"Make her gi' ye a buss[9] for it," said one of the fellows, laughing.

'An't were a pretty lass,' said the other, 'that a would; but a buss from such a little, ugly, ricketty witch, a'nt worth taking.'

Not all the philosophy of Bridgetina could support her any longer. Indignantly turning from the unenlightened rustic, she burst into tears, nor could she repress her sobs on the appearance of Mr. Myope and Mr. Glib, who had returned in search of her, and came up while she was still in conference with the pig-drivers, of whose behaviour she immediately began bitterly to complain.

"It was surely very rude to drive your pigs upon a lady," said Mr. Myope to the men.

'Did not she see un?' returned one of the fellows. 'The pigs were goying peaceably along the way, when she run her nose into the very midst o'em. Gin a had been as blind as a buzzard, a might ha' heard un squeak.'

Mr. Myope perceiving how little was to be gained by expostulation, gave the fellow a sixpence for the umbrella, and taking Bridgetina under his protection, conducted her in safety to her mother's door.

CHAP. II.

"With sense refin'd,
"Learning digested well, exalted faith,
"Unstudy'd wit, and humour ever gay."

THOMSON.[10]

---

[8] Tahiti.
[9] a kiss.
[10] James Thomson, *The Seasons* (1726-30), "Winter," lines 548-50.

IN the course of the ensuing fortnight,[11] Bridgetina had the happiness of enjoying frequent opportunities of meeting with the object of her tender hopes. For these opportunities she so indefatigably watched, that not one visit did Henry pay to the invalids at the farm, without his having the pleasure of being either accompanied, or followed, or met on his return by the love-inspired maiden; who took so little pains to conceal her passion, that he must have been very stupid indeed, if he remained ignorant of her partiality.

For all the multiplied proofs of tenderness which he every day received, we are sorry to confess that Henry was exceedingly ungrateful. So little did he know how to estimate the value of the metaphysical harangues with which Bridgetina always came prepared, that though previous to her entrance he had been only chatting on indifferent topics with Harriet Orwell, he seemed to regard her appearance as a very undesirable interruption.

Happy for Bridgetina her perception was not very acute! Having determined in her own mind that Henry should be her lover, she interpreted every part of his conduct in her own favour;[12] and persisted in believing, that notwithstanding his saying so little in favour of the new philosophy, its profound principles had made a sufficient impression upon his mind, which he was only deterred from acknowledging by the circumstances of his present situation; could that situation be fortunately changed, she had no doubt that he would gladly throw off the yoke of prejudice, and would in the philosophical galaxy become a star of the first magnitude. For this emancipation, the intended expedition to the coast of Africa would furnish him with a most favourable opportunity, which he would doubtless be happy to embrace. No longer bound in the adamantine chain with which the opinions of society cruelly fetters its unhappy slaves, his mind would then expand in all the energy of affection, and give a loose to the soul-touching tenderness of love.

She had not as yet thought proper to drop any hint of the proposed emigration; but by extravagant encomiums on the Hottentots, she sedulously prepared the way; and having prevailed on Henry to peruse the travels of Vaillant, she considered his praises of the work as a sufficient testimony of the impression it had made upon his mind.

The great plan, whose extensive consequences embraced no less an object than that of new modelling the human race, was now consider-

---

[11] Two weeks.

[12] This problem of females muddling fact and fiction recurs in educational treatises and is ascribed to indiscriminate novel reading. The liberal educationalist John Burton's description of how "young women, who apply themselves to this sort of reading, are liable to errors, both in conduct and conversation, from the romantic notions they will thence imbibe" (*Lectures on Female Education and Manners*, 1793, 1: 132) illustrates the common currency such views held.

ably advanced. Vallaton, who, after a few days confinement at the farm, returned to Mr. Glib's, entered into it with warmth. His superior activity entitled him to take the lead, and after a faint refusal, he was prevailed on to assume the conduct of the enterprize; to receive the money that should be raised for carrying it into execution, and to manage this common fund for the general benefit.

Mr. Myope, in quality of secretary, wrote a circular letter to the enlightened, of which the following is a faithful copy.

"To Citizen of

"Who is there deserving of the title of philosopher, that does not feel the aggravated evils which the present odious institutions of society impose on its wretched victim? Who is there among the enlightened, *the men without a God*, that does not wish to escape from this world of misery, where the prejudices of mankind are ever preparing for him the bitter draught of obloquy and contempt? Are not all our energies wasted in the fruitless lamentation of irremediable evils; and our powers blunted, and rendered obtuse, by the obstacles which the unjust institutions of society throw in the way of perfectibility?

"Who is there among us, whom the unequal distribution of property does not fill with *envy, resentment, and despair? Who is there among us, that cannot recollect the time when he secretly called in question the arbitrary division of property established in society, and felt inclined to appropriate to his own use many things, the possession of which appeared to him desirable?*★[13] And yet for these noble and natural sentiments, (when reduced to action) the unjust and arbitrary institutions of society have prepared prisons and fetters! The odious system of coercion is exerted to impose the most injurious restraints on these salutary flights of genius; and property is thus hemmed in on every side.

"Nor is the endeavour to get rid of the encumbrances by which we are weighed down, less abortive, or attended with consequences less deplorable.

"Has any of us, in the ferment of youthful passion, bound himself by marriage? In vain does he struggle to throw off the yoke; he is bound by the chains of this absurd and *immoral institution*, and restrained from seeking in variety the renovating charm of novelty, that rich magazine from which the materials of knowledge are to be derived.

"Who would not gladly escape from this scene of misery? Who would

---

[13] ★Pol. Jus.vol. i. 4to. edit. p.89.★ Godwin, *Political Justice*, Bk I, ch. iii, "Spirit of Political Institutions": "If among the inhabitants of any country there existed no desire in one individual to possess himself of the substance of another, or no desire so vehement and restless as to prompt him to acquire it by means inconsistent with order and justice, undoubtedly in that country guilt could scarcely be known but by report. If every man could with perfect facility obtain the necessaries of life, and obtaining them, feel no uneasy craving after its superfluities, temptation would lose its power."

not rejoice to anticipate that reasonable state of society, with all those improvements which true philosophy will, in the course of a few ages, generate throughout the world?

"Is he at a loss where to fly? Does he fear that the debasing restraint imposed by religion, and laws, and notions of government, will meet him in every direction, and pursue him to the farthest corner of the world? Let him rejoice to learn, that there is yet a refuge for philosophy; that there is now a region where the whole of our glorious system is practised in its full extent. In the interior parts of Africa an exalted race of mortals is discovered, who so far from having their minds cramped in the fetters of superstition, and their energies restrained by the galling yoke of law, do not so much as believe in a Supreme Being, and have neither any code of laws, nor any form of government!

"Let us join this pure and enlightened race! Let us hasten to quit the *corrupt wilderness of ill-constituted society, the rank and rotten soil from which every finer shrub draws poison as it grows.*[14] Let us seek in the philosophical society of the Hottentots that happier field and purer air, where talents and sentiments may *expand into virtue, and germinate into general usefulness.*

"Does any female citizen groan under the slavish and unnatural yoke of parental authority, or wish to shake off the chains of the odious and immoral institution, to which so much of the depravity of the world may be traced? Let her embrace the opportunity that is now offered, to obtain the glorious boon of liberty: let her hasten to become a member of that society, where her virtues will be duly honoured, and her energies expand in the wide field of universal utility.

"Is any philosopher thoroughly convinced of the truth of these gloomy representations of the present virtue-smothering state of society, which he has been at so much pains to propagate? In the bosom of the Gonoquais horde, let him seek an asylum from the oppressive hand of political institution, and from all *obligations to the observance of that common honesty which is a non-conductor to all the sympathies of the human heart.*[15]

"As in the dark and gloomy wilderness which we at present so unfortunately inhabit, there is no possibility of moving without money, a sum must of necessity be raised to freight a ship, and lay in requisites for the voyage. Contributions for this purpose will be received by Citizen Vallaton, who has generously undertaken the conduct of the important enter-

---

14 *See *Caleb Williams** Taken from the servant Caleb's final comment on his master Falkland's death in which he regrets the chain of events that led to Falkland being acknowledged as a murderer and Caleb as a wronged man: "But of what use are talents and sentiments in the corrupt wilderness of human society? It is a rank and rotten soil from which every finer shrub draws poison as it grows. All that in a happier field and a purer air would expand into virtue and germinate into general usefulness, is thus converted into henbane and deadly nightshade" (Godwin, *Caleb Williams*, 1794, 325-26).

15 *See Godwin's Enquirer* *Enquirer*, Part II, Essay VII, "Of Personal Reputation", 257.

prize. As it is probable that many philosophers may not be provided with specie, from such as have it not in their power to contribute their quota in cash, any sort of goods will be received that can be converted into articles of general utility. As an example worthy of imitation, we here think it necessary to inform our fellow-citizens, that Citizen Glib has bestowed the whole of his circulating library upon the society. The superfluous books, such as history, travels, natural philosophy, and divinity, are to be sold for the benefit of the fund. The novels and metaphysical essays are reserved for the instruction of the philosophers.

"By order of the Hottentotian Committee,
BEN. MYOPE, *Sec.*"

The recovery of Mr. Vallaton was sufficiently rapid, but still his mind suffered the most cruel apprehensions on account of his lovely mistress.

For the effects of the accident, he had now no reason to entertain any anxiety. He had received the pleasing assurance, that her recovery would be speedy and compleat. But as it was impossible for him to be admitted to an interview, he could not avoid some tormenting forebodings of the effect that so long a period of serious reflection might produce upon her mind. Her being constantly surrounded by the Orwells, he considered as a circumstance extremely inauspicious. Though personally unacquainted with any of the family, he was no stranger to the character of all its members, and greatly dreaded the baneful effects of their prejudices upon the susceptible heart of Julia.

The alarm of Mr. Vallaton was without foundation. Harriet Orwell had too much delicacy and good-sense officiously to obtrude her opinions, even upon her most intimate friends. She evidently saw that Julia had imbibed some notions which she considered to be erroneous; but so high an opinion did she entertain of the strength of her understanding, and the goodness of her heart, that she had no doubt but that a little observation and reflection would render her fully sensible of these errors, and open her mind to the reception of truths so consonant to the virtues of her disposition.

Had Miss Orwell been ever so much inclined to the conversion of Julia, she would not have considered the season of pain and languor as proper for the attempt. She thought it more conducive to the recovery of her friend to amuse than to perplex her; and by every engaging art endeavoured to raise her spirits, and to beguile the weary hours of confinement.

The mind of Julia, naturally grateful, tender, and affectionate, could not be insensible to the soothing attentions of the animated and ever-cheerful Harriet; but in vain did she endeavour to assume the appearance of that cheerfulness and serenity, which her friend so assiduously laboured to inspire. That she had deservedly forfeited the confidence of her father was ever present to her recollection, and brought with it a consciousness of degradation that oppressed her soul. Much did she long to acquaint Harriet with all that had passed, and to ask her advice concerning her future conduct; but the consciousness of having deserved disapprobation, and the dread of incurring contempt, deterred her from a confession of her errors; while her pride revolted at the idea of acknowledging, that the boasted principles of honour had not preserved her from being guilty of the meanness of a falshood.

Few days passed without a visit from the worthy rector, at whose appearance the delight that sparkled in the countenance of Harriet was sufficiently expressive of her filial love, while her whole behaviour indicated confidence, respect, and gratitude. She never spoke of him without emotion, nor could Julia without emotion listen to the effusions of her filial tenderness. One day, when talking upon this subject, Harriet, in the fulness of her heart, exclaimed, "Surely no sensation is so sweet as that a child enjoys from the fond affection of a worthy parent. How dreadful must it be to forfeit it! I do not think that any thing the world could offer, could recompense me for suffering one hour of my father's serious displeasure."

'And did you never incur his displeasure? said Julia.

"If ever I did, it was but for a moment," said Harriet; "and so exactly was his displeasure proportioned to the offence, that it only served to encrease my reverence and gratitude."

'I should not have been surprised at what you say,' replied Julia, 'if Doctor Orwell had been a necessarian; as no necessarian can, upon principle, ever be offended at any thing; but free-willers are generally passionate and vindictive.'[16]

"I know nothing about these things," said Harriet, "and never heard my father say whether he was an advocate for free-will or necessity; but this I know, that the rule he has laid down to himself for the government of his temper is an admirable one, and has effectually secured him from being guilty of the injustice of wrathful passion."

'And pray, my dear,' said Julia, 'what may this rule be?'

"Never to be offended at any thing that is not in itself immoral, and consequently subject to the Divine displeasure," rejoined Harriet. "What is no offence in the eye of GOD, is (he says) no subject for the sharp rebuke of man."

'I must own,' replied Julia, 'the voice of anger could not often be heard in a family, where every offence was measured by such a scale.'

"No," rejoined Harriet, "and we should indeed be wretches, if we were not truly sensible of our happiness."

'Well, but after all,' said Julia, 'it is still to your own goodness that you owe the forbearance of your father. Supposing that you were ever to have been guilty of aught that his prejudices taught him to consider as offen-

---

[16] Necessaritarians hold that all action is predetermined and freewill is impossible, while Free willers believe the opposite.

sive in the eyes of this Supreme Being, who is with him the ideal standard of perfection; that you had, for instance, (I only suppose it for the sake of argument) been guilty of artifice or—or falshood. Would he not, in such a case, have been very inexorable?'

"Inexorable! my dear Julia; no, surely! If you consider the spirit of the principle that inspired him, you will be convinced, that to be inexorable to the penitent was with him impossible. Considering the crime as an offence not against himself, but against GOD, could he refuse to accept of that which would not be rejected by the Most High? Could he, who served a Being whose first attributes are benevolence and mercy, be harsh or unforgiving to a penitent offender?"

'But why, I pray you, is this repentance to be a stipulated article in the treaty of forgiveness?' rejoined Julia.

"Because," said Harriet, "we are told, that without repentance there is no remission of sins; and without repentance there can surely be no hope of reformation. But here again my father looks to the example of his great Master; and by the mildness of entreaty, not the thunderings of indignation, calls sinners to repentance."

'Well, you must pardon me, but I declare I think there is something very mean in this slavish reference to the will of an unknown Being, of whose very existence we can, after all, never be thoroughly certain. How much more noble to be guided solely by the suggestions of reason and virtue in our own breasts!'

"Alas! my dear, we need not look into the page of history, we need not examine into the conduct of the world at large, but just only take an impartial view of what passes in our own breasts, to be convinced of the necessity of a higher standard of excellence than can be found in human nature. The contemplation of the immutability of the ALL-PERFECT, has a tendency to *fix* as well as to exalt our notions of virtue; while a consciousness of the infinite space between us and this Perfection annihilates the swellings of pride, and allays the ferment of imagination. Our reason, far from shining with unvaried lustre, is perpetually liable to be obscured by passion or prejudice, we cannot, therefore, always trust to its decision; but when we are in the constant habit of referring our actions to the judgment of a Being whose moral attributes are unchangeable, the clouds of passion and prejudice are dispelled, and reason again shines forth with steadiness and vigour. Oh! that I could explain to you the feelings that such contemplations have excited in my mind! feelings, which, instead of depressing, tend to expand and tranquillize the soul."

Julia smiled, 'Really, my dear, I did not think you had so much enthusiasm.'

"Call it not enthusiasm, my dear Julia; for besides these feelings which may, perhaps, depend in some measure upon constitutional sensibility, a constant reference to the Divine will, and an habit of modeling to it our thoughts and actions, cannot fail of having the happiest influence upon our conduct. Without having this Divine standard to refer to, how often should we be exposed by our passions to the most egregious mistakes! Mistakes, which pride would forbid us to acknowledge, and which, being unchecked by the believed presence of our future Judge, we might hope by artifice to conceal, or by ingenuity to defend."

Julia sighed. Her open and polished forehead was suddenly contracted, as if by some quick sensation of violent pain.

"What is the matter, my dear? I fear you have rashly moved your foot."

'I believe I have,' said Julia, recovering herself; 'but the pain is over, and I beg you would proceed. You argue so well, that I should like to hear you enter into a debate with some of my learned friends: upon the necessity of repentance, for instance. Ah, Harriet, you have no notion how soon that sweet eloquence of yours would be put to silence.'

"Very likely it might," rejoined Harriet. "If indeed I were bold enough to enter into a debate, from the hope that my eloquence could possibly convince a person skilled in argument, I should deserve the mortification I should probably meet with. But take notice, that my reasons for declining the colloquial combat arise from a knowledge of the weakness of my weapons, not from any distrust of the goodness of my cause."

'Well, but as your weapons are certainly at least equal to mine, suppose I give you a challenge? Let us take the ground upon the wisdom and efficacy of repentance. Which, dropping my gauntlet, I here aver to be the most mistaken notion in the world;—a mere prejudice, and a prejudice very inimical to the progress of virtue.'

"I accept your challenge, and only wish I had one of my father's wigs to equip me for the solemnities of the field: but here I take my ground, and prepare myself to receive your attack."

'Allons! then,' said Julia, raising herself up in her bed, and gracefully flourishing her fair hand; then extending it in the attitude of affirmation, she thus proceeded: 'If we form a just and complete view of all the circumstances in which a living or intelligent being is placed, we shall find that he could not, in any moment of his existence, have acted otherwise than he has acted. In the life of every human being there is a chain of causes generated in that eternity which preceded his birth, and going on in regular succession through the whole period of his existence; in consequence of which—'[17]

"Hold, hold," cried Harriet, "I proclaim a parley, and here enter my protest against using any words but your own. Plagiarism is an unlawful weapon in debate; and I never see it made use of, that I do not consider it as a proof of conscious weakness."

'Well, well, I shall, I make no doubt, be able to defend myself without its assistance. But there are some subjects on which one can speak so much better in the words of others than in one's own, that it is difficult to refrain from using them.'

---

[17] Julia is using Godwin's argument on "Freewill and Necessity" *(Political Justice*, Bk IV, ch. 7).

"Depend upon it, my dear Julia, that these are subjects which the mind has never thoroughly mastered. They will be found to have been driven into that little corner of the brain, which is said to be the storehouse of memory, by the arch witch imagination; and driven thither in such confusion too, in such higgledy piggledy order, that they have never passed under the close examination of judgment; and pop out they come again, just in the same manner that they got it. Oh! of all insufferables, a pedant with a good memory is the most insufferable!"

'But is not a good memory a great happiness? Is it not the parent of knowledge, the indispensible companion of science, the friend of wit and genius?'

"It is all you say, my dear, and a thousand times more than either you or I can ever say. The more excellent, the more capacious this grand repository, the more wise, the more virtuous, (if filled with motives to virtue) must we of course be. But if of this noble store-house judgment does not keep the key, if she does not arrange, and assimilate, and combine the materials that are placed in it, I think it is a great loss to have it too tenacious."

'A loss to have too good a memory! what a strange paradox. I wonder what Miss Botherim would say to you?'

"You may wonder what author she would quote, if you please; for of herself, poor dear, she could not say three sentences upon any given subject. Do you not think now, Julia, it would be better for poor Miss Botherim to have a memory rather less retentive, than to give you out, as she does, speech after speech from the author she has last read, without alteration or amendment, all *neat as imported*, as they say upon the sign-posts?"

'Indeed, poor Miss Botherim's quotations are, I confess, sometimes tiresome enough,' returned Julia; 'and I believe, as you say, that the capacity to retain, without the power to digest and combine, is of very little real advantage. But I have often observed, that Miss Botherim's power of retention is always confined to one side of the subject. While she remembers with accuracy all she herself has said, she forgets every word advanced by her opponent in the debate.'

"A proof of the truth of my father's observation, "said Harriet, "that we need only observe the sort of memory a person possesses, to have a certain key to the character."

'How so? I do not perfectly comprehend you.'

"I shall quickly explain myself. Memory, though an original faculty, is capable of improvement. It will be strong in proportion to the strength of the impression made upon it, and the impression most frequently recurring will of course become the strongest. Thus it happens, that trifling people are found only to remember trifles; that the vain and the selfish can so well recollect every minutiae of every circumstance in which they were themselves particularly concerned; and that even among those who pique themselves on superior taste, so many are found capable of retaining the *exact words* of a well-sounding author, while to the few is confined the more estimable power of impressing the *sense* and *substance* in the mind."

'I believe there is much truth in what you say,' rejoined Julia; 'but pray what has all this to say to our argument upon the necessity of repentance?'

"A great deal," returned Miss Orwell; 'for memory is certainly a very necessary agent in presenting to our view the works that occasion it: and perhaps, my dear Julia, it is never better employed than in tracing the rise and progress of our errors, in reminding us of how much we have come short of purposed excellence, how frequently led by the rapid violence of passion into self-deception, and how arrogantly we have decided upon subjects that now appear to us in a very different light."

'All this,' replied Julia, 'I allow. But when we consider that crime is nothing else than an error in judgment, a sort of miscalculation of consequences, in short, a mere mistake, and that (as I said before) every one is under the necessity of acting from the motive that is presented to him; it follows of course, that feelings of repentance for actions which it was impossible to avoid, are extremely absurd.'

"According to which doctrine, you would, I am to suppose, feel as much remorse at having lost a game at chess, as at having poisoned your father! And experience the same degree of compunction at having made up a cap in a bad taste, as at having deceived a friend, or betrayed the confidence of a parent. As I am not qualified to argue from books, I am under the necessity of appealing to your feelings. Consult these, my dear Julia, and I am sure they will declare themselves of a different party from your favourite authors. I am much mistaken, if they will not inform you that the pain, occasioned by the consciousness of any departure from moral rectitude, is a sensation of a very different nature from that which is produced by mere error of judgment.

'And pray what would you infer from this?'

"I would infer, that if our feelings, upon any lapse of moral rectitude, are different from those which we experience on any mere mistake of judgment in regard to other matters, they admonish us to a different sort of repentance."

'I wish you to illustrate your meaning by an example, and shall put a case for your decision. Supposing, that in order to ward some dreaded evil, you had been induced to deceive your father by a falsehood, how would you act upon being made sensible of your error?'

"Act! surely upon such an occasion I could not hesitate a moment how to act; I should instantly acknowledge it, ingenuously confess to him the whole truth, and think the mortification that must inevitably arise from this confession, a just punishment for my offence. How, till I had undeceived him, could I look up to the Searcher of hearts? Every prayer I offered up to my GOD under such circumstances, I should consider as a solemn mockery, and unpardonable presumption."

'I declare,' said Julia, with a smile which seemed to disown the heavy sigh that had just burst from her bosom, 'I declare,' said she, holding out her hand to Harriet, 'you are so charming an enthusiast, that you could almost make one believe that saying one's prayers was no bad preservative of virtue.'

The entrance of Mrs. Delmond put an end to the conversation; but the impression it made upon the mind of Julia was not to be easily effaced. After a few struggles with false shame and romantic tenderness, she adopted the resolution of throwing herself at her father's feet, as soon as she should be able to appear before him, and by a free and ingenuous acknowledgment of all that had passed between her and Vallaton, make an atonement for her past offence, and regain that confidence which she was miserable in having forfeited.

No sooner had this resolution taken possession of her mind, than she found herself restored to tranquillity. Vivacity once more sparkled in her eyes, and the elastic spirits of youth recovering their tone, bid defiance to the puny evil of confinement.

In order to relieve the anxiety of her father, she had every morning, since the fatal accident, been enabled, by an ingenious contrivance of Harriet's, to pencil a little billet to her father, without pain or change of posture.

So precious was this billet to Captain Delmond, and so anxiously did he watch for its arrival, that from early dawn his whole mind was occupied by an anticipation of its contents. If the messenger happened to be one minute beyond the usual time, he was filled with alarm; and if any considerable time elapsed, his agitation rose to such a height as to render him incapable of opening it for himself. When he saw the hand-writing of his darling Julia, when he read the assurance of her convalescence, his eyes filled with tears of paternal tenderness; and an involuntary ejaculation of thankfulness to the Being whose power had preserved his darling child, burst from his lips. So entirely had the remembrance of her offences been obliterated by fears for her safety, that a thought of Vallaton seldom came across his mind; and indeed so assiduously had he avoided the ungrateful subject, that it was almost forgotten, when a visit from Gen. Villers recalled it to his recollection.

The news of Julia's overturn was not long in finding its way to Castle-Villers. By the first accounts, both she and her companion were killed upon the spot. By the second, and it came from one who had his information from the best authority, it was announced to be only the horse and Mr. Vallaton that had suffered immediate death: Julia still survived, though with very little hopes of recovery. The death of Vallaton was particularly regretted by this detailer of grievances, on account of his leaving a disconsolate widow, and five fatherless children, to deplore his untimely fate.

The General was no sooner assured of Julia's being still alive, than he sent a messenger to Captain Delmond's, who brought such an answer to his enquiries, as very much relieved his mind, which had been severely shocked by the account of her misfortune. He from that time seldom omitted a daily enquiry at the farm, either personally or by message, for the health of Julia and her fellow-sufferer. Nor was he the only person at Castle-Villers that appeared to take an interest in her recovery.

The reader may recollect a Major Minden, who came with Miss Mordaunt, and appeared to Julia to be introduced by that young lady as an accidental visitor. This gentleman was in reality an old acquaintance of the General's, to whom he intended a visit of some weeks; nor was he altogether unknown to the father of Julia. Just before Delmond left the regiment, in which he served fourteen years as a lieutenant, Minden entered it a school-boy ensign. After having attained the rank of Major by purchase through every step, he took leave of the profession of a soldier, and set out on a tour through France and Italy; from which he returned, after an absence of three years, with the double acquirements of a taste for *vertû*, and an Italian mistress. This woman, of low birth and vulgar education, had engrafted upon a temper naturally proud, arrogant, and imperious, a degree of art and cunning, that so managed even the most repulsive qualities of her disposition, as to render them conducive to her interest. Over the weaker mind of her paramour she soon gained a compleat ascendency. He submitted to her caprice without reluctance, and bore all the violence of her temper with the most exemplary patience. Over himself, his servants, his house, and fortune, she reigned with the most despotic authority; nor did time seem to bring any diminution to her power.

But, alas! the vigilance of the most arbitrary government cannot always ward off the stroke of ruin; nor the compleatest despotism be proof against the mutability of all sublunary things. The poor Signora,

"Just when she thought, good easy soul, full surely,
"Her greatness was a ripening,"[18]

Received a formal notice of her deposition, with an order for her immediate departure from Minden-Place to a house which was taken for her by the friend to whom the Major had committed the management of this domestic revolution, and from whom she was informed a yearly stipend would hereafter be received.

After a noble but ineffectual struggle, for maintaining the possession of her post, she was obliged to retire on capitulation. The throne of the Major's heart having thus become vacant, he had determined to look out for a candidate worthy of filling the important situation in the quality of wife. He had not yet had time to make his election, when the sight of Julia fixed his resolution, which the result of every enquiry concerning her tended to confirm.

The love of Major Minden was not of that boyish sort, which timid delicacy endeavours to conceal; he soon informed the General of the honour he intended to do Miss Delmond, and in order to shew a prop-

---

[18] Shakespeare, *King Henry VIII*, III, ii 352. Modified to refer to a female rather than a male.

er respect for his future father-in-law, he proposed a visit to Capt. Delmond, to whom it was agreed the General should mention the intended overtures of his friend.

Captain Delmond was rejoicing over a pleasing billet from Julia, that seemed written in unusual spirits, when Gen. Villers and Major Minden arrived at his house. He was still in his bed-chamber, which he had often kept for whole days since the absence of his daughter, but gave immediate orders for having his chair wheeled into the adjoining room, into which the gentleman had been shewn.

There was somewhat in the air and figure of Capt. Delmond so indicative of *the gentleman*, that not all the disadvantages of sickness and infirmity could obliterate its traces. By the just proportions of the time-ruined pillar, an idea may be formed of the grandeur of the structure which it once adorned. Politeness and cordiality marked his manner of receiving his guests. With heart-felt satisfaction did he listen to their praises of his daughter; and while in answer to their enquiries he informed them, that in the course of ten or twelve days she would, it was expected, be able to come home, his once-brilliant eyes sparkled with delight.

General Villers enquired for the gentleman who had accompanied Miss Delmond.

The Captain felt a sudden repulsion of his blood at the unwelcome question, but possessed sufficient command over his feelings to answer in an easy way, that he heard he was nearly well.

"I am heartily glad of it," replied the General, "for the sake of his poor wife and family, who must have suffered much anxiety on his account."

Never did intelligence reach the ears of Capt. Delmond, that was half so welcome as this first account of the wife and family of Vallaton. It annihilated every suspicion that had preyed upon his heart; and by giving him the delightful assurance of Julia's being innocent of all clandestine intention, restored his confidence in her unsullied integrity and truth.

After a short conversation on indifferent topics, Major Minden, on pretence of calling at the post-office, took leave, and left the General to open the preliminaries of the proposed negociation.

Capt. Delmond received the notification of the honour that was intended his family with politeness, not devoid of dignity. "The esteem of Gen. Villers," he said, "was a sufficient recommendation to his favour; but however agreeable the connection might be to him, and however advantageous, in respect to fortune, it certainly was to his daughter, he must refer the Major entirely to her decision. It was an affair in which he might advise, but never would dictate."

The General coldly applauded the sentiments of Captain Delmond, but added, 'that he supposed there was very little reason to apprehend that Miss Delmond could be so blind to her own interest, as to decline the offer of so splendid an establishment.' After a few eulogiums on his friend, and having obtained permission for his visits, the General took leave, and left the anxious father not a little agitated by the subject of his conversation.

However firmly resolved that no consideration of *self* should interpose to prevent the establishment of his daughter, the idea of losing her society for ever overwhelmed his soul with involuntary sadness, nor was all his fortitude sufficient to support his spirits in the contemplation of the event. "But for what do I live?" said he, after some moments of bitterness, "for whom do I exist, but for this darling child? Is not her happiness far dearer to me than my own? O, yes! Let my Julia be but happy, and however forlorn I shall be, when she is from me, the certainty of her happiness will still afford a cordial to her father's heart."

CHAP. III.

"Stiff in opinion, always in the wrong."
POPE.[19]

ON the evening of the same day in which Capt. Delmond had received General Villers, Henry Sydney paid a visit to his fair patient at the farm. He had brought in his pocket a new publication, which, at the desire of Julia and her lovely nurse, he read aloud, giving by his remarks an additional spirit to the wit and humour of the author. He had been about half an hour thus employed, when casting a glance out of the window, he burst into a fretful exclamation, "Heavens! here is our evil genius coming to torment us in the shape of Miss Botherim. I wish to goodness that poor woman had any thing to do at home!"

'She is very kind,' said Harriet; 'but I do not know how it is, her visits are always, I think, *mal-apropos*.'

"To be interrupted in the middle of such an interesting story is very provoking," said Julia; "but we will make her hear it out."

Miss Botherim entered with an air of even more than usual solemnity. 'I am come,' said she, addressing herself to Harriet, 'to announce the necessity of your immediate return to your father's house: here is a note which will explain the cause.'

Harriet snatched the billet, which contained an account of her aunt's having been suddenly taken ill, for which reason she was desired to leave every thing to the care of Miss Botherim, (who had offered to supply her place with Julia) and to come directly home. Harriet, whose aunt had been to her as a mother, and who loved her with the sincerest affection, was equally shocked and afflicted by this intelligence; she lost not a moment in obeying the summons, but in the midst of her grief and agitation, preserved a sufficient presence of mind to give Miss Botherim every necessary instruction respecting her charge, and then affectionately embracing Julia, she hurried away.

---

[19] Wrongly ascribed to Pope. Actually John Dryden, *Absalom and Achitophel* (1681), 1.545: "Stiff in opinions, always in the wrong."

When Bridgetina observed Henry preparing to accompany her, 'There is no necessity for your going so soon, Doctor,' said she, making a motion for him to sit down; 'as you could not be found in time, Dr. Orwell sent for Mr. Gubbles, so that you need not hurry yourself; Miss Orwell, I dare say, can walk very well alone.'

Henry coldly declined her invitation, and in spite of her remonstrances he went with Harriet, who, indeed, stood very much in need of support and consolation.

In answer to the enquiries of Julia, Bridgetina informed her that she had received the information of Mrs. Martha Goodwin's illness, by happening to be with Maria Sydney when her brother was sent for; that she had instantly gone to the parsonage to see if they had found him, and had offered to take the note for Harriet, and inform Capt. and Mrs. Delmond that she would do herself the pleasure of remaining with Julia during the remainder of her confinement.

Julia returned to Bridgetina the warmest acknowledgments for her goodness; nor did it once occur to her, that the hope of a more frequent opportunity of enjoying the company of Henry Sydney was the inspiring motive that lurked at the bottom of Bridgetina's heart. Fearful of introducing a subject on which she found it dangerous to dwell, she did not once enquire for Vallaton, though Bridgetina had never yet payed her a visit without being freighted with some tender message from that gentleman; who, not being yet able to write, had no other method of conveying his sentiments, than through the medium of their mutual friend. These melting remembrances of his affection never failed to raise a soft commotion in the breast of Julia, where the idea of the sufferings of her lover occupied every thought, till some kind and tender billet from her father, or some fresh instance of his anxious solicitude concerning her, turned the current of her feelings, and gave her heart to filial duty and affection.

Bridgetina, perceiving the book which Henry had left upon the table, took it up, and eagerly began to run over the contents; which she continued to do in silence, notwithstanding the entreaties of Julia, which she silenced by declaring, 'that she never read aloud to any one.' After a few yawns, she at length threw down the book, pronouncing it to be a very poor performance.

"You surprise me," said Julia, "by saying so; it appeared to me to contain a great deal of genuine wit and humour."

'I do not care for wit and humour,' returned Bridgetina; 'they may serve to amuse the vulgar, but you know they are quite exploded by the new philosophy. The works of imagination which now enlighten the world, are all generated by system. The energies of philosophical authors are all expanded in gloomy masses of tenebrific shade. The investigators of *mind* never condescend to make their readers laugh.'

"I cannot altogether agree with you," replied Julia. "The authors most remarkable for wit and humour appear to have had no slight knowledge of the human heart. Do you think that Cervantes, or Moliere, or Fielding, were strangers to the study of the mind; or that they could possibly have delineated the minute features of the soul in the manner they have done, without an intimate acquaintance with its nature?"

'What is Cervantes, or Moliere, or Fielding,' replied Bridgetina, 'in the eye of a philosopher? What did they know of infinite causation, or of perfectibility; or of effects being equal to their causes, and causes antecedent to their effects? The wit of such men may amuse the vulgar, but is despised by the enlightened.'

"It is a subject on which people will pronounce according to their tastes," said Julia. "My father lays it down as a maxim, that the total incapacity for relishing humour is a sure proof of mental imbecility."

'A sentiment,' rejoined Bridgetina, 'very suitable to the ignorant prejudices of Capt. Delmond, but highly unworthy of a philosopher. I should not have been surprised to have heard it repeated by Harriet Orwell; but for you, you who have spent whole days, and weeks, and months, in studying the writings of the new philosophers, still to preserve a taste for wit! It is truly astonishing! I perceive the society of Harriet Orwell has perverted your mind.'

"Indeed," said Julia, "the society of Miss Orwell has been a very great happiness to me. She gives me new cause to love and to esteem her every hour. Never can I be forgetful of her goodness."

'Goodness!' repeated Bridgetina, with a sneer; 'from whence proceeds this boasted goodness? Does it flow from a conviction of general utility, pursued through the maze of abstract reasoning? If it does not, what I pray you is its value?'

"I confess," replied Julia, "I never heard Miss Orwell define the abstract nature of virtue; she rather appears to practice it from the spontaneous impulse of her heart. But though she may not be so enlightened by philosophy as we could wish, she is extremely well informed on other subjects; and reads a great deal, I assure you."

'I should not wish to be confined to books of her selecting,' replied Bridgetina; 'her taste and mine would not at all suit. Give me the wild extatic wanderings of imagination, the solemn sorrows of suffocating sensibility! Oh how I doat on the gloomy ravings of despair, or delicious description of the soul-melting sensations of fierce and ardent love! But alas! Julia, you are a stranger to the energetic extacies that pervade my soul. It is in a mind of great powers that strong passions predominate; and only people such as *I*, can taste the tender emotions of an importunate sensibility.[20] O Heloise! divine, incomparable Heloise! how, in perusing thy enrapturing page, have all my latent energies been excited? O Henry Sydney, Henry Sydney, the St. Preuse of my affections, how at the mention of thy name has a tide of sweet sensations gushed upon my heart!'

---

[20] cf. *Memoirs of Emma Courtney*, 61. See Appendix A.

"Henry Sydney!" repeated Julia, "can you be serious? Is it possible that Henry Sydney can really have engaged your affections?"

'Possible!" said Bridgetina, 'it is not only possible, but literally and demonstrably true. The history of my sensations are equally interesting and instructive. You will there see, how sensation generates interest, interest generates passions, passions generates powers; and sensations, passions, powers, all working together, produce associations, and habits, and ideas, and sensibilities. O Julia! Julia! what a heart-moving history is mine.'

It was almost impossible even for Julia to refrain from laughing at the figure of Bridgetina, as she pronounced these words. Every feature screwed into formality, and every distorted limb sprawling in affected agitation, she presented such an apparent antidote to the tender passion, that the mention of love from her lips had in it something irresistibly ridiculous. It was with some difficulty that Julia could sufficiently command her voice to desire her to proceed; which at length, after stretching her craggy neck, wiping the rheum from her eyes, and fixing them on the sharp point of her turned-up nose, she did as follows:

'The remoter causes of those associations which formed the texture of my character, might, I know, very probably be traced to some transaction in the seraglio of the Great Mogul, or to some spirited and noble enterprise of the Cham of Tartary; but as the investigation would be tedious, and, for want of proper data, perhaps impracticable, I shall not go beyond my birth, but content myself with arranging under seven heads (I love to methodise) the seven generating causes of the energies which stamp my individuality, observing, that it is by a proper attention to these fine and evanescent strokes, that the knowledge of *mind* is alone to be attained.'

'The first of these character-forming eras was the hour of my birth. The midwife who was to attend my mother, happening to be a mile or two out of town, her delay suddenly excited an energetic impetuosity which scorned to wait for her arrival, and generated a noble spirit of independence, which brought me into the world without assistance. About two hours after I was born, the germ of other passions was produced. The nurse, who from some early associations had acquired a habit of getting drunk, let me fall upon the floor. A torrent of resentment and indignation gushed upon my heart, and the bitter tears that followed were a certain indication of the important consequences which that accident was to have upon my future life.

'The third power-inspiring era is still more worthy of attention. It was, indeed, the fountain-head of all my feelings, the source of those sensibilities and propensities, which have been the springs of every action, the cause of every movement of my soul; it is therefore well worthy the attention of every philosophic mind, of every lover of minute investigation.

'Not to keep you in suspense, (a thing ill-suited to the energy of my character) I hasten to inform you, that my mother not being able to suckle me herself, a young woman was brought into the house to be my wetnurse, who some months before had borne a child to the parish-clerk. He kept a little day-school in Muddy-lane; and Jenny, whose education had been neglected in her infancy, had resorted to him to learn to read, and soon became so enamoured of literature, that from one of those associations so natural to the human mind, she conceived a tender passion for her instructor. "Imagination lent its aid, and an importunate sensibility, panting for good unalloyed, compleated the seduction."*[21] With her milk I greedily absorbed the delicious poison which circulated through every vein; and love of literature, and *importunate sensibility*, became from thenceforth the predominant features of my character.

'Early did the fruits of the associations thus formed expand to view: by the time I was four years old, I would have listened for hours to the story of little Red Ridinghood; and on a particular investigation of this important era, I have learned from an old domestic, that I could actually, at the age of five years, repeat the whole history of the *Glass Slipper*, without missing a single word![22]

'Having been a remarkably unhealthy child, I was even at this age so weak and rickety as to be scarcely able to walk; but as *physical causes are as nothing*,[23] I should not have mentioned this circumstance, but from the opportunity it afforded of expanding my powers in conversation. In my little chair I sat, talked, mused, cried, or fretted, according as events excited my sensibility. My father was so delighted with my premature eloquence, that he always kept me up to supper, and rewarded the exertion of my energies by a nice morsel of high-seasoned ragout or savoury pasty. During his life-time, my mother almost lived in the kitchen. But though her powers were expended in the science of cookery, she seldom had the good fortune to please; and the idea of her character, which from my father's contemptuous expressions I obtained, as it became a new source of action, may properly be termed a fourth operating principle of my mind.

'My father died when I had attained my ninth year, and my weakly constitution deterring my mother from sending me to school, I learned to read at home; I did not like my needle, and my mother (happily for me!) never controled the energies of my mind, or cramped its powers by a mean attention to domestic concerns. Thus at liberty, I quickly learned

---

[21] *See Emma Courtnay, a philosophical novel; to which Miss Botherim seems indebted for some of her finest thoughts.* Hamilton parodies the English Jacobin Mary Hays's novel *Memoirs of Emma Courtney* (1796), which is a fictional reworking of Hays's own experiences in love and philosophy. The passage quoted refers to the heroine's realisation that she has fallen in love with the absent son Augustus as a result of the mother's glowing comments and by staring at his portrait (61). See Appendix A.

[22] Hamilton satirises the child prodigy since Bridgetina's accomplishments are all normal.

[23] See Godwin, *Political Justice*, Bk VIII, ch. ix, Appendix, "Of Health and the Prolongation of Human Life", 770-77. See Appendix A.

to reason, to analize, to demonstrate; and lost no opportunity of improving these powers. Did she at any time desire me to ring the bell, to stir the fire, to fetch her keys from the next room, I had an ever-ready argument to offer against a compliance with her request. I examined its propriety, I investigated its origin, I pursued its consequences; till convinced by the subtlety of my reasoning, or fatigued with following me through a maze of argument, which her inferior capacity did not permit her to pursue, she gave up the point, and quietly rang the bell, stirred the fire, or fetched what she wanted for herself.

'The passion for literature to which I was pre-disposed by the antecedent propensities of my nurse, continued daily to encrease. I expanded my imagination by novels, I strengthened my energies by romances, and at length invigorated my powers by metaphysics.

'The manner in which my latent taste for the latter was brought into action, as it forms the fifth grand era of my history, deserves to be particularly narrated.

'My mother got a packet of brown snuff from London by the mail-coach; it was wrapped in two proof sheets of the quarto edition of the Political Justice.[24] I eagerly snatched up the paper, and notwithstanding the frequent fits of sneezing it occasioned, from the quantity of snuff contained in every fold, I greedily devoured its contents. I read and sneezed, and sneezed and read, till the germ of philosophy began to fructify my soul. From that moment I became a philosopher and need not inform you of the important consequences.

'Still my ardent sensibility led me back to novels. As I read each sweet, delicious tale, I reasoned, I investigated, I moralized. What! said I to myself, shall every heroine of all these numerous volumes have a lover, and shall *I* remain "a comfortless, solitary, shivering wanderer in the dreary wilderness of human society? I feel in myself the capacity of increasing the happiness of an individual;"[25] but where is he? does he live in this town? have I seen him? how shall I find him? does his breast sympathize with mine? An idea of young Mr. Gabriel Gubbles, the apothecary, came across my mind. Yes, said I, it must be he! I heaved a convulsive struggling sigh. Tears half delicious, half agonizing, gushed in torrents from my eyes. O Gubbles! Gubbles! cried I, my importunate sensibilities, my panting tenderness, are all reserved for thee!

'I hastily put on my cloak, and snatching up the umbrella, I walked forth to relieve the throbbing sensations of my too tender soul. A heavy cooling shower most opportunely at that moment fell. To quench the burning fervour I let down the umbrella, and was soon wet to the skin. I became somewhat more tranquil, more composed, and proceeded down the street.

---

[24] The suggestion is that Godwin's *Political Justice* did not sell well, so extra copies were used as wrapping paper.
[25] Mary Hays, *Memoirs of Emma Courtney* (1796), 116. See Appendix A.

I passed the shop of Mr. Gubbles; young Gabriel was there; he was looking into the mouth of an old woman, who sat upon the floor to have a tooth pulled out. The attitude was charming; the scene was interesting; it was impressive, tender, melancholy, sublime. My suffocating sensibilities returned. I pursued my walk, leaning at times upon the umbrella. Careless of the observations of the passengers, who, strangers to the fine feelings of an exquisitely susceptible mind, wondered at my keeping down the umbrella in such a heavy shower.

'Wet, dripping, draggled, dirty, I returned to the shop of Gubbles. The old woman was gone. Gabriel was pounding some drugs in the mortar, which sent forth a smell too powerful for my high-wrought frenzied feelings. I threw myself into a chair, and burst into tears. Gabriel Gubbles was astonished. Alarmed, terrified, distracted, at seeing me so ill, he took down bottle after bottle, and held to my nose; he poured out lavender and hartshorn, and presented them to me with a look so embarrassed, so full of feeling, that I exerted myself out of compassion to a sensibility which I observed to be already too much affected.

'He perceived my wet clothes, and in a voice of uncommon tenderness, begged me to have them changed. Unwilling to give him uneasiness, I promised to do as he requested, and retired.

'The tenderness of Gubbles inspired the most delightful hope. "The delicious poison circulated through every vein."[26] I gave myself up to the ardent feelings of a morbid imagination, and thus prepared for myself a cruel excess of wretchedness." O Julia! Julia! how will your tender soul sympathise with the sufferings of mine, when I tell you, that in one week from the interesting event I have just related, I heard of Gabriel Gubbles' marriage!'

Here Bridgetina took out her pocket-handkerchief. Having wiped her eyes, she thus proceeded:

'How shall I describe my sufferings! How shall I recount the salt, the bitter tears I shed! I yearn to be useful, (cried I) but the inexpressible yearnings of a soul which pants for general utility, is, by the *odious institutions of a distempered civilization*, rendered abortive. O divine Philosophy! by thy light I am taught to perceive that happiness is the only true end of existence. To be happy, it is necessary for me to love! Universal benevolence is an empty sound. It is individuality that sanctifies affection. But chained by the cruel fetters which unjust and detested custom has forged for my miserable and much-injured sex, I am not at liberty to go about in search of the individual whose mind would sweetly mingle with mine. Barbarous fetters! cruel chains! odious state of society! Oh, that the age of reason were but come, when no soft-souled maiden shall sigh in vain!

---

[26] cf. Edward Young, *Night Thoughts* (1742-45):
A man I knew who lived upon a smile,
And well it fed him; he look'd plump and fair,
While rankest venom foam'd through every vein ("Night", VIII, 336-38).

'In this joyless, comfortless, desponding state, I for some time remained. As I never at any time debased myself by houshold cares, never attended to any sort of work, I always enjoyed the inestimable privilege of leisure. Always idle, always unemployed, the fermentation of my ideas received no interruption. They expanded, generated, increased. The society of the philosophers gave a fresh supply to the fuel of my mind. I became languid, restless, impatient, miserable. But a mind of *great powers* cannot long remain in a state of inactivity; its sensations are ever ready to be called forth. *The romantic, frenzied feelings, of sensibility will soon generate an opportunity for their own exertion.*[27]

'Happening to visit Maria Sydney after the death of her mother, she shewed me a letter she had just received from Henry. The sentiments were so tender, so delicate, so affectionate, I perceived in every word the traces of a mind formed for the pure delightful congeniality of mutual tenderness. A thousand instances of his particular attention to me, the last time he was at home, rushed upon my mind. In going out to walk with his sister through the fields, I remembered having once stuck upon the top of a stile, which I vainly endeavoured to get over, till Henry sprung to my assistance, and with manly energetic fervour tore my petticoat from the stump in which it was entangled. Why did I not then perceive the tender emotion of his soul! why was I blind to such a proof of sensibility and affection! The letter, the important eventful letter, roused me from my lethargic slumber; every word thrilled through the fibres of my heart. It awaked the sleeping extacies of my soul. I inhaled the balmy sweetness which natural unsophisticated affection sheds through the human heart. O Henry! Henry! cried I, I perceive it is with thine my mind was formed to mingle. Thou art, from henceforth, the sovereign arbiter of my fate![28]

'The hour, the wished-for extatic hour of his return at length arrived. Excited by his sensations, he hurried to our house the morning after his arrival; and in his looks, his manner, gave the most unequivocal proofs of the tender sentiments that inspired his mind. But still a mysterious reserve seals his lips. Why does he not speak? Why does he not avow a passion so ennobling, so worthy, so natural, and ah! so fully returned! Female foibles, shrinking delicacies, why do you make me hesitate to begin the subject? Why should I blush to inform him of my affection? O dear, often-kissed relique! (pulling up something that was suspended by a ribbon from her bosom) precious deposit! chosen confidante of my tenderness! how often hast thou been witness to the convulsive struggling sigh! How often has thy bright face been dimmed by the dear, delicious, agonizing tears, which have stolen from my eyes!'

---

[27] Mary Hays, *Memoirs of Emma Courtney* (1796).

[28] A parody of Hays's Emma Courtney's love for Augustus, which has little to do with his actual behaviour towards her since she reads all courteous gestures as indications of his undying love for her.

"Is it Henry's picture!" said Julia; "how did you come by it? Did he present you with it himself?"

'Ah, no!' returned Bridgetina, sighing; 'it is a stolen memento; a theft of love. One day, on following his sister into his bed-chamber, while he was out, I cast my eyes upon his clothes, as they hung upon a horse; and perceiving a loose button, which dangled from the coat he had just thrown off, I took my scissars, and severed the thread by which it hung. I retired without being perceived, and pressed the button to my throbbing bosom. O button! button! cried I, in the delicious ardour of exquisite sensibility. Once the dear appendage of thy master's coat, thou shalt from henceforth be the companion of Bridgetina's bosom; the solace of her tender sorrows, the confidante of her afflictions! Yes; without reserve she shall murmur all her miseries to thee.'

Here Bridgetina ceased; and Julia (bewildered, as she often was, by the illusions of her own imagination) was struck with astonishment at the effects of a similar illusion on the mind of her friend. With regard to Bridgetina, she very quickly perceived the fatal consequences of yielding to the suggestions of a distempered fancy. She saw, that under the idea of cultivating *mind*, she had only been encouraging the mischievous chimeras of a teeming imagination; but never once did it occur to Julia, that she was herself the victim of the very same species of folly. So much easier is it for the mind's eye to pierce the faults of others, than to cast a retrospective glance upon its own.

The good-natured Julia, pitying the delusion of her companion, earnestly wished to save her from the mortification to which it must inevitably expose her. "My dear Bridgetina," said she, in a soft and gentle accent, "you have very much surprised me by the history of your feelings; but I wish—I fear—indeed, I cannot help being very much afraid—that with regard to Henry Sydney, you deceive yourself. If he loves you, why should he not declare it?"

'*If* he loves me!' repeated Bridgetina. 'Why that cruel *if*? Why should he not love me? What reason can he give? Do you think I have not investigated the subject? Do you think I have not examined every reason, moral and physical, that he could have to offer against returning my passion? Do not think I have learned to philosophise for nothing. But I perceive you are prejudiced,' continued she; 'you do not enter into the fine feelings of an exquisite susceptibility. O divine Heloife! (pulling two volumes from her pocket) thou art the friend, whose sentiments are ever soothing to the sensibilities of a too tender soul!' So saying, she put one volume into the hands of Julia, while she began to devour the contents of the other herself.

Julia perceiving how impenetrable she was to reason, took the book, and read till bed-time, without troubling her with any further remonstrance.

At the hour of retiring to rest, Julia first felt the misfortune of Harriet's absence. The settee on which she now reclined in the day, was to be wheeled into the bed chamber, and from thence she was to be lifted into bed; in which she had hitherto been so carefully assisted by Harriet, that she had never experienced the smallest inconvenience from the removal. Poor Bridgetina, unused even to assist herself, was too helpless to afford assistance to another; helpless and aukward she stood by, while the nurse and Julia's maid, a simple country girl, in so blundering a manner performed their task, that Julia was in some danger of slipping to the ground, and in attempting to assist herself, had the thumb of her right hand sprained in such a degree, that on the following morning she found herself totally incapable of writing the usual billet to her father. It was not without difficulty that she prevailed on Miss Botherim to become her amanuensis. Nor was this the only instance in which Julia was made to *feel* the absence of Miss Orwell. She now learned by contrast, how much she had been indebted to the judicious management of that active and ingenious young friend. She now first felt the full value of that series of small, quiet attentions, which, from the unostentatious manner in which they had been performed, had passed almost unnoticed; and now first began to suspect, that a well-informed mind, exerting its *powers* to promote the happiness and comfort of those within the reach of its exertions, might be little less usefully employed than in forming speculations upon *general utility*.

CHAP. IV.

"Blest are those,
"Whose blood and judgment are so well commingl'd,
"That they are not as pipes for fortune's finger,
"To play what stop she please."
　　　　　　　　　　　SHAKESPEARE.[29]

IN answer to the billet written by Miss Botherim, Julia received from her mother the following note:—

"My dear Julia,
"We are, you may believe, very much concerned at the unlucky accident which obliged you to make use of the pen of Miss Botherim; but hope, as she says it is only a very slight sprain, that it will soon be well; and beg that you may, for all our sakes, be sure to take proper care of yourself. I am sorry that my cold is still too bad to permit me to see you to-day, as I have something to communicate that particularly concerns you. It is the result of a conversation which General Villers had yesterday with your father, but I have not now time to enter into particulars. I have sent the

---

[29] Shakespeare, *Hamlet* III.ii.

things you mentioned, and with compliments to Miss Botherim, remain your very affectionate mother,
"E. DELMOND."

"P.S. Your father has had a very 'good night, and desires his blessing."

'Something to communicate that particularly concerns me,' repeated Julia, again examining the contents of the note, 'the result of a conversation which General Villers had with my father. Ah! too well do I know what the subject of that conversation was; the intelligence of Lady Page, concerning the mean, degrading employment which she believed to be the occupation of Mr. Vallaton, has doubtless been communicated to the General; and my father now believes me capable of carrying on a clandestine correspondence with a hair-dresser! What will he think of his Julia? How will his lofty spirit be wounded at the surmise of her baseness? Perhaps he at this moment loads my name with curses, and execrates me as the means of casting a foul blot upon his hitherto-unstained honour. Never, never will he listen to my explanation. Never will he be persuaded that it was but an idle frolic of Vallaton's youth, or that the man who could stoop to such employment had the soul of a gentleman. No, Vallaton! dear, excellent, unfortunate Vallaton! I must never see thee more. All hopes of reconciling my father to thy wishes are at an end. And must I indeed tear thy image from my heart? Must I never again have the pleasure of listening to thy conversation, never more be instructed by thy philosophy? O cruel, cruel fate! how flat and joyless will the heavy hours of existence now drag on. How –'

The mental soliloquy of Julia was here interrupted by the noise of steps in the passage: she listened: she heard her name pronounced by a well-known voice. The door opened, and Vallaton himself appeared before her.

An involuntary emotion of pleasure palpitated in the heart of Julia. In Vallaton's countenance she beheld the rapturous expression of unbounded joy. He knelt before her couch; he eagerly seized her extended hand, and pressed it to his lips in the same manner which Julia had so often seen described in her favourite romances.

"What an incident!" cried Bridgetina. "Ah! Julia, Julia! how happy are you in having such a lover! He is indeed a hero!"

After the first extravagant expressions of his joy were exhausted, Vallaton took a chair by Julia, and began to recount, in the most tender accents, the history of his own sufferings; the agony of his apprehensions for the life of his adored Julia; the torture of suspence; the pangs of absence. But then to have again the extatic felicity of beholding her, of seeing her so much recovered, of being once more permitted to converse with her, to enjoy her conversation without fear of interruption! It was an excess of happiness almost too exquisite for the present imperfect state of nature to support.

"How divinely he speaks!" cried Bridgetina.

Tears of mingled gratitude and tenderness suffused the eyes of Julia. How could she have the cruelty to injure that happiness, to destroy that sweet and exquisite taste of joy? Impossible. 'Ah! no. Let him enjoy the sweet delusion of hope for this one short visit! Let me not so soon, so very soon, give him back to all the shocking agony of despair! Who knows how dreadful might be the consequences?'

Thus reasoned Julia; and convinced by her own reasoning, that humanity and justice demanded of her this consideration for the *feelings* of Vallaton, she suffered not one word of her father, or the apprehension of his displeasure to escape her lips. She, however, *firmly* resolved not to permit another visit. This she thought a proper sacrifice to duty; but since it was to be the last time, why should she not ask him to stay to tea? Vallaton did not require that the invitation should be repeated.

At length, however, the hour of departure arrived.

Vallaton hoped he might be permitted the pleasure of enquiring after her health to-morrow? The beseeching look, the humble and submissive air with which he spoke, penetrated the gentle heart of Julia. It was probable her mother might not come to-morrow, if she did, it would be in the forenoon; why then might she not see Vallaton in the evening? She might then have an opportunity of acquainting him with her *determined* resolution of submitting to the will of her father. It was not only proper, it was absolutely necessary, that she should see him for that purpose.

During the moment of hesitation, while these thoughts rapidly hurried through her mind, a soft and involuntary sigh escaped from her bosom: with an expression of tender melancholy she raised her fine eyes to Vallaton, and in accents sweeter than the summer's breeze, she desired he would come to tea to-morrow.

He was no sooner gone, than Bridgetina launched out into the most extravagant encomiums on his person and manners, but above all on his *exquisite sensibility*. 'Happy Julia! thou hast *indeed* a lover! O Henry, Henry! when shall I see thee breathing the same tender accents at my feet? Wouldst thou wer't endowed with the sensibility of Vallaton!'

When Bridgetina spoke of Henry, Julia perceived nothing in her discourse but the ravings of a distempered fancy. She pitied the imbecillity of her judgment, and deplored the weakness of her perception; but when she uttered the praises of Vallaton, how sensible, how judicious, how just were her remarks! She appeared endowed with uncommon penetration, and was the friend whose congenial mind was most worthy of her confidence. She, she knew, would oppose her intention of sacrificing her inclination to duty, if such a sacrifice should be required; but by combating her arguments, she might herself become more enlightened. She had been told by the philosophers, that views ought to be for ever changing, and that there was nothing so pernicious as *fixed principle*. Perhaps she might have been too hasty in her determination? There could be no harm in canvassing it. If right, it would bear the test of argument; if wrong, it had better be given up. Julia needed not to have given herself the trouble of discussing the propriety of consulting Bridgetina on her affairs. Bridgetina was too much occupied by her own *feelings* to give her the hearing. With various conjectures concerning the motives of Henry's unusual absence, concerning his future plans and prospects, and the reasons which induced his silence, while tender passion, *it was evident*, preyed upon his heart, the tongue of Bridgetina continued to vibrate, till the hour of rest procured for Julia a cessation from its monotonous and unmusical sound.

It was, indeed, the first day that Henry had omitted to enquire for Julia since her unfortunate confinement. The dangerous illness of Mrs. Martha Goodwin might well have accounted for his absence; but of Mrs. Martha, or of the necessity of his attendance upon her, Bridgetina never thought. The life of a *prejudiced* old woman was, in her estimation, of little value, when compared with the *importunate sensations of exquisite sensibility*. These ought to have brought Henry to the farm; nor should the illness of any old woman, whose life could not promote the grand object of *general utility*, have detained him for a moment.[30]

Henry was of a different opinion. He had from early infancy experienced from this good lady so much kind attention, that the simple recollection of the notice she took of the *school-boy*, would have been sufficient to have ensured the gratitude of the *man*; but to this were added a thousand remembered proofs of the benevolence of her heart, and the excellence of her understanding. She was, besides, the aunt of Harriet; and had to her supplied the place of a mother. From all these united considerations, he felt for Mrs. Martha a sort of filial affection and esteem; and with filial sorrow did he now perceive that her disorder was far beyond the reach of human skill.

One evening as she returned from having spent the day with Julia and her niece, she caught cold, by being exposed to a sudden shower; but though she continued indisposed for the whole of the following week, she would not suffer Harriet to be made acquainted with her indisposition. Ever accustomed to consider others more than herself, the thought of the loss that Julia would sustain in being deprived of the society of Harriet, had repressed the desire of her heart, which yearned for the company of her favourite niece—a solace which a strong presentiment assured her she should not long enjoy.

Even when Harriet was (as we have seen) at length sent for, her good aunt was so apprehensive of her being too much alarmed on her account, that she earnestly intreated Mary Anne to go to the pianoforte, that the sound of musick, reaching Harriet's ear on her first entrance into the

---

[30] Hamilton has already satirised Godwin's idea that the action of best general utility is preferable. Godwin controversially argued in *Political Justice* that the person of most use to society should be rescued from a burning house before a loved one. See note 39.

house, might dispel all gloomy apprehensions. Her stratagem in part succeeded, and would have done so most compleatly, had not Harriet flown to the music-room, where she beheld her sister touching the instrument with her fingers, while her eyes streamed with tears, which, as she did not stop to wipe, fell fast upon her hands. At sight of her sister, the young heart of the tender Marianne, unused to suppress its emotions, swelled almost to bursting. She flew into the arms of Harriet, and wept and sobbed without restraint upon her neck.

Dr. Orwell entered unperceived. He gently threw his arms round both his lovely daughters, and fondly pressed them to his heart. "My dear girls, (said he) I cannot wonder at your affliction, but your aunt still lives; and it is our duty, as I am persuaded it is your wish, to promote the ease and happiness of her remaining term of life, whatever that may be. To do so effectually, we must suppress the selfish indulgence of our own feelings. We must dry our tears. We must, however painful the task, exert our resolution."

'And is there, then, no hope?' cried Harriet.

"While life remains, there must be some, my love;" replied her father. "But it would embitter the existence of my sister to see you thus. If you would not materially injure her, you must conquer these strong emotions of sorrow—you must be calm."

'I will, I will,' said Harriet; 'lead me to her, and you shall see how well I will behave.'

When they entered the apartment of Mrs. Martha, Henry was sitting at a table by the door, writing a prescription. His countenance betrayed his fears.

'What is my aunt's disorder?' said Harriet eagerly, in a low voice, keeping in her breath while she listened for his answer.

"It is an inflammation on her lungs," replied Henry. "She must be kept very quiet; strong emotion would be injurious to her. Therefore, dear Harriet, be composed."

The feelings of Harriet were naturally acute. Her sensations of pain and pleasure, of grief and joy, were keen and lively; but education and habit had now so well taught passion to submit to the control of reason, that she was ever mistress of herself. The alteration which she perceived in the countenance of her beloved friend, gave her the severest shock she had ever yet experienced. She, however, neither screamed, nor fainted, nor fell into hysterics, but sat down quietly by her aunt's bedside, and attentively listened to every word she uttered, and watched every motion of her eyes, as well as the tears, which she could not restrain, but which fell in silence, would permit. She sat up with her all night, which her aunt (who was sensible she would have suffered more by leaving her) did not oppose.

At the request of her aunt, Harriet read to her a select portion of the New Testament; it was the last discourse of our Saviour to his disciples, as recorded by St. John.[31] When she had finished, "My dear Harriet," said

---

[31] *John* 17.

the dying aunt, in a voice which seemed inspired with new energy as she spake, "My dear, dear Harriet! if ever, in the course of life, a sceptical doubt should be suggested to your mind under the false colour of philosophy, *think of this night*. Recollect the comfort your dying friend received from these last words of her beloved Master. Remember, how in these awful moments she was supported by the firm hopes of immortality. Oh, my sweet child! could I but make you sensible of the peace, the ineffable peace, that at this moment soothes my heart, you would not be so selfish as to weep. I would, indeed, for your sake, have been contented to have lived a little longer. You are in a situation that requires the guiding hand of experience; but I leave you under the protection of an all-powerful GOD, who has given you a father, worthy not only of your filial affection, but of your unbounded confidence and friendship. I have, however, in the prospect of the event that I feel will now soon take place, employed the leisure moments of the last three days in arranging upon paper my thoughts upon a subject which nearly concerns your peace. Read it with attention. It is the last memento of affection. Do not grieve so, my sweetest, best of girls! do not murmur at a change which is for me full of hope and joy! I would say more—but am fatigued, and must try to obtain repose."

Harriet found it very difficult to suppress her emotion, but she nevertheless succeeded, and did not disturb the succeeding silence by one articulate sigh.

In the morning Doctor Sydney found his patient so very ill, that he earnestly recommended sending to a town, about eight miles distant, for further medical advice. His desire was immediately complied with by Doctor Orwell, and about two o'clock the same day the physician, who was a gentleman of great and deserved celebrity, arrived. He no sooner saw the patient, than he frankly declared there were no hopes. 'Doctor Sydney had (he said) already ordered every possible remedy; and all he could now do, was to recommend a repetition of what had been already done.'

The sentence was as afflictive to the affectionate friends of the good old lady, as if it had been wholly unexpected. In the deep sorrow painted upon every countenance, she plainly read the opinion of the physician; but it had upon her a very different effect from that which it had produced upon her friends. She became more animated, more cheerful, and collected.

"Who would have thought, (said she, smiling) that all this concern should appear about a poor, solitary old maid? Alas! how abortive are the designs and desires of mortals! How many may join in the song of Mary, and say, 'Behold, the hungry are filled with good things, and the rich are sent empty away!'[32] How many have married from the apprehension of

---

[32] *Luke* 1: 53.

a desolate old age, have had their hopes crowned by a numerous family, and yet have had their eyes closed by the unfeeling hand of a mercenary or a stranger. Whilst I!—O my gracious GOD! how different hast thou made my lot!—Yes, my children, I feel all your affection, all your tenderness; it is a cordial, a balmy cordial to my heart."

'Oh, my aunt!' cried Harriet, kissing her cold hand; 'my more than mother! what do we not owe you!'

Marianne, unable to stifle the loud sobs which rose from her tender heart, hid her face in the bed-clothes, and gave vent to her feelings. It was a first-fruit offering to sorrow, ardent and sincere. Her aunt perceived, but saw it would be in vain to check her emotions; and therefore did not seem to observe them. She asked for drink, which, when Harriet reached, she found her own hands unable to raise to her head. Harriet held the cup to her lips, she drank it off, and then with a pleasant smile, said, "And now, my good friends, tell me how much the better should I at this moment be, if I had been born heiress to fifty thousand pounds? Or if double that sum were now in my possession, would my bed be easier, or my beverage taste the sweeter? I was born to no fortune. I never was mistress of any. Cordial friendship has been my rich inheritance, and my patrimony the protecting favour of the Most High! Blessed be the name of that merciful GOD, who from my earliest youth has been my hope, and my stay, and who is now about to be my portion for ever! Amen, amen!" As she said these words, she clasped her hands upon her bosom, and shutting her eyes, remained as if in mental prayer.★[33] Henry alone perceived that she was gone for ever.

We shall pass over the succeeding scene in silence. To those whose hearts have already been lacerated by the last sigh of a friend, the description would be superfluous. By those who have never witnessed a scene of sorrow, it would not be understood. Suffice it then to say, that a more sincere or tender tribute of grief was never paid to the memory of excellence.

Maria Sydney flew to the consolation of her friends. She had herself lately mourned the loss of a parent; and what so well qualifies us for the tender offices of sympathy, as the experience of affliction? Her good father was never a stranger in the house of mourning; and as for Henry, his tears mingled with the tears of Harriet, and his whole heart seemed to share in her sorrow. Nor was his sympathy confined to Harriet, neither did she entirely engross his attention: he was to Dr. Orwell, upon this occasion, as a son; and never are the tender offices of friendship so gratefully acknowledged by the heart, as when pride and vanity (those repellers of social affection) are annihilated by the stroke of sorrow. If the

---

[33] ★Such, my young reader, is the picture of a death-bed; not drawn from imagination, but from *real life*. It is a faithful transcript taken from the record of memory. Who can read it, and not exclaim with the son of Balak, "let me die the death of the righteous, and let my last end be like his!"★ *Numbers* 23: 10.

heart of the father were penetrated by the tender attentions of Henry, could the heart of the daughter be insensible to their value? Surely not: our readers will not suppose it.

The letter, mentioned by Mrs. Martha, was found in her bureau, addressed to Harriet; but it was not till after the elapse of several days, that she could prevail upon herself to read it. At length, shutting herself up in her own apartment, she took it out, dropped a tear upon the seal, opened it, and read as follows:

"Before my beloved Harriet peruses this paper, the hand that writes it will have been sent to mingle with its parent dust; the heart that dictates, will have ceased to beat; but the spirit, which animates and informs it, will still exist; and no idea of any state of existence can I at present form to my mind, in which the interest I take in the happiness of those now so dear to my heart, can be forgotten. If recollection and intelligence remain, that interest can never cease. Perhaps I may still be permitted to watch over my darling child. Perhaps—but in vain do I endeavour to penetrate the veil so wisely drawn; in vain I weary myself with conjectures; a little, a very little time will put me fully in possession of the awful secret.

"Certain, however, that whatever you may be to me, to you I must inevitably be soon, as to this life, lost—I would employ the little strength that is yet left me, in the manner that may best obviate that loss to my dear children.

"Offspring of a beloved sister! dear pledges of her affection! committed to my care by her dying breath; ye are witnesses of the manner in which I have endeavoured to supply to you a mother's care, a mother's tenderness. From the mansions of the blessed she now beholds you, pure as her own unspotted soul! She sees the amiable dispositions that inspired her own breast, renewed in yours; and if aught below can add to the happiness of angelic spirits, hers is increased by the promise of your virtues!

"You, my Harriet, are now arrived at a period which may possibly fix the happiness of your future life. Hitherto all has been the sunshine of peace, the uninterrupted serenity of domestic bliss. But I now behold you about to launch upon a dangerous ocean, where hidden rocks and quicksands may shipwreck all your hopes. Consider this letter as a chart by which you may so steer your course, as to avoid the most fatal dangers of the voyage.

"Your mind is cultivated, your heart is sincere. Pious, affectionate, benevolent, and pure, the love of virtue now reigns the ruling passion of your breast. But the love of virtue, however ardent and sincere, will not always be sufficient to keep us in her true and proper path. Imagination is for ever raising a bewildering mist, which distorts every object in such a manner, that the path of passion is often mistaken for the road of virtue; nor is the mistake discovered, till cruel disappointment and bitter sorrow point out, too late, the fatal error. A philosopher, who, it may be presumed, spoke from experience, tells us 'that when the heart is barred against the passions while they present themselves in their own form, they put on the mask of wisdom to attack us by surprise; they borrow the language of reason to reduce us from her maxims.'★[34]

"Our sex is more particularly exposed to this illusion. Our whole course of education is, in general, calculated to give additional force to the power of imagination, and to weaken, in a correspondent degree, the influence of judgment. You, my Harriet, have in this respect an advantage over many of your sex. You have been early instructed in the necessity of submitting the passions to the authority of reason; you have learned to control the throbbing tumult of the heart, when it beats for selfish sorrows; and by directing your attention to the real sufferings of others, you have been taught to estimate your own, not by the exaggerated representations of self-love, but by the eternal rules of impartial truth and justice. Your mind has not been suffered to run wild in the fairy field of fiction; it has been turned to subjects of real and permanent utility. And yet, my Harriet, with all these advantages on your side, much I fear me, that passion has already gained an influence over your heart, which may cost you many pangs to break. That conscious heart (if I am not much mistaken) at this moment anticipates the mention of Henry Sydney's name. Yes, my dearest niece, I have seen the progress this amiable young man has made in your affections; nor can I wonder, that a disposition and virtues so similar to your own should have made an impression on your unguarded heart.

"Henry, I confess, is worthy of you; I know no man so truly worthy of my Harriet (and how in higher terms can I speak his eulogium?) But, alas! my dear, the beautiful union of congenial souls is a sight seldom to be beheld on earth!

"Henry is genteelly educated, he is respectably connected; but Henry is *poor*—he cannot marry without a fortune; it would in him be folly in the extreme to do so, as certain ruin must be the inevitable consequence.

"What then, supposing it to be mutual, is to become of this romantic passion?

"Experience bids me tell you, that if Henry leave W —— without any declaration of his love, he will, like many other men, equally amiable and equally beloved, in the bustle of the world, lose by degrees this (at present) strong impression, and at length in other connections forget the attachment of his youth.

"If, impelled by passion, he seeks before his departure to bind you in the solemn tie of an engagement, how injurious to the future peace of both may this imprudent engagement prove? That mixture of affection, gratitude, and esteem, which constitutes the greater part of the passion in the breast of woman, is a sentiment increased by absence, and fostered by imagination in the bosom of retirement. But, alas! in the other sex as the passion is generally less pure, so it is naturally less permanent. Whatever

---

[34] ★Rousseau★. *Emile* (1762) iv.

engagements Henry forms, I make no doubt a principle of honour will compel him to fulfil. But on such terms could my Harriet be happy? Could she be happy in being united to a man who, perhaps, at the very moment of that union was the prey of regret, or at least who had exchanged the sensations of tenderness for the chilling cold of indifference? I know she could not.

"I have proceeded upon the supposition of Henry's attachment being at present real and sincere; but even in this respect, my Harriet, we may be mistaken. Henry may prefer your society to that of any other young woman in the small circle of W —, and yet be far from harbouring any sentiment warmer than esteem. Should you be convinced of this, (and you are not so much the slave of vanity as to repel the conviction) I have little to fear for you. Every sentiment of delicacy would, in this case, aid the dictates of judgment; and passion, all powerful as it is by imagination represented to be, would quickly be annihilated.

"If love is to be thus easily conquered by the suggestions of pride, why should it resist the remonstrances of reason? Alas! because self-love rejects her salutary counsel. Self-love, ever the advocate of the present passion, represents her dominion as eternal, and her overthrow as impossible. Listen not to her delusive voice, or believe any thing impossible to virtue.

"Instead of supinely deploring the circumstances which render the encouragement of this passion improper, exert your mind to consider them with attention. Let not imagination alter their form, or under the specious but false hope of some unforeseen behest of fortune, divert your attention from the contemplation of reality. If power were granted me to make you happy in the way your heart would dictate, how should I rejoice in procuring for you the accomplishment of your wishes! But is, then, your Heavenly Father less benevolent and kind? No: his goodness is infinite; but his wisdom is infinite also! What to my weak and limited apprehension might appear the means of happiness, Divine Wisdom may perceive to be the very reverse. Before Him lies the whole succession of events, which are to fill up your existence. It is in his power to arrange and model them at his pleasure; and so to adapt one thing to another, as to fulfil his promise of making all *work together for good to those who love Him*.[35] Were this life intended for our ultimate scene of enjoyment, we may from the provision we see made for the inferior creation, be convinced that our innocent inclinations should not be thwarted in their course. But can we who believe it only a probationary state, in which we are to be fitted and prepared for the enjoyment of a superior one, can we be surprised, if here we do not meet the fruition of our wishes? If resignation were not a necessary trial of our virtue, can we believe that we should be so frequently called on to resign?

"Doth wisdom, then, exact a gloomy dereliction of the pleasures of life? Because the cup of enjoyment be not always filled exactly as our

---

[35] *Romans* 8: 28.

foolish fancies would direct, are we with peevishness to dash it from our lips? Ah! no. The heart that is properly impressed with a sense of the Divine goodness, and firmly persuaded of the Divine superintendence, will not refuse to taste of the blessings by which it is surrounded, because the fancied good on which imagination doated, has been withheld. It is pride and infidelity that produce the querulous murmurs of discontent. By resigning the events of our life to Him whose all-seeing eye can alone survey the whole of our existence, we double every enjoyment, we enhance the value of every blessing. In teaching our hearts to yield a ready acquiescence to *his* will, we equally divest of its sting the dart of death, and the sharper (O how much sharper!) arrow of disappointment!

"Think not that this is the language of declamation. No, my Harriet, it is the sober dictate of experience. Time has not taught me to forget the cruel pang of disappointed love, but it has taught me to rejoice in the disappointment that cost me once so dear. Nor is it only in this awful moment, when "standing on eternity's dread brink," the objects of former interest necessarily lessening on the view, that this conviction has been impressed upon my heart. No; it has for years been the subject of my gratitude and thankfulness to the Supreme Director of events. I have seen, that, in spite of myself, I could be blessed; and have been long taught to acknowledge the possibility of being made happy in another way besides my own; nay, happy in the very loss of that in which I foolishly imagined all happiness to be comprised. I do not say that this was the work of a moment; but I can say with truth, that I attribute much of the tranquillity and real happiness of my after life to a proper improvement of my disappointment.

"*Sweet are the uses of adversity.*"[36]

"By struggling with passion, I invigorated my virtue; by subduing it, I exalted the empire of reason in my breast. I learned to take a different view of life and its pursuits. I no longer cherished the idea, that all happiness was comprised in prosperous love; and that the lives of such as were united by the tender bonds of mutual affection, must inevitably be crowned with *unclouded felicity*. A course of visits to two or three couples of my acquaintance, who had *married for love*, sufficiently convinced me of the fallacy of this opinion.

"Still the forlorn state of celibacy, the neglect, the ridicule to which it is exposed, threw at times a temporary damp upon my spirits, and might, perhaps, have betrayed me into that discontent, which is, alas! but too often visible in ancient maidens, had not I learned fairly to look my situation in the face, and boldly to examine how far the opinion of the world (that is to say, of the silly, the thoughtless, and the insignificant) ought to affect my happiness.

---

[36] Shakespeare, *As You Like It*, II.i.12.

"I perceived, that the conscious dignity of the being who endeavours to fulfil the duties of humanity, and to make progressive improvement in knowledge and in virtue, ought to be superior to situation; and by degrees lost all anxiety about *appearing happy*, in the consciousness of being really so. In the approbation of my own conscience; in the endearments of friendship; in the gratitude of those I have endeavoured to serve, or to comfort; and in that undisturbed peace which is the exclusive privilege of the unmarried; I have found an ample recompence for the mortification of hearing myself called *Mrs. Martha*.

"Think not, my Harriet, that by any thing I have said, it is my intention to recommend to you a determined resolution of remaining in the single state. All I mean is, to convince you that it is not simply in *situation* to make us either happy or miserable; to impress upon your mind a conviction of the possibility of conquering the most deeply-rooted and fondly-cherished passion; and to assure you, that the notion of its being impracticable is both false and foolish.

"If, upon a candid and impartial view of the circumstances to which I have alluded, you perceive the necessity of banishing from your bosom a passion which may lead to the destruction of your peace; I trust you have more strength of mind, more real virtue, fortitude, and courage, than to shrink from the painful task. Depending on this, I shall not throw away the time that is now to me so precious, in adducing any further arguments to prove the necessity of this direliction of your present affection; but shall, while strength permits, give you a few instructions concerning the most efficacious mode of proceeding, in order to ensure a victory.

"In the first place, I would earnestly advise you never to make a confidante of the passion prudence bids you conquer. At the description of our own feelings, imagination takes fire, while the appearance of sympathy feeds the consuming and destructive flame. Few, very few, have sufficient virtue to oppose the current of a friend's desires; nor is it probable, that those who have will be often chosen for bosom confidantes. In disburthening our hearts, we seem rather more solicitous to obtain a sanction to our passions, than to be put upon a method of conquering them; and I can say from experience, in looking back upon my past life, that I never did any thing which on cool reflection I had reason to regret, to which I was not spurred on by the injudicious advice of some too zealous friend.

"I would, therefore, recommend to my dear girl to avoid the dangerous condolence of a tender and sympathetic mind. Should your heart ever feel depressed from struggling with its emotions; should your spirits be inclined to sink, and imagination prompt you to believe that your own sufferings exceed the sufferings of your fellow-mortals; seek not to dissipate this gloom in scenes of amusement, which will only increase your melancholy—but turn your steps to the house of sorrow—fly to comfort the afflicted—to bind up the wounds of the broken in heart; and when you contemplate the real miseries of life, you will blush at having grieved for fancied ills. Oh, may never deeper sorrow wound the heart of my beloved child!

"Since the events of life are placed beyond our reach, since it is so seldom in our power to regulate them to our wishes, it is the wisest part we can pursue, to regulate our desires in such a manner as may prevent our becoming the prey of discontent, and losing the enjoyment of the blessings that are left us, in perverse and abortive murmurs at inevitable destiny. I have heard many different methods of obtaining this desirable frame of mind recommended to our use; but upon trial have found all to fail, except an humble and heart-felt confidence in the over-ruling providence of our great Creator.

"Fear not, then, my beloved child, to commit the events of your life to the care of that Heavenly Father, without whose knowledge even a sparrow falls not to the ground. If your desires are fulfilled, accept it as a boon from Him who alone can turn it to a blessing. If your wishes are disappointed, by the previous solemn dedication of your will disappointment will be divested of its bitterness. In the struggle of contending passions, the heart that is determined to submit to no law but that of duty, will ever come off victorious; but the victory will be doubly easy, when the prevailing motive is armed with the strength of the Most High.

"I know there are, who in the hey-day of health and spirits, would scoff at this, as the mere effusions of enthusiasm; but when these shall arrive at the close of life—when, like me, they shall stand on the threshold of eternity—when,

"—from the tomb
"Truth, radiant goddess! sallies on their soul,
"And puts Delusions's dusky train to flight,"[37]

depend on it, their derision will be at an end.

"My strength is exhausted. I can hold my pen no longer. Adieu! dearest, best of girls! adieu. May we meet in the regions of everlasting felicity! and till then may the GOD of mercies take thee under his protection!

"Amen! and farewell! M.G."

CHAP. V.

"Lovers and madmen have such seething brains,
"Such shaping fantasies, that apprehend
"More than cool reason ever comprehends."
                                    SHAKESPEARE.[38]

---

[37] Edward Young, *Night Thoughts* (1742-45), V. 327-28.
[38] Shakespeare, *A Midsummer Night's Dream*, V.i.

"YOUR cold is better, this morning, my dear;" said Captain Delmond to his wife, as she poured out his chocolate.

'I think it is;' replied Mrs. Delmond.

"The day appears to be remarkably fine;" said Captain Delmond, looking towards the road that led to the farm.

'It is a very good day;' answered his wife.

"I think a walk would be of service to you, my dear;" said the Captain.

'Perhaps it might;' replied Mrs. Delmond.

"It is a long time since you have seen poor Julia;" said the Captain.

'It will be a week on Thursday;' said Mrs. Delmond.

If the reader never has had any acquaintance with the race of the *Torpids*,[39] he will naturally conclude, that dear Mrs. Delmond was either so intent upon making breakfast, or had her mind so occupied by some subject of importance, that the meaning of her husband in all these several hints concerning the weather, &c. entirely escaped her observation.

Mrs. Delmond, however, was neither absent nor stupid. She was perfectly well acquainted with her husband's meaning from the first, and before she came to breakfast, had determined to visit Julia as soon as it was over. But the frank communication of her design would, perhaps, have afforded too much pleasure to her husband, and might have produced that unclouded cheerfulness, which at the time of meals is by many people deemed so prejudicial to health. Forming our opinion from observation, we should believe it to be a part of the medical creed of many wise personages, that the motion of the juices of the stomach, so necessary to the process of digestion, is happily augmented and assisted by a due proportion of what is called *fretting*. Nor can we sufficiently admire the tender care that is taken by many heads of families, in the due administration of this powerful stimulant, to all who have the happiness of sharing in their family repasts.

Whether Mrs. Delmond had actually studied this theory, we have never been able to learn; but as far as her powers could extend, she frequently put it in practice. These powers, it is true, were very circumscribed. She could not, by breaking into a violent passion because the fowls had got three turns too much or too little, promote the digestion of those who had the pleasure of sitting at her table. She could neither fret nor fume, nor swear at the cook for the health of her friends, (a privilege reserved for us lords of the creation;) she could only contrive to smother the blaze of cheerfulness; by a look of pensive sadness, or an apropos reprimand to the attendant, in the very middle of some good story of her husband's, or some lively sally of her daughter's, to which she saw him attending with uncommon glee. She now observed, that he

---

[39] Torpids is a rowing race in which the boats set off at spaced intervals and attempt to catch, and, if necessary, bump, the boat ahead of them.

wished to talk of Julia; and though her own inclination would have led her to the same subject, she, out of pure regard (no doubt) to his digestion, resolved to baulk his intention, and to introduce some other topic of discourse. She talked of the soot having fallen down the kitchen chimney. "Why, then, I suppose it is time to have it swept," said the Captain.

'It is but a month since it was swept,' said Mrs. Delmond, 'and I do not see the good of having it swept again.'

"What, then, would you have done with it?" said Captain Delmond.

'I do not know, indeed,' replied the lady.

"I wish," said the Captain, "you would take a walk to visit Julia to-day. I have been thinking of her all night. This proposal of Major Minden's—"

'Pray pull the bell,' said Mrs. Delmond.

"For what?" said the Captain, somewhat testily.

'Only to take the things,' replied Mrs. Delmond.

"The things may stand," said the Captain, taking his hand from the bell. "I was speaking of this proposal of Major Minden's: it is a serious business, the happiness of our dear girl's life may depend upon it. His fortune is great, his family is honourable; but I cannot help wishing that we knew something more of his temper and dispositions. His manners are pleasing, and his countenance has the appearance of much good-humour: don't you think so, my dear?"

'I did not take much notice of it,' said Mrs. Delmond.

"Do you think it will be proper to mention the affair to Julia?" said the Captain.

'I really do not know,' said Mrs. Delmond.

"I think it will," said the Captain, "I have ever disliked concealment. It appears to me to have something in it disingenuous and dishonourable, and is seldom, very seldom necessary. It is the mean trick of timid and dastardly minds, and does more mischief in the world than ever was achieved by blunt sincerity. Inform her, then, my dear; but at the same time assure her that—" Here the maid entered, Mrs. Delmond continued to address her in an under-voice, while she cleared the breakfast-table, and then getting up, bade her husband good-bye, and went to prepare herself for her walk.

She found Julia wonderfully better than when she had seen her last, though her spirits were now more languid than she had at that time observed them.

Julia, who expected every moment that her mother would mention Vallaton, found her heart palpitate as often as she observed her about to open her lips. She soon perceived, however, that the presence of Bridgetina presented an obstacle to Mrs. Delmond, who was not well enough acquainted with that young lady to speak of family matters before her without restraint. Julia, therefore, delicately hinted to her friend, that she wished to have some conversation with her mother in private—but in vain. Every hint was lost on Bridgetina, whose mind was so completely occupied in discussion and investigation of abstract theory, as to be totally lost to the perception of all that was obvious to common observation. Just as those whose opticks, by being constantly employed on distant objects, lose the power of seeing whatever comes close to the eye.

Perceiving that Bridgetina would not move, Julia had recourse to whispering, and at length, in a very low and tremulous voice, asked Mrs. Delmond whether she had not something to communicate?

"Yes," replied her mother, "I have a great many things to tell you, but not before Miss Botherim."

'She is reading,' said Julia, 'and will not take any notice.'

"You are then going to be married," said Mrs. Delmond, in a long whisper.

'Heavens!' said Julia, 'what, my dear mother, do you mean? Indeed, indeed, you do me injustice; I never will do any thing without my father's full and free consent.'

"But he has your father's consent," whispered Mrs. Delmond.

'Has!' repeated Julia in extacy, 'has my father's consent! impossible. How? where? which way did it come about? It is surely all a dream, an enchanting vision: O tell me quickly how it happened.'

"General Villers brought him yesterday to our house," replied Mrs. Delmond, "and spoke of him so highly to your father, when he proposed the business to him—"

'General Villers then proposed it!' exclaimed Julia.

"Yes," returned her mother, "it was General Villers that spoke for him; and got your father's consent that he should visit you as a lover. So you must make haste and get well, for you see what awaits you."

'It is wonderful!' said Julia. 'But how good it was of the dear General! and how delicate to make sure of my father's consent, before he made any direct proposals to myself.'

"It was very proper, to be sure;" said Mrs. Delmond.

'It is false reasoning;' cried Bridgetina aloud, throwing down the book with great vehemence upon the window-seat. 'Julia has done nothing wrong; nothing that is not, on every abstract principle of virtue, laudable, and praise-worthy, and meritorious.'

"And pray, who says any thing against her?" said Mrs. Delmond.

'Yes,' replied Bridgetina, 'the false prejudices of the world condemn her conduct. Nor is she herself sublimed and purified from every taint of the odious prejudices of society. Else, why this remorse, why these tears?'

"I hear of no remorse; I see no tears;" said Mrs. Delmond.

'It is plain, Madam, you have never read the second volume with attention.'

"The second volume of what?" replied Mrs. Delmond.

'The second volume of the divine Heloise;' said Bridgetina.

"Indeed I never read a word of it;" said Mrs. Delmond. "I declare I thought you meant my Julia."

'No,' said Bridgetina; 'Julia is to be sure very much enlightened, but she has not yet attained the sublime heights of Heloise.'

"I know nothing about her," said Mrs. Delmond. "But I perceive it is time for me to think of returning home; so, farewell, Julia! I shall tell your father that you are not averse to the subject mentioned by the General."

'Tell him,' said Julia, 'that my heart is penetrated with his goodness, and that I am ready to do whatever he pleases. Never can I be ungrateful for his tenderness—for his dear concern for my happiness!'

Mrs. Delmond was no sooner gone, than Bridgetina began a dissertation upon the mistaken notion of gratitude; wondering how a person, so well-informed as Julia, could be guilty of such a monstrous error.

'I know I have been convinced again and again, by the arguments of philosophy,' replied Julia, 'that gratitude is contrary to the principles of justice, which alone ought to govern our conduct; but I cannot tell how it is—it seems to spring so naturally to my heart, that I know not how to conquer it.'

Mr. Vallaton, punctual to the appointed hour, presented himself in the evening. The fine eyes of Julia sparkled at his approach. The roses which had been banished by confinement from her cheeks, revived with redoubled lustre, and gave fresh animation to one of the most expressive and beautiful countenances the hand of nature ever formed. The tumult of her spirits was not now, as on the day before, excited by a mixture of tender regret and bitter self-reproach. The sanction of her father's approbation had chased every painful emotion from her heart; and the flutter of spirits with which she expected the eclaircissement from Vallaton's lips, was, perhaps, the most pleasurable sensation she had ever in her life experienced.

Vallaton was, on his part, highly gratified by the manner of his reception; and resolving to improve the present favourable disposition of his mistress, urged the subject of his passion with all the eloquence of which he was master. He was equally surprised and delighted to find that Julia no longer opposed his suit by the apprehended displeasure of her father. She, indeed, never mentioned her father's name; for perceiving how it was avoided by Vallaton, and attributing his silence to the exquisite delicacy of his affection, which would be indebted to her heart alone for success, she resolved to indulge him at the expence of her curiosity, which burned to know by what means he had induced the General to plead his cause.

While Julia in sweet confusion listened to her lover's vows, of which in silent modesty she smiled her approbation, the heart of Bridgetina swelled with vexation, not unmixed with envy, at the superior happiness of her friend. Finding the attention of Vallaton too much engrossed by his fair mistress, to give her any hopes of a metaphysical argument, she betook herself to the garden; and there in sweet soliloquy she gave a vent to the tender sorrows of her gentle bosom.

"Ah! miserable, deplorable, odious, and wretched state of society! (cried she) in which every woman cannot find a lover equally ardent and equally amiable. Sweet sensibilities! delicious tenderness! Why do I sigh for you in vain? Ah! why was my cruel lot cast in such a dismal country? Why was I doomed to come into the world in such an age? Why was I born when an absurd, an unnatural institution ties up the hearts of men, and every nobler feeling becomes petrified, and worm-eaten, and mouldy, on the uncomeatable shelf of marriage? This is the cause, ye gods! this is the cause—"

Here a seasonable shower of tears came to her relief; and seating herself down upon the bank of a small stream that ran at the bottom of the garden, she increased its waters by the pearly torrent from her eyes, in as sensible a degree as ever brook was swelled from a similar source. For an exact measurement of the height to which rivers have been swoln by such incidents, and other minute description of the phœmena, we refer our readers to the poets; and shall content ourselves with observing, that in this, as in similar instances, it happened that the peccant humours which had risen to the eyes, from the region of the heart, were no sooner carried fairly down the stream, than the patient experienced relief.

It would be unpardonable to neglect the opportunity that now presents itself of offering a hint to our very much respected friends, the experimental philosophers; to whose serious consideration we would very earnestly recommend a minute investigation of the facts so often recorded in the works of celebrated writers. From these authors sufficient data may be obtained for an exact calculation of the greatest height to which any river was ever known to rise by the fall of a single shower of tears; but much subject for investigation will still remain. It is not enough to know how far the waters upon such occasions actually do rise; it is still to be ascertained, by a set of repeated thermometrical observations, what is the exact increase of heat that it experiences from the said shower. And a very careful analyzation must likewise be performed, to know *with certainty* the difference of the component parts of *salt tears*, and *bitter tears*, and *sweet tears*, and *sweet-bitter tears*, and *salt-delicious tears*, and *tears half-delicious, half-agonizing*, &c. &c. upon which a very pretty neat course of experiments might undoubtedly be made; and if recorded with philosophical accuracy, and ornamented with a sufficient quantity of technical terms, (distinguishing, for the benefit of the unlearned readers, the phlogistic from the antiphlogistic)[40] would make a very learned, useful, and entertaining pocket volume. With this hint, for which we are conscious of meriting the thanks of our fellow-citizens, we shall conclude the chapter.

---

[40] Inflammatory, fiery, heated, inflamed.

CHAP. VI.

> "His words replete with guile,
> "Into her heart too easy entrance won -
> "Impregn'd
> "With reason to her seeming, and with truth."
>
> MILTON.[41]

WHEN Mrs. Delmond returned to her own house, she found Mrs. Gubbles with the Captain, who was amusing himself with the domestic anecdotes of a neighbouring family; a species of information for which he could not have applied to a superior source. No one, however, could have half the pleasure in hearing any piece of news, that this generous woman experienced in communicating it. The delight she took in adding to the general stock of information was, indeed, so great, so truly disinterested, that it was not all affected by the nature of the intelligence she had to give; as whether that was sorrowful or pleasant, it was communicated by her with equal alacrity and cheerfulness.

No sooner did the account of Mrs. Martha Goodwin's death reach her ears, than hastily throwing on her cloak, which always hung upon a nail in the corner of the room to be in readiness upon such occasions, she sallied out to communicate the news of the mournful event to her neighbours.

She first called on Mrs. Botherim; but, alas! she was there too late; Mrs. Botherim had heard of it before. So, after settling with her the day of the funeral, and debating for some time upon the exact age of the deceased; the amount of her little fortune; the number of her gowns, petticoats, and stockings; and the probability that the maid would come in for a good share of these articles of apparel; which, no doubt, the Miss Orwells would be too proud to wear; she took her leave, and proceeded to Captain Delmond's, where she had the satisfaction of being the first to relate the loss the society of W— had sustained in the death of one of its worthiest members.

"She was an excellent woman," said the Captain, "and will be a very great loss to the family. She has been quite a mother to the young ladies, and was deservedly beloved by them."

'Oh yes, to be sure she was;' said Mrs. Gubbles. 'She was indeed a very good sort of a body, though a little particular in her way. I always thought it was a mighty odd whim, her never playing at cards; for my part, I have never no ideer of them there particularities; for, says I, what is it that can make any one make themselves so particular, says I, but pride?'

"She used to excuse herself on account of the weakness of her eyes," said Captain Delmond.

---

[41] John Milton, *Paradise Lost*, Book ix.

'Take my word for it, that was all a sham;' replied Mrs. Gubbles. 'Her eyes, indeed! why she could pore upon books for the matter of a whole morning. Never tell me that she could not have played at cards every bit as well, if she had had a mind. No, no; it was all nothing but the pride of being thought wiser than other people.'

"She was very kind to the poor," said Captain Delmond. "I have heard of her visiting their cottages, and kindly soothing their afflictions by her sympathy, when she could in no other way relieve them."

'Ay, poor body,' said Mrs. Gubbles, 'she had nothing else to do. People who have families to look after must spend their time, aye and their money too, in another guess way. But what do you think of young Mr. Churchill's good-luck?'

"I know nothing of it," said Captain Delmond.

'Have you not heard of his old grand-uncle's death?'

"No, I never heard a word of it," replied the Captain.

'Bless me! well, now, that is surprising. I could have told you of it a week ago. Yes, yes, the old miserly hunks is gone at last. He never did no good to nobody when living; but he has left a pretty fortune behind him, I warrant you; as good as fifteen hundred pounds a year in landed estate, besides a mint of money in them there funds, as they are called. It all goes, every farthing of it, to the young gentleman; and a very pretty, sweet young gentleman he is, as I ever seed in my life. Well, well, we shall see, but *I* know what I expects. If he is not over head and ears in love with your daughter Miss Julia, I give you leave to say I knows nothing.'

"With my daughter, Julia?" repeated Capt. Delmond. "How do you come to think so?"

'O,' returned Mrs. Gubbles, 'let me alone; I saw it all well enough, I warrant ye. When he was down last summer, and so much with young Dr. Sydney, though he was no doctor then, neither; I saw well enough how much he was taken with Miss Julia. Did I not see them together, when they came with a heap of other company to the fruit-gardens, at the Old Abbey, of a Sunday evening? Did not I perceive how the young gentleman singled out Miss Julia, and went always round to her side, and chose out the very nicest of the plumbs and the apricots for her?'

"Pugh! that's a great while ago," said Capt. Delmond.

'Long as it is,' rejoined Mrs. Gubbles, 'the young gentleman has not forgotten it, I warrant ye. It was but a few days before his grand-uncle died, that he came post from London, and the very next day he came to our shop himself to give orders about some medicines. He no sooner saw me, than he bowed, and spoke so genteelly, not pretending, as many of our saucy fine gentlemen would have done, to forget my name. "But, Mrs. Gubbles, says he, I think, says he, Mrs. Gubbles, I had the pleasure of seeing you at the Abbey gardens last summer; it is a very charming spot, says he." 'Yes, says I, sir, that it is to be sure, says I; I dare say, says I, you remember Miss Delmond? Poor, dear young lady, what a terrible misfortune has befel her!' "A misfortune! says he;" 'and as I live he turned as white as my apron; and when I told him all the particulars of the whole business, he looked so sorrowful and so melancholy! He clean forgot his grand-uncle, and would have gone away without the medicines he was in such haste for when he came in, if the boy had not run after him on purpose.'

Here the entrance of Mrs. Delmond changed the subject of the conversation, which, however, made a deep impression on the Captain's mind. Mrs. Gubbles had no sooner taken her leave, than he anxiously enquired in what manner Julia had received the intelligence of Major Minden's declaration.

'She seemed quite delighted with it,' said Mrs. Delmond. 'I never saw her look so pleased at any thing in my life: she was even thankful to the *dear General*, as she called him, for speaking in the Major's favour; and to you she sent her duty, and bid me tell you of her grateful sense of your goodness.'

"It is very strange!" said the Captain, after a short pause. "It is very strange, how the idea of rank and fortune operates upon the mind. She never, that I know of, saw this gentleman but once; and tho' he is a very well-looking man, I do not see any thing about him that one should think so captivating to a girl's fancy. Perhaps, however, he was at Castle-Villers in the spring; when Julia, you know, spent a fortnight there. Do you think he was, my dear?"

'I do not know, indeed,' returned Mrs. Delmond.

"Well," said the Captain, "her choice shall be mine; though if I could give any credit to what Mrs. Gubbles has been telling me, and could hope that young Churchill really was attached to her, the excellence of his character, his known merit, and his residence too in the very neighbourhood, would give him in my mind a decided preference. But I have told her, that a negative in this affair was all I would ever claim; and never shall my child reproach me with a breach of promise. But she is so well, you say, as to be able to sit up upon the sopha. The dear girl! would that I could once see her! She surely may soon be removed without danger."

Mr. Gubbles, it seems, advises another fortnight's confinement;' returned Mrs. Delmond.

"It can't be helped!" said the Captain, sighing; "but if the weather be fine, you, my dear, may see her every day."

The weather, however, was not fine; it was for above a week perversely adverse to the Captain's wishes. No possibility of Mrs. Delmond's visiting Julia in all that time. But though the rain prevented Mrs. Delmond, it was no obstacle to Mr. Vallaton: he lost not a single day, and every day blessed him with increased conviction of the complete influence he had obtained over the tender heart of Julia.

He mentioned to her the travels of Vaillant; described in romantic terms the beauty of the country in those unfrequented regions that daring traveller had explored; and spoke of the innocence and amiable simplicity of its virtuous inhabitants with enthusiastic rapture. Julia listened with delight to his description. When he perceived her imagination begin to glow: "Yes, dear Julia," said he, "these are scenes where true happiness might indeed be found. Freed from the galling chains of a corrupt and depraved society, the mind might there have room to expand to virtue, with a companion endeared by similarity of taste and sentiment, a congenial soul, a noble spirit which had strength and energy to soar above each vulgar prejudice, and to fly from a society unripe for the improvements of philosophy. How blest, how tranquil, might the delicious moments move!"

'It would be very charming, to be sure,' said Julia.

"Charming!" repeated Vallaton, "all that enthusiasts have ever preached concerning the joys of Paradise, would be more than realized."

'O extatic state of bliss!' cried Bridgetina, 'dear delirium of delight! O that we were all among the Hottentots! And we shall be among them too, ere long, I trust. But Julia knows nothing of the glorious scheme. Pray tell her, Mr. Vallaton, all about it; she will make a charming addition to the party.'

Vallaton, who would rather have told Julia in his own way, was a little disconcerted by this abrupt interruption. He had, however, the art to turn it to his own advantage; and Julia, who instantly thought of Prior's Emma, considered all he said as a trial of her love. Yes, thought she, like the artful lover of the nut-brown maid,

"By one great trial he resolves to prove
"The faith of woman, and the force of love."[42]

I am aware of his intention; it is at once a proof of the sincerity and the delicacy of his attachment. Nor shall I be less sincere than the faithful Emma:

"Alphonso too shall own,
"That I, of all mankind, could love but him alone."[43]

We should be extremely happy to oblige the dear boarding-school angels by a faithful repetition of every word that passed in these interesting conversations betwixt Julia and her happy lover; but as we have no doubt that their own sprightly imaginations will amply supply the deficiency, we leave it to fancy to paint the particulars of each tender scene, and content ourselves with observing, that by attributing to her lover a refinement of delicacy, which, though congenial to her own mind, was very foreign to his thoughts, Julia became the dupe of her own romantic imagination.

Anxious to remove from his mind every tender doubt, she scrupled not to engage herself by the most solemn promises to be his, and to follow his fortunes through the world.

---

[42] Matthew Prior, *Henry and Emma, A Poem, upon the model of the Nut-Brown Maid* (1709), 188-90.

[43] Matthew Prior, *Henry and Emma*, 323-24.

Vallaton received this convincing proof of her affection with extacy; but still, to Julia's great surprise, persevered in his silence with regard to her father. What could be his motive? What, but an intention of making her happy, by giving her an agreeable surprise? She would not for the world baulk his intention, and, therefore, not only carefully concealed her knowledge of what had passed, but became extremely anxious, lest by some *mal-apropos* discovery of her having been acquainted with it, the merit of the frank acknowledgment of her attachment should be lessened in its value.

The week passed on without affording any variety of amusement; yet notwithstanding the unfavourable state of the atmosphere, so injurious to delicate nerves, and notwithstanding the sameness of the scene, the spirits of Julia did not sink, but on the contrary, were never observed to be better than in this rainy week, which she declared to be the shortest she had ever passed in her life.

Bridgetina was of a different opinion. To her it seemed to creep with slow and lagging pace. Day after day she expected to behold Henry Sydney, and day after day closed in disappointment. She considered his conduct in all points of view; she discussed every possible motive that could induce him to forbear gratifying himself in her society; she divided and subdivided every argument in his favour; she reasoned, she investigated, and always concluded with proving, in the most satisfactory manner, that she was right, and that, therefore, Henry must inevitably be wrong.

As she was one morning sitting with Julia, who could now, with very little assistance, come from her own room into the parlour, she was interrupted in the sixth head of her argument by a loud knock at the door. She was still in her morning dishabille, which, to confess the truth, was none of the most elegant, and would willingly have been excused from being seen by Henry in a dress so very unbecoming; but to escape was now impossible: so folding over the laps of her wrapper, pulling up the heels of her shoes, and settling the bow of her morning cap, which she in vain endeavoured to adjust to the middle of her head, she snatched up a book, and reclining her head upon her hand, while her arm rested on the arm of the chair, she fixed herself in a meditating attitude, truly becoming the character of a female philosopher.

She had scarcely time to arrange her posture, when the door opened, and discovered—not Henry Sydney, but Mrs. Botherim; who, unable longer to support the absence of her dear Bridgetina, had bid defiance to every obstacle in order to satisfy her impatient desire of seeing the sole object of her affections.

"And is it *only* you?" cried Bridgetina, in the querulous tone of disappointment, as her mother entered the room.

'*Only me?*' repeated Mrs. Botherim, 'and very well it is that you see me alive, after all I have come through.'

Julia, with her wonted sweetness, endeavoured to make amends by the kindness of her expressions, for the abrupt manner of Bridgetina; at which, however, the good lady appeared neither hurt nor surprised. Accustomed to her petulance, she never felt its impropriety; but with a blind partiality, which converted every foible into a perfection, she thought every word her daughter uttered was, at all times, "wisest, discreetest, best." After having, at the earnest entreaty of Julia, taken some refreshment, the old lady began to expatiate upon the ever-ready topic of the weather; declaring she had never seen such continued rains in her life, or was ever out in such a day.

"I hope, however," said Julia, "that your health will not suffer from it."

'Nobody's health ought to suffer from any physical cause;' said Bridgetina. 'Rain, wind, tempest, hurricane, are mere trifles to a reflecting and investigating mind. It is nought but the weak prejudices of society that makes them be regarded in the light of evils. Let the rain beat, and the storm rage; can rain or storm be so pernicious or destructive, as the cruel state of protracted and uncertain feelings?'

"It is mighty fine talking," said Mrs. Botherim, "and mighty easy talking, too, in a good dry warm room; but let me tell you, Biddy, it is no such easy matter for a person at my time of life to carry about a great umbrella, and to tug a heavy pair of pattens[44] through the mud for two long miles, in such a day. Well, what does it signify? I am quite well, now that I see you; for I have been dreaming of you at such a rate."

'What foolish notions you have about dreams;' said Bridgetina. 'I don't know how often I have explained to you their whole theory; but you never can remember any abstruse point.'

"Indeed, I never can;" returned the old lady. "You know I never pretend to dispute with you in any point of learning; as, indeed, why should I? But it does my heart good to hear you talk, and I have been so tired, and the house has been so lonesome since you have been away, that you can't think."

'I am extremely sorry,' said Julia, 'to have deprived you of Miss Botherim for so many days, and very sensible of my obligation to you, as well as to her for the favour of her company.'

"Alas! my dear Miss," said Mrs. Botherim, "I have but little of her company at any time. She is always so taken up with them there wise books as she reads on from morning to night, that I often don't get a single word out of her the length of a whole day. But then it is a pleasure for me to see her, and to do all her little jobs, while she is making herself wise. Did you ever know any one with such a memory as my Biddy?"

'Few, indeed,' returned Julia, 'have the advantage of a memory so retentive.'

"Few!" said Mrs. Botherim; "I don't believe there is the like on't. She will talk you out of any book she has been reading, for the length of a

---

[44] A kind of overshoe worn to raise the ordinary shoes out of the mud or wet.

whole hour, and never once put in a word of her own. It is a fine thing to have such a genius! I wonder, for my part, who she takes after. Dear Mr. Botherim was, to be sure, a very learned man, but he kept it all to himself."

'My father was no philosopher,' said Bridgetina; 'he cultivated no sensations but those of the palate; his distinguishing taste in cookery shewed, however, that he was not totally destitute of *powers*. Had these *powers*, by some early combination of circumstances, taken a metaphysical direction, he might, doubtless, have enlightened the world.'

"See, now," cried Mrs. Botherim, "what it is to reason! There have all the people in our town been wondering for this week past at the learned pig;[45] when, if they had known any thing of them there *powers* and *combinations of circumstances* that Biddy speaks of, the learning of the pig would have been accounted for at once."

Julia could not forbear smiling at the simplicity of the fond mother; but found something so pleasing in the expression of maternal affection, that though thus united to weakness, she could not behold it with indifference. She exerted herself to entertain the old lady by her own and Bridgetina's conversation; for to Julia was Mrs. Botherim indebted for every sentence that was uttered by her daughter, who conceived it to be great loss of time to converse with one who was incapable of canvassing the nice points of her extraordinary system.

As Mrs. Botherim took leave, another visitor to Julia was announced. It was the faithful old Quinten, her father's servant, who had been on a six weeks' leave of absence into Yorkshire, from whence he had returned the preceding evening. Captain Delmond himself was not more shocked at the first accounts of Julia's misfortune, than was this affectionate creature. He could not get it from his mind all night. 'If I had not gone on this fool's journey, now, (said he) this accident would never have happened. I would have attended Miss myself, and taken care that no harm had come on her. I would ha' died sooner than that she should have been so hurt. I wish I had been at home.'

Thus did the poor fellow continue to lament over the misfortune of his young mistress, which he entirely attributed to his own absence; and in the morning, much as his wearied limbs demanded repose, he intreated permission to go to see her with so much earnestness, that Captain Delmond could not refuse his request.

"Welcome home again, my good Quinten!" cried Julia, as he entered,

---

[45] The "learned pig" appeared in London 1785 at no. 55 the Admiralty, opposite Charing Cross, under the direction of a Mr. Nicholson. The intelligent porcine told time, distinguished colours, cast accounts by means of typographical cards, and read the thoughts of ladies in the audience (see Ricky Jay, *Learned Pigs and Fireproof Women* New York: Villard, 1987). References to the "learned pig" occur in Sarah Trimmer's *Fabulous Histories* (1784), Mary Wollstonecraft's *Vindication of the Rights of Woman* (1792) and Boswell's *Life of Johnson* (1791).

holding out her hand to the old veteran, who advanced respectfully towards her. "I hope you have been well since you left us, and I am indeed very glad to see you safe returned."

'God bless thee, dear lady!' said Quinten, the tears running down his furrowed cheeks, 'God Almighty bless thee! I shall never forgive myself for going away at such a time. If I had been at home, I should ha' prevented it; I know I should.'

"Indeed, my good Quinten, no one could have prevented it;" said Julia.

Quinten shook his head. 'Who can tell, Miss,' said he, 'what one might ha' done? Old as I am, I'm not yet so feeble but that I might ha' stopped the horse; or, perhaps, saved your fall—or—Well, well! it was the very devil himself that contrived these cursed gigs, that's for certain. They are more dangersome, and do more mischief in the course of one summer, than any one of our best field-pieces in a whole campaign. There was a gentleman and his wife nearly killed t'other day out of them whirligigs, as I passed through Newark. May I be shot for a coward, if I would not sooner march up to the very muzzle of the enemy's guns, than venture into one of them.'

"A great many accidents are occasioned by them, to be sure," said Julia; "but I shall soon get the better of mine; I am almost well already."

'Thank God you are!' said Quinten; 'but I shall never be happy, till I see you tripping it about again, as you used to do. It breaks my heart to think what his Honour must ha' suffered in bearing you so long from his sight. Before he ever saw you, Miss, it was the joy of his heart to hear what a pretty baby you were. I remember, it was just as we were recovering from the third fever we had in that vile pestilence of a place, on the very morning that Ensign Wilson died; Captain More and Lieutenant Danby had been buried the day before; and in the course of the week seventeen of the stateliest fellows in our company had all dropped off, and made such a blank in our ranks, that it shook the bravest spirit of us all; had they met their death in the field, it would have been nothing; but to die without having fired a shot—without having so much as seen the enemy—t'was enough to vex the bravest man alive! Well, just at this time I heard of the arrival of the packet; and though scarcely able to crawl out of my room, I went as fast as my limbs would let me, to see if there were any letters for my master. I got one, and came back with it so joyfully! I thought no more of my weakness. Here, (said I) please your Honour, here is a cordial for your Honour's heart, that will do it more good than all the drugs in the medicine-chest. Had you but seen, Miss, how his sunk eyes revived at the sight! "It is a letter from my wife!" said he, as he took it from me with his wasted hand; and holding it to his heart, he wept just like a baby. As he read it, I stood at the foot of the bed, and when I saw how happy he looked, (though the tears still stood in his eyes) I could have cried for joy too. 'I knew it would be a cordial to your Honour's heart'; said I. "It is indeed, Quinten, (said my master) a very great one.

And Quinten, (said he) here is a crown to drink my wife and daughter's health. My dear girl comes on charmingly; (said he) by all accounts, she will make as great a beauty as her mother." And would you believe it, Miss, from that very hour he recovered, and had it not been for another fever, in which no letter from England arrived to comfort him, he might ha' been as well now as ever.'

"You are a kind-hearted soul," said Julia, "and I hope you have been made happy with your friends. How did you find them?"

'Oh, Miss, (returned Quinten) I have no friends in Yorkshire now. Death had struck every soul off the muster-roll that either cared for me, or that I cared for. My two brothers, my uncles, my cousins, all were dead. Not even an old school-fellow remained in the place, excepting one who was the son of the shoe-maker, a top man in the village, worth a deal of money, and kept as warm a house as any man in his station in all the Riding. But see the chance of war! What man can be sure that his son will maintain his post in the same condition in which he leaves it to him? Poor Jack is now, in his old age, obliged to go upon the parish; but the honest fellow has a heart still. He was as glad to see me, Miss, as if I had been his brother; related the history of all our old school-mates; and told me that I had still a near relation left—my brother William's son, who had got greatly up in the world, and was a manufacturer at Halifax, he said. So I thought I would go to see him, out of respect to his father's memory, who I loved very dearly. I little thought that the son of my brother would be ashamed to own me; but the pitiful dog is so puffed up with pride, that he scorned to call an honest soldier uncle. Well, (said I) thank GOD! I have the house of my own dear master to return to. He knows that I am no sneaker. Under his command I have fought for my king and country; we have battled it together with the world these thirty years past, and when marching orders for heaven shall arrive, I know his Honour won't refuse to let these old bones be placed in the ranks along-side with his own. So, Miss, here I am; and please GOD I shall never go from home again as long as I live.'

Julia, who had a great affection for this faithful domestic, listened to his garrulous prattle with much complacency. Observing how much he had been fatigued, she made him sit down, and ordered him a glass of wine and some biscuit. Nor did she make any apology to Bridgetina for taking this liberty, as she thought it would have been a sarcasm on her principles to have supposed the possibility of her taking offence from such a circumstance. Great was, therefore, her surprise, on observing the face of Bridgetina to redden with displeasure, as the old veteran retired to a chair at the further end of the room. He stood a moment after he had reached it, and on Julia's beckoning him to be seated, he put his hand upon his heart, and bowing with an expression of respect, humility, and gratitude, he sat down.

'Upon my word, Miss Delmond,' said Bridgetina, starting from her seat, 'this is a liberty to which I have not been accustomed.' And then, before Julia could possibly make any reply, she suddenly left the room.

Julia, though much disturbed at perceiving the emotion of Bridgetina, would not suffer Quinten to depart till her maid had brought him the refreshments she had ordered. She then dismissed him with a long and tender message to her father, who, since the departure of Miss Orwell, had through the medium of verbal messages alone heard of her welfare; Miss Botherim being too much engaged, either in studying or in talking, to have leisure to think, far less to write, upon any one's affairs but her own.

On the departure of Quinten, Bridgetina re-entered the room. As the traces of displeasure were still visible in her countenance, Julia began an immediate apology for the liberty she had taken in desiring the old domestic to sit down. "I thought," said she, "that when you considered the long journey the poor fellow has so lately had, and observed how much he appeared to be worn out with fatigue, you could not possibly have been displeased."

'How much soever I admire the beautiful system of perfect and compleat equality,' said Bridgetina, 'I hold every partial and premature attempt at introducing it to be improper, and therefore must declare my opinion of its impropriety.'

"Indeed," replied Julia, "I had no thoughts of introducing equality at all. I only wished to rest poor old Quinten's legs for a few minutes. I am sorry it offended you; but surely, if philosophy teaches us that the difference of ranks is an obstacle to perfectibility, it cannot be truly philosophical tenaciously to adhere to the imaginary distinctions that so unfortunately separate us from our fellow-creatures. Have not I a thousand times heard you lament the present miserable state of things, and pathetically mourn over the wretched depression of the lower ranks?"

'Oh, yes' said Bridgetina; 'in a general view, nothing to be sure is so deplorable. But the age of reason is not yet far enough advanced for people to desire their servants to sit down in the same room with them. The time will come, to be sure, when all the unhappy distinctions of station, and rank, and sex, and age, shall be abolished; when all shall be equally wise, and equally poor, and equally virtuous. Oh, happy period! Oh, much wished for aera of felicity!'

"But pray how is this blessed state to be brought about," said Julia, "if every one pertinaciously refuses to descend, and proudly prohibits the exaltation of his inferiors?"

'It will all be brought about by the dissemination of philosophy,' said Bridgetina. 'All will be then enlightened; but at present—'

"Well," cried Julia, "here comes Mr. Vallaton to decide upon our dispute—which of us have been in the right he shall now determine."

Vallaton was no sooner seated, than Julia informed him of the incident which had occurred, dwelling much upon the virtues of the old domestic, for whom she expressed much kindness and attachment.

"As to desiring the person you mention to sit down," said Vallaton, "you certainly did it from a principle of benevolence, and as such it cannot be very severely reprehended; though upon investigation, it may appear to have been founded upon mistake. True benevolence, or rather real virtue, (for there is, strictly speaking, no such thing as benevolence) gives no preference to any object, but for the sake of certain beneficial qualities which really exist in that object. Now what beneficial qualities can possibly exist in a man who, for thirty years, has been in a state of servitude and depression? How long must every nobler power of the soul have been lost in the degrading habitude of submission? *If the hopelessness of his condition have not long ere now, blunted every finer feeling of his mind, giving him for the habits of his reflection slavery and contentment, must he not cherish in his bosom a burning envy, an unextinguishable abhorrence against the injustice of society?*★[46] Such a person cannot, therefore, be a proper object of regard."

'But, indeed,' said Julia, 'honest Quinten is the very reverse of all this; he is quite a noble-minded creature; indeed he is. The affectionate attachment he has shewn to my father and his family is beyond all description. And so disinterested is his regard, that when my father would, on coming home, have dismissed him from his service, as thinking it inconsistent with his plan of economy to keep a man-servant in his house, Quinten, on his knees, besought him to suffer him to stay without wages, which he said his Chelsea pension[47] rendered now superfluous. I shall break my heart if I leave you, (said the poor fellow, with tears in his eyes) and what good will this pension do me then? I could not bear the thoughts of your honour's being without a servant now, when you stand more in need of one than ever; indeed I could not, said he, with so beseeching a look, that my father could not resist it. He wept as much as Quinten, while I climbed up on his knees, and casting my arms about his neck, My dear papa won't let the good Quinten leave us, cried I, I'm sure he won't. A speech for which poor Quinten has ever since been so grateful, that I am persuaded he would lay down his life to serve me!'

"Is it possible that the enlightened mind of my lovely Julia does not perceive, that all she has said tends rather to confirm than to rebut the force of my argument, which goes to prove that, as a servant, this person *must inevitably be destitute* of the best characteristics of a rational being. This blind affection, this degrading gratitude, which, it would seem, has excited your regard—how dark and ignoble is the source from whence it springs! But this fellow has not only been a servant, he has been a soldier. *He has learned ferocity in the school of murder. His mind has been familiarized to the most dreadful spectacles. He is totally ignorant of the principles of human nature. Whatever appearance he may wear, depend upon it he is at bottom mean, base, cruel, and arrogant; since it is impossible that a soldier should not be a depraved and unnatural being."*★[48]

---

[46] ★See the Enquirer, by Godwin★ *The Enquirer*, Part II, Essay IV, "Of Servants", 209.

[47] A Chelsea Pensioner is a resident of the Chelsea Royal Hospital (founded in 1682) for old or disabled soldiers.

[48] ★See Enquirer★ This is excerpted from Godwin's discussion about soldiers in the *Enquirer*, Part II, Essay V, "Of Trades and Professions", 233-37. See Appendix A.

'They may be so in general,' replied Julia; 'but I am sure both Quinten and his master are exceptions to the general rule. They, I am certain, have of each them hearts as good, and tender, and humane, as any human being ever yet possessed.'

"Impossible!" cried Vallaton; "utterly impossible! It is only, believe me, charming Julia, it is only from having been so fatally accustomed to their prejudices, that you view them with indifference. Could you divest yourself of that weak partiality, which so unhappily throws its delusive mist before your eyes, you would view with just and noble abhorrence those very persons who are now the objects of your much-mistaken regard. There is no point of philosophy more difficult of acquirement, than that which teaches us to make a proper estimate of the merits of individuals. This never can be done till we consider them, not with regard to ourselves, but to general utility. When our minds, purified from every narrow and illiberal prejudice, are enabled to take this enlarged and comprehensive view, our regards will be no longer influenced by the mean consideration of friendship or affection; we shall no longer admire any casual virtue; but in exact and just proportion to the talents, the powers, and capacity of the object, will be our reverence and esteem."

'Alas!' said Julia, 'how few are capable of this discernment! How few possess the strength of mind necessary for exerting it!"

"Few, to be sure, in the present depraved state of society," said Vallaton; "but it is only the regard of those few that possesses any real value. What is the indiscriminating affection of a parent, whose weak and selfish fondness blindly doats upon a child, because, forsooth, he believes it to be his own? What is it, when put in comparison with the dignified regard of an enlarged and philosophic mind, which has attentively weighed its merits? How many beauties, how many excellences do I discover in the soul of Julia, which were never discerned by the eye of her father? From an accurate examination of the powers of her mind, I bow before her as the first of human beings; while her father merely loves her for the obedience that has been subservient to his will, and beholds in her an object that at once soothes his pride, exalts his consequence, and gratifies his ambition."

Julia sighed deeply at this mortifying view of the motives of her father's tenderness; and Vallaton, perceiving the impression he had made, continued his attack upon her prejudices, which he carried on in so masterly a manner, that Julia, though she could not easily pluck from her heart the deeply-rooted sentiments of filial tenderness, was too much ashamed of her weakness to give encouragement to their growth. Finding herself incapable of refuting the arguments of her logical admirer, she readily admitted the belief that refutation was impossible; and so artfully did he contrive to mingle argument with flattery, that vanity and self-love were too much interested in the truth of his representations to render her solicitous of having them contradicted.

CHAP. VII.

"Fancy! thou busy offspring of the mind;
"Thou roving, ranging rambler, unconfin'd;
"Pleasing, displeasing, aping, marring, making;
"Oft right for wrong, and wrong for right mistaking."[49]

BRIDGETINA, to whom every day became more and more insupportable, was at length gratified by the appearance of Henry Sydney. The cruel youth, taking no notice of her soft embarassment, totally regardless of the faint scream she uttered, or of the soft languishment of her non-bewitching eyes, only made her a slight bow, and advanced to enquire for Julia, to whom, and whom alone, he thought it necessary to make any apology for his absence.

While he addressed himself to Julia, Bridgetina regarded him with much attention; she observed that an air of melancholy overspread his countenance, that he looked pale and thoughtful, and that the quick intelligence of his dark and brilliant eyes was exchanged for heavy languor and listless dejection.

The heart of Bridgetina beat quick at the discovery. "It is evident, said she to herself, "that the dear youth has been made miserable by this cruel separation, Yes; the pangs of absence have been more than he could bear. Delightful sensibility! enchanting tenderness! how amiably interesting do ye make him now appear!" Then addressing herself to Henry. "How much must it grieve the friends of Doctor Sydney," said she, "to behold him thus the prey of sorrow? It is but too evident that some tender sensation preys upon his heart. Could he but consider me as worthy of his confidence, with what delight would I soothe each tender emotion of his troubled mind."

'You are very good, Madam,' said Henry, smiling. 'I really did not know that my feelings had been quite so apparent; but you will not wonder that I should be a little out of spirits, when I inform you that I leave W—— to-morrow; and that it is probable I shall never more return to it as a place of residence.'

"Good heavens!" exclaimed Bridgetina, "is it possible! Can you really be so cruel, so barbarous, so insensible to the affection—"

'I am certain,' said Julia, (interrupting her friend, for whom she blushed nearly as deeply as Henry had done from the force of her expressions, which he was convinced could only allude to one object) 'I am certain,' said Julia, 'that the friends of Dr. Sydney must, indeed, suffer much from the loss of his society. I pity poor Maria from my heart.'

"What is the affection of Maria," exclaimed Bridgetina, "or of a thousand Marias, in comparison of that heart-bursting emotion—those

---

[49] not found.

romantic, high-wrought, frenzied feelings, which are inspired by fierce and ardent love? Doctor Sydney must know that he leaves behind him one person, and one alone, who is capable of such a tide of tenderness."

'Good GOD!' cried Henry, in amazement, 'what is it you mean?' Then recollecting himself, 'What a fool I am,' said he, 'not to perceive your intention of making a jest of me.'

"Me jest!" said Bridgetina, "no one can say that I ever made a jest, or so much as laughed at one in the course of my whole life. On a subject so serious, in a moment of such impression, it is not likely that I should speak lightly. Ah! too well you know the truth, the cruel truth of the circumstance to which I allude."

'You astonish me beyond measure,' said Henry. 'But do not thus play with my feelings, I beseech you: for heaven's sake be more explicit.'

"It is you that ought to be more explicit, I think" returned Bridgetina. "Why, acting under the influence of false delicacy, of erroneous prejudices, do you forbear to come to an explanation with her whose happiness, whose fate is in your hands? What right have you by suspense to destroy her peace, by delay to protract her utility?"

'You astonish me more and more,' said Henry, in the greatest agitation. 'But since you have so unaccountably discovered the secret of my heart, in justice to myself, I think I am bound to explain to you the motives of my conduct. The passion that inspires my breast, I have indeed laboured to conceal. Alas! I now find how ineffectually. But when I considered the narrowness of my fortune, the precariousness of a profession, in which neither assiduity nor abilities can ensure success, I thought it would be ungenerous and base to seek to bind by an engagement the hand and heart of her whose happiness is, and ever will be, dearer to me than thy own. No, never will I be so vilely selfish; she shall be free, though to her I am bound in ties indissoluble and eternal!'

"And do you really feel for her so much affection?" cried Bridgetina, softening her shrill voice as much as possible. "And do you think," continued she, "that she is less generous, less noble-minded than yourself? Ah! no; be assured she is at this moment ready and willing to sacrifice to you all the false prejudices of a depraved and misjudging world. What is the world to her who exists, who lives, who breathes but for you alone?"

'Dear Miss Botherim,' said Henry, 'you at once delight and grieve me by what you say. Dear as the flattering idea of being beloved is to my heart, it but renders the cruelty of my situation the more intolerable. Shall I take advantage of such endearing sensibility? Shall I involve a generous and exalted woman in my misfortunes? Good heavens, how miserable is my situation!'

"And why miserable?" returned Bridgetina. "Why is your situation to be deplored. It is this depraved and distempered state of civilization, that alone puts present happiness beyond your reach; but this is not an evil without a remedy. Leave this corrupt and barren wilderness, where the rank weed of prejudice spreads pestilence and perdition through the tainted air, and in a region uncorrupted by the baleful institutions of society, enjoy the delicious delirium of sweet and mutual love."

Henry stared at this speech, which was to him totally incomprehensible. Before he had time to ask for any explanation, the entrance of Mr. Gubbles put an end to the conversation.

Henry, deeply agitated by what he had heard from Bridgetina, now gave himself up to joy at the discovery of Harriet's affection; and again relapsed into the most gloomy melancholy from the cruel recollection of the barrier which remained, and might long remain, to oppose their union. His resolution of leaving W— without making any declaration of his passion began to waver. It was the idea of her happiness that had determined his silence, but now that he had been so plainly informed of her tenderness for him, he thought it would be equally cruel and dishonourable to leave her in any suspense concerning his sentiments.

Bridgetina, on the entrance of Mr. Gubbles, thought it necessary to retire, in order to conceal her emotion; which was, however, observable to no eyes but of Julia, as in truth she was the only person who either looked at or thought of her at all. She had not yet returned, when Henry, impatient to be gone, hastily took leave of Julia; who, much astonished at his whole behaviour, asked if he would not stay to see Miss Botherim. 'She will have the goodness to excuse me,' said he, 'as my time is now so limited;' and then again repeating his wishes for Julia's speedy and compleat recovery, he departed.

With hasty steps he proceeded to Dr. Orwell's. As he drew near the house, a thousand different emotions crouded on his mind; much as he was flattered by the pleasing certainty of Harriet's attachment, his delicacy was in some degree hurt by her making a confidante of Miss Botherim.

'What a perverse, what an inconsistent being is man!' said he to himself, with a deep sigh. 'How miserable did I deem the anxiety of doubt! how often have I trembled with the apprehensions of Harriet's indifference! and now that I have nought to fear, I am less happy, less contented than ever! Oh, had I wooed the confession from her own lips, how blessed would it have made me! But is not this vile, is it not ungrateful? Yes, dear Harriet, I ought, and I shall love you more than ever.'

He entered the house without ceremony, and proceeded to the saloon; where he beheld Harriet sitting at a small worktable which stood near the window. Her clasped hands rested on a folded letter which lay on the table, on the direction of which her eyes seemed to dwell with that unconscious fixedness which denotes deep and painful meditation. Tears trickled fast down her lovely cheeks, and a long and heavy sigh heaved her bosom. On perceiving Henry, she instantly took up the letter, and hastily putting it in her pocket, endeavoured to resume an air of cheerfulness and serenity.

'I fear I intrude upon you,' said Henry, 'but I know your goodness will pardon my intrusion, when I tell you that the long-dreaded hour of my departure is arrived; that short is the time I can now enjoy the society most dear to me; soon, very soon must I be torn from it, perhaps for ever.'

"I am extremely sorry to hear it," said Harriet, with much composure in her looks, but in accents scarcely articulate; "though, as I hope it will be for your advantage, your real friends ought rather to rejoice than grieve at the event."

'And can Miss Orwell part with her old friend thus coolly?' said Henry.

"No one can take a deeper interest in the happiness of their friends than I do," replied Harriet. "Could my friendship be of service to you, you should find that it was neither lukewarm nor insincere. For your kind attentions to this family in our late affliction, I can never be either ungrateful nor forgetful; but—" Here her voice totally failing her, she stopped a moment; and then, as if recollecting herself, said, "I must acquaint my father with your being here; he too, I know, will wish to return you his grateful acknowledgments, and will be sorry to lose a moment of your company."

'Cruel Harriet!' said Henry, 'in a moment such as this to talk of thanks for the common offices of humanity! When my full heart is bursting with anxiety to communicate to you the sensations which agitate it almost to madness, will you refuse to me the consolation of a hearing?'

"Doctor Sydney," said Harriet, with a look of mingled dignity and sweetness, "do not think me either insensible or capricious. You can have nothing to communicate to me to which I ought to listen, that you may not freely speak in presence of my father."

Often (thought Henry) have I heard of the caprice of the sex, but never did I imagine that in Harriet Orwell I should behold a proof of it. 'And do you,' said he, 'indeed prohibit me to make use of this last, this only opportunity of declaring to you the state of my heart!—,

"Indeed," said Harriet, interrupting him, "it is very foolish, very improper to have any conversation of this kind." And then hastily pulling the bell, she desired the servant, who immediately entered, to acquaint her father that Doctor Sydney wished to see him.

Vexed, mortified, and disappointed, Henry stood for some moments silent. "Am I in a dream?' at length he exclaimed. 'Is it from Miss Orwell's lips I hear these words? Has she then no regard, no pity, no feeling for me? Vain illusion! (continued he, in great agitation, striking his hand against his forehead) oh, how fully is my temerity and presumption punished!'

"I am truly grieved," said Harriet, in great confusion, "I am sorry, I am distressed to see you so much agitated. But if the assurance of my *friendship*—my sincere and lasting friendship, can afford you any consolation, it ever has been—it ever will be yours."

Her trembling lip and faltering voice, as she pronounced these words, proclaimed the agitation of her heart. Hearing her father's step in the passage, she arose, and holding out her hand to Henry, who seized it in a speechless agony of amazement and despair, "Farewell!" said she, "may happiness—" She could proceed no further; but as her father entered at one door, she hurried out at the other, and running to her own apartment, gave vent to the emotions she could no longer suppress.

Harriet had been in some degree prepared for the intended departure of Henry, of which she had heard about an hour before he came to take his leave of her. Her heart had sunk within her at the intelligence, and her agitated spirits had been forced to seek relief in a burst of involuntary sorrow. Far, however, from giving indulgence to these feelings, she had summoned up all her resolution to suppress them; she knew that Henry would certainly call to take leave, and prepared her mind to sustain the parting scene with dignity. When she had a little composed herself, she went to her bureau, took out the last letter of her beloved aunt, and endeavoured to fortify her mind by a perusal of its contents. She then bathed her eyes in cold water to take away the vestiges of her tears, and proceeded to the saloon, whither she knew Henry would be shewn; again she read over the last advice of her venerable friend, and with an enthusiasm kindled by the high-wrought emotion of her spirits, she vowed to obey her wise instructions.

How well she performed her resolution has been already seen. Her heroism was, however, pretty nearly exhausted by the time she reached her own apartment; she threw herself into a chair, and for some minutes gave way to the feelings of her deeply-wounded heart. She now regretted not having listened to Henry's declaration. "How cruel, how unfeeling must he now think me!" cried she; "his esteem, at least, I might surely have retained: O why did I, by the appearance of such pride, deprive myself of a regard so precious?" Thus did she for some time add to the weight of sorrow by the bitterness of self-accusation. But her understanding was too good to be long warped by the influence of passion. She soon perceived, that to have acted in any other manner would have brought on all the evils which her aunt had so forcibly pointed out; and no sooner did a consciousness of the propriety of her conduct reach her mind, than it comforted and soothed her. By an act of ardent and sincere devotion, she fortified her resolution; and while her innocent soul was poured out to heaven in earnest supplications for her lover's happiness, that serenity which is the companion of elevated sentiment, took possession of her mind.

Let us now return to the mortified and disappointed Henry, who remained, for some time after she left the saloon, in such a state of stupefaction, that he was almost insensible to the presence of her father. He was at length roused from his reverie by the repeated questions of Dr. Orwell, and forced, in reply to them, to give him an account of the cause of his sudden departure from W——; which was occasioned by advice that morning received from his patroness Mrs. Fielding, through whose interest he hoped to be appointed physician to the ——Hospital, vacated by the death of Dr.——.

Dr. Orwell very sincerely congratulated his young friend on so flattering a prospect, and highly approved of his fixing in London in preference to the country, where, though his virtues would be esteemed, his talents would be lost.

Henry in reply said, 'that he merely went in conformity to the opinion of his father, who did not wish to disoblige Mrs. Fielding by a non-compliance with her request. For my own share,' continued he, 'I am perfectly contented with the country, I have no wish to quit it; never shall I be so happy in any other place as I have been here; never, from the hour I leave this, shall I know a moment's peace.'

"I hope you will soon have too much business upon our hands to give you time for vain regrets," said Dr. Orwell, smiling. "Greatly, however, shall we all miss you—much have we been obliged to your attention; and wherever you are, the best wishes of me and of my family will attend you. Surely Harriet did not know that you were going away so soon, or she would not have run away without bidding you farewell. But, poor girl, you must excuse her; she has now a great many domestic concerns to look after. I can assure you she wishes you well, and will never forget your kind attention to her aunt."

Henry, much distressed by this speech, and unable to carry on the conversation any farther, suddenly started up, and shaking hands with his good old friend, bid him farewell, and went away as fast as possible. The behaviour of Harriet had astonished as much as it had mortified him. Prepossessed with the idea of Miss Botherim's being in her confidence, (for how else could she attain the knowledge of the disposition of her heart?) he could not doubt of her affection. From whence, then, proceeded this unnecessary and vexatious reserve? Why to Miss Botherim so free and open in the acknowledgement of her attachment, and to himself so backward as not even to deign to listen to his vows? "Alas! it is but too evident," cried he; "pride and ambition have stifled the voice of love: it is at the suggestion of those accursed passions that she rejects the man her heart approves. O Harriet, Harriet! how opposite to the exalted generosity of thy sentiments, is thy present conduct? If excellence such as thine be found imperfect, in whom may we hereafter confide?" Thus did he continue to upbraid the gentle Harriet for a behaviour, which could he but have read her heart, and seen its real motives there displayed, would have rendered her more estimable, more amiable in his eyes than ever.

And here, kind reader, of whatever age or gender thou mayest haply chance to be, we entreat thee to make one moment's pause; and to be so obliging as to give a glance towards the person whose conduct thou hast last condemned. Believe it certain, that with all thy penetration thou mayest, peradventure, have mistaken the intentions of his heart. Mitigate, therefore, the fierceness of thy wrath. Retract the harshness of thy censure, and so shalt thou, when the secrets of all hearts shall be revealed, escape the bitterness of remorse for the cruelty of injustice.

CHAP. VIII.

"With too much thinking to have common thought."
POPE.[50]

WHEN Bridgetina returned to the parlour, and found that Henry had departed without taking leave of her, she was beyond measure disconcerted. She had the day before received from Mr. Glibs a new novel, the declamatory stile and quaint phraseology of which had so highly pleased her, that anxious to dress her thoughts on the present occasion to the very best advantage, she had retired to refresh her memory with a few of the most striking passages; she now returned fraught with three long speeches, so ardent, so expressive, so full of energy and emphasis, that it would have grieved a saint to have had them lost.[51]

"And is he gone?" cried she, in a voice that at once denoted her surprise and mortification. "Was his sensibility too great to bear the sad—sad scene of separation? It was not his own feelings but mine, of which he was thus tender. Ah! the delightful excess of morbid sensibility!"

Julia, perceiving the astonishment of Mr. Gubbles, felt very much ashamed; and afraid lest Bridgetina should still further expose herself, begged her, in a whisper, to say no more upon the subject at present, as they should have an opportunity of talking it all over when they were alone.

"I know your meaning," replied Bridgetina aloud, "You would have me basely conceal my sentiments, in conformity to the pernicious maxims and practices of the world. But what so much as the dread of censure has cramped the energy of the female mind? Have not the first of female characters despised it? And do you think the odious fetters of a depraved society shall shackle me?"

'Indeed, Miss Botherim,' said Mr. Gubbles, "I must make bold to tell you, that if you mean, (for I cannot pretend to say that I very well understand you) but if you mean to say, that you intend to be above the censures of the world, I can assure you I never knew any good come of such notions.'

"What are the censures of the world to me?" said Bridgetina. "Do you think I have not sufficient philosophy to despise them?"

'Well, well,' returned Mr. Gubbles, 'I hope it will not be your case, Miss; but I must needs say, that in the long course of my practice, I never knew any one that began in despising the censures of the world, that did not conclude in deserving them.'

Mr Gubbles then took his leave, and was no sooner gone, than Bridgetina informed Julia of her intention of following Henry to London. "Good heavens!" exclaimed Julia, "you cannot, surely, be so very

---

[50] Alexander Pope, *To A Lady: of the Characters of Women* (1735), 98.

[51] Presumably a copy of Hays's *Memoirs of Emma Courtney*.

imprudent as to harbour a design of this sort now? Think of the consequences to your character. Think of the distress of your mother! Nay, to Henry himself such a circumstance could not fail at present to be inconvenient and distressing to the last degree."

'To answer your objections methodically,' said Bridgetina, '(for you know I love to methodize) they are, I think, three-fold. First, with regard to my character; secondly, in respect to my mother; and thirdly, in respect to Henry himself. These are your objections; they may all, however, be answered in one word—*general utility*. What is the use of character to an individual, when put in competition with the interests of general utility? By what moral tie am I bound to consult the inclinations of my mother? The only just morals are those which tend to increase the bulk of enjoyment: my enjoyment can never be increased by living with my mother, consequently living with her is adverse to the grand end of existence—general utility. As to Henry, will not my presence increase his happiness? And is not happiness and pleasure the only true end of our being?*[52] When we attain these, do we not then best promote general utility? These are the sublime principles of philosophy, and all that opposes it is the fable of superstition.'

"But I am not convinced, that by following Henry to London, before he has had time to arrange his affairs, or even to enter upon the profession on which he depends for his support, that you will contribute either to his happiness or your own," said Julia.

'What obstinacy of prejudice!' cried Bridgetina. 'Was not melancholy painted upon his countenance? Was not his misery, at the thoughts of leaving me, evident to the most careless observer? And shall not his happiness at again beholding me be equally apparent? Yes; I feel in myself a capacity for increasing his happiness, and my powers shall not be lost. Our souls shall mingle, our ideas shall expand together. Sensations! emotions! delicacies! sensibilities! O how shall ye overwhelm us in one great torrent of felicity!'

"Still," said Julia, "I wish—indeed, my dear Bridgetina, I wish—that with regard to Henry, you may not labour under some mistake. Forgive me, but I think it would be wrong to conceal from you, that I have still some doubts—"

'Doubts! after what you have heard him say?' cried Bridgetina, interrupting her. 'Was ever declaration more explicit? Was ever confession more sweetly candid or sincere?'

"He did indeed confess that he was in love with somebody," returned Julia; "but as he spoke in the first person, the object of his passion might, I think, be with greater probability supposed absent than present."

---

[52] *See Emma Courtney* A modification of Hays's heroine Emma's several statements "that *happiness* is, surely, the only desirable *end* of existence! (*Memoirs of Emma Courtney*, 85, 116). See Appendix A. Hays in turn echoes Godwin's notion of happiness in *Political Justice*, "Summary of Principles", 75.

The rage of Bridgetina, at a supposition so injurious to her wishes, and so destructive of her hopes, was for some time too great for utterance. She at length, however, gave vent to her wrath, and loaded poor Julia with the bitterest reproaches, mixed with many sarcastic observations on her want of penetration. Julia was at great pains to appease her, in which she at length happily succeeded; and though she could by no means prevail upon her to relinquish the plan of following Henry to London, she extorted from her a promise of delay.

Bridgetina then entered into a very long, and doubtless a very instructive, investigation of the nature of mind; proving, by a thousand irrefragable arguments, the utter impossibility of Henry's having continued insensible to the charms of her mental qualifications; and concluded her oration by an observation so full of novelty and wisdom, that it alone were sufficient to immortalize her name. 'Having proved,' said she, 'that mind is superior to matter, and never more superior than when the faculties are in the full vigour of youth, it necessarily follows, that were man, uncorrupted by the prejudices of society, to act from the pure impulse of nature, he would, in the wild career of energetic youth, despise the trifling disadvantages of ugliness and decrepitude. Regardless of the mere forms of matter, he would leave the unnatural admiration of beauty to the old, the dull, and the insensible; and seek for the object of his affection a discussing, a reasoning, and an investigating mind. This is the true course of nature! This is the most sublime proof of the perfectibility of man!"

CHAP. IX.

"Alike in ignorance, his reason such,
"Whether he thinks too little or too much;
"Chaos of thought and passion, all confus'd,
"Still by himself abus'd, or disabus'd."
POPE.[53]

JULIA was now so far recovered, as to be able to walk across the room with very little help. She could sit up the whole day, without experiencing any inconvenience; and, certain that she could well bear the motion of a carriage, she would no longer have delayed her removal to her father's house, had it not been for the earnest intreaties of Vallaton.

She asked him, with a smile, if any thing was to prevent his seeing her there as frequently as he did in her present situation? "Alas!" returned Vallaton, "I may, indeed, have there the pleasure of beholding you, of hearing the music of your voice; but can I pour out my soul to you in the presence of your father, as I do now in this blessed retirement? Ah! dear-

---

[53] Alexander Pope, *Essay on Man* (1733-34), Epistle 1, line 12.

est Julia, do not so soon deprive me of the exquisite happiness I have of late enjoyed. If you have any regard for me, you will not hesitate to prolong the period of my felicity."

Julia, who was herself too happy in the uninterrupted enjoyment of her lover's conversation to be very solicitous of change, consented to remain for some days longer. Meantime the sky brightened up, the sun again shone forth, the floods abated, and Vallaton on his next visit brought such an account of the dryness of the road, as induced Bridgetina, who was all impatience to learn some tidings of the young physician, to propose walking to her mother's, leaving Vallaton *tête à tête* with Julia, till her return. Her proposal met with no opposition from either of the parties, and she immediately set out.

By incessantly ruminating on her own situation, she had worked her mind into a state of effervescence, whose airy fumes so compleatly filled the light balloon of fancy, that judgment and common-sense (like the adventurous brothers*[54] of aerostatic memory) suffered themselves to be carried along by its wild career.

Full of distinguishing herself by some bold step that should immortalize her fame, she walked on with precipitation, unheedful of every object, careless of every observer; sometimes stopping to make a soliloquy, sometimes trotting along as fast as the shortness of her legs would permit; till, when about half-way to the town, she was stopped by Mrs. Delmond, who was thus far on her road to visit Julia. Mrs. Delmond was surprised by seeing her, and immediately enquired for her daughter. Bridgetina only stayed to say, that she would find Julia very well; and then, careless of Mrs. Delmond's intreaties that she would be so good as to take up her gown, which trailed after her upon the dirty road, she set off with redoubled speed.

A few steps from her mother's door she was met by Mr. Glib. "How d'ye do, citizen Miss?" cried he, as soon as he observed her. "Exerting your energies, I see. That's it! energies do all. Make your legs grow long in a twinkling. Won't then sweep streets with your gown. All owing to this d****d good-for-nothing state of civilization. No short legs in an enlightened society. All the Hottentots tall and strait as May-poles."

'Certainly,' said Bridgetina, bridling, 'if a person of energetic mind chooses to be tall, there is nothing to hinder it; mind, we all know, being despotic over matter; but I see no good in being tall, for my share, and would much rather remain as I am.'

"As you are, Miss?" cried Glib, grinning. "No, no; change your mind, when you get among the Gonoquais. Grand scheme goes bravely on. Four new philosophers agreed to go already. Nothing at our house but preparations. Shut up shop to-morrow. Ship to be freighted soon. Only

---

[54] *Stephen and Joseph Montgolfier* Two brothers who constructed the paper and fabric hot-air balloon used in the first manned flight over Paris on 21 Nov 1783.

want the cash. Philosophers all sadly out at elbows. Depend on you for five hundred."

'Yes,' replied Bridgetina, 'and I hope to bring an acquisition to the party of more real value than fifty times five hundred." She had now reached her mother's door, but finding her not at home, she proceeded without delay to the house of Mr. Sydney.

Maria was at home, and alone; her spirits dejected by parting with her brother, who had ever been the object of her fondest affection—an affection now increased by the stronger ties of tender friendship, unbounded confidence, and exalted esteem. She would willingly have been excused from the painful talk of talking on common topics with such visitors as chance might send her, at a time when her full heart was occupied by its own feelings; but as she had early learned too great a respect for truth to command a domestic to commit a breach of it, she did not assume the privilege of being denied. Nor did she, like some pretenders to sanctity, make amends to herself for the self-denial practised in one instance, by the indulgence of peevishness or ill-humour in another; but repressing her mortification at being thus unseasonably disturbed, she received our heroine, if not with the dissembled smile of pleasure, with the urbanity of real hospitality.

Bridgetina instantly enquired for Henry. When she heard that he had set off early in the morning, she burst into an exclamation of sorrow. "And is he gone?" cried she. "Gone, without one tender adieu? Cruel Henry! why didst thou thus leave me? why deny me the delicious agony of a parting embrace? But thy feelings were too much awakened! thy manly soul struggled with the suffocating sensations of sorrowing sensibility! Tell me, Maria! tell me, I conjure you, every word he said. Did he not murmur at his cruel fate? did he not sigh? did he not appear extremely wretched?"

'If you mean my brother,' said Maria, 'it cannot be doubted that he was very sorry to part with us. He has too much feeling to leave his friends with indifference.'

"Feeling!" cried Bridgetina, "Oh, he is all feeling, all sensibility, and softness, and interesting melancholy. But grieve not for him, Maria; soon shall I soothe his sorrows with the tender assiduity of unsophisticated and affective love; soon will I clasp him to my throbbing bosom; soon—"

'Indeed, Miss Botherim,' said Maria, 'you talk very wildly. I suppose you mean to rally me for my dejection; but indeed, this not the way to increase my spirits.'

"Has your brother then not told you of our loves?"

'Why, my dear Miss Botherim, will you persist in this absurd way of speaking? Indeed it is not kind; my spirits are by no means equal to it.'

"Why will you persist," returned Bridgetina, "in believing me not to be serious? Never was I more so, I do assure you, in my life. Henry was wrong in concealing from you his long and tender attachment; but since upon the formation of our first attachment depends the colour of our future life, happy may you be that existing circumstances led him to such an object. Yes, Maria, rejoice that your brother loves one who glories in returning his tenderness; who, with inexpressible yearnings, pants to convince him of the power he has obtained over her heart."

'For heaven's sake,' cried Maria, 'to what do you allude? To whom is my brother thus attached? How did you come by his confidence?'

"To whom is your brother attached?" repeated Bridgetina; "to whom should he possibly be attached, but to me? Yes; long the fierce consuming fire has flamed in secret; nor till yesterday morning did it get vent in the dear interesting channel of a full explanation. Oh, Maria, how did our souls then mingle! how delicious was the sympathetic tenderness that heaved our throbbing hearts!"

Amazed, yet doubting, Maria stared upon Bridgetina; at length, recovering herself, 'I see, Miss Botherim,' said she gravely, 'you have a mind to amuse yourself by an experiment upon my credulity; but I am not so easily deceived. Believe me, we have had enough of this foolish conversation, and had better change the subject.'

Bridgetina, much offended at a speech which insinuated a doubt of her being the object of Henry's affection, retorted with some warmth; and by a minute detail of the conversation that had taken place the preceding day, laboured to enforce the conviction, while she increased the astonishment of his sister.

In repeating what had been said by Henry, Bridgetina followed the method observed by many worthy people, who, from a benevolent desire of making whatever they recount appear to the best advantage, take the trouble of translating every sentence into their own language, and thus kindly bestow upon their friends their own peculiar turn of expression. So effectually, in the present instance, did Bridgetina pursue this admirable plan, that she made the declaration of Henry appear, even to the prejudiced mind of his sister, as full and unequivocal as it had done to her own. Every word she uttered filled the breast of Maria with an increasing portion of astonishment and dismay.

That Henry, the brother in whom her hopes were fondly centered; he, to whom, in her opinion, belonged all excellence and perfection; whose sentiments were so delicate, whose observation was so penetrating; that *he* should make choice of such a woman as Miss Botherim! It was equal subject of mortification and amazement! Yet when she considered the evident perturbation of his mind, when she recollected how anxiously he had sought for an opportunity of speaking to her unobserved by their father, which many little cross accidents had interposed to prevent; and that he had been forced to depart without an opportunity of communicating to her what seemed to hang so heavy on his mind; the recollection seemed to confirm the truth of the extraordinary tale. Bridgetina proceeded to mention her intention of immediately following Henry to London, and taking out her tablet, desired his address.

"Impossible!" cried Maria, reddening with vexation; "It is impossible you can be so ridiculous as to harbour a thought of following my brother to London."

'I not only think of it,' returned Bridgetina, 'but am determined upon going. You, my dear, who are the child of prejudice and superstition, would, perhaps, startle at the idea of following a lover. You have not strength of mind to devote yourself to that *moral martyrdom* which every female, who enters upon the grand path of true philosophy, must, in this depraved and corrupt state of civilization, be certain to encounter.'

"Indeed, indeed, Miss Botherim, these fine theories do very well to talk about," returned Maria; "but believe me, they were never meant for practice. Think but for a moment on the consequences that must ensue both to yourself and my brother, from persisting in a project so wild—so ridiculous. And I am sure you have too much sense to proceed any farther in a scheme that must bring ruin to you both."

'My scheme,' said Bridgetina, 'is too extensive for any but a mind of great powers to comprehend. It is not bounded by the narrow limits of individual happiness, but extends to embrace the grand object of general utility. Your education has been too confined to enable you to follow an energetic mind in which passions generate powers, and powers generate passions; and powers, passions, and energies, germinate to general usefulness. I see you do not understand this; it is, indeed, beyond the comprehension of a vulgar mind; but when I have more leisure I shall be happy to enter with you into an investigation of the subject. As I know the address of Mrs. Fielding, it is of little consequence whether I have your brother's or not; so good-bye!'

"Do not go, I beseech you," cried Maria, "do not go, dear Miss Botherim, till I talk to you a little further upon this subject. You would not, sure you would not wish to injure the interests of my brother, whose principal dependence is on the friendship of Mrs. Fielding. What would she think of seeing a lady come after him to London? What could she think, that would not be injurious to the honour and character of both?"

"If she be a person of such vulgar prejudices, her opinion is of little consequence,' answered Bridgetina. 'But make yourself easy, Maria, I have for Henry a scheme of happiness in view, which will make the friendship of Mrs. Fielding very immaterial.' So saying, Bridgetina hurried away without listening to any further expostulation, leaving poor Maria a prey to the most harassing perplexity and vexation.

Greatly she now regretted the absence of her father, who had gone to pay a visit to a gentleman in the country, in order to procure from him an introduction to his numerous connections in London in favour of Henry; and as this gentleman's house was ten miles distant from W—, she thought it probable he might not return till the following day. Upon this emergency, she determined to consult her friend Miss Orwell; and if she found that Bridgetina still persisted in her extraordinary plan, resolved to apply to Dr. Orwell himself for his interference; as his voice, she thought, would be effectual for its prevention.

She instantly hurried to the parsonage, where she found Harriet busily employed in preparing baby-linen for the wife of a poor labourer, who had that morning been brought to-bed of twins, and was altogether unprovided for this double demand upon her tiny wardrobe. The other children, whose noisy prattle disturbed the mother's repose, Harriet had brought home with her in the morning, and found their company very efficacious in driving away the troublesome companion—*thought*.

She dismissed her little guests on the entrance of Maria, whose countenance betrayed such symptoms of agitation, that it struck dismay to her inmost soul. She took Maria's hand, and with faltering voice, enquired if any thing had befallen her. "Has your brother—has any accident—Oh! for heaven's sake, speak."

'My brother, I hope, is well,' returned Maria; 'but he has lost himself—has thrown himself away—has—oh! Harriet, how shall I tell you?—he has engaged himself to Miss Botherim.'

"To Miss Botherim!" repeated Harriet, staring wildly upon Maria, whose feelings were now so overcome, that she could no longer refrain from tears, but throwing her arms round her lovely friend, for some time wept in silence on her neck. Harriet, stupified by the information she had received, made no attempt to interrupt her. Yet though tears are sometimes it is said infectious, not one found its way to the eyes of Harriet. She neither moved nor spake, till Maria, her voice half choaked in sobs, exclaimed, "O Harriet! the sister of my heart, how often have I flattered myself that you, you were the object of my brother's love. You, indeed, were formed to make him happy—but Miss Botherim!—O what sorcery has bewitched him?"

Whether it was the extreme tenderness of Maria's accent, as she pronounced these words, that touched some unison in Harriet's heart, or whether it was the words themselves that struck the chords of feeling, we know not; but they produced upon Harriet the instantaneous effect of sympathy. She strained Maria to her bosom, and mingled her tears with hers. After the first emotions of both had a little subsided, Maria proceeded fully to relate what she had learned from Miss Botherim, and by her relation, excited in Harriet feelings still more poignant than those she had herself experienced.

Harriet had indeed still more reason for astonishment: for though Henry had never talked to her of love, he had, by a long series of minute and delicate attentions, given her such unequivocal proofs of his partiality, that she could as soon have entertained doubts of her own existence as of the sincerity of his affection. As Maria proceeded in her narration, a thousand recollected proofs of tenderness rushed upon her mind. She remembered, too, how uneasy he had ever appeared in the presence of Miss Botherim, for whom he seemed to entertain an unconquerable dislike. Could this be affectation? Could it be a mask to conceal his real sentiments from observation? In any other instance Harriet would not have hesitated to have pronounced a firm negative to those unworthy suspicions. But where is the judgment which, under the influence of passion, can coolly exercise its undiminished powers? Where the candour that jealousy cannot bias? Where the firmness that suspicion cannot shake?

> "Such tricks hath strong imagination,
> "That if he would but apprehend some joy,
> "*It* comprehends some tringer of that joy;
> "Or in the night imagining some fear,
> "How easy is a bush supposed a bear?★[55]

The entrance of Dr. Orwell and Marianne, put a stop to the conversation, and restored to Harriet the liberty of ruminating in silence on the strange event, which, in spite of all she had heard, she scarcely knew how to believe.

The Doctor spoke to Miss Sydney of her brother, in whose welfare he took the most sincere and friendly interest. He talked of his journey, of his prospects, of the probability of his success in the capital; and mingled all he said respecting him with such discriminating, yet ardent praise, as would at any other time have kindled the flame of gratitude in the breasts of more than one of his auditors. In the midst of his panegyrick, a loud knock at the door announcing the approach of a visitor, Maria, who was in no spirits for seeing company, would have retired; but before she could get away, Mrs. Botherim hastily entered the room.

Breathless, pale, and trembling, the poor old lady sunk into the chair that was offered her, and hiding her face with the corner of her cloak, she burst into a flood of tears. The sight of age, venerable in itself, is doubly venerable in affliction. The hearts of these amiable young people bowed before it; and each, forgetful of her own particular sorrow, turned her whole attention towards those of the unhappy mother, the cause of whose distress they were at no loss to conjecture.

"Oh! Dr. Orwell," cried she, taking out her handkerchief to wipe away her tears; "you know what it is to be a parent, and will not wonder at what I feel, when I tell you that I have lost my child! Yes, she leaves me! she deserts me! In my old age she forsakes me! She will make my grey hairs go with sorrow to the grave!"

Miss Botherim about to leave you!' said Dr. Orwell in astonishment, 'where is she going? Does she leave you for a husband? If so, you know, my dear madam, it is what parents must lay their accounts with.'

"Oh! it is no such thing as for a husband," returned Mrs. Botherim; "it is for madness, for ruin, for misery! She says as how that young Dr. Sydney and she are going to live among the Hottentots. And Mr Glib is going, and all them there philosophers are going. And this is what at last comes of all her fine learning, and all her argufications out of them there

---

[55] ★Shakespeare, *Midsummer Night's Dream*★, V.i.7.

wise books. To run from her poor mother, and to go a harloting among the Hottentots! Oh! that I should ever live to see it!"

Much as Dr. Orwell was affected by the good lady's distress, at the mention of the Hottentots, he could not help smiling. A scheme so wild was, he thought, in no danger of being put in practice. 'Into what absurdities Mr. Glib or his friends may be led, I know not,' said he; 'but I think I can answer for Dr. Sydney, that his principles are built upon a rock, that gives security for the steadiness of his integrity and discretion.'

"Oh, you know nothing of him at all," returned Mrs. Botherim. "Who would have thought that he had been all this time slily a courting o' my daughter, and 'ticing her to follow him to London, with no other view but to make her his concubine? For she told me to my face they were to live together without being married.[56] Think of this, Dr. Orwell! think what a blow it is to my heart! oh, I shall never survive it."

'Depend upon it, Mrs. Botherim, there is some mistake in this,' rejoined the Doctor. 'That Doctor Sydney should take a fancy to Miss Botherim, as there is no accounting for tastes, is not impossible; but that he should be guilty of the arts of base seduction is so inconsistent with the whole tenor of his conduct, with the manly generosity of his sentiments, with the soundness of his principles, that it is utterly incredible. The best of men, it is true, act not at all times with consistency. By the impulse of sudden passion, all are liable to be sometimes betrayed; but the transient erratic wanderings of a noble mind never reach the confines of baseness. The man who entertains exalted conceptions of the Being to whom he believes himself accountable, is not likely to lose the transcript of his image on his heart, by an act of deliberate perfidy and wickedness. Henry Sydney, I repeat it, is incapable of being the seducer of innocence."

Harriet grasped her father's hand; tears of gratitude and pleasure glistened in her eyes. Her looks spoke more than words could have conveyed, and her approbation of his opinion was by no means indifferent to Doctor Orwell, who knew the generous warmth of her feelings, and highly esteemed the soundness of her judgment.

"How greatly is my brother honored by your esteem, sir," said Maria, with great emotion; "but indeed you do not think more highly of him than he deserves."

'I know not what he deserves,' cried Mrs. Botherim; 'no, not I. If he takes away my daughter, he deserves every thing that's bad; and I should not have thought that any body would have given countenance to such doings. My poor Biddy! little did I think what all her learning was to come to! Seeing my late dear Mr. Botherim consider me as nobody,

---

[56] The shocking suggestion that Bridgetina does not desire marriage is attributed by many to the precedent set by the behaviour of women such as Mary Wollstonecraft and Helen Maria Williams. Amelia Opie sympathetically explores the problems facing women following such actions in her novel *Adeline Mowbray* (1804).

because I was not book-read, I thought I would take care to prevent my daughter's meeting with such disrespect from her husband; and so I encouraged her in doing nothing but reading from morning till night. Proud was I when they told me she was a philosopher; for few women, you know, are philosophers; and so I thought she must surely be wiser than all her sex, and that all the men of sense would be so fond of her! And to be sure she was fit to talk with e'er a judge or an archbishop in the kingdom; and often have I thought, that if some of them great wise men had but heard her—'

"If your daughter have gained the affections of such a man as Henry Sydney," said Dr. Orwell, interrupting her, "you have nothing to regret. In a son-in-law so superior in talents, so unexceptionable in character, any reasonable parent may rejoice."

'I don't say any thing to disparage the young gentleman,' returned Mrs. Botherim; 'no, not I. And though I cannot say that I should much have liked her marrying a dissenter, (seeing that the late dear Mr. Botherim hated that very name o'em) yet I might have been brought to give my consent to their lawful marriage, had he courted her for that purpose; but to think of his 'ticing her to leave her mother's house, without being married at all! I wonder how you can have the conscience to take his part; it is not like a man of your cloth, Doctor; and what I should never have believed of you.'

The Doctor explained, and justified his opinion of young Sydney by many striking instances of noble and virtuous conduct, altogether incompatible with the crime alledged against him, and of which, for these reasons, he persisted in believing him incapable.

'Ah!' cried Mrs. Botherim, shaking her head, 'you don't know what them there presbyterians are capable of. The late dear Mr. Botherim used to say as how they were all as cunning and deceitful as Satan himself; and not one of them would he so much as speak to; no, nor give a farthing to one of their beggars, though in ever so much need of it, because it was encouraging a schism in the church; but the honour of the church was indeed ever next his heart. Poor dear gentleman! hard would it have been upon him, had he but known that he was to fall from his horse at a dissenter's door, and breathe his last in a dissenter's house!'

"And can there, my dear madam, be any stronger argument against the entertainment of such unchristian prejudices, than that which you have now adduced. The behaviour of Mr. Sydney, upon the unhappy occasion you have mentioned, evinced him to be a true disciple of the meek and forgiving JESUS; and from such let not the vile partition of sect or party separate our hearts. The truly religious, the truly good, are children of one family, by whatever names they may be distinguished. They ought, therefore, to love as brethren, to be united in affection; and, instead of harbouring the spirit of animosity, to *bind fast the bond of peace*.[57] But

---

[57] cf. *Ephesians* 4:3 "Endeavouring to keep the unity of the Spirit in the bond of peace."

where is Miss Botherim? I should like to have a little conversation with her, and perhaps may be able from it to procure you satisfaction."

'It was just for that that I came,' replied Mrs. Botherim. 'I wish you to come and speak to her, and try if you can make her listen to reason; for she minds me no more than nothing at all. I may speak, and speak my heart out, all to no purpose; she dumb-founds me in such a way, by talking out of them there wise books, that I know not how to answer her. But you can speak in print like herself. Do, then, good Doctor, come with me, and try to persuade her past this vile notion of going to see them there Hottentots; and if she will have Dr. Sydney, let her be but honestly married, and I won't contradict her. Indeed, I never contradicted her in my life: she knows I did not, and it a'nt time to begin now.'

Dr. Orwell very readily agreed immediately to try the force of his arguments upon Bridgetina, and set out with Mrs. Botherim for her house, entertaining no doubt of his success.

CHAP. X.

"Assaying by his dev'lish arts to reach
"The organs of her fancy—Thence raise
"At least distemper'd, discontented thoughts,
"Vain hopes, vain aims, inordinate desires,
"Blown up with high conceits, ingend'ring pride."
                                            MILTON.[58]

GREATLY to Mrs. Botherim's delight, and not a little to the satisfaction of Dr. Orwell, did they learn, from the servant who opened Mrs. Botherim's door, that Miss, fearful of being too late upon the road, had set out on her return to Miss Delmond. The Doctor had an easy task in convincing the fond mother, that her fears for the misconduct of her daughter were founded in mistake; and having soothed and quieted her mind, by his mild and ever-instructive conversation, he returned to his own house.

Bridgetina, mean time, inflamed by the opposition she had met with from her mother, and alarmed by a hint, that had dropt from her in the heat of argument, of detaining her by force, if reason could not prevail upon her to give up her extraordinary plan, resolved not to lose a moment's time in carrying it into effect. Instead of returning to Julia, she went directly to the house of Mr. Glib, from which she could take the stage-coach the following morning; and having declared her intention to the philosophers, whom she found assembled in the back parlour, intreated their secrecy and assistance.

---

[58] John Milton, *Paradise Lost*, Book iv.

Her resolution was applauded by Mr. Glib in terms of high encomium. 'What! hast left old Poke-about for good and all?' cried he, rubbing his hands with an air of infinite satisfaction. 'Now that is something excellent, indeed. Live with no one one does not like. Love no one but for what is in them. That's it! that's the way to perfectibility! What is it but loving one's own child, or one's own mother, or one's own wife, better than other people's, that obstructs the progress of morals? Leave them all. Let them all shift for themselves.[59] Make them exert their energies. That's it! Bring on the age of reason in a twinkling. Warrant though, the old lady take on at a great rate. Poor soul! knows nothing of philosophy. What is she then good for?'

"Mrs. Botherim, indeed," said Mr. Myope, "has a mind of such limited powers, that she cannot be expected to do much towards general utility; and she has certainly no right to deprive the world of the vast advantages of Miss Botherim's conversation and example; which, nevertheless, must have been in a great measure lost to society, if she had continued to live immured in her house. When such talents as hers are exerted in a wider field, and have the advantage of a happier soil and purer air, who can say how far they may extend, or what distant regions may not be meliorated by their fruits? To the event of Miss Botherim's leaving her mamma may the future Mandarins of China be indebted for their knowledge; and Tartars and Otaheitans, yet unborn, may from it experience, through channels that will never be discovered, an incitement to their virtue."

Bridgetina had too much philanthropy in her nature, not to rejoice in the prospect of being so extensively useful; and pleased with the approbation of minds so congenial, she regarded herself with even more than usual complacency. Having procured a messenger from Mr. Glib's, she dispatched a short note to Julia, informing her "that the urgency of her affairs permitted her not to return to her again, but that she should hear from her as soon as she reached London; and in the mean time begged to have her things from the farm; which, as her mother had sent her three times more than there was the least occasion for, would serve her for some time after she went to town. Hoping that Julia would soon follow her example, she concluded with wishes for her happiness."

The situation of Julia, at the time this note arrived, was by no means an enviable one. The reader will recollect, that we left Mrs. Delmond on the road to the farm, where she soon after arrived. Her voice was heard by Julia, enquiring for her of the farmer, who was clipping the straggling plumage of a yew-tree peacock that grew before her window.

"Hush!" said Julia, (withdrawing her hand from Mr. Vallaton, and gently tapping his shoulder, while her eyes were lighted up with an arch and charming smile) "Here comes my mother, to whom you, I suppose, are quite a stranger."

---

[59] Crude reading of Godwin's *Political Justice*, Bk II, ch. ii, "Of Justice", 170-73.

'Had I not better make my escape?' cried Vallaton.

"Certainly," returned Julia, still smiling ironically; "she must be *vastly* surprised at seeing you here. But as you must now inevitably meet her, you may as well sit still."

'I wish,' cried Vallaton, greatly disordered, 'I wish I could get off.'

"Now, indeed," said Julia, "this is carrying the jest too far." Here Mrs. Delmond entered, and Julia, with a look of infinite satisfaction, rose to receive her. "I can now," said she, holding out her hands, "I can now, you see, receive my dear mamma with proper respect. I cannot yet, indeed, make a handsome curtesy, but Mr. Vallaton here shall make a bow for me; for which I shall bye and bye make him two curtesies in return. What say you to the bargain?"

Vallaton, who, on the entrance of Mrs. Delmond, had made a hasty retreat from the side of Julia to a chair at the further end of the room, made a stiff and formal bow. Mrs. Delmond, with an air still more stiff and embarrassed, coldly returned his salute. —So seldom were the impressions made upon the mind of this sweet lady strong enough to form an index of her countenance, that Julia was thunderstruck on observing displeasure and surprise to be now written upon it in the most legible characters. She took the seat which Vallaton had lately occupied, and remained for a few moments silent. Mortified and perplexed by a behaviour which to her was wholly unaccountable, Julia hesitated on what subject to address her; but longer silence being utterly insupportable, she at length asked, whether she had met Miss Botherim?

'Yes;' returned Mrs. Delmond. Another pause ensued.

"I hope she will come back to tea;" said Julia. "Did she not tell us that she would?" looking to Vallaton.

'I believe so,' said Vallaton; 'yes, she certainly promised, now that I remember. I think that I had better go and meet her. Perhaps, as she is so bad a walker, she may be glad of my assistance.'

Julia bowed her assent; and Vallaton, seemingly rejoicing in the excuse, quickly hurried away.

"Good heavens! my dear mother," cried Julia, as soon as he was out of the room, "how strange you looked upon Mr. Vallaton! What is the matter with you? You seem as if you had never seen him before."

'I never did see him,' returned Mrs. Delmond, 'and very little expected to find him here. He is a sort of person with whom, I am sure, your father would be highly displeased with you for cultivating any acquaintance.'

"My father," repeated Julia, raising up her hands, "displeased with Mr. Vallaton! What does this mean? What has happened, my dear mother, since you were last here, to occasion this change?"

'Since I was last here, child! I really do not understand you.'

"Ah! do not, my dear, dearest mother! for heaven's sake, do not perplex me. Did you not tell me that my father approved of Mr. Vallaton?

that he had promised General Villers to—to give his consent to—Oh! my mother, why do you look so astonished?"

'Why? because I *am* astonished. What had General Villers to do with this man? Or how should your father come to talk of such a person to the General? You seem to me to be quite in a dream. Really, child, I wish you would recollect yourself.'

The heart of Julia sunk within her at this speech. The vermillion tint which had so lately flushed her lovely cheek, making her brilliant eyes still more brilliant, gave place to the pale livery of despair. She could scarcely retain command enough of her voice faintly to say, as she grasped her mother's hand, "Have I indeed been in a dream? Did I not hear of General Villers's visit to my father, and of his introducing—"

'Major Minden as your lover,' said Mrs. Delmond.

"Major Minden!" faintly repeated Julia, her eyes fixed in a ghastly stare. "Then—then, indeed, am I wretched for ever!"

'Indeed, Julia, you are very strange,' said Mrs. Delmond. 'You seemed mightily pleased with his proposal when I first told you of it: you were then all smiles and acquiescence. What now I wonder has made such an alteration in your sentiments? If this Mr. Vallaton were not a married man, I declare I should think that he had got hold of your heart.'

"Is Mr. Vallaton a married man?" said Julia, without being at all conscious of what she said.

'Yes, to be sure,' returned her mother; 'don't you know that he has a wife and five children?'

"I had forgot that," said Julia, with a vacant smile.

'Why, child, what is the matter with you? You appear quite stupified—bless me, how pale you are! are you sick?'

"Yes; very, very sick!" uttered Julia, sinking upon the arm of the sopha, and immediately fainting away.

Her mother, who happily was not subject to violent alarms, quietly went to the kitchen to desire some water. 'Julia is in a fainting fit,' said she to the maid, in the same voice she would have said, Julia has put on her gloves, or Julia wants her slippers; and then, with equal composure, added, 'you had better come to see if you can help her.' The girl stood in no need of the injunction; for no sooner did she hear of her young mistress's having fainted, than forgetful of the respect due to her superior, she sprung past Mrs. Delmond, and was in a moment on her knees by the side of Julia, sprinkling water in her face, and trying all the usual methods of recovery.

Julia at length recovered, but it was to more cruel sufferings than her sickness had occasioned. She at one glance perceived the dreadful consequences of the fatal mistake into which the equivocal expressions of her mother, aided by her own sanguine imagination, had so unfortunately plunged her. Her virgin heart, her plighted vows were given to Vallaton; while her father's promise was passed to the General in favour of a man whom she scarcely recollected to have seen, but whom she was thoroughly convinced it was utterly impossible she should ever love. Thus was she on the eve of one of those cruel persecutions with which so many heroines have been tormented. Often, indeed, had she wondered at having escaped so very common a calamity for such a length of time; and often in imagination had she approved of the spirit with which she was resolved to act upon such an occasion. Already did she behold Major Minden, with the determined and selfish obstinacy of the hateful Solmes,[60] persisting in seizing her reluctant hand; while her father, with all the cruelty of all the Harlowes, attempted to force her to the hateful union. But never, (she resolved) never would she disgrace the principles she had adopted, by a base submission to the will of an arbitrary tyrant. Her fate was cruel, but it was not unexampled. From all that she had read, she had rather cause to esteem herself peculiarly fortunate in being so long exempted from the common misfortune of her sex. Few novels furnished an example of any young woman who had been permitted to attain her nineteenth year, without having been distressed by the addresses of a numberless train of admirers, all equally odious and disagreeable as this Major Minden. Where was the female, possessed of any tolerable share of beauty, who had not been persecuted by a cruel hard-hearted father, in favour of some one of the detested wretches by whom she was beset? Why, then, should she complain? Her sufferings were only such as, in the present depraved state of society, were the inevitable lot of her unhappy sex!

Such were the reflections of Julia, on recovering her recollection. But before she had sufficient time to consider the plan of conduct it would be proper to adopt on this momentous crisis of her fate, she was roused from her reverie by Mrs. Delmond, who peremptorily desired to know, what had occasioned the violence of her emotions? The tone in which the question was put, though it had in reality acquired its emphasis from astonishment and curiosity, appeared to Julia a sufficient indication of the determined exertion of despotic authority; she therefore took care to arm herself against the weapons of tyranny and injustice by an evasive answer.

'The weakness of your spirits!' rejoined Mrs. Delmond, repeating the concluding words of her daughter. 'It is strange that your spirits should be so much weaker, now that your health is almost quite established; and still stranger, that Major Minden should appear so much more disagreeable to you now than at the time I first mentioned him.'

"Major Minden! ah, dearest Madam, have mercy on me, I beseech you, and repeat not his odious name. It is worse than death to me to hear it. No sound was ever half so hateful to my ears! It thrills my inmost soul with horror! Oh wretched, miserable, and unhappy girl that I am! Why was I doomed to survive the late accident? why was I reserved for this much more unhappy fate? Never, surely, was any one so truly unfortunate! Never was the misery of mortal equal to mine!"[61]

---

[60] Solmes is the detested suitor chosen by the heroine's family in Samuel Richardson's *Clarissa* (1748).

[61] Julia now speaks using the jargon and cliches of a persecuted heroine—language presumably imbibed from her novel reading.

'Julia! why Julia, have you lost your senses? I know not for my life what to think, what to make of all this nonsense. I wonder what your father would say, if he were to hear you! But I would advise you to beware of talking in this ridiculous strain to him.'

"And can my father be so determined against me? Can he be so cruel, so hard-hearted to his Julia, as to force her to a hated union with the man she most detests? Will he not be moved by my prayers? Will he not be touched with pity by my distress? Will he behold the misery of his poor unfortunate Julia, without one feeling of compassion? Oh yes, yes; his heart is steeled by the cruel prejudices of society, and I am doomed to add one to the numerous victims of a depraved and unnatural state of civilization!"

'Really, Julia, while you speak such nonsense, you do not deserve an answer. Let me tell you, Miss, your father is too good to you by half, and has compleatly spoiled you by his indulgence.'

"And is my mamma too become the advocate of this detested man? Does she too join in the cruel persecution of her poor unhappy Julia? Oh, my dear mamma, on my knees, if I could, on my knees would I conjure you to spare me—to save me from this cruel, cruel fate."

'Surely,' cried Mrs. Delmond, rising, 'nothing was ever so provokingly absurd as this ridiculous behaviour. I cannot stay to listen to such jargon, which, I suppose, you have learned from Miss Botherim, who has made herself the town-talk with her nonsense.'

"Oh Madam, dear Madam! dear, dear Mamma! do not leave me in displeasure."

'Why should I stay, if you are resolved not listen to any thing I say? I had, indeed, many things to communicate to you, not only concerning Major Minden, but about young Mr. Churchill, from whom we have had a visit. He made a polite offer of his carriage to fetch you home, which your father has accepted. Indeed, if we had known where to procure one, we should have contrived to have had you carried home a week ago, notwithstanding the opinion of Mr. Gubbles; but as the General's family had gone to Brighton races,[62] and are not to return till the end of the week, we knew not where to apply. Mr. Churchill, however, has saved us from all further trouble on this head; and has so pleased your father by his behaviour, that if you really give him the preference to the Major, I do not believe your choice will meet with any opposition. The—'

"Dear Madam, let me—"

'Nay, do not interrupt me; I will hear no more of your nonsense. The chariot will be here to-morrow afternoon about five o'clock, which your father thinks the best time for your removal. He is so much taken up by the thoughts of seeing you, that I do not believe he will get a wink of sleep to-night. Indeed, Julia, you can never shew enough of gratitude to

---

[62] A famous English horse-race track on the south coast.

so good a father, who loves you as his very soul. I shall not say a word to him of your behaviour this evening, as it would only serve to vex him; and I hope to find you in a better frame to-morrow."

Julia again attempted to speak, but Mrs. Delmond, with more firmness than it was usual for her to exert, prevented her reply; and after giving some directions to the servants, departed, not a little dissatisfied with the conduct of her daughter.

Soon as her mother was out of hearing, Julia burst forth into a pathetic exclamation on the hardship of her destiny. Her calamity had now assumed an hydra form; in the shape of Churchill, another persecutor appeared! And though two were a trifling number, to be sure, compared with the *hosts* which disturbed the repose of the Lady Seraphinas and Angelinas, over whose distresses she had shed so many tears, her imagination could even from these have extracted enough of food for terror and alarm, had no such person as Vallaton been in existence. At present, however, it must be confessed, that in the encouragement she had given to that gentleman's addresses; in the interest he had obtained in her affections; and in the utter destruction of the hopes she had been led to entertain of her father's approbation of his suit; she was not without real cause of uneasiness and disquiet.

She bitterly reproached herself, for having been duped by her own ardent imagination into a mistake, which she now perceived she might have seen through on a moment's reflection. But still more bitterly did she bewail those false prejudices which influenced her father's mind; prejudices, which engendered the wish of seeing her united to a man of established character and independent fortune; and which erroneously concluded, that the want of either of these in the object of her choice would be an obstacle to her felicity.

"Unhappy state of civilization!" cried she; "deplored constitutions of society! I am doomed to add to the number of your wretched victims! While things continue in the present miserable situation, fathers will be often led into the fatal error of thinking themselves in some instances wiser than their children! Oh, that I had not been born, till truth had enlightened the world!"

In this manner did Julia continue to deplore herself, till the entrance of Mr. Vallaton; who, having watched the departure of Mrs. Delmond, was no sooner assured of her being out of sight of the house, than he eagerly returned to renew the interesting conversation which her appearance had so unseasonably interrupted.

'In tears, my Julia!' exclaimed her astonished lover: 'What has occasioned your uneasiness? From whence proceed these looks of soft dejection?'

"Ah! Mr. Vallaton, you see before you the most unfortunate of human beings! My cruel father—"

'What of him? Has he forbidden you to see me? Has he been so—"

"Alas! he knows not of your visits; but he has formed the dreadful resolution of uniting me to a man my soul detests!"

'And will you tamely submit to this outrage upon the first principles of justice? Will you, from an immoral and slavish deference to the man who calls himself your father, sacrifice the first rights of humanity—the right of following your own inclination? What magic is there in the name of father, that can sanctify so base a direliction of duty?'

"No, my best, my only friend," cried Julia; "be assured I would sooner die than break the promise I have made to you. My father shall never prevail upon me to do that; but I dread the thoughts of what I have to encounter in braving his displeasure."

'As to your promise,' returned Vallaton, 'you know, that by the principles of our true philosophy, all regard to promises is utterly discarded. In the eye of a philosopher no promise is, or ought to be, binding. All scrupulosity about fulfilling the engagements into which we have entered, is childish and absurd. It is not, therefore, because you have *promised* to be mine, that you ought to become so;★[63] but because by an union with me you can best promote the grand end of life—general utility.'

"Dear, generous Vallaton, how noble are thy sentiments! How charmingly disinterested—how purely virtuous!"

'They are simply the deductions of truth. If the person that is chosen for you by your father, should, upon investigation of his principles, be found more enlightened; if he should be possessed of superior powers; if he should be more capable of energizing; if, as a percipient being, he should be endowed with a keener sensibility of your superior merit; should be able to make a higher estimate of the extraordinary powers of your mind; then it becomes my duty to yield to him, who shall in this case be proved a being of greater moral worth.'

"Ah! Vallaton, where shall the man be found possessed of such an exalted way of thinking as yourself? How mean, compared to yours, would be the selfish sentiments of either of the gentlemen, (for there are two pretenders to my favour) whose addresses are encouraged by my father! But as to them my mind is perfectly made up."

'Why, then, this cruel agitation of your spirits? Why this dismay and apprehension?'

"And would you have me, without dismay, behold the approach of our separation! I go home tomorrow; and long, very long may it be, before we can have an opportunity of seeing each other again."

'And why go home to-morrow, my adored Julia? Why obey the arbitrary mandate of a tyrant father? Why return to the base controul of unjust and usurped authority? Let me at least conjure you to examine the consequences of your return, that so your conduct may be governed by proper motives.'

"Alas! what can I do? what apology can I offer for delay? He knows I am now able to bear a much longer journey."

---

[63] ★See Pol. Jus★ Godwin, *Political Justice*, Bk III, ch. iii, "Of Promises", 216-30.

The eyes of Vallaton sparkled with extacy as, seizing her hand, he eagerly exclaimed, 'Then take that longer journey, my beloved Julia; take it under the protection of a man who prefers you to all your sex, because of your *real, intrinsic,* and *imperishable* excellence; who loves you as virtue personified; and whose love must, of necessity, be lasting as the adamantine foundation on which it stands.'

"Good heavens! Mr. Vallaton, what is it you propose? Elope with you! no more to see my father! Ah, no; it would too surely break his heart. I cannot think of taking so very unjustifiable a step."

'Unjustifiable!' repeated Vallaton; and upon what principles unjustifiable? If, indeed, you can prove your father to be a being of more moral worth, (and that therefore his happiness ought to be promoted in preference to mine) I have nothing further to urge.'

"Alas!" returned Julia, sighing, "how incapable am I of estimating the moral worth of two individuals so opposite in their sentiments, and of characters so totally different. May not both, in their way, be equally estimable?"

'Impossible!' retorted the philosopher; 'utterly impossible. To one of us you must give an immediate and decided preference. Let us be judged by the correct and infallible criterion of philosophy. Consider which of us is most likely to benefit the species by the exertion of powers, and energies, and talents; which of us has the most distinct perception of the nature of happiness, and the clearest views of the progress of mind?—For this alone is virtue.'

"Alas!" said Julia, "my poor father knows nothing of the new philosophy; but notwithstanding his unhappy prejudices, he is one of the worthiest of men."

'How can one, of my lovely Julia's very superior understanding admit of such contradictions? You confess his ignorance, (for one who knows not the new philosophy must, of course, be ignorant) you own him the victim of narrow and illiberal prejudice, and yet you speak of his worth! What is the worth of any being, but as it tends to general utility? In what respect can such a person as your father benefit society? And what is the force of that claim which he pretends to have upon you?'

"Has he then no claims upon his daughter?"

'How can the well-informed, the philosophically-instructed Julia put such a question? Does she not know that the progress of mind— the virtue, the happiness, the perfection of the human race, depends upon abrogating these unnatural and fastidious distinctions, which aristocratical pride and selfishness have interwoven in the constitutions of society? Has it not been to demonstration proved, that the prejudices of *filial duty,* and *family affection, gratitude to benefactors,* and *regard to promises,* are the great barriers to the state of perfect virtue?[64] These

---

[64] Godwin, *Political Justice*, Bk II, ch.2, "Of Justice".

obstacles to perfection it is the glory of philosophy to demolish, and the duty of every person, impressed with a sense of perfectibility, to remove. In the present instance, you, my Julia, are called to the energetic conflict by another motive, which involves a duty of a very serious nature. It is in your power to promote the happiness of an individual, whose talents and virtues may be either called forth "to energise, according to the flower and summit of their nature;" or, blasted by the ravages of passion, and withered by the canker of disappointment, may become lost to the grand purpose of general utility. Oh, Julia, let me beseech you to consider—'

Here the note from Bridgetina was put into the hands of Julia by her maid, and amply repaid Mr. Vallaton for the temporary interruption it had occasioned, by the opportunity it afforded him of reinforcing his arguments from the authority of so illustrious an example.

When Miss Botherim had first intimated her intentions of following Henry to London, the scheme appeared to Julia to be fraught with romantic absurdity, improper, disgraceful, and ridiculous. But now that it was displayed in its proper colours by the eloquence of Vallaton, she perceived in it the grand effort of a noble mind, that rose superior to the vulgar prejudices of an ill-constituted society.

We shall not fatigue our readers by the particulars of the conversation that ensued. Suffice it to say, that the opposition of Julia to the proposal of her eloquent admirer became fainter and fainter; till, convinced by his arguments, or overcome by his persuasion, she finally consented to set an example of moral rectitude, by throwing off the ignoble chains of filial duty, and to contribute her share to the general weal, by promoting the happiness of one of the most zealous of its advocates.

CHAP. XI.

———— "Becoming my critical foe,
"Has declar'd that my stile is *exceedingly low*;
"*That facts are mistated, assertions untrue;*
"*That I give her not half of the praise which is due.*
"But if the said speeches seem not very good,
"I will swear I detail'd them as well as I cou'd."
SIMKIN'S LETTERS.[65]

THE peaceful village of W— was still hushed in the silence of repose, when just as the steeple-clock repeated the hour of four, Citizen Glib gave notice to Bridgetina of the arrival of the stagecoach. She immediately hastened with him to the inn at which it changed horses, and for-

---

[65] Ralph Broome, *Letters from Simkin the Second to his Dear Brother in Wales* (1789), Letter vi, "The Real Simon in Wales to Simkin the Second in London."

tunately found a vacant seat in the heavy-laden vehicle, into which she was helped by the worthy citizen; who, while he pushed her in, gave his usual advice to exert her energies, to which he was adding some other wise instructions, when the coachman smacked his whip, and drove off.

Little was spoken by any of the party during the ensuing stage, but from what passed at breakfast, our heroine discovered so much of her companions, as to learn that two of them were gentlemen of the law, returning from the assizes,[66] and that the third was a farmer or grazier from her own neighbourhood. They all treated her with great civility, but spoke chiefly to each other concerning affairs to which she was a total stranger, so that a considerable time elapsed before she found an opportunity of joining in the conversation. At length, however, she burst upon their astonished senses in an harangue, by which if they were not greatly edified, the fault must have lain in their own stupidity, or rather, perhaps, in those prejudices which rendered them invulnerable to the weapons of truth. In vain did she labour to convince the two lawyers of the inutility of the law, and of the immorality of every species of coercion. In vain did she conjure up all the flowers of rhetoric, to persuade them to give up a profession which she described to be one uniform mass of error and absurdity.

The two lawyers were not a little astonished to hear such a stream of eloquence flow from so unexpected a source. They for some time thought it inexhaustible, but on putting some pertinent queries to the fair orator, they discovered that her eloquence, like the little coach and horses to be seen in the shew-box at the fair, ran always the same round. In vain did they endeavour to make it trace a wider circle; it could neither stop, nor turn, nor go strait forwards, nor move in any other direction than that in which it had at first attracted their curiosity. After exciting it to take two or three rounds over the same ground, they were perfectly satisfied as to the extent of its powers; and in order to give it leisure to run quietly down, they composed themselves to sleep. The honest farmer had resigned himself to Morpheus in the beginning of the debate, so that Bridgetina was left to enjoy the pleasure of her own meditations for the greater part of the journey.

Of all the accumulated evils with which the present unnatural state of civilization is so fully fraught, none is more severely felt by the modern biographer than that facility of communication established throughout all parts of the kingdom; whereby the possibility of adventures upon the road is almost entirely cut off. In former times, an heroine could not travel twenty miles, without encountering so many strange incidents, that the reader no sooner had notice of her having mounted her horse, than his imagination was upon the spur for some great event. Every inn was a

---

[66] A court sitting at intervals in each county of England and Wales to administer the civil and criminal law.

scene of action; and every stage so fruitful of adventures, that the judicious writer had some difficulty in compressing them within the limits of his volume. But now that maids and matrons of every rank and station, from the dame of quality who dashes in her chariot and six, to the simple adventress, who from the top of the heavy coach looks down upon her Grace, all may travel from one end of the kingdom to the other, without let, hindrance, or molestation, an author might as reasonably expect to pick up a purse of gold upon the road as an event worth narrating. It I do not this minute take care, Bridgetina will be at the end of her journey before I finish my digression. Allons, then, my good reader, let us hasten to the inn-door, to be ready to receive her. We are just in time; for here, at the Golden-Cross, you may behold her just alighted.

Impatient as our heroine may be supposed to be to fulfil the great purport of her journey, she found herself so oppressed by fatigue, (this being the first time of her having travelled ten miles from her native village) and so utterly incapable of further exertion, that she resolved to recruit herself by a night's repose. She was, at her own desire, conducted to a bed-chamber, but did not find it so easy a matter to get the bed prepared for her reception. The chambermaid prudently resolving, that if she did not choose to eat supper, it should not be for want of time, left her for a full hour to enjoy the benefit of her own reflections. In vain did she ring her bell; in vain did she poke her head out into the passage, at the sound of every footstep, and repeat to every waiter an account of her distress. No one seemed to trouble themselves about her; and she saw no alternative, but either to pass the night in her chair, or to throw herself on the bed as it was. She preferred the latter; but just as she was laying down, the chambermaid appeared.

"You ought to have known, young woman," said Bridgetina, "that man has not as yet arrived at that degree of perfection that can render him insensible to the languor of fatigue. I do not say that you ought to have returned to make my bed, because you promised, but because what you promised you ought to have performed, whether you had promised it or not."

'I came as soon as I could get away;' replied the girl pertly. 'There is no being in twenty places at a time.'

"What you say is indeed just, in the present state of society;" returned Bridgetina. "No one has as yet been capable of energizing in such an extraordinary degree. But who can say what future improvements may not yet take place? Who can set bounds to the attainments of a perfectible being? Or who, that knowing mind to be as all, and matter to be as nothing, will dare pronounce what is, or what is not, possible to its exertions?"

The girl stared, and on surveying our heroine more minutely, wondered that she had not sooner discovered the proofs that were now so evident of her insanity. Perceiving, however, no symptoms of outrageous phrenzy, she went on with her work, but determined to acquaint her mistress with the discovery she had made.

Bridgetina, perceiving that she had attracted the servant's attention, fatigued as she was, would not lose the favourable opportunity of impressing the mind of a percipient being with the important truths of philosophy. "I see," said she, raising her voice, "I see, by the attention you have given to my discourse, that you are not destitute of moral sensibility. Perhaps, notwithstanding your lowly station, you may, in this house of public reception, have been favoured with an opportunity of listening to the discourses of enlightened men? Perhaps some philosopher, by addressing the common sympathies of our nature, has awakened the dormant powers of your mind. Perhaps the germ of intellect has been aroused. If so, by adding the improvement of to-day with the progress of the day before, you may (though a servant) be no longer destitute of the best characteristics of a rational being."

'You had better get into bed, Ma'am,' said the girl; 'you will be much the better for a night's sleep.'

"Till the progress of mind is further advanced, sleep is, as you say, a necessary restorative to the bodily organs. But if, as I suppose, you have had an opportunity of listening to the deductions of truth, you cannot be ignorant, that the time approaches when sleep shall be no longer necessary. Oh, that to that chain of events, which has been generating from all eternity, some link had been added that would have brought me into the world at a more advanced period! Oh, that I had lived at an aera when one's bones could have borne the jolting of a stage-coach for a hundred miles without being sensible of fatigue! But in the present distempered state of civilization it is impossible to energize so effectually. We are only, as you know, my good girl, perfectible, but not perfect beings. And notwithstanding the illustrious examples, recorded in the annals of some celebrated modern romances, of heroines who have energized in so extraordinary a manner, as after having travelled for hundreds of miles on the hard backs of mules or horses, without either stop or refreshment, to have alighted so little wearied with their journey as to have no occasion for the vulgar restorative of sleep, we may depend upon it such instances are yet but rare."

Bridgetina had no sooner stepped into bed, than the chambermaid hurried to her mistress with the very unwelcome intelligence, that a person of deranged intellects had got possession of one of her apartments.

"Who is she? From whence did she come?" asked the mistress.

'I do not know who she is,' replied the girl; 'but from the manner in which she preachified, I should suppose her to be a Methodist.'

"Oh, if she be Methodist, she will be taken care of," said the mistress, much relieved by this part of the girl's information. "If she does not get so well as to leave us in the morning, I shall inform some of the congregation, and I know that at least they will not let her want."

In the morning, as soon as Bridgetina's bell gave notice of her being awake, the landlady herself attended her; not, however, without the precaution of placing the chambermaid at the door of the apartment, to be ready in case she should find it necessary to call further assistance. The hostess found the young lady up and dressed; and though the extraordinary manner in which her clothes were put on confirmed, in her opinion, the account of the chambermaid, she did not now speak in such a manner as to ratify the suspicion. After answering the civil enquiries of her hostess, she said "she should be glad to have breakfast immediately, as she was impatient to fly to her friends; some of whom she expected would be overwhelmed with rapture at her arrival."

'I know some of your friends very well,' returned the landlady, 'and must needs declare, that let people say of them what they will, I, for my share, have always found them to be very worthy people.'

"Yes," said Bridgetina, "they are, to be sure, the destined long-looked-for saviours of the human race; the expungers of ignorance and error; the eradicators of prejudice; the—"

'Pray, Ma'am, is Mr. Timothy Tottenham of your acquaintance? He, I am told, is a very powerful preacher.'

"I know no preachers;" retorted Bridgetina, with an air of superlative contempt.

Poor lady! (thought the landlady) she is deranged, sure enough. 'You have, you say, Ma'am, some friends in London, whom you now propose to visit; and if I may presume to advise, I think the sooner you put yourself under their care the better."

"I shall, you may depend upon it," replied Bridgetina, "lose no time in accomplishing the great end of my journey. Pray do you know Mrs. Fielding of Hanoversquare? It is through her I must obtain the direction to him who is the object of my journey; with whose mind my soul yearns to mingle its sentiments of congenial purity."

One of the fathers of the congregation, no doubt, thought the landlady. He has evidently touched this poor lady's conscience, by some very awakening discourse; then curtesying to Bridgetina, she took her leave, kindly wishing that the friend she was in search of might speak comfort to her wounded spirit.

Before we accompany Bridgetina to the house of Mrs. Fielding, it is necessary to give the reader a previous introduction to her acquaintance. A variety of methods presents itself for this purpose. We might either, according to the plan we have hitherto pursued, select from the authorities before us the necessary materials, and then give them to the reader of our own good pleasure, without deigning to account for the manner in which the said materials came into our possession; or we might place him in some convenient situation to hear the good lady recount her own history to some female confidante, who, though perhaps for years an inmate of her family, must yet be profoundly ignorant, not only of the incidents of her life, but of her temper and dispositions, the names of her connections, and the rank and situation she has always held in society. As this method has the greatest number of precedents in its favour, we should not hesitate to adopt it, did not another present itself, which, while it indulges the indolence of the writer, will be equally conducive to our purpose of instruction. This is no other than transcribing, for our reader's perusal, a letter written some time previous to the period to which we have brought our history, from Mr. Sydney to his son. For which letter we shall refer the reader to the following chapter.

CHAP. XII.

"I venerate the man whose heart is warm,
"Whose hands are pure, whose doctrine and whose life,
"Coincident, exhibit lucid proof
"That he is honest in the sacred cause.
"To such I render more than mere respect,
"Whose actions say that they respect themselves."
COWPER.[67]

Letter from the Reverend Mr. Sydney to his Son.

"I Can neither be offended nor surprised, my dear Henry, at your expressing a desire to be acquainted with the origin of that friendship which has so long subsisted betwixt me and your benefactress. You have a natural claim upon my confidence, and the terms upon which, from your boyish days, we have lived together, may prove to you how fully I acknowledge it.

"If I have hitherto been more reserved upon this subject than upon any other, it has only been because where the feelings of another were concerned, I did not find myself at equal liberty to be explicit. I detest the affectation of mystery, and think the necessity for secrecy is seldom any other than imaginary. But where silence is no infringement on the duty of sincerity, where it does not interfere with the law of truth, it is a debt due to delicacy, the payment of which is guaranteed by sensibility and honour.

"Without the consent of Mrs. Fielding, therefore, I should have declined a compliance with your request; but it is at her own desire, that I now proceed to give you a sketch of her little history.

"You know the degree of our relationship, which is just near enough to authorise a poor cousin to claim kindred with a rich one, and sufficiently distant to afford the latter an excuse for forgetting the connection. Her father was a clergyman of the church of England, and possessed a very good living, but which was inconsiderable when compared to his expectations. These looked to the first preferments in the church, to which he was so certain of succeeding, that he thought it proper to post-

---

[67] William Cowper, *The Task* (1785), Book II, "The Time-Piece", 372-77.

pone the thoughts of making any provision for his family till they were actually in his possession. The deanery of —, worth fourteen hundred a year, was only withheld from him by the life of an infirm old man, who had long been wasted to a shadow by the severe attacks of a chronic asthma. Nothing could be more precarious than such a tenure of existence, except those air-build speculations upon futurity, whose rapid extinction so often mocks the hopes of man. Two years before the death of this confirmed valetudinary, a fever of a few days carried off his appointed successor, by whose death his only daughter, then in her nineteenth year, was left destitute of all provision, and doomed to undergo the mortifying trials of dependence.

"A few months previous to the death of Mr. Fielding, I had, in consequence of a recommendation from Professor *****, under whose auspices I had finished my studies at the college of Glasgow, been appointed tutor to the sons of Lord Brierston. I had entered the family with no great predilection in favour of such a situation; but in the politeness of his lordship's manners, and in the good dispositions of my pupils, I found a counter-balance to the mortifications which petulent affluence is ever ready to bestow on humble poverty. Lady Brierston, his lordship's second wife, was the widow of an eastern nabob,[68] who had left to her the whole of his immense fortune, which, during the period of her own life, and in case of surviving his lordship, she still reserved in her own disposal. This lady was first-cousin to Mr. Fielding, and to her protection, at the death of her father, was Maria Fielding consigned.

"Never shall the day of her arrival at Brierston be effaced from my memory. Never shall I forget the dignified humility, the modest and graceful propriety with which she answered the unfeeling interrogatories of her haughty kinswoman.

Lady Brierston soon felt, but could not so soon pardon, the superiority of her dependent cousin. From a knowledge of what passed in her own mind, she considered pride as the necessary concomitant of every advantage, natural or acquired; and to mortify this imaginary pride, she concluded to be equally wise and meritorious.

"In the execution of this plan of mortification, her ladyship had abundance of auxiliaries.

"It is the peculiar misfortune of those who move in a certain sphere, to have their worst propensities so flattered as to render it almost impossible for them to escape the snare of self-delusion. The possessors of rank and fortune are every one surrounded by a sort of atmosphere of their own, which not only distorts and obstructs the view of external objects, but which renders it difficult for them to penetrate the motives of their own hearts. Such was the situation of Lady Brierston. As her charity and benevolence, in taking the orphan daughter of her cousin under her pro-

---

[68] Nabobs were men who made their fortune and often reputation in British India.

tection, was the theme of daily praise; she could not doubt that she had exerted a very extraordinary degree of those amiable qualities. And no sooner did she, by a sarcastic sneer at the superior information and extraordinary talents of her cousin, declare the birth of jealousy and envy, than she received such encomiums on her *wisdom* and *prudence* in checking the conceit of a young creature who had been quite spoiled by indulgence, as perfectly satisfied her of the propriety of her conduct.

"When her ladyship formed the resolution of wounding the spirit of her too amiable relation, by attacks upon her supposed vanity, she was ignorant of the character with which she had to deal. The mind of Maria Fielding was too great for the abode of vanity. Her ideas of excellence were too grand, too exalted, to permit her to view her own attainments through any other medium than that of unfeigned humility. She perceived the unkindness of her cousin, and grieved at the proofs of it, as they appeared to bear witness against the heart of one she wished to love; but she was not to be mortified by sneers against learned ladies, while conscious she could make no pretensions to the character of *learned*, or hurt by allusions to that state of poverty to which she had never attached the idea of disgrace, and of which, therefore, she knew not how to be ashamed. In short, the real dignity of Miss Fielding's character rose above every assault; and at last so far conquered even the selfish arrogance of her proud protectress, that she gradually became less assiduous in her efforts to torment her, and finally suffered herself to reap the advantage of those talents which she had so long pretended to despise.

"Miss Fielding was not long an inhabitant of Brierston, till my heart did homage to her virtues. The similarity of our tastes, sentiments, and dispositions, was of itself sufficient to create a sympathy bewixt us, which was perhaps increased by the similarity of our situations. In short, my son, for I feel it painful to dwell upon the subject, our mutual esteem was soon increased to the ardency of a sincere and mutual passion, which, during the two years that we lived under the same roof, was the source of the sweetest pleasure, the most delicious hope, and the most anxious solicitude.

"At length the hour of trial arrived. Lord Brierston, who had for some time entertained suspicions of our attachment, questioned me upon the subject. I had too great an abhorrence of duplicity to deny the justice of his suspicions. He heard my confession in silence, and left me without any expression either of censure or approbation. A week passed without any alteration in the behaviour of his lordship, which was at all times polite, distant, and reserved. At the end of that period he one morning entered my apartment with a look that denoted unusual satisfaction; and desiring his sons to leave the room, told me he was exceedingly pleased at having it in his power effectually to promote my happiness. I need not, to a young man like you, tell how my heart throbbed at this intelligence, or describe with what tumultuous joy it bounded at the idea of being united to the dear object of my affections? For such was the interpretation I gave to the designs of his lordship: nor was I deceived in my conjectures. He told me that from the moment he had perceived the mutual affection that substituted between me and his amiable cousin, he had conceived a plan for our union, which, though it had at first met with some opposition from his lady, was now honoured with her full approbation. It was fully ripe for execution. I had nothing to do but to take orders, and the living of —, worth more than six hundred a year, waited my acceptance, Nor should the cousin of Lady Brierston be suffered to enter into any family as a beggar. Her ladyship had that morning sealed to her a gift of two thousand pounds, which they should both think very well bestowed upon one whose whole character and conduct was so worthy of their esteem. "You make no reply, Mr. Sydney," said his lordship, perceiving the contending emotions that struggled in my breast. "Is there any thing disagreeable to you in my proposal?"

"What reply can I make to generosity so noble—to goodness so unmerited? And yet, forgive me, my Lord; forgive me, if, in the tumult your lordship's unexpected proposal has excited, I am deprived of the power of deciding. Yet why should I hesitate? The moment that makes passion the conqueror of conscience, renders me unworthy of your esteem; unworthy of the affection of her who is dearer to me than every thing but duty."

'I really do not understand you;' returned his Lordship, with apparent pique. 'Your conscience is of a very extraordinary nature, indeed, if it stand betwixt you and a good living.'

"Are there not, my Lord, certain preliminaries necessary to qualify me for that preferment? Am I not by these to declare my solemn assent to explanations and points of doctrine which either I do not understand, or cannot approve?[69] And should I do so with one remaining doubt upon my mind, must I not incur the heavy guilt of perjury?"

'And pray, Mr. Sydney, do you consider yourself as so much wiser and so much better than all the learned and worthy men who every day make the declaration at which you scruple? Are all who enter the church to be considered as perjured?'

"God forbid! Various are the views, which, with equal integrity of intention, may be taken of the same subject. That which I cannot reconcile to myself, another may fully approve. The arguments which carry conviction to my mind, may to his appear nugatory and futile. No honest man will condemn another for differing from him in opinion; but who can approve the hypocrite, who, from views of interest or ambition, makes public profession of opinions which privately he condemns? No; rather let me eat the bread of misery, and drink the tears of affliction, than purchase the enjoyment of every earthly bliss at the expence of sincerity."

---

[69] A living was offered by the patron who originally endowed it after approval by the Bishop. Gordon Rupp explains how "among the richer livings wealth, family influence and patronage prevailed" (*Religion in England 1688-1791*, Clarendon Press: Oxford, 1986, 489). Mr. Sydney is a Dissenter and thus unable to take up the living unless he becomes a member of the Church of England.

"His Lordship, far from being convinced by my arguments, was not a little displeased at my presumption. In daring to think for myself, he thought I had assumed a right to which I had no proper title. His prejudices, from birth, education, and habit, were strong, but his heart was still benevolent. He wished me to overcome scruples he considered as ridiculous; and did not doubt, that upon reflection I would open my eyes to my true interest. He gave me two days for deliberation, at the end of which I was either to be considered as the future husband of Miss Fielding, or take my leave of Brierston, and all that it contained, for ever.

"You, my dear Henry, are yet a stranger (oh! may you long be so) to the wild impetuosity of an extravagant and domineering passion. An union with Miss Fielding had long comprised in it every idea of earthly bliss. Honours I could have spurned; fortune I could have despised; but to reject the chosen mistress of my affections was an effort of virtue to which my feeble soul was hardly equal.

"While his Lordship was conversing with me, Lady Brierston, willing to take to herself as much merit in the affair as possible, had communicated to Miss Fielding the whole scope of the generous plan that had been formed for our future happiness. Judge, then, what must have been her feelings in beholding me; when, instead of the ardent lover, transported into extacy at the blissful prospect that had been opened to him, she beheld a trembling wretch, writhing with the torture of contending emotions, and pale from the agony of despair! I saw how keenly the disappointment pierced her gentle soul. I could not bear the sight, but hastily getting up from table as soon as the cloth was removed, buried myself for the rest of the day in my own apartment.

"To leave me at perfect liberty to pursue my deliberations, his Lordship had sent my pupils on a visit to their grandfather, so that I was master of my own time; but far from being able to employ it in investigation and argument, I supinely yielded to the stupor that had stolen upon my senses, and had not yet found courage to determine in what language to address my patron, when I was roused from my painful lethargy by a message from Miss Fielding. She desired to see me in the library, and thither with trembling steps I instantly attended her. She, too, was in agitation; but it was not the agitation of doubt. An air of heroick fortitude mingled with the native meekness and gentleness that characterised her manners. She held out her hand to me when I entered. 'Noble, excellent Sydney,' said she; 'I have ever thought you worthy of my esteem, and now shall I be for ever exalted in my own for having distinguished your merit. But why, my friend, this perturbation? Is it possible that you can hesitate? Can you entertain a doubt about how you are to proceed? Tell me, I beseech you; to me you may safely intrust the secrets of your soul; you shall find that I am worthy of your confidence.'

"I know not what answer I returned, but it sufficiently betrayed the irresolute state of my mind, and discovered to her how much I stood in need of the support she so generously bestowed.

'Has your reason been convinced?' returned she, with the most unshaken firmness. 'Does GOD and your conscience bear witness that it has? You cannot say so. Ah! then never, with such tremendous witnesses against you, will I be the partner of your bosom. Sooner would I beg my bread with you through the world, than share with you a throne purchased at a price so dear.'

"It would be injustice to this admirable woman, to pretend to give a minute detail of the arguments she adduced to fix my wavering resolution, and to give effect and vigour to my hitherto unshaken principles. Far less can I convey any idea of the dignity and sweetness of her manner, while she endeavoured to soothe the struggling emotions of my troubled soul; and by distant hope to alleviate the pangs of present disappointment. Even at this distance of time I find the subject too much for me. I shall therefore quit it for the present, and renew it in my next letter. Adieu."

Second Letter of Mr. Sydney.

"MY DEAR HENRY,
"You express so much impatience for the remainder of Mrs. Fielding's story, that I can no longer delay to gratify your curiosity.

'You cannot imagine how I could ever enter into any other connection.'

"At your time of life the surprise is natural, and I freely pardon the reproach that is implied in it. When you arrive at my age, your notions of eternal constancy may, perhaps, be somewhat less sanguine. But though the object of a first affection may be lost, and time may so far reconcile us to the loss, as to supply the vacancy by another love, never will the heart become totally indifferent to the first object of its tenderness.

"It is, I suppose, from a consideration of this fact, that women, who are in general much better casuists in these matters than we are, seem to be universally agreed in treating those whom they suspect of having (at however distant a period) once possessed a share in their husband's affections, with hatred, jealousy, and aversion. Not so your excellent mother. Greatly superior to the mean jealousy of little minds, she felt a peculiar complacency for every object that had ever been dear to that faithful husband whose affections she knew to be now her own. But to return to the promised conclusion of my narrative.

"Strengthened by the fortitude of my charming friend, I was enabled calmly to review the arguments that had formerly occurred to my mind upon the subject in question. Every objection remained in full force. They might, perhaps, have been removed to me, as they have been to others, by some new light or satisfactory explanation; but I did not think myself at liberty upon this *peradventure* to stake my integrity and honour.

"In a letter to his lordship I gave such an explanation of my sentiments as I hoped might have proved satisfactory; but I was mistaken. It must be a mind of no common greatness, that can bear to have its intentions thwarted by those on whom it meant to confer obligation, and not take offence. His lordship felt my refusal as ingratitude, and treated my objections as the wild dreams of fanatacism, or the pretended scruples of hypocrisy.

"The censures of his Lady were still more severe; her indignation was unbounded. From her lips I received the dreadful assurance, that the least attempt on my part to see or correspond with Miss Fielding would be the means of sending that young lady destitute into the world, and for ever depriving her of the favour of her present protectors. For the contumely of pride, and the bitterness of reproach, I came prepared to the conference; but this, this was a sentence equally severe and unexpected. I however made no difficulty in engaging my promise never to enter into any clandestine correspondence with Miss Fielding; but the privilege of taking leave of her, either in person or by letter, I would by no means relinquish. Seeing me firm and resolute in my purpose, her Ladyship at length gave her reluctant consent to my writing one letter before I left Brierston, which should be delivered on my departure; but the happiness of seeing her was a blessing which I was destined never more to enjoy.

"On leaving Brierston, I returned to the university of Glasgow, and in the pursuit of science sought to obtain the restoration of tranquillity. My slender finances might have been augmented from the small fund raised by subscription for the support of the sons of our clergy; but I could not in conscience accept of a bounty which was intended for the assistance of the indigent and the helpless. In my learning and talents I found a more worthy resource.

"Under the patronage of the Professors, I formed a class for classical reading, which was chiefly attended by young men of fortune, who wished to facilitate the progress of their knowledge and information.[70] Mr. Campbell was one of my pupils, and it was at this time that strong friendship was cemented, which was only dissolved by his death. My attachment to him would have afforded me a sufficient inducement to accept of his proposal of accompanying him to the Continent, without the prospect of any pecuniary advantage; but with a firmness and generosity peculiar to himself, he peremptorily insisted on my acceptance either of a large salary during our tour, or of a life-annuity at its conclusion; an alternative which had been formerly offered by his guardian to another gentleman. The idea of Maria Fielding rushed upon my mind, and I immediately accepted of the latter, in the fond hopes that it might one day be shared by her who was still mistress of my heart.

"Two years and a half had then elapsed from the period of my leaving Brierston, nor had I in all that tedious space heard one word of intelli-

---

[70] Since sons of Dissenters were denied access by law to Oxford and Cambridge Universities they founded their own institutes of higher learning. Godwin himself attended Hoxton Academy near the Dissenting centre of Norwich.

gence concerning its inhabitants. On the morning we arrived at Dover, happening to run my eye over a London newspaper that lay on the table, my attention was arrested by the following paragraph: 'On Tuesday last was married by special licence, at the house of Lord Brierston, in Piccadilly, Sir William Danvers, bart. to Miss Maria Fielding, cousin to Lady Brierston.' I shall not attempt describing to you my feelings upon this occasion; they were, perhaps, beyond what the disappointment of any earthly hope ought to have inflicted upon a rational being. Of the truth of the intelligence I could not entertain a doubt. Little did I imagine, that information given to the public in this authentic form could be a forgery! Little did I conjecture, that a wanton ebullition of female malice could have produced the wicked and accursed lie; or that a refutation of it was to be given in the next paper. That paper, however, I did not see; for before it reached Dover, a favourable wind had wafted us to the Gallic shore.

"Deep, very deep, was the wound which this intelligence gave to my heart. But, thanks to the goodness of Providence, the wounds of the heart are not by nature intended to be indelible; nor do they ever resist the healing influence of time, except when the will, acted upon by an overheated imagination, resists the salutary assistance of reason. Severe as was the conflict, I struggled not in vain to teach my heart submission to irremediable evil. The time spent in our long tour assisted my endeavours, and an incident which occurred on our way back to England, gave a new turn to my ideas, and presented a new object to my affections.

"On our return from Italy, through the south of France, we happened one day to be detained by accident at a small village, remarkable for the salubrity of its air, and the poverty of its inhabitants. On taking a walk through the village, as I stopped at the door of one of the houses to speak to a poor creature who solicited my charity, I observed a female come out of the house in tears.

'She is dead! said she to a person who met her in the street; the good lady is dead, and I believe the dear creature will die with grief too; it almost breaks my heart to see her.' The other observed, that "it was no wonder the poor young lady should be afflicted; it was very hard to lose both father and mother in a strange country."

"I could no longer forbear enquiring into the circumstances of a case that appeared so interesting, and was informed that the person of whom they spake was a young lady from my own country, who had accompanied her parents to the south of France, which they induced to visit on account of the declining state of the old gentleman's health: that he had died six weeks before; and that his widow and daughter were preparing for their return to England, when the former was seized with a fever, which had that morning put a period to her existence.

"I was so much affected by the idea of the young stranger's situation, that I involuntarily advanced towards the door of her lodgings, but afraid of hurting her feelings by abruptly intruding upon her affliction, I there hesitated. I knew not, indeed, how to proceed. At length recollecting myself, I enquired for her maid. Alas! she had no maid; she had herself been the only attendant of both father and mother. I prevailed upon the woman of the house to carry up a message, informing the fair mourner, that an English gentleman was below and wished to see her. The fond remembrances that rushed upon her mind at this unexpected intelligence, occasioned such a powerful revulsion of feeling as to overcome her senses. The fortitude that had supported her through all the trying scenes of sorrow, now so entirely forsook her, that she fainted away. The woman called to me for help, and I hastily entered the apartment. How striking was the scene that there presented itself to my view! The poor afflicted girl had sunk upon the bed that supported the lifeless body of her mother. Her cheek, pale as that of the corpse, pressed the clay-cold hand of her departed parent, while her snowy arm, thrown over the body, seemed in death to cling to the protectress of her youth. The old woman being too feeble to give any effectual assistance, I took up the lovely creature in my arms, and carried her into the adjoining room, where I had at length the pleasure of seeing her restored to life and recollection.

"Such, Henry, was my first interview with your dear, beloved, and ever-to-be lamented mother! Her gentle, generous, and grateful heart magnified the common exertions of humanity into deeds of extraordinary merit. I could not be unconscious of the interest I had in her affections, or remain insensible to the value of such a treasure. By a sympathy of tastes, views, and sentiments, our hearts were soon so firmly united, that the arrangements for our future life were formed without difficulty. Immediately after our nuptials we retired to my native village, where, having received ordination, I became the pastor of my father's little flock, who I humbly hope will one day witness for me, that my endeavours to promote their temporal and eternal happiness have neither been lukewarm nor ineffectual!

"I need say nothing of our domestic felicity to the dear boy who has at once shared and augmented every pleasure of his parent's heart; but shall only hint to you, that the full value of the home-felt happiness you have hitherto witnessed, will not probably be truly known till a more enlarged knowledge of the world shall enable you to make comparisons. Then, when you behold the misery of family dissensions, the heart-burnings of contention, and all the little gnawing sorrows which opposition of sentiments and difference in opinion create in the generality of houses, you will look back to the cheerful fire-side of your father, and say, with the wise king of Israel, surely, "Better is a dinner of herbs where love is, than a stalled ox and hatred therewith."[71]

"On my return to England, I had forborne to make any enquiry about the supposed Lady Danvers; and the retirement in which we lived, precluded us from the possibility of receiving any intelligence concerning

---

[71] *Proverbs* 15:17.

people who were in every respect so far removed from our own situation. When you were about five years old, I was called to the melancholy office of attending my friend Mr. Campbell in his last illness. I had been absent about a fortnight, when your mother was one day surprised by a carriage driving up to the door. As it was the first that had ever stopt at it, she was thrown into a considerable degree of alarm, and dreaded that something had befallen me, for of a visitor to herself she had not the least idea. A lady begged to see her, who was immediately admitted to the parlour. She at first appeared a little embarrassed; but soon recovered herself, and with a peculiar air of sweetness and affability informed my wife, that she was a near relation, and had formerly been an acquaintance of her husband's, and having been accidentally led to that part of the country, could not resist the inclination she felt of introducing herself to the partner of his affections, and embracing his little family. You soon caught her attention, and the ardour with which she pressed you to her bosom, while tears stole from her eyes, convinced my wife that she had a more than ordinary interest in him from whom you sprung.

"May I," asked my wife, with hesitation, "May I enquire the name of the lady who does my boy so much honour?"

'My name is, I suppose, quite unknown to you, Madam. *You* never, I day say, heard of Maria Fielding?'

"Is it, then, Lady Danvers that I behold?" returned my wife, in astonishment.

'No,' said Miss Fielding, equally astonished at such a supposition, 'my name never has, nor ever will be changed.'

"A mutual explanation immediately took place. I need not tell you, how affecting to both these amiable women such an explanation must necessarily be. Equally noble, and equally generous, the sympathy of their affections served but to endear them to each other. Assured that my absence was still to be prolonged for another fortnight, Miss Fielding frankly accepted of my wife's invitation to remain with her for a few days; and in that time made her the confidante of all that had befallen her since the hour of our separation. When they parted, it was with mutual regret, softened by the promise of punctual correspondence.

"Soon as Miss Fielding's carriage was out of sight, you flew to your mother to shew her a pretty book with which she had presented you, when, at her desire, you had crept up to the carriage to give her another parting kiss. On opening it, a paper dropped out, addressed to *Master Henry Sydney*; it contained two bank-notes for a hundred pounds each, and these words—*An annual gift from the most affectionate of friends to the child of her adoption.* You know the punctuality with which this annuity has ever since been paid, but you do not know the difficulty I made to accept of it, or the delicacy of the methods employed by this generous woman to reconcile me to the thoughts of *my* son's becoming the object of her bounty. We at length compromised the matter; I giving my consent to your receiving the annuity till you had finished your education;

and Mrs. Fielding promising on her part to withdraw it as soon as you were established in a profession.

"I shall now satisfy your curiosity with regard to all that befel Miss Fielding from the period of my leaving Brierston:—

"When I so rashly credited the report of her marriage, I did not sufficiently consider the nature of love in such a breast as that of Maria Fielding's. In a mind like hers, this pure and delicate sentiment exalts the object of its attachment so far above the rest of the human race, that the idea of all that is deserving of esteem, admiration, or affection, becomes associated with its form. Mere passion is in its nature fickle and transitory, but an attachment such as I have described will bid defiance to time; and though it may submit to the control of reason, will, long after all the *passion* with which it was first connected has been obliterated, retain its influence over the breast. The woman who can *suddenly* and *lightly* change the object of her affections, may make what pretensions to sentiment and delicacy she pleases, but is in reality the slave of passions modesty would blush to own.

"Not such was the pure and affectionate heart of Maria Fielding. In vain, after my departure did Lady Brierston load me with epithets of reproach, and endeavour to influence the mind of her cousin in my disfavour. She, with modest firmness, persisted in justifying my conduct, which, she candidly confessed, had not only gained her approbation, but rivetted her esteem. The confession of continued regard for me, was construed by her Ladyship into insolence and ingratitude; it aggravated her harshness, and rendered the capricious petulance of a temper, arrogant by nature, and callous from prosperity, every day more and more intolerable. All this Miss Fielding continued to endure with that christian meekness which blunts the arrows of malignity, and is the only true shield against the insults of the proud, and the sneers of the scornful. Instead of bemoaning the situation that subjected her to the bitterness of dependence, she considered it as an opportunity afforded by Providence for extending her knowledge of the human heart; and exerted herself to improve it into an increasing fund of wisdom and virtue.

> "Happy the mind,
> "That can translate the stubbornness of fortune
> "Into so quiet and so sweet a style!"[72]

"Notwithstanding the contempt which her ladyship affected for the understanding of her cousin, she yet frequently felt herself obliged to yield to its ascendancy. This ascendancy was invariably made use of by Miss Fielding to promote the interests of the humble children of poverty, whose situations she frequently had it in her power to represent in

---

[72] Shakespeare, *As You Like It*. II.i.

such a light as procured for them that relief which may be wrung from unfeeling affluence by addressing its pride, when application would be made in vain to its charity.

"This consideration would, probably, have retained Miss Fielding at Brierston, had not her refusal of the addresses of Sir William Danvers inflamed the resentment of her Ladyship to such a height, as rendered their separation inevitable. She then retired to a small village in the neighbourhood of —, where she was received as a boarder into the family of a respectable farmer.

"Even here she found means of employing her time to the advantage of the little circle by which she was surrounded. By her instructions she improved the young; by her sympathy she consoled the unfortunate; and by her example of unrepining patience, humility, and piety, she edified all who came within the sphere of her observation. To raise a little fund for deeds of charity, she had recourse to her pen; and in this retirement she composed several little treatises, chiefly intended for the benefit of her own sex, and calculated to restore that intellectual vigour which the whole course of their present mode of education tends so effectually to destroy.[73]

"Thus did she, by the exertions of a superior mind, transmute evil into good; and in a situation in which most of her sex would have indulged in a listless and low-spirited despondency, continue to give dignity to herself by the employment of her faculties, while she promoted the virtue and the happiness of others.

"From this place she was recalled by the accounts of the melancholy situation of Lady Brierston. Her Ladyship, now in the second year of her widowhood, had, by a paralytic stroke, entirely lost the use of one side, and was become such an object of compassion, that the delicate nerves of her *friends* were too much shocked to bear the sight of her distress. She was, indeed, no sooner incapable of contributing to the amusement, or flattering the vanity of her former associates, than she found herself deserted and forlorn. Even the formal enquiries by which she was for some time mocked, were by degrees neglected; and she was left, without the consolation of beholding one pitying tear shed over her calamity, to the care of mercenaries, and the comfort of her own reflections.

"In a heart like Miss Fielding's, the sufferings of a fellow-creature never fail to annihilate the feelings of resentment. On the wings of gratitude and affection she flew to the consolation of her former benefactress. She attended her with unceasing assiduity thro' the remaining tedious course of her disorder; bore with unshrinking patience the peevishness of a bad temper, rendered still more irascible by the pressure of disease; and cheerfully complied with all the whims and caprices to which a mind weakened by such a malady is subject.

---

[73] Hamilton herself had "recourse to her pen" writing treatises and novels.

"At length the death of her noble kinswoman released her from this very painful situation, and she was preparing to return to her former retirement; when, very unexpectedly, on examining her Ladyship's will, it was discovered that the assurances she had from every quarter received of having been cut off from all share in her fortune, were without foundation; but that, on the contrary, she was left sole heiress of all her great possessions.

"Of the use she had made of the noble fortune thus bequeathed her, you have heard too much of her deeds of charity to be ignorant. May the prayers for her life that are every day put up from the grateful hearts of the indigent and afflicted, ascend to the throne of the Most High! and long may she continue to bless the world by her example; and to furnish it with a living instance of the efficacy of *fixed* and *steady* principles of virtue!

"Adieu, my dearest Henry. GOD bless you, and make me sensible of the blessing he has in you bestowed on your affectionate father,

H. S."

CHAP. XIII.

"Deep vers'd in books, and shallow in himself."
MILTON.[74]

THE hour of dinner at Mrs. Fielding's had just been reported by the hall clock, as Henry Sydney knocked at the door. He found his patroness in the drawing-room, surrounded by a select party of friends, to all of whom she particularly presented him. Dinner being then announced, the company moved to the parlour, where it was some time before the attention due to her guests permitted Mrs. Fielding to address her young friend. At length she took an opportunity of enquiring whether he had seen the lady from W——, who had that morning enquired for him at her house?

"You greatly astonish me, Madam!" said Henry; "I know of no lady from W ——, nor have I been at my lodgings since twelve o'clock."

'Did the lady leave any message for Doctor Sydney?' enquired Mrs. Fielding.

"No, Madam," answered the servant, "she neither left any message, nor would she give her name; though the second time she called, I told her that as Doctor Sydney was to dine here, she might depend on my punctually delivering either."

'She then called twice.' said Henry. 'How do you know, Mr. Wethersby, that she came from W——?'

---

[74] John Milton, *Paradise Regained*, Book iv.

"She said so herself," returned the butler; and that she need not leave her name, as you, sir, would not fail to discover it by the power of *tender sympathy*."

The confusion of Henry was not a little augmented by observing the universal simper occasioned by these words. Mrs. Fielding herself could scarcely forbear laughing: she, however, would not add to the evident distress of Henry, by giving way to the impulse. The same delicacy did not operate upon Mr. Sardon, the gentleman who sat opposite to Henry, who looking earnestly in his face, exclaimed, "And by the power of tender sympathy Dr. Sydney has discovered it. Oh, a parish-certificate could not have described the fair lady in language more intelligible! But pray, sir, is this the common stile of your visiting-cards in the country."

Henry replied in some vexation, 'that really his question was as unintelligible as the lady's message; he confessed he could comprehend neither the one nor the other.'

"No!" returned Mr. Sardon; "and have you really no sort of guess who the dear creature is? Are there, then, so many from whom you would expect a similar message? What a happy man you are!"

'Upon my honour,' returned Henry, (whose earnestness to clear himself made the affair appear still more ridiculous) 'I declare I have not the least conception of who the lady is—and suppose it will all turn out to be a mere mistake.'

"Poor lady!" cried Mr. Sardon, "she little thought that eight and forty hours of London air could destroy the power of *tender sympathy* so effectually!"

In this manner did Mr. Sardon continue to amuse himself at the expence of Henry, during the time of dinner; just as the desert was put upon the table, a hackney-coach stopped at the door. "Ah," said Mr. Sardon, observing how anxiously Henry listened to the voices in the hall, "I see, Doctor, the tender sympathies are not quite extinguished; they were only dormant—but spring to life at the knock of a hackney-coachman—as I live, here she comes!"

At that moment the voice of Miss Botherim distinctly reached the ears of Henry, who heard her saying to the servant as he offered to conduct her to another room. 'I tell you I will go to him wherever he is, and have no objection to see Mrs. Fielding.' Petrified with astonishment he beheld her enter, when, after making a formal curtsey at the door, she immediately made up to him, saying, 'So, I have found you out at last!' The distress of Henry, as she approached towards him, is not to be described. He involuntarily shrunk from her approach. 'I knew you would be surprised,' said she, in a tone of tenderness; 'you were not prepared for the pleasure of seeing me so soon.'

"The pleasure is indeed very unexpected," said Henry, in great confusion. "Pray is Mrs. Botherim in town?"

'She in town?' cried Bridgetina, 'no, no; but I shall reserve all the interesting particulars of my leaving W— for your private ear, in the mean time pray introduce me to Mrs. Fielding.'

Henry would rather have undertaken a journey to the Antipodes, but perceiving the astonished looks of his patroness, he thought it best to lose no time in announcing to her who Miss Botherim really was.

Mrs. Fielding, whose politeness flowed from a deeper source than the established rules of etiquette, and the fictitious forms of ceremony, received Miss Botherim not only with good-breeding, but with that complacency which is the offspring of good-nature. The very strange appearance of Miss Botherim, the deformity of her person, the fantastic singularity of her dress, rendered more conspicuous by the still stranger singularity of her manners, were to her benevolent heart so many motives to pity, and seemed alike to claim her compassion and protection. The abruptness of her intrusion she attributed to ignorance, and the extraordinary mode of her addressing Henry to simplicity, neither of which were, in her eyes, subjects of ridicule; whose only true province she considered it to be to expose the arrogant pretensions of vanity, and to unmask the insiduous designs of sophistry and deceit. She ordered a chair for Miss Botherim near her own, to the great relief of Henry, who was not a little ashamed of his very unwelcome visitor, whose unexpected appearance he was totally at a loss to explain. The behaviour of Mrs. Fielding gave the ton to her guests, some of whom were very much inclined to indulge their risibility at the appearance of Miss Botherim, till the stile of Mrs. Fielding's reception convinced them of the impropriety of such a behaviour. Mr. Sardon, indeed, could not forbear slily congratulating Henry on his uncommon felicity, and when the ladies retired, he still more unmercifully rallied him upon his enviable conquest.

Bridgetina, whom total want of observation rendered unconscious of any breach of the established forms and customs of society, felt no pain from either bashfulness or embarrassment. She did not wait for an invitation to accompany the ladies to the drawing-room; but bent upon the prosecution of her plans with regard to Henry, she resolved without ceremony to remain at Mrs. Fielding's the rest of the evening.

Mrs. Fielding knew not what to make of her; she was distressed at the poor girl's thus exposing herself to the derision of her guests, but so unwilling to hurt her feelings, that she could not bring herself to wear the appearance of wishing for her departure. The gentleman very soon followed the ladies to the drawing-room, where the circle was enlarged by additional visitors, it being an evening on which Mrs. Fielding was always known to be at home.

Henry was extremely vexed at perceiving Miss Botherim still of the party. Taking care to place himself at as great a distance from her as possible, he entered into immediate conversation with the person next him, avoiding to look the way she was; and though her eyes were fixed upon him from the moment of his entrance, happily for Henry no one could possibly follow their oblique glances to the object on which they darted their most tender beams.

"You are fond of the country, I presume, Madam;" said Mr. Sardon, placing his chair by Bridgetina. "I am greatly mistaken, if you will find the society of London at all congenial to your feelings."

'Why so, sir?'

"Because it is seldom agreeable to a person of refined sensibility."

Bridgetina drew up her head, with a look of much approbation. Mr. Sardon continued: "In shady groves and purling streams there is something so soothing to a susceptible mind, so—"[75]

'A mind of great powers, Sir,' said Bridgetina, bridling and interrupting him, 'is superior to the operation of physical causes. It is in no case to be influenced by surrounding objects. *A person of talents, in the midst of the most crouded street, can give full scope to his imagination.* I make no doubt, you, Sir, who appear to be possessed of no common abilities, have experienced the truth of this. Have you not *laughed, and cried, and entered into nice calculations, and digested sagacious reasonings, and consulted by the aid of memory the books you have read, and projected others for the good of mankind, while taking a walk from Charing-Cross to Hyde-Park Corner;*[76] and done it too as much at your ease as in the middle of your study?

"Really, Madam, I cannot say that I have."

'No! Then I am mistaken in your character.'

"Perhaps," rejoined Mr. Sardon with a smile, "the mistake is mutual; but I should be glad to know from what instance you do me the honour to infer me capable of such compleat abstraction?"

'From no particular instance, but merely because such employment of the mind is common to every man of talents in walking the streets. *The dull man, indeed, goes straight forward; he observes if he meets with any of his acquaintance; he enquires respecting their health and their family; he glances at the shop-windows, and sees shoe-buckes and tea-urns.* But a man of genius observes none of his acquaintance, makes no enquiries respecting their health or their families, looks at no shop-windows, nor sees either buckles or tea-urns, should they be ever so much in his way.'

"Bravo!" cried Mr. Sardon; "What an excellent criterion by which to judge of genius! But did you not say something about laughing and crying?"

'Oh yes,' returned Bridgetina, 'I said the man of talent, in walking the streets, gives full scope to his imagination. He laughs and cries. *Unindebted to the suggestions of surrounding objects, his whole soul is employed. In imagination he declaims or describes; impressed with the deepest sympathy, or elevated to the loftiest rapture.*'[77]

---

[75] cf: Congreve's *Way of the World* (1700) in which Lady Wishfort suggests to Mrs Marwood that they "retire to deserts and solitudes, and feed harmless sheep by groves and purling streams" (V.i.132-34).

[76] *See Godwin's Enquirer* This exchange comes directly from Part I, Essay V, "Of an Early Taste for Reading" (31-32), which details the man of talents' thoughts when walking. See Appendix A.

[77] *See Enquirer* Godwin, *The Enquirer* Part 1, Bk V, 30-34. See Appendix A.

Mr. Sardon was astonished at the fluency of her expression. He began to consider her as a very extraordinary character, and willing to pursue the conversation, expressed himself highly satisfied with her very accurate delineation of the different ways in which a dull man and a man of genius employed themselves while walking the streets. He then begged to know how they were to be distinguished in the country. Here, alas, Bridgetina was soon run aground. She had gone to the very end of her lesson; and was running away from the subject in a very unaccountable manner when it was taken up by a lady near her, who had attentively listened to the conversation.

'I know not how to account for it,' said Mrs. Mortimer, 'but I have generally remarked that men of distinguished talents, who have always resided in the country, seldom deign to be agreeable in conversation; while in town, one daily meets with men of the first-rate abilities, who seem so totally unconscious of their own superiority, that one is neither pained by their reserve, nor mortified by their condescension.'

"You do not consider, my dear Madam," said Mr. Sardon, "that the value of a commodity rises in proportion to its scarcity. The greatest scholar in the parish is too extraordinary a personage to demean himself after a common manner. When he deigns to speak, every word is law, and every sentence the *ipse dixit* of infallibility. And would you expect such a sage as this to descend to chit-chat with a lady?"

'Oh, it is when he *descends*, that he offends me most,' rejoined Mrs. Mortimer. 'I could bear the most pompous display of his learning far better than the arrogance of his stupid and affected reserve, or the conceited air with which he lets himself down to the level of a female understanding.'

"The observation of Mrs. Mortimer (severe as it is) may, perhaps, be often applicable to mere scholars," said Mrs. Fielding; "but I believe it will seldom be found deserved by men of refined taste, or real genius, however remote their situation. The cultivation of taste bestows a polish upon the mind, that seldom fails to form the manners to urbanity; but upon the whole, I must allow, that men of superior talents or information are generally much improved by mutual collision."

'I never mind the learned bears, for my share,' said a young lady who sat by Bridgetina. 'What I detest in the country is, the coterie of censorious old maids, established in every little town, who are everlastingly making their ill-natured remarks upon all that passes.'

"Permit me to rectify your mistake," said Bridgetina; "and to inform you, that the censure of which you complain is the very perfection of human reason; and the persons who exercise it are the enlightened friends of the human race. When laws are abrogated, and governments dissolved, these old maids, whose censures are, from the depraved state of a distempered civilization, rendered unpalatable to a multitude of the present race of mankind, will keep the whole world in a moral dependence upon reason. Nor will old maids be then permitted to make a monopoly of censoriousness. A censure will then be exercised by every individual over the actions of his neighbour; a promptness to enquire into and judge them, will then be universal;★[78] and every man will enjoy the advantage of deriving every possible assistance for correcting and moulding his conduct, by the perspicacity not of a few solitary old maids only, but of all his neighbours. Oh, happy time! Oh, blessed aera of felicity!"

'Oh wise, judicious, and enlightened maidens!' cried Mr. Sardon, 'who have given the world such convincing proofs of the efficacy of censure, as have enabled the philosopher to make an estimate of its value! How greatly are mankind indebted to the accuracy of your observations, and the curious minuteness of your research!'

Though Mr. Sardon spake this in a tone sufficiently ironical, Bridgetina, totally unconscious of the irony, was much delighted with having such a champion to support her; and was taxing her memory for another harangue, when looking up, she observed Henry Sydney slipping out of the room.

"Doctor Sydney, Doctor Sydney," cried she, out of breath with terror and perturbation, "you do not, I hope, intend to go away?"

'I am obliged to go, Madam;' returned Henry, still receding.

"What! leave me without one tender interchange of congenial sentiment! without giving me an opportunity of disburthening my full heart of one of the many thousand, thousand things I had to say!"

'If you leave your address, I shall do myself the honour of waiting on you before you leave town;' said Henry, hastily opening the door, and making his retreat as quickly as possible.

"Before I leave town!" repeated Bridgetina, following him to the head of the stairs. "And is this like your protestations of affection? Is this conduct in unison with the ardour of your declaration of fervid love?"

Henry had reached the first landing-place, but at these words he turned. 'Miss Botherim,' said he rather sternly, 'this is not the first time that you have seemed to make a point of teizing me. I must now, once for all, desire to know what your extraordinary conduct means?'

"Ah! Henry, too charming Henry, it is your conduct that is extraordinary; mine is the natural result of deep investigation, and the true principles of morals. Though you had never disclosed your passion, I should have followed you to town all the same; I—"

'Heavens! Miss Botherim, what is it you mean?' exclaimed Henry, who now saw with horror the mistake into which he had been betrayed. 'You follow me to London, and follow me on pretence of my having disclosed a passion for you! A passion for *you*, Miss Botherim; I really have not patience for any thing so absurd.'

"And can you deny all that you said at our last tender interview at the

---

[78] ★see Pol. Jus Vol. ii★ Godwin, *Political Justice*, Bk VI, ch i, "General Effects of the Political Superintendance of Opinion".

farm? What is become of that charming morbid excess of sensibility and tenderness, with which you then confessed the fervour of your fierce consuming flame? Oh, how greedily I absorbed the delicious poison that flowed from the soft tongue of tender love! Oh!—"

'Miss Botherim, this is really too ridiculous. I well remember when we last met, that I was weak enough to suffer myself to be led into a confession of my attachment, not for you, indeed, but for one with whose sentiments you pretended to be intimately acquainted. It is impossible, utterly impossible that you could apply any thing I then said to yourself. The supposition is too injurious to your understanding. Why then pursue me in this manner? Why persist in tormenting me?'

"And is it, then, not with me that you are in love after all? How can I believe it *compatible with the nature of mind, that so many strong and reiterated efforts have produced no effect?*[79] Is it possible that you can intend to leave me a comfortless, solitary, shivering wanderer, in the dreary wilderness of human society? Ah! cruel Henry!"

'Really, Madam, if you take my advice, you will not long remain in the wilderness of London. You shall have my hearty wishes for your good journey back to the country. Pray shall I now desire Mrs. Fielding's footman to call a coach to take you home to your lodgings?" Without waiting for her permission, he instantly called the footman, and telling him to conduct Miss Botherim into the parlour till he could fetch her a coach, he hurried off in spite of her earnest entreaties to prolong the conference. It was fortunate for Bridgetina that Henry had presence of mind enough to prevent her return to the drawing-room, where she certainly would have done her utmost to expose both herself and him.

She no sooner heard the hall-door shut upon Henry than she threw herself into a chair, and to use her own expression, gave a vent to the high-wrought frenzied emotions of her troubled spirit. She bitterly bemoaned her unparalleled misfortunes, to which she applied every epithet in the vocabulary of sentimental misery, and was still struggling with the full tide of melancholy emotions, when the servant returned with the coach, "Tell Mrs. Fielding," said she to the footman, as he attended her to the coach; "tell her that I shall see her to-morrow, when I will repose my sorrows in her friendly bosom."

'Did you drop your bosom-friend, Ma'am?' said the footman, who thought he had not rightly heard her. 'Give me leave to fetch it.'

"Ah! you cannot fetch him!" said Bridgetina, heaving a deep sigh; "he will not come for you; he is hard and impenetrable as the marble rock; but I shall find a way to soften the obduracy of his flinty heart!"

The footman stood aghast; and when she told the coachman to drive to Charing-Cross, 'Better drive to Bedlam, I think!' exclaimed he;

---

[79] According to Godwin's reasoning about persuasion considered in relation to the doctrine of necessity, Henry should see the necessity of returning Bridgetina's love. See *Political Justice*, Bk IV, ch. viii, "Inferences from the Doctrine of Necessity". See Appendix A.

'for sure I am, many honest souls are put in there that are not half so mad!'

CHAP. XIV.

HENRY Sydney, extremely anxious to exculpate himself to Mrs. Fielding from having any concern in the intrusion of Miss Botherim, impatiently hurried through the business of the morning, and presented himself at Hanover-square before three o'clock.

"Your coming is very apropos," said Mrs. Fielding, "as I was just going to send for you. But, bless me! how very much fatigued you look; from your appearance one might suppose you had not been in bed since I saw you last."

'I must own I have had a sleepless night, though I was in bed the usual time,' replied Henry; 'but as I have, since leaving it, paid my respects to half the governors of the hospital, and been as far as Hackney and Homerton to deliver letters of introduction, my jaded appearance may be well accounted for. I should, indeed, have gone home to dress before I did myself the pleasure of waiting on you, had I not been impatient to make some apology for the extraordinary visit of Miss Botherim.'

"It was on this very account I wished to see you," returned Mrs. Fielding. "She has been with me half the morning, and I must confess has not a little surprised me by what she has communicated."

'I know not what she has communicated to you, Madam,' said Henry; 'but I know I never was more astonished in my life than at her appearance; and, indeed, can neither account for that nor any part of her behaviour in any other way, than by supposing a degree of mental derangement.'

"If it be madness, yet there is method in it," rejoined the lady. "Bizarre as she evidently is, and ridiculous as many of her notions appear to me, I must acknowledge, that if the account she this morning gave me of your conduct be founded in truth, you appear to me to have acted in a very indefensible manner."

'It wounds me to the soul to find that you, Madam, can believe me capable of acting in a reprehensible manner in any instance; but with regard to Miss Botherim I solemnly assure you—'

"I need no assurances as to your intentions, Dr. Sydney; I can readily believe that you never meant any that were serious with regard to Miss Botherim, but I fear—I fear you are not to be so easily acquitted of the crime of amusing yourself with her credulity: a crime, which, however light and trifling it may appear, is in reality the very height of cruelty and injustice."

'Believe me, it is a conduct I have ever reprobated. You, Madam, cannot hold it in more abhorrence than I do. But had I even been inclined to practise it, Miss Botherim is the last woman in the world whom I should have thought of for furnishing amusement in any way.'

"You may certainly think I have no right to catechise you; but you must pardon me for putting you in mind of the last conversation you had with her before you left the country. Am I to believe that what she told me was all her invention?"

Henry coloured, hesitated, took up Mrs. Fielding's work-bag, examined the embroidery, opened, and then drew the strings; opened and drew them again; then hastily throwing it aside, 'I can give you no answer, Ma'am, that will not convict me of folly, credulity, and presumption. Yet as I would rather bear the imputation of weakness, than be thought capable of the conduct Miss Botherim has ascribed to me, I shall frankly confess to you, that I suffered myself to be betrayed by her into a mistake which—which—'

"I perceive that the subject grows painful to you, and should be very sorry to distress you. I shall only, before we call another, beg leave to assure you, that it was not with a view to gratify an idle and impertinent curiosity that I introduced it. I am truly sorry for the dilemma into which you have drawn yourself; and in spite of her folly, cannot help being sorry for the poor girl, who is, indeed, likely to be the greatest sufferer. I hope, however, you have not gone so far as to wound your honour by retracting."

'You, if you please, Madam, shall yourself be judge.—I have scarcely ever met with Miss Botherim since my return to W—, without receiving some obscure hint of her knowledge of the situation of my heart. "The galled deer winces," and I shall not conceal from you, that I could not deny the justice of her suspicions. I frequently met the lovely girl, who ever has, and ever will be the sole object of my affections, in her company. And, though I cautiously endeavoured to conceal my heart-felt preference, found I had not done it so effectually as to escape the penetration of Miss Botherim. I contrived to parry her attacks upon the subject of my passion, till the day before I left W—; when, on hearing of my design of coming to London, she so roundly taxed me with cruelty in leaving one who was deservedly dear to me, in a state of suspence, that she extorted from me an avowal of my love, and a detail of the reasons that had hitherto sealed my lips upon the subject.'

"But how could Miss Botherim take this to herself?"

'As to that, Madam, Miss Botherim alone can tell. Happily, the conversation passed in the presence of a third person, who, I make no doubt, will exculpate me from saying a word to Miss Botherim, that credulity itself could construe into anything beyond bare civility. My weakness, in having been duped into believing her the confidante of a woman of uncommon sense and penetration, it is not such an easy matter to vindicate.'

"That I may not be led into a similar mistake with poor Miss Botherim," said Mrs. Fielding, smiling, "I must beg to know the lady's name who is likely to be the innocent cause of so much mischief."

'Oh, that I could have the honour of introducing her to you, not only by name but in person,' returned Henry. 'Young as she is, and inferior as she may be deemed in point of situation, I glory in the proud certainty that you would in her's acknowledge a kindred mind.'

"The greatest compliment that I have received these twenty years, without doubt;" replied Mrs. Fielding, bowing. "To be thought to have any resemblance to a young man's mistress, is an honour for which I cannot be too grateful. But you have not yet told me who this paragon is."

'Her name is, I believe, unknown to you. She is the rector of W——'s eldest daughter.'

"Daughter to Dr. Orwell?"

'Yes; the same.'

"I remember the Doctor well. He was only in deacon's orders at the time of my father's death, but had for three months done duty as his curate. He was a young man remarkable for piety and learning, and an excellent preacher; is he not?"

'Without appearing to aim at the graces of oratory, he possesses its essentials, and I believe was never heard with indifference. His sermons are of a piece with all his actions; they bear the sterling mark of sound wisdom, unaffected piety, and genuine benevolence.'

"What fortune does he give to his daughter?"

'His private fortune is, I believe, nothing; and his living (in order to avoid all disputes with his parishioners) he put it out of his power to raise. It is little more than three hundred a year; out of which he cannot be supposed to have saved much for his family.'

"And pray, Sir, what right had you to fall in love with any lady without a fortune?"

'Alas! no right. But how is it possible to shield the heart from the admiration of excellence? Conscious, however, that a knowledge of my affection could but serve to involve the object of it as a sharer in my distress, in case I should have the misfortune of passing any considerable length of time unestablished in my profession, I determined to keep the secret locked within my bosom, till a tolerable prospect of success should enable me to reveal it without the imputation of temerity or presumption.'

"Mighty heroick, to be sure! And pray, were your looks and actions equally well guarded as your lips?"

'It is impossible for me to answer for them. In spite of my endeavours, perhaps, it was sometimes impossible to avoid betraying a preference so strongly felt.'

"And so you could play with this poor girl's feelings; to gratify the inclination, or rather the vanity of the moment, you could excite her tenderness by a behaviour which might convince her of your decided partiality; and after having insidiously betrayed the affections of a grateful heart, you can satisfy your conscience, because, forsooth, you never spoke of love! Oh, 'Brutus is an honourable man!' So are ye all—all honourable men!"

Henry looked somewhat embarrassed. After a short pause, he resumed the conversation. 'If I had not preferred her happiness to my own,' said he, 'I should certainly not have left W— without endeavouring to engage her hand. But in my situation, what right had I to do so?'

"Then, my good friend, you had surely no right to behave in such a manner, as to give her reason to believe herself mistress of your affections. Looks and actions are frequently as unequivocal as words. Where they are known, and intended to be so, I do not see why in honour they ought not to be deemed as binding."

'With pleasure should I ratify every engagement mine have ever made; but, alas! far from having any reason to conclude that my attentions have made any impression on her heart, I have now much cause to fear that she will never listen to my vows.'

"Have you ever made the experiment?"

'In the belief that to Miss Botherim she had confessed some sentiments in my favour, (for so, fool that I was, did I construe what fell from that bundle of absurdity) I flew to Harriet, with a full intention of laying open to her my whole heart. She received me with her usual sweetness; but when I would have talked of love, she absolutely refused to hear me, and having called her father, left me with a cold assurance of her continued friendship.'

"And pray, if she had listened to you, what would have been the consequence? Years may elapse, before your profession enables you to maintain a wife in a stile of common decency. If you think of marrying till you are at least in possession of a clear five hundred a year—I cannot help being your relation—but remember, you are no longer to reckon me in the number of your friends."

The solemn and positive manner in which Mrs. Fielding pronounced these words, seemed to prohibit all reply. Henry deeply sighed, and was silent. After a short pause, Mrs. Fielding, resuming her usual tone of affability, again reverted to the subject of Miss Botherim, in which she had not far proceeded, when the entrance of some visitors put a stop to the conversation, and gave Henry an opportunity of retiring. He immediately proceeded to his lodgings, which he entered with a heavy heart. He was so wrapt in thought, that it was a considerable time ere he perceived that two letters lay for him upon the table. One was directed by his sister's hand; with the other he was unacquainted. He gave the preference to the former, precipitately broke the seal, and read as follows.

CHAP. XV.

"Is there in human form that wears a heart,
"A wretch, a villain, lost to love and truth,
"That can with study'd, sly, ensnaring art
"Betray sweet Julia's unsuspecting youth?
"Curse on his perjur'd arts! dissembling, smooth!
"Are honour, virtue, conscience, all exil'd?

"Is there no pity, no relenting ruth,
"Points to the parents, fondling o'er their child,
"Then paints the ruin'd maid, and their distraction wild!"
BURNS.[80]

"*To Henry Sydney, M.D.*

"MY DEAREST BROTHER,

"SURELY the post was this morning much longer coming in than usual. I thought it never would have arrived. The long-wished-for sound of the little urchin's horn no sooner gave notice of his approach, than I threw on my shawl, and flew down to the post-office to demand the expected letter. I might as well have staid at home; for the bag could not be unsealed till the post-master had made an end of dipping. I was almost suffocated with the steams, but there in the little box cribbed from a corner of the tallow-chandler's shop,[81] and dignified with the name of *Post-Office*, did I stand for half an hour, till the master of the ceremonies, begreased from head to foot, appeared. Nasty as he was, I believe I could have kissed him for my letter if he had given it me immediately; but quite insensible to my impatience, there did the wretch stand taking out letter by letter, spelling and putting together the names on every stupid scrawl, till at length, and at the very bottom of the bag, he pulled out your epistle in his dirty paw.

"That's mine!" cried I; "that's my brother's letter!"

'Stay, Miss, till I read the direction;' said he, wiping his spectacles with the most provoking composure. 'To Miss—Miss, Sydney—Sydney; aye, I believe it is your's.'

"I threw down the postage, snatched it from his hand, and hastily ran over the contents. Then, returning to my father, I enjoyed the sweetest of all pleasures—that of talking of the dearest object of my affection to one to whom the subject is no less grateful, no less interesting, than to myself.

"I hope we are not too sanguine with regard to your prospects, when we pronounce them more than tolerable; but upon his subject your father intends to write you more at large; and to him I shall leave the ample discussion of your plans, contenting myself with hearty wishes and ardent prayers for their success.—Happy am I in the heart-felt assurance that it is not in the power of time or absence, of prosperity or adversity, no, not even of that general damper of brotherly affection—a wife, to deprive me of the place I hold in my dearest brother's love.

"Apropos, of a wife. You cannot imagine how I have been alarmed by this strange unaccountable girl, Miss Botherim, who yesterday evening

---

[80] Hamilton modifies Robbie Burns' *The Cotter's Saturday Night* (1786), stanza 10, changing the maiden's name from Jenny to Julia.

[81] A maker or vendor of candles and soap made from refined harder animal fats.

very gravely assured me you had paid your addresses to her. I at first thought she was only in jest, but she continued to insist upon it so seriously, that I confess she made me very uneasy. I went to Harriet Orwell, to consult her upon the subject, and was indeed much relieved by her endearing sympathy. She felt for me as if the case had been her own. Indeed, if you had been her own brother, she could not have been more affected. But what friend must not have felt concern at the thoughts of your throwing yourself away? Forgive me, but I really am not yet quite easy on the subject, and beg you will give me a full explanation of it in your next. I am called down to Harriet, who comes to take me out, so must bid you adieu till to-morrow; when, in the language of novelists, I shall resume my pen.

"I do not wait for to-morrow. I cannot. My heart is too full. And as I know my spirits are at present too much agitated to permit me to sleep, I shall try if by writing I cannot weary them into a state of greater tranquillity.

"O Henry, what a scene have I just now witnessed! Poor Captain Delmond! you may imagine better than I can describe the agony of his soul, when I tell you that he has lost his daughter! Yes, poor Julia is, as I greatly fear, lost to herself and to her friends for ever.

"On going down to Harriet Orwell, I found she wished me to accompany her to the farm to enquire for Julia; we immediately set out, but had not advanced many steps when we were met by Mrs. Gubbles, who informed us that Julia was expected home; and that it was indeed probable she might already have arrived at her father's. We then thought it proper to change our route, and turned down to Capt. Delmond's. The Captain heard our voices in the hall, and sent down old Quinten to beg us to walk up to the dining-room, where we found him sitting in his wheeled chair, giving directions to the servants about placing a new sopha which had been just brought home, intended, as he told us, for the accommodation of Julia. 'The dear girl may, perhaps, be fatigued from her little journey,' said the fond and anxious father; 'and she may here repose herself without depriving us of the pleasure of her company' and then made us walk into his dressing room, which you know looks into a garden; there a field bed had been put up for Julia, to save her the trouble of going up and down stairs; and of that, and all the other little arrangements made for her reception, we were obliged to give our opinion, and highly did we delight him by our approbation. Mrs. Delmond was then out at market; she was to go for Julia after dinner, when the Captain intreated we would return to him, and by our presence add to the pleasure poor Julia could not fail to experience, in returning home after so long and melancholy an absence.

"We did not hesitate to accept of the old gentleman's invitation, and went a little after five o'clock. With the Captain we found young Mr. Churchill, in whose carriage Mrs. Delmond was gone for Julia. He appeared little less interested than the Captain in the return of the fair invalid, and listened with no less assiduity for the signal of her approach. At length Quinten opened the dining-room door with a joyful countenance. "The carriage is coming, sir; I see it; 'tis turned the corner of Job's field, and will be here in a minute." Capt. Delmond was in the middle of a sentence but could not proceed. He clasped his hands and listened, looking towards the window with an earnestness of expectation and pleasure, that it is impossible to describe. The carriage rattled along the pavement. 'They should not drive so quick,' cried the Captain; they will shake the poor girl to pieces.'

"Mr. Churchill flew down stairs, as the carriage drove up to the door. Harriet followed him; I too involuntarily arose, but on a moment's reflection, returned to the Captain, whom I thought it would be cruel in us all to leave, and resumed my seat beside him. The dining-room door was left open, so that we could distinctly hear all that passed below.

"The first sound that reached our ears was the voice of old Quinten, exclaiming in the most melancholy accent, "Good God! what is become of my young mistress? Where is Miss Julia? Why is she not returned?"

"Captain Delmond sunk back in his chair. "Oh! they have deceived me!' cried he, in the most sorrowful voice; 'my dear girl is not well enough to come home. Alas! I see she has been worse—much worse than they ever told me!'

"I would have assured him he was mistaken, but my attention was attracted by the voice of Mrs. Delmond. What she said was too much broken by sobs to be distinctly heard. I trembled with apprehension and anxiety, but could not leave the unhappy father in order to satisfy myself. He pulled the bell again and again, but no one answered. It seemed as if every one was afraid of approaching him; too sure a proof of how unwelcome were the tidings they so much dreaded to announce. At length Quinten appeared; but oh, how altered was the expression of the old man's countenance! When he attempted to speak, his pale lips quivered with a sort of convulsive motion, and the big drops chased each other down his weather-beaten cheeks.

'On your peril let me know the worst!' said Captain Delmond, in a voice scarcely articulate. 'Is Julia ill! Is she dying!'

"Oh, no, thank God! she is not ill; but—but—she is gone off!"

'Gone off! How? Where? With whom?'

"Gone off to London, I suppose," returned Quinten; "with a sweetheart, 'tis most likely. Heavens grant he may be made of true stuff; and then all may be well again, please your Honour, soon."

"Captain Delmond raised his hands and eyes to heaven, and threw himself back into the chair in speechless agony. Quinten proceeded: "Don't let your Honour take it so to heart. Miss is indeed gone off without leave; but what then? If she has done half as well as your lady her mother did, when she ran off with your Honour, no one need pity her."

"Captain Delmond took no notice of what he said; he did not even seem to hear him, but hastily enquired why he did not see his wife?

Quinten then confessed, that his mistress was so ill as to be obliged to be carried into the parlour. Leaving Quinten with his master, I then ran down stairs to enquire after Mrs. Delmond; who, as I entered the front parlour, was just recovering from a violent hysteric fit. She was sensible only for a few minutes, when she relapsed into another more severe, and of longer duration than the former. Had it not been for the judicious and well-directed endeavours of the dear sensible Harriet, I question whether it might not have been nearly fatal. Soon as I beheld her open her eyes, I flew back to Captain Delmond, to inform him of her recovery. 'You are very good, my dear,' he said in a sort of hollow voice; 'you, I hope, will never be the murderer of him who gave you being.'

"Tears now for the first time found their way to the afflicted father's eyes; he wept bitterly. I stood in silence by his side; for what comfort had I to offer him? Could I desire him not to feel the wound that pierced his soul? Could I palliate the offence of her who had fixed the keen dart of anguish in a father's heart? Impossible! The attempt would have been impertinent as vain. I thought it best to let the first strong emotion have free course, and out of respect to his feelings, I after a little time again went down to Mrs. Delmond. While I was on the last stairs, a heavy sigh from the back parlour attracted my attention. I then for the first time recollected Mr. Churchill, and on opening the parlour door, I there found him sitting; his elbows resting upon the table, and his clasped hands supporting his forehead. I stood for a minute before he observed me; and when he looked up, "Mr. Churchill," said I, without seeming to notice his confusion, "in what distress has this rash step of Julia's involved this unhappy family! Poor Captain Delmond! I do not think he will ever get the better of it."

'What a wretch I am,' cried he, 'in such a case to think only of myself! I will go to Captain Delmond. But what can I say to comfort him? Is not Julia gone? Is she not the prey of a villain? Ah! Julia, it is not my happiness alone that thou hast destroyed; thine, thine too, is gone for ever! Heaven knows with what care I should have cherished it. Oh, Miss Sydney, you know not how dear this charming creature was to my heart! For her alone I prized this accession of fortune, that is now become to me a vile thing, of no earthly use. For her—but you will scorn me for this weakness—let me go to her father.' So saying, he passed me, and with slow steps proceeded to the dining room, while I went to Mrs. Delmond.

"I found her better, but she did not speak till after some time, when Quinten came down to beg, that as soon as she was able she might go up stairs to his master.

"What will become of me!" said she; 'oh, Miss Orwell, how shall I meet my poor husband! How shall I tell him the particulars of this sad affair!" She then threw herself on Harriet's neck, and wept in such a manner, that I feared she would have relapsed into another fit. Indeed, I never should have believed that Mrs. Delmond could have felt so strongly on any occasion whatever. But I see there are wounds which the most apathetic must feel; sorrows which touch the bosom of the most insensible.

"We would have had her to go up alone, but she insisted upon our accompanying her. When we entered the dining-room, your friend Churchill, pale and agitated, was leaning on the Captain's chair, in vain endeavouring to conceal the emotion that swelled his heart. Captain Delmond attempted to speak, but his voice was choked, and the words died away upon his lips; he held out his hand to his wife, who bathed it with her tears; we made her sit down beside him; but a considerable time elapsed before either could find utterance to the sensations that oppressed their souls.

"At length Captain Delmond begged to have a minute detail of all the circumstances concerning the event they so much deplored; and Mrs. Delmond, composing herself as much as possible, proceeded to relate, 'that the last time she had been to see Julia, she was surprised to find that fellow Vallaton with her.'

"Vallaton!" exclaimed Capt. Delmond; "Is it then that villain, that infernal villain, who has seduced my child! A married man, too! O distraction!—If there be vengeance in heaven, it will strike him—proceed no further. I cannot bear it. My heart-strings are cracked already." He heaved a convulsive groan, and I actually thought would have instantly expired. We with difficulty prevailed on him to taste of some cordial, which having a little revived him, he desired Mrs. Delmond to proceed.

"She related, that at the time above-mentioned she thought the behaviour of Julia extremely flighty and odd; but that considering Vallaton in the light of a married man, she entertained not the least suspicion of him; though now that she looked back upon all that passed, she wondered at herself for being so very blind. 'But how could I imagine,' cried she, 'that such a girl as Julia, so virtuous, so modest as she has ever been, so far from any forwardness or levity, should yet be capable of such vile wickedness? Oh, that I had died before she saw the light! Little did I think, that she, who was the pride of my heart, should live to become a curse to her that bore her!'

"Here poor Mrs. Delmond was again obliged to stop; and Julia's maid Nancy having come into the room, I took the liberty of hinting to Captain Delmond that the particulars he wanted might be learned of her, without putting Mrs. Delmond to the pain of recital.

"She accordingly was called, and briefly stated, that Mr. Vallaton, (who had, ever since Miss Botherim was with Julia, been her daily visitor) came in a post-chaise at nine that morning, and on stepping out, told her (Nancy) that he was come to fetch Miss Delmond home. He asked it her cloaths were packed? She told him no; for that Mrs. Delmond had informed her Miss was not to be sent for till the afternoon; but that she could put them up in a quarter of an hour. He desired her to make haste, and then went into the parlour to Miss Delmond, who was dressed, and ready for breakfast. She took in the tea-kettle some minutes after, and observed her young mistress in tears. Mr. Vallaton was speaking to her in a low voice, as if soothing her (or, in Nancy's own words, coaxing her) to do something she did not quite approve. She could not distinctly hear all that he said, but the words *general utility, right reason,* and *true philosophy,* frequently met her ear; and once, in answer to something that Julia seemed to urge concerning her father, Mr. Vallaton expressed his wonder that she had not got the better of such *foolish prejudices.* Then turning to Nancy, he again bade her make haste, and put nothing up at present but Miss Delmond's clothes, as every thing else would be sent for afterwards. When all was ready, he took Julia's hand to lead her to the carriage, but she had not advanced many steps, when she grew sick, and was obliged to have hartshorn and water twice before she could proceed; at length Vallaton took her up in his arms, and lifted her in, jumping in after her; he desired Nancy to follow, and they drove off.

"To her great surprise, when they came to the cross, instead of going on to W——, they turned into the London road. Julia then wept violently, and Vallaton, (the villain!) putting his arm round her waist, spoke to her in a low and soothing voice; he spoke in French, so that Nancy knew not what he said.[82] When they arrived at ——, he told Julia she need not leave the carriage, as fresh horses were ready to be put to it immediately, and that he should speak to the landlord to take care of Nancy till the arrival of the stage-coach, when she should be taken back to the farm.

"And is my mistress not to go back to W——?" cried the poor girl, in an agony of grief. "Oh, do not let me leave you, my dear young lady. Pray take me with you; I will attend you wherever you go, and I will go with you to the very world's end, if you will but permit me to serve you."

"Julia leaning over her to Vallaton, who had by this time stepped out of the carriage, 'Do, my good friend,' said she, (while the tears fell from her eyes) 'do permit her to go with us—pray do. I shall want her assistance, and should be glad to have her with me. It would be a comfort to me—indeed it would.'

"I tell you, my love," returned the wretch, "it is impossible; there are a thousand reasons against it. Come," said he, taking the girl's hand, and pulling her out of the carriage, "you only teize your mistress by your prate." Then dragging her into a parlour, he told her she must return to the farm by the stage-coach, and there wait the arrival of Mrs. Delmond, who would take her home in the evening.

'And what am I to say to my mistress!' cried Nancy. "How shall I look her in the face, after what has happened?'

"And what has happened?" returned the wretch fiercely. The rest of his speech was too much above Nancy's comprehension to enable her to detail it with exactness; she only knew it was about *the prejudices of society*, and that he called her master *an old licenced murderer,* and said, that 'it

---

[82] French is used by both Loyalist and conservative writers as the language of deceit and seduction. For example, Jane West in *Tale of the Times* (1799) has the heroine and her lover speak French to confuse the servants as they elope.

was Julia's duty to prefer his happiness to her father's, and that they were going to enlighten the world."—Such was the substance of Nancy's narration, which received many interruptions from the cross questions and bitter exclamations of the heart-wounded parents.

"When she had finished, a silence of some minutes ensued, which was only interrupted by the deep sighs of Mrs. Delmond. The feelings of her husband seemed too acute for utterance; but in his countenance the agony of his soul was pourtrayed in colours stronger than imagination can paint, or it is in the power of words to describe. The recollection is engraven on every fibre of my heart; and when I attempt to sleep, (which I have done for some hours since I began this) the figure of the unhappy father swims before my eyes, and harrows up my soul.

"Mrs. Delmond, though she continued for the most part to weep in silence, could not forbear now and then to utter a reproachful exclamation against the ingratitude of Julia. "Good GOD! that she should suffer herself to become the prey of such a wretch, a low fellow whom nobody knows! a man who is not, perhaps, even in the rank of a gentleman!" These exclamations called forth a fearful burst of passion from the lips of Captain Delmond. 'Let not the villain think he shall escape my vengeance!" cried he, in a voice of frantic rage; 'I shall pursue the base-born scoundrel, I shall make him answer for his villainy! I—'

"The recollection of his own enfeebled and helpless state then rushed upon his mind, and crushed his spirit to despair; he sunk back in his chair and burst into a flood of tears.

"Churchill eagerly seized his hand. "Permit me, sir," cried he, "to pursue the villain, give me your authority, and be assured you shall have a speedy account of him."

'And I too!' cried Quinten, all panting with eagerness. 'Permit me to attend his honour, and old as I am I may be of some service. I shall let him know what it is to call an honest soldier, that fights for his King and country, a licensed murderer. The cowardly thief! the sneaking, smooth-tongued scoundrel! he must have dealt with the devil to bewitch my dear young lady; so wise as she was, and so dutiful!'

"Mr. Churchill again urged his request, and taking the emphatic freeze which Captain Delmond gave his hand for a token of approbation, he flew down stairs, mounted his servant's horse, and ordering him to follow on one from the carriage, he rode off before any plan had been concerted for the conduct of his enterprize. Pray heaven he may not suffer from the generous forwardness of his gallant spirit!

"Oh, Julia, how have you thrown away your happiness! In the affections of Charles Churchill you might have been blessed indeed! But, poor, infatuated girl! what store of misery have you not prepared for yourself? When an awakened conscience tells you what you have inflicted on the authors of your being; when the remembrance of their thousand, thousand tender offices, their fond anxieties, their never-ceasing cares of love, shall tinge with deeper hue your black ingratitude, how must it sting your soul!

"Alas, Henry, while young, we little think—

"How sharper than a serpent's tooth it is,
"To have a thankless child!"[83]

But what shall we say to this sort of philosophy, which builds the fabrick of morals on a direliction of all the principles of natural affection, which cuts the ties of gratitude, and pretends to extend our benevolence by annihilating the sweet bonds of domestic attachment? Should this system prevail,—"Relations dear, and all the charities of father, son, and brother," would soon be no longer known. O for the spear of Ithuriel, whose potent touch made the lurking fiend appear in his proper shape, when, as I suppose, in the form of false philosophy, he attempts to instil into the heart of Mother Eve—

"Distemper'd discontented thoughts,
"Vain hopes, vain aims, inordinate desires,
"Blown up with high conceits engend'ring pride."[84]

"May we, my dear brother, never suffer ourselves to be seduced from the plain path of piety and peace: may the blessing of our heavenly Father knit the bonds of our affection on earth, and at length reunite us a family of love in heaven!

Adieu! Your's, most sincerely,

MARIA SYDNEY."

"P.S. I have just heard that Miss Botherim has likewise gone off to London. Surely, Harry—but it is impossible—you can have no interest in her. Yet I cannot help being very much disturbed by this intelligence. For heaven's sake, write immediately. I hope in GOD you can clear yourself; if not, O Harry, how miserable! but I cannot, will not suppose it. Poor Mrs. Botherim is quite beside herself. Captain Delmond too is, I hear to-day very ill. The gout is flown to his stomach, and the symptoms appear dangerous. Should he die, what must be the feelings of Julia! Your father will write to-morrow. He and Dr. Orwell have both been with Captain Delmond all the morning.—Once more adieu!"

Henry did not read his sister's letter without experiencing a considerable degree of emotion. Hoping the other might give him some further infor-

---

[83] Shakespeare, *King Lear*, I.iv.312.
[84] Milton, *Paradise Lost*, Book iv.

mation on the subject that had employed his sister's pen, he hastily opened it, and casting his eye to the end, saw the name of Bridgetina Botherim. He pronounced an emphatic pbob! and threw it down; but recollecting that she might possibly know something of the elopement of Julia, in whose fate he was most sincerely interested, he again took it up, and read as follows:

"YOU tell me I have no share in your affection. You even hint that you love another; but you are mistaken if you think this makes any alteration in the decided part I have taken. No:—I have reasoned, I have investigated, I have philosophised upon the subject; and am more than ever determined to persevere in my attacks upon your heart. The desire of being beloved, of inspiring sympathy, is congenial to the human mind. I will inspire sympathy; nor can I believe it compatible with the nature of mind, that so many strong and reiterated efforts should be made in vain. *Man does right in pursuing interest and pleasure. It argues no depravity. This is the fable of superstition.*★[85] My interest, my pleasure, is all centered in your affections; therefore I will pursue you, nor shall I give over the pursuit, say what you will. I know the power of argument, and that in the end the force of reason must prevail. Why should I despair of arguing you into love? Do I want energy? Am I deficient in eloquence?—No. On you, therefore, beloved and ah! too cruel Henry, on you shall all my energy and all my eloquence be exerted; and I make no doubt that in the end my perseverance shall be crowned with success. It is your mind I wish to conquer, and mind must yield to mind. Can the mind of my rival be compared with mine? Can she energize as I do? Does she discuss? Does she argue? Does she investigate with my powers? You cannot say so; and therefore it plainly follows she is less worthy of your love.

"The apprehension of embarrassment with regard to fortune may be another obstacle that you may haply start. But this, likewise, I can obviate. Read the inclosed; and you will perceive that there is a scheme on foot, which will accellerate the progress of happiness and philosophy through the remotest regions of the habitable globe. Fly this dismal, dirty hogstye of depraved and corrupt civilization; and let us join ourselves to the enlightened race, who already possess all those essentials which philosophy teaches us to expect in the full meridian of the Age of Reason. Let us, my Henry, in the bosom of this happy people, who worship no God, who are free from the restraint of laws and forms of government, enjoy the blessings of equality and love. You will not then need to 'look blank and disconsolate when you hear of the health of your friends.' 'Pain, sickness, and anguish, will not then be your harvest;' nor will you then, as now, 'rejoice to hear that they have fallen on any of your acquaintance.'★[86] There are no physicians among the Hottentots.—There you shall enjoy

---

[85] ★See *Emma Courtney*★ (116). See Appendix A.
[86] ★See the Characteristics of a Physician, in the Enquirer.★ Godwin explains that since "pain, sickness and anguish" are the physician's "harvest" he "rejoices to hear that they have fallen upon any of his acquaintance. He looks blank and disconsolate, when all men are at their ease" *The Enquirer*, Part II, Essay V, "Of Trades and Professions", 227. See Appendix A.

the blessing of leisure; and the powers of your mind, not blunted by application to any particular science, shall germinate into general usefulness. Oh, happy time! and in that time happy, thrice happy, shall be your
"BRIDGETINA BOTHERIM."

END OF THE SECOND VOLUME.

Vol. III.

CHAP. I.

—"His speech was an excellent piece
"Of patch-work, with shreds brought from Rome and from Greece;
"But should poets and orators try him for theft,
"Like the jackdaw of old—would a feather be left?"
                                           SIMKIN'S LETTERS.[1]

THE admirable epistle of our thrice-admirable heroine, with which we thought it proper to conclude the last chapter, was left by her at Henry's lodgings, on her way to Mrs. Fielding's. On her return from Hanover-square, she, in pursuance of her adopted plan, went to look for lodgings in the same street in which Henry had taken up his abode. Her attempt was unsuccessful.

Not a house in George's-street would receive her.

Her attack upon the heart of Henry was from this unfavourable circumstance prevented from being turned into a blockade; but still she resolved to carry on the siege; and happily for her purposes, on turning by chance into Conduit-street, she found a lodging exactly suited to her wishes. She fixed upon the first-floor, and asked the price.

"Two guineas a week, Ma'am, is the very lowest at which these lodgings were ever let."

'Two guineas a week!' cried Bridgetina, in astonishment. 'What! a hundred and four guineas a-year for two paltry rooms. You must be mistaken, good woman; I shall convince you that you are. In my mother's house at W—, for which she pays no more than twenty pounds a-year, there are seven better rooms than these! Do not think I am to be so easily imposed upon.'

"If you can suit yourself cheaper elsewhere, I have no objection, Ma'am," returned the mistress of the house, drily; "but I believe," added she, "you will find few such lodgings at the price (considering the situation) in London."

The situation was indeed desirable; not that Bridgetina would in itself have considered it as preferable to Hound's-ditch, or even to any of the noble avenues of Wapping; but its being in the vicinity of Henry gave it a value beyond all price. Finding it in vain to argue the good woman out of any part of her demand, she closed with her terms, and told her she should take immediate possession of the apartments. Mrs. Benton curtseyed, and after a little modest hesitation, informed Miss Botherim, that she made it a rule never to take any lodger without a reference for their character to some person of respectability.

"Mrs. Benton, for that I think is your name, I perceive you are a very

---

[1] Ralph Broome, *Letters from Simkin the Second to his Dear Brother in Wales* (1789), Letter VII, "The Real Simon in Wales to Simpkin the Second in London."

unenlightened person," said Bridgetina. "A regard to the character of any individual is one of the immoral prejudices of a distempered state of civilization. I shall soon instruct you better; and out of the choice writings of the most illustrious modern philosophers, convince you that there is no notion more erroneous than the false prejudice entertained against certain persons of *great powers*, who have happened to energize in a direction vulgarly called vicious. I, for my part, think it one of the peculiar advantages of this great metropolis, that it happily affords to the philosopher an opportunity of cultivating an intimacy with liberal-minded persons of this description; and shall be much obliged to you for an introduction to any heroine who has nobly sacrificed the bauble—reputation. Pray have you any acquaintance in this line?"[2]

Mrs. Benton stared—'I really do not understand you, Ma'am. My acquaintances are all people of unspotted reputation. Nor, though my lodgings should stand empty throughout the year, would I admit any person of suspected character into my house. I do not mean to insinuate any reflection upon you, Ma'am; but you are a stranger to me, and therefore I must again request a reference.'

"You are really strangely invulnerable to argument; but I hope I shall in time convince you of your mistake. Meanwhile you may apply to Mrs. Fielding, in Hanover-square, the only person I have yet visited in London; and as she is as much the slave of prejudice as yourself, her testimony will, I dare say, please you."

'Oh, Ma'am, if you visit Mrs. Fielding, I am more than satisfied. To be honoured with her acquaintance is a sufficient recommendation to me. She is the best, the most generous of women! To her goodness I am indebted for every comfort that I now enjoy. I should be base, indeed, if I did not with gratitude acknowledge that she has been the saviour of me and mine."

"Gratitude is a mistaken notion, Mrs. Benton; and if you feel any extraordinary regard towards Mrs. Fielding, on account of her being your benefactress, you act in direct opposition to the principles of justice and virtue."

'What! Not feel gratitude to my benefactress! Not feel a regard for her who rescued my husband from a prison! Who, like a ministering angel, brought relief to our extreme necessity! Who saved my babes from perishing, and has put us in a situation to earn our bread with comfort and with credit! O, if ever I cease to bless her, may tenfold misery be my portion!'

"I perceive you have imbibed all the pernicious prejudices of superstition; but notwithstanding your mistaken notions, I dare say you are a good sort of woman at bottom; and so I shall tell Mrs. Fielding, when I go to breakfast with her to-morrow morning."

Mrs. Benton curtseyed; and Bridgetina, desiring a coach to be called, stepped into it, and drove to the Golden-Cross for her things. Having paid her bill, and counted her remaining stock of cash, she found there

---

[2] A reference to women such as Mary Hays and Mary Wollstonecraft.

was only one guinea[3] and a half left; which having restored to her purse, she returned to Conduit-street, where she found her apartment diligently prepared by Mrs. Benton for her reception.

As she had not given any orders about dinner, Mrs. Benton naturally concluded it was her intention to dine abroad; while Bridgetina, never accustomed to pay any attention to the affairs of life, and ignorant of all the manners and habits of society, had taken it for granted that food was to be included with her lodging. At five o'clock, finding she could energize no longer, she pulled the bell, to enquire whether dinner was ready.

'Dinner! Ma'am?' said the maid-servant who attended her; 'I did not know that you were to have any. I received no directions to make market for you.'

"No!" returned Bridgetina; "I perceive, then, that your mistress has conceived too exalted an idea of my *powers*. In the present state of society, no one's energies can be so effectually exerted as to elude the physical necessity of eating. I therefore desire to have my dinner immediately."

The demand which followed for money to go to market, brought on an explanation by no means agreeable to Bridgetina, and which very little suited the state of her finances. After a learned expostulation on the part of our heroine, and a plain statement on that of Mrs. Benton, it was finally settled, that the maid should hereafter make provision for Bridgetina's meals; which were to be fixed to no regular hour, but taken *philosophically*,★[4] at what time the energies of her stomach required it.

"You will say it is more convenient for you, that I should dine at your table," said Miss Botherim; "and probably quote the example of the Spartans, who, by a law of the immortal Lycurgus, were obliged to common meals.[5] But when the progress of mind shall have carried us further on the road to perfection, all co-operation in butchery, in cookery, or in eating, shall be at an end. If, at that happy period, the animal œconomy should still continue (notwithstanding the advanced state of society) to demand a supply of food, every man will then, when he is hungry, knock down an ox for himself, and cutting out his own steak, will dress and devour it at the time and place best suited to his avocation and circumstances. Do you think the Gonoquais sit down to table, as we do? No, no; social meals (as they are vulgarly called) are an interruption to the sublime flights of genius, and ought to be discountenanced by every true philosopher."

---

[3] An English coin, not coined since 1813, first struck in 1663 with the nominal value of 20 shillings, but from 1717 until its disappearance circulating as legal tender at the rate of 21 shillings.

[4] ★See Pol. Jus. vol.ii. p.492★ *Political Justice*, Bk VIII, ch. VIII, "Objection to this System from the Inflexibility of its Restrictions", 756, 758.

[5] Reference to Lycurgus the Spartan, as mentioned in Godwin, *Political Justice*, Bk V, Ch. xv 497-98.

In this manner did Bridgetina endeavour to enlighten her humble and modest auditor; whose silence she interpreted into profound admiration of her extraordinary powers of eloquence, and on whose mind she firmly believed every word she spoke made a deep and lasting impression.

On the following morning, according to appointment, she attended Mrs. Fielding at breakfast; when, to her great mortification, instead of meeting with Henry, as she had fully expected, she received from his respectable friend a very warm expostulation on the impropriety of her conduct; which, though delivered with all possible gentleness of voice and manner, kindled in her mind the flame of deep resentment.

In vain did Mrs. Fielding endeavour to persuade her to return to W——. In vain did she urge the duty she owed her aged mother; the risque she ran of exposing her character to reproach, and her name to ridicule, by persisting in a conduct so utterly inconsistent with the laws of delicacy and decorum. Bridgetina was like the deaf adder, 'which refuseth to hear the voice of the charmer, charm he never so wisely,'[6] Mrs. Fielding was the slave of prejudice; her mind was fettered by superstition; her morals were built upon the false structure of religious principle. She looked to a future world for that state of compleat order, happiness, and perfection, which she weakly believed would never be found in this. She was not enlightened enough to conceive how the progress of mind could be accellerated by casting off all dependance on a Supreme Being, by contemning his power, or denying his existence; but on the contrary, adored his goodness, revered his wisdom, and firmly believed in his revelation. How, then, could she fail to be the scorn of our deep and enlightened philosopher! In truth, Bridgetina felt for her understanding the most sovereign contempt; and after an harangue, which had too little of novelty in it to afford the reader any amusement, she took her leave of the weak and prejudiced Mrs. Fielding, fully resolved never more to honour a person so full of prejudices with her confidence.

Her next attempt was to obtain a conference with Henry. She was informed by his servant that he was not at home. Leaving her address, and desiring the man to tell his master that she should be at home all the evening, she stepped into a hackney-coach,[7] and drove to the house of Sir Anthony Aldgate, in Mincing-lane.

Here, also, her evil stars seemed to preponderate. The knight, his lady, and daughter, were on a visit to Mr. Deputy Griskin, at his villa at Bow-Bridge, and were not expected home till the latter end of the week. This was very unwelcome intelligence to Bridgetina. Sir Anthony had been by her father's will appointed trustee for her fortune, which consisted of four thousand pounds stock in the four per cents. the whole of which was to continue under his management till the day

---

[6] *Psalms* 58: 4-5: "the deaf adder stoppeth her ears, and will not harken to the voice of the charmer, charm he never so wisely."

[7] A four-wheeled coach, drawn by two horses, and seated for six persons, kept for hire.

of Bridgetina's marriage; with power, however, to sell, or change the security, (with her consent) as might appear most eligible.

It was her intention to raise an immediate supply of five hundred pounds for her own expences; and to put five hundred more into the hands of Mr. Vallaton, as treasurer for the Gonoquais emigrants, with a promise of doubling the sum, should the subscription of the philosophers appear inadequate to the expences of the expedition.

Great was her vexation at the delay occasioned by Sir Anthony's absence, which not only protracted the glory she expected to reap from the applauses of the enlightened, but reduced her to the mortification of remaining for several days with an empty purse. O cheerless companion of philosophy! too well do we know the torpedo effects of thy chilling aspect: too often have we experienced the sickening languor which the contemplation of thy long, lank sides occasions, to refuse our sympathy to the luckless wight who has thee for a guest! Thy casual appearance is a trifling evil, but where thy form is permanent, thou art

"Abominable, unutterable, and worse
"Than fables yet have feign'd, or fear conceiv'd,
"*Gorgons*, and *Hydras*, and *Chimeras* dire."[8]

In all the calamities to which life is liable, there is no comfort equal to that which arises from being able to fix the blame upon that which has occasioned, or is supposed to have occasioned it. In the opinion of many wise men, it is one of the chief advantages of matrimony, that in every cross accident, a constant resource of this nature is provided for in the helpmate of the party aggrieved. Even the vexation arising from the loss of a game at cards is considerably alleviated by the privilege of finding fault with the play of a partner; so to Bridgetina was it no small consolation, that in her present perplexity she could relieve her mind by bitter invectives against the *distempered state of civilization*. Had it not been for the present depraved institutions of society, her father would not have had it in his power to make a will. She would not then have been fettered by the impertinent interference of this trustee; who had, indeed, by his management during her minority, considerably increased the capital of her little fortune, and thus, by adding to the wealth of an individual, had sinned against the glorious system of equality.

Her soliloquies upon this subject were not interrupted by any visitor. Henry did not appear; neither did he send any answer to her letter. She again wrote, but to no purpose. She repeatedly called at his lodgings, but still he was not at home. Another letter, conjuring him to enter into her arguments, and either reply to them on paper, or come to reason the subject with her in a personal interview, met with no better success than the former. Henry remained inexorable.

---

[8] Milton, *Paradise Lost*, Bk 1, 626.

Mrs. Fielding had, at his request, informed Bridgetina, that as it was impossible for him to answer her but in a way that must appear harsh and disagreeable, he begged leave to decline writing. In musing on this subject, and investigating in her usual method the motives of Henry, and the conduct of his patroness, it all at once occurred to her that Mrs. Fielding herself was the object of Henry's pursuit; and that it was in order to get rid of a rival, that that lady had so strongly pressed her return to the country. The longer her imagination dwelt upon all the circumstances which had occurred, the more strongly was she impressed with the truth of her suspicions. The glaring disparity in point of age was in her mind no obstacle, neither did she make any account of that nice propriety of sentiment and of conduct which marked the character of Mrs. Fielding, and rendered her eminently superior to the suspicion of weakness or absurdity. That she was attached to Henry, she thought was evident; and that she should wish to marry him was not (in her opinion) at all extraordinary. She therefore determined to change her plan, and to exert all her energies to persuade Mrs. Fielding that she ought in justice to resign her pretensions to one, who, by her superior powers, was more eminently qualified to promote the happiness of a deserving individual. She would immediately have written, but apprehensive that Mrs. Fielding, following the example of Henry, would leave the letter unanswered, she thought it better to discuss the subject in a personal interview; and set out for Hanover-square with all possible expedition.

As she entered the square, Mrs. Fielding's carriage drove from her door; she however proceeded to knock, and had the door opened to her by a maid-servant, from whom she learned, that Mrs. Fielding was not expected home till near dinnertime.

"Would she be at home in the evening?"

'Yes; but in the evening she was to have a party.'

This intelligence was extremely agreeable to Bridgetina, as she doubted not that Henry would be of the number of Mrs. Fielding's guests, of whom she also determined to make one; nor did the want of an invitation appear to her any obstacle, as that was a mere matter of form, which she thought might very easily be dispensed with.

It was now that Bridgetina for the first time felt the absence of her mother, who had from her cradle supplied the place to her of maid, milliner, and mantua-maker;[9] and though the good woman's fond wishes of setting off the person of her daughter to the best advantage were but ill seconded by her taste, her officious zeal had rendered the object of her affections so unaccustomed to do any thing for herself, that she was helpless as a baby. Her only resource was to consult Mrs. Benton, whom she accordingly sent for; and after telling her she was to go that evening to a party at Mrs. Fielding's, intreated her assistance in the nec-

---

[9] One who makes a loose gown worn by women in the 17th and 18th century.

essary preparations. Mrs. Benton very good-naturedly offered to do every thing in her power; and proposed sending immediately for a hair-dresser, as really she could not help observing that Miss Botherim's hair stood very much in need of cutting.

Bridgetina replied, that "all unnecessary co-operation was vicious, and that as Mrs. Benton and her maid had both offered their voluntary assistance, she would by no means purchase the service of a mercenary. Besides," added she, putting her hand to her forehead, and gently introducing her fingers betwixt her skull and the high frizzled locks that towered above, "my hair is much more easily dressed than you imagine. See, (cried she, taking off the wig) these curls want only a little combing, and then, as they are somewhat stiff, they must be well smoothed down with hard pomatum,[10] and covered over with a little powder, and they will do very well."

Mrs. Benton shook her head, but desiring Jenny to take the comb, and proceed by Miss Botherim's directions, she went on to the examination of the wardrobe, which Bridgetina displayed for her inspection. Having laid aside two or three printed callicoes, and many ordinary muslins, she at length arrived at a dress carefully pinned up in a large table-cloth. "How very fortunate," said she, "that my mother should by mistake have sent me this favourite dress, in which she always says I look so well. It is made up after her own fancy, and admirably suited to my complexion. Do you not admire it?"

'Indeed, Ma'am, the silk is very pretty, to be sure, but only—now that silks are so little worn, I fear it will look a little particular. The colour, too, so deep a rose is rather glaring, and I fear it will be thought unfashionable.'

"Oh, as to the fear of being particular, I despise it. The gown has been very much admired at W—, and the fancy of trimming it with these knots of deep blue ribbons has been greatly praised."

'I do not doubt it; but you know, Ma'am, that in London—indeed, believe me that you had better go to the Mrs. Fielding's in a plain muslin. I beg pardon for the liberty I take, but indeed I cannot help wishing you to consider, how odd such a dress as this will appear in a room full of company."

The predilection of Bridgetina for her favourite gown was not to be moved by the remonstrances of Mrs. Benton, though they continued to be urged with increasing vehemence till interrupted by Jenny, who declared the curls of the wig to be so intractable as to bid defiance to her utmost skill. Again Mrs. Benton hinted the necessity of procuring a hair-dresser; but as Bridgetina was obstinate in opposing it, she herself undertook to settle the inflexible tresses on one side of the wig, while Jenny tugged at the other. At length the labours of the toilette were concluded, and our heroine, having refused to permit Jenny to call a coach,

---

[10] See note 31.

tripped it on foot through George's-street, and reached Mrs. Fielding's door at the moment some ladies, who had just stepped from a coroneted carriage, were entering it. She followed them without hesitation up stairs. The names of Lady Caroline and Lady Juliet Manners were announced aloud; and immediately after, that of Miss Botherim was pronounced by the same sonorous voice. Mrs. Fielding started at the sound; she was still speaking to Lady Juliet at no great distance from the door, when it reached her ears. She instantly turned round, and in spite of her vexation, could scarcely forbear smiling at the strange appearance of the little *outr*é figure that approached her.

"Bless me," cried a young lady who stood up to speak to Lady Caroline Manners, "What masquerade figure has your ladyship brought in with you? I did not hear of any fancy ball this evening?"

'She did not come with us,' said Lady Caroline, 'nor can I imagine who she is; but she is dressed in character sure enough, though I am positive there is no masquerade. I dare say she is some oddity, for you know Mrs. Fielding does sometimes pick up queer people.'

Who is she? what can she be? where does she come from? reverberated twenty whispering voices at once. Some imagined her to be a foreigner, but of what nation no one could determine. Others sagaciously discovered it to be some one of their common acquaintance dressed up in disguise, and introduced by Mrs. Fielding for the amusement of the company; but the conclusion made by those best acquainted with Mrs. Fielding, and which in a short time became general, was highly in Bridgetina's favour, as it supposed her some person of extraordinary talents, whose soaring genius was above conformity to the common fashions of the world.

Time does not permit us at present to controvert the false notion upon which this opinion is founded, otherwise we should not despair of being able satisfactorily to prove, that the affectation of singularity, so far from being a concomitant of real genius, is a certain proof of a confined and little mind. But without waiting to discuss this subject any further, we return to Bridgetina, who, quite unconscious of the wonder her appearance excited, dressed her countenance in a gracious smile as she waddled up to Mrs. Fielding, who waited to be addressed by her without speaking.

"It was extremely fortunate that I heard you were to be at home this evening," said Bridgetina, after making her curtsey.

'I should have been extremely happy to have heard the same of you from W—,' replied Mrs. Fielding, attempting to look serious.

"I do not doubt that," returned Bridgetina; "but I know your motives, and have come with a view to convince you that they are erroneous. I wish to have an opportunity of communing with you for half an hour or so in private, and shall wait your time."

'It cannot possibly be this evening,' returned Mrs. Fielding, who hoped, by an absolute refusal, to prevail on her to depart; 'you see how I am engaged: I cannot have it in my power to speak to you for five minutes on any account whatever.'

"Ah!" said Mr. Sardon, who at that moment entered the room, "see how the *power of sympathy* attracts me to the spot that contains Miss Botherim. You cannot think, Ma'am," continued he, addressing himself to Bridgetina, from whom Mrs. Fielding had turned to receive some other company, "you cannot think what a convert you have made of me. I have twice walked from Charing-Cross to Hyde-Park corner, without casting one glance on either shoe-buckles or tea-urns; and though I must confess I neither laughed nor cried, I have had some flights of fancy that I hope will entitle me to be ranked among your men of genius."

'I make no doubt of your powers, sir,' returned Bridgetina, gravely. 'You seem a man capable of estimating, and of energizing in no common degree.'

Mr. Sardon bowed. "The approbation of a lady of your penetration is too flattering. How much does Mrs. Fielding oblige her friends by introducing among them a person so rarely qualified! But pray, do you not intend to enlighten this brilliant circle by a lecture on metaphysicks? You know no opportunity for instructing mankind ought to be lost; and I dare say there are many persons here present to whom your arguments would be strikingly original."

Mrs. Fielding, who overheard the latter part of Mr. Sardon's speech, here interposed. 'Miss Botherim has too much sense to believe you,' said she, gently tapping him with her fan. 'Though unaccustomed to town-circles, she knows that to give a lecture upon any subject in a mixed company would be very improper; though not so bad (whispering Mr. Sardon) as to lead a poor wrong-headed girl into the folly of exposing herself to the ridicule of a whole company.'

"No time can be improper for the promulgation of truth," said Bridgetina. "Mr. Sardon speaks like a philosopher. He knows it is our duty in every company to argue, to reason, to discuss. But to be sure," continued she, drawing up her head with an air of conscious triumph, "it is not every person that is qualified to enlighten the world by abstract speculation."

'Miss Botherim speaks like an oracle!' cried Mr. Sardon. He was going on, but was checked by a frown from Mrs. Fielding, who, observing the eyes of the whole room fixed on Bridgetina, desired her to sit down in a corner less exposed to observation. Thither she was followed by Mr. Sardon, who continued to amuse himself with her eccentricity; while the curiosity excited by the singularity of her appearance, and the pedantic formality of her manner, attracted round them a circle of ladies who were all eager to listen to their conversation.

Though cards were not excluded from the parties of Mrs. Fielding, they were generally declined by the majority of the company. Where persons qualified to relish the pleasures of conversation have an opportunity of enjoying it in perfection, they must, indeed, be the fettered slaves of custom, if they prefer an amusement in which fools may conquer, and knaves be crowned with victory, to the refined delight arising from the communication of ideas, the collision of wit, and the instructive observations of genius.

From the appearance of Bridgetina something very extraordinary was expected. Mrs. Fielding's taste for the conversation of people of talents was well known. Her solicitude to bring forward extraordinary genius from the depressing shade of obscurity had often been crowned with success; but though talents had her admiration, it was goodness and virtue that could alone ensure her approbation or esteem. Her situation in life gave her an opportunity of selecting her acquaintance, and her discernment and discrimination afforded her the means of employing this inestimable privilege to the best advantage. No sooner, therefore, was a new face seen in her drawing-room, than her friends anticipated a new source of pleasure or improvement; nor were they often disappointed. Sometimes, indeed, it would happen, notwithstanding the art she displayed in mixing her guests, that two learned men would get near enough to fall into a tedious argument concerning the etymology of a word, or some minute point in history or antiquity, for which not another soul but themselves could care a single straw; and sometimes a dispute in politicks would cast a temporary cloud over the good-humour of the disputants; but by the management of Mrs. Fielding these things rarely occurred. She was at such pains to provide the talkers with listeners, and the listeners with talkers, and to suit the subject of conversation to the general taste, that all enjoyed in some degree the pleasure of pleasing, and the happiness of being pleased.

Bridgetina was at first afraid to run on in the words of her favourite authors, as she could not doubt that the subject of her studies must be familiar to the greatest part of her well-informed audience. Great was her surprise, when she discovered that the books which she believed were destined to enlighten the whole world, and new-model the human race, had not been thought worthy of a reading by any one who heard her. She took advantage of the discovery to quote page after page, while any one would listen to her; but though the novelty of her arguments for some time excited attention, and her flow of language did not fail to obtain applause, she soon experienced the common fate of an haranguer, in wearying the patience of those she pretended to instruct. Fatigued with the monotonous sounds of her discordant voice, they turned from her, and gladly joined the different groupes where subjects of general literature, or of elegant criticism, gave every one an opportunity of contributing their quota to the fund of conversation.

Bridgetina was now, in her turn, obliged to become a listener, till her patience being quite exhausted, she arose, and walking across the room to where Mrs. Fielding sat, enquired aloud whether she might expect to see Dr. Sydney there that night? Mrs. Fielding told her she need not expect to see him, as he had another engagement.

"You are acquainted with his engagements!" cried Bridgetina. "You are the confidante of his bosom, the object of his passion! it is for you he rejects my love! but if you have any moral sensibility, if you are at all capable of energising, I do not despair of convincing you that you owe it to duty, you owe it to every principle of justice, you owe it to the happiness of an individual to relinquish your designs on the person of this amiable young man."

Mrs. Fielding, shocked beyond measure at a speech which so strongly indicated a disordered state of intellect, thinking it better to soothe than to irritate the mind of the speaker, in a voice of pity told her, that if she would, on the morning after the following, give her the pleasure of her company at breakfast, she would endeavour to give her satisfaction.

"I shall not fail to come," said Bridgetina; "and as truth is onmipotent, I make no doubt my arguments will prevail." So saying she took her leave, to the great delight of Mrs. Fielding, who, tho' she never made a practice of being denied, immediately ordered that Miss Botherim should never again be admitted with other company.

As Bridgetina retired, the servant stationed in the anti-room desired the footman below to call Miss Botherim's carriage. "I have no carriage, sir," said Bridgetina, "I disdain the use of a carriage, which is a contrivance of pampered luxury, and altogether unnecessary to a philosopher."

The man bowed, and again gravely advancing to the head of the stairs, 'Open the street-door to a philosopher,' cried he with the voice of a Stentor.[11]

Bridgetina, highly pleased with the compliment, thanked him, and descending, made her way through an avenue of grinning footmen, to whom her appearance afforded no small subject of merriment. The door was opened by the footman who had formerly conducted her to the coach, and who had the civility again to offer to procure her either coach or chair; but she declined his services, declaring there was nothing she so much loved as a solitary ramble by moon-light.

Unfortunately for Bridgetina, her reply to the footman was overheard by a couple of girls, who were on their way to Bond-street in search of adventures, and who eagerly seised the opportunity that presented itself, of venting the malignant spirit of mischief in that sort of outrage which is vulgarly denominated *fun*. They soon came up with Bridgetina, and getting her between them, addressed her with pretended gravity.

"Do you intend to take a long walk?" cried one.

'Yes, upon the tight-rope, as you may perceive by her dress,' cried the other.

"I intend to walk no farther than Conduit-street," said Bridgetina; "and am such a stranger in town, that I know not where such a walk as tight-rope is."

A loud laugh from her companions very much discomposed our heroine, who, greatly offended by their rudeness, begged they would leave her to her own reflections."

---

[11] A Greek warrior in the Trojan war noted for his voice—applied allusively to a man of powerful voice.

'Own reflections, pretty dear!' said the tallest of the girls. 'Do you know, Maria, where *own* reflections is?'

"I'll be hanged if I do," replied the other; "unless it be in Rag-fair, where she bought that quiz of a wig."

'My dress is no concern of yours,' said Bridgetina, angrily; 'and I must need tell you, it is rather uncivil to intrude upon me in this manner, when I wish to be alone.'

"Why don't you leave us," said one, giving her a push, and winking significantly to the other. "I am sure I don't wish to keep you."

'Nor I neither,' said the other; 'I would not be seen walking with such a trollopy quiz for the world.' So saying, she gave the unfortunate Bridgetina such a push towards her companion, that both were driven upon the rails. Bridgetina screamed, but before she could recover herself, was again pushed with such violence by the girl against whom she had last been driven, that after reeling a few paces she fell prostrate in the kennel.[12] The girls set up a shout of victory, while Bridgetina, forgetful of the immoral tendency of coertion, vociferated Murder! help! murder! as loud as she was able to bawl. In an instant the street, which was before still as midnight, was filled with a croud, which as few were seen to issue from the houses, seemed as if by inchantment wafted to the spot. The dread sound of the watchman's rattle gave the signal for alarm. Three or four guardians of the night were soon assembled, who, at the instance of Bridgetina, would have taken her companions into custody, had they not by a singular piece of effrontery contrived to turn the popular voice in their favour.

"What!" cried the one who had shoved Bridgetina into the kennel, "you are pretty watchmen, indeed! pretend not to know Poll Maddoc! the most notorious wench in London. There's ne'er a boy in St. Giles's that don't know squinting Poll. She was condemned at the Old-Bailey for picking the pocket of Jerry Wapping last 'sizes,[13] let her deny it if she dare; or that she nimm'd that wig from Moses the jew in Rag-fair; or that she is now kept by Peter Puff, the puppet-show man. She cry out murder, indeed, because we would not suffer her to walk the streets with us. Does she think that we would be seen in company with such a trull? No, no; it an't come to that yet; we will let her know that we are meat for her masters."

This oration quickly turned every voice against the hapless Bridgetina, who in vain protested that the orator had mistaken her person.

The sagacious watchman recognized her as an old acquaintance, and declared that he should provide her a night's lodging in the watch-house.

Bridgetina expostulated; she declared she was going home to her lodgings, when accosted by the two ladies who had given such an erroneous description of her person.

'Your lodgings!' cried the watchman with a sneer, 'you intended to

---

[12] See note 30.

[13] The sessions held periodically in each county of England, for the purpose of administering civil and criminal justice, by judges acting under certain special commissions.

sleep with master punch, did you? but we shall lodge you as safe as with the devil, and Doctor Faustus to boot; come along, we cannot stay for any more jabber.' So saying, he seised the reluctant arm of Bridgetina, but was stopped for a moment by his coadjutor, who, jogging the other arm of his prisoner, told her in a whisper, that 'if she would tip them half-a-crown, she might still regain her liberty.'

"Half-a-crown!" repeated Bridgetina, "I have not a single shilling in my pocket; but if you will call upon me to-morrow, I shall pay you the money with pleasure."

'To-morrow!' said the watchman; 'that's all my eye, d'ye see. D'ye think I'm such a simpleton as to trust your word?'

"I know," replied Bridgetina, "that promises are immoral, and ought not to be considered as binding; but in the present case—"

'No more palaver,' said the honest watchman; 'if you don't down with the ready, you must go.'

Bridgetina begged to be heard, but in vain. Each seizing an arm, they dragged her off; and had nearly reached the end of the street, when, to the unspeakable joy of the struggling, weeping Bridgetina, she perceived Henry Sydney advancing towards them.

Great was the surprise of Henry, on beholding the dismal plight of our heroine; of which, in a commanding voice, he instantly demanded the cause. He could not very easily understand either the story of the watchman, or the incoherent detail of Bridgetina, but found it no difficult matter to persuade the guardians of the peace of their mistake; who, receiving from his pocket some very convincing arguments in favour of their prisoner's innocence, did not hesitate to deliver up their charge.

'I hope, (said he) Miss Botherim,' as he conducted her to Mrs. Benton's door, 'this incident will convince you that London is a very improper place for you to remain in, while destitute of the protection of any friend. You see how your ignorance of the manners of the metropolis exposes you to insult. I am happy in having rescued you at present from a situation so terrible that I shudder to think of it; but another time you may not be so fortunate to meet a friend. Let me, therefore, intreat you to think of an immediate return to W—, where your mother is made miserable by your absence.'

"Cruel Henry!" returned the weeping Bridgetina; "but I now know the motive of your conduct. Let me but reason the matter with you in one single conference, and I shall be satisfied."

Henry, in hopes of being able to conquer her strange infatuation by argument, consented to drink tea with her the following evening; and having seen her under the protection of Mrs. Benton's roof, took his leave, and pursued his way to his own lodgings.

CHAP. II.

"Bring me a father that so lov'd his child,
"Whose joy of her is overwhelm'd like mine,
"And bid him speak of patience!
"No, no; 'tis all men's office to speak patience
"To those that wring under the load of sorrow;
"But no man's virtue nor sufficiency
"To be so moral when he shall endure,
"The like himself."
SOUTHEY.[14]

BEFORE we accompany Henry on his visit to Bridgetina, it may not be amiss to take a retrospective view of the manner in which he has been engaged from the time we left him reading the proposals of his enlightened and liberal admirer.

The ungrateful Henry, far from being elevated into rapture by the exalted sentiments and generous proposals of the philosophic maiden, having given her letter a hasty and peevish perusal, threw it on the ground; nor did he at that time vouchsafe to read the paper which had been inclosed in it, and which was no other than the circular letter addressed by Mr. Myope to his brethren the philosophers.

By the unfortunate fate of the amiable Julia, and the deep affliction of her wretched parents, the mind of Henry was so completely engrossed, that he had not a single thought to bestow on the tender woes of Bridgetina. Even the reflections upon his own situation were suspended; and selfish cares and selfish sorrows were absorbed in the benevolent feelings of compassion, or banished by disinterested regret. He flew to the lodgings of his friend Churchill, whom he found just arrived; his body worn out with fatigue, and his mind lacerated by disappointment. After many vexatious delays and interruptions, he had traced the fugitives to London; but there, having stepped from the post-chaise into the first empty hackney-coach that met them, they effectually eluded all further pursuit. Henry spent the remainder of the day with his friend, and devoted the greatest part of the succeeding ones to his assistance. Their endeavours were fruitless. The retreat of the lovers could not be discovered; and poor Churchill, at length submitting to the judgment of Henry, was persuaded to give over the hopeless research.

The day of the election of the physician for the hospital at length arrived; when the rival candidate having, in consequence of a private visit from Mrs. Fielding's agent, relinquished his pretensions, Henry was unanimously chosen to the vacant office; and thankfully rejoiced in his success, as a step towards that state of independency on which his dear-

---

[14] Wrongly ascribed to Southey, actually Shakespeare, *Much Ado About Nothing*, V.i.

est hopes of happiness seemed entirely to depend. Still were his prospects distant, far distant from such an income as would, in the present state of society, be deemed adequate to the support of a family. Many men of the first abilities in his profession had, he well knew, spent their lives in hopeless penury; and that he should be one of the fortunate few whom the caprice of fashion should introduce to fortune's favours, was a peradventure too precarious for hope to build on.

The peculiar advantage he enjoyed of being introduced by Mrs. Fielding into the houses of several families of distinction, does not appear to have been estimated by Henry at its full value. He was so ignorant as to imagine, that when people were sick, they would look more to the experience and abilities of the physician in whose hands they entrusted their lives, than to his rank in the scale of fashion. He did not think it possible that the vanity of a dying man could be flattered by having his prescription written by the same hand that had lately felt the pulse of a lord; or that his weeping wife and daughters could feel a superior gratification in telling their friends that the dear deceased had been visited by Doctor—, at the very time he was attending my Lady Duchess, than they should have experienced from the happy effects of any medical skill. Of the omnipotence of fashion Henry had as yet formed no adequate idea; and trusting to his own efforts, he resolved by exertion and unceasing assiduity to deserve the success he so ardently wished for.

Several days elapsed without bringing him another letter from W—; neither had Mr. Churchill received any intelligence from that quarter; so that the anxiety of both was wound up to the extreme; when Henry, on returning from his attendance on a new patient, a few hours previous to his chivalrous rescue of Bridgetina from the hands of the giant enchanters, found a letter from his sister, which had been brought by that morning's post. He eagerly broke the seal, and read as follows:

"BEFORE I enter upon subjects of a less pleasing though deeply-interesting nature, let me tell my dear Harry how my heart thanks him for the kind haste he made to rid me of my foolish fears. No; I did not, I could not, suspect you of loving such a woman as Miss Botherim; but I could not help entertaining some sort of apprehension that you might have left her room to construe some unmeaning speech into an avowal of tenderness. Even here I have been mistaken; and my heart exultingly repeats, that my beloved brother is now as ever free from the shadow of reproach. But the more unequivocal your conduct, the more shameful, the more absurd and preposterous appears that of this weak, bewildered girl, whose brain seems to have been turned by the wild ambition of standing forth a practical champion for doctrines which even in theory are sufficiently ridiculous.

"Would to GOD that she had been the only sacrifice to these extravagant opinions! But, alas! poor Julia! She too, it seems, was a convert to this new system, which teaches, that by cancelling the bonds of domestic affection, and dissolving the ties of gratitude, the virtue and happiness of the world is to be increased. Fatal delusion! how would it vanish from her mind, could she have but a momentary glance at the altered countenance of her dying father! For these last three days he has continued to suffer all that the most extreme agony of mind, added to the most acute bodily torture, can inflict. Dr. Orwell and my father have united their efforts to soothe his sorrows, and to alleviate the pangs of grief; but, alas! they cannot remove the dart which rankles in his bosom, or lead him to forget that it was planted there by the hand of his much-beloved child.

"The assurance obtained from Mrs. Glib, that Vallaton was not a married man, as had been reported, seemed to convey a short-lived relief; but it was followed by such an account of his character, and of the meanness of his station, (which, it seems, is that of a hair-dresser) as opened every wound of the father's heart. Unable to support the war of conflicting passions, his feeble frame seems nearly exhausted by the contest. In proportion as he becomes weaker, the more powerful emotions subside. Indignation gives place to pity, and the feelings of resentment are swallowed up in those of paternal tenderness. He even strives to form excuses for his daughter's conduct, and seems eager to transfer the blame from her to some other object.

"Yesterday as my father sat by his bedside, after a silence of some minutes. "Mr. Sydney," said he, "you are very good to bear with me; but you are yourself a father, though you cannot—oh, no; you cannot possibly know the sorrow that has pierced me. For the pride I took in this darling child, how severely am I now punished! In the foolishness of my heart, I believed her to be superior to all her sex. I encouraged her to throw off the prejudices of religion—to act from nobler motives than the hopes of an hereafter—to substitute the laws of honour for the laws of GOD; and to consult the dictates of her mind instead of the morality of the gospel. Oh if I have taught my child to err; if it is for want of more solid principles that she has been made an easy prey to the snares of a seducer—but I cannot bear the thought. Tell me, Mr. Sydney, O tell me that it is not *to me* she owes her fall! Say not that it was I who led my child to the precipice down which she has sunk!"

"You, Harry, who are so well acquainted with the benignity of our dear father's nature, may imagine how much he was affected: nor need I say, that he used every endeavour to soothe and comfort the poor unhappy man, who seemed thus to cling to him for support. You know how much it is his delight to heal the wounded spirit, and to speak peace to the broken in heart. I pray GOD that his endeavours may in this instance prove successful!

"Our amiable friend, Harriet Orwell, has done all in her power to supply the place of a daughter to poor Mrs. Delmond. While her attentions have been engrossed by her, I have devoted mine to Mrs. Botherim; who, ever since she heard of Biddy's departure, has been in a state little short of distraction. Nothing, to be sure, can be more ludicrous than the stile of her lamentations sometimes are; but the voice of sorrow ought to command respect, however mean or absurd the language in which it is conveyed. I am far, you may believe, from justifying a breach of filial duty; but surely the man does great injustice to his children, who gives them a mother so weak, or so ignorant, as to render her despicable in their eyes; not that to a well-regulated mind the weakness of a parent will ever be made the object of contempt; but how should the children of a fool come by the information necessary to point out the line of duty, or to fix the principles of filial piety in the heart?[15]

"Oh, my brother, if ever you marry, may your wife be one whose memory your children's children shall delight to honour; may she demand from her family, not merely the barren obedience of duty, but the grateful tribute of heart-felt veneration and esteem!

"At the conclusion of the last paragraph, I laid aside my writing, to enquire for Capt. Delmond; the answers sent by a servant are so little satisfactory, that I have generally contrived to go twice a-day myself, and from Harriet have learned the particulars for which I was so anxious.

"Very little alteration has taken place in his state of mind or health since yesterday, except that he is apparently weaker and more tranquil. Dr. Orwell accompanied me up street. As we approached the house of Mr. Glib the stationer, we perceived a croud about the door; and on enquiring into the cause, were informed that Mr. Glib had suddenly departed from W——, and that the creditors were then taking possession of the few effects he had left behind him. A person from the house requested of Dr. Orwell to step in for a few moments, as the presence of a justice of peace was necessary, in order to take the affidavit of Mrs. Glib about some matters, but I do not know what. While waiting for the Doctor, I was accosted in the rudest manner by two or three of the children, who were running about like so many ragged colts. To say they are in a state of nature would be doing little honour to our species, for never did I see imps so mischievous and impudent. They were happily attracted by the arrival of another stranger, an officer of dragoons, who was lately quartered in a neighbouring town, and whose attentions to Mrs. Glib have not escaped the notice of the scandal-loving coterie. This gentleman stepped up to Mrs. Glib's apartment without ceremony, and from the air of satisfaction that appeared in this manner, went, I hope, with the intention of affording relief to her misfortunes. In a few minutes Dr. Orwell returned to me, and brought with him a letter which Mrs. Glib had put into his hands. It was written by her husband, and left behind him as justification of his conduct. By this it appears, that in deserting his wife and children he acts *upon principle.* "Convinced," he says, "of the immoral tendency of matrimony, and that it is an odious and unjust institution—*a monopoly, and the worst of monopolies—which, by forbidding two human beings to follow the dic-*

---

[15] A sentiment expressed in Wollstonecraft's *Vindication of the Rights of Woman* (1792) 10.

tates of their own minds, makes prejudice alive and vigorous;★[16] he is resolved to dismiss the mistake he has so happily detected, and no longer seek, by artificial and despotic means, to engross a pretty woman to himself, but to restore to her that liberty, of which (by the despotic sanction of a foolish law) she had been unjustly deprived. As to the five children which she calls *his*, it is a matter of no importance to him whether they are so or no. He has neither the *aristocracy, self-love,* or *family pride*,★[17] that teaches prejudiced people to set a value upon a matter in itself so insignificant; and as they may, very probably, be no worthier than the children of any other man, it is not consistent with moral justice that he should devote to them the fruits of his labour.

"So far he seems to make use of the words of some author, who probably little imagined that his theory would ever meet with such a practical advocate.[18] In the conclusion, he makes use of his own peculiar jargon, which is often whimsical enough. Talks of Hottentots, who live according to the sublime system that is to be universally adopted in the *Age of Reason*, and hints at a design of emigrating to Africa!

"It is probable Miss Botherim may have been induced to become a party in this projected expedition. For the sake of her poor mother, I hope she will not carry her folly quite so far; and intreat you may do all you can to persuade her to an immediate return to W——.

"Adieu, my dearest brother. We have another frank for this day week,[19] which my father desires me to tell you he will fill; in the mean time he sends his blessing. In my opinion, the greatest we can have from Heaven, is a just sense of the happiness we enjoy in having such a parent. That he may be blessed in the prosperity and happiness of 'his heart's dear Harry,' is the never-ceasing prayer of

"Your truly affectionate sister,
 "MARIA SYDNEY."

A second letter from Maria was enclosed in the same cover. The contents were as follows:

"I HAVE opened the pacquet, to inform my dear Henry that the sorrows of Captain Delmond are at an end. They have at length broken the attenuated thread of his existence, and accellerated his departure to the

---

[16] ★See Pol Jus. vol.11 p.499★ Godwin, *Political Justice*, Bk VIII, Appendix, "Of Co-operation, Cohabitation and Marriage". See Appendix A.

[17] ★See Pol Jus★ *Political Justice*, Bk VIII, ch. i, "Preliminary Observations, of Property."

[18] Ironically Godwin himself denounced his daughter Mary's practical implementation of his writings when she eloped with the married Percy Byshe Shelley. See William St Clair, *The Godwins and the Shelleys* (London: Faber, 1989), 355-63.

[19] To superscribe (a letter) with a signature, so as to ensure its being sent without charge; to send or cause to be sent free of charge. MPs had free mail and so would frank other people's mail to save them the expense.

silent grave. Oh, Julia, Julia, what must be thy feelings, when informed of this event! The infatuation of passion may for a while stifle the voice of nature, but a time will come when the sword with which she has pierced her father's heart, shall deeply wound her own.

"The whole of yesterday the poor Captain was so much easier as to give some hopes of his recovery. He sat up great part of the day, and appeared to receive so much pleasure from the company of my father, that he spent the greatest part of it in his apartment. He more than once regretted that he had so long lived near two such men as my father and Doctor Orwell, without having attempted to cultivate their friendship. 'I now,' said he, 'perceive my error, in attributing to the spirit of the christian religion itself that gloomy illiberality which I have observed in some of its pretended votaries. I see that its priests are not necessarily either mercenary knaves or zealous bigots; and begin to apprehend, that while I piqued myself on being superior to prejudice, I have in reality been its dupe.'

"The endeavours used by my father to soothe and tranquillize his mind appeared to be effectual; and he left him in such a composed and happy state, as seemed to promise a night of undisturbed repose. No sooner, however, was he left to his own meditations, than his thoughts' appear to have recurred to the subject of his uneasiness. He became restless, impatient, and not unfrequently delirious. Sometimes he uttered the wildest threats against the villain who had deprived him of his daughter; and sometimes he called upon her name, and in the tenderest and most supplicating voice, adjured her not to leave him. Towards morning he called upon the nurse to assist him in changing the posture of his head; and while she did so, 'Oh, Julia! Julia!' he murmured in a feeble voice, 'I looked to thy dear hand to smooth my death-bed pillow—but I forgive thee!' His voice failed, he sunk down upon the bed, and in a few moments expired.

"Mrs. Delmond, being worn out with fatigue and grief, had, by the persuasion of Harriet, (who has indeed acted like an angel) lain down to take some rest. She had fallen into a profound slumber, from which she would have been hastily awakened by the nurse; but Harriet, satisfying herself that all was over, would not permit the slumbers of the poor widow to be disturbed. By her wise precaution, Mrs. Delmond regained some strength of mind as well as of body; and, supported by her soothing tenderness, has been enabled to bear her afflictions with more fortitude than could have been expected.

"A message from General Villers has just arrived, requesting Mrs. Delmond's permission to take upon himself the charge of the funeral; which he wishes to be performed in a manner suitable to the birth and merit of his deceased friend.

"Your letter is this moment put into my hand. Ah! in what just colours does it paint the amiable Churchill! What noble generosity of sentiment! What affecting sensibility! That Julia should have known him, should have seen (and how could she be blind to a partiality so visible) the

impression she had made upon his heart, and yet give her preference to a wretch like Vallaton, is a mystery to me inexplicable. Adieu! dearest Henry, my spirits are so depressed I can say no more, but that I am ever affectionately your's,
"M.S."

Henry had no sooner perused his sister's letter, than he hastened to his friend Churchill to inform him of the contents. As the quickest method of doing so, he gave it him to read, a breach of delicacy which we can by no means excuse. If Henry had given a moment's consideration to what the feelings of Maria would have been, could she have seen the eye of Churchill gazing on her letter, and devouring, with an appearance of more than common interest, those passages concerning himself, which she would least of all have exposed to his perusal, Henry would not have given the letter out of his own hand.

Churchill returned it to him with a sigh. "What a charming girl is your sister," said he. "How clear her understanding! How just her sentiments! Happy had it been for poor Julia Delmond had her mind been formed like hers. But the death of the poor father—how very shocking it is! He deserved a better fate. I foolishly flattered myself that I should have had it in my power to contribute to his happiness, and promised myself much pleasure in performing to him the duty of a son. That is over. And I can now only shew the respect I bear his memory, by assisting at the last offices of humanity, and following his body to the grave."

Henry, finding it in vain to oppose this sudden design of his friend, left him to follow his inclination. To say truth, had he been at liberty to consult his own, he would much rather have encountered the fatigue of a midnight journey, to accompany him to W—, than have gone to the splendid party to which he was engaged.

It was on his return from this party, that he discovered our heroine in the deplorable situation from which he had the good fortune to rescue her. He now reproached himself for the little pains he had taken to persuade her of the folly and impropriety of her remaining in London, and resolved to lose no time in urging the necessity of her immediate return to W—. He next morning communicated his intention to Mrs. Fielding, when, by her own appointment, he waited on her to report the situation of some poor patients she had recommended to his attention. On receiving from her an account of all that had passed the preceding evening, his hopes of success became rather less sanguine; but the necessity there appeared to him of making some effort to rescue the poor girl from a situation exposed to so many evils, made him resolve on making the experiment. While canvassing the subject with Mrs. Fielding, her carriage drove up to the door, in which, accompanied by Henry, she set off on a tour of visits; and strange to tell, set off with a certain assurance of receiving, wherever she appeared, a hearty welcome!

CHAP. III.

"Come hither, out-cast one! and call her friend,
"And she shall be thy friend more readily,
"Because thou art unhappy.
"Art thou astonish'd, maid,
"That one, though powerful, is benevolent!
"In truth, thou well may'st wonder!"
                                        SOUTHEY.[20]

"A welcome!" repeats some lovely fair one, as with a yawn she throws down the book at the conclusion of the last chapter. "La! how vulgar! What a bore to find one's friends at home! I am fatigued to death at the very thoughts of it. What odd notions these low authors have of the manners of the fashionable world!"

Stay, dear lady, and be convinced that we are not so ignorant, or so little accustomed to the world of fashion, as you seem to imagine. Well do we know, that in dropping your tickets at the splendid dwellings of the *dear friends*, whose names ye in return expect to swell your porter's list, ye have neither end nor object in view, but the gratification of your own vanity; a vanity which might be somewhat humbled, were ye obliged to witness the mortification that would be inflicted on your *dear friends* by your tiresome and insipid company. Wisely, therefore, do ye keep your insignificance concealed; and trust the gratification of your pride and vanity not to your own intrinsic merits, but to those of the honest artisans, whose united labours have clothed your equipage with splendor. But never, when rolling in that splended equipage, did the loud thundering of your well-drest footman at the door of a duchess, not even when it has disturbed half a street, touch your conscious heart with half the extacy that Mrs. Fielding experienced, when after walking down a dirty lane, too narrow for her coach to enter, her gentle tap at the door of a decayed house was opened by a face beaming with gratitude, and her presence hailed as that of a superior being, the dispenser of happiness and joy!

It happened that this obscure retreat of wretchedness was not above a hundred yards remote from the residence of a man of fashion, at whose house Mrs. Fielding was engaged to dine the day of her first visit to its starving inhabitants. Her heart was still full of the scene she had witnessed. The ghastly figure of the wretched father of the family, stretched upon a pallet in one corner of the room in the agony of a rheumatic fever, was still before her eyes; the appearance of his wife, not four and twenty hours delivered, sitting up in bed, and with her feeble hands stretching out some pieces of muslin which a lady had in charity sent her to clear-starch, and in which she was assisted by the eldest little girl, a

---

[20] Robert Southey, *Joan of Arc* (1796) Bk.v., 63-65, 90-92.

half-naked and more than half-starved creature of nine years old, who worked with eagerness in hopes of sharing in the bread to be thus procured, and for which four other little mouths now vainly clamoured, still dwelt on Mrs. Fielding's imagination; when she took her place at the loaded board of the voluptuous baronet, who was equally remarkable for the irascibility of his temper, and the epicureanism of his table.

In vain had the ingenuity of the purveyor, and the art of the cook, been employed to please the sickly appetite of this son of luxury. Every dish afforded him a subject of inquietude and vexation. It was upon a fine turbot that he particularly vented the ebullition of his wrath. The sauce had not been made to please him, and sauce and turbot were ordered from the table, with directions that they might be thrown to the dunghill, as they were not fit even for the dogs.

An involuntary exclamation, which at that moment escaped the lips of Mrs. Fielding, reached the angry gentleman's ears. He immediately asked her pardon for his violence, but urged the impossibility of keeping his temper on an occasion so provoking.

"You need make no apology to me, sir," said Mrs. Fielding; "for *me* your behaviour has not insulted."

'I hope I have insulted no one;' returned the Baronet, attempting to resume his cheerfulness, while his fiery eye and contracted forehead indicated the rage that still possessed his breast.

"Pardon me, sir," said Mrs. Fielding, "if I differ from you."

'I really do not understand you, Madam,' rejoined the Baronet; 'to whom has my sending away that execrable dish given offence?'

"To the image of GOD in your fellow-creature, now starving at your very door!" returned Mrs. Fielding. "To the famished wretches, who, while you are gorged to loathing, have not even bread for their mouths. Within a hundred yards from where you now sit, have I this morning seen a family of eight souls, to whom the price of that very dish you have spurned from your table would have afforded luxuries for a week. It is the pardon of *such as these* you should solicit, for to misery such as theirs your conduct is an insult."

Mrs. Fielding felt her energy in the cause of humanity not a little strengthened by the striking contrast this day afforded her, betwixt the sickly caprice of voluptuousness and the eagerness of hungry poverty.

It was to give his medical advice to the father of this little family of wretchedness, that she carried Henry to their habitation, which now wore a very different aspect from that which on her first visit it had presented. The children were now clothed; the furniture, which had been by piece-meal sent to pawn, was now replaced; the wife with maternal tenderness pressed the infant to her bosom, whose birth she had deplored as an aggravation to her misfortunes; and even the poor husband, relieved from the torture of beholding his family perishing before his eyes for the want of that food which sickness rendered him unable to procure, felt half the acuteness of his malady removed, and with tears of gratitude implored the best blessing of Heaven upon his worthy benefactress.

After a few visits of a similar nature, Mrs. Fielding carried our young physician to a large house destined for the reception and temporary abode of such of her own sex as, from being destitute of friends in London, were (when by sickness or misfortune thrown out of employment) in danger of being driven, through fear of want, into habits of infamy. The incident that gave rise to this plan of charity in Mrs. Fielding's mind, is sufficiently interesting to claim the attention of those of our readers who really believe people of an inferior station to be composed of the same materials with themselves.

It happened one cold evening in December, that on returning from the theatre, through a narrow street, an accident which befel a preceding carriage occasioned a stop of many minutes to the line of carriages which followed. Mrs. Fielding let down the glass to enquire the cause; and having learnt it, was about to pull it up and patiently wait the event, when her attention was attracted by an object of wretchedness, who with looks of deep humility implored alms at the door of the coach which was immediately before her's in the line. She heard the glass violently drawn up, and saw at the same moment the trembling emaciated wretch who had presumed to supplicate, receive a blow for her impertinence from the rattan of the laced footman who stood behind. Mrs. Fielding, who could not help feeling indignant at an insult offered to misery, even when coupled with vice, was about to offer the poor wretch a compensation for what she had endured, when she saw her familiarly accosted by a bold-looking fellow of the order vulgarly called *shabby-genteel*. The lamp now shone full upon the object of her attention, and displayed a countenance that had once been handsome, but apparently wasted by sickness and famine. She seemed to shrink from the person who addressed her, but yet wanted resolution to resist his importunity. She suffered him to take one of her hands, while with the back of the other she wiped the tears which trickled down her pallid cheek. The coach moved a step or two nearer. Mrs. Fielding distinctly heard the ejaculation, 'Oh, GOD, forgive me! if to save myself from starving—' She could hear no more. The obstruction to the proceeding of the further carriage being now removed, it drove on with fury, and Mrs. Fielding's, with the rest that followed it, suddenly darted forward in full speed.

Mrs. Fielding's sensibility was not of that nature which can content itself with dropping a graceful tear to the misery which an active exertion of benevolence has power to relieve. She hastily pulled the check-string, and having called the footman, "Run, Thomas, run with speed, I beseech you, after that poor woman, whom yonder wretch is dragging away. Desire her to come hither; fly—"

Thomas hesitated. 'I presume, Madam, you do not know that she is'

"No matter what she is—I must speak to her."

Thomas obeyed; and no sooner did the poor forlorn creature hear the welcome message, than struggling from the man who had hold of her, she hastened as fast as her trembling limbs could carry her, to the coach-door over which Mrs. Fielding leaned.

"You appear to be in great misery, young woman;" said Mrs. Fielding, in a voice of pity.

'I am, indeed, Madam! in misery that is inexpessible.'

"But is taking to a course of vice the proper way to procure relief? Would it not be better by honest industry to seek a livelihood, than by continuing in the path of infamy, to—"

'Ah, Madam! I am not the wretch you take me for. I am, indeed, I as yet am virtuous; but I am starving. I have not one farthing to get either food or lodging. I wish I had courage to die! I know it would be better; and that I ought to die, rather than be wicked—but I am *so hungry!*—'

Her weak and hollow voice here became quite inarticulate; it died away in short convulsive sobs, a shivering came over her, and she would have sunk to the ground, had she not been supported by Thomas; who, having caught the contagion of pity from his mistress, was now as zealous to relieve the poor unfortunate, as he was before unwilling to go after her. What was to be done? To leave her in her present situation, was to leave her to perish. A heavy shower came on, which instantly determined Mrs. Fielding. She ordered Thomas to open the coach-door, and to lift the poor exhausted wanderer into the carriage, where she supported her with her own arms all the way to Hanover-square. A few mouthfuls of biscuit soaked in wine restored the sinking powers of nature; and Mrs. Fielding, who administered the cordial with her own hands, had the pleasure of beholding the colour return to the faded cheek, and an expression of sensibility reanimate the sunken eye.

'Are you an angel?' cried the poor miserable, grasping Mrs. Fielding's hand, as she held out to her a bit of biscuit. 'Yes, yes, you must be an angel! no great lady could be so condescending, so very, very good.'

"Alas!" said Mrs. Fielding, "that the common duties of humanity, in a world where misfortune in one shape or other is the lot of all, should be so rare as to be thus over rated!"

The salutary refreshment she had received, aided by a night's repose, had so far restored the poor woman, that when she appeared before Mrs. Fielding on the following morning, she could hardly believe it was the same person.

In answer to Mrs. Fielding's interrogatories, she informed her, that she was the daughter of a Northumbrian peasant: that an elder brother, who had come up to London some few years before, had got so good a place as shopman at a druggist's, that on her father's death she was tempted to come up to town likewise—hoping, through her brother's interest, to procure a place as maid of all work in some creditable family. On arriving in London, she found that her brother had died of the small-pox the week before, and his master (who was a batchelor) had been appointed surgeon in the army, and was then on the eve of embarking for the West-Indies. He however had the goodness, before his departure, to recommend her to a lady and gentleman from Devonshire, who had taken lodgings in Suffolk-street, where they had the use of a back-kitchen. From breathing the pure air of the Northumberland mountains, she was transferred to this unwholesome dungeon, where she had not been confined for many weeks when she was seised with a fit of illness, forced to leave her place, and with the small pittance of wages she had acquired in her short service, to pay for a lodging, food, and physic. On recovering from her fever, which lasted many weeks, she found herself deep in her landlady's debt, who had the *goodness* to accept of all the remains of her little wardrobe in lieu of cash; and having stripped her of every thing but the rags in which she used to do her dirty work, *humanely* turned her out to the street. A stranger in London, and without friends, to whom could she apply for relief? Who would listen to the tale of her misfortunes? Who would accept her services, or open their doors to receive a wretch that had none to help her?

At the time she was seen by Mrs. Fielding, she had been eight and forty hours without food. Her virtuous principles revolted at the proffered wages of prostitution, till hopeless of succour, and over-powered by the repulse she had met with from the sentimental Lady Mary Mildmay and her powdered footman, she gave way to the impulse of despair, and would probably, if the interposing hand of Mrs. Fielding had not been held out to save her, soon have added one other wretched female to the thousands who yearly perish by disease and want, in the streets of the most wealthy, the most charitable, and the most munificent city in the world.

"Surely," said Mrs. Fielding, "there is something wrong in this. There ought to be a reputable receptacle established for affording temporary shelter to those who are willing to eat the bread of honest industry. The government ought—but, alas! I cannot dictate to the government. I have not the power to influence the makers of our laws. But cannot I do something towards the relief of a few of these unhappy individuals? Let me see—"

She then began to make calculations. Gradually, and with deep reflection formed her plan; appropriated a sum to carry it into execution; and at the time she carried Henry to her asylum, she could exult in the reflection, that without injury to her fortune, without assistance from the public, or aid from the purse of any individual, she had, in the five years that had elapsed since the commencement of her scheme, afforded relief to above a thousand destitute females, of whom many were snatched from the jaws of ruin, and saved from courses that would have led to infamy or death.

At first the number admitted was very limited. She had now fourteen beds constantly occupied by as many women, whose willing industry was employed to such advantage in needle-work of various descriptions, that they entirely cleared the price of their maintenance. These were chiefly composed of servants, who by sickness, accident, or misfortune, had been thrown out of employment, and who were willing by their diligence to procure the recommendation of the house to creditable places. The unhappy female abandoned by the seducer, for whom she had quitted the protection of her friends, here found the shelter she dared not to implore from her offended family; and if inclined to acquire habits of industry, was soon put in a way of earning a comfortable subsistence, and of regaining the invigorating stimulus of self-approbation. Even the wretched outcast of society, such as are every sessions disgorged from our prisons, and after having been acquitted by a jury of all crime, are charitably sent forth either to *steal* or *perish*, was admitted here; not indeed to the superior apartment, but to one provided with every necessary for their accommodation, where works of an inferior nature were carried on, the profits accruing from which were all appropriated to cloathing the poor wretches who here found shelter.

Three hundred a year was the sum first designed by Mrs. Fielding to be expended in this charity. It gradually increased to five, and would have been much greater, had she not found means to engage an American merchant in her interest, who opened a store in Charlestown for the sale of ready-made linen garments; and would have taken off her hands, at a good price, more than she was able to supply.

"Five hundred a year!" cries Lady Racket; "bless me, what a sweet masked ball one might give every winter with such a sum! It is true, Mrs.★★★'s and Lady★★★'s, cost twice the money; but with five hundred pounds well managed, one might give a very pretty, dashy, stileish sort of an entertainment for a single evening. Do'nt you think so?"

CHAP. IV.

"This *forager* on others' wisdom, leaves
"Her native farm, her reason quite untill'd.
"With mixt manure she surfeits the rank soil,
"Dung'd, but not dress'd; and rich to beggary,
"A pomp untameable of weed prevails."
                                    YOUNG.[21]

MRS. Fielding and Henry were so deeply engaged in conversation as the carriage went down Holborn, they perceived not Bridgetina paddling along the dirty street. They did not, however, pass unobserved by her. "Yes!" cried she aloud, "there they are, side by side, tasting the balmy sweetness, drinking the delicious poison, which unsophisticated effective love sheds through the human heart! Perhaps they are now going to be married. O odious institution! nurse of depravity! foe to energy and usefulness! Never shall I prevail upon the prejudices of Henry to break thy galling chain. But why should I despair? Is not truth omnipotent? Must not my reiterated efforts in the end prevail? What though he should be

---

[21] Edward Young, *Night Thoughts: The Complaint* (1742-45) "The Relapse" Night v.

married?[22] May I not convince him of the immoral tendency of all engagements? May I not demonstrate from the divine principles of philosophy, that promises are not, ought not, to be binding?"

Though the busy croud of passengers were too much occupied by their own concerns to take notice of her soliloquy, it met with numerous interruptions from the jostlings of hawkers, porters, draymen, &c. &c. who, careless of all before them, pushed their way in a manner so rude, as would frequently have provoked an expostulation from our heroine, had they not quickly got out of the reach of her voice. At the bottom of Holborn-hill the throng was so great, that she was unable to resist its impetuosity; but hurried along by the torrent, was forced to make a retrogade movement of several steps. On another occasion she was carried forward with a rapidity as much beyond her strength as contrary to her inclination: gasping for breath, she attained the steps of a shopdoor, where she stood for a few moments to recover herself. "Ah!" said she to herself, "how great must be his genius, who, in walking through a street like this, *can enter into nice calculations, can digest sagacious reasonings, can declaim or describe, impressed with the deepest sympathy, or elevated to the loftiest rapture!*[23] Oh, that I could energize in such a manner!"

'You seem at a loss, Ma'am;' said a tolerably well-dressed man, who at that moment passed. 'Can I be of any service to you, in shewing you your way?'

"I should be sorry to task your urbanity, sir,' returned Bridgetina; "but if you are going to Mincing-lane, I shall willingly accept of your assistance."

The stranger declaring he should have pleasure in escorting her, Bridgetina laid hold of his offered arm, and ascended Snow-hill, not a little satisfied with her polite conductor. They had proceeded to the middle of Newgate-street, Bridgetina all the while loading with praises the benevolence of the stranger; when, to her utter astonishment, giving her a push into the middle of the street, he darted off, and was out of sight in a moment.

"Look to your pockets;' cried a butcher's boy. She did so, and to her no small dismay perceived they had been both turned inside-out. Happily, a pocket-handkerchief and an empty purse was all she had to lose; but her spirits were so much fluttered by the accident, that she was glad to get into a coach, in which she hoped to return loaded with too considerable a sum to trust to the mercy of another benevolent stranger.

Sir Anthony Aldgate was at home; and our heroine, by her own desire, was conducted into his office, (a little, dismal, dirty-looking hole, where

---

[22] Wollstonecraft's propositioning of a married man became public knowledge following her husband Godwin's *Posthumous Works* (1798). Hays also advertised her own advances in *Memoirs of Emma Courtney* (1796).

[23] *Enquirer* Godwin, *The Enquirer*, Part I, Essay V, "Of an Early Taste for Reading". See Appendix A.

every thing wore the appearance of wretchedness and penury.) Here were several young men of no despicable parentage, no vulgar education, and no mean abilities, destined to pass the flower of their days in summing up pounds, shillings, and pence. But though every new combination increased the owner's wealth, it increased not the comforts of one of his dependants. Sir Anthony himself had no idea of any comfort but that of accumulation; and this place, which had been the scene of his successful negociations, was in his eyes beauteous as the gates of Paradise, and cheerful as the garden of Eden.

Bridgetina, who had never seen the knight but in his dress-suit and tie-wig, was surprised at the appearance he now made, in a scarlet flannel night-cap, and night-gown of green stuff, lined throughout with crimson flannel. A small black silk handkerchief was tied tightly round his neck, but quite hid from observation by the enormous mass of joller[24] which overhung it. He was seated at the desk when our heroine entered, from which having raised his small black eyes, "My cousin Biddy Botherim!" cried he, "is it possible? I am glad to see you, my dear. But where is your mother? Up stairs, with my wife and daughter, I suppose. Well, better go up to them, and I shall be with you presently. Good-bye."

'My business at present is only with you,' rejoined Bridgetina; 'and I must request an immediate audience.'

"Business with me, my dear; and pray what about? I really did not think you knew any thing about business."

'My business is of some importance,' rejoined Bridgetina; 'I am to inform you that I have immediate use for a thousand pounds, and to request that you would let me have that sum as soon as possible.'

"What! are you then really going to be married!" cried Sir Anthony. "I declare I should not have thought of that; but I hope your mother has taken care of the main chance: a good warm man—hey?—"

'I neither wish my mother, or any one else, to concern themselves in my affairs,' said Bridgetina; 'and desire you would put yourself to no farther trouble, than to make over to me the sum I mention.'

"Fair and softly, cousin," rejoined Sir Anthony; "don't you know that my consent in this business is absolutely necessary? And do you think that I will give my consent to any person that does not choose to settle your fortune upon you and your lawful issue?"

'I shall have no lawful issue,' cried Bridgetina angrily, 'I hate lawful issue, and every thing that is lawful. Persons of enlightened minds ought not, by giving their sanction to an odious institution, to retard the progress of intellect. I never shall marry.'

"No!" returned Sir Anthony, archly measuring with his little optics the figure of our heroine, "I believe not, my dear, till you get an offer, he, he, he—what, sour grapes, Miss Biddy, hey?"

---

[24] Variant of jowl.

'Whether I have an offer or not, sir, is no concern of yours. All you have to do is, to let me have a thousand pounds of my own fortune, which I can now dispose of in a way that will reflect lasting honour on my name, and effectually operate towards the grand end of life, general utility.'

"A thousand pounds!" cried Sir Anthony, in amazement. "What d—ned fools these people in the country are; they know no more of the price of stocks than what's doing in the moon. Time of war, time of peace, loan or no loan, all's the same to them. I'd lay ten pounds to a sixpence, thou can'st not tell what consols were done for any time these three months; and yet ye would sell out, would ye? A pretty ignoramus, truly! You may thank your stars, my dear, that your father left ye in better management. A thousand pounds, indeed! And pray, how would your wise head speculate with a thousand pounds?"

'Your perceptions,' returned Bridgetina, with a contemptuous sneer, 'your perceptions are too obtuse to penetrate the scope of the grand design in which I am about to engage. The virtues of the philosophers of Africa, with whom I intend shortly to associate, are too sublime for the comprehension of a vulgar mind. The—'

"What! going to speculate in Sierra-Leona shares, Miss Wisehead, are ye? But what, indeed, poor thing, should you know of such matters? Be thankful, again I tell you, be thankful that your father wisely put you into better hands. No man upon 'Change can tax me with having ever lost a farthing upon idle speculation. I remember in the year sixty-seven—no—I believe it was in the year sixty-nine—aye, now I think of it, it was sixty-nine, for it was the very day after Mr. Alderman Pruen gave his grand feast on being elected to the ward of —; I remember it well; the turtle soup was the very best I ever ate in my life. I say it was in the year sixty-nine, just as—"

Here Bridgetina made an attempt to interrupt the knight, but in vain; he thus proceeded:

"You shall hear—you shall hear—I hate to be tedious. Just, I say, as I turned the corner of 'Change-alley, who should come up to me but Mr. Peter Purdy, brother to Purdy of Yarmouth, the great speculator in whale-blubber. He was a Scotchman; so was Peter. Aye, aye; they were both Scotsmen; a shrewd fellow, I warrant ye. Thought to take me in! But you shall hear. As I was saying, just as I turned the corner of 'Change-alley, up comes Peter. Now you must know, stocks had been done for 87 3/4 for the January account. I was then a bull—I remember it well—Nib, of Bartholomew-lane, was a lame duck, and Tom—"

'I never concern myself with any body's ducks,' cried Bridgetina, impatiently, 'I leave the care of the poultry entirely to my mother, and to her you may talk of such matters with propriety; but my energies are directed to nobler objects. Unhappy state of civilization! Odious laws, that put it in a man's power to secure his property to his children! If it had not been for them my fortune should have been, ere now, disseminated in a direction which—'

"Aye, aye, you may thank your father's will for having one shilling to rub upon another, I see that. It would all have gone else to sharpers and swindlers. Your father did well in consulting me; did he not? But, indeed, my cousin Botherim was a man of sense; he never took any step without consulting me. Who, do you think, advised his marriage with your mother? Ah! it was an excellent speculation! Six thousand pounds for a young curate, whose whole stock lay in the Greek and Latin funds, was no bad job, let me tell ye. I knew how old Pasty would cut up. There was not a better frequented cookshop in London than his. No one made better vermicelli soup. I well remember going there once with old Drugget of Lombard-street, father to Drugget of the Borough; he was partner to Bingley the broker, and did a monstrous deal of business. As I was saying, we went one day to old Pasty's, your grandfather's—"

'What is my grandfather to me?' cried Bridgetina; 'an illiterate drudge, whose energies were all directed to the sordid purposes of accumulation. I once for all desire to have a categorical answer. Will you, or will you not, let me have a thousand pounds of my fortune to dispose of at my own pleasure?'

"A thousand pounds! no, nor a thousand pence neither; no, nor a single shilling while you remain a spinster, on any pretence whatever; so there's your answer, Miss; will that please you?"

'No, it does not please me; but what can be expected in a state of society so depraved? so—'

"GOD help the foolish girl, how she talks. Prythee, my dear, where didst thou pick up all this jargon? This is all along of them there foolish books your mother suffers you to read. If I ever caught my daughter so much as opening a book, it should be the dearest day she ever saw. But she is better taught, I promise ye; I don't believe she has looked in one since she came from school; don't know how she should, for not a book has ever been within these doors, but the Book of Common-Prayer, and old Robin's almanack. Trust me for that. I know better what to do with my money."

'If you persist in refusing my request of the thousand pounds, I hope at least you will not deny me the trifling sum of twenty guineas for immediate necessaries?'

"What! your last dividend all gone already? It is shameful extravagance. I shall not encourage such profusion, such a squandering of property; at a time, too, when it might be laid out to such advantage! It is monstrous. I tell you I shall not encourage it. Want money to buy books, I suppose—do ye? Is that the way you have spent all that I paid you in August?"

'Yes, man of narrow mind. That sum, which would have been spend in useless luxury by a weak, or vilely hoarded by an ignoble, spirit, was by me bestowed to promote the grand object of general utility.'

"General Fiddlestick!" exclaimed Sir Anthony.

Bridgetina, without noticing the interruption, went one. 'It was given to the enlightened Citizen Glib to enable him to import from France several valuable treatises on philosophy and atheism.'

"Philosophy and atheism!" repeated Sir Anthony in a fury. "Hell and confusion, who ever heard the like of this? What has made the stocks fall forty per cent. but philosophy and atheism? What has raised the price of insurance, and burthened the nation with such a load of new taxes, but philosophy and atheism? Tell me that? Why have we raised such an army, aye and such a navy too, but to keep these vile French principles out of the kingdom?[25] And yet this here idle girl, this fool, this little viper, shall be the means of importing in a box, four feet square, all the principles that it has cost us so many millions of money, and so many hundred thousand lives to keep out of the kingdom! Away, I say, and never see my face; I would inform on you for a farthing.[26] Was it not for my cousin Botherim's memory, I should give you lodgings you little think of; but you shall have no harbour here, d'ye mind me! Never again darken my doors, I desire you. Never come here again on such an errand."

'Wretched mortal!' cried Bridgetina, 'how deplorable is thy ignorance! Yet,' continued she, in a tone that sufficiently indicated the violence she did in suppressing her resentment: 'yet thou hast energies, which, if properly directed, might produce glorious effects. Think not, however, by thy intemperance to intimidate me. He that would adorn himself with the most elevated qualities of a human being, ought to come prepared for encountering obloquy and misrepresentation. When thou art willing to listen to information, I shall be happy to instruct thee, till then I take my leave.' So saying, she tottered in great agitation to the coach, while the knight returned to his seat with an intention of communicating to Mrs. Botherim a full account of the behaviour of her daughter, with a severe censure upon herself for permitting it.

Bridgetina, having given the coachman orders to drive to Conduit-street, pulled up the glasses, and throwing herself into a corner of the coach, gave way to a burst of passion, which was the more violent for having been so long suppressed.

Anger and disappointment so entirely occupied her mind, that the door was opened for her at Mrs. Benton's, before she recollected that she had not any means of paying the coachman. Her embarrassment was soon removed by her good-natured landlady; to whom, though she was already indebted more than Mrs. Benton's slender finances could bear without inconvenience, she did not scruple to owe a still farther obligation.

---

[25] England was at war with France from February 1793-March 1802 and then again from May 1803-June 1815.

[26] Reference to the Loyalist Address Movement which arose from King George III's proclamation on May 21st 1792 that "divers wicked and seditious writings had been circulated throughout the kingdom which might excite tumult and disorder." The King urged subjects "to avoid and discourage proceedings, tending to produce riots and tumults and instructed magistrates to forward any information about seditious activities to the central government." See Robert Dozier, *For King, Constitution and Country: The English Loyalist and the French Revolution* (Lexington: UP of Kentucky, 1983).

The idea of seeing Henry Sydney in the evening soon banished every disagreeable impression from her mind. Now, at length, she was to have an opportunity of combating all his objections; now she should have the glory of arguing him into love. A speech which had long been conned, twice written over in a fair hand, and thirteen times repeated in private, was now to prove its efficacy. It was taken from her pocket; the heads again run over; and for the help of memory, in case of interruption, a sort of index taken of the contents, which she thus read aloud, while the maid cleared the table after dinner. *Moral sensibility, thinking sensibility, importunate sensibility; mental sensation, pernicious state of protracted and uncertain feeling; congenial sympathy, congenial sentiment, congenial ardour; delicious emotions, melancholy emotions, frenzied emotions; tender feeling, energetic feeling, sublimised feeling; the germ, the bud, and the full-grown fruits of the general utility, &c. &c.*[★27] "Yes," cried she, in extacy, when she had finished the contents, "this will do! Here is argument irresistible; here is a series of calculations, enough to pour conviction on the most incredulous mind. Henry overcome shall cry—Bridgetina, thou hast conquered!"

'*Let not him that girdeth on his armour, boast as he that throweth it off;*' said a wise king of Israel.[28] The victory was not quite so decisive on the side of Bridgetina as she expected. The prejudices of Henry were invincible. Instead of acknowledging the force of her arguments, he laughed at their absurdity. What she called the sublime deductions of recondite and abstract truth, he termed the pernicious delusions of sophistry; and so perversely erroneous were his sentiments, that instead of admiring the contempt of chastity as an exalted proof of female heroism and virtue, he persisted in reprobating the principles that could lead to such an idea, as destructive of the peace, the happiness, and the well-being of society.

Bridgetina, having gone twice round the circle of her arguments, was at length compelled to give an unwilling hearing to those of Henry. He began by assuring her of his friendship, and as the best proof he could give her of his good wishes for her happiness, pointed out to her in the strongest terms the consequences of her present conduct; and earnestly urged the necessity of her immediate return to W—, as the only means of saving her from mortification and misfortune. He had at first laughed very heartily at her strange notion of his being in love with Mrs. Fielding; but apprehensive lest the old lady should be hurt by a hint of any thing so ridiculous, he took some pains to convince Bridgetina of her

---

[27] ★Note, for the benefit of Novel-writers.—We here generously present the fair manufacturers in this line with a set of phrases, which, if carefully mixed up with a handful of story, a pretty quantity of moonshine, an old house of any kind, so that it be in sufficient decay, and well tenanted with bats and owls, and two or three ghosts, will make a couple of very neat volumes. Or should the sentimental be preferred to the descriptive, it is only leaving out the ghosts, bats, owls, and moonlight, and the above phrases will season any tender tale to taste★.

[28] 1 *Kings* 20: 11.

mistake as to the object of his passion; at the same time declaring, that though delicacy prevented him from mentioning the name of her who possessed his affections, they were for ever fixed.

"Who can promise for ever?" cried Bridgetina. "Are not the opinions of a perfectible being for every changing? You do not at present see my preferableness, but you may not be always blind to a truth so obvious. How can I believe it compatible with the nature of mind, that so many strong and reiterated efforts shall be productive of no effect? Know, therefore, Doctor Sydney, it is my fixed purpose to persevere. I shall talk, I shall write, I shall argue, I shall pursue you; and if I have the glory of becoming a moral martyr, I shall rejoice that it is in the cause of general utility."

'If you are resolved to be a martyr to your own folly, Miss Botherim,' said Henry, rising, 'I am determined your friends shall not have me to blame in the business. I solemnly assure you, this is the last time I shall ever speak to you, unless you shew, by your immediate return to W—, that you have recovered a sense of what you owe to yourself and to your sex. Good night.'

Bridgetina called after him in the soft tone of persuasion, but in vain. The hard-hearted youth hurried down stairs, and opening the street-door for himself, was out of hearing in a moment.

To paint the feelings of our heroine, on the abrupt departure of her beloved swain, is a task less suited to the pen than the imagination. To the imagination of our readers we shall therefore leave it; and content ourselves with observing, that as it is one of the prime advantages of *system* to be able to twist, and turn, and construe every thing to its own advantage, defeat produces as potent a stimulus to perseverance as victory.

The three following days were employed by Bridgetina in the composition of a letter, which she determined should be a master-piece of fine writing. It was, indeed, the very essence of philosophy, and flower of eloquence. The stile was sublime and energetic, adorned in every sentence by strings of double and treble epithets, and all the new coined noun-verbs and verb-nouns that have of late so much enriched the English language. As to the arguments, the reader must have formed a very inadequate idea of Bridgetina's powers, if he does not believe them to be unanswerable. After having carefully taken a copy, which she resolved should on some future day be generously presented to the public, she consigned the letter to the care of Jenny, with instructions to give it into Henry's own hand, and diligently to observe the expression of his countenance while he perused it.

The twenty minutes of Jenny's absence appeared an age to Bridgetina. She took her station at the window, and at length had the happiness of seeing her messenger of love appear, loaded to her wish, with a packet still larger than her own. "He has written! He has written!" cried she, in an extacy. "He has at length deigned to enter into a discussion on the important truths it has been my glory to promulgate. My *powers* shall be again called forth in an answer. Our correspondence shall be printed. It shall be published. It shall be called *The Sweet Sensations of Sensibility, or the Force of Argument*.[29] But here she comes. Give me the letter. But before I open it, let me know how he received mine? I see by this it must have arrived in a moment of impression. Did he not kiss the seal? Did he not in trembling extacy press it to his throbbing bosom? Tell me, tell me all, I conjure you."

'He did not kiss a bit of it, that I saw, Ma'am,' returned Jenny. 'He only took it out of my hand, and said Pshaw.'

"Pshaw! What does Pshaw signify? What is its etymology? From whence its derivation? I must look to the dictionary. But did you mark his looks, as he perused the important pages? Did you observe where he changed colour, where he appeared struck with admiration, and where thrilled with delight?"

'I could see nothing of all which you says, Ma'am; for though I told him as how that you desired me to see him pruse it, he only said Phoh! and walked into his closet."

"Charming delicacy! But here, here it is that I shall view the portrait of his soul. Here the high-wrought frenzied emotions of his bosom are doubtless pourtrayed. Here—"

'Bless me, Ma'am, how pale you look! Aye, that is the very letter I carried to the gentleman, sure enough. The seal not so much as broken! I'll be bound he never read a word on't. Well now, I vow I never saw a more ungenteeler thing done in all my life; and if I was you, Ma'am, (thos to be sure, you must know best) but I should ha' my fingers burnt before I should write another sullebul to such a grumpish sort of a gentleman.'

"My epistle of fourteen pages, my precious essay on philosophy and love, returned without a perusal—returned in a blank cover! O hideous perversion of intellect! O prejudices, obstinate and invincible! Has he no sense of justice, no sense of the duty he owes society, that he thus deprives of her usefulness one of its most valuable members? O Jenny, Jenny, I can energize no longer. The freezing frost of frigid apathy chills my powers. The morbid excess of a distempered imagination choaks the germ of general utility! I shall become a wanderer in the barren wilderness of society, an useless plant in the populous desart of human life! Leave me, leave me to myself, that I may in apt soliloquy give vent to the palpitating perturbation of my woe-struck fancy."[30]

'Good la! what a power o' fine words you ha, Ma'am, just at your fingers' ends too, as a body may say. I never did hear so fine a spoken lady

---

[29] Bridgetina positions her love for Henry within the tradition of love letters such as those between Eloise and Abelard, Julie and St Preux. Her indebtedness to Godwin's theory of Necessitarianism is reflected in the title.

[30] Like Hays's heroine Emma, whose correspondence is often unread or unanswered by the man she loves and who laments "Should I, at length, awake from a delusive vision, it would be only to find myself a comfortless, solitary, shivering, wanderer, in the dreary wilderness of human society" (*Memoirs of Emma Courtney*, 1796, 116).

in all my life. But, well-a-day! the men care no more for a woman's words, if so be as how that she happens to be a little ordinary or so, than for the squeaking of a pig. But I would despise the fellors, so I would—and so I does. I walors not e'er a man in the world the walor of a rush!'

Bridgetina again signified her pleasure to be left alone, and Jenny, not a little pleased with having been so far admitted to her confidence, hastened to disburthen herself of all she knew of the late transaction, to the very first person that would give her the hearing.

While Bridgetina was eloquently bemoaning the indignant treatment of her letter in the drawing-room, and Jenny expatiating on the same subject (though, perhaps, in terms not exactly similar) in the kitchen; the whole soul of Henry was entirely occupied, not with Bridgetina, nor with her love, nor with her letter, but with the contents of one he had just received from his father; and in the perusal of which he had been interrupted by Miss Botherim's messenger. The old gentleman's epistle was as follows:

"*My dear Henry,*

"IT would be superfluous to dwell upon the pleasure your letters have afforded to those most dearly interested in your happiness. Though far from considering fortune as the "one thing needful," the exclusive object of pursuit, I cannot but with thankfulness contemplate your opening prospects of honourable independence. May the Giver of all good bestow upon you *a heart to enjoy*, a mind superior to the restlessness of ambition, and stranger to the gnawings of discontent. For the attainment of these happy dispositions, without which increase of fortune is but increase of sorrow, I know no better means (next to an habitual dependence on the Divine favour) than the pursuit of science, particularly those branches of it that are most intimately connected with your profession.

"I am delighted with the success of your chemical experiments, and still more highly satisfied with the ingenuous frankness you display in so candidly acknowledging your former errors. But such must ever be the consequence of directing our researches, not into the wild and fruitless regions of idle speculation, where the chimeras of fancy are mistaken for realities, and bold conjecture assumes the authoritative tone of truth; but into those laws of nature that, by being objects of sense, and subject to the investigation of experiment, are within the grasp of our limited and feeble minds.

"Such speculations have, indeed, a direct tendency to influence the moral character of man. It is this that stamps them with their real value; for to whatever height we ascend in tracing the causes which regulate the system of the world, our views must at last terminate in an uncaused Being, in whom all the beauty and order, all the wisdom and power, displayed throughout the universe, are centered. "When we look around us," says an amiable philosopher, in the conclusion of a volume that presented a valuable discovery to the world, "When we look around us, we perceive that every part of the material world is governed by general laws; and when we reflect that in this vast system of things, a race of beings exists, to whom the Deity has communicated a portion of his intelligence and activity, we cannot avoid concluding, that laws must have been ordained for the government of such beings, as well as for that of all other parts of the universe."★[31]

"Thus does the study of Nature lead us up to Nature's GOD. Thus does the material world itself give evidence to the probability of a revelation, and to those whose minds have been expanded by the contemplation of the union of grandeur and simplicity in the works of creation, it must be peculiarly delightful to observe the same union of grandeur and simplicity characterising the gospel of Jesus Christ.

"Yes, my son, believe me, the more you study the life and precepts of our great Master, the more forcibly will you be struck with the congruity at which I have already hinted. But, alas! as in the infancy of natural philosophy, the ill-directed diligence of the chemist was wasted upon trifles, while the grand laws of nature were unnoticed and unknown; so in the Christian world, has the zeal of believers been more strenuously exerted in the support of non-important forms and dogmas, than in the promulgation of those grand and simple truths which are marked with the signet of Nature's GOD.

"I need not apologize to you, my dear Harry, for being led into a subject which, though the most important, as well as the most exalted, of which human beings can treat, it is, I know, deemed a breach of politeness to hint at even to a friend; but shall confess, that the impression made upon my mind by the conversation I held with Captain Delmond on his deathbed, has given an unusual degree of solemnity to the train of my ideas. Indeed the misfortunes of that unhappy family, as well as the misery that has overtaken some others of this place, so evidently originate in false impressions received of religion, as a gloomy and illiberal system of superstition, that I cannot cease from deploring the neglect of early information on this important point, as the foundation of those mistaken prejudices that are fraught with consequences so fatal to the happiness of society.

"While Captain Delmond was taught to idolise the name of *honour* as the palladium of human virtue, religion was presented to his mind as a mean and inferior principle, incapable of inspiring noble sentiments in the soul of a gentleman. Had not the avenues to investigation been thus pre-occupied by prejudice, he would have discovered that *honour*, which is nothing more than a nice susceptibility to the censure or applause of mankind, is neither so grand in its views, so extensive in its operation, nor so noble in its object, as that principle which teaches the heart to appeal

---

[31] ★Treatise on Animal Heat and Combustion. By Adair Crawford, M.D.★ Adair Crawford, *Experiments and Observations on Animal Heat, and the Inflammation of Combustible Bodies; being an Attempt to Resolve these Phenomena into a General Law of Nature* (London: J. Murray, 1779).

for its purity and integrity, not to the purblind judgment of our fellow-mortals, but to a Being of infinite purity and perfection. While performing a part on the busy stage of life, Captain Delmond found honour competent to the purpose of gaining him the flattering approbation of the multitude, which was reverberated by self-applause; but when he proposed it as the sole principle of action to his daughter, when he deprived her mind of the supporting aid of religion, and desired her to consider the intrinsic excellence of virtue as its own sure and only reward, he was not aware how liable she was to be taught by sophistry a definition of virtue very opposite to his. Had a proper value for the morality of the Gospel, enhanced by its gracious promises and elevated views, been instilled into her tender mind, his child, his darling Julia, would not have brought the grey hairs of her father with sorrow to the grave.

"The remains of this unhappy gentleman were yesterday consigned to their parent dust in military state, and with a degree of magnificence, an ostentatious parade of pomp and grandeur, that, in my opinion, was ill-suited to the occasion. After the conclusion of the ceremony, Gen. Villers and a Major Minden, (a man of large fortune, who, it seems, had made proposals to Miss Delmond) politely waited on the poor forlorn and disconsolate widow, and took their leave of her in terms of the most courtly civility. I expected that the General, who was no stranger to the poverty to which she was reduced, would have come forward with some generous offer of pecuniary assistance. But no: the General's generosity was completely expended in producing the parade of a half an hour's procession; and I greatly question, whether he ever does Mrs. Delmond the honour of another visit.

"After the departure of these great gentlemen, I was called out of the room by Quinten, the Captain's old domestick, on whose face was painted the sincerity of sorrow; he beckoned me into the back-parlour, and having once or twice, with a stroke of his hard hand, driven away the tears that fell upon his furrowed cheek, "I thought, sir," said he, "when I saw the lid of the coffin screwed down upon my good master, that I had lived too long. When I heard the hammer knock upon the last nail, my heart so sunk at every stroke, it made a coward of me; and I should have been glad to have skulked to the quiet garrison of death. But then, when I thought on my poor mistress, and remembered how my poor dear master loved her, I scorned to be so cowardly as to desert my post, when, by fighting with life a little longer, I might save her from being stormed by want. I know all I can do is but a trifle—a nothing, as a body may say, to folks that are any way above the world, but it may be of use to her for all that; and so, as I hear you are going to look into my master's papers, and to see what can be made out for my poor mistress, I thought it best to tell you to take my pension into the account."

"Your pension, Quinten! and what do you reserve for yourself?"

'Nothing but what I can earn by my own labour. Thank GOD, I am not yet past working. You see how well I have dressed the Captain's garden. It was I that made that pretty serpentine walk for Miss Julia, and planted all them flowers, of which she used to be so fond. Alas! that I should ever live to see the day of her deserting them! Oh, who would have thought it! such a pretty creature as she was, and so mild-spoken, and so good to every body, that she should after all go for to break her father's heart!'

"Well, but, honest Quinten, you do not consider that you are now in the decline of life, and cannot long be able to labour as you have done."

'I know it, sir. I am growing old apace, but Sam Smith, the old gardener at Bensfield, is ten years older than I am, and he still keeps his place. I am a stouter man than he at any time. And so, dy'e see, I am determined not to touch a farthing of this here Chelsea pension while I am able to lift a spade. Did not I get it by the good word of my master; and who, then, has so good a right to it as his widow? Here are twelve guineas besides, which I humbly beg, you would fall on some means to make her accept; for I know she would not touch it, if she thought it came from me. So pray don't let her know who sent it; for folks in affliction ought to be mighty tenderly dealt with, so as not to hurt their pride—*feelings*, I believe, my young mistress would have called it, but I am not learned enough to know the difference.'

"Honest, worthy Quinten!" cried I, grasping his hand, "thou hast a heart that doth honour to thy species, and principles that are more estimable than all the learning in the world. At a period when neither talents nor learning shall avail, thy gratitude and thy virtues shall exalt thee to glory!" I was so struck by the nobleness of this poor fellow's behaviour, that I could not avoid giving you the conversation in detail. I shall be more brief with regard to what followed, though for the honour of your friend I ought there likewise to be particular.

"On examining the books and papers of the deceased, it appeared, that all which remained to the widow was the house and furniture, and twenty-five pounds a year from an annuity-association, of which her husband had been a member. I had planned an application to Mrs. Fielding for doubling this sum, when Mr. Churchill generously stepped forward, and with a delicacy that enhanced the merit of his generosity declared, that though the transaction did not appear in any of the Captain's papers, he was trustee for an annuity of an hundred pounds to Mrs. Delmond, which as long as she remained a widow, should be regularly paid at the terms of Lady-Day and Michaelmas.[32]

"I know how you will rejoice in the noble conduct of your friend, but I believe I should have left the description of it to your sister, whose lively sensibility to all that is great and excellent would have done that justice to the subject of which my tired pen is now incapable. From her

---

[32] Lady Day: 25th March, day of annunciation of the Virgin; Michaelmas 29th September, festival of St. Michael, a quarterly rent day.

own lips, however, you will shortly have an opportunity of receiving it; and I do not think she will suffer any circumstance that attended it to lose in the recital.

"Sadly shall I feel the dear girl's absence, whose company is the solace of my heart. The sweetness of her temper, the harmonious cheerfulness of her disposition, might soften the rugged breast of a tyrant, and soothe the most boisterous passions into peace; to me they are enhanced by a mind of quick intelligence, whose cultivation has been the sweetest and the easiest task of my whole life. I must, however, carefully conceal from her the pain her absence shall occasion me; as otherwise, I know all the pleasure Mrs. Fielding has prepared for her would be destroyed. She and her friend Miss Orwell are now busily employed in preparing for their purposed expedition, to which they look forward with the happy ardour of juvenile expectation. The kind consideration of Mrs. Fielding, in inviting Miss Orwell to partake with Maria in the scenes of novelty and amusement, where their reciprocal feelings of surprise and pleasure must enhance their mutual delight, is a new proof of the goodness of her heart. Harriet does not, however, express her relish for the journey in the same manner as Maria. The emotion with which she now speaks of it, is less gay, and apparently more constrained. When first informed that her father had given his consent to her acceptance of Mrs. Fielding's invitation, she, indeed, appeared agitated in a greater degree than I should have expected from a girl of her understanding; but that I suppose was from the mere love of novelty, a charm that never fails to operate strongly on the youthful breast. This day fortnight is fixed on for the day of their departure, Dr. Orwell is himself to be their escort, and Mr. Churchill likewise proposes being of the party; Mrs. Botherim has delayed her journey, in order to have their company upon the road, so that they will fill two chaises, and, if no accident interposes, have the promise of a pleasant journey.

"Meantime I shall be left to the enjoyment of my own reflections; but, thank GOD, these are not disagreeable companions. I can look upon the past with comfort, and to the future without dismay. In the happiness of my children I am more than happy. O may this dearest of all felicities be my companion and my solace through all the short space that now remains for me to tread! May they never cause me a sigh of sorrow, as, thanks to Heaven, they have never tinged my cheeks with the blush of anger or of shame. GOD bless thee, my dear Harry, prays your tenderly affectionate father,

"H. SYDNEY."

P.S. I find I have committed a sad blunder, in telling you of the intended journey to London. It was to have been a secret, it seems, and much pleasure did the girls promise themselves in your surprise. It is in vain I preach to Maria about the sin it would be to deprive you of the pleasure of anticipation, which, alas! makes up such a mighty part of the small sum of human happiness. They insist upon my writing the last part of my letter over again, but my fingers are already cramped, so it must go; and when you read it, you may go to your glass, and tell them how you looked when you see them; for it is their curiosity as to this important point, that I now find to be their reason for secrecy. GOD help them! poor things! Adieu!

CHAP. V.

> "—He was a shrewd philosopher,
> "And had read every text and gloss over.
> "Whate'er the crabbed'st author hath,
> "He understood b'implicit faith.
> ...
> "All which he understood by rote,
> "And as occasion serv'd, wou'd quote."
> BUTLER.[33]

'HARRIET Orwell coming up to town by invitation from Mrs. Fielding!" exclaimed Henry. "How extraordinary! Is it in order to gratify my wishes, or to try my prudence, that she at this juncture brings her to London? No matter which; I shall see my Harriet; I shall hear her sweet voice; I shall have the delight of being near her almost continually. Dear Mrs. Fielding, how I bless thee!'

In the midst of this delirium of pleasure, Henry was interrupted by the arrival of Miss Botherim's letter. Of the manner of its reception it is unnecessary to repeat the particulars, as they have already been given so minutely by Jenny, whose faithful report of all that fell from Henry's lips upon the occasion, justly entitles her to our applause. No sooner had he re-delivered the important packet into the hands of Bridgetina's messenger, than he stept to Mrs. Fielding's, on pretence of informing her of the contents of his father's letter, but in reality to endeavour to penetrate into her motives for inviting Miss Orwell to accompany his sister to London. In vain did he watch her countenance, while she perused that part of the epistle which had caused him such extreme emotion; he only saw it lighted up with a benignant smile. "How much is Maria, how much are we all indebted to your goodness!" cried he; "how happy have you made me—I—mean, how—"

'You mean, I suppose, that it was good-natured of me to provide your sister with a companion, that she might not be altogether confined to the society of an old woman, which you know from experience to be sufficiently tiresome. You see how well I can explain for you.'

"The society of Mrs. Fielding must ever—"

---

[33] Samuel Butler, *Hudibras* (1663) First Part, Canto 1, 125-36.

'Be superior in your opinion to that of a young and pretty girl, I suppose; but as Maria may be of a different way of thinking, I imagined a companion of her own age would be no disagreeable circumstance to her; and as I wished to pay my old acquaintance, Dr. Orwell, a compliment, I thought I could not do it at an easier rate than by inviting his daughter to spend a few weeks in London. But, pray, who is this Mr. Churchill? He seems a character that is worth the knowing, and I must desire you would introduce him to me whenever he comes to town.'

"I shall have a pride in presenting him to you as my earliest and dearest friend; and one I can, with confidence, pronounce worthy of the honour of your acquaintance."

'Does he reside at W——?'

"He was brought up by a rich uncle, whose estate surrounds the village, but who was such a miser, that, though Churchill was his only near relation, and a deserved favourite, he could hardly be prevailed upon to afford him the education of a gentleman. My friend's genius was rather stimulated than repressed by the obstacles which his uncle's avarice threw in the way of his improvement. His intimacy with me brought him frequently to our house, where his thirst after knowledge was encouraged and gratified by the lessons of my father. The expences attending an university education would for ever have deterred the old gentleman from permitting him to prosecute his studies in a professional manner, had it not fortunately occurred to him, that by having a lawyer in his own family, he might gratify his love of litigation without the expence of a fee."

'Admirably calculated! He took care, I presume, that the young gentleman's studies should not be interrupted by those ingenious contrivances for getting rid of superfluous cash, that occupy so much of the time and talents of our young gentlemen of fashion at the university!'

"Alas! poor Charles! His ingenuity was, indeed, very differently employed. His most rigid economy was necessary to preserve the appearance of a gentleman; and the purchase of books, and attending lectures on such subjects of literature or science as were not immediately connected with his profession, was all stolen from his slender allowance of pocket-money. Yet these circumstances, then considered as so mortifying, he now regards as fortunate. But for these he might have been drawn into the vortex of dissipation, and in the wild career of pleasure have lost his taste for science, and regard to virtue."

'Too truly observed,' said Mrs. Fielding; 'and in my opinion, the abundance of pocket-money, with which every schoolboy is now furnished, has done as much towards the rapid progress of depravity, as any circumstance whatever. I hope your friend's success at the bar has been equal to his merit.'

"It has at least far exceeded his most sanguine expectations," returned Henry. "But the honour that has accrued to him from undertaking the cause of a helpless family, who, but for his generous aid, might have perished in obscurity and want, has deservedly raised his reputation into celebrity. Indeed, his whole conduct has given an ample proof that the profession of the law is not necessarily a narrower of the human heart."

'Narrow and illiberal must be his heart, that can so pronounce of it,' returned Mrs. Fielding. 'It is, like other professions, open to men of unprincipled, as well as to virtuous, minds; and the selfish passions have there, perhaps, as wide a field for their operation as in any other. But, thank heaven, we need not go to the records of former ages for illustrious instances of lawyers, whose eminent talents have been more than equalled by their exalted virtues.'

Henry again endeavoured to turn the conversation to the subject that engrossed his thoughts, but in vain. He could not obtain from Mrs. Fielding the smallest satisfaction relative to Miss Orwell's visit: she so sedulously avoided coming to any explanation, that he left her without being able in the least degree to penetrate her intentions.

Leaving Henry to pursue

"The idle phantasies of love,
"Whose miseries delight,"[34]

we return to Bridgetina. Her abstract reasoning and most profound reflections on the unenlightened conduct of her lover, received a very unseasonable interruption from Mrs. Benton. That good woman, after a modest preface of many apologies for the liberty she was compelled to take, presented her an account of the sum due for a fortnight's lodging which, together with what had been disbursed for other necessaries, amounted to seven guineas.

"Seven guineas!" said Bridgetina; "it is an unnatural state of civilization, in which seven guineas can be spent so soon. But my mind cannot at present descend to the vulgar concerns of common life. You may leave your bill, however, and when the present romantic, high-wrought, frenzied emotions of my perturbed spirit have a little subsided, I shall enter into an examination of the contents."

'I am extremely sorry to disturb you, Madam,' returned Mrs. Benton, 'but shall be really much obliged to you, if you can possibly make it convenient to settle it at present. I make a point of paying all our trades-people so regularly, that I shall be quite distressed at not being able to discharge the butcher's bill, and he is to return for the money in the evening.'

"Regularity," rejoined Bridgetina, "is a characteristic of common honesty, that *non-conductor to all the sympathies of the human heart*; that *infallible proof of mediocrity, to which it is impossible that any thing great, magnanimous, or ardent, can be allied*."★[35] Punctuality in the discharge of one's debts is

---

[34] James Thomson, *Seasons* (1726-30) "Spring", 1074-5.
[35] ★See Enquirer★ *Enquirer*, Part II, Essay VII, "Of Personal Reputation", 256.

held in deserved contempt by the illustrious and eccentric part of mankind; in whose eyes common honesty is a nuisance, reprobated and abhorred."

'It is, indeed, as you say, Ma'am, but common honesty to pay one's debts; and too often is it neglected by those who ought to set a better example. Oh, if my daughters and I were but regularly paid for our embroidery by the fine ladies for whom we work, we should then be but too happy, for we should then have nothing to care for. But great folks do not know the degree of misery they often inflict by their carelessness; they are too highly exalted out of the sphere (as one may say) of their fellow-creatures to cast a thought upon the difficulties of those who are to earn their bread by labour. I myself know ladies who never refuse to open their purses to charity, but who, if they had paid their tradesmen with punctuality, might have preserved some honest families from ruin."

"*Want of punctuality has for time immemorial supplied materials for invective against great and extraordinary characters,*★[36] returned Bridgetina. It is, as I said before, a breach of common honesty; and greatly is it to be regretted, that common honesty should so long have gained the applause of an injudicious world. But when mankind shall have been sufficiently enlightened by philosophy, utterly to discard the ignoble prejudices of religion, regard to common honesty will cease. Blessed æra! when a fair character shall be no longer deemed essential! When promises shall be no longer binding! And when men who have *practically proved themselves the pests and enemies of their species*, shall be estimated according to their energies; and for acts, which would in the present distempered state of civilization, be deemed worthy of the gallows, receive the applause due to their *eminent talents and uncommon generosity!*"[37]

'I cannot express myself so finely as you do, Ma'am, but I believe what you observe is very just; that though morals are badly enough attended to at present, God knows, yet if religion were banished from the world, (which Heaven forbid!) it would be far worse.' Again laying the bill before Bridgetina on the table, she begged her to peruse it at her leisure, and after making a second apology for her intrusion, left the room.

"Unnatural state of civilization!" cried Bridgetina, as soon as she was alone, "Odious and depraved society, where every thing one eats, or drinks, or wears, must necessarily be paid for! Oh, wise and enlightened Hottentots! ye alone of all mankind have attained to that state of perfection so charmingly described by the philosopher! where the evils of co-operation are avoided, where pecuniary rewards for labour are unknown, and a blessed state of equality gives vigour to the intellect, and rouses the sublime energies of the soul. Oh, that I were in the midst of the Gonoquais horde! There no mercenary demand for the rent of my lodgings,

---

[36] ★See Enquirer★ *Enquirer*, Part II, Essay VII, "Of Personal Reputation", 265.

[37] *Enquirer*, Part II, Essay VII, "Of Personal Reputation", 272.

no fares to hackney-coachmen, no bills from laundresses, nor butchers, nor bakers, nor grocers, nor shoe-makers, nor chandlers, nor glovers, would interrupt the sublime speculations of my towering fancy; but each congenial Hottentot, energizing in his self-built shed, would be too much engrossed by forming projects for general utility to break in upon my repose!"

Some hours were thus spent by our heroine in deprecating the odious institutions of the society in which it was unhappily her lot to live, before she thought of any method of extricating herself from her present embarrassment. It at length, however, very fortunately occurred to her recollection, that she had, on the day of her fruitless application to the city knight, observed the words *Money Lent* inscribed upon the doorposts of a shop in Oxford-street.

"Happy circumstance!" cried she, as soon as the thought occurred; "How fortunate was it, that by taking that road to the city, I should become acquainted with the abode of this philanthropist. Thus it is that events generate each other! Had Alexander the Great never bathed in the Cydnus, Shakespeare would never have written.★[38] Had I gone by the Strand, I might not have known, that even in this depraved and unnatural state of civilization, men are to be found, who, convinced of the immoral tendency of accumulation, promote the glorious aera of equality by distributing their superfluous wealth. Let me hasten to the abode of this enlightened person, who will doubtless deem it a duty to supply my wants."

Delighted with this idea, she hastily threw on her cloak, and proceeded without delay to the place where the advertisement had arrested her attention. The place was easily found. She entered, and instantly demanded an audience of the enlightened personage who had notified the generous intention of lending money. His wife was the person to whom she addressed herself; who told her, that Mr. Poppem was then engaged with a customer in the parlour, but that she could do her business equally well.

"My business," replied Bridgetina, "is to converse with the man you call your husband; for that he is your husband I can scarcely suppose, as it is little likely that a philosopher, who is convinced of the immoral tendency of accumulation, should give encouragement to a monopoly so pernicious as marriage."

'Dy'e mean to tell me, that I am not an honest woman?' cried the shopkeeper's in an enraged voice.

"An honest woman is a very mean and vulgar appellation for a person who acts upon principles of abstract virtue," rejoined Bridgetina. "I make no doubt that your virtues are sublime; and it is the high idea I have conceived of Mr. Poppem's, that now brings me here. Pray let him know, that a person of no mean energies wishes to converse with him."

---

[38] ★See Pol. Jus.★ *Political Justice*, Bk II, ch. v, "Of Rights", 193.

The sight of Bridgetina's large gold watch, which, in spite of the change of fashion, she still wore suspended from her apron-string by its massy chain of the same precious metal, operated as a more powerful pacifier of the good woman's resentment than all the arguments of philosophy. Without farther hesitation, she conducted our heroine to the inner chamber of Mr. Poppem, a place peculiarly dedicated to the mysteries of his profession; where, like a bronze statue that has been accidentally pushed into some ill-assorted wardrobe, he sat half-hid from view by piles of gowns, petticoats, great-coats, &c. A wretched-looking female stood before him, with a half-starved infant in her arms.

"And will you really give no more?" cried the supplicant, in a feeble voice.

'No more!' returned Poppem; 'no, not a shilling more, if it was to save you from the gallows. There's ne'er a pawnbroker in London would ha' gi'n you the half on't on that there trash; so you may take up your money, and be gone.'

"I must so!" returned the woman, with a heavy sigh; and taking up a few shillings that lay on a small table, she pressed her infant to her breast. "Yes, dearest," said she, "you shall now have bread!" The child turned up its languid eyes to her pale face, which was bedewed with tears. She again pressed it to her bosom, and departed.

'I beg your pardon, Miss,' cried Mr. Poppem, on perceiving Bridgetina. 'I purtest I have been so bothered by that there woman, and her tales of a cock and bull, that I did not observe you. These sort of paupers are such troublesome people to have any dealings with, that for my share, I declare I never wish to see one of them enter my shop. But pray, what is your demand, Miss?'

"I come, enlightened citizen," replied Bridgetina, "I come to inform myself of your motives, to enquire into your principles, and to convince you that I am entitled to a share in the property which, I make no doubt, it is your study to distribute according to the unerring rules of moral justice."

'Justice!' returned the pawn-broker; 'What d'ye mean by justice? I never was before any justice, but Justice Trap, in all my life; and then no one dared to say that black was the white of my eye. I stands upon my character. I deals upon the fair and the square. All open and above-board. I am no resetter of stolen goods—no abettor of robbery—no—'

"I understand you," said Bridgetina, interrupting him. "The unequal distribution of property may, undoubtedly, be termed a robbery; and *all existing abuses are to be deprecated only as they serve to increase and perpetuate the inequality of conditions.*★[39] When mankind are sufficiently illuminated, every person, possessed of property, will act as you, Mr. Poppem, now do. What I want particularly to know, is your mode of estimating the worth

---

[39] ★See Pol. Jus. vol.ii.★ *Political Justice*, Bk VIII, "Of Property."

of individuals; or, in other words, the criterion by which you judge of capacity?"

'Produce the pledge, Miss,' said Mr. Poppem; 'and if I don't estimate it as fairly as e'er a pawn-broker in London, you shall ha' the money for nothing.'

"What proof of powers or energies can the narrow limits of one short conversation afford?" returned Bridgetina. "I am, however, prepared to discuss, to investigate, to argue, to energize, to—"

Here the voice of a person in the front-shop attracted the attention of our heroine. She stopped to listen, and instantly recognized the peculiar dialect of her townsman, Mr. Glib. "How fortunate!" cried she, opening the slight door that separated the place she was in from the outer shop. "See how events generate each other!" holding out her hand to Mr. Glib.

'Ha! Citizeness Botherim!' cried Glib. 'How do, chuck? Glad to see you. Didn't think to meet ye here, though. Dost not come to Pop, surely?'[40]

Bridgetina immediately informed her brother illuminé of the motives of her visit to Mr. Poppem, at which he laughed so immoderately as to incur no small degree of our heroine's resentment.

'Can't help it, for my soul,' cried Glib, breaking into another immoderate fit of laughter. 'Take a pawn-broker for a philosopher! How comical! But never mind; better than us come for cash. Can'st help me to any? Cursedly out at elbows. Citizen Vall no better than a scoundrel. Sold my books to Lackington,[41] and gone off with the cash. Left me without a sixpence. Can lend me five pounds, I hope!'

"No, really," returned Bridgetina, "I have not at present so much as five shillings in my possession, and came here in hopes of receiving a supply for myself."

'So you can,' returned Glib. 'Get it on your watch. No watches among the Hottentots. No baubles, nor trinkets, nor gewgaws, in a reasonable state of society. Give it to me. Get you the money in a twinkling. How much dost want?'

"Ten guineas will do for my immediate exigences," replied Bridgetina, putting the watch into his hands.

'Say no more,' cried Glib. 'Shalt have it in a moment.' Then skipping across the shop, he entered Mr. Poppem's apartment without ceremony, and in a few minutes returned with fifteen pounds, and a duplicate.[42] The latter he put into the hands of Bridgetina, with the ten-pound note. 'Ten will serve your turn,' said he, and five is just what I want myself. Shall pay it in a trice.'

"But when? cried Bridgetina, perceiving him about to leave her. "When shall I see you? I shall want the money in a few days, and you do'nt know where to find me."

---

[40] To pawn something.
[41] A famous circulating library.
[42] Receipt for a pawned article.

'Never mind promises,' cried Glib. 'Nothing so immoral. Damps my energies to see a creditor. Preserve your energies, my dear. That's it! Energies do all!' So saying, he skipped out of the shop, and mingling with the croud, was quickly out of sight.

Bridgetina, forgetting at that moment the immoral tendency of punctuality, was extremely disconcerted by the sudden departure of Glib without a promise of repayment. The illuminated citizen's contempt of common honesty she knew to be as far superior to her own, as practice is to theory; but though she ought, upon her own principles, to have made a point of conceding to him the larger sum, as being the more deserving individual, yet either through the operation of some latent prejudice, or of some pre-disposing causes generated in the eternity that preceded her birth, she felt more inclined at that moment to relieve the pressing difficulties of her own situation, than to pay attention to the probably still more pressing difficulties by which he was embarrassed. Replete with chagrin and disappointment, she slowly returned to her lodgings; and having discharged Mrs. Benton's bill, retired to her own apartment, to muse in solitude and silence on the many miseries that overspread the barren wilderness of society.

CHAP. VI.

"He little recks the woes which wait.
"To scare his dreams of joy;
"Nor thinks to-morrow's alter'd fate
"May all those dreams destroy."
MRS. HANNAH MORE.[43]

SLOWLY, in the opinion of Henry, did the hours move on, till the day that brought his sister and her fair companion to London. At length the sun arose that was to light them on their journey, and never did astronomer with more anxiety watch its progress on the day of the transit of a planet, than did Henry on this occasion. He had formed the design of meeting them at Barnet, and having ordered his servant to procure horses, mounted about three o'clock, and set off full speed, in hopes of surprising them by his appearance at the Red-Lion, which he expected to reach before their arrival.

The day had been unusually fine for the season, but by the time he had got to Highgate, the sky became obscured, and a thick fog gradually spread over the face of the country. Cheered by the prospect in his "mind's eye," he pushed forward, and having obtained the rising ground in the middle of Finchley-Common, observed with palpitating delight the approach of

---

[43] Hannah More, *Sir Eldred of the Bower, a Legendary Tale* (1775), Part II.

two post-chaises, which he doubted not contained the friends he was in quest of. Riding briskly up to the first of the carriages, the glasses of which were all up, he called to the postillion to stop. The postboy obeyed. Immediately the front glass was let down, and the kindly greetings of Henry answered by the firing of a pistol! At the same moment two persons leaped from the carriage, and holding their pistols to the supposed highwayman, laid hold of the bridle, which had dropped from his hand.

"Have you enough?" cried one of the gentlemen.

'Yes,' returned Henry; 'and when you have discovered your mistake, you will probably think I have had too much.'

Henry's servant being neither so well mounted as his master, nor inspired with an equal degree of impatience, had fallen considerably behind. He darted forward at the report of the pistol, and seeing his master (as he imagined) in the hands of footpads,[44] he called out for help.

The gentleman who had fired the pistol, had, from the appearance of Henry, and still more from his manner of speaking, begun to have some apprehensions of his mistake. The appearance of the servant gave additional strength to his surmises.

"Wherefore did you stop the carriage?" cried he, in a voice rather less violent than his former tone.

'I expected to meet with friends,' said Henry, 'and confess I owe the accident entirely to my own imprudence. Whatever may be its consequences, you, sir, are acquitted of all blame.'

"Curse on my rashness!" cried the gentleman; "but I hope, sir, you are not much hurt?"

'Not mortally, I trust,' returned Henry. 'From my feelings, I should suppose the ball to be lodged in my shoulder: the wound in my arm will signify nothing.'

"A brave fellow, by my shoul!" exclaimed a person who at that moment came up from the second carriage. "I hope you will soon be after settling the matter honourably, my dear, and be able to call him to account for taking a highwayman for a jontleman."

'I can only blame my own imprudence,' said Henry.

"*You* may forgive me," said the gentleman, grasping Henry's hand; "but I never shall forgive myself. But let us not delay. My servant shall ride your horse, while you take his place in the carriage with me. I shall be miserable till the wound has been examined. Pray let us make haste."

'The jontleman may do as he plases,' said the other traveller, 'but by my shoul, my dear, when you travel through the county of Galway you had better take care how you pop at a jontleman, without giving him a chance of returning your fire!'

"I shall accept your offer with pleasure, sir," said Henry, without paying any attention to his observation, "and hope I shall have reason to rejoice in the accident, as giving me the acquisition of a friend."

---

[44] A highwayman who robs on foot.

The Irishman shrugged up his shoulders, and returned to his chaise; while Henry, with the assistance of the stranger, dismounted from his horse, and had placed his foot upon the step of the chaise, when the rattling noise of carriages advancing quickly towards them attracted his attention. It was now so dark, that they were quite near before they could be distinctly seen.

'Has any accident happened?' cried a voice, which Henry knew to be Doctor Orwell's.

"None that is of any consequence," said Henry, approaching the carriage.

'It is Doctor Sydney!' cried Harriet.

'It is Doctor Sydney!" repeated her father; "I hope no disaster—"

'A slight accident only,' said Henry: 'which I shall inform you of at leisure, if you will have the goodness to make room for me.'

"Yes, surely!" said they both at once. "Maria is behind," added the Doctor, "your appearance will alarm her, so pray step in immediately."

Henry assented; and taking a hasty leave of the stranger, placed himself by the side of Harriet, whose emotion was too apparent to escape the penetrating eyes of love. In a voice expressive of the tenderest solicitude, she enquired into the nature of the accident that had befallen him. Henry gave an evasive answer to her interrogatories, and turned the conversation; which, in spite of the pain he suffered, he continued to support with all that spirited animation the presence of a beloved object naturally inspires.

In the middle of a sprightly sally, he was stopped by a scream from Harriet. 'Ah! Sydney,' cried she, 'you are wounded! you are desperately wounded. My cloak is covered with blood.'

Henry, finding it was in vain any longer to attempt deceiving her, gave a faithful account of all that had happened; and was amply repaid for the anguish of his wound, by the interest Harriet evidently took in his misfortune.

On stopping at the door of Henry's lodgings, whither it had been agreed to drive, the stranger, whose rashness had occasioned the unlucky accident, presented himself, and with him an eminent surgeon, with whom Sydney was well acquainted; and who was the very person he had thought of sending for on the occasion.

Such generous ardour to repair an injury he had unintentionally committed, excited the admiration of Sydney, who, in suitable terms, thanked him for his attention; and then proceeded with him and Doctor Orwell to his own apartment, to submit the wound to the examination of the surgeon.

Harriert's heart sunk within her, at the idea of the pain he must necessarily undergo; in vain did she endeavour to exert her fortitude. When the carriage stopped in Hanover-square, she was too much agitated to alight. The second chaise drove up, and Maria, Mr. Churchill, and Mrs. Botterim had descended from it and come up to her, before she had sufficiently recollected her scattered spirits, to be able to form any excuse for her father's absence.

Alarmed at the appearance of her emotion, Maria earnestly entreated to know the cause; but without taking any notice of her questions, she hastily followed Mrs. Botherim into the house, where Mrs. Fielding received them with that happy mixture of cordiality and politeness which denotes the union of good-breeding and benevolence.

Henry's servant had communicated the news of his master's misfortune at Mrs. Fielding's a few minutes before the arrival of his friends, and had thereby excited a degree of alarm and anxiety, which was still visible in that good lady's countenance. The similar feelings of Harriet did not escape her notice; and by exciting a degree of interest and compassion, gave a stronger impression in her favour than all the graces of her person, or beauty of her countenance, could have produced.

The shock which Maria received from the intelligence was sufficiently severe, though mitigated by the confidence she reposed in the veracity of her friends; which she knew to be of too genuine a nature to admit of their imposing upon her by any of those *kind lies*, which are often so liberally dispensed upon similar occasions. Doctor Orwell's report was extremely favourable. The ball, he told them, had been extracted without difficulty, and the wound, in the opinion of the surgeon, so little serious, that it would only occasion a few days confinement.

Maria's anxious desire to visit her brother was indulged by Mrs. Fielding, who kindly ordered her own chair to attend her. Mr. Churchill, as he handed her into it, whispered a wish that it had been a more sociable conveyance; Maria did not frown, nor was she, possibly, much displeased at seeing him walk beside it to Henry's door.

While Maria and Churchill were on this charitable visit, poor Mrs. Botherim was employed in giving Mrs. Fielding a circumstantial detail of all she had suffered from Bridgetina's absence; interspersed with many bitter reflections on the wicked people, and still more wicked books, that had led her daughter astray. "Yes," cried she, "Ma'am, as I was telling you, I now knows for certain it is all along of them there people as comes to Mr. Glib's, who I thought, all the time, (GOD help me) to be the most learned and the most wisest people in the world. It is true, I did not understand much of the meaning of what they said; for what should I know of perfebility, and cowsation, and all them there things? But had I known that they meant to make children unnatural, and undutiful to their parents, they should never have been uttered in my house, I promise ye."

'It is, indeed, to be regretted,' said Mrs. Fielding, 'that Miss Botherim should have been so unfortunate in the choice of her books and friends. It could not be expected from Miss Botherim, that with her limited opportunities of information she should be able to detect the pernicious tendency of the opinions she so unhappily embraced.'

"Ah! Madam," returned Mrs. Botherim, "you have no sort of notion how learned she was. I do assure you, she has read as many books as e'er a parson in the kingdom. The histories of lords and counts, and colonels and ladies of quality, was what she pored on from morning till night. And then she got them there Metam Physics in whole volumes, as big as the church bible; all written, as she told me, by that *General Utility*, as she called him. I'm sure I shall hate the name of him as long as I live."

Mrs. Fielding could not help smiling at the simplicity of this account. 'I am afraid, my good Madam,' said she, 'that the sort of reading you first alluded to, was a very bad preparative for the latter. To an imagination enflamed by an incessant perusal of the improbable fictions of romance, a flight into the regions of metaphysicks must rather be a dangerous excursion. I am afraid Miss Botherim has gone too far astray in the fields of imagination to be easily brought back to the plain path of common sense.'

"I should hope," said Doctor Orwell, "that a little reflection would make her sensible of the fallacy of opinions, which have invariably proved fatal to all who have so far adopted, as to make them a principle of action."

'Yes, my dear Madam,' said Mrs. Botherim, 'do pray tell her of the consequences. Bid her think of poor Miss Delmond, who has been ruinated, and deluded, and ticed away by a fellow, who, for all his fine talk, is no better than a shabby hair-dresser. And—'

Here the entrance of Bridgetina, who had been sent for by Mrs. Fielding, put an end to the good lady's harangue. Her affection for her daughter so far outweighted her resentment, that the former only appeared in her reception. Throwing her arms round her neck, she exclaimed in broken accents, while tears flowed from her eyes, 'My Biddy! my dear Biddy! you will not leave your poor mother again? No, no, you cannot be so cruel. You shall do just whatever you please, and have the command of all I have in the world, if you will but stay with me to comfort my old age. I am sure,' added she, sobbing, 'I am sure I never contradicted you in my life—you cannot say that I did.'

"It would have been quite counter to the proper order of things, if you had," returned Bridgetina. "To a perfectible being every species of coercion is improper, and as contradiction is a species of coercion, it necessarily follows that—"

'There!' cried Mrs. Botherim, holding up her clasped hands in agony, 'there, now! she is at it again! Just the old story! all them there fine words over again, as pat as the day she first learned them. O, Biddy! Biddy! would ye but speak in a way that a body could understand!'

"If I were to speak to your comprehension, mother," returned Bridgetina, "I must descend indeed! A mind that is illumined like mine—"

'Come, come, Miss Botherim,' said Doctor Orwell, 'don't think you will add to your dignity by lessening your parent. I, for my share, know no good of any illumination that does not shew itself in the conduct. And in that, my dear, your mother has the advantage of you; as she has never been guilty of any glaring impropriety.'

"The person, sir, who would energise in no vulgar manner must prepare herself for encountering obloquy and censure" retorted Bridgetina.

'And pray, my dear, what entitles you to be superior to obloquy and censure? What right have you to think, that a line of conduct, condemned by the general suffrage of mankind, and which, if it were universally to prevail, would prove destructive to the peace and happiness of society, should escape reprehension?'

"The prejudices which spring from the odious institutions of an ill-constituted society," said Bridgetina, "ought to be despised by every person capable of soaring to a sublime morality, founded on abstract reasoning."

'And it is this sublime morality, founded on abstract reasoning, which teaches you to neglect, or to despise, the performance of every duty belonging to your situation?' returned the Doctor. 'It is *it* which teaches you to forsake an indulgent parent, who has made your happiness the study of her whole life; and in return for the tender care she has bestowed on your infancy and youth, to leave her old age to solitude and sorrow. It is this sublime morality, founded on abstract reasoning, which has likewise, I suppose, taught you to break through every law of delicacy and decorum, and shamelessly to offer yourself to prostitution? Such have been the fruits of this *sublime morality*, which arrogantly pretends to excell that of the Gospel!'

"I have somewhere heard reasoning termed *the arithmetick of words*," said Mrs. Fielding. "Where the sum total is so monstrous, I think we may confidently pronounce that there has been some error in the calculation. Of this, I have no doubt, Miss Botherim will become fully sensible, when she takes a wide and impartial view of the consequences."

'Aye!' cried Mrs. Botherim, 'let her take a view of Mr. Glib's poor ragged children in the parish workhouse, whom their father has left to starve, because, forsooth, a man should have no regard for his own flesh and blood! And let her see what is become of their mother—gone off, like a hussey, with a recruiting officer! Pretty consequences, truly! To say nothing of the death of that worthy gentleman, Captain Delmond, who died of a broken heart, if ever man did; and I am sure I do not wonder at his doing so, for what touches the heart of a parent equal to the undutifulness of a darling child? Woe is me that I should live to speak this from experience! But, indeed, Biddy, I shall never recover your unkindness.'

Notwithstanding the philosophy of Bridgetina, she could not help being affected by the tears of her mother. Mrs. Fielding, perceiving the impression that they made upon her, thought it best to leave them some time to themselves. She arose, and taking a hand of each, led them to the adjoining apartment, saying, "that after so long a separation they had probably many things to communicate, that would be best discussed in a *téte-a-téte*."

The endeavours of Mrs. Fielding to reconcile our heroine to return to her mother were forcibly seconded by the mortifying circumstances of her situation. Without money, without friends, without any remaining hopes of success in the great object of her wishes, she began to think that she had rather been too precipitate in her anticipation of the practices of *The Age of Reason*; and that in the present deplorable state of things, a young woman might be excusable in remaining under the protection of her relations, though she escaped the glory of moral martyrdom by doing so.

A thousand times since she left W— had she sensibly felt the want of those little tender attentions, which her fond mother had ever been so ready to bestow. She had been sick—and found no one interested in her recovery. Mrs. Benton had, indeed, attended her as much as her business would allow; but her attentions fell far short of the anxious solicitude of a parent, who, on the slightest indisposition, had been alarmed for her safety. Nor had she been able to eradicate from her breast the feelings of filial affection; feelings, which the unexpected meeting with her mother had powerfully revived. And as she had now little prospect of soon seeing any of those who were sufficiently enlightened, to condemn her for this returning weakness, she was easily prevailed upon to oblige the old lady, by consenting to accompany her back to W—.

Overjoyed at this instance of condescension, Mrs. Botherim willingly undertook to discharge all the debts contracted by her daughter; and having gratefully thanked Mrs. Fielding for her kind attention, departed with Bridgetina to Mrs. Benton's.

CHAP. VII.

"Beware of Jealousy!"

SHAKESPEARE.[45]

MRS. Fielding's intention of sending to enquire for Henry on the following morning was anticipated by Doctor Orwell, whose report was so favourable as to infuse cheerfulness into the countenances of the circle, now assembled at breakfast.

In talking over the disaster of the preceding evening, Dr. Orwell mentioned the gentleman who had been the unfortunate occasion of it, by the name of Carradine.

"Has he ever been in India," asked Mrs. Fielding, eagerly.

'I believe he has,' returned the Doctor.

"Then," said Mrs. Fielding, "I make no doubt he is the son of one of my oldest and most intimate friends. Through the interest of Lady Brierston I procured this boy a cadet's appointment on the Bengal establishment, about fourteen years ago; but of me, it is probable, he now retains not any remembrance."

---

[45] Shakespeare, *Othello*, III.iii, 165.

Mrs. Fielding was mistaken. While she yet spoke, Mr. Carradine was announced. He had, through Henry Sydney, heard of her living in London, and no sooner heard it, than with all that ardour which was the prominent feature of his character, he hastened to pay his respects to his acknowledged benefactress. Mrs. Fielding received this testimony of his gratitude with a satisfaction equal to the interest she took in the welfare of the son of her friend. She heard with pleasure of his success in India, which had far exceeded his most sanguine expectations; and was still more highly gratified by learning, that that success had enabled him to make a handsome provision for two orphan sisters. He had come over to pay a visit to the eldest of these, upon her marriage, and his leave of absence being now nearly expired, was on the eve of again taking his departure for the East.

In speaking of the misfortune occasioned by his rashness the preceding evening, he expressed himself with so much feeling on account of Henry, and such a generous condemnation of his own impetuosity, as not only reconciled Mrs. Fielding, but even divested Maria of all inclination to impute to him the least degree of blame. Harriet was, on this occasion, somewhat behind her friends in point of generosity. As the person by whom the life of Henry had been exposed to danger, she could not help viewing Mr. Carradine with a degree of dislike; nor was her dislike diminished by finding herself the object of his particular attention. That she so was, was evident almost from the very moment of his entrance; and the avidity with which he accepted Mrs. Fielding's invitation to dinner, might, perhaps, be as justly attributed to the power of attraction as to the impulse of gratitude.

This young man, whose quick and lively feelings had, by early indulgence, been fostered into uncontrollable impetuosity, was the willing slave of impulse; but though frequently led astray by his capricious guide, his errors were more than compensated by the virtues of his heart. Open, generous, and sincere, he was still more fervent in his friendships than in his enmities; and equally prompt to confer an obligation, as to resent an injury. The impression made upon his mind by the first appearance of Miss Orwell, was augmented into intoxication before the end of the evening; nor was this delirium of love in the least checked by the apparent coldness of her manners. Little accustomed to intercourse with the sex, he was a stranger to the delicacy of sentiment which renders an union of minds essential to happiness; and having gathered from conversation in the course of the day, that Miss Orwell's fortune consisted chiefly in her charms and virtues, he retired elate with hope, and fully confident of success.

On the following morning he returned to escort the ladies to an exhibition of paintings, to which Mrs. Fielding had mentioned an intention of carrying her young friends on the preceding evening. Harriet would willingly have been excused, but she was such a novice in the modern school of female manners, that she did not consider herself at liberty to indulge every wayward humour, or to disconcert the pleasure of a party for the gratification of her own feelings. She therefore concealed her repugnance, and only begged Maria not to quit her side. Maria promised, and no doubt intended to comply with her request; but Mr. Churchill knew so well the paintings that were particularly suited to her taste, and took such pains to point them out, that in the fervour of her admiration of the pieces to which he directed her attention, she was insensibly drawn to another part of the room. Dr. Orwell and Mrs. Fielding were mean time engaged in conversation, so that Harriet found herself left to the care of Mr. Carradine; who, without considering the character to whom he addressed himself, employed the opportunity thus afforded him to pour out that profusion of exaggerated compliment, which he had been taught to consider as the most acceptable offering to the ear of beauty.

Tired by his assiduity, and provoked by his perseverance, she hastened to where Mrs. Fielding and her father had procured seats. Just as she approached them, Dr. Orwell resigned his to an elderly lady, whom he heard complain of fatigue. The same complaint was heard by several young men of fashion, who lounged upon the same bench, but heard without producing on their part the smallest effort for her accommodation. The eyes of the same party were now turned on Harriet, who involuntarily shrunk from their familiar stare, and gladly entered into a conversation with Mrs. Fielding, in order to relieve her embarrassment.

The conversation naturally turned on the paintings, on which Harriet gave her opinion with all that ingenuousness and simplicity which belonged to her character. Accustomed to think for herself, she did not hesitate to speak from her feelings; and as she made no pretensions to connoisseurship, would not have been at all mortified at finding that she had been pleased with a piece that was not stamped with the approbation of a connoisseur.

"You seem fatigued, my dear," said Mrs. Fielding; "I wish we could make room for you," looking at the gentlemen, who still kept their seats.

'I beg the young lady may take mine;' said the elderly lady whom Doctor Orwell had accommodated. Harriet declined the offer, and the subject of the paintings was renewed.

"I confess," said Mrs. Fielding, "that I receive peculiar pleasure from such paintings as afford an exercise to the mind. I am not connoisseur enough to be long enraptured with all the charms of light and shade; and though I admire the beauty of that St. Cecilia, I dwell with much more satisfaction on its companion, which gives such a lively representation of the manners of a former age and distant country."

'Tasteless must they be, who can turn their eyes to painted canvass, while animated beauty demands their admiration!' whispered Carradine.

"You are right," said Dr. Orwell to Mrs. Fielding; "and that view of the savages, which hangs opposite to us, has afforded me particular pleasure, from the train of ideas it has excited. No one can view it, and look around, without being convinced how nearly the extremes of barbarism and civilization are united. Do but mark the expression of stupidity and indolence in the countenance of that savage who sits at the door of the hut. Methinks he wants but a tooth-pick to make him quite a modern fine gentleman; he seems almost as much insensible to all the moral, natural, and social feelings and enjoyments, as any beau in the room. See with what listless indifference his companion views the females who are placed beside him. How vacant his stare! How rude and brutish does it speak his manners!"

While Dr. Orwell was speaking, Mrs. Fielding accidentally turned her eye from the picture upon the gentlemen who sat beside her. 'An't you tired of this horrid place?' said one.

"Tired!" returned his companion; "I have been fatigued to death this half-hour." So saying, they rose with one consent, perhaps determined never more to take their place at an exhibition beside a portrait of savages.

On their return home, Mrs. Fielding stopped the carriage at Henry's door. While Doctor Orwell and Maria were stepping out to enquire for him, 'Tell him' said Mrs. Fielding, 'that we shall all pay him a visit together, the first evening he is well enough to receive us. Maria soon returned, with earnest intreaties from her brother that the kind promise might be fulfilled that very evening. The request was seconded by Dr. Orwell, on whose judgment Mrs. Fielding so much relied, that she was easily prevailed upon to acquiesce in the proposal.

In the evening they accordingly went, and were received by Henry with the most rapturous gratitude. To Mrs. Fielding he was profuse in his acknowledgments, for her goodness and condescension. To Harriet his eyes only spoke, but they required not any interpreter. In answer to the interrogatories concerning his wound, he declared it to be a mere scratch, not worth mentioning; and only that it obliged him to keep on his night-gown, would not confine him to his room another day. While Mrs. Fielding was congratulating him on the fortunate issue of an event which had appeared so big with danger, and Harriet smiling delight at the certainty of his recovery, Mr. Carradine entered the room. He instantly seized the vacant chair by the side of Harriet, and to her so exclusively devoted his attentions, that he did not seem to have either eyes or ears for any other object. Unaccustomed to disguise his feelings, he sought not to conceal them; tho' the evident distress of Harriet might have convinced him, that whatever gratification he enjoyed from this open avowal of his partiality, he enjoyed at her expence. In vain did she endeavour by monosyllable answers to weary out his patience, or by frequently addressing Mrs. Fielding or Maria, to turn his attention to the conversation of her friends. He could speak but to her alone, and made such frequent allusions to what passed either in the course of the morning, or during his visit to Mrs. Fielding on the preceding day, as must have impressed any listener with an idea of their being on terms of long-established intimacy.

Trifling was the pain of the wound his hand had given, in comparison of that which his conduct now inflicted on the heart of Henry. He now first felt the torturing pang of jealousy, nor did the behaviour of Harriet quiet his apprehensions. He knew her delicacy, he knew her prudence; and to prudence and delicacy did he solely attribute her seeming indifference to the too evident partiality of her new admirer. But would she continue indifferent to a man, who, emboldened by prosperity, addressed her in the stile of confident success? Would she scorn the allurements of ambition, and refuse the offer of affluence from one whose personal accomplishments alone might make an impression on any female heart? "She will," said Hope. 'No, no;' said trembling Apprehension, 'you have no right to expect it.' "Then she is lost to you for ever!" said Despondency.

The pale hue that succeeded the feverish flush on the cheek of Henry, was not unobserved by Mrs. Fielding. "Sydney," said she, "I fear you have over-rated the progress of your recovery. Your wish to see your friends has led you to an exertion beyond your strength; but we must be no longer parties in your indiscretion." She then ordered her carriage, and while Henry endeavoured to assure her that her fears were without foundation, she was, by the changes of his colour, and the faltering of his voice, fully persuaded of their reality.

When Doctor Orwell went to enquire for his young friend on the following morning, he met the surgeon coming out of his apartment, and from him (to his great disquietude) received intelligence of Henry's increased indisposition. A considerable degree of fever had already taken place, which in the course of the day became so alarming, that the surgeon on his next visit in the afternoon proposed calling in the assistance of an eminent physician. Next day he was still worse, and Maria, in anguish of heart, dispatched a messenger to her father with the melancholy tidings.

All the bright visions of expected happiness, with which Maria and her friend had indulged their imaginations while preparing for their jaunt to London, were now compleatly annihilated; and in their place melancholy reflections on the past, or gloomy forebodings of the future, took possession of their minds. From the pressure of these Maria was somewhat relieved by active exertion; but Harriet had no such resource. She had not even the privilege of communicating the sufferings of her anxious heart. They did not, however, escape the penetrating eye of Mrs. Fielding, who, by the most soothing attention, endeavoured to alleviate as much as possible the pain she well knew how to estimate.

A still severer task awaited her—it was the reception of Mr. Sydney; who instantly on the receipt of his daughter's letter had set off for London, and arrived on the day that Henry was pronounced to be in the utmost danger.

Though a period of thirty years had elapsed since Mrs. Fielding had last seen Mr. Sydney, it is probable that time had not so compleatly obliterated the remembrance of their parting scene, that she could now, without emotion, have gone through the ceremony of the first interview, had not every feeling been absorbed by the object of their mutual anxiety. The same cause would have been productive of the same effects at any period of their acquaintance; for in spite of the supreme dominion ascribed by poets and novelists to the God of Love, (who is represented as the prime mover of every human action, and the omnipotent governor of the breast of every person who has ever felt his power) he is, in fact, a mere sunshine visitor, who skulks away at the first appearance of calamity, and is driven from the heart at the approach of real evil.

Mrs. Fielding, who felt for Henry all the affection of a parent—feelingly participated in the parent's affliction. For some days after the arrival of Mr. Sydney, fearful suspence continued to rest on every brow, and to throb in every heart. Harriet, to whom the presence of Carradine had been so disagreeable, now watched for his knock at the door with sickening impatience; he, indeed, spent the greatest part of his time in going betwixt Hanover-square and George-street; and by the lively interest he took in Henry's recovery, raised himself not a little in the opinion of his mistress.

Above a week was thus spent. At the end of that period a change took place, which his medical friends pronounced to be a favourable crisis. Harriet was sitting with Mrs. Fielding in her dressing-room, the door of which had been left open, to facilitate the communication of intelligence. Twice had she gone to it on tip-toe, on hearing two several knocks at the hall-door, but was each time disappointed by the appearance of visiting-tickets in the servant's hands.

While he was delivering the last of these to Mrs. Fielding, Carradine rushed in.—"He is out of danger!" cried he; "the physicians declare he is out of danger! But Miss Orwell, why do you not speak? You are not sorry, sure, to hear that Sydney is out of danger? why do you not rejoice?"

'I—I do rejoice!' said Harriet, and burst into a violent flood of tears.

"Good heavens!" exclaimed Carradine, "I thought it would have made you happy to hear the poor fellow was out of danger; but had I known how differently it was to affect you, I would sooner have been shot from the mouth of a cannon than have told you a word of the matter."

'Good as well as bad news may be declared too abruptly,' said Mrs. Fielding. Then, in order to divert his attention from Harriet, she proceeded to ask a number of questions concerning the opinion of the physicians, and the symptoms on which that opinion was founded. Mr. Carradine was but ill qualified to give her information concerning these particulars; but the simple fact that Henry was pronounced out of danger, was a solace to her friendly heart.

CHAP. VIII.

"Reader, attend: Whether thy soul
"Soars Fancy's flights beyond the pole,
"Or darkling grubs this earthly hole,
  "In low pursuit;
"Know prudent, cautious, self-control,
  "Is Wisdom's root."

BURNS.[46]

THE recovery of Henry was not rapid, but it was unattended by any relapse. No sooner did returning health begin to re-brace the unstrung nerves, and re-invigorate the feeble frame, than the mind reverted to the objects of its former interest; and though (contrary to the usual practice of lovers in similar circumstances) he had not during his delirium once mentioned the name of Harriet, her image now reassumed its wonted place in his breast.

"Maria," said he one day to his sister, as she set by his bedside, which he was yet too feeble to leave for more than half an hour at a time, "you confine yourself too much to my apartment. Besides the risk of injuring your health, you must embitter the happiness of Miss Orwell by thus perpetually depriving her of your society. But, perhaps, she sees enough of company at Mrs. Fielding's to solace her for the absence of her old friends?"

'No, indeed,' returned Maria, 'Mrs. Fielding has received no visitors since you were taken ill; I do not believe that any stranger, except Mr. Carradine, has been within her door.'

"And has Mr. Carradine been often there?"

'O yes, two or three times at least every day.'

"He is, then, quite on a familiar footing in Hanover-square?" said Henry, in a tremulous voice.

'Entirely so,' returned Maria. 'He goes in and out just like one of the family. Indeed, I believe the interest he took in your recovery, and the sensibility he evinced in the time you were thought to be in danger, has more endeared him to Mrs. Fielding than if he had been the son of twenty friends. That deep sigh tells me, that I must not yet indulge you in talking; but if you please I shall now read to you a little—'

"I think I had rather sleep," said Henry. Maria drew the curtain, and remained in silence.

The convalescence of Henry was no sooner ascertained, than Doctor Orwell began to think of returning home. And no sooner did Carradine hear of his intention, than he hastened to communicate to him such proposals concerning his daughter as he was well assured could not fail to meet his approbation. Having entered the Doctor's dressing-room in a

---

[46] Robert Burns, *A Bard's Epitaph* (1786) 25-30.

manner sufficiently abrupt to have created some alarm in a person of weak nerves, he thus opened the conference. 'Doctor Orwell, your daughter is a charming girl! By my soul, I do not believe there is such a lovely girl in England!'

"You do my daughter great honour, sir," said the Doctor, smiling at his odd manner of expressing a truth which he himself had, however, no difficulty in believing. "Harriet is surely much obliged to you for the compliment."

'Not at all,' returned Carradine, 'not obliged to me at all. I would not love her if I could help it, but I cannot help it; and I do love her with all my heart. Ten thousand pounds is what I mean to settle on her. Tell me, if that will answer your expectations?'

"Really, sir, I do not well understand you. Your proposal is made in a manner so abrupt, and was so truly unexpected, that you must forgive me if I cannot give it an immediate answer."

'Nothing can be plainer than my proposal,' rejoined Carradine. 'I love your daughter, and will marry her without a shilling, making her a settlement of ten thousand pounds, which shall be entirely at her own disposal.'

"And is it with Harriet's knowledge that you now apply to me on this business?"

'No. Miss Orwell, notwithstanding we have now been acquainted for almost a fortnight, has never yet given me an opportunity of talking to her on the subject.'

"And do you really think, that on a fortnight's acquaintance the character of any person can be sufficiently developed, to warrant entering with them into a connection that is indissoluble?"

'A fortnight! Why I have known many very happy marriages take place in Bengal upon an acquaintance of less than half the time. I remember the time, when every fresh cargo of imported beauties used to go off as fast as they were seen. Now, to be sure, the market is rather overstocked; and many a fine girl remains on hands for the length of a whole season. But as to making up one's mind upon the business, that can be done in half an hour as well as in half a century.'[47]

"You astonish me!" cried Dr. Orwell. "I have indeed heard of young women's going out to India with a view, no doubt, to get established in marriage. But that whole cargoes should go out in that manner, as to a regular market, I really should not, but from good authority, have credited. Surely they can only be some poor, unfortunate, and friendless girls, who have neither parents nor protectors at home, that are driven to such desperate methods of obtaining a provision?"

'Pardon me,' replied Carradine, 'the greatest number who now come

---

[47] Hamilton declined her brother's invitation to India with the probable reward of a husband in 1783.

out are sent by their parents and protectors; and, in general, the speculation is not a bad one.'

"Is it possible," cried Doctor Orwell, "that any parent should be so depraved, as to expose his child to a situation so humiliating! How lost to all that conscious dignity which enhances every female charm; how lost to every sentiment of delicacy must she become, who is thus led to make a barter of herself! My mind revolts at the idea!"

'Does the distance of the market, then, make such a mighty difference?' said Carradine. 'Really, my dear sir, that is an objection merely imaginary. The voyage is a trifle; and as to the conscious dignity, and all that, I do assure you, that so far from its being lost by going to India, I have there seen many a girl who, at an English watering-place, would have been glad to flirt with an ensign, get so proud and saucy in the space of a few weeks, that she would not deign to speak to a subaltern! The reason is plain—in India the number of European ladies is still so small, in proportion to the gentlemen, that they are *there* of some consequence. But here they are hawked about in such quantities at every place of publick resort, that if the poor things did not lay themselves out to court attention, they would have no chance of being taken notice of.'

"Better remain unnoticed for ever, than be so degraded!" said Doctor Orwell, with vehemence. "For my part," continued he, "though the increasing prevalence of luxury and false pride, and false notions of true dignity, tend to render poverty an evil of mighty magnitude to a helpless female, I had rather see my daughters reduced to the necessity of earning their bread, than behold them raised to the highest pinnacle of fortune by such methods as you have described."

'*Your daughter!* my dear sir. Oh she is a being of a superior order. Tell me but that you consent she shall be mine, and by all that's sacred she shall be as happy a woman—aye, and trust me, as much respected as the wife of any man in Europe.'

"I must repeat it again," replied the Doctor, "that I am no friend to hasty connexions. We are frequently taught by experience, that where the general character is on both sides good, an unconformity of temper, or dissimilarity of taste, is sufficient to embitter the tenor of existence. And how on a short acquaintance can we form that knowledge of the disposition which prudence requires, in order to give a chance for happiness?"

'As to temper, I do assure you no one ever found fault with mine. Let Miss Orwell enquire of my friends, and they will tell her that I am the best-natured fellow in the world. A little hasty, or so, perhaps, but then it is over in a moment; and I vow to God I never shall be in a passion with her. How could I, with such an angel! Believe me, sir, we shall be one of the happiest couples in the world.'

Doctor Orwell smiled. "Well, but Mr. Carradine, if you had my consent, pray have you any reason to conclude that Harriet's is certain?"

'No, I really cannot say that I am sure of that. But when she knows how good a husband I shall make, and sees that you are very much inclined to the match, I do not despair of prevailing on her to make me happy. She is so sweet, and so compassionate, that I do not think she could have the cruelty to inflict misery upon any mortal. I never saw any creature possessed of a heart so tender! Why she could not even hear mention made of what poor Sydney suffered, without always changing colour; and I have more than once observed the silent tear steal softly down her cheek, even while a smile sat upon her countenance. And what is the anguish of a thousand fevers, in comparison of what I should feel in losing her?'

"I hope, that if my daughter should be so cruel," said Doctor Orwell, "there is little reason to apprehend any *danger* from the misfortune; and that in the smiles of some other beauty all your wounds will soon be healed."

'I shall never speak to another beauty in my life;' replied Carradine, warmly. 'I shall embark for India in the first ship; and do you think, that after having contemplated the unaffected loveliness of Miss Orwell, endeared by sweetness, and exalted by the utmost refinement of sentiment and gracefulness of manners, I shall have any taste for the insipid morsels of foil and froth that I am there likely to meet with? No, no; if I return to India without a wife, I shall go back to poor Mirza; tho' besides the burthen of so many dingy brats, there is plaguy little comfort in a connexion that affords neither friendship nor society.'

Here the conversation was interrupted by the sudden entrance of Mrs. Botherim, who, with a heavy heart, came to complain to Doctor Orwell of the untoward disposition of her daughter. As many years had elapsed since the good lady had visited London, she had thought it proper to take the present opportunity of renewing her acquaintance with the few friends of her childhood who were still in existence; and had accepted an invitation to take up her residence, while she remained in town, at the house of a relation, for whose family she anxiously wished her daughter to cultivate an affection. It was of her behaviour to these friends that she now came to complain, which she did with great bitterness; and concluded with intreating Doctor Orwell to visit them, and point out to Bridgetina the impropriety of her behaviour towards people whose character she represented as extremely amiable, and whose conduct had in some respects been highly meritorious. The Doctor readily promised compliance with her request, and as soon as she departed, hastened to Harriet's apartment, to talk to her about the proposals of Carradine.

The subject did not bear much discussion. It was decided by Harriet in a moment. Her objections were pointed out with so much judgment, and supported with so much firmness, as left no room to expect a change of sentiment.

"Well, my dear," said the Doctor, "I cannot say that I am sorry for your refusal of this young man; particularly, as I do not believe your refusal of him proceeds from any romantic notions of getting a more advantageous proposal hereafter. If I considered marriage as absolutely necessary to your happiness, I should regret your losing such an opportunity of establishing yourself; for with a fortune that will be no more than adequate to your support in a very retired situation, small will be your chance of any other offer. But your mind has, I trust, too much of the dignity of independence, to be absolutely at the mercy of extrinsic circumstances for happiness."

While Doctor Orwell was thus conversing with his daughter, her impatient lover who had left the room on Mrs. Botherim's entrance, in hopes of finding his adorable alone in the drawing-room, went immediately thither in search of her. No one was there but Mrs. Fielding; and Carradine, who had at that time little relish for her society, very speedily put an end to his visit.

His impatience to know how Harriet would receive his proposals, was quite insupportable. Still hope predominated; and with spirits highly exhilarated, notwithstanding their agitation, he suddenly darted into Henry's apartment, who was sitting pensive and alone over the dying embers of his fire, the decline of which had entirely escaped his observation.

"What! moping all alone?" cried Carradine, on entering. "Have you had no visit from your sister to-day?"

'No, indeed,' returned Henry; 'she, I believe, is assisting Miss Orwell in making some preparations for this ball, to which they have been invited. You, I suppose, mean to accompany them?'

"Me! oh, without a doubt. I would accompany Miss Orwell to the end of the world! Is she not a charming creature? Tell me now, Sydney, did you ever see a more lovely girl? Don't you think a man might fancy himself in paradise with such an angel? Oh, if she be ever mine!"

'Your's!' exclaimed Henry, in a voice which his parched tongue could scarcely render audible.

"Yes, mine!" gaily answered his happy rival. Perhaps to-day—perhaps in an hour—in less than an hour, I may hear from her sweet lips, that I am the happiest fellow in Christendom! Zounds, Sydney, you have no notion what a happy fellow I shall be!"

The elder Mr. Sydney then coming in excused Henry from making any reply. Carradine asked him, whether he had been at Mrs. Fielding's? To which the old gentleman returned for answer, that he had called there to speak with Doctor Orwell, but found him engaged in his daughter's apartment; and as he thought they might be consulting about some family business, he did not interrupt their *tête à tête*.

"Fine old fellow!" cried Carradine. "I see he did not lose a moment. But the conference must be over by this time. I fly to know my fate. Good morning." Grasping Henry's hand, which he squeezed with great violence, "Dear Sydney, wish me success!" and then, without making any observation on the altered countenance of Sydney, or imagining him in the least interested in the subject, he precipitately left the room.

No sooner was Sydney alone with his father, than the latter, observing his unusual gravity, and anxious to amuse him in the best manner possible, began to enter into a minute description of a cabinet of natural history, which he had that morning had the pleasure of examining. In vain did he give a detail of all the wonders it contained; in vain did he describe, with the most minute exactness, the discriminating marks that distinguished the peculiar genus of every butterfly and every beetle. The delight he had received, he did not find it in his power to communicate; and he saw with regret, that the mind of Henry had not sufficiently recovered its tone to enter with avidity into this favourite subject. So fully was the old gentleman occupied in his description, that it was a considerable time before he observed the distracted and absent air of his son.

At length, having for some moments fixed his eyes on Henry's face, "Henry," said he, in a voice full of paternal tenderness, "What is the matter with thee, my son? I plainly perceive that something has perturbed thy mind. But am I not worthy of thy confidence?"

'You are, you are, sir,' replied Henry, 'most truly worthy of it; but my mind is at present in such a distracted state that I can scarcely make you comprehend my feelings—this fellow—this Carradine has undone me!'

"Carradine! did you say Carradine? And do you then apprehend any further bad consequences from the wound? If so, let me go instantly for the surgeon. Not a moment shall be lost. I—"

'Stop, my dear father,' cried Henry, 'Carradine has indeed inflicted a wound that is incurable; but it is beyond the surgeon's reach. He has torn my heart, and deprived my life of every hope that was dear to it. Oh! look not on me with contempt, accuse me not of folly, when I tell you, that in Harriet Orwell I had treasured up the happiness of my existence!'

"And has Miss Orwell deceived you? Has she scorned your poverty, and forsaken you for a wealthier lover? If so—she is unworthy of my son; she never deserved to share a heart like thine."

Though the feelings of Henry would have made his heart believe that Harriet did him injustice, reason told him she was blameless; and love and honour equally impelled him to exculpate her from the charge. He, therefore, with great eagerness proceeded to vindicate the conduct of Harriet, and to attribute to his own want of merit, and deficiency in address, the disappointment that now overwhelmed him. To his father he freely opened his whole heart, and found from his soothing and tender sympathy all the consolation of which he was at present susceptible.

From the mutual confidence established in the family of the Sydneys, it was rather surprising that a subject, which had so long engrossed his mind, should not sooner have been communicated. His naturally open and generous temper was formed for confidential intercourse with kindred minds. He was equally a stranger to the coldness of reserve, and the pride of concealment. Whenever he could give pleasure, or even afford amusement by what he communicated, he did it with a frankness at once so natural, and so engaging, that it endeared him to every heart. It was of selfish cares and selfish sorrows that he was alone a churl. These, which are by most young gentlemen deemed the only subject of family confidence, Henry often devoured in secret, or carefully concealed in the recesses of his own bosom. The knowledge of his attachment to Harriet would, he knew, create anxiety in the affectionate hearts of his father and sister, to whom his happiness was too dear to render the completion of his wishes an object of indifference. Now that anxiety was lost in despair, he did not sullenly refuse the consolations of sympathy, but happy in being now able to speak to his best friend without reserve on a subject that occupied his whole soul, he willingly conceded to his proposal of sending an apology to Mrs. Fielding's, that he might have his company for the rest of the evening.

CHAP. IX.

"Truth weeping tell, the mournful tale,
"How pamper'd Lux'ry, Flatt'ry by her side,
   "The parasite empoisoning her ear,
   "With all the servile wretches in the rear,
"Looks o'er proud property extended wide,
   "And eyes the simple rustic mind;
"Whose toil upholds the glittering show—
   "A creature of *another kind,*
   "Some coarser substance, unrefin'd,
"*Placed for her lordly use, thus far, thus vile below!*"

BURNS.[48]

FEARFUL of meeting with Carradine, and anxious to avoid an interview that must have been mutually embarrassing, Harriet Orwell proposed accompanying her father on an immediate visit to Miss Botherim; and understanding that Mrs. Botherim intended calling at their late lodgings, she hastened thither in hopes of finding her, while her father wrote a few lines to Carradine, intimating her determined rejection of his suit. Doctor Orwell then stepped into the carriage which waited for him, and taking up his daughter and Mrs. Botherim at Mrs. Benton's, proceeded with them to the city.

No sooner were they seated in the carriage, than the old lady renewed her lamentations concerning Bridgetina's conduct. "See," said she, presenting Mrs. Benton's bill to Doctor Orwell, "see what a sum I have just now paid for her. But this is nothing! Oh, just nothing at all, in comparison to the disgrace of pawning her watch! Oh, think of that, Doctor Orwell! Think of that! The very watch that had cost me so many tears to

---

[48] Robert Burns, *A Winter Night* (1786) 50-58; Hamilton's italics.

coax from my father on my marriage. Not that I should have cared a pin about it, but that the Miss Pickles never let alone telling me of the fine things our neighbour, Miss Dough, the biscuit-maker's daughter, had got upon her wedding. And my poor dear father, who did not like to see me fret, resolved that I should be as fine as the best of 'em! Little did he think that it was ever to come to a pawnbroker's shop!—"

Here the poor lady gave way to a burst of sorrow and indignation, which her companions did all in their power to pacify. After it had somewhat subsided, she thus proceeded: "Nothing could be kinder than our reception from our poor cousin Biggs's; for though they have had a hard struggle with the world, and gone down in fortune, their hearts are as warm and as good as ever. I hoped that Biddy would have taken to them, and that she would ha' been the better of seeing what some folks have to do to get through life; but, alas! they are not book-learned enough for her. And she looks so down upon them that you can't think. But how (says I) should they have found time for study? Cousin Peggy, who is the eldest, was but eighteen years of age when her father died. In half a year after his death their house was burnt to the ground, and in making their escape from a two-pair of stair window, their mother's back was broke, so that she has been bed-ridden ever since; and their brother, then a fine promising lad of fourteen, received a hurt upon his head which reduced him to the condition you now see. The poor lad is quite an idiot, and the most melancholiest object in the world. Think, Biddy, (says I) think what a charge this was to the poor girls! And do but see how they have fulfilled it. Finding what they had left of the wreck of their father's fortune insufficient for their maintenance, they set up a tea-shop; and as they were well beloved by all the neighbourhood, and every one pitied their misfortunes, they succeeded wonderfully. But what betwixt their attendance on their mother, and on their business, their time to be sure has been too fully occupied to have any leisure for your abstract reasoning, as you call it. They cannot talk about *duties*, I must own, as fine as you do; for how should they, when their whole lives have been employed in performing them?

"Alas, sir, I might as well talk to the stone wall. Biddy just minded me no more than nothing; and when I would make any remark on the kindness with which they treated their poor brother, whom they even seem to love the better for the misfortune that deprived him of the notice of every one besides, or on their attention to their poor miserable parent, who has been so many years a burthen to them, she stops my mouth by asking what all this has to do with *General Utility?* Poor thing! I am sure it was a bad day for her that ever she heard his name; so it was!—"

The carriage now drew up at Mrs. Biggs's door; and while Doctor and Miss Orwell waited in the shop, through which lay the only entrance to the apartments, Mrs. Botherim went up to prepare Bridgetina for their reception. The mind of Harriet had been so early and so deeply embued with a respect for virtue, that she could not divest herself of a degree of reverence in approaching Miss Biggs, such as no external circumstance of rank or splendour could have excited. She willingly accepted of a seat by her, and entered into conversation with a cheerfulness and unaffected humility, very different from that species of condescension which certain people so kindly assume, when addressing themselves to those whose situation is in any respect inferior to their own. Their conversation was soon interrupted by the entrance of some ladies, who issued from a splendid carriage. Harriet retired to make way for them, while Miss Biggs stood to receive their orders. To her, however, they were in no haste to speak, but continued their conversation to each other, without deigning to observe her.

At length, one of the ladies, seeming to recollect herself, exclaimed, "La! what a shocking place! I vow I cannot breathe in it a moment longer. I beg, young woman, you would make haste."

Miss Biggs modestly requested to know with what article she would be served?

"Did not I tell you it was Indian toys?" returned the lady; then addressing herself to one of her companions, "I declare, these people in the city are so stupid, it is quite a bore!"

The counter was by this time covered with various articles of japan, mother-of-pearl, &c. which the ladies examined and cheapened, making such remarks on the replies given to their questions, as plainly charged the dealer with want of truth and common honesty. At length, after they had sufficiently amused themselves with looking over the things, and were about to depart, the lady first-mentioned happened to lift her veil, and discovered to Doctor Orwell the face of Mrs. General Villers. She either did not see, or tended not to see, the Doctor; and he on his part, was by the scene that had just occurred, inspired with such a sovereign contempt for the actors, that he felt no wish to recognize any of them as an acquaintance. When they were gone, he asked Miss Biggs if they had really made no purchase.

"No, sir," returned Miss Biggs, "nor had they the least intention to make any. It is what we often meet with."

'But I hope,' rejoined Doctor Orwell, 'you do not often meet with such unprovoked rudeness, such unfeeling insolence?'

"Oh, yes, sir;" said Miss Biggs, smiling, "people of fashion reserve all their good-breeding for their equals; they never consider their inferiors as entitled to the smallest share."

'Then,' said Doctor Orwell, 'people of fashion know not what true good-breeding is. A consideration for the feelings of those with whom we converse, and a quick perception of what those feelings are, is true politeness; and those who have it not, whatever be their rank, are *vulgar*.'

"I am afraid, sir," said Miss Biggs, "that your definition of politeness is not taught at any modern school. At least, if I am to judge from what has fallen under my own observation, I should imagine that a consideration for the feelings of inferiors in any situation is thought not only unnecessary, but absurd."

'I am sorry to hear you say so,' said Harriet, 'as you have such an opportunity for making observations upon character, that I cannot doubt the justice of your remarks.'

"Yes, Madam," replied Miss Biggs, "we have indeed an opportunity of observing an infinite variety in the tempers and dispositions of those who to their equals appear uniformly amiable. In the common intercourse of civilities little of the real character appears; but if one would know the world, it is necessary to be dependent."

'Ah!' returned Harriet, 'would the gay and the giddy but bear in their recollection, how often they may be looking down upon their superiors in all that is truly estimable, in all that will one day appear so even to themselves, it would check the insolence of pride, and lower the arrogance of presumption.'

Mrs. Botherim, who had been all this time assisting Bridgetina to dress, now came to lead Doctor and Miss Orwell to the dining-room. Bridgetina received them coldly, and before they had time to enter into any conversation with her, the poor lad, of whose unhappy situation Mrs. Botherim had informed them, ran into the room. Harriet was shocked at his appearance, but would not suffer disgust to enter her bosom at the sight of misfortune incident to humanity. He quickly approached her, and seized the large sun-fan which she held in her hand. Instantly conquering the involuntary flutter which his sudden motion had occasioned, she spoke to him with great gentleness, offering to teach him how to open and shut it. He seemed sensible of her indulgence, and after playing with it for some time, restored it with an appearance of great satisfaction. His youngest sister then came in, and made many apologies for his intrusion. She desired him (not in the tone of authority, but with the voice of affection) to go with her to their mother's apartment, who was then getting her dinner; and at length, by the promise of some sweetmeats which she shewed him, prevailed on him to leave the room.

"How amiable," said Harriet, "how respectable is the conduct of these young women! I shall ever esteem myself obliged to Mrs. Botherim for introducing me to their acquaintance."

'And pray,' cried Bridgetina, 'what is the worth about which you make such a mighty rout? Is not knowledge essential to virtue? And what knowledge have they to boast of?'

"That knowledge," said Dr. Orwell, "without which all other knowledge is an empty boast—*the knowledge of their duty.* The knowledge which leads not to this one point, is, to the individual who possesses it, futile and nugatory."

'And pray,' retorted Bridgetina, 'how is society benefited by the sort of knowledge you talk of? What is the knowledge good for, that only benefits the individual?'

"Surely," repled Dr. Orwell, "you cannot *ask* that question seriously! The mere knowledge of our duty is, I grant you, of little consequence, if it does not lead to the practice of it; but when, as in the present instance, it eminently does so, who can say how far the benefit may extend? The active virtue of these young women, their filial piety, their sisterly affection, their kind and humane attention to their unfortunate brother, and the many self-denials they must have undergone in the performance of these duties, added to the conspicuous exertions they have made to enable them to perform them, is such an example of virtue as is not to be contemplated without bettering the heart. Believe me, Miss Botherim, one such example speaks more home to the feelings, and is of greater consequence to society, than volumes of philosophy."

'I trust,' said Harriet, 'the impression it has made on my heart shall never be obliterated.'

"Nor do I make any doubt," continued Dr. Orwell, "that many have viewed it with feelings of a similar nature. Who knows how often the example of these young women may have silenced the murmurs of discontent? how often it may have produced reflection in the careless, and excited gratitude in the unthinking? We commit a great mistake, when we confine the influence of example to the higher ranks of society. It is an influence of which people in every rank and in every situation are in some degree possessed. Happy they who make such a use of it as the family of whom we are now speaking."

'You, sir,' said Bridgetina, 'have so many prejudices, that it is impossible to argue with you. It may, to be sure, be very well for old Mrs. Biggs and her son, that her daughters were not philosophers; but you will never make me believe, that if they had been taught "to energize according to the flower and summit of their nature," they would not have done more for general utility.'

'And who is this General Utility?' cried Mrs. Botherim, 'whose name is for ever in Biddy's mouth? She is always in a pet when I ask her, as if I should know all about him as well as she; but I am sure she may well know I never seed a General but General Villers, in all my life."

'General Utility, my dear madam,' said Dr. Orwell, smiling, 'is an ideal personage, a sort of Will o' the wisp, whom some people go a great way out of the road to find, but still see him shining in some distant and unbeaten track; while, if they would keep at home, and look for him in the plain path of christian duty, they would never miss their aim.'

The entrance of Lady Aldgate and her daughter put an end to the conversation, and gave to Doctor and Miss Orwell an opportunity, of which they willingly availed themselves, of taking leave.

CHAP. X.

"Let reason teach what passion fain would hide,
"That Hymen's bands by prudence should be tied;
"Venus in vain the wedded pair would crown,
"If angry fortune on their union frown."
LYTTLETON.[49]

---

[49] 1st Baron George Lyttleton, "Advice to a Lady" (1773) 87-90.

GREATLY had the sanguine spirit of Carradine been mortified, by the unfavourable report that had been made to him of the sentiments of his mistress. That report had, however, been given by her father in terms so obliging, as though it greatly damped, did not entirely extinguish every hope. Perhaps her heart might be melted by a love-letter. He had heard of such things, and resolved to try the experiment. Writing, it is true, was not poor Carradine's sort; but tasks more difficult would at this time have appeared trifling to his ardent mind. After spending the whole of the evening and great part of the night in writing and re-writing the important scroll, he at length produced an epistle, which, if not a first-rate piece of oratory, contained at least as much good-sense as any love-letter we have ever had the pleasure of perusing.

It was received by Harriet at such an early hour, as gave her sufficient time to answer it before breakfast. By being delivered in presence of her friend, it laid her under the necessity of breaking the silence she had hitherto observed to Maria on the subject of Carradine's addresses. Superior to that mean vanity which leads little minds to exult in exposing to the view of others the mortification of a rejected lover, she considered every principle of delicacy and honour as engaged in keeping his secret. To have made the affections of any human being the object of her ridicule, she would have deemed in the last degree cruel and unjustifiable. The behaviour of many of her companions had, in this particular, appeared odious in her eyes; and so far was she from following their example, that till the introduction of Carradine's letter, (when any longer concealment would have worn the appearance of mystery) she had not even given her bosom-friend a hint upon the subject.

In her answer to Carradine, she united firmness to delicacy, and candour to politeness. She did not consider the circumstance of her being singled out from among her sex, as the person with whom he would wish to spend his days, as giving her any right to treat him with scorn or indignity; but at the same time had too much regard for her own honour and his repose, to give him a hope which she did not mean to realize.

Poor Carradine had no sooner dispatched his letter, than he repented him of his rashness. It then occurred to him, that through the medium of Mrs. Fielding he might more effectually have pleaded his cause; and the instant the idea was started he resolved to pursue it, hoping that the interest of Mrs. Fielding might still be so far exerted in his favour, as to prevent Miss Orwell from extinguishing his hopes by a positive refusal. He flew to Hanover-square on the instant, or rather would have flown if wings could have been procured, but for these a hackney-coach is, alas! a sorry substitute. In vain did he swear at the coachman, in vain did he anathematize the horses; neither coachman nor horses could be prevailed on to keep pace with his impatient spirit. At length arrived, he sprung to the door, and told the servant who opened it, that he must see Mrs. Fielding on a business of importance immediately.

"My mistress is not yet up," replied the footman; "but if you will step into the breakfast-parlour, I dare say she will be down in less than an hour."

'An hour!' 'sdeath, an age! For heaven's sake, at least desire her maid to inform her that I am here, and greatly wish to see her.'

The man obeyed, and in less than half and hour Mrs. Fielding was with him. He abruptly informed her of the purport of his visit, and vehemently besought her interest in his favour; intreating her to go immediately to Miss Orwell, to urge her to grant him the favour of an interview.

While he yet spoke, he heard the voice of Harriet on the stairs, and involuntarily opening the door, he saw the answer to his letter in the hands of the servant, to whom Miss Orwell had just delivered it. He impatiently snatched it from him, and casting his eye over the contents, gave way to an agony of despair.

Mrs. Fielding, having perused the letter, told him, that after such a candid declaration of her sentiments, it would be offering an insult to the delicacy of Miss Orwell to persevere in his suit. The woman (she observed) who after such a positive rejection could be flattered into a change of mind, must be the imbecile child of vanity. Such, she was certain, was not Harriet Orwell. She therefore advised him to bear with manly firmness an evil that could not be remedied, and to endeavour by absence to wear off the impression.

Carradine listened to her for a short time in silence, and then coldly thanking her for her advice, abruptly took his leave. There was a certain fermenting principle in his mind, which, laying hold of whatever happened to be the present object of interest, worked it up to such a state of effervescence, as rendered it absolutely necessary for him to have a confidant to receive the overflowings of his heart.

Finding solitude intolerable, he bent his way to Henry Sydney, in order to vent to him those feelings of chagrin and disappointment which he no longer had patience to confine to his own breast. Henry was alone, and not (as many of our fair readers doubtless will expect) confined to his bed by a relapse of fever, or raving in a beautiful delirium of despair; but pensively sitting by the fire-side with a book in his hand. We are sensible that a dangerous fit of illness would in his circumstances have been vastly more becoming, and much more natural, in the hero of a novel. We do not presume to say, that youth and a good constitution ought to be admitted as any apology for his persevering in convalescence at such a time, but simply own the fact. That he may not, however, entirely lose the interest we hope he has obtained in the hearts of our fair readers, we must not omit adding that he looked as melancholy as possible. Soon, however, was his melancholy dissipated by Carradine; who, after a few incoherent sentences, and as many exclamations, of which Henry could not guess the meaning, put into his hands the letter of Harriet, which had been to him as the sentence of never-ending misery.

Henry perused it with an emotion even superior to his own. "Charming, charming Harriet!" cried he, after having with his eye devoured the contents; "How disinterested! how noble! how generous!"

'Generous!' cried Carradine; 'one would think you were glad she had refused me!'

"Forgive me, Carradine!" said Henry, offering him his hand; "but you are yourself so generous and so open, that I should hate myself if I deceived you. I love Harriet Orwell. I have long loved her. Even from infancy our hearts have been united in the bonds of the tenderest friendship. Want of fortune has alone prevented me from urging her to unite her fate with mine. Judge, then, if I can say I am sorry at a circumstance which revives my hopes, and raises me from the very brink of despair."

Carradine started back, and regarded him for a moment with a look of frenzy. Then hastily turning from him, he strided four or five times up and down the room, and at length retiring to the further window, stood for some minutes silent. Henry reproached himself for having inflicted an additional wound in the breast of his rival. He was afraid to speak, lest whatever he should say might wear the appearance of triumphing in his disappointment. The silence was at length broken by Carradine, who coming up to Henry, and taking the hand he had before rejected, 'Sydney,' said he, 'you are a happy fellow! but don't think me the wretch to repine at your felicity. No. If I had known you had a prior claim to her affections, curse me if I would have interfered with it. I would perish sooner than do any thing so base!'

Henry spoke the effusions of his heart, in giving him the praise his generosity so truly merited; and assured him, that though her refusal of an offer so advantageous, from a character so unexceptionable, gave him some cause for hope, he was far from being certain of success. So well in the conversation that ensued did Henry manage the ardent temper of Carradine, that he left him in a great measure reconciled to a disappointment, which, but an hour before, he had considered in the light of an event that was to tinge the colour of his future days with misery.

The recovery of Henry was now so rapid, that on the very following day he surprised his friends by an unexpected visit. Though dinner had been some time over, the ladies had not yet retired to the drawing-room, when Henry made his appearance. Mrs. Fielding received him with joy, and welcomed his return with an embrace that spoke the feelings of maternal affection.

"Thank Heaven! that my brother, my dear brother is again restored to us!" exclaimed Maria, affectionately retaining one hand, while Dr. Orwell and Mr. Churchill alternately took the other. Harriet alone did not advance to meet him in the general joy; her voice only was unheard, but the congratulations which her faltering tongue could not pronounce, beamed from her eyes in a look of ineffable delight, while pleasure and surprise suffused her glowing cheek with crimson. When he came up to where she stood, she held out her hand with a complacency which seemed to assure Henry that his presence did not displease her; and though the few words she stammered out were perfectly unintelligible to every one besides, it would appear that he sufficiently understood their meaning.

The remainder of the evening was exclusively devoted to friendship; Mrs. Fielding giving orders that no visitor should be admitted to intrude upon the social circle. And though neither cards nor scandal were introduced, we do not find that time appeared particularly tedious to any of the party.

While Henry was again enjoying a happiness, rendered doubly dear to him from the sufferings he had lately endured, his father, full of anxious solicitude for his felicity, was making every effort to render it compleat. He took the earliest opportunity of informing Doctor Orwell of his son's attachment to his daughter, and found the Doctor more pleased than surprised at the information. He had in truth long ago observed the growing passion, and as it was the happiness, not the affluence, of his child, that was the object of his wishes, nothing was more desirable in his eyes than to behold her united to a man of Henry's sense and virtue.

Since the time that these old gentlemen had entered into the married state, they had lived so secluded from the world, that the rapid progress of luxury had almost escaped their observation. In an humble mediocrity of fortune, they had themselves found happiness; and it did not readily enter into their imaginations to conceive, why beginning the world with a splendid establishment was more necessary to their children than it had been to themselves. To the mind of Mr. Sydney a monopoly of wealth and power appeared an evil of mighty magnitude; and far from wishing his children to become accessaries, in continuing a system to which, in his opinion, might be fairly attributed the greater part of the miseries that have scourged the human race, he had laboured to impress their minds with a sense of its turpitude and injustice. Political science had long been his favourite study; and though a perfect equality of conditions he considered to be impracticable and absurd, the advantages that would result to society from such a dissemination of the wealth of a country as should render the extremes of wealth and poverty unknown, appeared to him so obvious, that he wondered how it could escape the observation of an enlightened mind. He had himself written a tract upon the subject, which he addressed to the great landed proprietors of Great-Britain; clearly demonstrating it to be their bounden duty, by making an equal division of their property among their children, to begin that gradual and rational reform, which would ultimately be productive of an increase of publick happiness and virtue.

Doctor Orwell, though less inclined to abstract speculation than his friend, perfectly coincided with him in principle. With respect to the happiness of their children their sentiments were in unison; and to promote their union they readily agreed to give up, on both sides, such a part of their present income as they deemed sufficient to establish the young people in some degree of comfort.

The result of their consultations was immediately communicated to Henry by his father, who informed him, that he was now at full liberty to disclose his sentiments to Harriet, since the consent of her father had given a sanction to his wishes.

With some confusion Henry was obliged to confess, that he had anticipated the permission so graciously bestowed. Harriet was already mistress of every secret of his heart. Attracted by the sound of the harpsichord to Mrs. Fielding's music-room, he had there found Harriet alone; the opportunity was irresistible. The apprehension of her father's displeasure, the threatened loss of Mrs. Fielding's friendship, the imprudence of marrying without a fortune, all were at that moment forgotten; and the dread of suffering from the horrid idea of another and perhaps more fortunate rival, appeared to him a consideration paramount to every other. His father listened to his apology with a smile, that told him he had no great difficulty in pronouncing his pardon. He moreover promised to speak to Mrs. Fielding on the subject, and hoped to be able to avert her displeasure at such a very direct breach of her injunctions.

Mr. Sydney was as good as his word; he told her of the plan agreed to by Dr. Orwell and himself for the union of their families, and begged to have her opinion concerning it.

"I must speak to Miss Orwell on the subject before I can reply to your question," said Mrs. Fielding; and stepping to the next room, where she knew Harriet was then employed in writing to her sister, "I come, my dear," said she, "to speak to you on matters of such importance to your happiness, that I shall not apologize for interrupting you." Harriet, anticipating the subject on which she intended to interrogate her, bowed in some confusion. Mrs. Fielding proceeded—"I am afraid you will set me down for an intermeddling old woman; but I do assure you, it is not from the desire of gratifying an old maidish curiosity that I am prompted to ask you some questions, which I hope you will have the good-nature to forgive, and the ingenuousness to answer."

Harriet again bowed assent.

"The reasons you gave me for refusing the addresses of Mr. Carradine were all calculated to do you honour. They were such as I could not but approve; but tell me, my dear, was there no other little lurking motive?—Ah! that blush is a sufficient reply, and I shall require no other. Had Henry Sydney a fortune equal to Carradine's, I should not be surprised at your preferring him; but my dear Miss Orwell, do you consider what you are about to do? Have you duly weighed the consequences?"

'I hope I have, Madam; but if you see any objections—if you—pray go on, I shall be much obliged to you for your opinion and advice.'

Mrs. Fielding resumed:—"Though we are all the poor dependents on futurity, and though it be our sanguine hope of future felicity that makes up the greater part of our present enjoyment, yet do we almost always err by making the estimate of that felicity from present feeling. While inspired by youthful passion, we think that love alone will constitute the happiness of our future days; the evils of poverty are then despised, and when viewed at a distance are perhaps converted by fancy into a charming addition to romantic tenderness. If imagination have thus deceived you, let me beg of you, before it is too late, to dismiss the vain illusion, and take a real view of the cares and vexations that may await you."

'I am fully sensible of the truth of all you have said,' returned Harriet, 'as well as of your goodness in reminding me of it. The subject is not new to my reflections; if I had been brought up in the lap of luxury and sloth, or accustomed to place my happiness in the gratification of vanity, I am aware of the misery that would await a change of circumstances. But all my habits have been those of active industry, and all my hopes of happiness been taught to rest in the bosom of domestic peace. For myself I have therefore nothing to fear; but for Henry—'

"You are a charming girl!" cried Mrs. Fielding, tenderly embracing her, "and truly deserving of the happiness that I hope awaits you. But here comes Henry, and I must now talk a little with him; so pray step into the next room for a few minutes. Well, sir," continued Mrs. Fielding, addressing herself to Henry as Harriet retired, "I see the friendship of an old woman is not so valuable in your eyes as the affections of a young one. Nay, nay, don't offer any apology, you must hear me out. I told you, I never should consent to your marrying without a fortune adequate to your support; and I shall keep my word. Here," continued she, taking a bundle of papers from her pocket, and presenting them to Henry, "on perusing these you will perceive, that I then addressed myself to a man who was his own master. Forgive me for having prolonged the term of your probation, but I too well knew the danger of habits of luxury and dissipation, not to wish to save the child I had adopted from their dominion. It was on this account I directed you to the choice of a profession which, while it afforded an immediate object to your mind, and prevented the rust of idleness from corroding your faculties, put it in your power to be useful to your fellow-creatures. The man without employment is a cypher in society; dependent upon others for an adventitious value, he is in himself contemptible. May you, my son, (for as such I shall ever consider you) so employ your fortune and your talents, as to make them instrumental to your eternal happiness. And in the dear girl you have chosen for a wife, may you receive as great a reward as this world can bestow. So GOD bless you!"

Henry seized the hand that she held out to him, and involuntarily dropping on his knees, pressed it to his lips. His emotion was too great for utterance; and Mrs. Fielding, wishing to escape the effusions of his gratitude, immediately left the room.

It was some time before Henry could sufficiently compose himself to proceed to the examination of the papers she had left with him; when he did, he found a deed of gift for ten thousand pounds, made on the day he had attained his fifth year. The sum had been at that period lodged in the hands of trustees, who received the interest, which they laid out in the funds, and regularly accounted for the stock thus accumulated. The principal was now, even after deducting the two hundred a year allowed for his education, nearly doubled; so that he saw himself in possession of one thousand pounds a year, independent of his profession.

Harriet, who had in the adjoining apartment watched the departure of Mrs. Fielding, and expected Henry would instantly join her, was not a little disappointed at his delay. She began to persuade herself that the arguments urged by prudence had prevailed upon his mind, and that he, perhaps, at that moment was struck with repentance for the rashness of his declaration. A small spark of latent pride began to operate upon her mind. She would no longer be the cause of his uneasiness; she would free him from the fetters of an engagement, of which it was plain he already began to feel the weight. Impressed with this idea, she gently opened the door that separated the two apartments, the first view she took of Henry confirmed her suspicions; but the first sentence he uttered banished them from her heart for ever!

CHAP. XI.

"Will you not now the pair of sages praise,
"Who the same end pursued by different ways?
"One pity'd, one condemn'd, the woeful times;
"One laugh'd at follies, one lamented crimes."
DRYDEN'S TRANS. OF JUV. SAT. X. 28.[50]

AS lovers are of all people in the world those whose company we have found most insupportably insipid, we shall not tire our readers by confining them to it for too great a length of time, but briefly inform them, that Mr. Churchill having found in the charms of Maria a consolation for his late disappointment, obtained her father's consent to lead her to the alter at the same time that Henry and his bride were to exchange their vows. While the preparations were going on for the double nuptials, Doctor Orwell found it necessary to return to W——, but proposed coming up with his youngest daughter before the ceremony took place. Mr. Sydney, having procured a young clergyman to officiate in his absence, readily consented to remain in London till he could be accompanied to the country by his children. While fixing on houses for their future residence, giving directions about repairs, purchasing furniture, plate, &c. &c. occupied the mornings of the young people, Mr. Sydney employed his at the Museums of Natural History, which particularly attracted his attention. In these he found a never-failing source of

---

[50] John Dryden, *The Tenth Satire of Juvenal* (1692) 41-44.

amusement, and was only mortified on perceiving the little interest the young people seemed to take in his elaborate descriptions. Even Maria, who in the country had listened to the subject with so much complacency, had apparently lost much of her relish for plants and butterflies, since her residence in London. Hoping, however, that her taste was not as yet quite lost, he one day brought her home a small chrysalis of uncommon beauty, with which a friend had presented him; while she complacently expressed her admiration Churchill entered the room, and perceiving how she was engaged, peeped over her shoulder at the object of her contemplation.

"Is it not very beautiful?" said she, looking up to him with an enchanting smile.

'It is, indeed,' replied he, dashing with his finger and thumb the little chrysalis into the fire, but still keeping his eyes fixed upon the paper.

"Bless me!" exclaimed Maria, "what have you done? Where is the chrysalis? Why did you throw it away?"

'Indeed, sir,' said Mr. Sydney, gravely, 'I shall take care how I permit such a treasure to come into your way again.'

"What have I done?" cried Churchill, in amazement; "of what treasure do you speak? I have not surely injured the poem Maria was looking at, which, if not a first rate performance, is certainly not destitute of merit, if there be merit in truth."

Maria, though vexed at the mortification it occasioned her father, could scarcely forbear laughing at her lover's mistake. The chrysalis was happily not irrecoverably lost. After having carefully picked it from the ashes, and restored it to him who best knew its value, she examined the lines that had attracted the attention of Mr. Churchill, and at his request read them aloud.

TO SELFISHNESS.

No, Selfishness, thou art not Nature's child!
Of proud and pamper'd Lux'ry thou wer't born!
   Not in the rural vale, or desart wild,
But 'mid those polish'd scenes where Plenty pours her horn.

Behold that youth, in whose soul-beaming eye
Sits Sympathy, and each affection kind;
   His bosom swells with Pity's tender sigh,
And at another's bliss warm glows his gen'rous mind.

No cold distrust hath ever chill'd his heart,
No blank reserve his truth-taught lips hath seal'd;
   Ardent he seeks his feelings to impart,
And to the friend he loves his inmost soul's reveal'd.

    Is there who cheer'd him in the hour of woe,
Who from his eyes has wip'd Affliction's tear?
    Pure Gratitude's full stream doth ceaseless flow,
Enhancing, as it runs, each obligation dear.

    Doth rude Necessity's imperious law
In toilsome business half his hours employ?
    From sleep, from pastime, still he time can draw,
To aid the precious fund of dear domestic joy.

    His soul a sister's fond affection charms,
He joys to meet maternal love's mild beam;
    The bliss of blessing all his bosom warms,
And dear doth his pure heart the social circle deem.

    Such is the youth in Nature's bosom bred,
While yet a stranger to the polish'd world;
    Behold him now in Fashion's gay walks tread,
And in the vortex vile of Dissipation whirl'd.

    As Knaresborough's rills★[51] arrest the silken zone,
And drop by drop insidious works its change,
    Till the gay flutt'rer, stiff'ning into stone,
In form alone escapes the transformation strange;

    So love of Pleasure of degrees devours
Each nobler, finer feeling of the heart;
    So Pride and Vanity's transforming pow'rs
Doth callous Selfishness e'en to its core impart.

    See him, who erst with Sympathy's warm zeal
Explor'd the rhet'rick of the asking eye;
    Who with the poor would share his scanty meal,
And at soft Pity's call could his own wants deny;

    Now press'd by wants that Nature never knew,
(Fantastic wants! imperious as vain)
    He for himself finds Fortune's gifts too few,
Nor at soft Pity's call will one wild wish restrain.

---

[51] ★Alluding to the petrefaction of ribbons so quickly effected by the dropping-well of Knaresborough★ Knaresborough, a small town in the north of England, known for its wishing well into which people drop ribbons and pennies.

He, whose warm heart with sympathetic glow
Shar'd all the bosom-feelings of a friend,
 Now in gay crouds, or at the public shew,
In heartless, joyless pomp prefers his hours to spend.

No more the social fire-side circle charms,
No more a mother's smiles he joys to meet;
 Fraternal love no more his bosom warms,
Nor thoughts of giving joy imparts one rapture sweet.

No, Selfishness, thou art not Nature's child;
Of proud and pamper'd Lux'ry thou wer't born;
 Not in the rural vale, or desert wild,
But in those polish'd scenes where Plenty pours her horn.

Though the name of Carradine was never mentioned at Mrs. Fielding's, he was not forgotten by any of the party. The generous heart of Henry felt for the mortification of his rival, and finding that he did not come again to him, he took the earliest opportunity of calling at his lodgings. He there learned that Carradine had set off for Bath the day after he had last seen him, and from thence he soon after received from him the following letter:

"MY DEAR SYDNEY,"

"IMMEDIATELY on leaving you, I met with a party of friends who, like myself, were on the wing for India; but as the fleet will not be ready to sail for a few weeks, they resolved to take a dash to Bath in the interim. I liked the thought, and was glad to accompany them; and here we are beating about like so many spaniels in a rabbit-warren. No cessation from amusement. Morning, noon, and night, all here are on the scent of pleasure; but for what is called *pleasure* I find I have lost somewhat of my relish, for I now find living in a croud to be abominably insipid. Poor Doctor Orwell was shocked at the idea of girls of character going to the Indian market; but had he come to Bath, he might have beheld a perpetual fair, where every ball-room may be considered as a booth for the display of beauty to be disposed of to the highest matrimonial bidder. Having been introduced to some very pleasant fellows, all of them men of large fortune and high connexions, I have through them had an opportunity of making what acquaintance I chose. The mothers have all smiled upon me, and I have had no reason to complain of my reception from the daughters. I have admired the beauty of several, and do not know, had it been less pressed upon my observation, what effect it might have had upon my heart. But what one sees morning, noon, and night, soon ceases to interest; and in a society where intimacy takes place without acquaintance, the mind can never rivet the chain which is forged by the senses.

"Harriet Orwell would not, I think, like Bath. No; she likes *conversation*, and here is only *talk*. But were Harriet Orwell here, she would, I make no doubt, soon discover some congenial souls, who form a more rational society than that which has come within the sphere of my observation. But why do I mention Harriet Orwell? Why, to shew you that I can do it without pain; and to convince you that my heart has been made the better, and not the worse, for its admiration of excellence.

"From the tenor of my letter, you will perceive that this trip has been of use to my spirits, and if you are the generous fellow I take you for, you will entirely restore them. To do this, you must permit me to contribute to your happiness. I am at present looking out for some person in whose hands I can deposit two thousand pounds. It is the remainder of the sum I brought with me from India. I am perfectly careless about the interest, nor would the loss of the principal affect me; so that it is no compliment to say that the use of it is very much at your service. I hate the lawyers, and am an enemy to the stamp-act;[52] I shall therefore have nothing to say to bonds or parchments, but leave you to manage the sum I have mentioned entirely as you please, till my return to Europe; and am, &c. &c.

BASIL CARRADINE.

The reader's heart, if he have one, will be at no loss to suggest the reply which Henry made to the friendly offer of his truly generous rival. Another letter of the same date, received from Dr. Orwell, assigned to him a task of a more unpleasant nature. Tidings of Mr. Glib's having been arrested and thrown into prison had reached W—; and the good Doctor, who never remembered the faults of the unfortunate, intreated his friends to interest themselves in his behalf, and if possible, to extricate him from the horrors of confinement.

Following the directions they had received, Mr. Sydney and his son proceeded to Newgate; where, in a gloomy and desolate apartment, they found the unhappy Glib, a prey to the most abject dejection. The flippancy of his manner was now exchanged for an air of despondency, which, however, a little brightened up on being informed of the purport of their visit. In order to know how far there was a possibility of serving him, it was necessary to have an accurate account of the state of his affairs; in giving which he was obliged to confess himself the dupe of Vallaton, against whom he now poured forth all the bitterness of invective.

Mr. Sydney was at much pains to turn the current of his wrath from the man to the principles on which he had acted; these the old gentleman was at great pains to pourtray in their proper colours. What he learned from Glib of the conduct of Vallaton, impressed him with a deep

---

[52] Acts of parliament for regulating the stamp duties on various products, salt, newspapers; especially that of 1765 for levying stamp duties in the American colonies.

sorrow for the fate of poor Julia, and gave him a fresh anxiety concerning her situation; and finding that Glib, though he could not himself furnish any information concerning them, suspected Mr. Myope of being acquainted with the place of their concealment, he resolved immediately to apply to that gentleman on the subject.

While Henry remained to take in writing the statement which Glib had given of his affairs, his father proceeded to Myope's lodgings, and had the good fortune of finding him at home, and alone. He introduced himself without difficulty, but found the philosopher very little inclined to gratify him on the subject of his enquiries. After receiving some evasive answers to his plain questions, Mr. Sydney with some indignation said, "After the accounts I have just received from a person whom the perfidious villainy of this man has involved in ruin, I cannot wonder that he should skulk in concealment; but from you, sir, I should expect better than to protect a man who, as far as I can learn, has acted like a scoundrel in every thing."

'Scoundrels, sir,' said Mr. Myope, 'are frequently, indeed almost always, men of talents, and great talents are great energies; and great energies cannot but flow from a powerful sense of fitness and justice. You allude, I suppose, to Mr. Vallaton's conduct as treasurer of the Hottentonian committee, from which conduct Mr. Glib has been a sufferer. But, sir, Mr. Vallaton no doubt perceived a degree of fitness in appropriating those sums to himself, which a man of more confined intellect might not have discovered.'

"Is it possible, sir," cried Mr. Sydney, "that a man of your seeming gravity can be the apologist of such crimes?"

'There is no such thing as crime,' replied Myope; 'and though Mr. Vallaton may, perhaps, in some instances have acted erroneously, yet it is incontestibly proved, that as a man of talents he cannot be destitute of virtue.'

"The Devil himself is represented as possessed of talents," returned Mr. Sydney, "and of him the doctrines you have mentioned are truly worthy."

'The Devil!' rejoined Mr. Myope; 'why, my dear sir, the Devil is the first of heroes! I cannot conceive a greater compliment than to be compared to the Devil. You do not know in what high estimation his character is held by modern philosophers. It is possible that his energies, like those of Mr. Vallaton, centered too much in personal regards; but take him all in all, his is the first of imaginary characters that it ever entered into the heart of man to conceive. Oh, the virtues of the Devil are inestimable!'

"Mr. Vallaton has indeed proved a very close imitator of the arch apostate," said Mr. Sydney; "and I am afraid Miss Delmond, like our general mother, will find that she has listened to the voice of this black seducer to be

"Despoil'd of innocence, of faith, of bliss!"[53]

Can you, sir, inform me (for, from the infamous character of the man, I have my doubts) whether he and Miss Delmond are really married?"

'I cannot speak to a certainty,' replied Myope; 'but all I can say is, that I do not think Mr. Vallaton a man likely to sanction by his example an institution so immoral and injurious to the interest of society.'

Mr. Sydney looked aghast. "Is it possible," cried he, "that vice should thus audaciously assume the name of virtue?"

'And pray, sir,' returned Myope, 'what is virtue, but another name for happiness? Is not happiness the only true end of existence?'

"That happiness in the only true end of existence, I grant you," said Mr. Sydney; "and if you can point out a single instance where an encrease of happiness has been the result of this new system of morals, I shall allow your argument to have some weight."

'The new morality is too sublime for the present depraved and distempered state of human society,' rejoined Mr. Myope. 'The experiments that have been made in it have been rather premature, and therefore cannot expect to have been followed with advantageous consequences to the individuals, who have nobly stemmed the torrent of prejudice to make them.'

"A proof to me," replied Mr. Sydney, "of the superiority of those principles which are adapted to every state of society, and to every circumstance in which a human being can be placed; which, by governing the passions and regulating the affections of the heart, bring peace to the soul, and are equally calculated for enhancing the enjoyment of prosperity by preserving from its temptations, and of allaying the bitterness of adversity by saving from despair."

A contemptuous smile, which overspread the countenance of Mr. Myope as Mr. Sydney pronounced the last sentence, indicated a sneering reply; but a letter, which was at that moment put into his hands by his servant, gave a new expression to every feature, and for the supercilious smile of scorn, substituted the frown of fury and revenge. 'Vallaton is indeed a villain!' exclaimed he, stamping his foot in a paroxysm of rage. 'Insidious serpent! *He* seduce my Emmeline! *He* entice her to leave me in this manner! Ungrateful wretch! To act thus by *me*! It is intolerable!' In this incoherent manner did he run on for some time, before Mr. Sydney could at all comprehend the cause of his inquietude. At length, however, he discovered that Mr. Vallaton had that morning set off for France with *the Goddess of Reason*, of whom it now appeared he had long been the favoured lover.

It may perhaps be expected, that Mr. Sydney should with avidity avail himself of so favourable an opportunity of triumphing in the discomfi-

---

[53] John Milton, *Paradise Lost*, Bk IX.

ture of an opponent; so far, however, was Mr. Sydney from doing so, that the expressions which would so naturally have slid to the tongue of many good people in similar circumstances, never once found their way to his. Observing the mind of Mr. Myope too much agitated for a discussion on principles, he only staid with him until he obtained an address to the lodgings Vallaton had lately occupied; and thither the old gentleman instantly hurried, in hopes of gaining some information concerning the injured and now forsaken Julia. His solicitude was fruitless. Vallaton and Julia had left these lodgings a fortnight, nor could the people of the house furnish him with any clue to their next place of abode. Oppressed by fatigue, and overwhelmed with regret, he returned to Mrs. Fielding's, where happiness beamed on every countenance, and the sweet flutterings of youthful hope, or the more delicious feelings of internal satisfaction, dwelt in every heart. In the contemplation of such a scene every selfish sorrow would have been annihilated. The heart of Mr. Sydney swelled with gratitude to the Giver of all good, for making him a witness of the happiness of his children, but had been too deeply wounded in the course of the morning to admit of an immediate return of its wonted serenity.

CHAP. XII.

"Then gently scan your brother man,
   "Still gentler, sister woman;
"Though they may gang a kennin wrang,
   "To step aside is human.
"Who made the heart, 'tis he alone
   "Decidedly can try us;
"He knows each *chord*, its *various tone*,
   "Each spring, its various bias:
"Then at the balance let's be mute,
   "*We never can adjust it*;
"What's done we partly may compute,
   "*But never what's resisted.*"

BURNS.[54]

BY the zeal of Mr. Sydney, the liberality of Mrs. Fielding, and the active exertions of Henry, the affairs of Mr. Glib were put into such a train, that in the course of a few days he was set at liberty. Putting himself under the direction of his benefactors, and abjuring all connection with his former associates, he set out for W— to re-enter upon the possession of his house and shop, to re-assemble his children round his own fire-side, and

---

[54] Robert Burns *Address to the Unco Good or the Rigidly Righteous* (1787) 48-51, 56-63.

to receive back his repentant wife, who now forsaken by her gallant, was left a prey to the miseries of poverty, or the still greater miseries of vice. Having been mutually to blame, Mr. Sydney strongly recommended to them the duty of mutual forgiveness; and such weight had his advice, from the acts of beneficence with which it was prefaced, that they did not scruple to adopt it. New ideas of duty, and new perceptions of happiness, began to open on their minds; attention to business occupied the hours that had formerly been devoted to the study of new theories in philosophy; and instead of descanting on general utility, they now seriously applied themselves to the education of their own children.

Glib, being now convinced that there is no immorality in gratitude, scruples not to declare, that he owes to his benefactors not only the re-establishment of his credit, but the existence of his happiness. Nor let the proud reader murmur at our thus transgressing the order of our history, to give this concluding sketch of the adventures of a simple tradesman. It is the affected perogative of selfish prosperity to consider as mere automatons all who move not in its own exalted sphere; but it is the privilege of philosophy to view human nature from a still more lofty eminence, from which the paltry distinctions of situation are lost to the eye, and the interests of humanity exert an equal claim to the feelings of the heart.

To return to our narrative. The preparations for the nuptials were now completed; the day fixed on for their celebration was at hand. It was expected by the parties with that chastened hope, which in well-regulated minds attends the often-clouded prospect of earthly felicity. They felt the fulness of satisfaction, but were taught by reason to set bounds to the wild extravagance of joy.

The friendship of the two young ladies, which had been knit by a sympathy of taste and sentiment, was strengthened by a similarity of situation; nor would the happiness of either have been compleat, if it had not been shared by the other.

"Surely," said Harriet, one day that she was sitting alone with her friend, "surely, Maria, we are highly favoured of Heaven; if our gratitude were proportioned to its gifts, I believe we should do nothing but pray and sing psalms from morning to night. Well, I wish to GOD that all the world was as happy as we are!"

'And that wish, my dear girl,' said Mrs. Fielding, who then entered the room, 'is of itself a song of thanksgiving more acceptable than a thousand psalms. But where is Henry? I have got some business for him, and expected to find him here.'

"He will be here soon, I will answer for him," said Maria, "and here he is."

'Here, however,' said Mrs. Fielding, 'I cannot at present permit him to remain.'

She then put into his hands a billet she had just received from the matron of her asylum, informing her of the admission of an unfortunate young woman, who was so very ill as to require immediate medical assistance. Her appearance, she added, was extremely interesting, and plainly indicated something very superior to her present situation.

'Come,' said Mrs. Fielding, when Henry had read the note, 'let us hasten 'to this poor unfortunate. The carriage is already at the door; and not to mortify you too much by taking you away, the girls shall accompany us. What say you, ladies, to my proposal?"

Their assent was readily accorded, and the coachman, obeying the orders of his mistress, drove full speed to the asylum. On alighting, the young ladies went into the work-room, where they were already known and beloved; while Mrs. Fielding and Henry followed the matron to the chamber of the young stranger. There, reclining on the bed in a state of almost torpid insensibility, they beheld a young person, whose face was concealed from view by a mass of pale brown hair, which uncombed and unarranged flowed over it in wild disorder. The inimitable beauty of her hand and arm attracted their instant observation; Henry gazed for a moment in silence, and then suddenly advancing, "Is it possible!" cried he, in a smothered tone. "Is it Miss Delmond, Julia Delmond, that I see thus?"

At the sound of that name she hastily raised her head; and with a wild and sudden motion putting back her hair, franticly gazed on Henry for a moment, then uttering a loud scream, fainted away. When she recovered, she found herself supported in the arms of Mrs. Fielding, and her face bathed with the tears which fell fast from that good lady's eyes. 'Where am I?' cried she, in a quick and hurried voice. 'And who are you? And why do you weep? Did *you* know my father? But be comforted; *you* did not kill him; you did not break his heart. Ah! no, no, no!' then striking her hand against her forehead, she hid her face in Mrs. Fielding's bosom.

"Do not afflict yourself thus, my dear child,' said Mrs. Fielding; "you are ill, and must take care of yourself, and here is you old friend and physician, Doctor Sydney, who begs leave to attend you, and I dare say will join me in entreating you to dismiss every uneasy thought from your mind. You are not among strangers, but surrounded by your best and most affectionate friends."

'Yes,' said Doctor Sydney, affectionately taking her hand, 'yes, dear Miss Delmond, you do not know how much pleasure your recovery will give to many hearts.'

A deep sigh burst from her bosom, but as if afraid to look on Henry, she clung to Mrs. Fielding to conceal her face from his observation.

"Perhaps," said Mrs. Fielding, "Miss Delmond would better like to see her friend Harriet Orwell."

'Harriet Orwell!' repeated Miss Delmond; 'ah! no, no, Harriet Orwell would now disdain to look on the poor forlorn Julia!'

"My Julia! my dear Julia! my sweet friend!" cried Harriet, who had only waited for a signal to approach her, and clasping her in her arms, imprinted an affectionate kiss on her pale cheek; "Never, never will your friend Harriet forsake you!" Sighs and tears choked her utterance; while

Julia, with all the strength she had left, strained her to her bosom. She attempted to speak, but voice was denied her; the words died away upon her parched and pallid lips, and again she was near fainting, when a timely shower of tears seemed in some measure to relieve her swoln heart.

It was the relief of nature, and her friends were too judicious to seek to stop the salutary effusion. Harriet, indeed, shed tear for tear; and Maria, who stood at a distance, apprehensive of overpowering the poor timid mourner, by the appearance of so many people at once, had her full share of the affecting scene.

At length Mrs. Fielding observed, that they must not too far indulge their feelings. That ill as Miss Delmond evidently was, she thought she might now be removed to her house without danger. "And when there," said she, "I hope, under the care of so many kind nurses, she will soon be well. Come, my love," she added, kindly pressing Julia's hand, "do not too much give way to this emotion, but let me prevail upon you to rally your exhausted spirits, and to take some refreshment to enable you to bear the fatigue of the ride."

Again Julia attempted to speak, but her words were not yet audible. With difficulty she swallowed the cordial Doctor Sydney had ordered, which seeming to restore some degree of animation to her languid frame, Mrs. Fielding took the opportunity of again urging their immediate departure. Henry begged leave to support her to the carriage. 'And I too,' said Harriet, putting her arm round her waist, 'I too will be the supporter of my dear Julia.'

She passively permitted them to raise her from the chair, when, as if recollecting herself, she shrunk suddenly from their assisting arms, exclaiming, "Oh! never, never, never shall the house of Mrs. Fielding be contaminated by the reception of a wretch like me. Here let me hide myself from a world that will despise me, and here let me die in peace." The effort she made in pronouncing these words shook her whole frame; her eyes rolled wildly round, and she seemed speedily relapsing into the same disordered state from which she had so lately recovered.

In vain did Harriet second Mrs. Fielding's kind intreaties with all the soothing eloquence of friendship. She made no other reply than by clinging to the bedpost, and several times repeating, in a hollow tone, "No, no, here, here," and some other disjointed words, all, however, plainly indicative of her determined resolution of not being removed.

Henry at length put an end to the contest by declaring, that it would be injurious in her present state to persist in it any further.

'Here then, my love, you shall stay for to-day,' said Mrs. Fielding, 'provided you will suffer yourself to be put immediately to bed, and take whatever Doctor Sydney orders for you.'

It was then agreed, that she should be left to the care of Harriet, who would on no account leave her. Nor did Henry require the motive of Harriet's presence to determine him to devote as much of his time as was not engaged by other patients, to the relief of this unhappy girl; though as his hopes rested more upon the efficacy of confidential friendship than on the exertion of medical skill, they depended on Harriet still more than on himself. After the departure of Mrs. Fielding and Maria he withdrew, telling Harriet she would find him in the parlour whenever she thought his attendance necessary. Harriet smiled her approbation of his kind solicitude, and as soon as he was gone, urged Julia to permit herself to be immediately undressed. Julia made no opposition to her proposal, and as Harriet observed her uneasiness at the approach of strangers, she herself performed the office of her maid. While she endeavoured to confine within the small cap, the matron had provided for her, those beautiful tresses which she had so often seen adorned with the nicest care, and remembered how proud Captain Delmond used to be of their luxuriant growth, she was so forcibly struck with the contrast the present moment presented, that she could not restrain the falling tear. Julia perceived the tender emotion; and seizing Harriet's hand, pressed it to her lips.

"My good, my gentle Harriet!" said she, in a low and tremulous voice, "you alone, of all the world, will have compassion on me. It is your innate virtue only that will not fear contamination from a wretch like me. Oh that my father had had such a child!" Then leaning her head against Harriet's shoulder, she burst into a fresh agony of tears. It was a considerable time before Harriet's utmost efforts could restore her to any degree of composure; at length she was conveyed to bed, and a soporific draught soon gave a temporary oblivion to her sorrows.

Towards the close of the evening, Henry, who shared with his amiable mistress the task of watching the slumbers of their unhappy friend, was called out of the room. He soon returned, followed by his father, who, to Miss Orwell's great surprise, led in his hand the almost forgotten Bridgetina. She took no notice of Harriet, but with trembling steps followed Mr. Sydney to the bed-side. On beholding the face of Julia, she started, and laying hold of Mr. Sydney's arm, 'Why,' said she, 'did you not tell me she was dead!'

"Nay, shrink not from this sight," said Mr. Sydney, without noticing her mistake, "but in that pale face and altered form contemplate the fruits of your boasted system of happiness and virtue. Lovely, indeed, very lovely was this fallen flower! and long might it have bloomed the delight of every heart, had it not been deprived of those supports which GOD and Nature had assigned it. Sweet innocent! how cruel was the spoiler that laid thy glory in the dust! how detestable the arts that led to thy destruction!"

Bridgetina, though not remarkable for the quickness of her feelings, was affected. She sobbed aloud. In pity to her distress, and in apprehension that Julia might be disturbed by her noisy grief, Harriet took pains to comfort her. She told her they had every reason to hope for Miss Delmond's speedy recovery. "Even the wound which her peace of mind has received is not mortal," said she; "she will apply to the balm of consolation, and the principles of religion will aid the power of time, and restore her to tranquillity."

'She is not then dead!' cried Bridgetina, eagerly pressing forward. 'She breathes! I see she breathes. Look how she smiles! but ah! how ghastly is that smile! how unlike the playful smile of Julia! What has wrought this change?'

"It has been wrought," said Mr. Sydney, "by the same delusive principles that have seduced you from the path of filial duty. Had nature bestowed upon you a form as beautiful, or a face as fair, you too would have been the prey of lust, and the victim of infamy. Be thankful that you have escaped a fate so dreadful. Repent of ever having dared it; and by your future behaviour to your fond mother, strive to make amends for your past conduct."

Bridgetina wept bitterly, but did not refuse her hand to Mr. Sydney, who led her out of the room, without having given the least disturbance by their presence to the profound slumbers of Julia.

In order to account for the appearance of our heroine at this juncture, it is necessary to mention the proceedings of Mr. Sydney subsequent to the interview with Mr. Myope, which has been already related. Mr. Sydney (though a clergyman) was neither *dictatorial, impatient of contradiction, harsh in his censures*, nor *illiberal in his judgments*.★[55] He saw the prejudices of Myope with compassion; he felt for the situation in which his false principles had plunged him, with the acutest sensibility; and was impelled by his benevolence to exert every power of his soul for the restoration of his peace.

The mind of Mr. Myope was now in a state peculiarly favourable to the reception of new impressions. The ardour with which he had embraced the new theory of morals was somewhat abated. Circumstances had occurred, which even before the desertion of his friend and mistress, had considerably cooled his zeal. This event had given a new turn to his reflections, and he began to doubt whether the recent discoveries in morality were likely to be attended with all the beneficial consequences to mankind, which, in the moment of enthusiasm he had so fondly predicted. The antipathy he had imbibed against the clerical character, made him receive the first advances of Mr. Sydney with reluctance; but he soon found that zeal is not necessarily accompanied with arrogance, and that a preacher of christianity is not always of consequence *dogmatical and intolerant*.[56]

As Myope had been a zealous leader of several different sects of religionists, it may be supposed that Mr. Sydney could offer him no new arguments in support of christianity; but however strange it may appear, so it was, that the light in which the truths of natural and revealed religion were placed by Mr. Sydney, were such as never before had been pre-

---

[55] ★See Enquirer, p. 232★ *Enquirer*, Part II, Essay V, "Of Trades and Professions", 232. See Appendix A.

[56] *Enquirer*, Part II, Essay V, "Of Trades and Professions" 232. See Appendix A.

sented to the mind of the philosopher. He sought not to perplex by logical definitions; he betrayed no zeal for peculiar tenets; he treated the various explanations of particular passages of scripture as of very small importance; and seemed only anxious for the establishment of great and fundamental truths. The God of Mr. Sydney was a God of mercies—a God of consolation—"the God of lights, with whom there is no variableness, neither shadow of changing." His gospel, the perfection of benevolence, proclaiming "peace on earth, and goodwill towards men."

The enthusiasm of Mr. Myope kindled as he spoke, but it was not the design of Mr. Sydney to excite enthusiasm. He represented it as the business of religion to regulate the emotions of the heart, to allay the effervescence of the spirits, and to watch over the peculiar tendency of the temper. Its office to conduct the activity of an ardent mind into proper channels, where, instead of being expended in vain speculations, it may be productive of real and substantial good. Far from loading with indiscriminate abuse all the opinions which formed a part of Mr. Myope's system, Mr. Sydney allowed all the merit that was due to the spirit of philanthropy which breathed in his notions of benevolence, and gave to his doctrines of sincerity the warmest and most decided applause. But while he applauded the abstract notions entertained of each of these noble principles, he plainly demonstrated their inutility in the direction Mr. Myope had given them; and proved that to these, as well as to every other virtue, the principles of christianity were the best, the only support. "I do indeed admire and applaud the zeal with which you espouse the cause of the poor and oppressed part of our species," said Mr. Sydney; "it does honour to your heart. But what does your system do for them? What does it propose to do?"

'It proposes,' replied Mr. Myope, 'by enlightening the public mind, to render an equality of conditions, by the voluntary cession of property, universal.'

"Supposing this to be practicable," returned Mr. Sydney, "(though how a person who is at all acquainted with the world or with human nature can make the supposition, I am at a loss to imagine) still it does not appear that happiness is the natural and necessary result. Does the experience of those who are most exempt from the physical evils of life, lead us to form such a conclusion? I am sure it does not. And what is the present consequence of such doctrines to the objects of your benevolent regard? To infuse additional gall into the bitter cup of poverty, to add to the burden of human miseries a load of discontent! How different that system of equality preached by Him who emphatically announced himself the friend of the poor and needy! What are riches, or honours, or even the less equivocal blessings of liberty and independence, compared with the glorious certainty of the favour of GOD, and the enjoyment of immortal happiness? By this hope have millions been supported under the pressure of calamities which your system could never reach; for in it alone is found a cure for the sorrows of the heart. The love of glory and the desire of fame have sometimes, it is true, animated their votaries into a contempt for the evils of pain, and even of death itself; but from the influence of this principle the many must ever be excluded. The man who cherishes it, and is by his situation thrown into obscurity, where his sufferings are unnoticed, or regarded with contempt, must be miserable; but absolute misery can never in any situation be the lot of the christian."

After some little hesitation, the truth of Mr. Sydney's assertion was acknowledged by Mr. Myope; still, however, the enormous evils attendant on the present state of society afforded him an ample field for expatiation and censure. These Mr. Sydney canvassed one by one, as they were pointed out by the philosopher. Some he traced to causes very different from those from which Mr. Myope had deduced them; some he proved to have consequences less injurious than those assigned them; and others he candidly gave up, as subjects of regret and mortification to every thinking mind; while he evidently shewed, that not an evil complained of could have existence in a society, where the sprit of christianity was the ruling principle of every heart.

The impression he made upon his learned adversary was gradual, but it was strong; and at every successive conversation he found him less tenacious of his former theory, and more inclined to admit the proofs of the truth of that doctrine which alone,

"Amid life's pains, abasements, emptiness,
"The soul can comfort, elevate, and fill;
"Which only, and which amply this, performs;
"Lifts us above life's pains, her joys above!
"Their terrors those, and these their lustre lose;
"Eternity depending covers all."★[57]

It was on his return from one of these conferences that Mr. Sydney learned the situation of Julia. It immediately occurred to him, that an incident so striking was more likely to produce an effect on the mind of Bridgetina than any argument that could possibly be made use of. Mrs. Fielding readily entered into his views, and impatiently waited to know the result of the interview they then projected, and from which they expected the most salutary effects. How far their expectations were answered shall appear hereafter.

---

[57] Edward Young, *Night Thoughts* (1742-45) VI, 574-79.

CHAP. XIII.

"Prostrate fell
"Before him reverent, and there confess'd
"Humbly their faults, and pardon begg'd with tears,
"Watering the ground; and with their sighs the air
"Frequenting, sent from hearts contrite, in sign
"Of sorrow unfeign'd, and humiliation meek."
MILTON.[58]

THE slumbers of Julia were not refreshing. She awoke languid and oppressed, but perfectly restored to her recollection. Harriet, for whom a bed had been provided in an adjoining room, had retired to snatch a short repose; and Henry had some hours before been obliged to go to the other end of the town, so that on awaking, the nurse was the only person near her. To her she addressed herself in low and trembling accents, "Pray, pray, good woman, be so kind as to inform me where I am. I thought I came to the Asylum of the Destitute. Yes, I remember the name— the Asylum of the Destitute.[59] Is it there I am?"

'Yes,' replied the nurse, 'this is the Asylum of the Destitute.'

"Thank GOD!" said Julia, "I am then safe. I am under the protection of the virtuous. I believe my head has been disturbed. It has been sadly confused. I thought some dear friends were with me; but it was all a dream. I now see it was a dream."

'Miss Orwell sat up with you the greatest part of the night,' said the nurse.

"Miss Orwell! Harriet Orwell! Dear amiable girl! And shall I not see her again?"

'She is only lain down to take a little rest. Dr. Sydney insisted on it before he would go away.'

"Henry Sydney too here! Yes, I think I remember seeing him. But how extraordinary is all this! I believe my head is still strangely bewildered, for I can account for nothing."

'It is only the effects of your sleeping draught, Madam. You had better keep quiet for a little time, and it will soon go off;' replied the judicious nurse, drawing the curtains.

Julia followed her advice, and remained silent till the light footsteps of Harriet attracted her attention. She then quickly withdrew the curtains, and raising herself up in the bed, held out both her hands to her fair friend, who, tenderly embracing her, made anxious enquiries after her

---

[58] John Milton, *Paradise Lost*, Book X.
[59] Hamilton managed the Edinburgh House of Industry which afforded assistance to "aged females of respected character, when thrown out of employment, and of training the young to habits of industry and virtue" (Benger, *Memoirs of the Late Mrs. Elizabeth Hamilton*, 1818, 193-94).

health. "Ah, Harriet! how good, how very good you are! But your kindness overpowers me. When last I saw you, how little did I think I should now be the humbled wretch I am!"

'Do not distress yourself, my dear Julia, by too keen a recollection of past events. Over these we have no control. Let us occupy our minds by the present and the future; and if we do so properly, be assured there is no evil of which good may not be the result.'

"Alas! for me no good remains. No, no; for me all is the darkness of despair, the gloom of misery! My father!—Oh, Harriet, you know the circumstances of his death; tell me then, nay do not conceal it; tell me, if with his latest breath he did not curse his Julia?"

'No, my dear, your father expired in a better frame of mind; his last words were to implore a blessing on you. He never spoke of you with resentment, but pitied your delusion, and I believe from his heart forgave it.'

"Did he, indeed! and did he bless me! Oh, my dear, dear papa! how could I—" Here she was interrupted by a flood of tears, which for some time rendered her incapable of holding further converse.

'Do not, my dear Julia,' said Harriet, 'do not, I beseech you, dwell so much upon the past. Much as I wish to know the particulars of all the cruel circumstances that have led to our present meeting, I will not now permit you to enter upon the sad detail. We shall have sufficient time for this hereafter, as I hope you will find yourself well enough this morning to accompany me to Mrs. Fielding's, in whom, I can assure you, you will find a tender and affectionate friend; she will be as a mother to you, till the arrival of your own; and I hope I may this morning have the pleasure of informing Mrs. Delmond, that you are under such respectable protection.'

"Alas! alas! it is impossible. Never can I appear at Mrs. Fielding's; never more can I enjoy the pleasures of society. No, Harriet; I have been a vain, guilty, infatuated creature; but never will I add to my self-condemnation by the meanness of imposture. In retirement, deep retirement, will I bury myself from the notice of the world. Even from you, my kind, my estimable friend—even from you must I hide myself; lest your fair fame should suffer by your deigning to pity such a wretch as I. Oh, I am indeed a wretch!

"Have I not steep'd a mother's couch in tears,
"And ting'd a father's dying cheek with shame?"

Oh, for me there is no comfort."

'And think you, Julia, that I am a slave to the *letter*, and a stranger to the *spirit* of virtue! That you have erred, I regret; but that you are sensible of your error, gives you a claim not only to my esteem, but my admiration. For how much less effort does it require to keep in the onward path of virtue, than to recover it when gone but a single step astray? Amply, I am assured, shall your future life compensate the fault of inexperienced youth. Cheer up, then, my Julia; and believe that you may yet be doubly dear to all who ever loved you.'

"Ah, Harriet! your words are a cordial (what a cordial!) to my drooping heart." Here she fervently pressed the hand of Harriet to her lips; then dropping it, and looking timidly in her face, while a burning blush shot over her pallid cheek, "But you—you know not all my shame. You know not that it *must be public*. I see you are shocked, greatly shocked. Did I not say, that even you would scorn to own me?"

'I am shocked, my love, I confess; but it is with the idea that your sufferings are not yet to have an end. Let us not talk more of this circumstance at present; permit me only to confide it to Mrs. Fielding, on whom you may rely for advice, and in whose tenderness you will find consolation.'

"To Mrs. Fielding! Alas, yes, it must be so—but yet—why, Harriet, after all that has befallen me, should false shame bring this cold sweat upon my forehead? But I will conquer it. Do I not deserve the censure I shall meet with? And why should I shrink from my deserts? Tell her, however—pray tell her, that I did not fall a prey to depraved inclination; that my judgment was perverted by argument, not seduced by flattery; and that when I yielded to the specious reasonings of my betrayer, I thought I was setting an example of high-souled virtue, which soared above the vulgar prejudices of the world. It is to vanity—yes, Harriet, I now see it is to vanity (though not the vanity of beauty) that I owe my ruin!"

Here she paused for a little, but Harriet only answering her by a sigh, she thus renewed the conversation. "My mind is still perplexed and bewildered. I have acted upon the sublimest principles of morality; I have been inspired by the most elevated sentiments of virtue. But virtue is happiness—and I am miserable! Is it owing to the prejudices of society that I am so? Ah! no. My father!—my unhappy father!—Had my heart received no other wound, his death would have transfixed a dagger in its inmost core. But how has it been wounded by another hand! How cruelly torn! O Harriet! my sufferings have been multiplied. I have passed through scenes which would freeze your soul with horror—but I dare not think of them. No, no, let me not think of them. I must avoid distraction—I—"

Harriet, perceiving the agitation of her mind, and fearful of its consequences, tenderly interrupted her, and used every endeavour to soothe her into composure. Henry soon after came in, and while he made his enquiries after Julia's health, Harriet stepped down to Mrs. Fielding, who was below in the parlour. She there informed her of all that had passed in the late conversation. They then consulted together on what was now to be done with the poor unfortunate, and as Harriet gave it as her opinion, that she would not be prevailed upon to remove to Mrs. Fielding's house, it was agreed, that she should remain where she was until the arrival of her mother, who was immediately to be sent for. Mrs. Fielding then begged leave to wait upon her; Julia would have excused herself, on account of her being still in bed; she had attempted to rise but had fainted in the attempt, and was advised by the Doctor not to get up till the evening, when he hoped she would find herself restored to greater strength. Mrs. Fielding waved the apology, and though her first appearance threw Julia (who conjectured the subject of her conversation with Harriet) into the deepest confusion, the sympathetic tenderness of her address was so truly maternal, that it quickly re-assured her confidence, and restored her serenity.

The natural openness and candour of Julia's mind suggested the propriety of giving her friends a faithful relation of all that had befallen her; but neither strength nor feelings were equal to the task. Mrs. Fielding and Harriet, perceiving that the bare recollection of some of these events was attended with a degree of horror that shook her tender frame, united their endeavours to recall her from the subject. They spoke of her health, and of the means necessary for its restoration; of these Mrs. Fielding mentioned country air as the most efficacious. She said, she had upon her estate in Hertfordshire a charming cottage, where Mrs. Delmond and Julia might enjoy all the advantages of retirement, and remain as long as they pleased unnoticed and unknown. When convenient for them to quit it, if they chose to remove to Ireland, she had there some friends to whom she could introduce them in such a manner as would procure their welcome reception into a very agreeable circle of society.

"I understand your kind hint, my dear Madam," said Julia, "I perfectly understand it; but you must not think me an ungrateful creature if I decline your generous offer. I would live—yes, it is now my wish to live, that by my future life I may make some amends for my past misconduct. But I greatly fear I have, in a moment of despair, of heart-rending agony, shortened the period of my existence. O that I could recall that moment! O that I may not have been a double murderer! My father! and my child! Nay, I pray you do not look upon me with such horror! I cannot bear that look!" covering up her head with the bed-clothes.

'Fear not the looks of us, thy frail fellow-mortals,' rejoined Mrs. Fielding; 'to the Searcher of hearts thy humility and thy penitence will be acceptable. And shall we, who know now how little of our boasted virtue we can call our own—we, who are ignorant of the temptations that have assailed thee, dare to pronounce thy condemnation? No, my dear Miss Delmond; far other sentiments, believe me, at this moment inspire our breasts. But if you feel my presence too much for you, I will retire and leave you with your friend Miss Orwell, to whom you may safely unburthen every feeling of your heart.'

Again Julia lifted up her head, and pressing Mrs. Fielding's hand, which had kindly taken hold of her's, "Surely," said she, "there is a GOD, a Providence, a reward hereafter for goodness such as your's. But if there be a GOD, if there be an hereafter, what must my situation be?"

'That GOD, my dear, who in the things that are made hath not left himself without a witness, is, by the Gospel of Jesus Christ, revealed to us as a father and a friend. Surrounded as we are by the glorious proofs of a Supreme Intelligence, it is scarcely possible for a sane mind to doubt the existence of a GOD. But our peculiar happiness is to have our vague and imperfect ideas upon this subject cleared and explained by Him who brought life and immortality to light; our great master came into the world "not to condemn the world, but that the world through him might have life."[60] He addressed not himself to the perfect. He professed not to call the "righteous (or those who proudly deemed themselves such) but sinners to repentance," and revealed to them the Almighty as a GOD of hope and consolation. Do not then, my sweet girl, encourage the language of despair. Acquaint yourself with the promises of the Gospel, and when the world withdraws its consolations, these shall support your soul. I hope, however, that you have not—no, assuredly you have not, done any thing with a wilful intention of shortening your existence?'

"Oh! yes, yes! If there be guilt in seeking to fly from a miserable existence, I am guilty! In a moment of frenzy and desperation I swallowed poison, I hoped it would have rid me of a wretched being, and buried my woes in the dark abyss of annihilation; but no sooner had I done the dreadful deed, than Nature recoiled, and death, which had long been the only object of my wishes, appeared horrible to my view. Oh! how my soul then struggled within me! What palpitations, what terrors laid hold of my distracted mind! 'Twas then, then I first suspected the possibility of my having cherished false opinions; then that I first began to fear, that there *might* be reality in those I had been taught to despise. The conversations I had held with you, my Harriet, rushed upon my recollection; we had each of us acted upon the principles we had adopted; but, oh! how different was the result! These and a thousand other agonizing reflections tore my throbbing heart, while momentarily I expected its beating pulse to be arrested by the cold hand of death. In this I was disappointed; cold shiverings, indeed, came upon me, and a numbness, which has not yet left me, seized my limbs, but death came not. I fear, however, the consequences will still be fatal—if not to myself, to—"

Here she stopped, and Mrs. Fielding kindly renewed those soothing assurances of divine aid, and divine mercy, which, however lightly thought of in the gay hours of prosperity, are found a cordial to the sinking heart.

Mrs. Fielding's zeal was not disgraced by bigotry, nor was it enflamed by superstition; she did not seek to overwhelm the already broken spirit by aggravating the colour of past offences, but rather made it her endeavour to re-assure her confidence in the possibility of future happiness from future exertions of virtue.

It was her opinion, that the support of reputation being found to be a strong additional motive to virtue, it ought not to be put out of the power of the unfortunate female, who, conscious of her error, is desirous to retrieve it by her after conduct. On this account, in the next conversation she held with Julia, she was led again to propose the plan she had suggested for her going first into the country, where she could enjoy all

---

[60] *John*: 13.17.

the privacy her circumstances required; and then removing to a situation, where the past incidents of her life might remain for ever buried in oblivion.

Julia listened to her proposal with respectful attention, and then, though in faltering accents, with a look and manner that denoted the utmost firmness and composure, she thus replied:—"I am fully, I am gratefully sensible of the goodness of your intention; your kind consideration for my reputation is the suggestion of pure benevolence, and believe me, I feel it as I ought. Do not, therefore, my dear Madam, attribute to perverseness or pride my opposition to your proposal; but it is a subject on which I have deeply thought; on which I have fully made up my mind. If you will have the goodness to listen to my reasons you will, I flatter myself, acknowledge the force of the arguments that have determined me."

Mrs. Fielding affectionately intreating her to speak without reserve, she thus proceeded:—"the peculiar disadvantages under which our sex is doomed to labour, early appeared to me so enormous, that it made me listen with avidity to the reveries of the new theorists, whose doctrines promised emancipation from the tyranny of prejudice; and seemed to offer the rights of equality to the hitherto degraded part of the human race. Independence I considered as essential to virtue. But what was the independence to which I had resort?—Alas! to throw off the gentle, the endearing restraints of parental authority for the yoke of a domineering passion, which bowed my soul in subjection to a man who has since proved the most barbarous and unworthy of the human race! In the height of my enthusiasm for the new doctrines I had embraced, I was intoxicated with the idea, that for me it was reserved to point out to my sex a new and nobler path to glory than the quiet duties of domestic life. To convince them, that equal to man in all the most noble qualities of the mind, we ought to scorn the meanness of confining our notions of virtue to one point; and that it was to our giving way to the prejudices of society in this particular, we owed the degradation and misery of our sex. You, Madam, will wonder at my strange delusion, when I confess that I considered the loss of my honour as a sacrifice to principle, and that in this idea I struggled to overcome the instinctive repugnance of that delicacy which Nature had implanted, and education cherished, in my breast. I was taught to glory in having asserted the prerogative of human nature in a free and independent choice; but when I expected the meed of fame, I was plunged into the depth of misery, and goaded by the stings of remorse. Alas! what idea can *words* convey of what I have suffered!— Robbed, betrayed, deserted, by the man on whom my foolish heart rested as lover, counsellor, and friend! The cruel certainty of his unworthiness would have been sufficient to have made me miserable for ever. But this, even this, was light to what I suffered, when in the den of demons, to which I was betrayed, I saw in an old newspaper, put as a wrapper about some writing-paper, the account of my father's death. Then, indeed, the excess of horror seized my soul. The wretches that surrounded me were to me no longer objects of hate or terror. On myself, on my own guilty head all my execrations were poured. The vilest of the vile, compared with me, I thought was innocent. In the frenzy of despair I endeavoured to escape existence; but no sooner had I swallowed the deadly potion, than the death I so ardently had wished for became dreadful to my imagination. Oh! the struggles of that moment! But they are not to be described. Blessed be GOD! that however dreadful, they were salutary. In the violence of the conflict the strength of contending passions seemed to have been exhausted. A sort of gloomy tranquillity succeeded, which was not interrupted, save by my renewed apprehensions of the wicked designs of the people of the vile house, where I knew myself to be a prisoner. Many were my plans for escape which accident had rendered abortive. At length, on the certainty that violence was intended me, and that the wretched woman had actually received the price of my person from a man of seeming gravity, who, while he kept what is called a fair character in society, and was himself the father of daughters, whose honour he would have protected with his life, would not have scrupled to gratify his own brutal passions at the expence of the temporal and eternal happiness of a poor young creature destitute of all protection. I collected all the vigour of my mind, and determined to run every risk, in order to effect my escape. Having taken my resolution, I affected a degree of composure, and even of cheerfulness, that my design might be the less suspected; and the moment that I found myself unobserved, in pursuance of my plan, I hastened up to the garret, got out of the window upon the leads, and as fast as my benumbed limbs would permit, slowly crept upon my hands and knees along the different houses, till I reached that at the end of the street. There I likewise found the garret-window open; with some difficulty I entered, and quickly shutting after me, retired into a corner, where leaning against the wall, I stood grasping for breath, and trembling in every limb.

"A little kitten had, without my perceiving it, crept in at the half-open door. A boy of about four years old came in pursuit of it; but seeing me, screamed and fled. New terrors then seized upon me, as I made no doubt he would alarm the family, and that I should be treated as a thief, perhaps consigned to the horrors of a prison; but as no prison was so dreadful in my eyes as that I had just quitted, I resolved to bear my destiny with patience. Part of my apprehensions were soon fulfilled. The mistress of the house, followed by her maid-servant and a lad of about fourteen, armed with a huge stick, came up to me, and almost in one voice demanded how I came there?

"I came hither for protection—for deliverance! O save me, dear Madam," said I, dropping on my knees; "save me from death, and worse than death!"

'Where did you come from?' said the mother of the little boy, who now ventured to approach me.

I told her. She at first seemed to doubt my veracity, but did not hesitate (before her doubts on this head were removed) to assure me of temporary protection.

'Whether what you say be true or no,' said she, 'you are young, and evidently unfortunate. I have children of my own, and who knows what may yet befal them! So, poor thing, I will not betray you. Here, however, these wretches may soon trace you; and how can a poor widow defend you? I would therefore advise you to put yourself under the protection of a magistrate, who will put you in a way of returning to your friends.'

"Alas!" said I, "I have no friends! Oh GOD! what will become of me!"

'Take courage, Miss,' said the servant-maid, taking my hand with an appearance of sympathy for which my heart shall never cease to be grateful, 'there is a refuge for you, a blessed refuge—*The Asylum of the Destitute*. There I myself was saved from misery and destruction. There you will be received, and treated with kindness and humanity; and if you appear to be a proper-behaved person, will have every encouragement to continue in a virtuous course."

"Where," cried I, "oh, where is this blessed retreat? Let me fly to it instantly. I will do any thing, I will submit to any thing—only to get permission to live among the good and virtuous. I care not how humble, how lowly—for I am truly humbled."

I would instantly have set out, but the good people, observing how ill I was, proposed my remaining there till the evening, and that in the mean time I should take some refreshment and repose; and much, indeed, did I stand in need of both. They supported me between them to a bed-chamber on the first-floor; and there, by their advice, I was about to lay me down, when a loud knocking at the door called away both mistress and maid, and threw me into fresh trepidation. I listened, and heard a man's voice. It was loud and terrible. A thief, he said, had escaped from justice, and must have contrived to hide herself in some house on that side of the street; he therefore advised them to secure their doors, as if they permitted her to get off, they would be considered as accessaries in her crimes. I could not hear what reply was made by the mistress of the house, and dreadful was the suspence I remained in till she returned to me. She came, but suspicion was not in her looks.

'Alas! poor thing,' said she, 'you must depart from hence immediately. I have sent Hannah for a coach, and in it she shall conduct you to the Asylum; for I believe, yes, I *do* believe you innocent.'

I had no power to reply. She wrapped me in a long cloak, and put her own bonnet and veil upon my head, to conceal me from the people who might be watching for me in the street. I happily got into the coach without observation, and supported by the kind-hearted Hannah, reached this blessed place in safety. Ah! how little did I then imagine who I was here to meet with! The agitation I had undergone, together with the want of food and sleep, affected my brain; I was sensible that it was affected. One image took possession of my mind—the image of my dying father. I conceived myself doomed to suffer as his murderer, and that all I had undergone, all I yet might have to undergo, was in expiation of this foul offence. Alas! the return of reason, though it enables me to methodize my thoughts, takes not from the bitterness of this reflection. But how have I wandered from the subject on which I designed to have explained myself! Forgive me, dear Madam, for I now fear I shall exhaust your patience."

'Not my patience, dear Miss Delmond, but your own strength, is in danger of being exhausted by the continuance of the conversation. If, however, you do not feel yourself too much fatigued, I shall be glad to hear the plan you intend to adopt, and the reasons you have for thinking it preferable to mine; which was intended to save your character from obloquy, and to restore to society one whose many virtues may still eminently adorn it.'

"For your good intentions, I thank you—from my heart I thank you," replied Julia; "but low as I am now sunk in my own estimation, sensible as I am of the faultiness of my conduct, and humbled under the consciousness, as my soul truly is, I must shrink still lower than I am, not to feel myself degraded by the practice of any species of imposture. Whether the unrelenting laws of society with regard to our sex are founded in injustice or otherwise, is not for me to determine. Happy they who submit without reluctance to their authority! But first to set them at defiance, and then under false pretences to shrink from the penalty, what is this but to add hypocrisy to presumption—to add an unjustifiable (because deliberate) crime to an error, which perhaps may receive some mitigation on the score of human frailty? Forgive me, Madam, for speaking in this manner on a subject you have evidently considered in a different light; but I know you are too generous to find fault with me for differing from you."

'Find fault with you, my dear!' said Mrs. Fielding; 'no, I honour you in my heart for your noble sentiments, so full of integrity and honour. I do not pretend to combat them, but in justification of myself shall only mention the motives that led to my proposal. On unsullied character, not only our reception in society, but our usefulness in life depends. The woman who is suspected of having made a false step, but who, by assiduously concealing it, shews some regard for reputation, will ever meet with more indulgence from the world than she, who by openly avowing it, seems to brave its censures. In the latter case she becomes a mark for public scorn to point the finger at; all the virtues she may possess are of no avail, or rather they are considered by the world, what certain dogmatists affirm of the virtues of the unregenerate, as so many *shining sins*. Her dishonour attaches not merely to herself alone, but extends to all with whom she is connected. Should her future conduct be ever so circumspect, nay should it be ever so exemplary over those of her own sex who are most inclined to applaud it, the fetters of public opinion will still exert a restraining influence, and very few will dare to own her. Men alone will presume to express for her any friendship; and thus thrown upon the protection of men, while her heart beats indignant at what she considers as injustice, who can answer for the consequences? From all these evils who would not wish to preserve a character so estimable? Have not your errors been already sufficiently expiated by your sufferings? Why then should you be lost to society at a period of life when you might enter it with every advantage? You are yet but in the very early morning of your life; by removing to another kingdom, you may in a manner recommence its course. Nor can the concealment of the past be properly termed imposition; that belongs to false pretences only, and I am convinced the conduct of your future life will vindicate the reality of your claim to respect and veneration.'

Julia's languid eyes were suffused with tears of gratitude. "How generously do you endeavour to reconcile me to myself," she exclaimed; "but it cannot be. Hope of future happiness can never reanimate my heart. On me the sun of joy is set for ever. The only ray of peace or consolation that can ever shine upon me, must be from the approbation of my own mind, reverberated and confirmed by the approbation of those to whom it is fully known. Mortifying to me would be the applause, oh! very mortifying the expressions of esteem I might receive from strangers;. who, if they knew the circumstances I must then labour to conceal, would spurn me from them with contempt. No, my dear Madam; my place in society I have forfeited; nor will I endeavour to regain it by clandestine means. I will not add to my trangression by relinquishing the duties I have still to perform. If I am the means of bringing a helpless being into the world under circumstances the most deplorable, I will not desert it. Oh, no! Cruelly, very cruelly has it already been deserted by one parent! and shall its mother, for the sake of preserving a false appearance to the world, act a part equally inhuman? Never! never! The infamy I have brought upon its innocent head I shall freely share; and devote my future life to making it what recompence is in my power, for the inauspicious circumstances under which it is for ever doomed to labour." As she thus spoke, her fine eyes regained a momentary lustre, heightened by the vivid blush that gleamed on her pale cheek wet with tears.

Mrs. Fielding gazing on her as she spoke, felt for her a degree of admiration mingled with pity and regret, that caused sensations too big for utterance. She folded her maternal arms round her, and pressed her to her heart. 'You are, indeed you are, an admirable creature!' she at length exclaimed. 'Your arguments make me ashamed of the comparative meanness of my own sentiments upon this subject; and approbation is too poor a word to express the sense I have of your magnanimity.'

"Alas!" replied Julia, "how little am I deserving of such praise! Were all my tears tears of penitence for past misconduct, and did my heart possess sufficient firmness to throw from its affections the man who has proved himself unworthy of its esteem, then indeed I might boast some little portion of magnanimity. But ah! how feeble are the sentiments of virtue, when they prove so ineffectual in subduing the strength of an unhappy passion!"

'Let not this consideration too much discourage you,' said Mrs. Fielding. The affections of love are much more warm and vivid than those of friendship; and yet even in friendship, where it has been misplaced, the heart is long, very long in receiving the conviction that is forced upon it by reason. Affection still lingers in the bosom, even after esteem has taken its everlasting flight; nor does it finally forsake it, till the mind has experienced the most exquisite degree of anguish in the contest. Still, where the love of virtue reigns, the love of its opposite will in the end be conquered. Take courage, then, my dear, and employ your mind, not so much in ruminating on the past, as in forming plans for your future conduct.'

The entrance of Harriet and Maria, who just then returned from an airing which Mrs. Fielding had prevailed on them to take, put an end to the conversation. A kind contest then took place between the two friends about which should remain with Julia, who was a length called upon to determine it. Affectionately pressing the hand of each, "Between two such cordials," said she, "it is difficult for me to choose; but here is my physician, and to his decision I shall leave it."

Henry had come with the secret hope that Harriet would return to Hanover-square with him and Mrs. Fielding. Since the arrival of Julia at the Asylum, he had enjoyed little of Harriet's company, and his heart was deeply sensible of the privation; but when he met the eyes of Julia, and read in them the wish for Harriet's stay; when he reflected on their greater intimacy, which must afford to Julia the pleasure of unreserved confidence, he checked the prompt wish of selfishness, and declared that Harriet should remain.

And here, lest the reader should not be inclined to give to the conduct of Henry all the merit it deserves, we beg the favour of him to pause for a moment, and give a candid answer to the few following questions.

Pray, sir, have you ever been in love? If not, you may go on to the next chapter.

"You have." Well then, be so obliging as to say how often you have sacrificed the slightest gratification of passion to the calls of friendship or benevolence? Pray, how often have you disobeyed the dictates of selfishness, from the consideration of conferring pleasure on any individual of your acquaintance? What have you sacrificed to the interests even of the object of your passion? One selfish desire?

"No. Passion was too powerful."

Justly, then, may you appreciate the nobleness of Henry Sydney's heart; which, filled with a passion as strong and pure as ever warmed a human breast, was yet sufficiently capacious to have room for the sentiments of friendship, and the feelings of benevolence.

CHAP. XIV.

" A wrench from all we *love*, from all *we are*;
" A sun extinguish'd! a just-opening grave!
" And oh! the last, last what? (can words express?
" Thought reach?) the last, last *silence* of a friend."[61]

IT is high time to return to Bridgetina, to whom, as the ostensible heroine of these memoirs, it is our duty to attend. The inauspicious career of her *quondam* friends, if it did not effect a sudden change in her opinions, considerably damped the ardor of her zeal. Neither the reasonings of Mr. Sydney or Mrs. Fielding were calculated for making a convert of one, who to a very limited understanding united an active imagination; but they were so unanswerable that they abated the confidence of self-conceit, and tempered her dislike to the doctrines of Christianity.

Though this were all that was expected by Mr. Sydney, it did not perfectly satisfy Mrs. Fielding. "It is very extraordinary," said she, in speaking to Mr. Sydney on this subject, "it is very extraordinary that Miss Botherim should be so obstinately blind, as not to perceive the shocking consequences of the erroneous opinions she has adopted. Does she not see to what they have already led? How can she refuse assent to demonstration so strong, so full as that you have just now been delivering? And to what is she thus wedded?—to a system that annihilates every future hope, and reduces us to a level with the beasts that perish! I can no way account for such obstinacy of unbelief."

'My dear Madam,' replied Mr. Sydney, 'you do not sufficiently attend to the nature of the human mind. Not to mention the tenaciousness of pride, which naturally revolts at the acknowledgment of conviction, we must, I fear, make greater allowances than you seem inclined to do, for the strength of early association. Among those who were eye-witnesses of the miracles of our Saviour, we are told that many doubted—of what? Not of the miracles, for these they do not appear to have attempted to deny. The unbelief of the Jewish sceptics were by *their early prejudices* directed to a different point; they acknowledged the miracle, but doubted whether it was of GOD, or proceeded from the power of some demon. In embuing the minds of our children with notions of religion, we too often represent to them not only the great and leading truths of revelation, but every minutia of our own peculiar tenets, as inseparable links of one great chain, of which no one can be broken without destroying the whole. The early association which we thus create, is frequently productive of the most unhappy consequences. By it a long range of outworks of unequal strength are exposed to the attack of the enemy, where, if one be found untenable, the whole must of course surrender. In con-

---

[61] Edward Young, *Night Thoughts* (1742-45) II, 655, 659-61.

versing with Miss Botherim, I have more than once had occasion to remark the truth of the above observation. But let us not expect too much at once; time, her ripened judgment, reading, and observation, may effect a change in her mind of greater consequence than a sudden conviction could possibly produce.

Mrs. Fielding acquiesced in this opinion, and leaving Bridgetina's conversion to Mr. Sydney, and the means by him prescribed, she entirely occupied herself in the concerns of the more amiable and more unfortunate Julia.

Doctor Orwell and his youngest daughter were on the eve of setting out for London to attend Harriet's nuptials, when they received the account of Julia's reappearance, which Doctor Orwell was begged to communicate to Mrs. Delmond. He did so, but found the poor lady in no situation for undertaking an immediate journey. Ever since her husband's death a slow fever had preyed upon her constitution, which gradually increasing, had at length brought her to the very brink of the grave. Till the elopement of Julia her mind had never experienced the dominion of a strong emotion; she was, therefore, unequal to its control. Incessantly dwelling on the ingratitude of her daughter, who had been the object of her pride as much as of her affections, her grief was embittered by resentment; which, from the taciturnity and reserve of her temper, being denied a vent, preyed inwardly, and consumed the vital flame. And here it is worthy of remark, that while Captain Delmond execrated the seducer, and his wife bitterly arraigned the conduct of the seduced, neither one or other ever once cast a retrospective glance upon what they themselves had done. The aunt of Mrs. Delmond had been little less hurt by her conduct, than she was by that of her daughter. But *her* resentment she had deemed unreasonable and absurd; so different is the allowance self-love permits us to make for the feelings of others, and for our own!

Till informed by Doctor Orwell, Mrs. Delmond had not the most distant idea of Julia's being still unmarried. The intelligence aggravated the feelings of resentment and despair. And after a silence, occasioned by the excess of agitation, she broke out into the bitterest reproaches, not only against Julia, but against all who should receive or countenance her. In vain did Doctor Orwell preach up to her the doctrine of christian charity and forgiveness. She told him, that if he gave such encouragement to wickedness, she thought his own children would do well to put his charity to the proof; and concluded by declaring, that were she even able to undertake the journey, nothing should induce her to go to see a wretch, whose infamous conduct had brought disgrace on all connected with her.

After having exhausted her strength by venting the feelings of resentment, she apparently sunk into her usual state of torpid apathy. But it was only in appearance, for a variety of contending emotions continued to struggle in her breast; where, though grief, anger, and resentment were first in place, they could not overcome the yearnings of the mother in her heart. The struggle was too much for her weak frame to support, and an increase of fever was the fatal consequence. Dr. Orwell was no sooner informed by Mr. Gubbles of her danger, than he dispatched a messenger for the nearest physician; but ere he could arrive Mrs. Delmond was no more.

Having given the necessary directions for the interment, the Doctor was urged by his daughter Marianne to set out immediately on their intended journey, as they would now have little enough time to reach London before the wedding.

"You are mistaken, my dear," said Dr. Orwell, "so much must the news of this event add to the misery of the wretched Julia, and so much will she now require the soothing support of friendship, that I know not Harriet's heart, if it have not the generosity to defer her own happiness, in order to alleviate the pressure of another's anguish. There is no fear, therefore, of our not being in time to the wedding; but to gratify you, we shall set out to-morrow."

They accordingly did set out, and arrived at Mrs. Fielding's the evening of the following day. There they found only servants to receive them, and from them they learned, that Mrs. Fielding and her guests had spent the greater part of the day at the Asylum, from whence they were not yet returned. Thither Dr. Orwell, after committing Marianne to the care of Mrs. Fielding's housekeeper, directly drove.

He was shewn into a small parlour, where the first object that struck his eye was old Quinten, leaning against the window, and with the hand that pressed upon his forehead covering his eyes, so that he did not perceive the Doctor's approach.

"Quinten!" cried Doctor Orwell, "is it you? How came you here? I did not know you had left W——."

'Ah! sir,' said Quinten, 'could I hear that my master's daughter was ill, and in distress, and not come to offer her my poor services? Susan no sooner told me of the news you had brought my mistress, which, by reason of her being in the next room, she could not avoid hearing, than I begged her leave to march, and set out that very Thursday evening; though she did not seem overpleased at my coming, I know she will thank me afterwards, when—'

"You do not then know that Mrs. Delmond is dead?" said Doctor Orwell interrupting him.

'My mistress dead?' exclaimed Quinten. 'Oh! that is heavy news indeed! But Miss Julia will never hear it! Oh! no. She will never know that her mother died without forgiving her; but GOD will be more merciful. He will receive the penitent to his bosom, and the dear child shall be an angel of light in heaven!'

"Is Miss Delmond then so very ill?" asked Doctor Orwell.

'Ill, indeed,' replied Quinten. 'But here is Miss Orwell, and she will tell you all.'

Quinten then retired, while Harriet, rushing into the room, threw her arms round her father's neck, and wept and sobbed aloud upon his bosom.

"Be calm, my love," said Dr. Orwell, "my darling child! How should I bow in gratitude to that Providence whose grace has been so liberally bestowed upon you; every action of your life endears you still further to my heart." Then fondly kissing her, he wiped away the tears that still continued to flow from her eyes, and again begged her to be composed. "I am afraid to ask for Julia," said he; "from your tears I fear it is all over."

'No,' replied Harriet, 'she yet lives, but that is all that can now be said. The night before last she was seized with spasms and other symptoms, which the Doctor immediately pronounced fatal. Since then she has suffered the extreme of pain; but suffered with a patience, a meekness, and resignation, that deserve a higher term than fortitude, for fortitude is sometimes the effort of despair. Her's is the effect of sincere penitence, and lively hope in the mercies of GOD through that Saviour to whom she has been brought, effectually, I trust, brought through sufferings. But you must see her. I can place you where you will be unperceived, for the sight of you would make her, perhaps, renew her enquiries concerning her mother, and she knows nothing of her death. It would be cruel to disturb her last moments by the intelligence.' So saying, she took her father's hand, and silently led him into Julia's room.

Accustomed as Doctor Orwell was to the sight of a death-bed, he never without awe could approach the solemn scene,

"Where darkness brooding o'er unfinish'd fate,
"With raven wing incumbent, waits the hour,
"Dread hour! that interdicts all future change."[62]

But never were his feelings more sensibly impressed than on the present occasion. The first object that presented itself was old Mr. Sydney, sitting in an arm-chair by the bedside, his hands clasped, and his eyes directed towards Heaven in mental prayer, while a few unbidden tears stole down his venerable cheeks. Mr. Churchill knelt by the bed, and pressed one of the cold hands of the dying Julia between both of his; while Maria, sitting behind her on the bed, supported in her arms her feeble frame. She was still addressing herself to Mr. Churchill, but in a voice too low and broken to be distinctly heard. To what she said Churchill was too much affected to permit him to make any other reply than by kissing her hand, and bathing it with his tears. After a short pause— "Heaven will, in this dear virtuous girl," said she, attempting to join Maria's hand to his, "amply reward you for your goodness. She too will act the part of a child to my poor mother—alas! a more deserving child than I have been towards her! Oh, that I could recall the past! But it cannot be. Penitence is all I now can offer—and that I hope GOD and she will accept of. Farewell, sir! may GOD reward you for your goodness to my mother! He only can."

---

[62] Edward Young, *Night Thoughts* (1742-45) III, 256-58.

Again Churchill kissed her hand with emphatic tenderness, and covering his face with his handkerchief, hastily withdrew to give vent to the feelings he could not control. Maria's eyes followed him to the door with looks of tender sympathy, which seemed eager to express how much his sensibility endeared him to her heart.

Julia observed her looks, and tenderly taking her hand, "You will be happy, dear Maria," said she, "and you deserve to be so. Harriet too, my dear Harriet, she will be happy with her worthy Sydney; doubly happy even here, for having kept constantly in view the happiness of hereafter. Where is Miss Botherim? I think I have now strength to speak to her, and it may not be so long. I should like now to see her."

Harriet instantly went out, and returned leading in Bridgetina, who seemed to enter with some reluctance. She appeared pale and frightened, and seemed to dread the solemnity of a dying scene—a scene she had never yet witnessed. "You must come near her," said Harriet, as she drew Bridgetina on; "it would distress her too much to speak to you at this distance."

Julia attempted to hold out her feeble hand as she approached her, which Bridgetina took in her's without speaking.

"You tremble, my dear!" said Julia. "Does it then so greatly shock you to see me thus? Ah, Bridgetina! could I indeed impress you with a sense of what my mind now feels, I should not die in vain. You see me now on the threshold of eternity—that eternity, of which we have made a jest, but which we must acknowledge was never by any argument to a certainty disproved; improbable we were taught to believe it, but *impossible* by mere man it could never be pronounced. I am now convinced, oh! thoroughly convinced, of its awful truth. I believe that I shall, ere the lapse of many hours, appear before the throne of GOD! that GOD whose will I have despised, whose providence I have arraigned, nay, whose very being I have dared to deny! Blessed be his mercy, that did not leave me to perish in my iniquity!"

After a pause, occasioned by want of breath, she thus proceeded. "You believe Jesus Christ to have been a moralist and philosopher. Examine, I beseech you, the morality he preached, and you will acknowledge its teacher could not lay the foundation of such a system in imposture. Well did he say of future teachers, *By their fruits ye shall know them.*" What, my Bridgetina, are the fruits of the doctrines we have so unhappily been led to embrace? *In me you behold them!* [63] In vain will you exclaim, in the jargon to which we have been accustomed, against the *prejudices of society*, as if to them were owing the load of misery that sinks me to a premature grave. Ah! no. Those prejudices, against which we have been accustomed so bitterly to rail, I now behold as a salutary fence, which, if I had never dared to overleap, would have secured my peace. Were those barriers bro-

---

[63] *Matthew* 7: 16-20.

ken down, and every woman encouraged by the suffrage of universal applause to act as I have acted, fatal, my dear Bridgetina, very fatal to society, would be the consequence! In my friends here, these dear friends whom Heaven has in mercy sent as ministering angels to smooth the path of death, see the fruits of a firm adherence to the doctrines we have despised! If, like them, I had been taught to devote the actions of every day to my GOD; and instead of encouraging a gloomy and querulous discontent against the present order of things, had employed myself in a vigilant performance of the duties of my situation, and a scrupulous government of my own heart and inclinations, how very different would my situation now have been! Think of these things, Bridgetina; and if ever you should meet with—but I will not disturb the serenity of my soul by mentioning his name.—Yet why? I carry not with me any resentments to the grave. Tell Vallaton, then, that as a christian I forgive him, and pray GOD to turn his heart. If mine had been fortified by principle, he never could have seduced it by his sophistry. No. It was not he, it was my own pride, my own vanity, my own presumption, that were the real seducers that undid me. My strength fails. Farewell, my poor Biddy! Nay, do not weep so much. I have now hopes of happiness more sweet, more precious, than aught the world can bestow! Go home to your mother, my Biddy; and in the sober duties of life forget the idle vagaries which our distempered brains dignified with the name of philosophy."

Bridgetina weeping withdrew.

Julia, exhausted by speaking, reclined her head on Maria's bosom, and remained for some minutes silent. She then with a quick motion raised her head, and looked around the room. "Who is now here?" said she. "Methinks I do not see distinctly. This I know is Harriet's hand. Dear Harriet, oh, when you draw near the close of your life, may the remembrance of the comfort you have bestowed on me be a fund of joy and consolation to your heart! My sweet instructor, my monitress, my guide to the path of salvation, how shall I thank you? Your Sydney too I would thank. How much have I been indebted to his friendly attention! Let me join your hands, that with my dying lips I may bless you both."

While Henry and Harriet knelt in silent sorrow by the side of the bed, endeavouring as much as possible to suppress their feelings, in order to catch every world that fell from Julia, a loud groan was heard from the opposite side of the room. Julia instantly caught the sound. "It is honest Quinten," said she, "let him come near me. Do not, my good Quinten, do not grieve for me thus. GOD has for me ordered all things graciously—I rejoice in his decrees. Death has now for me no terrors."

'O that I should have lived to see this day!' sobbed the old soldier. 'Would to GOD I could die for thee, my dear young lady! But surely there is yet hope. So young as you are—so very young!'

"Death is no respector of persons, my good Quinten! you may yet see many younger than me laid in their graves. Return to my poor mother, and continue to be attentive to her. She has been ill; do not wound her by the excess of your sorrow. I know my death will grieve her; but tell her, I beg she would consider it as a blessing."

'This is too much!' cried Quinten. 'I cannot, cannot stand it.' Then striking his hand upon his furrowed brow, he turned away to conceal the anguish of his heart. On a slight motion made by Mrs. Fielding he lifted up his eyes, and beheld the lifeless hand of Julia sunk upon Maria's bosom.

A silence, more expressive than the loudest lamentations of clamorous sorrow, closed the solemn scene.

Maria continued still to clasp in her arms the inanimate form of her lovely friend, lovely even in death; and learning over her, bedewed the pale face with her fast-falling tears. Henry and Harriet still knelt by the bedside, and still continued to press the hand whose last office had been uniting theirs. While the old domestic, the venerable Quinten, wringing his hands in silent anguish gazed upon the corpse, and seemed insensible of the tears which coursed each other down his hard and weather-beaten face. Mrs. Fielding, who sat by the bedside assisting and supporting Maria, made an effort to speak, but could not. Doctor Orwell was the first who broke the emphatick silence. "It is enough, my children," said he, "all is now over. The solemn scene is now closed—happily closed, I trust in GOD, for the dead; and usefully for us who are of the living, if we have grace *to lay it to heart.*

CONCLUSION.

"Domestic Happiness, thou only bliss
"Of paradise that has survived the fall!
"Though few now taste thee unimpaired and pure;
"Or tasting, long enjoy thee—too infirm,
"Or too incautious, to preserve thy sweets
"Unmixt with drops of bitter, which neglect,
"Or temper, sheds into thy crystal cup.
"*Thou art the nurse of virtue.*"

COWPER.[64]

THE serious part of our readers may, perhaps, be of opinion, that with the last chapter our history ought properly to have concluded; as whatever we now can add must tend to destroy the impression it was calculated to produce. It may be so. But how could we have the heart to disappoint the Misses, by closing our narrative without a wedding? A novel without a wedding is like a tragedy without murder, which no British audience could ever be brought to relish. A wedding, a double wedding, we shall with pleasure and alacrity announce; but from us our fair readers must not expect too much. Willing as we are to oblige them, we can-

---

[64] William Cowper, *The Task* (1785) Bk III, "The Garden", 41-48; Hamilton's italics.

not possibly contrive to marry every individual of our dramatis personae in the last scene.

"And pray, why not?" exclaims a pretty critic. "All the young ones at least, you must certainly provide for; is it not always done?"

'Yes,' cries another, 'to be sure it is; and nothing should have tempted me to wade through the book, but to see who Bridgetina was to have at the last. Had I thought she was to have remained unmarried after all, I give you my word I should never have read three pages.'

"Nor I," repeats a third; "and during the half of the last volume, I have been doing nothing but thinking whether Mr. Vallaton or Mr. Myope was to be the happy man. Vallaton is a sad wretch, to be sure; but then he might have been made to *reform all at once*; nothing is *so* common; and who, except this stupid author, but would have made him out to be the son of some great Lord?"

'If Bridgetina can't have him' cries the other, 'she surely may have Myope at least. His poverty is no obstacle; for what so easy, as to make him have some rich uncle come home from the East-Indies, or to give him a prize in the lottery; or—oh, there are a thousand ways of giving him a fortune in a moment; and if Bridgetina be not married either to him or Vallaton, I shall be out of all patience.'

"And I," rejoins another fair judge, "shall condemn the book without mercy, if Mrs. Fielding be not married to her old lover Mr. Sydney. It must be so, to be sure. After being in love with each other for thirty years, it would be *so* romantic! and they must of course be *so* happy! As for Henry and Harriet, there is nothing interesting in their story. Such matches take place every day. Had they married to live in a cottage upon love, or had they been raised to all the splendour of the high ton, it might have been charming either way. But to give them competence in middle life is quite a bore, and shews the author to be a mere quiz. Churchill and Maria, too, are tame creatures. What woman of spirit would put up with being a man's *second love?*[65] When I marry—"

Stay, dear young lady. Make no rash promises; and till experience have convinced you that romantic passion is the only true foundation for matrimonial felicity, do not condemn the conduct of Maria Sydney. To the observations of your sister critics we shall reply in order, and obviate (as much as it is in our power to obviate) the force of their objections.

First, then, with regard to the disposal of our heroine. We are very sorry to confess that she is still unmarried. But this is far from being our fault; and if you will have the goodness to recollect that she is neither *rich* nor *handsome*, it will cease to appear so very extraordinary. Mr. Vallaton might, it is true, have been reformed for her, as you propose; he might,

---

[65] Jane Austen jokes about "second attachments" in *Sense and Sensibility* (1811). Colonel Brandon despairs to Elinor of making her sister Marianne ever consider being someone's second attachment (Penguin, 1969: 87, 367).

likewise, for aught we know, have been recognized as the offspring of some noble Lord, had it not unfortunately happened, that before either of these events could take place, a period was put to his existence by the perfidious contrivance of the very woman for whose sake he had robbed and abandoned the unfortunate Julia. This wretched woman, whose principles Vallaton had made it his boast to form, had the art so far to insinuate herself into his affections, as to reign absolute mistress of his heart. His passion for Julia gave but a short-lived interruption to her authority. Though the beauty of Julia excited his admiration, his heart was too depraved to feel the full force of her charms. The delicacy of her pure and uncorrupted mind laid him under a restraint so disagreeable, that had not the power over her fortune been attached to the possession of her person, he would soon have desisted from the pursuit. Nor when success had crowned his arts, did the tender affection of Julia touch his soul. The mind and manners of the profligate Emmeline were so much more congenial to his own, that he found her conversation a relief from the insipid innocence of Julia's; and though in personal attractions there could be no comparison made between them, he preferred to youth, modesty, and beauty, the sophisticated blandishments of a time-worn wanton. So perverse is the taste of sensual depravity! which, in the well-known language of our immortal bard,

"Though to a radiant angel link'd,
"Will prey on garbage."[66]

With a degree of art beyond the conception even of the artful Vallaton, did this infamous woman employ the influence she had obtained to his destruction. At her instigation he took Julia to the house from which she so fortunately escaped to Mrs. Fielding's Asylum; and as the wickedness of even the worst of men seldom equals the wickedness of woman, it was by her contrivance that Julia was there robbed of the sum he had intended to leave her for the supply of her immediate exigencies. The plan of their elopement to France was likewise her's, and the execution of it she contrived to accellerate by the introduction of a pretended friend from that kingdom, who appeared as a private agent for the sale of the confiscated estates of the exnobles; and who fired the avarice of Vallaton by the description of a seigniory which he offered him upon terms so advantageous that it would have been folly to let slip the opportunity of so highly advancing his fortune.

On arriving at Paris, where the purchase was to be compleated, some obstacles occurred of which the London agent had not been sufficiently aware; hopes were however given that these might be overcome, and the negociation was still going forward, when Vallaton was arrested as a spy

---

[66] Shakespeare, *Hamlet*, I.v.53.

and agent of the royalists. It was not till after his trial and condemnation that he discovered the name of his accuser, or the nature of the evidence on which he had been condemned. Sharper than the instrument of death was the anguish that pierced him, when made sensible that he had been betrayed by the wretched partner of his guilt. On his way to the scaffold he gave vent to his rage by curses and imprecations, which he continued to pour forth till the last minute drew on. He then paused, and by the expression of his countenance seemed to cast a retrospective glance on the events of his past life. A convulsive groan of horror and despair then burst from his agitated bosom; he started from the grasp of the executioner, but after a short and ineffectual struggle, was forced to submit to the fatal blow.

To offer any comment upon the circumstances of this catastrophe would be impertinent. As we do not presume to imagine, far less to take it for granted, that our readers are less capable of reflection than we are ourselves, we shall not trouble them with obvious deductions from the circumstances we relate; but content ourselves with having fully explained the reasons that rendered it impossible for us to gratify our fair readers by making up a match between Mr. Vallaton and our heroine Bridgetina.

Why Mr. Myope did not marry her is, perhaps, not quite so easily solved. He might, indeed, as has very properly been observed, have made an excellent husband for her; but it unfortunately so happened, that having *no* rich uncle coming home from abroad, and having got *no* prize in the lottery, and having moreover become acquainted with a rich widow, (a disciple of Swedenburg's,[67] by whom he was made a convert to the New Jerusalem faith) he sealed his conversion by uniting himself to his instructress; and is now employed in writing a quarto volume to prove the possibility of an intercourse with the world of spirits. He has already had some admirable visions; but Bridgetina, though much inclined to adopt his new opinions, has not yet been so highly favoured. She continues to live with her mother, and notwithstanding the dissimilarity of their pursuits, begins to find that the consciousness of contributing to the happiness of a parent is a *pleasurable sensation*.

As for Mrs. Fielding, we shall in her own words explain to you her reasons for declining an union with Mr. Sydney, when proposed to her by some friends who knew the length and sincerity of their mutual attachment.

"It is observed by Solomon," said Mrs. Fielding, 'that *there is a time for all*

---

[67] Swedenborgians, members of the Church of the New Jerusalem, founded on the teachings of Emanuel Swedenborg (1688-1772), Swedish scientist, mystic and theologian. Swedenborgian chruches follow an almost Anglican liturgy, baptize, worship the glorified Christ as the embodiement of the Trinity, observe the Lord's Supper and believe in redemption by works as well as faith. In 1787 the New Church was established in London by five Wesleyan preachers.

things;' among the rest '*a time to marry.*' This *time* is surely not in the autumn of life, when the habits are formed, and the mind has lost that ductility which renders it capable of yielding to, and even of coalescing with, the humours of its partner. Without solid and mutual esteem, no marriage can be happy. The love that has it not for its basis, is, as Solomon observes of the laughter of fools, '*like the crackling of thorns;*'[68] a blaze that is soon extinguished. But cold esteem is not sufficient. Love too must lend its aid; and what can be more ridiculous than a Cupid in wrinkles! No, no, my friends; I shall not so expose myself. I still feel for Mr. Sydney the most lively affection, but it is not the affection that would now lead me to become his wife. From the day I heard of his marriage, I have devoted myself to a single life. I have endeavoured to create to myself objects of interest that might occupy my attention, and engage my affections. These I have found in the large family of the unfortunate. My plan has been successful in bringing peace to my bosom; and peace is the happiness of age—it is all the happiness of which on this side the grave I shall be solicitous."

Such was the decision of Mrs. Fielding, which no intreaty could prevail on her to alter. To our fair readers we shall leave it to pronounce upon its propriety.

In the affectionate and endearing attention of her children (for so she calls Henry Sydney and his wife) she receives as great satisfaction as ever parent experienced. She is a daily witness of their happiness, and perhaps, in the consciousness of having been instrumental in promoting it, experiences a happiness that is little inferior.

Mr. and Mrs. Churchill, (who reside great part of the year in the country) though they could not prevail upon Mr. Sydney to relinquish his house at W——, or give up the paternal care of his little flock, enjoy a great deal of his company, and have the pleasure, by a thousand tender attentions, of increasing his comfort, and augmenting his felicity. In their journies to town, where Mr. Churchill is obliged to spend a part of every winter, they have hitherto prevailed on Mr. Sydney to accompany them; and that he may have an additional inducement for continuing to do so, Mr. Churchill has fitted up a small museum of natural history, which it is the old gentleman's delightful business to fill with the choicest specimens. The museum has, however, of late occupied a less share of his attention than formerly. Since the little Maria Churchill has been able to lisp the name of *grand-papa*, and Harry Sydney to climb upon his knee, the beetles and butterflies have been frequently neglected; nor is it a slight gratification to the smiling parents to perceive how much the endearing caresses of his little favourites gain upon his heart.

"Oh speak the joy, ye whom the sudden tear
"Surprises often, while ye look around,
"And nothing strikes your eye but sights of bliss,

---

[68] *Ecclesiastes* 3: 1.

"All various nature pressing on the heart;
"An elegant sufficiency, content,
"Retirement, rural quiet, friendship, books,
"Ease, and alternate labour, useful life,
"Progressive virtue, and approving Heav'n!
"These are the matchless joys of virtuous love,
"And thus their moments fly. The seasons, thus
"As ceaseless round a jarring world they roll,
"Still find them happy—"[69]

Happy even in *"this corrupt wilderness of human society,"*[70] where any degree of happiness is, in the dark and gloomy dogmas of modern philosophy, represented as impossible. Impossible, however, it never will be found by those who seek for it in the right path of regulated desires, social affections, active benevolence, humility, sincerity, and a lively dependance on the Divine favour and protection.

"What cause for triumph, where such ills abound?
"What for dejection, where presides a Pow'r
"Who call'd us into being—*to be blest!*"[71]

END OF THE THIRD VOLUME

---

[69] James Thomson, *Seasons* (1726-30) "Spring", 1161.
[70] Mary Hays, *Memoirs of Emma Courtney*, 116. See Appendix A.
[71] Edward Young, *Night Thoughts* (1742-45) viii, 760-62.

Appendix A: Contemporary Works

1. William Godwin

Godwin's *Enquiry Concerning Political Justice* and *The Enquirer* are quoted, paraphrased and put into practice by many of the characters in *Memoirs of Modern Philosophers*. Although Hamilton professes to have some regard for these works, she has no hesitation in lambasting the more philosophical and impractical conclusions that would result from an application of the proposed theories. The following excerpts are taken from the most cited and often mocked sections of Godwin's works.

A. *Enquiry Concerning Political Justice and its Influence on Modern Morals and Happiness* (1793) (Ed. Isaac Kramnick, Harmondsworth: Penguin, 1985)

i. Bk II ch. ii "Of Justice"
In a loose and general view I and my neighbour are both of us men; and of consequence entitled to equal attention. But, in reality, it is probable that one of us is a being of more worth and importance than the other. A man is of more worth than a beast; because, being possessed of higher faculties, he is capable of a more refined and genuine happiness. In the same manner the illustrious archbishop of Cambray[1] was of more worth than his valet, and there are few of us that would hesitate to pronounce, if his palace were in flames, and the life of only one of them could be preserved, which of the two ought to be preferred.

But there is another ground of preference, beside the private consideration of one of them being further removed from the state of a mere animal. We are not connected with one or two percipient beings, but with a society, a nation, and in some sense the whole family of mankind. Of consequence that life ought to be preferred which will be most conducive to the general good. In saving the life of Fénelon, suppose at the moment he conceived the project of his immortal Telemachus, I should have been promoting the benefit of thousands who have been cured by the perusal of that work of some error, vice and consequent unhappiness. Nay, my benefit would extend further than this; for every individual, thus cured, has become a better member of society, and has contributed in his turn to the happiness, information and improvement of others.

Suppose I had been myself the valet; I ought to have chosen to die, rather than Fénelon should have died. The life of Fénelon was really preferable to that of the valet. But understanding is the faculty that per-

---

[1] Archbishop of Cambray, François de Salignac de la Motte (1651-1715), also known as Fénelon, was the author of *Telemachus* (1699), a bitter satire of Louis XIV's rule.

ceives the truth of this and similar propositions; and justice is the principle that regulates my conduct accordingly. It would have been just in the valet to have preferred the archbishop to himself. To have done otherwise would have been a breach of justice.

Suppose the valet had been my brother, my father or my benefactor. This would not alter the truth of the proposition. The life of Fénelon would still be more valuable than that of the valet; and justice, pure, unadulterated justice, would still have preferred that which was most valuable. Justice would have taught me to save the life of Fénelon at the expense of the other. What magic is there in the pronoun "my", that should justify us in overturning the decisions of impartial truth? My brother or my father may be a fool or a profligate, malicious, lying or dishonest. If they be, of what consequence is it that they are mine?

"But to my father I am indebted for existence; he supported me in the helplessness of infancy." When he first subjected himself to the necessity of these cares, he was probably influenced by no particular motives of benevolence to his future offspring. Every voluntary benefit however entitles the bestower to kindness and retribution. Why? Because a voluntary benefit is an evidence of benevolent intention, that is, in a certain degree, of virtue. It is the disposition of the mind, not the external action separately taken, that entitles to respect. But the merit of this disposition is equal, whether the benefit were conferred upon me or upon another. I and another man cannot both be right in preferring our respective benefactors, for my benefactor cannot be at the same time both better and worse than his neighbour. My benefactor ought to be esteemed, not because he bestowed a benefit upon me, but because he bestowed it upon a human being worthy of the distinction conferred.

Thus every view of the subject brings us back to the consideration of my neighbour's moral worth, and his importance to the general weal, as the only standard to determine the treatment to which he is entitled. Gratitude therefore, if by gratitude we understand a sentiment of preference which I entertain towards another, upon the ground of my having been the subject of his benefits, is no part either of justice or virtue (169-71).

ii. Bk IV ch. viii: "Inferences from the Doctrine of Necessity"
In the life of every human being there is a chain of events, generated in the lapse of ages which preceded his birth, and going on in regular procession through the whole period of his existence, in consequence of which it is impossible for him to act in any instance otherwise than he has acted.

The contrary of this having been the conception of the mass of mankind in all ages, and the ideas of contingency and accident having perpetually obtruded themselves, the established language of morality has been universally tinctured with this error.... Man is in no case, strictly speaking, the beginner of any event or series of events that takes place in the universe, but only the vehicle through which certain antecedents operate, which antecedents, if he were supposed not to exist, would cease to have that operation.

...

According to this doctrine [of necessity] it will be absurd for a man to say, "I will exert myself", "I will take care to remember," or even "I will do this." All these expressions imply as if man were, or could be, something else than what motives make him. Man is in reality a passive, and not an active being. In another sense, however, he is sufficiently capable of exertion. The operations of his mind may be laborious, like those of the wheel of a heavy machine in ascending a hill, may even tend to wear out the substance of the shell in which it acts, without in the smallest degree impeaching its passive character. If we were constantly aware of this, our minds would not glow less ardently with the love of truth, justice, happiness and mankind. We should have a firmness and simplicity in our conduct, not wasting itself in fruitless struggles and regrets, not hurried along with infantine impatience, but seeing actions with their consequences, and calmly and unreservedly given up to the influence of those comprehensive views which this doctrine inspires.

...

The less I am interrupted by questions of liberty and caprice, of attention and indolence, the more uniform will be my constancy. Nothing could be more unreasonable than that the sentiment of necessity should produce in me a spirit of neutrality and indifference (351-56).

iii. Bk VIII Appendix: "Of Co-operation, Cohabitation and Marriage"
From these principles it appears that everything that is usually understood by the term co-operation is, in some degree, an evil. A man in solitude is obliged to sacrifice or postpone the execution of his best thoughts, in compliance with his necessities, or his frailties. How many admirable designs have perished in the conception, by means of this circumstance? It is still worse when a man is obliged to consult the convenience of others. If I be expected to eat or to work in conjunction with my neighbour, it must either be at a time most convenient to me, or to him, or to neither of us. We cannot be reduced to a clockwork uniformity.

...

Another article which belongs to the subject of cooperation is cohabitation. The evils attendant on this practice are obvious. In order to the human understanding's being successfully cultivated, it is necessary that the intellectual operations of men should be independent of each other. We should avoid such practices as are calculated to melt our opinions into a common mould. Cohabitation is also hostile to that fortitude which should accustom a man, in his actions, as well as in his opinions, to judge for himself, and feel competent to the discharge of his own duties. Add to this, that it is absurd to expect the inclinations and wishes of two human beings to coincide, through any long period of time. To oblige them to act and to live together is to subject them to some inevitable portion of thwarting, bickering and unhappiness. This cannot be otherwise, so long as men shall continue to vary in their habits, their preferences and their views. No man is always cheerful and kind; and it is better that his fits of irritation should subside of themselves, since the mischief in that case is more limited, and since the jarring of opposite tempers, and the suggestions of a wounded pride, tend inexpressibly to increase the irritation. When I seek to correct the defects of a stranger, it is with urbanity and good humour. I have no idea of convincing him through the medium of surliness and invective. But something of this kind inevitably obtains where the intercourse is too unremitted.

The subject of cohabitation is particularly interesting as it includes in it the subject of marriage. It will therefore be proper to pursue the enquiry in greater detail. The evil of marriage, as it is practiced in European countries, extends further than we have yet described. The method is for a thoughtless and romantic youth of each sex to come together, to see each other, for a few times and under circumstances full of delusion, and then to vow eternal attachment. What is the consequence of this? In almost every instance they find themselves deceived. They are reduced to make the best of an irretrievable mistake. They are led to conceive it their wisest policy to shut their eyes upon realities, happy, if, by any perversion of intellect, they can persuade themselves that they were right in their first crude opinion of each other. Thus the institution of marriage is made a system of fraud; and men who carefully mislead their judgments in the daily affair of their life must be expected to have a crippled judgment in every other concern.

Add to this that marriage, as now understood, is a monopoly, and the worst of monopolies. So long as two human beings are forbidden, by positive institution, to follow the dictates of their own mind, prejudice will be alive and vigorous. So long as I seek, by despotic and artificial means, to maintain my possession of a woman, I am guilty of the most odious selfishness. Over this imaginary prize, men watch with perpetual jealousy; and one man finds his desire, and his capacity to circumvent, as much excited as the other is excited to traverse his projects, and frustrate his hopes. As long as this state of society continues, philanthropy will be crossed and checked in a thousand ways, and the still augmenting stream of abuse will continue to flow.

The abolition of the present system of marriage appears to involve no evils. We are apt to represent that abolition to ourselves as the harbinger of brutal lust and depravity. But it really happens, in this, as in other cases, that the positive laws which are made to restrain our vices irritate and multiply them. Not to say that the same sentiments of justice and happiness which, in a state of equality, would destroy our relish for expensive gratifications might be expected to decrease our inordinate appetites of every kind, and to lead us universally to prefer the pleasures of intellect to the pleasures of sense (758-63).

B. *The Enquirer: Reflections on Education, Manners, and Literature in a Series of Essays* (1797) (Reprints of Economics Classics. New York: Augustus Kelley, 1965)

i. Part I. Essay V: "Of an Early Taste for Reading"
The chief point of difference between the man of talent and the man without, consists in the different ways in which their minds are employed during the same interval. They are obliged, let us suppose, to walk from Temple Bar to Hyde-Park-Corner. The dull man goes straight forward: he has so many furlongs to traverse. He observes if he meets any of his acquaintance; he enquires respecting their health and their family. He glances perhaps the shops as he passes; he admires the fashion of a buckle, and the metal of a tea-urn. If he experience any flights of fancy, they are of a short extent; of the same nature as the flights of a forest-bird, clipped of his wings, and condemned to spend the rest of his life in a farm-yard. On the other hand the man of talent gives full scope to his imagination. He laughs and cries. Unindebted to the suggestions of surrounding objects, his whole soul is employed. He enters into nice calculations; he digests sagacious reasonings. In imagination he declaims or describes, impressed with the deepest sympathy, or elevated to the loftiest rapture. He makes a thousand new and admirable combinations. He passes through a thousand imaginary scenes, tries his courage, tasks his ingenuity, and becomes gradually prepared to meet almost any of the many-coloured events of human life. He consults by the aid of memory the books he has read, and projects others for the future instruction and delight of mankind. If he observe the passengers, he reads their countenances, conjectures their past histories, and forms a superficial notion of their wisdom or folly, their virtue or vice, their satisfaction or misery. If he observe the scenes that occur, it is with the eye of a connoisseur or an artist. Every object is capable of suggesting to him a volume of reflections. The time of these two persons in one respect resembles; it has brought them both to Hyde-Park-Corner. In almost every other respect it is dissimilar (31-32).

ii. Part II. Essay V: "Of Trades and Professions"
To what calling, or profession shall the future life of my child be devoted?—Alas! I survey them all; cause each successively to pass in review before me: but my mind can rest upon none: there is not one that a virtuous mind can regard with complacency, or select with any genuine eagerness of choice! What sort of a scene then is that in the midst of which we live; where all is blank, repulsive, odious; where every business and employmeny is found contagious and fatal to all the best characteristics of man, and proves the fruitful parent of a thousand hateful vices?

[Those in Trade]
Trade in some form or other is the destination of the majority of those, to whom industry is either in part or in whole made the source of pecuniary income. Let us analyse the principles of trade....

Avarice is not so thoroughly displayed in the preservation, as in the accumulation, of wealth. The chief method by which wealth can be begun to be accumulated by him who is destitute of it, is trade, the transactions of a barter and sale.

The trader or merchant is a man the grand effort of whose life is directed to the pursuit of gain. This is true to a certain degree of the lawyer, the soldier and the divine, of every man who proposes by some species of industry to acquire for himself a pecuniary income. But there is a great difference in this respect. Other men, though, it may be, their first object in choosing their calling was the acquisition of income, yet have their attention frequently diverted from this object, by the progress of reputation, or the improvements of which they have a prospect in the art they pursue. The trader begins, proceeds and concludes with this one object constantly in view, the desire of gain.... His whole mind is buried in the sordid care of adding another guinea to his income.... There is one thing that stands out grossly to the eye, and respecting which there can be no dispute: I mean, the servile and contemptible arts which we so frequently see played off by the tradesman. He is so much in the habit of exhibiting a bended body, that he scarcely knows how to stand upright. Every word he utters is graced with a simper or a smile. He exhibits all the arts of a male coquette; not that he wishes his fair visitor to fall in love with his person, but that he may induce her to take off his goods.

...

Yet this being, this supple, fawning, cringing creature, this systematic, cold-hearted liar, this being, every moment of whose existence is centred in the sordid consideration of petty gains, has the audacity to call himself a man. One half of all the human beings we meet, belong, in a higher or lower degree, to the class here delineated. In how perverted a state of society have we been destined to exist.

[The Physician]

Pain, sickness and anguish are his harvest. He rejoices to hear that they have fallen upon any of his acquaintance. He looks blank and disconsolate, when all men are at their ease. The fantastic valetudinarian is particularly his prey. He listens to his frivolous tale of symptoms with inexplicable gravity. He pretends to be most wise, when he is most ignorant. No matter whether he understand any thing of the disease; there is one thing in which his visit must inevitably terminate, a prescription. How many arts have been invented to extract ore from the credulity of mankind? The regular and the quack have each their several schemes of imposition, and they differ in nothing so much as in the name.

[The Divine]

It is the singularity of [a clergyman's] office, that its duties principally consist in the inculcating certain opinions. These duties cannot properly be discharged, without an education, and, in some degree, a life, of study.

It is surely a strange and anomalous species of existence, where a man's days are to be spent in study, with this condition annexed, that he must abstain from enquiry. Yet abstain he must, for he has entered into a previous engagement, express or implied, what his opinions shall be through the course of his life. This is incompatible with any thing that deserves the name of enquiry. He that really enquires, can by no means forsee in what conclusions his enquiry shall terminate.

One of two consequences is especially to be apprehended by a man under these circumstances.

He will perhaps arrive at sceptical or incredulous conclusions, in spite of all the bias impressed upon him at once by pecuniary considerations, and by the fear of losing the friendship and admiration of those, to whom his habits perhaps had chiefly attached him, and who were the principal solace of his existence. In that case he must determine for the rest of his life, either to play a solemn farce of hypocrisy, or, unless his talents be considerable, to maintain his integrity at the expence of an obscure and solitary existence.

...

A second disadvantage incident to the clerical profession is the constant appearance of sanctity, which a clergyman, ambitious of professional character, is obliged to maintain. His sanctity does not rise immediately from spiritual motives and the sentiments of the heart; it is a certain exterior which he finds himself compelled to preserve. His devotion is not the result of devout feelings; he is obliged equally to affect them, when he experiences them least. Hence there is always something formal and uncouth in the manners of a reputable clergyman. It cannot be otherwise. His continual attention to a pious exterior, necessarily gives a constrained and artificial seeming to his carriage.... Thus the circumstances of every day tend to confirm in him a dogmatical, imperious, illiberal and intolerant character. Such are the leading features of the character which, in most instances, we must expect to find in a reputable clergyman. He will be timid in enquiry, prejudiced in opinion, cold, formal, the slave of what other men may think of him, rude, dictatorial, impatient of contradiction, harsh in his censures, and illiberal in his judgments. Every man may remark in him study rendered abortive, artificial manners, infantine prejudices, and a sort of arrogant infallibility (213-33).

2. Mary Hays, *Memoirs of Emma Courtney* (1796)

Hays's novel *Memoirs of Emma Courtney* is central to Hamilton's work since Bridgetina not only quotes verbatim from it but also models her actions upon those of the heroine Emma. Emma's actions in turn were largely autobiographical since Hays incorporated much personal material and many experiences into her fictional work. The following excerpts typify Emma's character and point to the behaviour that Hamilton so mercilessly parodies in *Memoirs of Modern Philosophers*.

i. Rouse the nobler energies of your mind; be not the slave of your passions, neither dream of eradicating them. Sensation generates interest, interest passions, passion forces attention, attention supplies the powers, and affords the means of attaining its end: in proportion to the degree of interest, will be that of attention and power. Thus are talents produced. Every man is born with sensation, with the aptitude of receiving impressions; the force of those impressions depends on a thousand circumstances, over which he has little power; these circumstances form the mind, and determine the future character. We are all the creatures of education; but in that education, what we call chance, or accident, has so great a share, that the wisest preceptor, after all his cares, has reason to tremble: one strong affection, one ardent incitement, will turn in an instant, the whole current of our thoughts, and introduce a new train of ideas and associations (Letter to Augustus Harley, 8).

ii. In the course of my researches, the Heloise of Rousseau[2] fell into my hands.—Ah! with what transport, with what enthusiasm, did I peruse this dangerous, enchanting, work!—How shall I paint the sensations that were excited in my mind!—the pleasure I experienced approached the limits of pain—it was tumult—all the ardour of my character was excited.—Mr Courtney, one day, surprised me weeping over the sorrows of the tender St. Preux. He hastily snatched the book from my hand, and, carefully collecting the remaining volumes, carried them in silence to his chamber; but the impression made on my mind was never to be effaced—it was even productive of a long chain of consequences, that will continue to operate till the day of my death (ch. VIII, 25).

iii. The small pittance bequeathed to me was insufficient to preserve me from dependence.—*Dependence!*—I repeated to myself, and I felt my heart die within me. I revolved in my mind various plans for my future establishment.—I might, perhaps, be allowed to officiate, as an assistant, in the school where I had been placed in my childhood, with the mistress of which I still kept up an occasional correspondence; but his was a species of servitude, and my mind panted for freedom, for social intercourse, for scenes in motion, where the active curiosity of my temper might find scope wherein to range and speculate.... Cruel prejudices!—I exclaimed—hapless woman! Why was I not educated for commerce, for a profession, for labour? Why have I been rendered feeble and delicate by bodily constraint, and fastidious by artificial refinements? Why are we bound, by the habits of society, as with an adamantine chain? Why do we suffer ourselves to be confined within a magic circle, without daring, by a magnanimous effort, to dissolve the barbarous spell (ch. XI, 31-2).

---

[2] A reference to Jean-Jacques Rousseau's novel *Julie, ou La Nouvelle Héloïse* (1761) in which the heroine Julie has an illicit affair with her tutor St. Preux.

iv. I reflected, meditated, reasoned, with myself—"That one channel, into which my thoughts were incessantly impelled, was destructive of all order, of all connection." New projects occurred to me, which I had never before ventured to encourage—I revolved them in my mind, examined them in every point of view, weighed their advantages and disadvantages, in a moral, in a prudential scale.—Threatening evils appeared on all sides—I endeavoured, at once, to free my mind from prejudice, and from passion; and, in the critical and *singular* circumstances in which I had placed myself, coolly to survey the several arguments of the case, and nicely to calculate their force and importance.

"If, as we are taught to believe, the benevolent Author of nature be, indeed benevolent" said I, to myself, "he surely must have intended the *happiness* of his creatures. Our morality cannot extend to him, but must consist in the knowledge, and practice, of those duties which we owe to ourselves and to each other.—Individual happiness constitutes the general good:—*happiness* is the only true *end* of existence;—all notions of morals, founded on any other principle, involve in themselves a contradiction, and must be erroneous. Man does right, when pursuing interest and pleasure—it argues no depravity—this is the fable of superstition: he ought only to be careful, that, in seeking his own good, he does not render it incompatible with the good of others—that he does not consider himself as standing alone in the universe. The infraction of established *rules* so precise and determinate, as to be alike applicable to every situation: what, in one instance, might be a *vice*, in another may possibly become a *virtue*:—a thousand imperceptible, evanescent, shadings, modify every thought, every motive, every action, of our lives—no one can estimate the sensations of, can form an exact judgment for, another" (ch. VI, 115-16).

Appendix B: The Hottentots

Hamilton's choice of the Hottentots of Africa as the chosen destination of the Modern Philosophers is significant. She correlates the supposed sexuality of English philosophers (such as Mary Wollstonecraft and Mary Hays) with the findings of contemporary studies (by Georges Cuvier)[1] and travelogues (such as Vaillant's)[2] that the female Hottentot was associated with extreme and primitive sexuality. It is ironically appropriate to Hamilton that the Modern Philosophers should look for their counterparts not in a progressive society but one contemporary studies defined as primitive and backward. Hamilton's inference is that Westerners have evolved beyond the primitive state represented both by the Hottentots and desired by the philosophers.

An aspect of particular interest and fascination to Western readers was the Hottentot Venus. This term was originally applied to Saartjie Baartman, a twenty-year old Khoe Khoe woman exhibited in London and Paris from 1810 to 1815, and later to a second African woman displayed at a Parisian ball by the Duchess of Berry[3] in 1829. In his study "Black Bodies, White Bodies" (*Critical Inquiry* 12, 1985) Sander Gilman explains that "the antithesis of European sexual mores and beauty is embodied in the black, and the essential black, the lowest rung on the great chain of being, is the Hottentot. The physical appearance of the Hottentot is, indeed, the central nineteenth-century icon for sexual difference between the European and the black." Gilman shows that widely familiar illustrations and caricatures represented the "Hottentot Venus" in profile or rear view with exaggeratedly large buttocks (and, after her death and dissection by Cuvier) with supposedly "aberrant" genitalia, referred to as the "Hottentot Apron".

The following illustrations would have been available to Hamilton and her contemporaries. Three are original illustrations from Vaillant's *Travels from the Cape of Good-Hope into the Interior Parts of Africa* which the New Philsophers read with such interest at the end of volume one of *Modern Philosophers*.

---

[1] Georges Cuvier, anatomist, professor of natural history at the Collège de France from 1798. Cuvier originated the natural system of animal classification and from this established the sciences of palaeontology and comparative anatomy.

[2] François Le Vaillant, *Voyage dans l'interieur de l'Afrique*. Various English translations were available including *Travels from the Cape of Good-Hope into the Interior Parts of Africa*, translated by Elizabeth Helme. 2 vols. Lane: London, 1790.

[3] Marie-Caroline, daughter of the King of Naples, married the Duke of Berry, son of Count Artois in 1816 to become the Duchess of Berry. She witnessed his assassination on the steps of the Paris Opera, in February 1820 but renewed hopes for the Bourbon line when she gave birth to a son seven months later. In "February 1829 she gave a costume ball, reminiscent of the court of Francis II" (de Savigny, Guillaume de Bertier. *The Bourbon Restoration*. Translated by Lynn M. Case. Philadelphia: University of Philadelphia Press, 1966) 261.

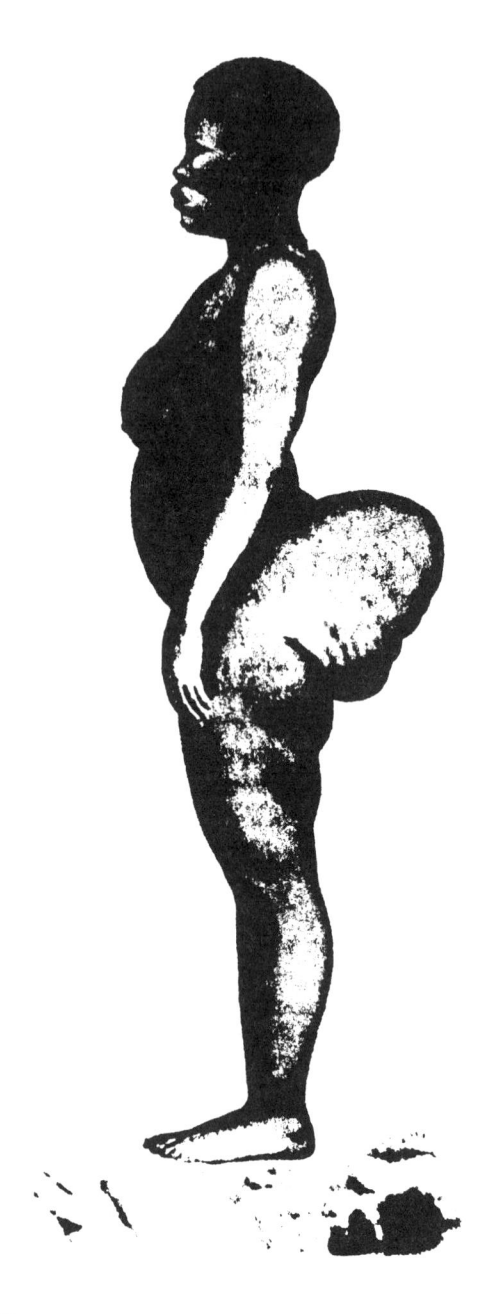

Fig 1: The "Hottentot Venus." George Cuvier, *Extraits d'observations faire sur le cadavre d'une femme connue à Paris et à Londres sous le nom de Vénus Hottentote*, 1817.

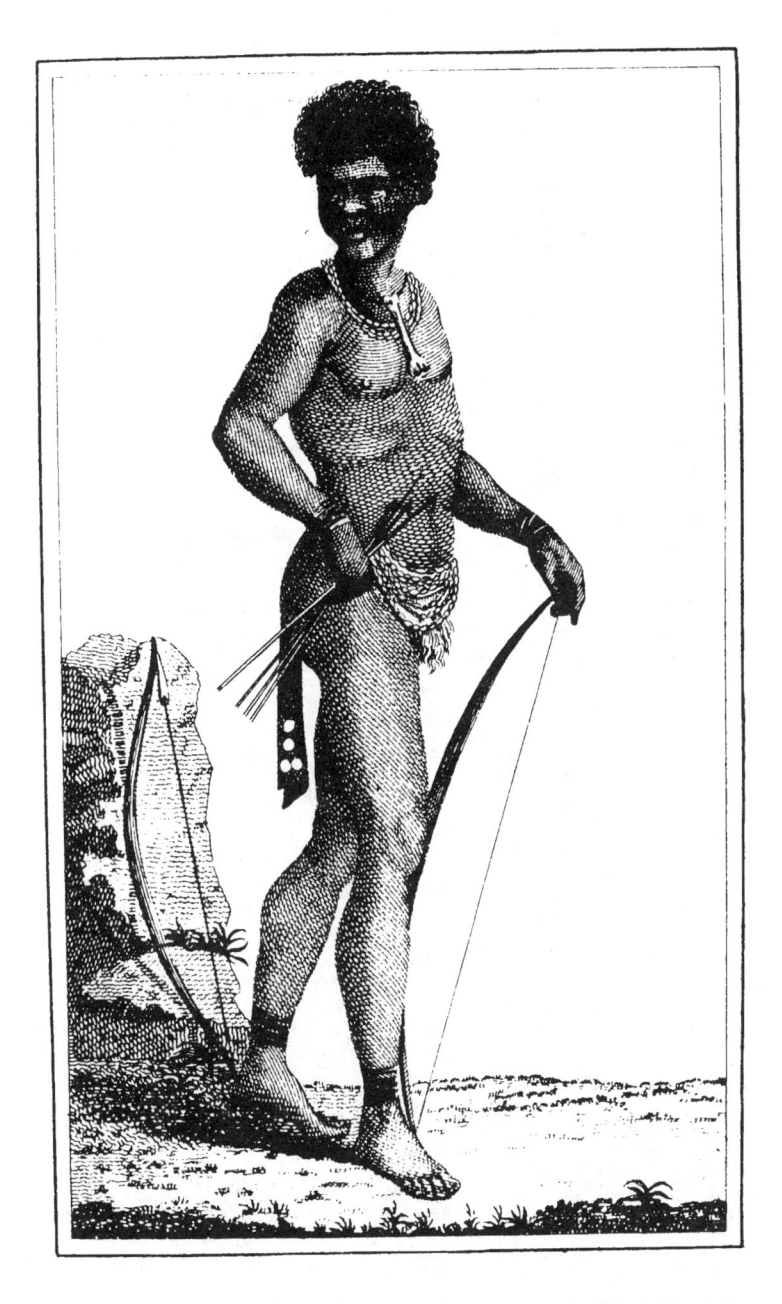

Fig 2: A Gonoquais Hottentot. Illustration from François Vaillant's *Travels from the Cape of Good-Hope into the Interior Parts of Africa.*

Fig 3: KLAAS, "The Author's Favourite Hottentot." Illustration from François Vaillant's *Travels from the Cape of Good-Hope into the Interior Parts of Africa.*

Fig 4: Female Hottentot. Illustration from François Vaillant's *Travels from the Cape of Good-Hope into the Interior Parts of Africa*.

Appendix C: Reviews of Memoirs of Modern Philosophers

(Original spelling and punctuation has been retained.)

i. *Critical Review*, May 1800, vol 29 pp 311-13.
The shafts of lively and ingenious satire have been frequently leveled at the paradoxical metaphysics of Mr. Godwin, and his brethren of what is called the new school of philosophy. In the present work, some leading principles in the writings of that eccentric author are represented as influencing the conduct of Julia, an amiable and accomplished female, and of Bridgetina, a compound of garrulity, ignorance, and affectation. The vehicles of this new light are Glib, a shallow and loquacious apothecary; Myope, a speculative metaphysician; and Vallaton, a low and unprincipled adventurer: the last, by the jargon of the new philosophy, obtains an ascendancy over the romantic mind of Julia, whom he persuades to elope from her parents, and to enter into a connexion superior to the *contemptible formality* of marriage. Julia is soon abandoned by her *philosophical* protector to infamy and distress, and expiates her errors by repentance and a premature death. Vallaton, who, among other villainies, had supplied the French revolutionary tribunal with an innocent victim, is finally, with due dramatic justice, conducted to the guillotine at Paris. Myope, whom we suppose to be intended as the type of Mr. Godwin, recants many of his metaphysical doctrines, as in some respects too pure for the present conditions of mankind, and as calculated in other points to interfere with the practice of the social and domestic virtues which constitute so large a proportion of the happiness of the species.

The satirical part of this novel is, upon the whole, conducted with ability; but we think Vallaton too deficient in talents and deportment for the place assigned to him by the author. The character of Bridgetina might have been made the vehicle of an agreeable vein of satire on the female converts to the new philosophy, but it is grossly and farcically overcharged.—The following circular letter from the Hottentotian committee affords a favourable specimen of the humour of the work.
... [quotes letter detailing emigration to Hottentots] ...

Some domestic scenes in this novel are delineated with the pencil of truth and nature; and, while the characters of captain and Mrs. Delmond gratify the penetration of the sagacious reader, those of Dr. Sydney and Harriet Orwell will delight the amiable feelings that sympathize with the progress and the reward of virtue.

ii. *British Critic* 16 (October 1800), 439–40.

The Vagabond, written by Mr. Walker,[1] and formerly commended by us (Brit. Crit. vol. xv, p. 432) and this Novel of the Modern Philosophers, are formed upon the same design; that of ridiculing the extravagancies of several pretenders to wisdom in the present times, particularly of Mr. Godwin. The wild and almost incredible absurdities of that author's Political Justice (exposed by us with some care in our first volume, p.307, &c) afford so fair and open a subject for ridicule, that no man possessing any share of humour could fail to raise a laugh, if so disposed, at the expence of the fanatical speculator. In this respect, both these publications are abundantly successful; though we cannot but think the humour of the Vagabond the more delicate and refined. Bridgetina in the present Novel, is such a caricature as exceed all probability, and almost all patience; and Mr. Glib talks only the cropped cant of the Road to Ruin,[2] and such stuff; the pleasantry of which consists in leaving out articles and pronouns. Mr. Myope greatly resembles the sublime Stupeo,[3] but is drawn with less vigour. On the other hand, the villainy of Vallaton is well designed, and highly finished. As a regular novel, the present has much more plot and more interest than the Vagabond. The good characters are given with admirable skill, and form a useful and a striking contrast to the bad. Many of the serious parts are of high merit. The catastrophe of Julia in particular is tremendous, but touched with a most judicious hand. Yet the triumph of the amiable girl over the superficial philosopher, in the Vagabond, gave us more pleasure, and has in our opinion more probability, than the strange and unaccountable lapse of Julia. We have heard it surmised, probably from its being printed at Bath, that the present Novel proceeds from the pen of the venerable Mr. Graves, author of the Spiritual Quixote,[4] Euphrosyne, &c. Some passages seem to us a little to contradict that opinion; but we would not be too positive. Much of the work is certainly worthy of that able author. The Modern Philosophers appear to us to have attracted the public attention more than the Vagabond; we have therefore been careful to compare them. Were we to add another feature to the comparison, we should say that Mr. Walker more completely exposes the authors he attacks than the present writer. His account of emigration to America is useful, because touched with truth; and his imaginary society of philosophers is managed with a vein of high humour. Both novels however will be read, and both deserve it.

---

[1] George Walker, *The Vagabond; or Practical Infidelity* (London: G. Walker, Lee and Hurst, 1799).
[2] Thomas Holcroft's radical play *The Road to Ruin* (1792) was first performed at Covent Garden Theatre in February 1792.
[3] A character in Walker's *Vagabond*.
[4] Richard Graves, *The Spiritual Quixote, or the Summer Ramble of Mr Geoffrey Wildgoose* (1773).

iii. *Anti-Jacobin Review and Magazine* 7 (Sept. 1800), 39-46; 7 (Dec. 1800), 369-76.

We will endeavour to offer to our readers something like an outline of the story of this excellent work; in doing which we shall occasionally make such extracts as will afford them an opportunity of forming their own judgement, on what we esteem the first novel of the day.

Bridgetina Botherim, daughter of the late Rector of —, is the heroine of the tale. She is described as one of those young ladies, who, disregarding all the old-fashioned female excellencies by which the women of this country have been so eminently distinguished, has devoted herself to the study and practice of Godwinian and Wollstonecraftian philosophy. In the midst of a party, collected at the house of Mrs. Botherim, rushes Mr. Glib, the philosophizing bookseller of the village, who—

"skipping at once up to Bridgetina, 'Good News!' cried he, 'citizen Miss. Glorious news! We shall have rare talking now! ...'"

[Excerpt describing arrival of Mr. Myope, the Goddess of Reason, and Mr. Vallaton]

At Mr. Glib's she finds Mr. Myope, and Mr. Vallaton, two steady promoters of the new system of things; the former accompanied by the strumpet who officiated at Paris as the Goddess of reason; the latter, whom we presume is intended for the hero of the story, appears to be attracted into the country by his passion for the person, or property, or both, of Julia Delmond, the daughter of an officer in the neighbourhood, whose affections he has gained by first perverting her understanding. As this young lady makes a melancholy and prominent figure in the work, we give the following extract, as characteristic of her, as well as of Vallaton. During a conversation between Glib and the latter,

[Initial conversation between Vallaton, Julia, and Glib]

By such a wretch was the wretched, unsuspecting, Julia betrayed to ruin, misery, and death; but we will not anticipate. His history, to this time of his appearance, is given with great ability, and proves him in a higher degree worthy the appellation of an adept in modern philosophy.

Vallaton having informed Julia that he was found, by the lady who had educated him, "in a white basket, lined with quilted pink satin," and that "on his infant robes" were embroidered the letters A.V. she conceives the romantic idea of introducing him to General Villers and his lady, as their long lost son. To accomplish this, she proposes to her father that she should call upon the General, and secretly determines within herself to take Vallaton with her. This scheme, to the great discomfiture of Julia, ends as might be expected, in the detection of Vallaton by one of the party at the General's, who declares him to have exhibited formerly in the character of a hair-dresser. This unfortunate discovery occasions them immediately to quit the house; and, in driving her home, the philosopher's mind being too deeply engaged to attend to his horse, he overturns the chair, by which accident both are so bruised as to be under the necessity of being carried to a farmhouse. Here we must leave them, to introduce to our readers some other characters of a different complexion, and these are Dr. Orwell, the rector of —, and his daughters, and Mr. Sydney the dissenting minister, residing in the same place, and his son Dr. Henry Sydney, a young physician. These excellent people strictly performing the duties of religion and morality are admirably contrasted, with the unprincipled disciples of Godwin and his wife. Henry Sydney is the lover of Harriet Orwell, and is beloved by her: Bridgetina is, also, to make the character of a true female citizen complete, anxiously desirous to be *useful*, and sighs in her turn for Henry. Her various schemes and amorous advances for the accomplishment of her purpose form a most interesting and amusing portion of the work.

In a visit of Mrs. Botherim and Bridgetina to Mr. Sydney's, where the whole party are met, there is some well supported conversation in which the heroine shines with her usual lustre. Walking afterwards into the hayfield, "where every face wore the appearance of chearfulness and contentment, Bridgetina thus addresses the happy rustics:
[Exchange between Bridgetina and rustics]

It is not necessary to say that these stupid plagiarisms of the heroine are combated by Mrs. Martha, the sister of Dr. Orwell, with sound sense, and irrefutable argument.

Having thus shortly given our readers some idea of the other personages of the drama, we return to Julia, who, attended by Dr. Sydney, and nursed by Harriet Orwell, is confined at the farm-house to which she was at first carried—happy had it been for her had a broken limb been the only evil brought upon her by her attachment to modern philosophers. This day so unhappy to Julia, was by Bridgetina marked as the most auspicious of her existence. Among a variety of books received by Glib from his correspondent in London, was a copy of Valliant's tour in Africa. This work produced, among the party at Glib's, the following conversation:
[Discussion of plan to live with the Hottentots]

We have not given here the whole of this very admirable illustration of Godwinian philosophy; for however desirous we might be to do it, it would occupy too much of our Number fully to gratify, even with our own wishes on the subject. In our opinion it is a consistent and true picture, and we give the author our best thanks for his very happy exposition of its absurd and wicked doctrines. The discussion concludes with the determination of the whole party "to embark for the only place to which, in this distempered state of civilisation, a philosopher can resort with any hopes of comfort. "Let us seek," said he, "an asylum among those kindred souls. Let us form a horde in the neighbourhood of Haabas; and, from the deserts of Africa, send forth those rays of philosophy which shall enlighten all the habitable globe."
[The review is continued here in the Dec. 1800 issue of the *Anti-Jacobin Review*]

The confinement of Julia at the farm-house, from under the protection of her father, gave the insidious Vallaton full opportunity of effecting his nefarious purposes. Proposals of marriage being made to Captain Delmond for her union with Major Minden, assist the designs of the hero. The tyranny of parental authority, and the glory of being among the number of those who resist the institutions of a "distempered state of civilization," are the motives which he urges for the renunciation of all filial duties. The struggle is great, and extremely well supported; but love and vanity finally prevail, and she flies to his arms and, of course, to misery.

The scheme of sailing to the Cape still appears to proceed. We shall give the circular letter of Citizen Myope, in quality of secretary.
"*To Citizen* ———— *of* ————"
[Excerpt of letter detailing emigration to the Hottentots]

In the mean time, the heroine of the tale is tormenting herself, and Henry Sydney, with her passion, the origin of which is most admirably well given by herself in a conversation with Julia. Part of it we offer to our readers as an excellent imitation of that vicious and detestable stuff which has issued from the pen of M—y H—s. Indeed the whole character of Bridgetina so strongly resembles that of this impassioned Godwinian, that it is impossible to be mistaken.
[Bridgetina describing her love for Henry to Julia]

She then proceeds to state some other trifling circumstances, among which is her attachment to an apothecary, on whose marriage to another she thus describes her own sensations.
[Importance of philosophy to Bridgetina and history of Henry's love for her]

Our readers will, perhaps, think that our extracts from this novel are already of sufficient length; of this we are ourselves aware; but we could not resist the inclination of affording to our friends, who are not in the habit of perusing works of this description, an opportunity of knowing that *all* the *female* writers of the day are not corrupted by the voluptuous dogmas of Mary Godwin, or her more profligate imitators.

We shall, as briefly as possible, relate the remainder of the story of this work. Dr. Sydney proceeds to London to pursue his profession; to which place, in the true spirit of the modern doctrines, he is followed by Bridgetina. Like Mr. F—d, he declines all her advances; and she, in imitation of M— H—s,[5] writes to him the following philosophical love-letter:
[Love letter written to Henry]

After a variety of interesting adventures, natural, and well related; this work concludes with the marriage of Dr. Sydney with Harriet Orwell, and the return of Bridgetina to her mother. Poor Julia, having been seduced and deserted by Vallaton, (who is guillotined in Paris) dies by poison of her own administering. It seems to be the intention of the author to exhibit here the fallacy of all principles which have not their

---

[5] Referring to Hays's unrequited love for William Frend, the Cambridge mathematician.

foundation in religion. Had the education of Julia been grounded on the doctrines of Christianity, instead of the vapid rules of modern honour, instilled into her by her father; with such an understanding as she possessed, she would neither have been overcome by the plausible inanity, and the superficial reasoning of such a wretch as Vallaton, nor would she have attempted to expiate the crimes of filial ingratitude and prostitution by the commission of suicide. Among the rest of the characters all due poetical justice is distributed; but as they are not *immediately* concerned in the *main* design of the work, they necessarily excite not that interest which is produced by the philosophical portraits.

Since writing the first part of this review, we have learnt the name of the author of the work. The public, that part of it, at least, with whom novels form the great portion of amusement, is infinitely obliged to *her* for this admirable exposition of Godwinian principles, and the more so, for her having given it in the form of a novel; for the same means by which the poison is offered, are, perhaps, the best by which their antidote may be rendered efficacious. It will in this shape find its way into the circulating libraries of the country, whence is daily issued such a pestiferous portion of what are termed enlightened and liberal sentiments. We could without difficulty point out for whom, in our opinions, the characters were delineated; but conceiving that we have no possible right to involve the fair author in the evils that might arise from such a declaration, we shall leave it to each to discover his, or her own face, in the glass. The *gentle* and *tender* original of Bridgetina once thus addressed the author of Political Justice—

"Pray Mr. G— when will the nation be ruined? I want some vivid emotions:"—To your sampler, to your sampler; poor wretched, infatuated creature, an by honourable and becoming exertions endeavour to acquire that peace of mind which you can never attain in your present worthless, nay, unprincipled, pursuits. We have been thus particular in our notice of this last character, because we know that some lamentable effects have arisen from her novels.

This work is written in an excellent stile, and altogether does great credit to the literary acquirements of the author. We should be happy to meet her again, and on the same subject. The philosophical harvest is great; and the hand that thus condescends to the irksome, though meritorious, labour of plucking up and burning the weeds, deserves the thanks of her country, and the honour of being classed with the most unexceptionable female writers of the times★[6]

We are sorry to see a publication calculated to be so eminently beneficial, charged so high as one guinea; not that we think the sum beyond the value of the work, but that it will check the extent of its circulation, and of course impede its progress towards "general utility."

---

[6] ★Hannah More.

iv. Anna Laetitia Barbauld. Introductory Essay, *British Novelists* (1810) 1: 56-57.

No small proportion of modern novels have been devoted to recommend, or to mark with reprobation, those systems of philosophy or politics which have raised so much ferment of late years.

... On the other side may be reckoned *The Modern Philosophers*, and the novels of Mrs Jane West.[7] In the war of systems these light skirmishing troops have often been employed with great effect; and, so long as they are content with fair, general warfare, without taking aim at individuals, are perfectly allowable. We have lately seen the gravest theological discussions presented to the world under the attractive form of a novel, and with a success which seems to show that the interest, even of the generality of readers, is most strongly excited when some serious end is kept in view.

---

[7] A popular Loyalist novelist who used her early works (*Advantages of Education*, 1793, *A Gossip's Story*, 1796 and *A Tale of the Times*, 1799) to denounce revolutionary sentiments.

Select Bibliography

Works by Elizabeth Hamilton

Translation of the Letters of a Hindoo Rajah; Written Previous to, and During the Period of his Residence in England; To Which is Prefixed a Preliminary Dissertation on the History, Religion, and Manners of the Hindoos. 2 vols. London: G.G. & J. Robinson, 1796.

Memoirs of Modern Philosophers. 3 vols. Bath: R. Crutwell, for G.G & J. Robinson, London, 1800.

Letters on Education. Bath: R. Crutwell, for G.G. & J. Robinson, London, 1801. Republished as *Letters on the Elementary Principles of Education.* 2 vols. Bath: R. Crutwell, for G.G. & J. Robinson, London, 1801; Alexandria, Va: Printed by Cotton & Stewart for S. Bishop, 1803.

Memoirs of the Life of Agrippina, Wife of Germanicus. 2 vols. Bath: R. Crutwell, for G.G. & J. Robinson, London, 1804.

Letters, Addressed to the Daughter of a Nobleman, on the Formation of Religious and Moral Principle. 2 vols. London: T. Cadell & W. Davies, 1806.

The Cottagers of Glenburnie: A Tale for the Farmer's Ingle-nook. Edinburgh: Manners and Miller and S. Cheyne; London: T. Cadell & W. Davies, and William Miller, 1808; New York: Printed for E. Sargent, 1808.

Exercises in Religious Knowledge; for the Instruction of Young Persons. Edinburgh: Manners and Miller; London: T. Cadell & W. Davies, 1809.

A Series of Popular Essays, Illustrative of Principles Essentially Connected with the Improvement of the Understanding, the Imagination, and the Heart. 2 vols. Edinburgh: Manners and Miller; London: Longman, Hurst, Rees, Orme & Brown; and T. Cadell & W. Davies, 1813; Boston: Wells & Lilly, 1817.

Hints Addressed to the Patrons and Directors of Schools: Principally Intended to Shew, That the Benefits Derived from the New Modes of Teaching May Be Increased by a Partial Adoption of the Plan of Pestalozzi; To Which Are Subjoined Examples of Questions Calculated to Excite, and Exercise the Infant Mind. London: Longman, Hurst, Rees, Orme & Brown, 1815.

Examples of Questions Calculated to Excite and Exercise the Infant Mind. London: Longman, Hurst, Rees, Orme & Brown, 1815; Salem: Foote & Browne, 1829.

Other Primary Sources

Benger, Elizabeth. *Memoirs of the Late Mrs. Elizabeth Hamilton with a Selection from Her Correspondence, and Other Unpublished Writings,* 2nd ed., 2 vols. London: Longman, 1819.

Burke, Edmund. *Reflections on the Revolution in France*. Ed. Connor Cruise O'Brien. Harmondsworth: Penguin, 1968.

Gregory, John. *A Father's Legacy to his Daughters, by the Late Dr. Gregory*. London: W. Strahan, 1774.

Hamilton, Charles (trans. and ed.). *An Historical Relation of the Origin, Progress, and Final Dissolution of the Rohilla Afghans in the Northern Provinces of Hindostan; Compiled from a Persian Manuscript and Other Original Papers*. London, 1787.

—. (trans. and ed.). *The Hedaya, or Guide: A Commentary on the Mussulman Laws*, 4 vols. London: T. Bensley, 1791.

Hays, Mary. *Memoirs of Emma Courtney*. Ed. Eleanor Ty. London: Oxford University Press, 1996.

Knox, Vicesimus. *Essays, Moral and Literary*. 2 vols. London: Dilly, 1782.

More, Hannah. *Essays on Various Subjects, Principally Designed for Young Ladies*. London: J. Wilkie and Cadell, 1777.

—. *Strictures on the Modern System of Female Education: With a View of the Principles and Conduct Prevalent Among Women of Rank and Fortune*. 2 vols. London: Cadell and Davies, 1799.

Paine, Thomas. *Rights of Man*. Ed. Eric Foner. London: Penguin, 1984.

Roberts, William. *Memoirs of the Life and Correspondence of Mrs. Hannah More*, 3rd rev. ed., 2 vols. London: Thames Ditton, 1835.

West, Jane. *Letters to a Young Lady, in which the Duties and Character of Women are Considered, Chiefly with a Reference to Prevailing Opinions*. 3 vols. London: Longman, 1806.

Wollstonecraft, Mary. *Vindication of the Rights of Woman*. Ed. Carol H. Poston. 2nd edition. New York: Norton, 1988.

Secondary Sources

Boulton, James T. *The Language of Politics in the Age of Wilkes and Burke*. London: Routledge, 1963.

Butler, Marilyn. *Burke, Paine, Godwin, and the Revolution Controversy*. Cambridge: Cambridge UP, 1984.

Cage, R.A. *The Scottish Poor Law 1745-1845*. Edinburgh: Scottish Academic Press, 1981.

Cannon, Garland. *Oriental Jones: A Biography of Sir William Jones 1746-1794*. Bombay: Indian Council for Cultural Relations, 1964.

Collier, Jane Fishburne. "Women in Politics." *Woman, Culture, and Society*. Ed. Michelle Zimbalist Rosaldo and Louise Lamphere. Stanford, CA: Stanford UP, 1974, 89-112.

Cone, Carl B. *The English Jacobins: Reformers in Late 18th Century England*. New York: Scribner, 1968.

Dickinson, Harry T. *Liberty and Property: Political Ideology in Eighteenth-Century Britain*. London: Methuen, 1979.

Doody, Margaret. "English Women Novelists and the French Revolution." *La Femme en Angleterre et dans les Colonies americanes aux XVIIe et XVIIIe siècles*. Pub. de l'Universite de Lille: Lille, 1976. 176-98.

Dwyer, John. *Virtuous Discourse: Sensibility and Community in Late Eighteenth-Century Scotland*. Edinburgh: John Donald, 1987.

Felski, Rita. *Beyond Feminist Aesthetics: Feminist Literature and Social Change*. London: Hutchinson Radius, 1989.

Goodman, Dena. "Enlightenment Salons: The Convergence of Female and Philosophic Ambitions." *Eighteenth-Century Studies*, 22 (Spring 1989) 329-50.

Grogan, Claire. "The Politics of Seduction in British Fiction of the 1790s: The Female Reader and Rousseau's *Julie, ou La Nouvelle Héloïse*." *Eighteenth-Century Fiction* 11: 4 (July 1999).

—. "Mary Wollstonecraft and Hannah More: Politics, Feminism and Modern Critics," *Lumen* 13 (1994) 99-108.

Hellmuth, Eckhart., ed. *The Transformation of Political Culture: England and Germany in the Late Eighteenth Century*. Oxford: Oxford UP, 1990.

Hobsbawm, Eric J. *Nations and Nationalism since 1780: Programme, Myth, Reality*. Cambridge: Cambridge UP, 1990.

Homans, Margaret. *Bearing the Word: Language and Female Experience in Nineteenth-Century Woman's Writing*. Chicago: University of Chicago Press, 1986.

Hone, J. Ann. *For the Cause of Truth: Radicalism in London 1796-1821*. Oxford: Clarendon Press, 1982.

Innes, Joanna. "Politics and Morals: The Reformation of Manners Movement in Later Eighteenth-Century England." *The Transformation of Political Culture: England and Germany in the Late Eighteenth Century*. Ed. E. Hellmuth. Oxford: Oxford UP, 1990. 57-118.

Jones, Vivien. "The Seductions of Conduct: Pleasure and Conduct Literature." *Pleasure in the Eighteenth-Century*. Ed. Roy Porter and Marie Mulvey-Roberts. New York: New York UP, 1996. 108-32.

Kelly, Gary. *English Fiction of the Romantic Period 1789-1830*. London: Longman, 1989.

—. *Revolutionary Feminism: The Mind and Career of Mary Wollstonecraft*. London: Macmillan, 1992.

—. *Women, Writing, and Revolution 1790-1827*. Oxford: Clarendon Press, 1993.

—. "Women Novelists and the French Revolution Debate: Novelising the Revolution/Revolutionizing the Novel." *Eighteenth Century Fiction* 6: 4 (July 1994) 369-88.

Gallagher, Catherine and Thomas Laqueur, eds. *The Making of the Modern Body: Sexuality and Society in the Nineteenth Century*. Berkeley: University of California Press, 1987.

Goodwin, Albert. *The Friends of Liberty: The English Democratic Movement in the Age of the French Revolution*. London: Hutchinson, 1979.

Kramnick, Isaac. *Republicanism and Bourgeois Radicalism: Political Ideology in Late Eighteenth-Century England and America*. Ithaca, NY: Cornell UP, 1990.

Landes, Joan B. *Women and the Public Sphere in the Age of the French Revolution*. Ithaca, NY: Cornell UP, 1988.

Levine, Philippa. *Victorian Feminism: 1850-1900*. London: Hutchinson, 1987.

Mahood, Linda. *The Magdalenes: Prostitution in the Nineteenth Century*. London: Routledge, 1990.

McKendrick, Neil, John Brewer and J.H. Plumb. *The Birth of a Consumer Society: The Commercialization of Eighteenth-Century England*. London: Hutchinson, 1982.

Messer-Davidow, Ellen. "'For Softness She': Gender Ideology and Aesthetics in Eighteenth-Century England." *Eighteenth-Century Women and the Arts*. Ed. Frederick M. Keener and Susan E. Lorsch. New York, 1988, 45-55.

Mukherjee, S.N. *Sir William Jones: A Study in Eighteenth-Century British Attitudes to India*, rev. ed. London: Sangam, 1987.

Mullan, John. *Sentiment and Sociability: The Language of Feeling in the Eighteenth Century*. Oxford: Clarendon Press, 1988.

Myers, Sylvia Harcstark. *The Bluestocking Circle: Women, Friendship, and the Life of the Mind in Eighteenth-Century England*. Oxford: Clarendon Press, 1990.

Newman, Gerald. *The Rise of English Nationalism: A Cultural History 1740-1830*. London: Weidenfeld & Nicolson, 1987.

Ortner, Sherry B. "Is Female to Male as Nature is to Culture?" *Woman, Culture, and Society*. Ed. Michelle Zimbalist Rosaldo and Louise Lamphere. Stanford, CA: Stanford UP, 1974, 67-87.

Outram, Dorinda. *The Body and the French Revolution: Sex, Class and Political Culture*. New Haven, CT: Yale UP, 1989.

Paulson, Ronald. *Representations of Revolution 1789-1820*. New Haven, CT: Yale UP, 1983.

Philp, Mark., ed. *The French Revolution and British Popular Politics*. Cambridge: Cambridge UP, 1991.

Prochaska, Frank K. *Women and Philanthropy in Nineteenth-Century England*. Oxford: Clarendon Press, 1980.

Rajan, Tilottama. "Autonarration and Genotext in Mary Hays' *Memoirs of Emma Courtney.*" *Studies in Romanticism* 32: 2 (Summer 1993) 149-76

—. "Wollstonecraft and Godwin Reading the Secrets of the Political Novel" *Studies in Romanticism* 27: 2 (Summer 1988) 221-51.

Rendall, Jane. *The Origins of Modern Feminism: Women in Britain, France and the United States 1780-1860.* London: Macmillan, 1985.

Rosaldo, Michelle Zimbalist and Louise Lamphere., eds. *Woman, Culture, and Society.* Stanford, CA: Stanford UP, 1974.

Spencer, Jane. *The Rise of the Woman Novelist: From Aphra Behn to Jane Austen.* Oxford: Blackwood, 1986.

Spender, Dale. *Mothers of the Novel: 100 Good Women Writers before Jane Austen.* London: Pandora, 1986.

Stanton, Judith Phillips. "Statistical Profile of Women Writing in English from 1660 to 1800." *Eighteenth-Century Women and the Arts.* Ed. Frederick M. Keener and Susan E. Lorsch. New York, 1988, 247-54.

St Clair, William. *The Godwins and the Shelleys: The Biography of a Family.* London: Faber, 1989.

Summers, Anne. "A Home from Home—Women's Philanthropic Work in the Nineteenth Century." *Fit Work for Women.* Ed. Sandra Burman. London: Croom Helm, 1979, 33-63.

Taylor, Barbara. *Eve and the New Jerusalem: Socialism and Feminism in the Nineteenth Century.* London: Virago Press, 1983.

Thaddeus, Janice Farrar. "Elizabeth Hamilton's Domestic Politics." *Studies in Eighteenth Century Culture.* 23 (1994), 265-84.

Todd, Janet. *The Sign of Angellica: Women, Writing, and Fiction 1660-1800.* London: Virago Press, 1989.

Tompkins, Joyce M.S. *The Popular Novel in England 1770-1800.*

Ty, Eleanor. "Female Philosophy Refunctioned: Elizabeth Hamilton's Parodic Novel." *Ariel.* 22: 4 (Oct. 1991) 111-29.

Walkowitz, Judith. *Prostitution and Victorian Society: Women, Class, and the State.* Cambridge: Cambridge UP, 1980.